EXCITED ACCLAIM FOR DAN SIMMONS'S

The

TERROR

"I am here to tell you that this tale of a doomed expedition is the best and most unusual historical novel I have read in years. Based on real events and historical figures, it extrapolates from them to provide a haunting, precisely imagined fictional solution to one of history's most disquieting mysteries." — Katherine A. Powers, *Boston Globe*

"*The Terror* is nothing less than a revelation. Dan Simmons is a giant among novelists, and I am in awe of his achievement."
— Lincoln Child

"Simmons is a master of horror, suspense, characterization, and description. This true story gives him an opportunity to demonstrate these talents." — Mark Graham, *Rocky Mountain News*

"Dan Simmons takes the mysterious fate of Arctic explorer John Franklin and his crew and spins it into a bone- and spine-chilling novel." — *Minneapolis Star-Tribune*

"A historical thriller that reads like a collaboration among Henry James, Peter Straub, and Sebastian Junger."
— Dorman T. Shindler, *St. Louis Post-Dispatch*

"*The Terror* is the sort of rich, character- and plot-driven novel that provides thrills while fulfilling the desire for a substantial, intellectually satisfying read." — *Milwaukee Journal Sentinel*

"Simmons, an accomplished writer of horror and sci-fi, is predictably adroit in his deployment of terror, but the greatest pleasure of the novel lies in the sharp and sympathetic portrayals of Captain Francis Crozier, who assumes command of the expedition after Franklin's death, and Dr. Harry Goodsir, the mild yet determined ship's physician." — *The New Yorker*

"In the hands of a lesser writer than the Hugo Award–winning Dan Simmons, *The Terror* might well have dissolved into a series of frigid days and three-dog nights. But Simmons is too good a writer to ignore the real gold in his story — its beleaguered cast." — *BookPage*

"The most impressive achievement of this brilliant historical novel about the Franklin expedition is that the author manages to account plausibly for all the known facts. . . . *The Terror* is a tour de force." — Ken McGoogan, *Toronto Globe & Mail*

"Guaranteed to have readers pulling their covers up to their noses, *The Terror* will make for a blood-freezing bedtime read this winter — and any season thereafter." — *Pages*

"Brutal, relentless, yet oddly uplifting, *The Terror* is a masterfully chilling work." — Gilbert Cruz, *Entertainment Weekly*

"*The Terror* makes some keen observations about man and nature, civilization and savagery." — Matt Crenson, *San Francisco Chronicle*

"First-rate historical fiction." — Jeff Baker, *Portland Oregonian*

"Dan Simmons does not need comparison with anybody else. He is very much his own man, and now, with this chilling — in every way — thriller, he is set to break big." — Bill Bell, *New York Daily News*

"Simmons's prose is as sharp and dazzling as the ice of which he writes." — Dorman T. Shindler, *Denver Post*

"A literary thriller that reads like a cross between Charles Dickens and Robert B. Parker. . . . *The Terror* will have readers rushing to the end as they huddle beneath their bedcovers." — *Newark Star-Ledger*

"This mix of historical realism, Gothic horror, and ancient mythology is a difficult walk on fractured ice, and anyone without Simmons's mastery of narrative craft would have undoubtedly fallen through." — David Masiel, *Washington Post Book World*

"A brilliant fictional saga. . . . The novel works most of all because of the complicated, ever-changing interaction between the men. Adversity brings out the best and the worst in human nature. The men reveal themselves as savage, brave, loyal, pusillanimous, or barking mad amid the stark, unforgiving white landscape." — Deirdre Donahue, *USA Today*

"Dan Simmons's new novel, *The Terror,* may be the best thing he's ever written: a deeply absorbing story that combines awe-inspiring myth, grinding horror, and historically accurate adventure." — Nisi Shawl, *Seattle Times*

"Simmons is a remarkably versatile storyteller, and *The Terror* allows him the opportunity to employ his many narrative skills. He marshals a huge quantity of historical data and extrapolates from it a richly textured thriller." — Michael Berry, *San Francisco Chronicle*

"Gripping. . . . The book metes out one hard lesson after another, yet its palpable adversities occasionally give way to moments of real beauty and transcendence. It's hard to imagine a more perfectly judged Arctic novel." — Scott Tobias, *The Onion*

The

TERROR

A Novel

DAN SIMMONS

BACK BAY BOOKS

Copyright © 2007 by Dan Simmons

Back Bay Books / Little, Brown and Company
Hachette Book Group
1290 Avenue of the Americas, New York, NY 10104
littlebrown.com

Originally published in hardcover by Little, Brown and Company, January 2007
First Back Bay paperback edition, December 2007
First Back Bay media tie-in paperback edition, March 2018

The publisher is not responsible for websites (or their content) that are not owned by the publisher.

Library of Congress Cataloging-in-Publication Data
Simmons, Dan.
The terror: a novel / Dan Simmons.
p. cm.
ISBN 978-0-316-01744-2 (hc) / 978-0-316-01745-9 (pb) /
978-0-316-48609-5 (media tie-in pb)
1. Survival after airplane accidents, shipwrecks, etc.—Fiction.
2. Shipwrecks—Fiction. 3. Sea monsters—Fiction. I. Title.
PS3569.I47292T47   2007
813'.54—dc22   2006014608

10 9 8 7 6

LSC-C

Book design by Fearn Cutler de Vicq
Maps by Jeffrey L. Ward

Printed in the United States of America

This book is dedicated, with love and many thanks for the indelible Arctic memories, to Kenneth Tobey, Margaret Sheridan, Robert Cornthwaite, Douglas Spencer, Dewey Martin, William Self, George Fenneman, Dmitri Tiomkin, Charles Lederer, Christian Nyby, Howard Hawkes, and James Arness.

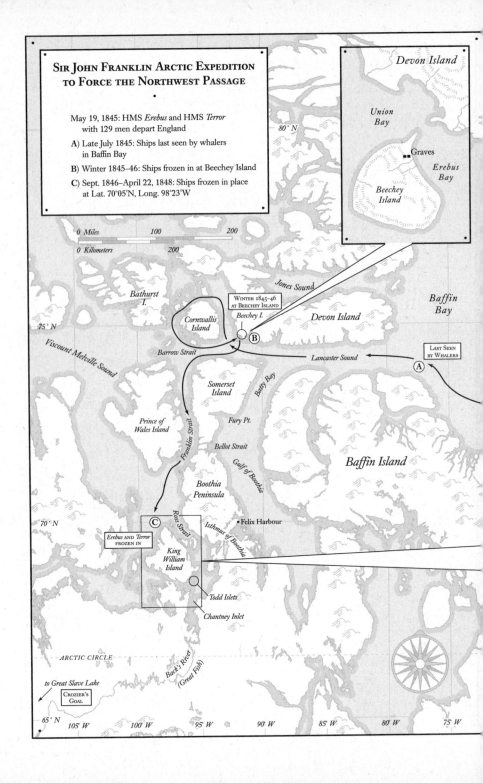

SIR JOHN FRANKLIN ARCTIC EXPEDITION TO FORCE THE NORTHWEST PASSAGE

•

May 19, 1845: HMS *Erebus* and HMS *Terror* with 129 men depart England

A) Late July 1845: Ships last seen by whalers in Baffin Bay

B) Winter 1845–46: Ships frozen in at Beechey Island

C) Sept. 1846–April 22, 1848: Ships frozen in place at Lat. 70°05'N, Long. 98°23'W

Devon Island

Union Bay

Graves

Erebus Bay

Beechey Island

0 Miles — 100 — 200
0 Kilometers — 200

Jones Sound

Bathurst I.

WINTER 1845–46 AT BEECHEY ISLAND

Beechey I.

(B)

Devon Island

Baffin Bay

Cornwallis Island

75° N

Viscount Melville Sound

Barrow Strait

LAST SEEN BY WHALERS

Lancaster Sound

(A)

Somerset Island

Batty Bay

Prince of Wales Island

Franklin Strait

Fury Pt.

Bellot Strait

Gulf of Boothia

Baffin Island

Boothia Peninsula

70° N

Erebus and *Terror* FROZEN IN

(C)

Ross Strait

Isthmus of Boothia

• Felix Harbour

King William Island

Todd Islets

Chantrey Inlet

ARCTIC CIRCLE

Back's River (Great Fish)

to Great Slave Lake

CROZIER'S GOAL

65° N

105° W — 100° W — 95° W — 90° W — 85° W — 80° W — 75° W

80° N

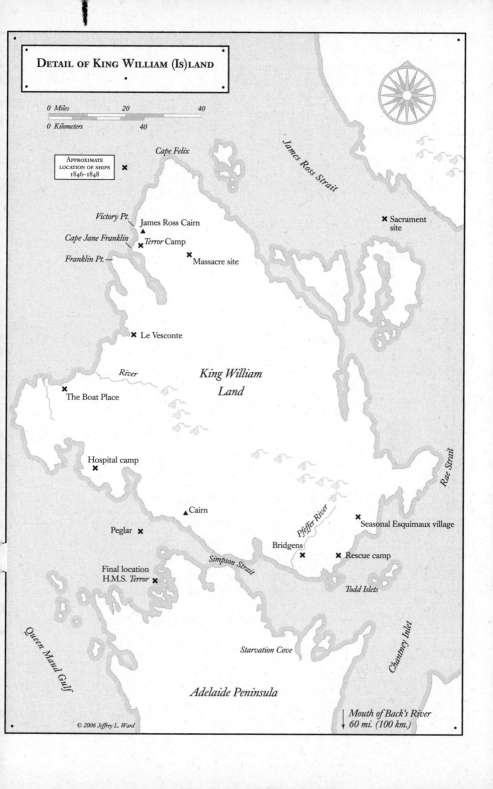

DETAIL OF KING WILLIAM (IS)LAND

0 Miles 20 40
0 Kilometers 40

APPROXIMATE
LOCATION OF SHIPS ✕
1846–1848

Cape Felix

James Ross Strait

Victory Pt.

James Ross Cairn ▲

✕ Sacrament site

Cape Jane Franklin

✕ Terror Camp

Franklin Pt.

Massacre site ✕

✕ Le Vesconte

River

King William Land

✕ The Boat Place

Hospital camp ✕

▲ Cairn

Rae Strait

Peglar ✕

Pfeffer River

✕ Seasonal Esquimaux village

Bridgens

✕ ✕ Rescue camp

Final location
H.M.S. Terror ✕

Simpson Strait

Todd Islets

Queen Maud Gulf

Starvation Cove

Chantrey Inlet

Adelaide Peninsula

Mouth of Back's River
60 mi. (100 km.)

© 2006 Jeffrey L. Ward

This elusive quality it is, which causes the thought of whiteness, when divorced from more kindly associations, and coupled with any object terrible in itself, to heighten that terror to the furthest bounds. Witness the white bear of the poles, and the white shark of the tropics; what but their smooth, flaky whiteness makes them the transcendent horrors they are? That ghastly whiteness it is which imparts such an abhorrent mildness, even more loathesome than terrific, to the dumb gloating of their aspect. So that not the fierce-fanged tiger in his heraldic coat can so stagger courage as the white-shrouded bear or shark.

— HERMAN MELVILLE
Moby Dick (1851)

The

TERROR

1

CROZIER

Lat. 70°-05' N., Long. 98°-23' W.
October, 1847

Captain Crozier comes up on deck to find his ship under attack by celestial ghosts. Above him — above *Terror* — shimmering folds of light lunge but then quickly withdraw like the colourful arms of aggressive but ultimately uncertain spectres. Ectoplasmic skeletal fingers extend toward the ship, open, prepare to grasp, and pull back.

The temperature is −50 degrees Fahrenheit and dropping fast. Because of the fog that came through earlier, during the single hour of weak twilight now passing for their day, the foreshortened masts — the three topmasts, topgallants, upper rigging, and highest spars have been removed and stored to cut down on the danger of falling ice and to reduce the chances of the ship capsizing because of the weight of ice on them — stand now like rudely pruned and topless trees reflecting the aurora that dances from one dimly seen horizon to the other. As Crozier watches, the jagged ice fields around the ship turn blue, then bleed violet, then glow as green as the hills of his childhood in northern Ireland. Almost a mile off the starboard bow, the gigantic floating ice mountain that hides *Terror*'s sister ship, *Erebus,* from view seems for a brief, false moment to radiate colour from within, glowing from its own cold, internal fires.

Pulling up his collar and tilting his head back, out of forty years' habit of checking the status of masts and rigging, Crozier notices that the stars overhead burn cold and steady but those near the horizon not only flicker but shift when stared at, moving in short spurts to the left, then to the right, then jiggling up and down. Crozier has seen this before — in the far south with Ross as well as in these waters on earlier expeditions. A scientist on that south polar trip, a man who spent the first winter in the ice there grinding and polishing lenses for his own telescope, had told Crozier that the perturbation of the stars was probably due to rapidly shifting refraction in the cold air lying heavy but uneasy over the ice-covered seas and unseen frozen landmasses. In other words, over new continents never before seen by the eyes of man. Or at least, Crozier thinks, in this northern arctic, by the eyes of white men.

Crozier and his friend and then-commander James Ross had found just such a previously undiscovered continent — Antarctica — less than five years earlier. They named the sea, inlets, and landmass after Ross. They named mountains after their sponsors and friends. They named the two volcanoes they could see on the horizon after their two ships — these same two ships — calling the smoking mountains Erebus and Terror. Crozier was surprised they hadn't named some major piece of geography after the ship's cat.

They named nothing after him. There is, on this October winter's dark-day evening in 1847, no arctic or antarctic continent, island, bay, inlet, range of mountains, ice shelf, volcano, or fucking floeberg which bears the name of Francis Rawdon Moira Crozier.

Crozier doesn't give the slightest God-damn. Even as he thinks this, he realizes that he's a little bit drunk. *Well,* he thinks, automatically adjusting his balance to the icy deck now canted twelve degrees to starboard and down eight degrees by the bow, *I've been drunk more often than not now for three years, haven't I? Drunk ever since Sophia. But I'm still a better sailor and captain drunk than that poor, unlucky bastard Franklin ever was sober. Or his rosy-cheeked lisping pet poodle Fitzjames, for that matter.*

Crozier shakes his head and walks down the icy deck forward to the bow and toward the only man on watch he can make out in the flickering light from the aurora.

It is short, rat-faced Cornelius Hickey, caulker's mate. The men look all the same out here on watch in the dark, since they're all issued the same cold-weather slops: layers of flannel and wool covered with a heavy waterproof greatcoat, bulbous mittens protruding from voluminous sleeves, their Welsh wigs — heavy watch caps with floppy ears — pulled tight, often with long comforters — scarves — wrapped around their heads until only the tips of their frostbitten noses are visible. But each man layers or wears his cold-weather slops slightly differently — adding a comforter from home, perhaps, or an extra Welsh wig tugged down over the first, or perhaps colorful gloves lovingly knit by a mother or wife or sweetheart peeking out from under the Royal Navy outer mittens — and Crozier has learned to tell all fifty-nine of his surviving officers and men apart, even at a distance outside and in the dark.

Hickey is staring fixedly out beyond the icicle-sheathed bowsprit, the foremost ten feet of which are now embedded in a ridge of sea ice, as HMS *Terror*'s stern has been forced up by the ice pressure and the bow is pushed lower. Hickey is so lost in thought or cold that the caulker's mate doesn't notice his captain's approach until Crozier joins him at a railing that has become an altar of ice and snow. The lookout's shotgun is propped against that altar. No man wants to touch metal out here in the cold, not even through mittens.

Hickey starts slightly as Crozier leans close to him at the railing. *Terror*'s captain can't see the twenty-six-year-old's face, but a puff of his breath — instantly turning into a cloud of ice crystals reflecting the aurora — appears beyond the thick circle of the smaller man's multiple comforters and Welsh wig.

Men traditionally don't salute during the winter in the ice, not even the casual knuckling of the forehead an officer receives at sea, but the thick-clad Hickey does that odd little shuffle and shrug and head dip by which the men acknowledge their captain's presence while outside. Because of the cold, the watches have been cut down from four hours to two — God knows, thinks Crozier, we have enough men for that on this overcrowded ship, even with the lookouts doubled — and he can tell just by Hickey's slow movements that he's half-frozen. As many times as he's told the lookouts that they have to keep moving on deck — walk, run in place, jump up and down if they have to, all the while keeping their attention on the ice — they still tend to stand immobile for the majority of their watch, just as if they were in the South Seas wearing their tropical cotton and watching for mermaids.

"Captain."

"Mr. Hickey. Anything?"

"Nothing since them shots . . . that one shot . . . almost two hours ago, sir. Just a while ago I heard, I think I heard . . . maybe a scream, something, Captain . . . from out beyond the ice mountain. I reported it to Lieutenant Irving, but he said it was probably just the ice acting up."

Crozier had been told about the sound of the shot from the direction of *Erebus* and had quickly come up on deck two hours ago, but there'd been no repetition of the sound and he'd sent no messenger to the other ship nor anyone out on the ice to investigate. To go out on the frozen sea in the dark now with that . . . *thing* . . . waiting in the jumble of pressure ridges and tall sastrugi was certain death. Messages were passed between the ships now only during those dwindling minutes of half-light around noon. In a few days, there would be no real day at all, only arctic night. Round-the-clock night. One hundred days of night.

"Perhaps it was the ice," says Crozier, wondering why Irving hadn't reported the possible scream. "The shot as well. Only the ice."

"Yes, Captain. The ice it is, sir."

Neither man believes it — a musket shot or shotgun blast has a distinctive sound, even from a mile away, and sound travels almost supernaturally far and clearly this far north — but it's true that the ice pack squeezing ever more tightly against *Terror* is always rumbling, moaning, cracking, snapping, roaring, or screaming.

The screams bother Crozier the most, waking him from his hour or so of sound sleep each night. They sound too much like his mother's crying in her last days . . . of that and his old aunt's tales of banshees wailing in the night, predicting the death of someone in the house. Both had kept him awake as a boy.

Crozier turns slowly. His eyelashes are already rimmed with ice, and his upper lip is crusted with frozen breath and snot. The men have learned to keep their beards tucked far under their comforters and sweaters, but frequently they must resort to hacking away hair that has frozen to their clothing. Crozier, like most of the officers, continues to shave every morning, although, in the effort to conserve coal, the "hot water" his steward brings him tends to be just barely melted ice, and shaving can be a painful business.

"Is Lady Silence still on deck?" asks Crozier.

"Oh, yes, Captain, she's almost always up here," says Hickey, whispering now as if it made a difference. Even if Silence could hear them, she couldn't understand their English. But the men believe — more and more every day the thing on the ice stalks them — that the young Esquimaux woman is a witch with secret powers.

"She's at the port station with Lieutenant Irving," adds Hickey.

"Lieutenant Irving? His watch should have been over an hour ago."

"Aye, sir. But wherever Lady Silence is these days, there's the lieutenant, sir, if you don't mind me mentioning it. She don't go below, he don't go below. Until he has to, I mean. . . . None of us can stay out here as long as that wi— . . . that woman."

"Keep your eyes on the ice, and your mind on your job, Mr. Hickey."

Crozier's gruff voice makes the caulker's mate start again, but he shuffles his shrug salute and turns his white nose back toward the darkness beyond the bow.

Crozier strides up the deck toward the port lookout post. The previous month, he prepared the ship for winter after three weeks of false hope of escape in August. Crozier had once again ordered the lower spars to be swung around along the parallel axis of the ship, using them as a ridgepole. Then they had reconstructed the tent pyramid to cover most of the main deck, rebuilding the wooden rafters that had been stowed below during their few weeks of optimism. But even though the men work hours every day shoveling avenues through the foot or so of snow left for insulation on deck, hacking away ice with picks and chisels, clearing out the spindrift that has come under the canvas roof, and finally putting lines of sand down for traction, there always remains a glaze of ice. Crozier's movement up the tilted and canted deck is sometimes more a graceful half-skating motion than a stride.

The appointed port lookout for this watch, midshipman Tommy Evans — Crozier identifies the youngest man on board by the absurd green stocking cap, obviously made by the boy's mother, that Evans always pulls down over his bulky Welsh wig — has moved ten paces astern to allow Third Lieutenant Irving and Silence some privacy.

This makes Captain Crozier want to kick someone — everyone — in the arse.

The Esquimaux woman looks like a short round bear in her furry parka, hood, and pants. She has her back half turned to the tall lieutenant. But Irving is crowded close to her along the rail — not quite touching, but closer than an officer and gentleman would stand to a lady at a garden party or on a pleasure yacht.

"Lieutenant Irving." Crozier didn't mean to put quite so much bark into the greeting, but he's not unhappy when the young man levitates as if poked by the point of a sharp blade, almost loses his balance, grabs the iced railing with his left hand, and — as he insists on doing despite now knowing the proper protocol of a ship in the ice — salutes with his right hand.

It's a pathetic salute, thinks Crozier, and not just because the bulky mittens, Welsh wig, and layers of cold-weather slops make young Irving look something like a saluting walrus, but also because the lad has let his comforter fall away from his clean-shaven face — perhaps to show Silence how handsome he is — and now two long icicles dangle below his nostrils, making him look even more like a walrus.

"As you were," snaps Crozier. *God-damn fool,* he mentally adds.

Irving stands rigid, glances at Silence — or at least at the back of her hairy hood — and opens his mouth to speak. Evidently he can think of nothing to say. He closes his mouth. His lips are as white as his frozen skin.

"This isn't your watch, Lieutenant," says Crozier, hearing the whip-crack in his voice again.

"Aye, aye, sir. I mean, no, sir. I mean, the captain is correct, sir. I mean . . ." Irving clamps his mouth shut again, but the effect is ruined somewhat by the chattering of his teeth. In this cold, teeth can shatter after two or three hours — actually explode — sending shrapnel of bone and enamel flying inside the cavern of one's clenched jaws. Sometimes, Crozier knows from experience, you can hear the enamel cracking just before the teeth explode.

"Why are you still out here, John?"

Irving tries to blink, but his eyelids are literally frozen open. "You ordered me to watch over our guest . . . to look out for . . . to take care of Silence, Captain."

Crozier's sigh emerges as ice crystals that hang in the air for a second and then fall to the deck like so many minuscule diamonds. "I didn't mean every *minute*, Lieutenant. I told you to watch her, report to me on what she does, to keep her out of mischief and harm's way on the ship, and to see that none of the men do anything to . . . compromise her. Do you think she's in danger of being compromised out here on deck, Lieutenant?"

"No, Captain." Irving's sentence sounds more like a question than an answer.

"Do you know how long it takes for exposed flesh to freeze out here, Lieutenant?"

"No, Captain. I mean, yes, Captain. Rather quickly, sir, I think."

"You should know, Lieutenant Irving. You've had frostbite six times already, and it's not even officially winter yet."

Lieutenant Irving nods dolefully.

"It takes *less than a minute* for an exposed finger or thumb — or any fleshy appendage — to freeze solid," continues Crozier, who knows that this is a load of horse cobblers. It takes much longer than that at a mere fifty below, but he hopes that Irving doesn't know this. "After that, the exposed member will snap off like an icicle," adds Crozier.

"Yes, Captain."

"So do you *really* think there's any chance that our visitor might be . . . *compromised* . . . out here on deck, Mr. Irving?"

Irving seems to be thinking about this before replying. It's possible, Crozier realizes, that the third lieutenant has put far too much thought into this equation already.

"Go below, John," says Crozier. "And see Dr. McDonald about your face and fingers. I swear to God that if you've gotten seriously frostbitten again, I'll dock you a month's Discovery Service pay and write your mother to boot."

"Yes, Captain. Thank you, sir." Irving starts to salute again, thinks better of it, and ducks under the canvas toward the main ladderway with one hand still half raised. He does not look back at Silence.

Crozier sighs again. He likes John Irving. The lad had volunteered — along with two of his mates from the HMS *Excellent,* Second Lieutenant Hodgson and First Mate Hornby — but the *Excellent* was a damned three-decker that was old before Noah had fuzz around his dongle. The ship had been mastless and permanently moored in Portsmouth, Crozier knew, for more than fifteen years, serving as a training vessel for the Royal Navy's most promising gunners. *Unfortunately, gentlemen,* Crozier had told the boys during their first day aboard — the captain had been more than usually drunk that day — *if you look around, you'll notice that while* Terror *and* Erebus *were both built as bombardment ships, gentlemen, neither has a single gun between them. We are, young volunteers from* Excellent *— unless one counts the Marines' muskets and the shotguns secured in the Spirit Room — as gunless as a newborn babe. As gunless as fucking Adam in his fucking birthday suit. In other words, gentlemen, you gunnery experts are about as useful to this expedition as teats would be on a boar.*

Crozier's sarcasm that day hadn't dampened the young gunnery officers' enthusiasm — Irving and the other two remained more eager than ever to go get frozen in the ice for several winters. Of course, that had been on a warm May day in England in 1845.

"And now the poor young pup is in love with an Esquimaux witch," Crozier mutters aloud.

As if understanding his words, Silence turns slowly toward him.

Usually her face is invisible down the deep tunnel of her hood, or her features are masked by the wide ruff of wolf hair, but tonight Crozier can see her tiny nose, large eyes, and full mouth. The pulse of the aurora is reflected in those black eyes.

She's not attractive to Captain Francis Rawdon Moira Crozier; she has too much of the savage about her to be seen as fully human, much less as physically attractive — even to a Presbyterian Irishman — and besides that, his mind and lower regions are still filled with clear memories of Sophia Cracroft. But Crozier can see why Irving, far from home and family and any sweetheart of his own, might fall in love with this heathen woman. Her strangeness alone — and perhaps even the grim circumstances of her arrival and the death of her male companion, so strangely intertwined with the first attacks from that monstrous entity out there in the dark — must be like a flame to the fluttering moth of so hopeless a young romantic as Third Lieutenant John Irving.

Crozier, on the other hand, as he discovered both in Van Diemen's Land in 1840 and again for the final time in England in the months before this expedition sailed, is too old for romance. And too Irish. And too common.

Right now he just wishes this young woman would take a walk out onto the dark ice and not return.

Crozier remembers the day four months earlier when Dr. McDonald had reported to Franklin and him after examining her, on the same afternoon the Esquimaux man with her had died choking in his own blood. McDonald said, in his medical opinion, the Esquimaux girl appeared to be between fifteen and twenty years old — it was so hard to tell with native peoples — had experienced menarche, but was, by all indications, *virgo intacta*. Also, Dr. McDonald reported, the reason that the girl had not spoken or made a sound — even after her father or husband had been shot and lay dying — was because she had no tongue. In Dr. McDonald's opinion, her tongue had not been sliced off but had been chewed off near its root, either by Silence herself or by someone or something else.

Crozier had been astonished — not so much by the fact of the missing tongue, but from hearing that the Esquimaux wench was a virgin. He'd spent enough time in the northern arctic — especially during Parry's expedition, which wintered near an Esquimaux village — to know that the local natives took sexual intercourse so lightly that men would offer their wives and daughters to whalers or Discovery Service explorers in exchange for the cheapest trinket. Sometimes, Crozier knew, the women just offered themselves up for the fun of it, giggling and chatting with other women or children even as the sailors strained and puffed and moaned between the laughing women's legs. They were like animals. The furs and hairy hides they wore might as well be their own beastlike skins as far as Francis Crozier was concerned.

The captain raises his gloved hand to the bill of his cap, secured under two wraps of heavy comforter and therefore impossible to doff or tip, and says, "My compliments to you, madam, and I would suggest you consider going below to your quarters soon. It's getting a bit nippy out here."

Silence stares at him. She does not blink, although somehow her long lashes are free of ice. She does not, of course, speak. She watches him.

Crozier symbolically tips his hat again and continues his tour around the deck, climbing to the ice-raised stern and then down the starboard side, pausing to speak to the other two men on watch, giving Irving time to get below and out of his cold-weather slops so that the captain doesn't seem to be following hard on his lieutenant's heels.

He's finishing his chat with the last shivering lookout, Able Seaman Shanks, when Private Wilkes, the youngest of the Marines aboard, comes rushing out from under the canvas. Wilkes has thrown on only two loose layers over his uniform, and his teeth begin chattering even before he delivers his message.

"Mr. Thompson's compliments to the captain, sir, and the engineer says that the captain should come down to the hold as quick as you might."

"Why?" If the boiler has finally broken down, Crozier knows, they are all dead.

"Begging the captain's pardon, sir, but Mr. Thompson says that the captain is needed because Seaman Manson is near to mutiny, sir."

Crozier stands up straight. "Mutiny?"

" 'Near to it' were Mr. Thompson's words, sir."

"Speak English, Private Wilkes."

"Manson won't carry no more sacks of coal past the Dead Room, sir. Nor go down in the hold no more. He says he respectfully refuses, Captain. He won't come up, but he's sitting on his arse at the bottom of the man-ladder and won't carry no more coal back to the boiler room."

"What is this nonsense?" Crozier feels the first stirrings of a familiar dark Irish anger.

"It's the ghosts, Captain," says Marine Private Wilkes through chattering teeth. "We all hear 'em when we're hauling coal or fetching something from deep stores. It's why the men won't go down there below orlop deck no more unless the officers order 'em to, sir. Something's down there in the hold, in the dark. Something's been scratching and banging from *inside* the ship, Captain. It ain't just the ice. Manson's sure it's his old mate Walker, him . . . it . . . and the other corpses stacked there in the Dead Room, clawing to get out."

Crozier checks his impulse to reassure the Marine private with facts. Young Wilkes might not find the facts so reassuring.

The first simple fact is that the scrabbling noise from the Dead Room is almost certainly the hundreds or thousands of large black rats feasting on Wilkes's frozen comrades. The Norway rats — as Crozier knows better than the young Marine — are nocturnal, which means that they're active day and night during the long arctic winter, and the creatures have teeth which constantly keep growing. This, in turn, means the God-damned vermin have to keep chewing. He has seen them chew through Royal Navy oak barrels, inch-thick tins, and even lead plating. The rats are having no more trouble down there with the frozen remains of Seaman Walker and his five unlucky comrades — including three of Crozier's finest officers — than a man would have chewing on a strip of frigid salted beef.

But Crozier doesn't think it's only the rats that Manson and the others are hearing.

Rats, as Crozier knows from the sad experience of thirteen winters in the ice, tend to eat one's friends quietly and efficiently, except for their frequent screeching as the blood-maddened and ravenous vermin turn on one another.

It's something else making the clawing and banging noises down on hold deck.

What Crozier decides not to remind Private Wilkes of is the second simple fact: while the lowest deck would normally be cold but safe there beneath the waterline or winter line of frozen sea ice, the pressure from the ice has forced *Terror*'s stern more than a dozen feet higher than it should be. The hull there is still locked in, but only by several hundred heaped tons of jagged sea ice and the added tons of snow the men have piled alongside to within a few feet of the railings so as to provide more insulation during the winter.

Something, Francis Crozier suspects, has dug down through these tons of snow and tunneled through the iron-hard slabs of ice to get at the hull of the ship. Somehow the thing has sensed which parts of the interior along the hull, such as the water-storage tanks, are lined with iron, and has found one of the few hollow outside storage areas — the Dead Room — that leads directly into the ship. And now it's banging and clawing to get in.

Crozier knows that there's only one thing on earth with that much power, deadly persistence, and malevolent intelligence. The monster on the ice is trying to get at them from below.

Without saying another word to Marine Private Wilkes, Captain Crozier goes below to sort things out.

2

FRANKLIN

He was — and always would be — the man who ate his shoes.

Four days before they were to sail, Captain Sir John Franklin contracted the influenza that had been going around, getting it, he was sure, not from one of the common sailors and stevedores loading the ships at London's docks, nor from any of his one hundred and thirty-four crew members and officers — they were all healthy as dray horses — but from some sickly sycophant in one of Lady Jane's circles of society friends.

The man who ate his shoes.

It was traditional for the wives of arctic heroes to sew a flag to be planted at some point farthest north, or in this case raised upon the completion of the expedition's transit of the North-West Passage, and Franklin's wife, Jane, was finishing her sewing of the silken Union Jack when he came home. Sir John came into the parlour and half collapsed onto the horsehair sofa near where she sat. Later he did not remember removing his boots, but someone must have — either Jane or one of the servants — for soon he was lying back and half dozing, his head aching, his stomach more unsteady than it had ever been at sea, and his skin burning with fever. Lady Jane was telling him about her busy day, never pausing in her recital. Sir John tried to listen as the fever carried him off on its uncertain tide.

He was the man who ate his shoes, and had been for twenty-three years, ever since he returned to England in 1822 after his first, failed overland expedition across northern Canada to find the North-West Passage. He remembered the sniggers and jokes upon his return. Franklin had eaten his shoes — and he'd eaten worse on that botched three-year journey, including *tripe-de-roche,* a disgusting gruel made from lichen scraped from rocks. Two years out and starving, he and his men — Franklin had dazedly divided his troop into three groups and left the other two bands to survive or die on their own — had boiled the uppers on their boots and shoes to survive. Sir John — he was just John then, he was knighted for incompetency after a later overland voyage and botched polar expedition by sea — had spent days in 1821 chewing on nothing more than scraps of untanned leather. His men had eaten their buffalo sleeping robes. Then some of them had moved on to other things.

But he had never eaten another man.

To this day, Franklin doubted whether others on his expedition, including his good friend and chief lieutenant Dr. John Richardson, had succeeded in resisting that temptation. Too much had happened while the parties were separated as they stumbled through the arctic wastes and forests, desperately trying to get back to Franklin's little improvised Fort Enterprise and the real forts, Providence and Resolution.

Nine white men and one Esquimaux dead. Nine dead out of the twenty-one men young Lieutenant John Franklin, thirty-three years old and pudgy and balding even then, had led out of Fort Resolution in 1819, plus one of the native guides they'd picked up along the way — Franklin had refused to let the man leave the expedition to forage for himself. Two of the men had been murdered in cold blood. At least one of them was, without doubt, devoured by others. But only one Englishman died. Only one real white man. All the rest were mere French *voyageurs* or Indians. This was success of a sort — only one white Englishman dead, even if all the others had been reduced to gibbering, bearded skeletons. Even if all the others survived only because George Back, that confounded, oversexed midshipman, had snowshoed 1,200 miles to bring back supplies and — more important than supplies — more Indians to feed and care for Franklin and his dying party.

That confounded Back. Not a good Christian at all. Arrogant. Not a true gentleman, despite his later being knighted for an arctic expedition sailing on this very same HMS *Terror* that Sir John now commanded.

On that expedition, Back's expedition, *Terror* had been flung fifty feet into the air by a rising tower of ice, then thrown down so violently that every oak plank in the hull sprang a leak. George Back brought the leaking boat all the way back to the coast of Ireland, beaching it just hours before it would have sunk. The crew had wrapped chains around it to squeeze the boards tight long enough for the vessel to get them home. All the men had scurvy — black gums, bleeding eyes, teeth falling out of their heads — and the madness and delusions that went with scurvy.

They'd knighted Back after that, of course. It's what England and the Admiralty did after you returned from a polar expedition that failed miserably, resulting in appalling loss of life; if you survived, they gave you a title and a parade. After Franklin returned from his second coastal-mapping expedition in the far north of North America in 1827, he was personally knighted by King George IV. The Geographical Society of Paris gave him a gold medal. He was awarded captaincy of the beautiful little 26-gun frigate HMS *Rainbow* and ordered to the Mediterranean, a destination to which every captain in the Royal Navy prayed nightly for posting. He proposed marriage to one of his dead wife Eleanor's dearest friends, the energetic, beautiful, and outspoken Jane Griffin.

"So I explained to Sir James over tea," Jane was saying, "that my darling Sir John's credit and reputation are infinitely dearer to me than any selfish enjoyment of my husband's society, even if he must be gone for four years . . . or five."

What was the name of that fifteen-year-old Copper Indian girl that Back was going to fight a duel over at their winter quarters of Fort Enterprise?

Greenstockings. That was it. Greenstockings.

That girl was evil. Beautiful, yes, but evil. She had no shame. Franklin himself, despite all efforts never to look her way, had seen her slip out of her heathen robes and walk naked across half the length of the cabin one moonlit night.

He was thirty-four years old at the time, but she was the first naked human female he had ever seen and even now the most beautiful. The dark skin. The breasts already heavy as globed fruit but also still those of an adolescent, the nipples not yet raised, the areolae strange, smooth dark-brown circles. It was an image Sir John had not been able to eradicate from his memory — try and pray as he might — in the quarter of a century since then. The girl had not the classic V of pubic hair that Franklin had later seen on his first wife, Eleanor — glimpsed only once, as she prepared for her bath, since Eleanor never allowed the slightest light to illuminate their rare lovemaking — or the sparser but wilder wheat-coloured nest that was part of the aging body of his current wife, Jane. No, the Indian girl Greenstockings had only a narrow but pure-black vertical escutcheon above her female parts. As delicate as a raven's feather. As pitch black as sin itself.

The Scotsman midshipman, Robert Hood, who had already fathered one bastard with a different Indian woman during that endless first winter at the cabin Franklin had named Fort Enterprise, had promptly fallen in love with teenaged Copper squaw Greenstockings. The girl had previously been lying with the other midshipman, George Back, but with Back gone hunting, she'd shifted her sexual allegiance to Hood with the ease known only to pagans and primitives.

Franklin could still remember the grunts of passion in the long night — not the passion of a few minutes, as he had experienced with Eleanor (never grunting or making a noise, of course, since no gentleman would do that), or even two brief bouts of passion, such as on that memorable night on his honeymoon with Jane; no, Hood and Greenstockings went at it half a dozen times. No sooner would Hood's and the girl's noises stop in the adjoining lean-to than they would begin again — laughter, low giggles, then soft moans, leading again to the louder cries as the brazen girl-woman urged Hood on.

Jane Griffin was thirty-six years old when she married the newly knighted Sir John Franklin on December 5, 1828. They honeymooned in Paris. Franklin did not especially like the city, nor did he like the French, but their hotel had been luxurious and the food very good.

Franklin had been in a sort of dread that during their travels on the continent they might run into that Roget fellow — Peter Mark, the one who gained some sort of literary attention by preparing to publish that silly dictionary or whatever it was — the same man who had once asked for Jane Griffin's hand, only to be rejected like all the other suitors had been in her younger years. Franklin had since peeked into Jane's diaries from that era — he rationalized his crime by thinking that she wanted him to find and read the many calfskin-bound volumes, why otherwise would she have left them in such an obvious place? — and saw, in his beloved's tight, perfect hand, the passage she had written on the day Roget had finally married someone else — "*the romance of my life is gone.*"

Robert Hood had been making noises with Greenstockings for six endless arctic nights when his fellow midshipman George Back returned from a hunting party with the Indians. The two men arranged a duel to the death at sunrise — around 10:00 a.m. — the next morning.

Franklin had not known what to do. The corpulent lieutenant was unable to exert any discipline over the surly *voyageurs* or the contemptuous Indians, much less able to control the headstrong Hood or the impulsive Back.

Both midshipmen were artists and mapmakers. From that time on, Franklin had never trusted an artist. When the sculptor in Paris did Lady Jane's hands and the perfumed sodomite here in London had come for almost a month to paint her official oil portrait, Franklin had never left the men alone with her.

Back and Hood were meeting at dawn for a duel to the death and there was nothing John Franklin could do but hide in the cabin and pray that the resulting death or injury would not destroy the last vestige of sanity in his already compromised expedition. His orders had not specified that he should bring *food* on the 1,200-mile arctic overland, coastal sea, and river trek. Out of his own pocket, he'd provided enough supplies to feed the sixteen men for one day. Franklin had assumed the Indians would then hunt for them and feed them adequately, just as the guides carried his bags and paddled his birch-bark canoe.

The birch-bark canoes had been a mistake. Twenty-three years after the fact, he was willing to concede that — to himself, at least. After just a few days in the ice-clogged waters along the northern coast, reached more than a year and a half after their departure from Fort Resolution, the flimsy vessels had started to come apart.

Franklin, his eyes closed, his brow burning, his head throbbing, half-listening to the uninterrupted stream of Jane's chatter, remembered the morning when he'd lain in his heavy sleeping bag and squeezed his eyes shut as Back and Hood had stepped off their fifteen paces outside the cabin, then turned to fire. The confounded Indians and confounded *voyageurs* — equally savage in many ways — were treating the duel to the death as entertainment. Greenstockings, Franklin remembered, was radiant that morning with an almost erotic glow.

Lying in his bag, his hands over his ears, Franklin still heard the call to pace, the call to turn, the call to aim, the command to fire.

Then two clicks. Then laughter from the crowd.

During the night, the old Scottish seaman calling the pacing, that tough and ungentlemanly John Hepburn, had unloaded charge and balls from the carefully prepared pistols.

Deflated by the unceasing laughter of the mob of *voyageurs* and knee-slapping Indians, Hood and Back had stalked off in opposite directions. Shortly after that, Franklin ordered George Back to return to the forts to purchase more provisions from the Hudson's Bay Company. Back was gone most of the winter.

Franklin had eaten his shoes and had subsisted on lichen scraped from rocks — a slime meal that would make a self-respecting English dog vomit — but he had never partaken of human flesh.

A long year after the forestalled duel, in Richardson's party after Franklin's group had separated from it, that surly, half-mad Iroquois on the expedition, Michel Teroahaute, shot the midshipman artist and mapmaker Robert Hood in the centre of his forehead.

A week before the murder, the Indian had brought back a strong-tasting haunch of meat to the starving party, insisting that it had come from a wolf that had either been gored to death by a caribou or killed by Teroahaute himself using a deer horn — the Indian's story kept changing. The ravenous party had cooked and eaten the meat, but not before Dr. Richardson noticed a slight hint of a tattoo on the skin. The doctor later told Franklin that he was certain that Teroahaute had doubled back to the body of one of the *voyageurs* who had died that week on the trek.

The starving Indian and the dying Hood were alone when Richardson, off scraping lichen from the rocks, had heard the shot. *Suicide,* Teroahaute had insisted, but Dr. Richardson, who had attended on more than a few suicides, knew that the position of the ball in Robert Hood's brain had not come from a self-inflicted gunshot.

Now the Indian armed himself with a British bayonet, a musket, two fully charged and half-cocked pistols, and a knife as long as his forearm. The two non-Indians remaining — Hepburn and Richardson — had only a small pistol and one untrustworthy musket between them.

Richardson, now one of the most respected scientists and surgeons in England, friend of the poet Robert Burns, but then only a promising expedition surgeon and naturalist, waited until Michel Teroahaute returned from a foraging trip, made sure his arms were full of firewood, and then lifted his pistol and cold-bloodedly shot the Indian through the head.

Dr. Richardson later admitted to eating the dead Hood's buffalo robe, but neither Hepburn nor Richardson — the only survivors of their party — ever mentioned what else they might have eaten in the next week of arduous trekking during their return to Fort Enterprise.

At Fort Enterprise, Franklin and his party were too weak to stand or walk. Richardson and Hepburn seemed strong in comparison.

He might be the man who had eaten his shoes, but John Franklin had never . . .

"Cook is preparing roast beef tonight, my darling. Your favorite. Since she's new — I am certain that the Irish woman was padding our accounts, stealing is as natural as drinking to the Irish — I reminded her that you insist that it must be rare enough to bleed at the touch of the carving knife."

Franklin, floating on an ebbing tide of fever, tried to formulate words in response, but the surges of headache, nausea, and heat were too great. He was sweating through his undershirt and still-fixed collar.

"Admiral Sir Thomas Martin's wife sent us a delightful card today and a wonderful bouquet of flowers. She's the last to be heard from, but I must say the roses are beautiful in the foyer. Did you see them? Did you have much time to chat with Admiral Martin at the reception? Of course, he is not that important, is he? Even as Controller of the Navy? Certainly not as distinguished as the First Lord or First Commissioners, much less your Arctic Council friends."

Captain Sir John Franklin had many friends; everyone liked Captain Sir John Franklin. But no one respected him. For decades, Franklin acknowledged the former fact and avoided the latter, but he now knew it to be true. Everyone liked him. No one respected him.

Not after Van Diemen's Land. Not after the Tasmanian prison and the botch he had made of that.

Eleanor, his first wife, had been dying when he left her to go on his second major expedition.

He knew she was dying. She knew she was dying. Her consumption — and the knowledge she would die from it long before her husband would die in battle or on expedition — had been with them like a third party at their wedding ceremony. In the twenty-two months of their marriage, she had given him a daughter, his only child, young Eleanor.

A small, frail woman in body — but almost frightening in spirit and energy — his first wife had told him to go on his second expedition to find the North-West Passage, this trip by land and sea to follow the North American coastline, even while she was coughing up blood and knowing that the end was near. She said that it would be better for her if he were elsewhere. He believed her. Or at least he believed that it would be better for himself.

A deeply religious man, John Franklin had prayed that Eleanor would die before his departure date. She hadn't. He left on February 16, 1825, wrote his darling many letters while in transit to Great Slave Lake, posted them in New York City and Albany, and learned of her passing on April 24, at the British Naval station at Penetanguishene. She had died shortly after his ship left England.

When he returned from this expedition in 1827, Eleanor's friend Jane Griffin was waiting for him.

The Admiralty reception had been less than a week ago — no, just precisely a week ago, before this confounded influenza. Captain Sir John Franklin and all his officers and mates from *Erebus* and *Terror* had attended, of course. So had the civilians on the expedition — *Erebus*'s ice master, James Reid, and *Terror*'s ice master, Thomas Blanky, along with the paymasters, surgeons, and pursers.

Sir John had looked dashing in his new blue swallow-tailed coat, blue gold-striped trousers, gold-fringed epaulettes, ceremonial sword, and Nelson-era cocked hat. The commander of his flagship *Erebus,* James Fitzjames, often called the handsomest man in the Royal Navy, looked as striking and humble as the war hero he was. Fitzjames had charmed everyone that night. Francis Crozier, as always, had looked stiff, awkward, melancholic, and slightly inebriated.

But Jane was wrong — the members of the "Arctic Council" were not Sir John's friends. The Arctic Council, in reality, did not exist. It was an honorary society rather than a real institution, but it was also the most select Old Boys club in all of England.

They'd mingled at the reception, Franklin, his top officers, and the tall, gaunt, grey members of the legendary Arctic Council.

To gain membership to the Council, all one had to do was command an expedition to the farthest arctic north . . . and survive.

Viscount Melville — the first notable in the long receiving line that had left Franklin uncharacteristically sweating and tongue-tied — was First Lord of the Admiralty and the sponsor of their sponsor, Sir John Barrow. But Melville was not an old arctic hand.

The true Arctic Council legends — most in their seventies — were, to the nervous Franklin that night, more like the coven of witches in *Macbeth* or like some cluster of grey ghosts than like living men. Every one of these men had preceded Franklin in searching for the Passage, and all had returned alive, yet not fully alive.

Did anyone, Franklin wondered that evening, *really* return alive after wintering in the arctic regions?

Sir John Ross, his Scotsman's face showing more sharp facets than an iceberg, had eyebrows leaping out like the ruffs and feathers of those penguins his nephew Sir James Clark Ross had described after his trip to the south arctic. Ross's voice was as rough as a holystone dragged across a splintered deck.

Sir John Barrow, older than God and twice as powerful. The father of serious British arctic exploration. All others there that night, even the white-haired septuagenarians, were boys . . . Barrow's boys.

Sir William Parry, a gentleman above gentlemen even when among royalty, who had tried four times to force the Passage only to watch men die and his *Fury* squeezed and smashed and sunk.

Sir James Clark Ross, newly knighted, was also newly wed to a wife who made him swear off any more expeditions. He would have had Franklin's job of commander of this expedition if he'd wanted it, and both men knew it. Ross and Crozier stood slightly separate from the others, drinking and talking as softly as conspirators.

That confounded Sir George Back; Franklin hated sharing sirdom with a mere midshipman who once served under him, and a womanizer at that. On this gala night, Captain Sir John Franklin almost wished that Hepburn hadn't taken the powder and shot out of the dueling pistols twenty-five years earlier. Back was the youngest member of the Arctic Council and seemed happier and smugger than any of the others, even after suffering the battering and near-sinking of HMS *Terror*.

Captain Sir John Franklin was a teetotaler, but after three hours of champagne, wine, brandy, sherry, and whiskey, the other men began to relax, the laughter around him grew stronger and the conversation in the grand hall less formal, and Franklin began to feel calmer, realizing that all this reception, all the gold buttons, silk cravats, gleaming epaulettes, fine food, cigars, and smiles were for *him*. This time, it was all about *him*.

So it was a shock when the older Ross pulled him aside almost abruptly and began to bark questions at him through the cigar smoke and the glint of candlelight off crystal.

"Franklin, why in hell's name are you taking one hundred and thirty-four men?" rasped the holystone across rough wood.

Captain Sir John Franklin blinked. "It's a major expedition, Sir John."

"Too bloody major, if you ask me. It's hard enough to get thirty men across the ice, into boats, and back to civilization when something goes wrong. A hundred thirty-four men . . ." The old explorer made a rude noise, clearing his throat as if he was going to spit.

Franklin smiled and nodded, wishing the old man would leave him alone.

"And your age," continued Ross. "You're sixty, for God's sake."

"Fifty-nine," Franklin said stiffly. "Sir."

The elder Ross smiled thinly but looked more like an iceberg than ever. "*Terror* is what? Three hundred thirty tons? *Erebus* something like three hundred seventy?"

"Three hundred seventy-two for my flagship," said Franklin. "Three hundred twenty-six for *Terror*."

"And a draft of nineteen feet each, isn't that right?"

"Yes, m'lord."

"That's buggering insane, Franklin. Your ships will be the deepest draft vessels ever sent on an arctic expedition. Everything we know about those regions has shown us that the waters where you're headed are shallow, filled with shoals, rocks, and hidden ice. My *Victory* only drew a fathom and a half and we couldn't get over the bar of the harbour where we wintered. George Back all but ripped his bottom out on the ice with your *Terror*."

"Both ships have been strengthened, Sir John," said Franklin. He could feel sweat running down his ribs and chest onto his portly belly. "They're now the strongest ice ships in the world."

"And what is all the nonsense about steam and locomotive engines?"

"Not nonsense, m'lord," said Franklin and could hear the condescension in his own voice. He knew nothing about steam himself, but he had two good engineers on the expedition and Fitzjames, who was part of the new Steam Navy. "These are powerful engines, Sir John. They'll see us through the ice where sail has failed."

Sir John Ross snorted. "Your steam machines aren't even maritime engines, are they, Franklin?"

"No, Sir John. But they're the best steam engines the London and Greenwich Railway could sell us. Converted for marine use. Powerful beasts, sir."

Ross sipped his whiskey. "Powerful if you're planning to lay down rails along the North-West Passage and take a God-damned locomotive across it."

Franklin chuckled good-naturedly at this, but he saw no humor in the comment and the obscenity offended him deeply. He often could not tell when others were being humorous, and he had no sense of humor himself.

"But not really so powerful," continued Ross. "That one-point-five-ton machine they crammed into the hold of your *Erebus* only produces twenty-five horsepower. Crozier's engine is less efficient . . . twenty horsepower, maximum. The ship that's towing you beyond Scotland — *Rattler* — produces two hundred twenty horsepower with its smaller steam engine. It's a *marine* engine, built for sea."

Franklin had nothing to say to that, so he smiled. To fill the silence he signaled a passing waiter carrying glasses of champagne. Then, since it was against all his principles to drink alcohol, all he could do was stand there holding the glass, occasionally glancing at the flattening champagne, and wait for some opportunity to get rid of it without being noticed.

"Think of all the extra provisions you could have crammed in the holds of your two ships if those damned engines weren't there," persisted Ross.

Franklin looked around as if seeking rescue, but everyone was in animated conversation with someone else. "We have more than adequate stores for three years, Sir John," he said at last. "Five to seven years if we have to go on short rations." He smiled again, trying to charm that flinty face. "And both *Erebus* and *Terror* have central heating, Sir John. Something I'm sure you would have appreciated on your *Victory*."

Sir John Ross's pale eyes gleamed coldly. "*Victory* was crushed like an egg by the ice, Franklin. Fancy steam heat wouldn't have helped that, would it?"

Franklin looked around, trying to catch Fitzjames's eye. Even Crozier's. Anyone to come to his rescue. No one seemed to notice the old Sir John and the fat Sir John huddled here in such earnest, if one-sided, conversation. A waiter passed, and Franklin set his untouched glass of champagne on his tray. Ross studied Franklin through slitted eyes.

"And how much coal does it take just to heat one of your ships for a day up there?" pressed the old Scotsman.

"Oh, I don't really know, Sir John," said Franklin with a winning smile. He really did *not* know. Nor especially care. The engineers were in charge of the steam engines and coal. The Admiralty would have planned well for them.

"*I* know," said Ross. "You'll use up to one hundred fifty pounds of coal a day just to keep the hot water moving to heat the crew's quarters. Half a *ton* of your precious coal a day just to keep steam up. If you're under way — expect about four knots out of those ugly bombardment ships — you'll be burning two to three *tons* of coal a day. Much more if you're trying to force your way through pack ice. How much coal are you *carrying,* Franklin?"

Captain Sir John waved his hand in what he realized was a dismissive — and almost effeminate — gesture. "Oh, somewhere around two hundred tons, m'lord."

Ross squinted again. "Ninety tons each for *Erebus* and *Terror,* to be precise," he rasped. "And that's when you're topped off in Greenland, before you cross Baffin Bay, much less get into the real ice."

Franklin smiled and said nothing.

"Say you arrive at where you winter in the ice with seventy-five percent of your ninety tons unburned," continued Ross, boring ahead like a ship through soft ice, "that leaves you what . . . how many days' steam under normal conditions, not ice conditions? A dozen days? Thirteen days? A fortnight?"

Captain Sir John Franklin had not the slightest idea. His mind, although professional and nautical, simply did not work that way. Perhaps his eyes revealed his sudden panic — not over coal but over appearing an idiot in front of Sir John Ross — for the old mariner clamped a steel vise grip on Franklin's shoulder. When Ross leaned closer, Captain Sir John Franklin could smell the whiskey on his breath.

"What are the Admiralty's plans for your rescue, Franklin?" rasped Ross. His voice was low. All about them was the laughter and chatter of the reception in its late hour.

"Rescue?" Franklin said, blinking. The idea that the two most modern ships in the world — reinforced for ice, powered by steam, provisioned for five years or more in the ice, and manned by crews handpicked by Sir John Barrow — would or could require rescue simply did not register in Franklin's brain. The idea was absurd.

"Do you have plans to cache depots along your way in through the islands?" whispered Ross.

"Caches?" said Franklin. "Leave our provisions along the way? Why on earth would I do that?"

"So you can get your men and boats to food and shelter if you have to take to the ice and walk out," Ross said fiercely, eyes gleaming.

"Why would we walk back toward Baffin Bay?" asked Franklin. "Our objective is to complete the transit of the North-West Passage."

Sir John Ross had pulled his head back. His grip tightened on Franklin's upper arm. "Then there's no rescue ship or plan in place?"

"No."

Ross grabbed Franklin's other arm and squeezed so tightly that the portly Captain Sir John almost winced.

"Then, laddie," whispered Ross, "if we've not heard from ye by 1848, I'll come looking for you myself. I swear it."

Franklin slammed awake.

He was soaked with sweat. He felt dizzy and weak. His heart was pounding, and with each reverberation his headache tolled like a church bell against the inside of his skull.

He looked down at himself in horror. Silk covered the lower half of his body.

"What is this?" he cried in alarm. "What is this? There's a flag thrown over me!"

Lady Jane stood, aghast. "You looked cold, John. You were shivering. I put it over you as a blanket."

"My God!" cried Captain Sir John Franklin. "My God, woman, do you know what you've done? Don't you know they lay the Union Jack over a corpse!"

3

CROZIER

Captain Crozier descends the short ladder to the lower deck, pushes through the sealed double doors, and almost staggers in the sudden blast of warmth. Even though the circulating hot-water heat has been off for hours, body heat from more than fifty men and residual warmth from cooking have kept the temperature here on the lower deck high — just below freezing — almost 80 degrees warmer than outside. The effect on someone who's been out on deck for half an hour is the equivalent of walking into a sauna fully clothed.

Since he's continuing down to the unheated orlop and hold decks and thus keeping his cold-weather slops on, Crozier doesn't tarry long here in the heat. But he does pause for a moment — as any captain would — taking the time to glance around and make sure that everything hasn't gone to hell in the half hour he's been away.

Despite the fact that this is the only berthing, eating, and living deck on the ship, it's still as dark as a working Welsh mine with its small skylights snowed over in the daytime and the night now twenty-two hours long. Whale-oil lamps, lanterns, or candles throw small cones of illumination here and there, but mostly the men make their way through the gloom by memory, remembering where to dodge the innumerable half-seen heaps and hanging masses of stored food, clothing, gear, and other men sleeping in their hammocks. When all the hammocks go up — fourteen inches allowed per man — there will be no room to walk at all except for two 18-inch-wide aisles along the hull on either side. But only a few hammocks are up now — men catching some sleep before late watches — and the din of conversation, laughter, cursing, coughing, and Mr. Diggle's inspired clankings and obscenities is loud enough to drown out some of the press and moan of the ice.

The ship's diagrams show seven feet of clearance, but in reality, between the heavy ship's timbers overhead and the tons of lumber and extra wood stored on racks hanging from those timbers, there's less than six feet of headroom on this lower deck and the few truly tall men on *Terror,* like the coward Manson waiting below, have to walk in a perpetual hunched-over posture. Francis Crozier is not that tall. Even with his cap and comforter on, he doesn't have to duck his head as he turns.

To his right and running aft from where Crozier stands is what looks to be a low, dark, narrow tunnel, but it is actually the companionway leading to the "officers' quarters," a warren of sixteen tiny sleeping cubicles and two cramped mess quarters for the officers and warrant officers. Crozier's cabin is the same size as the others' — six feet by five feet. The companionway is dark and barely two feet wide. Only one man can pass at a time, ducking his head to avoid hanging stores, and heavy men have to turn sideways to shuffle down the narrow passage.

The officers' quarters are crammed into 60 feet of the 96-foot length of the ship, and since *Terror* is only 28 feet wide here on the lower deck, the narrow companionway is the only straight-line access aft.

Crozier can see light from the Great Cabin at the stern, where — even in this Stygian cold and gloom — some of his surviving officers are relaxing at the long table, smoking their pipes or reading from the 1,200-volume library shelved there. The captain hears music playing: one of the metal disks for the hand organ playing a tune that had been popular in London music halls five years ago. Crozier knows that it's Lieutenant Hodgson playing the tune; it's his favorite, and it drives Lieutenant Edward Little, Crozier's executive officer and a lover of classical music, absolutely mad with irritation.

All apparently being well in officers' country, Crozier turns and glances forward. The regular crew's quarters take up the remaining third of the length of the ship — 36 feet — but into it are crammed 41 of the surviving able-bodied seamen and midshipmen from the original ship's muster of 44.

There are no classes being taught tonight and it's less than an hour until they will unfurl their hammocks and turn in, so the majority of the men are sitting on their sea chests or heaps of stowed material, smoking or talking in the dim light. The centre of the space is taken up by the gigantic Frazer's Patent Stove, where Mr. Diggle is baking biscuits. Diggle — the best cook in the fleet as far as Crozier is concerned and a prize, most literally, since Crozier had stolen the obstreperous cook right off Captain Sir John Franklin's flagship just before the expedition departed — is always cooking, usually biscuits, and curses and bangs and kicks and berates his assistants all the while. Men are literally scuttling near the giant stove, disappearing down the scuttle there to bring up stores from the lower decks, hurrying to avoid Mr. Diggle's voluble wrath.

Frazer's Patent Stove itself appears, to Crozier's eye, almost as large as the locomotive engine in the hold. Besides its gigantic oven and six large burners, the bulking iron contraption has a built-in desalinator and a prodigious hand pump to bring water in from either the ocean or the rows of huge water-storage tanks down in the hold. But both the sea outside and the water in the hold now are frozen solid, so the huge pots bubbling on Mr. Diggle's burners are busy melting chunks of ice chipped out of the water tanks below and hauled up for that purpose.

The captain can see, beyond the partition of Mr. Diggle's shelves and cupboards where forward bulwarks had once stood, the sick bay in the forepeak of the ship. For two years there had been no sick bay. The area was stacked from deck to beams with more crates and casks and those crewmen who needed to see the ship's surgeon or assistant surgeon at 7:30 a.m. lubber's time did so near Mr. Diggle's stove. But now, with the amount of stores depleted and the number of sick and injured men multiplying, the carpenters had created a more permanent and separate section of the forepeak to serve as sick bay. Still, the captain could see the tunnellike entrance through the crates where they'd made a space for Lady Silence to sleep.

That discussion had taken the better part of a day last June — Franklin had insisted that the Esquimaux woman not be allowed on his ship. Crozier had accepted her, but his discussion with his executive officer, Lieutenant Little, as to where to berth her had been almost absurd. Even an Esquimaux wench, they knew, would freeze to death on deck or on the lower two decks, which left only the main lower deck. She certainly could not sleep in the crew's berthing area, even though they had empty hammocks by this time thanks to that thing out on the ice.

In Crozier's day as a teenaged lad before the mast and then as a midshipman, women smuggled aboard were put in the lightless, almost airless stinking hawser room in the lowest and most forward part of the ship, within reach of the fo'c'sle for the lucky man or men who smuggled her aboard. But even last June, when Silence appeared, it was below zero in HMS *Terror*'s hawser room.

No, berthing her with the crew was not an idea to be considered.

Officers' country? Perhaps. There were empty cabins, with some of his officers dead and torn apart. But both Lieutenant Little and his captain had quickly agreed that the presence of a woman just a few thin partitions and sliding doors away from the sleeping men would be unhealthy.

What then? They couldn't assign her a sleeping place and then post an armed guard over her all the time.

It was Edward Little who'd come up with the idea of shifting some stores to make a little cave of a sleeping area for the woman in the forepeak where the sick bay would have been. The one person awake all night, every night, was Mr. Diggle — dutifully baking his biscuits and frying his breakfast meats — and if Mr. Diggle had ever had an eye for the ladies, it was apparent that day had long passed. Also, reasoned Lieutenant Little and Captain Crozier, the proximity to the Frazer's Patent Stove would help keep their guest warm.

It had succeeded in that, all right. Lady Silence was made sick by the heat, forcing her to sleep stark naked on her furs in her little crate-and-cask cave. The captain discovered this by accident and the image stayed with him.

Now Crozier takes a lantern from its hook, lights it, lifts the hatch, and goes down the ladder to the orlop deck before he starts to melt like one of those blocks of ice on the stove.

To say it's cold on the orlop deck would be the kind of understatement Crozier knows he used to make before he first voyaged to the arctic. A drop of six feet of ladder down from the lower deck has dropped the temperature at least sixty degrees. The darkness here is almost absolute.

Crozier takes the usual captain's minute to look around. The circle of light from his lantern is weak, illuminating mostly the fog of his breath in the air. All around him is the labyrinth of crates, hogsheads, tins, kegs, casks, coal sacks, and canvas-covered heaps crammed deck-to-beams with the ship's remaining provisions. Even without the lantern, Crozier could find his way through the dark and rat-screech here; he knows every inch of his ship. At times, especially late at night with the ice moaning, Francis Rawdon Moira Crozier realizes that HMS *Terror* is his wife, mother, bride, and whore. This intimate knowledge of a lady made of oak and iron, oakum and ballast, canvas and brass is the one true marriage he can and will ever know. How could he have thought differently with Sophia?

At other times, even later at night when the ice's moaning turns to screams, Crozier thinks that the ship has become his body and his mind. Out there — out beyond the decks and hull — lies death. Eternal cold. Here, even while frozen in the ice, there continues the heartbeat, however faint, of warmth and conversation and movement and sanity.

But traveling deeper into the ship, Crozier realizes, is like traveling too deeply into one's body or mind. What one encounters there may not be pleasant. The orlop deck is the belly. This is where the food and needed resources are stored, each thing packed away in the order of its presumed need, easy to hand for those driven down here by Mr. Diggle's shouts and blows. Lower, on the hold deck where he's headed, are the deep guts and kidneys, the water tanks and the majority of the coal storage and more provisions. But it's the mind analogy that bothers Crozier the most. Haunted and plagued by melancholia much of his life, knowing it as a secret weakness made worse by his twelve winters frozen in arctic darkness as an adult, feeling it recently triggered into active agony by Sophia Cracroft's rejection, Crozier thinks of the partially lighted and occasionally heated but livable lower deck as the sane part of himself. The brooding mental lower world of the orlop deck is where he spends too much of his time these days — listening to the ice scream, waiting for the metal bolts and beam fastenings to explode from the cold. The bottom hold deck below, with its terrible smells and its waiting Dead Room, is madness.

Crozier shakes such thoughts away. He looks down the orlop-deck aisle running forward between the piled casks and crates. The lantern's gleam is blocked by the bulkheads of the Bread Room and the aisles on either side constrict to tunnels even narrower than the officers' country companionway on the lower deck above. Here men must squeeze between the Bread Room and the sleeves holding the last sacks of *Terror*'s coal. The carpenter's storeroom is forward there on the starboard side, the boatswain's storeroom opposite on the port side.

Crozier turns and shines his lantern aft. Rats flee somewhat lethargically from the light, disappearing between casks of salt meat and crates of tinned provisions.

Even in the dim lantern's glow, the captain can see that the padlock is secure on the Spirit Room. Every day one of Crozier's officers will come down here to fetch the amount of rum needed for that day's doling out of the men's noonday grog — one-fourth pint of 140-proof rum to three-fourths pint of water. Also in the Spirit Room are stored the officers' wine and brandy, as well as two hundred muskets, cutlasses, and swords. As has always been the practice in the Royal Navy, scuttles lead directly from the officers' mess and Great Cabin overhead to the Spirit Room. Should there be a mutiny, the officers would get to the weapons first.

Behind the Spirit Room is the Gunner's Storeroom with its kegs of powder and shot. On either side of the Spirit Room are various storage and locker spaces, including chain cable lockers; the Sail Room, with all its cold canvas; and the Slop Room, from which Mr. Helpman, the ship's clerk, issues their outdoor clothing.

Behind the Spirit Room and the Gunner's Storeroom is the Captain's Storeroom, holding Francis Crozier's private — and personally paid for — hams, cheeses, and other luxuries. It is still the custom for the ship's captain to set the table from time to time for his officers, and while the victuals in Crozier's storeroom pale in comparison to the luxurious foodstuffs crammed into the late Captain Sir John Franklin's private store on *Erebus,* Crozier's pantry — almost empty now — has held out for two summers and two winters in the ice. Also, he thinks with a smile, it has the benefit of containing a decent wine cellar from which the officers still benefit. And many bottles of whiskey upon which he, the captain, depends. The poor commander, lieutenants, and civilian officers aboard *Erebus* had done without spirits for two years. Sir John Franklin was a teetotaler and so, when he was alive, had been his officers' mess.

A lantern bobs toward Crozier down the narrow aisle leading back from the bow. The captain turns in time to see something like a hairy black bear squeezing its bulk between the coal sleeves and the Bread Room bulkhead.

"Mr. Wilson," says Crozier, recognizing the carpenter's mate from his rotundity and from the sealskin gloves and deerskin trousers which had been offered to all the men before departure but which only a few had chosen over their flannel and woolen slops. Sometime during the voyage out, the mate had sewn wolf skins they'd picked up at the Danish whaling station at Disko Bay into a bulky — but warm, he insisted — outer garment.

"Captain." Wilson, one of the fattest men aboard, is carrying the lantern in one hand and has several boxes of carpenter's tools tucked under his other arm.

"Mr. Wilson, my compliments to Mr. Honey and would you ask him to join me on the hold deck."

"Aye, sir. Where on the hold deck, sir?"

"The Dead Room, Mr. Wilson."

"Aye, sir." The lantern light reflects on Wilson's eyes as the mate keeps his curious gaze up just a second too long.

"And ask Mr. Honey to bring a pry bar, Mr. Wilson."

"Aye, sir."

Crozier stands aside, squeezing between two kegs to let the larger man pass up the ladder to the lower deck. The captain knows he might be rousing his carpenter for nothing — making the man go to the trouble of getting into his cold-weather slops right before lights-out for no good reason — but he has a hunch and he'd rather disturb the man now than later.

When Wilson has squeezed his bulk up through the upper hatch, Captain Crozier lifts the lower hatch and descends to the hold deck.

Because the entire deck-space lies beneath the level of outside ice, the hold deck is almost as cold as the alien world beyond the hull. And darker, with no aurora, stars, or moon to relieve the ever-present blackness. The air is thick with coal dust and coal smoke — Crozier watches the black particles curl around his hissing lantern like a banshee's claw — and it stinks of sewage and bilge. A scraping, sliding, scuttling noise comes from the darkness aft, but Crozier knows it's just the coal being shoveled in the boiler room. Only the residual heat from that boiler keeps the three inches of filthy water sloshing at the foot of the ladder from turning to ice. Forward, where the bow dips deeper into the ice, there is almost a foot of icy water, despite men working the pumps six hours and more a day. The *Terror*, like any living thing, breathes out moisture through a score of vital functions, including Mr. Diggle's ever-working stove, and while the lower deck is always damp and rimed with ice and the orlop deck frozen, the hold is a dungeon with ice hanging from every beam and meltwater sloshing above one's ankles. The flat black sides of the twenty-one iron water tanks lining the hull on either side add to the chill. Filled with thirty-eight tons of fresh water when the expedition sailed, the tanks are now armored icebergs and to touch the iron is to lose skin.

Magnus Manson is waiting at the bottom of the ladder as Private Wilkes had said, but the huge able-bodied seaman is standing, not sitting arse-on-ladder. The big man's head and shoulders are hunched beneath the low beams. His pale, lumpy face and stubbled jowls remind Crozier of a rotten white peeled potato stuffed under a Welsh wig. He will not meet his captain's stare in the harsh lantern glow.

"What is this, Manson?" Crozier's voice does not hold the bark he unleashed on his lookout and lieutenant. His tone is flat, calm, certain, with the power of flogging and hanging behind every syllable.

"It's them ghosts, Cap'n." For a huge man, Magnus Manson has the high, soft voice of a child. When *Terror* and *Erebus* had paused at Disko Bay on the west coast of Greenland in July of 1845, Captain Sir John Franklin had seen fit to dismiss two men from the expedition — a Marine private and a sailmaker from *Terror*. Crozier had made the recommendation that seaman John Brown and Private Aitken from his ship also be released — they were little better than invalids and never should have been signed on for such a voyage — but on occasion since, he wished he'd sent Manson home with those four. If the big man was not feebleminded, he was so close to it that it was impossible to tell the difference.

"You know there are no ghosts on *Terror*, Manson."

"Yes, Cap'n."

"*Look* at me."

Manson raises his face but does not meet Crozier's gaze. The captain marvels at how tiny the man's pale eyes are in that white lump of a face.

"Did you disobey Mr. Thompson's orders to carry sacks of coal to the boiler room, Seaman Manson?"

"No, sir. Yes, sir."

"Do you know the consequences of disobeying any order on this ship?" Crozier feels like he's talking to a boy, although Manson must be at least thirty years old.

The big sailor's face brightens as he is presented with a question he can answer correctly. "Oh, yes, Cap'n. Flogging, sir. Twenty lashes. A 'undred lashes if I disobeys more than once. 'Anging if I disobey a real officer rather'n jus' Mr. Thompson."

"That's correct," says Crozier, "but did you know that the captain can also inflict any punishment he finds appropriate to the transgression?"

Manson peers down at him, his pale eyes confused. He has not understood the question.

"I'm saying I can punish you any way I see fit, Seaman Manson," says the captain.

A flood of relief flows over the lumpy face. "Oh, yes, right, Cap'n."

"Instead of twenty lashes," says Francis Crozier, "I could have you locked up in the Dead Room for twenty hours with no light."

Manson's already pale, frozen features lose so much blood that Crozier prepares to get out of the way if the big man faints.

"You . . . wouldn't. . . ." The child-man's voice quavers toward a vibrato.

Crozier says nothing for a long, cold, lantern-hissing moment. He lets the sailor read his expression. Finally he says, "What do you think you hear, Manson? Has someone been telling you ghost stories?"

Manson opens his mouth but seems to have trouble deciding which question to answer first. Ice forms on his fat lower lip. "Walker," he says at last.

"You're afraid of Walker?"

James Walker, a friend of Manson's who had been about the same age as the idiot and not much brighter, was the last man to die on the ice, just a week earlier. Ship's rules required that the crew keep small holes drilled in the ice near the ship, even when the ice was ten or fifteen feet thick as it was now, so that they could get at water to fight a fire should one break out aboard. Walker and two of his mates were on just such a drilling party in the dark, reopening an old hole that would freeze in less than an hour unless rammed with metal spikes. The white terror had come out from behind a pressure ridge, torn off the seaman's arm, and smashed his ribs to splinters in an instant, disappearing before the armed guards on deck could raise their shotguns.

"Walker told you ghost stories?" says Crozier.

"Yes, Cap'n. No, Cap'n. What Jimmy did was, 'e tells me the night before the *thing* killed 'im, 'e says, 'Magnus, should that 'ellspawn out on the ice get me someday,' 'e says, 'I'll come back in me white shroud to whisper in your ear how cold 'ell is.' So help me God, Cap'n, that's what Jimmy said to me. Now I 'ear 'im tryin' to get out."

As if on cue, the hull groans, the frigid deck moans under their feet, metal brackets on the beams groan back in sympathy, and there is a scraping, clawing noise in the dark around them that seems to run the length of the ship. The ice is restless.

"Is that the sound you hear, Manson?"

"Yes, Cap'n. No, sir."

The Dead Room is thirty feet aft on the starboard side, just beyond the last metal-moaning iron water tank, but when the outside ice stops its noise, Crozier can hear only the muffled scrape and push of the shovels in the boiler room farther aft.

Crozier's had enough of this nonsense. "You know your friend's not coming back, Magnus. He's there in the extra sail storage room securely sewn into his own hammock with the other dead men, frozen solid, with three layers of our heaviest sail canvas tied around them. If you hear anything from in there, it's the damned rats trying to get at them. You *know* this, Magnus Manson."

"Yes, Cap'n."

"There will be no disobeying orders on this ship, Seaman Manson. You have to make up your mind now. Carry the coal when Mr. Thompson tells you to. Fetch the food stores when Mr. Diggle sends you down here. Obey all orders promptly and politely. Or face the court . . . face *me* . . . and the possibility that you'll spend a cold, lanternless night in the Dead Room yourself."

Without another word, Manson knuckles his forehead in salute, lifts a huge sack of coal from where he's stowed it on the ladder, and hauls it aft into the darkness.

———

The engineer himself is stripped to his long-sleeved undershirt and corduroy trousers, shoveling coal alongside the ancient 47-year-old stoker named Bill Johnson. The other stoker, Luke Smith, is on the lower deck sleeping between his shoveling hours. *Terror*'s lead stoker, young John Torrington, was the first man of the expedition to die, on New Year's Day 1846. But that had been from natural causes. It seems Torrington's doctor had urged the 19-year-old to go to sea to cure his consumption, and he'd succumbed after two months of being an invalid while the ships were frozen in the harbour at Beechey Island that first winter. Doctors Peddie and McDonald had told Crozier that the boy's lungs were as solidly packed with coal dust as a chimney sweep's pockets.

"Thank you, Captain," says the young engineer between heaves of the shovel. Seaman Manson has just dropped off a second sack of coal and gone back for a third.

"You're welcome, Mr. Thompson." Crozier glances at Stoker Johnson. The man is four years younger than the captain but looks thirty years older. Every seam and wrinkle on his age-molded face is outlined in coal black and grime. Even his toothless gums are soot grey. Crozier doesn't want to reprimand his engineer — and thus an officer, although civilian — in front of the stoker, but he says, "I presume we'll dispense with using Marines as messengers, should there be another such instance in the future, which I very much doubt."

Thompson nods, uses the shovel to clang shut the iron grate on the boiler, leans on the tool, and tells Johnson to go above to get him some coffee from Mr. Diggle. Crozier's glad the stoker is gone but even happier that the grate is closed; the heat in here makes him slightly nauseated after the cold everywhere else.

The captain has to wonder at the fate of his engineer. Warrant Officer James Thompson, Engineer First Class, graduate of the Navy's steam factory at Woolwich — the world's best training grounds for the new breed of steam-propulsion engineers — is here stripped to his filthy undershirt, shoveling coal like a common stoker in an ice-locked ship that hasn't moved an inch under its own power now for more than a year.

"Mr. Thompson," says Crozier, "I'm sorry I haven't had a chance to talk to you today since you walked over to *Erebus*. Did you have a chance to confer with Mr. Gregory?"

John Gregory is the engineer aboard the flagship.

"I did, Captain. Mr. Gregory's convinced that with the onset of real winter, they'll never be able to get at the damaged driveshaft. Even if they *were* able to tunnel down through the ice to replace the last propeller with the one they've jury-rigged, with the replacement driveshaft bent as badly as it is, *Erebus* is going nowhere under steam."

Crozier nods. *Erebus* bent its second driveshaft while the ship was throwing itself desperately on the ice more than a year ago. The flagship — heavier, with a more powerful engine — led the way through the pack ice that summer, opening leads for both ships. But the last ice they'd encountered before being frozen in for the last thirteen months was harder than the iron in the experimental propeller screw and driveshaft. Divers that summer — all of who suffered frostbite and came close to dying — had confirmed not only that the screw had been shattered but that the driveshaft itself was bent and broken.

"Coal?" says the captain.

"*Erebus* has enough for . . . perhaps . . . four months of heating in the ice, at only one hour of hot-water circulation through the lower deck per day, Captain. None at all for steaming next summer."

If we get free next summer, thinks Crozier. After this last summer, when the ice never relented for a day, he's a pessimist. Franklin had used up *Erebus*'s coal supply at a prodigious rate during those last weeks of freedom in the summer of 1846, sure that if he could smash through those last few miles of pack ice, the expedition would reach the open waters of the North-West Passage along the northern coast of Canada and they'd be drinking tea in China by late autumn.

"What about *our* coal use?" asks Crozier.

"Perhaps enough left for six months of heating," says Thompson. "But only if we cut back from two hours a day to one. And I recommend we do that soon — no later than the first of November."

That is less than two weeks away.

"And steaming?" says Crozier.

If the ice relents at all next summer, Crozier plans to cram all the surviving men from *Erebus* aboard *Terror* and make an all-out effort to retreat the way they'd come — up the unnamed strait between Boothia Peninsula and Prince of Wales Island, down which they rushed two summers ago, past Walker Point and Barrow Strait, out through Lancaster Sound like a cork from a bottle, then rushing south into Baffin Bay with all sail set and the last coal being burned, going like smoke and oakum, burning extra spars and furniture if need be to get the last bit of steam, anything to get them into open water off Greenland where whalers could find them.

But he'll also need steam to fight his way north through the south-flowing ice to Lancaster Sound, even if a miracle occurs and they are released from the ice here. Crozier and James Ross once sailed *Terror* and *Erebus* out of the south polar ice, but they'd been traveling *with* the currents and bergs. Here in the damned arctic, the ships have to sail for weeks *against* the flow of ice coming down from the pole just to reach the straits where they can escape.

Thompson shrugs. The man looks exhausted. "If we cut off the heat on New Year's Day and somehow survive until next summer, we might get . . . six days steaming without ice? Five?"

Crozier merely nods again. This is almost certainly a death sentence for his ship, but not necessarily for the men of both ships.

There is a sound out in the darkened corridor.

"Thank you, Mr. Thompson." The captain lifts his lantern off an iron hook, leaves the glow of the boiler room, and heads forward in the slush and darkness.

Thomas Honey is waiting in the corridor, his candle lantern sputtering in the bad air. He is holding the iron pry bar in front of him like a musket, clutched in thick gloves, and hasn't opened the bolted door of the Dead Room.

"Thank you for coming, Mr. Honey," Crozier says to his carpenter.

Without explanation, the captain throws back the bolts and enters the freezing-cold storage room.

Crozier can not resist lifting his lantern toward the aft bulkhead where the six men's bodies have been stacked in their common canvas shroud.

The heap is writhing. Crozier expected that — expected to see the movement of rats under the tarp — but he realizes that he's looking at a solid mass of rats *above* the shroud-canvas as well. There is a solid cube of rats, extending more than four feet above the deck, as hundreds of them jostle for position to get at the frozen dead men. The squealing is very loud in here. More rats are underfoot, scuttling between his and the carpenter's legs. *Rushing to the banquet,* thinks Crozier. And showing no fear of the lantern light.

Crozier turns the lantern back to the hull, walks up the slight incline caused by the ship's cant to port and begins pacing along the curved, tilted wall.

There.

He holds the lantern closer.

"Well, I'll be God-damned to hell and hanged for a heathen," says Honey. "Pardon me, Captain, but I didn't think the ice would do this so soon."

Crozier doesn't answer. He crouches to investigate the bent and extended wood of the hull more closely.

Hull planks have been bent inward here, bulging almost a foot from the graceful curve elsewhere along the hull's side. The innermost layers of wood have splintered and at least two planks are hanging free.

"Jesus God Christ Almighty," says the carpenter, who has crouched next to the captain. "That ice is a fucking monster, begging the Captain's pardon, sir."

"Mr. Honey," says Crozier, his breath adding crystals to the ice already on the planks and reflecting the lantern light, "could anything but the ice have done this damage?"

The carpenter barks a laugh but stops abruptly as he realizes his captain is not making a joke. Honey's eyes widen, then squint. "Begging your pardon again, Captain, but if you mean . . . that's impossible."

Crozier says nothing.

"I mean, Captain, this hull was three inches of the finest English oak as it was, sir. And for this trip — for the ice, I mean, sir — it was doubled with two layers of African oak, Captain, each one and a half inches thick. And them African oak panels was wrought on the diagonal, sir, givin' it even more strength than if it were just doubled straight-like."

Crozier is inspecting the loose planks, trying to ignore the river of rats behind them and around them as well as the chewing sounds from the direction of the aft bulkhead.

"And, sir," continues Honey, his voice hoarse in the cold, his rum-tainted breath freezing in the air, "on top of the three inches of English oak and the three inches of diagonal-laid African oak, they laid on two layers of Canadian elm, sir, each two inches thick. That's four more inches of hull, Captain, and that wrought diagonal against the African oak. That's five belts of serious timber, sir . . . ten inches of the strongest wood on earth between us and the sea."

The carpenter shuts up, realizing that he's lecturing his captain on details of the shipyard's work that Crozier had personally overseen in the months before departure.

The captain stands and sets his mittened hand against the innermost planks where they have come free. There's more than an inch of open space there. "Set your lantern down, Mr. Honey. Use your pry bar to lever this loose. I want to see what the ice has done to the outer layer of hull oak."

The carpenter complies. For several minutes the sound of the iron bar prying at iron-cold wood and the carpenter's grunts almost drown out the frenzied gnawing of the rats behind them. The bent Canadian elm tears back and falls away. The shattered African oak is leveraged out. Only the inward-bent original oak of the hull remains now as Crozier steps closer, holding his lantern so that both men can see.

Shards and spears of ice reflect the lantern light through the footlong holes in the hull, but in the centre is something much more disturbing — blackness. Nothing. A hole in the ice. A tunnel.

Honey bends a piece of the splintered oak farther in so Crozier can shine his lantern on it.

"Holy fucking Jesus Christ fucking shit almighty," gasps the carpenter. This time he does not ask his captain's pardon.

Crozier has the temptation to lick his dry lips but knows how painful that will be here where it's 50 below in the dark. But his heart is pounding so wildly that he's also tempted to steady himself with one mitten against the hull the way the carpenter has just done.

The freezing air from outside rushes in so quickly that it almost extinguishes the lantern. Crozier has to shield it with his free hand to keep it flickering, sending the men's shadows dancing across decks, beams, and bulkheads.

The two long boards from the outer hull have been smashed and bent inward by some inconceivable, irresistible force. Clearly visible in the light from the slightly shaking lantern are huge claw marks in the splintered oak — claw marks streaked with frozen smears of impossibly bright blood.

4

GOODSIR

Lat. 75°-12' N., Long. 61°-6' W.
Baffin Bay, July, 1845

From the private diary of Dr. Harry D. S. Goodsir:

11 April, 1845 —

In a letter to my brother today, I wrote — "All the Officers are in great hopes of making the passage and hope to be in the Pacific end of next summer."

I confess that, however Selfish it is, my own hope for the Expedition is that it may take us a bit longer to reach Alaska, Russia, China, and the warm waters of the Pacific. Although trained as an anatomist and signed on by Captain Sir John Franklin as a mere assistant surgeon, I am, in Truth, no mere surgeon but a Doctor, and I confess further that as amateurish as my attempts may be, I hope to become something of a Naturalist on this voyage. While having no personal Experience with arctic flora and fauna, I plan to become personally acquainted with the life-forms in the Icy Realms to which we set sail only a month from now. I am especially interested in the white bear, although most accounts of it one hears from whalers and old Arctic Hands tend to be too fabulous to credit.

I recognize that this personal Diary is most out of the ordinary — the Official Log that I shall begin when we depart next month will record all of the pertinent professional events and observations of my time aboard HMS Erebus *in my capacity as Assistant Surgeon and as a member of Captain Sir John Franklin's expedition to force the North-West Passage — but I feel that something More is due, some other record, some more personal account, and* even if I should never let another soul read this after my Return, it is my Duty — to myself if no other — to keep these notes.

All I know at this point is that my Expedition with Captain Sir John Franklin already promises to be the Experience of a Lifetime.

Sunday, 18 May, 1845 —

All the men are aboard, and although last-minute Preparation is still going on around the clock for tomorrow's Departure — especially with the stowing of what Captain Fitzjames informs me is more than eight thousand cans of tinned food which have arrived only in the nick of time — Sir John conducted Divine Service today for us aboard Erebus and for as many of Terror's crew who wished to join us. I noted that Terror's captain, an Irishman named Crozier, was not in attendance.

No one could have attended the lengthy service and heard the very lengthy sermon by Sir John today without being deeply moved. I wonder if any Ship from any nation's Navy has ever been captained by such a Religious Man. There is no doubt that we are truly and safely and irrevocably in God's Hands on the voyage to come.

19 May, 1845 —

What a Departure!

Having never gone to sea before, much less as a member of such a Heralded Expedition, I had no Idea of what to Expect, but Nothing could have prepared me for the glory of this Day.

Captain Fitzjames estimates that more than ten thousand well-wishers and Persons of Importance crowded the docks at Greenhithe to see us off.

Speeches resounded until I thought we would never be allowed to depart while Daylight still filled the Summer Sky. Bands played. Lady Jane — who has been staying aboard with Sir John — went down the gangplank to a rousing series of Hurrahs! from we sixty-some Erebuses. Bands played again. Then the cheers started as all lines were cast off, and for several minutes the noise was so deafening that I could not have heard an order had Sir John himself shouted it in my ear.

Last night, Lieutenant Gore and Chief Surgeon Stanley were Kind enough to inform me that it is custom during sailing for the officers not to Show Emotion, so although only technically *an officer, I stood with the officers lined up in their fine blue jackets and tried to restrain all Displays of emotion, however manly.*

We were the only ones doing so. The Seamen shouted and waved handkerchiefs and hung from the ratlines, and I could see many a rouged dockside Doxie waving farewell to them. Even Captain Sir John Franklin waved a bright red-and-green handkerchief at Lady Jane, his daughter, Eleanor, and his niece Sophia Cracroft, who waved back until the sight of the docks was obstructed by the following Terror.

We are being towed by steam tugs and followed on this leg of our voyage by HMS Rattler, *a powerful new steam frigate, and also a hired transport ship carrying our provisions,* Baretto Junior.

Just before Erebus *pushed away from the docks, a Dove landed high on the main mast. Sir John's daughter by his first marriage, Eleanor — then quite visible in her bright-green silk dress and emerald parasol — cried out but could not be heard above the Cheers and Bands. Then she pointed, and Sir John and many of the Officers looked up, smiled, and then pointed out the Dove to others aboard ship.*

Combined with the Words spoken in yesterday's Divine Service, this, I have to assume, is the Best Possible Omen.

4 July, 1845 —

What a terrible Crossing of the North Atlantic to Greenland.

For thirty stormy days, even while under tow, the Ship has been tossing, rolling, and wallowing, its tightly sealed Gunports on each side barely four feet out of the water during the downward rolls, sometimes barely making Headway. I have been terribly seasick for Twenty-eight of the last Thirty days. Lieutenant Le Vesconte tells me that we never made more than five knots, which — he assures me — is a Terrible time for any ship merely under Sail, much less for such a Miracle of Technology as Erebus *and our companion craft,* Terror, *both capable of steaming along under the Impetus of their invincible Screws.*

Three days ago we rounded Cape Farewell at the southern tip of Greenland, and I confess that the glimpses of this Huge Continent, with its rocky cliffs and endless glaciers coming right down to the Sea, lay as heavily on my Spirits as the pitching and rolling did upon my Stomach.

Good God, this is a barren, cold place! And this in July.

Our morale is Top Notch, however, and all aboard trust to Sir John's Skill and Good Judgement. Yesterday Lieutenant Fairholme, the youngest of our lieutenants, said to me in Confidence, "I never felt the Captain was so much my companion with anyone I have sailed with before."

Today we put in at the Danish whaling station here in Disko Bay. Tons of supplies are being transferred from Baretto Junior, and ten live oxen transported aboard that ship were slaughtered this afternoon. All the men of both Expedition ships shall feast on fresh meat tonight.

Four men were dismissed from the Expedition today — upon advice of the four of us surgeons — and will be returning to England with the tow and transport ship. These include one man from Erebus — a certain Thomas Burt, the ship's armourer, and three from Terror — a Marine private named Aitken, a seaman named John Brown, and Terror's primary sailmaker, James Elliott. That brings our total muster down to 129 men for the two ships.

Dried fish from the Danes and a cloud of Coal Dust hang over everything this afternoon — hundreds of bags of coal were transferred from Baretto Junior today — and the seamen aboard Erebus are busy with the smooth-sided stones they call Holy Stones, scrubbing and rescrubbing the deck clean while the Officers shout encouragement. Despite the extra work, All Hands are in High Spirits because of the promise of Tonight's Feasting and extra rations of Grog.

Besides the four men to be invalided home, Sir John will be sending the June musters, official dispatches, and all personal letters back with Baretto Junior. Everyone will be busy writing the next few days.

After this week, the next letter to reach our loved ones will be posted from Russia or China!

12 July, 1845 —

Another departure, this time perhaps the Last One before the North-West Passage. This morning we slipped our cables and sailed west from Greenland while the crew of Baretto Junior *gave us three hearty* Hurrahs! *and waved their caps. Surely these shall be the last White Men we see until we reach Alaska.*

26 July, 1845 —

Two whalers — Prince of Wales *and* Enterprise *— have anchored nearby to where we have tied up to a floating Ice Mountain. I have enjoyed many hours talking to the captains and crewmen about white bears.*

I also had the distinct terror — if not Pleasure — of climbing that huge iceberg this morning. The sailors scrambled up early yesterday, chipping steps into the vertical ice with their axes and then rigging fixed lines for the less agile. Sir John ordered an Observatory be set up atop the giant berg, which towers more than twice as tall as our Highest Mast, and while Lieutenant Gore and some of the officers from Terror *take atmospheric and astronomical measurements up there — they have erected a tent for those spending the night atop the Precipitous Ice Mountain — our Expedition Ice Masters, Mr. Reid from* Erebus *and Mr. Blanky from* Terror, *spend the daylight hours staring west and north through their brass telescopes, seeking, I am informed, the most likely path through the near-solid sea of ice already formed there. Edward Couch, our very Reliable and Voluble Mate, tells me that this is very late in the Arctic Season for ships to be seeking any passage, much less the Fabled North-West Passage.*

The sight of both Erebus *and* Terror *moored to the iceberg below us, a maze of ropes — what I must remember to call "lines" now that I am an old nautical hand — holding both ships fast to the Ice Mountain, the two ships' highest crow's nests below my precarious and icy perch so high above everything, created a sort of sick and thrilling Vertigo within me.*

It was exhilarating standing up there hundreds of feet above the sea. The summit of the iceberg was almost the size of a cricket pitch and the tent holding our Meteorological Observatory looked quite incongruous on the blue ice — but my hopes for a few moments of Quiet Revery were shattered by the constant Shotgun Blasts as the men all over the Summit of our Ice Mountain were shooting birds — arctic terns, I am told — by the hundreds. These heaps and heaps of fresh-killed birds shall be salted and stored away, although Heaven Alone Knows where those additional casks shall be Stored, since both our ships are already Groaning and riding low under the weight of all their Stores.

Dr. McDonald, assistant surgeon aboard HMS Terror — my counterpart there as it were — has theories that heavily salted food is not as efficient and antiscorbutic as fresh or nonsalted Victuals, and since the regular seamen aboard both ships prefer their Salted Pork to all other meals, Dr. McDonald worries that the heavily salted birds will add little to our Defenses against Scurvy. However, Stephen Stanley, our Surgeon aboard Erebus, dismisses these worries. He points out that besides the 10,000 cases of preserved cooked meats aboard Erebus, our tinned rations alone include boiled and roast mutton, veal, all forms of vegetables including potatoes, carrots, parsnips, and mixed vegetables, wide varieties of Soups, and 9,450 pounds of Chocolate. An equal weight — 9,300 pounds — of lemon juice has also been brought as our primary antiscorbutic measure. Stanley informs me that even when the juice is sweetened with liberal dollops of sugar, the common men hate their daily ration and that one of our Primary Jobs as surgeons on the Expedition is to ensure that they swallow the stuff.

It was interesting to me that almost all of the hunting by the officers and men of both our ships is done almost exclusively with Shotguns. Lieutenant Gore assures me that each ship carries a full arsenal of Muskets. Of course, it only makes sense to use Shotguns to hunt birds such as those killed by the hundreds today, but even back at Disko Bay, when small parties went out hunting Caribou and Arctic Fox, the men — even the Marines obviously trained in the use of Muskets — preferred to take along Shotguns. This, of course, must be the result of Habit as much as Preference — the officers tend to be English Gentlemen who have never used muskets or Rifles in their hunting, and except for the use of single-shot weapons in Close Quarters Naval Combat, even the Marines have used Shotguns almost exclusively in their past hunting experience.

Will Shotguns be enough to bag the Great White Bear? We've not seen one of those Wondrous creatures yet, although every Experienced Officer and Hand reassures me that we shall encounter them as soon as we enter the Pack Ice, and if not then, certainly when we Winter Over — should we be compelled to do so. Truly the tales the whalers here tell me of the elusive White Bears are Wonderful and Terrifying.

As I write these words, I am informed that current or wind or perhaps the necessities of the whaling business itself have carried both whalers, Prince of Wales *and* Enterprise, *away from our moorings here at our Ice Mountain. Captain Sir John shall not be dining with one of the whaling captains — Captain Martin of* Enterprise, *I believe — as had been planned for this evening.*

Perhaps more Pertinent, Mate Robert Sergeant has just informed me that our men are bringing down the astronomical and meteorological instruments, striking the tent, and reeling in the hundreds of yards of fixed rope — line — which allowed my Ascent earlier today.

Evidently the Ice Masters, Captain Sir John, Commander Fitzjames, Captain Crozier, and the other Officers have determined our Most Promising Path through the ever-shifting pack ice.

We are to cast off from our little Iceberg Home within minutes, sailing Northwest as long as the seemingly endless Arctic Twilight allows us to.

We shall be beyond the reach of even the Hardy Whalers from this point on. As far as the World Beyond our intrepid Expedition is concerned, as Hamlet said, The rest is silence.

5

CROZIER

C rozier is dreaming about the picnic to the Platypus Pond and of Sophia stroking him under water when he hears the sound of a shot and comes crashing awake.

He sits up in his bunk not knowing what time it is, not knowing if it is day or night, although there is no line between day and night any longer since the sun has disappeared this very day, not to reappear until February. But even before he lights the small lantern in his berth to check his watch, he knows that it is *late*. The ship is as quiet as it ever gets; silent except for the creak of tortured wood and frozen metal within; silent except for the snores, the mumbles, and the farts from the sleeping men, and curses from Mr. Diggle the cook; silent save for the incessant groaning, banging, cracking, and surging of the ice outside; and, added to those exceptions to silence this night, silent but for the banshee screech of a high wind.

But this is no sound of ice or wind that wakes Crozier. It is a gunshot. A shotgun — muffled through the layers of oak planks and overlaying snow and ice, but a shotgun blast without doubt.

Crozier was sleeping with most of his clothes on and now has pulled on most of the other layers and is ready for his cold-weather slops when Thomas Jopson, his steward, knocks on the door with his distinctive soft triple rap. The captain slides it open.

"Trouble on deck, sir."

Crozier nods. "Who's on watch tonight, Thomas?" His pocket watch shows him that it is almost 3:00 a.m., civilian time. His memory of the month's and day's watch schedule gives him the names an instant before Jopson speaks them aloud.

"Billy Strong and Private Heather, sir."

Crozier nods again, lifts a pistol from his cupboard, checks the priming, sets it in his belt, and squeezes past the steward, out through the officers' dining cubicle that borders the captain's tiny cabin on the starboard side, and then quickly forward through another door to the main ladderway. The lower deck is mostly dark at this time in the morning — the glow around Mr. Diggle's stove the primary exception — but lamps are being lit in several of the officers', mates', and stewards' quarters as Crozier pauses at the base of the ladder to pull his heavy slops from the hook and struggle into them.

Doors slide open. First Mate Hornby walks aft to stand next to Crozier by the ladder. First Lieutenant Little hurries forward down the companionway, carrying three muskets and a saber. He's followed by Lieutenants Hodgson and Irving, who are also carrying weapons.

Forward of the ladder, seamen are grumbling from deep in their hammocks, but a second mate is already turning out a work party — literally tumbling sleeping men from their hammocks and shoving them aft toward their slops and the waiting weapons.

"Has anyone been up top yet to check out the shot?" Crozier asks his first mate.

"Mr. Male had the duty, sir," says Hornby. "He went up as soon as he sent your steward to fetch you."

Reuben Male is captain of the fo'c'sle. A steady man. Billy Strong, the seaman on port watch up there, has been to sea before, Crozier knows, on HMS *Belvidera*. He wouldn't have shot at phantoms. The other man on watch was the oldest — and in Crozier's estimation, the stupidest — of the surviving Marines, William Heather. At age 35 and still a private, frequently sick, too often drunk, and most frequently useless, Heather had almost been sent home from Disko Island two years before when his best friend Billy Aitken was discharged and sent back on HMS *Rattler*.

Crozier slips the pistol into the oversized pocket of his heavy woolen outer coat, accepts a lantern from Jopson, wraps a comforter around his face, and leads the way up the tilted ladder.

———

Crozier sees that it is as black as the inside of an eel's belly outside, no stars, no aurora, no moon, and *cold;* the temperature on deck registered sixty-three degrees below zero six hours earlier when young Irving had been sent up to take measurements, and now a wild wind howls past the stubs of masts and across the canted, icy deck, driving heavy snow before it. Stepping out from beneath the frozen canvas enclosure above the main hatch, Crozier holds his mittened hand alongside his face to protect his eyes and sees a lantern gleam on the starboard side.

Reuben Male is on one knee over Private Heather, who is lying on his back, his cap and Welsh wig knocked off and, Crozier sees, part of his skull knocked away as well. There seems to be no blood, but Crozier can see the Marine's brains sparkling in the lantern light — sparkling, the captain realizes, because there is already a sheen of ice crystals on the pulped grey matter.

"He's still alive, Captain," says the fo'c'sle chief.

"Jesus fucking Christ," says one of the crewmen crowded behind Crozier.

"Belay that!" cries the first mate. "No fucking profanity. Speak when you're fucking spoken to, Crispe." Hornby's voice is a cross between a mastiff's growl and a bull's snort.

"Mr. Hornby," says Crozier. "Assign Seaman Crispe to get below double-quick and bring up his own hammock to carry Private Heather below."

"Aye, sir," say Hornby and the seaman in unison. The pounding of running boots is felt but goes unheard over the wind screech.

Crozier stands and swings his lantern in a circle.

The heavy railing where Private Heather was standing watch at the base of the iced-over ratlines has been smashed away. Beyond the gap, Crozier knows, the heaped ice and snow runs down like a toboggan ramp for thirty feet or more, but most of that ramp is not visible in the blinding snow. There are no prints visible in the small circle of snow illuminated by the captain's lantern.

Reuben Male lifts Heather's musket. "It wasn't fired, Captain."

"In this storm, Private Heather couldn't have seen the thing until it was right on him," says Lieutenant Little.

"What about Strong?" asks Crozier.

Male points toward the opposite side of the ship. "Missing, Captain."

To Hornby, Crozier says, "Choose a man and stay with Private Heather until Crispe is back with the hammock and carry him below."

Suddenly, both surgeons — Peddie and his assistant, McDonald — appear in the circle of lamplight, McDonald wearing only light slops.

"Jesus Christ," says the chief surgeon, kneeling next to the Marine. "He's breathing."

"Help him if you can, John," says Crozier. He points to Male and the rest of the seamen crowding around. "The rest of you — come with me. Have your weapons ready to fire, even if you have to take your mittens off to do it. Wilson, carry both those lanterns. Lieutenant Little, please go below and choose twenty more good men, issue full slops, and arm them with muskets — not shotguns, muskets."

"Aye, sir," Little shouts over the wind, but Crozier is already leading the procession forward, around the heaped snow and vibrating canvas pyramid amidships and up the canted deck toward the port lookout station.

William Strong is gone. A long wool comforter has been shredded, and the tatters of it, caught in the man lines here, are flapping wildly. Strong's greatcoat, Welsh wig, shotgun, and one mitten are lying near the railing in the lee of the port privy where men on watch huddle to stay out of the wind, but William Strong is gone. There is a smear of red ice on the railing where he must have been standing when he saw the large shape coming at him through the blowing snow.

Without saying a word, Crozier dispatches two armed men with lanterns aft, three more toward the bow, another with a lantern to look beneath the canvas amidships. "Rig a ladder here, please, Bob," he says to the second mate. The mate's shoulders are hidden under heaps of fresh — that is, not yet frozen — rope he's carried up from below. The ladder goes over the side within seconds.

Crozier leads the way down.

There is more blood on the ice and snow heaped along the exposed port-side hull of the ship. Streaks of blood, looking quite black in the lantern light, lead out beyond the fire holes into the ever-changing maze of pressure ridges and ice spires, all more sensed than seen in the darkness.

"It wants us to follow it out there, sir," says Second Lieutenant Hodgson, leaning close to Crozier so as to be heard over the wind howl.

"Of course it does," says Crozier. "But we're going anyway. Strong might still be alive. We've seen that before with this thing." Crozier looks behind him. Besides Hodgson, only three men had followed him down the rope ladder — all the rest were either searching the upper deck or were busy hauling Private Heather belowdecks. There is only one other lantern here besides the captain's.

"Armitage," Crozier says to the gunroom steward, whose white beard is already filled with snow, "give Lieutenant Hodgson your lantern and you go with him. Gibson, you remain here and tell Lieutenant Little where we've headed when he comes down with the main search party. Tell him for God's sake not to let his men fire at anything unless they're sure it's not one of us."

"Yes, Captain."

To Hodgson, Crozier says, "George, you and Armitage head out about twenty yards that way — toward the bow — then stay parallel to us as we search south. Try to keep your lantern within sight of ours."

"Aye, aye, sir."

"Tom," Crozier says to the only remaining man, young Evans, "you come with me. Keep your Baker Rifle ready but only at half-cock."

"Aye, sir." The boy's teeth are chattering.

Crozier waits until Hodgson reaches a point twenty yards to their right — his lantern only the dimmest glow in the blowing snow — and then he leads Evans out into the maze of seracs, ice pinnacles, and pressure ridges, following the periodic smears of blood on the ice. He knows that a delay of even a few minutes will be enough to blow snow over the faint trail. The captain doesn't even bother to remove the pistol from the pocket of his greatcoat.

Less than a hundred yards out, just where the lanterns of the men on the deck of HMS *Terror* become invisible, Crozier reaches a pressure ridge — one of those great heaps of ice thrown up by the ice plates grinding and surging against each other beneath the surface. For two winters in the ice now, Crozier and the other men of the late Sir John Franklin's expedition have watched these pressure ridges appear as if by magic, rise with a great rumbling and tearing sound, and then extend themselves across the surface of the frozen sea, sometimes moving faster than a man can run.

This ridge is at least thirty feet high, a great vertical rubble of ice boulders each at least as large as a hansom cab.

Crozier walks along the ridge, extending his lantern as high as he can. Hodgson's lantern is no longer visible to the west. Nowhere around *Terror* is the view simple any longer. Everywhere the snow seracs, drifts, pressure ridges, and ice pinnacles block one's line of sight. There is one great ice mountain in the mile separating *Terror* and *Erebus* and half a dozen more in sight on a moonlit night.

But no icebergs here tonight, only this three-storey-tall pressure ridge.

"There!" shouts Crozier over the wind. Evans steps closer, his Baker Rifle raised.

A smear of black blood on the white wall of ice. The thing had carried William Strong up this small mountain of icy rubble, taking an almost vertical route.

Crozier begins climbing, holding the lantern in his right hand while he searches with his mittened free hand, trying to find cracks and crevices for his frozen fingers and already icy boots. He hadn't taken time to put on his pair of boots in which Jopson had driven long nails through the soles, giving traction on such ice surfaces, and now his ordinary seaman's boots slip and skitter on the ice. But he finds more frozen blood twenty-five feet up, just below the ice-jumbled summit of the pressure ridge, so Crozier holds the lantern steady with his right hand while kicking against a tilting ice slab with his left leg and leveraging himself up to the top, the wool of his greatcoat rasping against his back. The captain can't feel his nose and his fingers are also numb.

"Captain," calls Evans from the darkness below, "do you want me to come up?"

Crozier is panting too hard to speak for a second, but when he gets his wind back, he calls down, "No . . . wait there." He can see the faint glow of Hodgson's lantern now to the northwest — that team isn't within thirty yards of the pressure ridge yet.

Flailing for balance against the wind, leaning far to his right as the gale streams his comforter straight out to his left and threatens to topple him off his precarious perch, Crozier holds the lantern out over the south side of the pressure ridge.

The drop here is almost vertical for thirty-five feet. There is no sign of William Strong, no sign of black smears on the ice, no sign that anything living or dead has come this way. Crozier can't imagine how anything could have found its way down that sheer ice face.

Shaking his head and realizing that his eyelashes are almost frozen to his cheeks, Crozier begins descending the way he'd come, twice almost falling onto the rising bayonets of ice before slip-sliding the last eight feet or so to the surface where Evans is waiting.

But Evans is gone.

The Baker Rifle lies in the snow, still at half-cock. There are no prints in the swirling snow, human or otherwise.

"Evans!" Captain Francis Rawdon Moira Crozier's voice has been trained to command for thirty-five years and more. He can make it heard over a sou'westerly gale or while a ship is white-foaming its way through the Strait of Magellan in an ice storm. Now he puts every bit of volume he can muster into the shout. "Evans!"

No answer except the howl of the wind.

Crozier lifts the Baker Rifle, checks the priming, and fires it into the air. The *crack* sounds muffled even to him, but he sees Hodgson's lantern suddenly turn toward him and three more lanterns become dimly visible on the ice from the direction of *Terror*.

Something roars not twenty feet from him. It could be the wind finding a new route through or around an icy serac or pinnacle, but Crozier knows that it isn't.

He sets the lantern down, fumbles in his pocket, pulls the pistol out, tugs off his mitten with his teeth, and, with just a thin woolen glove between his flesh and the metal trigger, holds the useless weapon in front of him.

"Come on, God-damn your eyes!" Crozier screams. "Come out and try *me* instead of a *boy*, you hairy arse-licking rat-fucking piss-drinking spawn of a poxy Highgate whore!"

There is no answer except the howl of the wind.

6

GOODSIR

From the private diary of Dr. Harry D. S. Goodsir:

1 January, 1846 —

John Torrington, stoker on HMS Terror, died early this morning. New Year's Day. The beginning of our Fifth Month stuck in the ice here at Beechey Island.

His death was not a surprise. It has been obvious for several months that Torrington had been in the advanced stages of Consumption when he signed on the expedition, and if the Symptoms had manifested themselves just a few weeks earlier in the Late Summer, he would have been sent home on Rattler or even with the two whaling ships we encountered just before sailing west across Baffin Bay and through Lancaster Sound to the Arctic Waste where we now find ourselves wintering. The sad Irony is that Torrington's doctor had told him that going to Sea would be good for his health.

Chief Surgeon Peddie and Dr. McDonald on Terror treated Torrington, of course, but I was present several times during the Diagnosis stage and was escorted to their ship by several of Erebus's crewmen after the young stoker died this morning.

When his illness became Obvious in early November, Captain Crozier relieved the 20-year-old of his duties as stoker down in the poorly ventilated lowest deck — the coal dust in the air alone there is enough to asphyxiate a person with normal lungs — and John Torrington had been in a consumptive invalid's Downward Spiral since then. Still, Torrington might have survived for many more months had not there been an Intermediating Agent of his death. Dr. Alexander McDonald tells me that Torrington, who had become too weak in recent weeks even to allow his short Constitutionals around the lower deck, helped by his messmates, came down with Pneumonia on Christmas Day, and it had been a Death Watch since then. When I saw the body this morning, I was shocked at how Emaciated the dead John Torrington was, but both Peddie and McDonald explained that his appetite had been waning for two months, and even though the ship's surgeons altered his Diet more heavily toward Canned Soups and Vegetables, he had continued to lose weight.

This morning I watched as Peddie and McDonald prepared the corpse — Torrington in a clean striped shirt, his hair recently and carefully cut, his nails clean — binding the usual clean cloth around his head to keep the jaw from dropping, then binding him with more strips of white cotton at the elbows, hands, ankles, and big toes. They did this in order to hold the Limbs together while they weighed the poor boy — 88 Pounds! — and otherwise prepared his body for burial. There was no discussion of Postmortem Examination since it was obvious that Consumption accelerated by Pneumonia had killed the lad, so there was no worry of contamination reaching other crew members.

I helped my two surgeon colleagues from HMS Terror lift Torrington's body into the coffin carefully prepared for it by the ship's able Carpenter, Thomas Honey, and by his mate, a man named Wilson. There was no rigor mortis. The carpenters had left a residue of Wood Shavings along the bottom of the coffin, so carefully constructed and shaped out of standard ship's mahogany, with a Deeper Pile of shavings under Torrington's head, and because there was yet little Scent of Decay, the air was scented primarily by the wood shavings.

3 January, 1846 —

I keep thinking about John Torrington's Burial late yesterday.

Only a small contingent of us attended from HMS Erebus, but along with Sir John, Commander Fitzjames, and a few officers, I made the Crossing on Foot from our ship to theirs, and hence the extra two hundred yards to the Shore of Beechey Island.

I have not been able to Imagine a worse winter than the one we have suffered frozen into this small anchorage in the lee of Beechey Island itself, set in the cusp of larger Devon Island, but Commander Fitzjames and others have assured me that our Situation here — even with the Treacherous Pressure Ridges, Terrible Dark, Howling Storms, and Constantly Menacing Ice — would be a thousand times worse out beyond this anchorage, out where the Ice flows down from the Pole like a hail of Enemy Fire from some Borean god.

John Torrington's crewmates gently lowered his coffin — already covered with a fine blue wool — over the railing of their ship, which is Wedged High on its own pillar of ice, while other Terror seamen lashed the coffin to a large Sledge. Sir John himself draped a Union Jack over the coffin, and then Torrington's friends and messmates set themselves into Harness and pulled the sledge the six hundred feet or so to the ice-and-gravel shore of Beechey Island.

All of this was performed in near Absolute Dark, of course, since even at midday, the sun makes no Appearance here in January and has not done so for three months. It shall be another month and more, they tell me, before the Southern Horizon welcomes back our Fiery Star. At any rate, this entire procession — coffin, sledge, man-haulers, officers, surgeons, Sir John, Royal Marines in full dress concealed under the same drab Slops the rest of us were wearing — was illuminated only by bobbing lamplight as we made our way across the Frozen Sea to the Frozen Shore. Men from Terror had chopped and shoveled away at the several recently arisen Pressure Ridges which stood between us and the graveled beach, so there were few Deviations from our sad Route. Earlier in the Winter, Sir John ordered a system of Stout Poles, ropes, and Hanging Lanterns to line the shortest route between the Ships and the graveled isthmus where several Structures had been built — one to house much of the ships' stores, removed should ice destroy our vessels; another as a sort of emergency bunkhouse and Scientific Station; and a third housing the armourer's forge, set here so that the Flames and Sparks should not ignite our tindered shipboard Homes. I have learned that Sailors fear fire at sea above almost everything else. But this Course of wooden Poles and Lanterns had to be abandoned since the ice is constantly shifting, rising up, and scattering or smashing anything set out on it.

It was snowing during the burial. The wind was blowing hard, as it always does here on this godforsaken Arctic Waste. Just north of the burial site rose Sheer Black Cliffs, as inaccessible as the Mountains of the Moon. The lanterns lit on Erebus *and* Terror *were only the dimmest of glows through the blowing snow. Occasionally a fragment of Cold Moon would appear from between quickly moving clouds, but even this thin, pale moonlight was quickly lost in the snow and dark. Dear God, this is truly a Stygian bleakness.*

Some of the strongest men from Terror *worked almost without pause since the hours right after Torrington's death, using pickaxe and spade to excavate his Grave — a regulation five feet deep, as commanded by Sir John. The Hole had been dug out of the most Severely Frozen ice and rock and one glance at it revealed to me what Labour had gone into its excavation. The flag was removed, and the coffin was lowered carefully, almost reverently, into the narrow Pit. Snow immediately covered the top of the coffin and Glistened in the light from our several lanterns. One man, one of Crozier's officers, set the wooden headboard in place and it was driven down into the frozen gravel with a few slams of a giant wooden hammer wielded by a giant of a seaman. The words on that carefully carved headboard read*

SACRED

TO

THE MEMORY OF

JOHN TORRINGTON

WHO DEPARTED

THIS LIFE

JANUARY 1ST

A.D. 1846

ON BOARD OF

H.M. SHIP TERROR

AGED 20 YEARS

Sir John conducted the Service and spoke the Eulogy. It went on for some time and the soft drone of his soft voice was interrupted only by the Wind and by the stamping of Feet as the men tried to avoid frostbite of the toes. I confess that I heard little of Sir John's eulogy — between the howling wind and my own wandering thoughts, oppressed by the loneliness of the place, by the memory of the striped-shirted body, limbs bound, that had just been lowered into that Cold Hole, and oppressed most of all by the Eternal blackness of the cliffs above the graveled isthmus.

4 January, 1846 —

Another man is dead.

One of our own here on HMS Erebus, *twenty-five-year-old John Hartnell, an able seaman. Just after what I still think of as 6:00 p.m., just as the tables were being lowered on chains for the men's dinner, Hartnell stumbled against his brother, Thomas, fell to the deck, coughed blood, and was dead within five minutes. Surgeon Stanley and I were with him when he died in the cleared part of the forward area of the lower deck which we use for Sick Bay.*

This death stunned us. Hartnell had shown no symptoms of scurvy or consumption. Commander Fitzjames was there with us and could not hide his consternation. If this were some Plague or beginning of Scurvy moving through the crew, we needed to know at once. It was decided then and there, while the curtains were drawn and before anyone made ready to prepare John Hartnell for his coffin, that we would do a Postmortem Examination.

We cleared the table in the Sick Bay area, shielded our Actions further by moving some crates between the milling Men and ourselves, drew the curtain around our Labours as best we could, and I fetched my instruments. Stanley, although Chief Surgeon, suggested that I should do the work since I had studied as an anatomist. I made the initial Incision and began.

Immediately I realized that in my Haste I had used the inverted-Y incision that I had used in training on cadavers when I was in a rush. Rather than the more common Y, with the two arms of the incision reaching down from the shoulders and meeting at the base of the sternum, my upside-down Y incision had the arms of the Y starting near each hip and meeting near Hartnell's umbilicus. Stanley commented upon it and I was embarrassed.

"Whatever is faster," I said softly to my fellow surgeon. "We must do this quickly — the men hate knowing that bodies of their crewmates are being opened."

Surgeon Stanley nodded and I continued. As if to Confirm my statement, Hartnell's younger brother, Thomas, began shouting and crying from just the other side of the curtain. Unlike Torrington's slow decline on Terror, *giving his crewmates time to come to terms with his death, time to parcel out his belongings and prepare letters for Torrington's mother, John Hartnell's sudden collapse and death had shocked the men here. None of them could abide the idea that the ship's surgeons were cutting into the body. Now only the bulk, rank, and demeanor of Commander Fitzjames stood between the angry brother, confused seamen, and our Sick Bay. I could hear that the younger Hartnell's messmates and Fitzjames's presence were holding him back, but even as my scalpel cut through tissue and my knife and rib spreader opened the corpse for examination, I could hear the Muttering and Anger just a few yards beyond the curtain.*

First I removed Hartnell's heart, cutting away part of the trachea with it. I held it up to the lantern light, and Stanley took it and washed away blood with a dirty rag. We both inspected it. It looked normal enough — not visibly diseased. With Stanley still holding the Organ close to the light, I made one cut in the right ventricle, then one in the left. Peeling the tough muscle back, both Stanley and I reviewed the valves there. They seemed healthy.

Dropping Hartnell's heart back into his abdominal cavity, I dissected the lower part of the able seaman's lungs with quick strokes of my scalpel.

"There," said Surgeon Stanley.

I nodded. There were obvious signs of scarring and other indications of Consumption, as well as signs that the seaman recently had been suffering from pneumonia. John Hartnell, like John Torrington, had been tubercular, but this older, stronger — and according to Stanley — harsher and louder sailor had concealed the Symptoms, perhaps even from himself. Until today, when he keeled over and died just minutes before getting his salt pork

Pulling and cutting the Liver free, I held it under the light, and both Stanley and I believed that we noticed adequate confirmation of the consumption as well as indications that Hartnell had been too heavy a Drinker for too long a time.

Just yards away on the other side of the curtain, Hartnell's brother, Thomas, was shouting, furious, being held in check only by Commander Fitzjames's stern bark. I could tell from the voices that several of the other officers — Lieutenant Gore, Lieutenant Le Vesconte and Fairholme, even Des Voeux, the mate — had joined in calming and intimidating the Mob of sailors.

"Have we seen enough?" whispered Stanley.

I nodded again. There had been no sign of Scurvy on the body, on the face or in the mouth, or in the organs. While it remained a Mystery how the consumption or pneumonia or a combination of the two had been able to kill the able-bodied seaman so quickly, it was at least obvious that we had nothing to fear from some Plaguelike Disease.

The noise from the crew's Berthing Space was growing Louder, so I quickly thrust the lung samples, liver, and other organs back in the abdominal cavity with the heart, taking no care to set them in proper place, more or less squeezing them into a Mass, and then I returned Hartnell's chest plate roughly back in place. (Later I was to Realize that I had set it in upside down.) Chief Surgeon Stanley then closed up the inverted-Y incision, using a large needle and heavy sail thread with a quick, confident motion that would have done credit to any sailmaker.

Within another minute we had Hartnell's clothes back on — rigor mortis was beginning to be a problem — and we thrust the curtain aside. Stanley — whose voice is deeper and more resonant than mine — assured Hartnell's brother and the other men that all we had remaining was to wash their crewmate's body so that they could prepare it for burial.

6 January, 1846 —

For some reason this Burial Service was Harder on me than the first. Again we had the solemn Procession from the ship — with only Erebus *and its crew involved this time, although Dr. McDonald, Surgeon Peddie, and Captain Crozier joined us from* Terror.

Again the flag-covered coffin — the men had dressed Hartnell's upper body in three layers, including his brother Thomas's best shirt, but had wrapped his naked lower body in only a shroud, leaving the top half of the coffin open for several hours in the black-creped Sick Bay on the lower deck before the nails were hammered in for the burial service. Again the slow sledge procession from the Frozen Sea to the Frozen Shore, lanterns bobbing in the black night, although the stars were out this Midday and no snow fell. The Marines had work to do, since three of the Great White Bears came sniffing closer, looming like white wraiths out of the ice blocks, and the men had to fire muskets at them to drive them away — visibly wounding one bear in the side.

Again the Eulogy from Sir John — although shorter this time, since Hartnell was not as well liked as young Torrington had been — and again we walked back across the creaking, squeaking, moaning ice alone, under the stars dancing in the Cold this time, the only sound behind us the dwindling scrape of spades and pickaxes filling in the frozen soil in the new hole next to Torrington's nicely tended grave.

Perhaps it was the black cliff face Looming over All that murdered my Spirits this second burial. Although I deliberately stood where my back was to the Cliff this time, closer to Sir John so that I could hear the Words of Hope and Solace, I was always aware of that cold, black, vertical, lifeless and lightless slab of insensate Stone behind me — a portal, it seemed, to that Country from Which No Man Has Ever Returned. Compared to the Cold Reality of that black, featureless stone, even Sir John's compassionate and inspired words had little effect.

The morale on both ships is very low. We are not yet a Full Week into the new year, and already two of our Company have died. Tomorrow the four of us surgeons have agreed to Meet in a Private Place — the carpenter's room belowdecks on Terror *— to discuss what should be done to avoid more Mortality in what seems to be a Cursed Expedition.*

The headstone on this second grave read

SACRED TO THE MEMORY OF

JOHN HARTNELL, A.B. OF H.M.S.

EREBUS

DIED JANUARY 4TH, 1846

AGED 25 YEARS

'THUS SAITH THE LORD OF HOSTS, CONSIDER YOUR WAYS'

HAGGAI, I., 7.

The wind has come up in the last hour, it is almost Midnight and most of the lamps are out here on the lower deck of Erebus. *I listen to the wind howl and think of those two cold Low Heaps of Loose Stone out on that black, windy isthmus, and I think of the dead men in those two cold Holes, and I think of the Featureless Black Face of Rock, and I can imagine the fusillade of snow pellets already working to eradicate the letters on the wooden headstones.*

7

FRANKLIN

Lat. 70°-03'-29" N., Long. 98°- 20' W.
Approximately 28 miles NNW of
King William Land, 3 September, 1846

C aptain Sir John Franklin had rarely been so pleased with himself.

The previous winter frozen in at Beechey Island, hundreds of miles northeast of his present position, had been uncomfortable in many ways — he would be the first to admit that to himself or to a peer, although he had no peers on this expedition. The death of three members of the expedition, first Torrington and Hartnell so early in January, then Private William Braine of the Royal Marines on 3 April, all of consumption and pneumonia, had been a shock. Franklin was not aware of any other Navy expedition losing three men of natural causes so early in their endeavor.

It was Franklin himself who had chosen the inscription on the thirty-two-year-old Private Braine's headstone — *"Choose this day whom ye shall serve," Joshua, ch. xxiv, 15* — and for a short while the words had seemed as much a challenge to the unhappy crews of *Erebus* and *Terror,* not yet near mutiny but neither so far away from it, as it was a message to the nonexistent passersby of Braine's, Hartnell's, and Torrington's lonely graves on that terrible spit of gravel and ice.

Nonetheless, the four surgeons met and conferred after Hartnell's death and decided that incipient scurvy might be weakening the men's constitutions, allowing pneumonia and such congenital defects as consumption to rise to lethal proportions. Surgeons Stanley, Goodsir, Peddie, and McDonald recommended to Sir John that the men's diet be changed — fresh food when possible (although there was almost none except polar bear possible in the dark of winter, and they had discovered that eating the liver of that great, ponderous beast could be fatal for some unknown reason) and, failing finding fresh meat and vegetables, cutting back on the men's preferred salted pork and beef, or salted birds, and relying more on the tinned foods — vegetable soups and the like.

Sir John had gone along with the recommendation, ordering the diet on both ships changed so that no less than half the meals were prepared with tinned foods from stores. It seemed to have turned the trick. No more men died, or were even seriously sick, between Private Braine's death in early April and the day both ships were freed from their icy imprisonment within the harbor of Beechey Island in late May of 1846.

After that, the ice broke up quickly and Franklin, following the paths through the leads chosen by his two fine ice masters, steamed and sailed south and west, going, as the captains of Sir John's generation liked to say, like smoke and oakum.

Along with the sunlight and open water, animals, birds, and aquatic life returned in plenitude. During those long, slow, arctic summer days, where the sun remained above the horizon until almost midnight and the temperature sometimes rose above freezing, the skies were filled with migrating birds. Franklin himself could identify the petrels from the teals, eider ducks from the little auks, and the sprightly little puffins from all others. The ever-widening leads around *Erebus* and *Terror* were alive with right whales that would have been the envy of any Yankee whaler, and there was a profusion of cod, herring, and other small fish, as well as the large beluga and bowhead whales. The men put out the whaling boats and fished, often shooting some of the small whales just for sport.

Every hunting party came back with fresh game for the tables each night — birds, of course, but also those confounded ringed and harp seals, so impossible to shoot or catch in their holes in the winter, now brazen on the open ice and easy targets. The men did not enjoy the taste of the seals — too oily and astringent — but something about the blubber in the slimy beasts appealed to all their winter-starved appetites. They also shot the large bellowing walruses visible through telescopes tusking away for oysters along the shores, and some hunting parties returned with the pelts and flesh of the white arctic fox. The men ignored the lumbering polar bears unless the waddling beasts seemed ready to attack or contest the kill of the human hunters. No one really liked the taste of the white bears and certainly not when there was so much tastier game to be found.

Franklin's orders included an option: if he "found his way toward the Southern Approach to the North-West Passage blocked by Ice or other Obstacles," to turn north and to follow the Wellington Passage into "the Open Polar Sea" — in essence, to sail to the north pole. But Franklin did what he had done without question his entire life: he followed his primary orders. This second summer in the arctic, his two ships had sailed south from Devon Island, Franklin leading HMS *Erebus* and HMS *Terror* past Cape Walker into the unknown waters of an icy archipelago.

The previous summer, it had seemed as if he would have to settle for sailing to the north pole rather than finding the North-West Passage. Captain Sir John Franklin had reason to be proud of his speed and efficiency so far. During his shortened summer voyage time that year before, 1845 — they had departed England late and Greenland even later than planned — he had nonetheless crossed Baffin Bay in record time, passed through Lancaster Sound south of Devon Island, then through Barrow Strait, and found his way south past Walker Point blocked by ice so late in August. But his Ice Masters reported open water to the north, past the western reaches of Devon Island into the Wellington Channel, so Franklin obeyed his secondary orders and turned north toward what could be an ice-free passage into the Open Polar Sea and the north pole.

There had been no opening to the fabled Open Polar Sea. The Grinnell Peninsula, which might have been part of an unknown Arctic Continent for all the men of the Franklin Expedition knew, had blocked their way and forced them to follow open water north by west, then almost due west, until they reached the western tip of that peninsula, turned north again, and encountered a solid mass of ice that extended north from the Wellington Channel apparently to infinity. Five days of sailing along that high wall of ice convinced Franklin, Fitzjames, Crozier, and the ice masters that there was no Open Polar Sea north of the Wellington Channel. At least not that summer.

Worsening ice conditions made them turn south, around the landmass previously known as only Cornwallis Land but now understood to be Cornwallis Island. If nothing else, Captain Sir John Franklin knew, his expedition had solved that puzzle.

With pack ice quickly freezing in place that late summer of 1845, Franklin had finished circumnavigating the huge, barren Cornwallis Island, reentered the Barrow Strait north of Cape Walker, confirmed that the way south past Cape Walker was still blocked — now solid with ice — and sought out their winter anchorage at little Beechey Island, entering a little harbour they had reconnoitered two weeks earlier. They'd arrived just in time, Franklin knew, for the day after they anchored in the shallow water of that harbour, the last open leads in Lancaster Sound beyond closed up and the moving pack ice would have made any more sailing impossible. It was doubtful if even such masterpieces of reinforced iron-and-oak technology as *Erebus* and *Terror* would have survived the winter out in the channel ice.

But now it was summer and they had been sailing south and west for weeks, restoring their provisions when they could, following every lead, seeking out any glint of open water they could spy from the lookout's position high on the main mast, and every day smashing and forcing their way through the ice when they had to.

HMS *Erebus* continued to lead the way in the ice-breaking, as was her right as the flagship and her logical responsibility as the heavier ship with a more powerful — five horsepower more powerful — steam engine, but — confound it! — the long shaft to the screw had been bent by underwater ice; it would neither retract nor work properly, and *Terror* had moved into the lead position.

And with the icy shores of King William Land visible no more than fifty miles ahead of them to the south, the ships had moved out from under the protection of the huge island to their north — the one which had blocked their way directly to the southwest past Cape Walker, where his orders had directed him to sail, and instead had forced him south through Peel Sound and previously unexplored straits. Now the ice to the south and west had become active and almost continuous once again. Their pace had slowed to a crawl. The ice was thicker, the icebergs more frequent, the leads thinner and farther apart.

This morning of 3 September, Sir John had called a conference of his captains, top officers, engineers, and ice masters. The crowd fit comfortably into Sir John's personal cabin; where this space on HMS *Terror* served as a Great Cabin for the officers, complete with libraries and music, the width of the stern of HMS *Erebus* was Sir John Franklin's private quarters — twelve feet wide by an amazing twenty feet long, with a private commode "seat of ease" in a room to itself on the starboard side. Franklin's private privy was almost exactly the size of Captain Crozier's and all the other officers' entire cabins.

Edmund Hoar, Sir John's steward, had lengthened the dining table until it could accommodate all the officers present — Commander Fitzjames, Lieutenants Gore, Le Vesconte, and Fairholme from *Erebus,* Captain Crozier and Lieutenants Little, Hodgson, and Irving from *Terror.* Besides those eight officers seated on either side of the table — Sir John sat at its head near the starboard bulkhead and entrance to his private head — also present, standing at the foot of the table, were the two ice masters, Mr. Blanky from *Terror* and Mr. Reid from *Erebus,* as well as the two engineers, Mr. Thompson from Crozier's ship and Mr. Gregory from the flagship. Sir John had also asked one of the surgeons, Stanley from *Erebus,* to be in attendance. Franklin's steward had set out grape juice, cheeses, and ship's biscuits, and there was a short period of chatting and relaxing before Sir John called the conference to order.

———

"Gentlemen," said Sir John, "I am sure you all know why we are gathered here. Our expedition's advance the last two months, thanks to the graciousness of God, has been wonderfully successful. We have left Beechey Island almost three hundred and fifty miles behind us. Lookouts and our sledge scouts still report glimpses of open water far to our south and west. It still may be in our power — God willing — to reach this open water and to navigate the North-West Passage this very autumn.

"But the ice to our west is increasing, I understand, in both thickness and frequency. Mr. Gregory reports that *Erebus*'s main shaft has been damaged by ice and that although we can make headway under steam, the flagship's effectiveness has been compromised. Our coal supplies are dwindling. Another winter will soon be upon us. In other words, gentlemen, we must decide today what our course of action and direction shall be. I think it is not unfair to say that the success or failure of our expedition shall be determined by what we decide here."

There was a long silence.

Sir John gestured to the red-bearded ice master of HMS *Erebus*. "Perhaps it would be helpful, before we venture opinions and open discussion, to hear from our ice masters, engineers, and surgeon. Mr. Reid, could you inform the others of what you told me yesterday about our current and projected ice conditions?"

Reid, standing on the *Erebus* side of the five men at the end of the table, cleared his throat. Reid was a solitary sort and speaking in such exalted company made his face flush redder than his beard.

"Sir John, . . . Gentlemen . . . it ain't no secret that we've been God-da— . . . that is . . . darned lucky in terms of ice conditions since the ships was released from ice in May and since we left Beechey Island harbour around the first of June. While we was in the straits, we been plowing through mostly sludge ice. That ain't no problem. Nights — them few hours of darkness we have what's called nights up here — we cut through pancake ice, that's like what we been seeing the last week as the sea's always on the verge of freezing, but that ain't no real problem either.

"We been able to stay away from the young ice along the shores — that's more serious stuff. Behind that's the fast ice that'll tear the hull off even a ship as reinforced as this here and *Terror* in the lead. But as I say, we stayed away from fast ice . . . so far."

Reid was sweating, obviously wishing he hadn't gone on so long but also knowing that he hadn't fully addressed Sir John's question yet. He cleared his throat and continued.

"So with the moving ice, Sir John and your honours, we ain't had much problem with the brash ice and thicker drift ice, and the bergy bits — them little bergs what broke off from the real bergs — we been able to avoid them because of the wide leads and open water we've been able to find. But all that's coming to an end, sirs. What with the nights getting longer, the pancake ice is always there now and we're running into more and more of them growlers and hummocky flows. And it's the hummocky flows that's got Mr. Blanky and me worried."

"Why is that, Mr. Reid?" asked Sir John. His expression showed his habitual boredom at discussions of the different ice conditions. To Sir John, ice was ice — something to be broken through, gone around, and overcome.

"It's the snow, Sir John," said Reid. "The deep snow atop 'em, sir, and the tidemarks on the side. Such always signifies old pack ice ahead, sir, real screwed pack, and that's where we get frozen in, you see. And as far as we can see or sledge ahead to the south and west, sirs, it's all pack ice, except for the possible glint of open water way down south of King William Land."

"The North-West Passage," Commander Fitzjames said softly.

"Perhaps," said Sir John. "Most probably. But to get there we shall have to cross through more than a hundred miles of pack ice — perhaps as much as two hundred miles of it. I am told that the ice master of *Terror* has a theory about why the conditions worsen to our west. Mr. Blanky?"

Thomas Blanky did not blush. The older ice master's voice was a staccato explosion of syllables as blunt as musket fire.

"It's death to enter that pack ice. We've come too far already. The fact is, since we came out of Peel Sound, we've been looking at an ice stream as bad as anything north of Baffin Bay and it's getting worse every day."

"Why is that, Mr. Blanky?" asked Commander Fitzjames. His confident voice showed a slight lisp. "This late in the season, I understand that we should still have open leads until the sea actually freezes, and close to the mainland, say southwest of the peninsula of King William Land, we should have some open water for another month or more."

Ice Master Blanky shook his head. "No. This isn't no pancake ice or sludge ice, gentlemen, it's *pack ice* we're looking at. It's coming down from the northwest. Think of it as a series of giant *glaciers* — calving bergs and freezing the sea for hundreds of miles as it flows south. We've been protected from it, is all."

"Protected by what?" asked Lieutenant Gore, a strikingly handsome and personable officer.

It was Captain Crozier who answered, nodding at Blanky to step back. "By all the islands to our west as we've come south, Graham," said the Irishman. "Just as we discovered a year ago that Cornwallis Land was an island, we know now that Prince of Wales Land is really Prince of Wales Island. The bulk of it has been blocking the full force of the ice stream until we came out of Peel Sound. Now we can see that it's full pack ice being forced south between whatever islands are up there to our northwest, possibly all the way to the mainland. Whatever open water is down there along the coast to the south won't last long. Nor will we if we forge ahead and try to winter out here in the open pack ice."

"That is one opinion," said Sir John. "And we thank you for it, Francis. But we must decide now on our course of action. Yes, . . . James?"

Commander Fitzjames looked, as he almost always did, relaxed and in charge. He had actually put on weight during the expedition so his buttons appeared ready to pop from his uniform. His cheeks were rosy and his blond hair hung in longer curls than he'd worn in England. He smiled at everyone along the table.

"Sir John, I agree with Captain Crozier that to be caught out in the pack ice we're facing would be unfortunate, but I do not believe that will be our fate should we forge on. I believe that it is imperative that we get as far south as we can — either to reach the open water to realize our goal of finding the North-West Passage, which I think we shall do before winter sets in, or simply to find safer waters near the coast, perhaps a harbour where we can winter in relative comfort as we did at Beechey Island. At the very least, we know from Sir John's earlier expeditions overland and from previous Naval expeditions that the water tends to stay open much later near the coast because of the warmer waters coming in from the rivers."

"And if we don't reach open water or the coast by going south-west?" Crozier asked softly.

Fitzjames made a deprecating gesture. "At least we will be closer to our goal come the thaw next spring. What's our alternative, Francis? You aren't seriously suggesting returning up the strait to Beechey or trying to retreat to Baffin Bay?"

Crozier shook his head. "Right now we can as easily sail to the *east* of King William Land as to the west — more easily, since we know from our lookouts and scouts that there is still ample open water to the east."

"Sail to the east of King William Land?" said Sir John, his voice incredulous. "Francis, that would be a dead end. We would be shel-tered by the peninsula, yes, but frozen in hundreds of miles east of here in a long bay that might not thaw next spring."

"Unless . . . ," said Crozier, looking around the table, "unless King William Land is also an island. In which case we would have the same protection from the pack ice flowing from the northwest that Prince of Wales Island has been giving us the past month of travel. It would be probable that the open water on the east side of King William Land will extend almost to the coast, where we can sail west along the warmer waters there for more weeks, perhaps find a perfect harbour — perhaps at a river's mouth — if we have to spend a second winter in the ice."

There was a long silence in the room.

Erebus lieutenant H. T. D. Le Vesconte cleared his throat. "You believe in the theories of that eccentric Dr. King," he said softly.

Crozier frowned. He knew that the theories of Dr. Richard King, not even a Navy man, a mere civilian, were disliked and discarded, pri-marily because King believed — and had very vocally expressed — that such large Naval expeditions as Sir John's were foolish, danger-ous, and absurdly expensive. King believed, based upon his mapping and experience with Back's overland expedition years before, that

King William Land was an island, while Boothia, the ostensible island even farther to their east, was actually a long peninsula. King argued that the easiest and safest way to find the North-West Passage was to send small parties overland in northern Canada and to follow the warmer coastal waters west, that the hundreds of thousands of square miles of sea to the north were a dangerous maze of islands and ice streams that could swallow up a thousand *Erebus*es and *Terror*s. Crozier knew that there was a copy of King's controversial book in *Erebus*'s library — he had checked it out and read it and it was still in Crozier's cabin on *Terror*. But he also knew that he was the only man on the expedition who had, or would, read the book.

"No," said Crozier, "I'm not subscribing to King's theories, I am merely suggesting a strong possibility. Look, we thought that Cornwallis Land was huge, perhaps part of the Arctic Continent, but we sailed around it in a few days. Many of us thought that Devon Island continued north and west directly into the Open Polar Sea, but our two ships found the western end of it and we saw the open channels north.

"Our orders instructed us to sail directly southwest from Cape Walker, but we found that Prince of Wales Land was directly in the way — and what is more pertinent, that it is, almost without doubt, an island. And the low strip of ice we glimpsed to our east while heading south may well have been a frozen strait — separating Somerset *Island* from Boothia Felix and showing that King was wrong, that Boothia is not a continuous peninsula all the way north to Lancaster Sound."

"There is no evidence that the low area of ice we saw was a strait," said Lieutenant Gore. "It makes more sense to consider it a low ice-covered isthmus such as we saw on Beechey Island."

Crozier shrugged. "Perhaps, but our experience on this expedition has been that landmasses previously thought to be very large or connected have in truth been shown to be islands. I suggest that we reverse course, avoid the pack ice to the southwest, and sail east and then south down the eastern coast of what may well be King William *Island*. At the very least, we will be sheltered from this . . . seaborne *glacier* that Mr. Blanky talks about . . . and should we discover the worst, that it is a long, narrow bay, odds are very great that we could sail north again around the point of King William Land next summer and be right back here and none the worse for wear."

"Except for the coal burned and the precious time lost," said Commander Fitzjames.

Crozier nodded.

Sir John rubbed his round and well-shaved cheeks.

In the silence, *Terror*'s engineer, James Thompson, spoke. "Sir John, gentlemen, since the issue of the ships' coal reserves has been brought up, I would like to mention that we are very, very close to reaching — and I mean this quite literally — a point of no return in terms of our fuel. Just in the past week, using our steam engines to force a way through the fringes of this pack ice, we've gone through more than a quarter of our remaining coal reserves. We are now just above fifty percent of our coal remaining . . . less than two weeks of normal steaming, but only days' worth trying to force the ice as we have. Should we be frozen in for another winter, we will be burning much of that reserve just to heat the ships again."

"We could always send a party ashore to cut trees for firewood," said Lieutenant Edward Little, sitting at Crozier's left.

For a minute every man in the room except Sir John laughed heartily. It was a welcome break in the tension. Perhaps Sir John was remembering his first overland expeditions north to the coastal regions now to their south. The mainland tundra extended for nine hundred barren miles south from the coast before one would see the first tree or serious shrub.

"There is one way to maximize our steaming distances," Crozier said softly into the more relaxed silence following the laughter.

Everyone's head turned toward the captain of HMS *Terror*.

"We transfer all the crew and coal from *Erebus* to *Terror* and make a run for it," continued Crozier. "Either through the ice to the southwest or to reconnoiter down the east coast of King William Land or Island."

"Go for broke," said Ice Master Blanky into the now stunned silence. "Aye, that makes sense."

Sir John could only blink. When he finally found his voice, it still sounded incredulous, as if Crozier had made a second joke that he could not understand. "Abandon the flagship?" he said at last. "Abandon *Erebus?*" He glanced around as if just having the other officers look at his cabin would settle this issue once and for all — the bulkheads lined with shelves and books, the crystal and china on the table, the three Preston Patent Illuminators set into the width of the overhead, allowing rich late-summer light to stream into the cabin.

"Abandon *Erebus,* Francis?" he said again, his voice stronger but spoken in a tone of someone who wants to be let in on a rather obscure joke.

Crozier nodded. "The main shaft is bent, sir. Your own engineer, Mr. Gregory, has told us that it cannot be repaired, nor retracted any longer, outside of a dry dock. Certainly not while we are in pack ice. It will only get worse. With two ships, we have only a few days' or a week's worth of coal for the battle necessary to fight the pack ice. We'll all be frozen in — both ships — if we fail. If we freeze into the open sea to the west of King William Land, we have no idea where the current will move the ice of which we will be a part. The odds are great that we could be thrown into the shallows along the lee shore there. That means the destruction of even such wonderful ships as these." Crozier nodded around him and at the skylights above.

"But if we consolidate our fuel in the less damaged ship," continued Crozier, "and especially if we have some luck finding open water down the east side of King William Land, we will have much more than a month's fuel for steaming west along the coast as fast as we can. *Erebus* would have been sacrificed, but we might — we *will* — reach Point Turnagain and familiar points along the coast within a week. Complete the North-West Passage into the open Pacific this year instead of next."

"Abandon *Erebus?*" repeated Sir John. He did not sound cross or angry, only perplexed by the absurdity of the notion being discussed.

"Conditions would be very cramped aboard *Terror,*" said Commander Fitzjames. He seemed to be seriously considering the notion.

Captain Sir John turned to his right and stared at his favorite officer. Sir John's face was slowly assuming the cold smile of a man who has not only been left out of a joke on purpose but may well be the butt of it.

"Crowded, but not intolerably so for a month or two," said Crozier. "My Mr. Honey and your ship's carpenter, Mr. Weekes, will supervise the breaking down of interior bulkheads — all officers' quarters to be dismantled except for the Great Room, which could be turned into Sir John's quarters aboard *Terror,* and perhaps the officers' mess. That would give us ample room, even for another year or more on the ice. These old bomb ships have a great amount of space belowdecks, if nothing else."

"It would take some time to transfer the coal and ship's stores," said Lieutenant Le Vesconte.

Crozier nodded again. "I've had my purser, Mr. Helpman, work out some preliminary figures. You may remember that Mr. Goldner, the expedition's provisioner of canned foods, failed to deliver the bulk of his goods until less than forty-eight hours before we sailed, so we had to repack both ships to a great extent. We did so in time to meet our departure date. Mr. Helpman estimates that with both crews working through the long daylight, sleeping on half-watch schedules, that everything we can hold on one ship can be transferred to *Terror* in just under three days. We'd be a crowded family for some weeks, but it would be as if we're starting anew on the expedition — coal reserves topped off, food for another year, a ship in full working condition."

"Go for broke," repeated Ice Master Blanky.

Sir John shook his head and chuckled as if he had finally had enough of this particular joke. "Well, Francis, that is a very . . . *interesting* . . . speculation, but of course we shall not be abandoning *Erebus.* Nor *Terror* either, should your ship suffer some minor misfortune. Now, the one thing I've not heard at this table today is a suggestion to *retreat* to Baffin Bay. Am I correct in the assumption that no one is suggesting that?"

The room was silent. Overhead came the rumble and scrape of crewmen holystoning the decks for the second time that day.

"Very well then, it is decided," said Sir John. "We shall press forward. Not only do our orders direct us to do this, but as several of you gentlemen have pointed out, our safety increases the closer we get to the coast of the mainland, even if the land itself there is every bit as inhospitable as the dreadful islands we have passed up here. Francis, James, you may go tell your crews of our decision."

Sir John stood.

For a dazed second the other captains, officers, ice masters, engineers, and surgeon could only stare, but then the Naval officers stood quickly, nodded, and began filing out of Sir John's huge cabin.

The surgeon Stanley was plucking at Commander Fitzjames's sleeve as the men went forward along the narrow companionway and stomped up the ladder to the deck.

"Commander, Commander," Stanley said, "Sir John never called on me to report, but I wanted to tell everyone about the increasing numbers of putrid foodstuff we've been finding in the tinned goods."

Fitzjames smiled but freed his arm. "We'll arrange a time for you to tell Captain Sir John in private, Mr. Stanley."

"But I've told *him* in private," persisted the little surgeon. "It's the other officers I wanted to inform in case . . ."

"Later, Mr. Stanley," said Commander Fitzjames.

The surgeon was saying something else, but Crozier passed beyond earshot and waved to John Lane, his bosun, to bring his gig alongside for the sunny ride back up the narrow lead to where *Terror*'s bow was wedged in the thickening pack ice. Black smoke still poured from the leading ship's funnel.

———

Heading southwest into the pack ice, the two ships made slow headway for another four days. HMS *Terror* burned coal at a prodigious rate, using its steam engine to throw itself against the ever-thicker pack ice. The glint of possible open water far to the south had disappeared, even on sunny days.

The temperature dropped suddenly on 9 September. The ice on the long thin line of open water behind the trailing *Erebus* covered over with pancake ice and then froze solid. The sea around them was already a lifting, surging, static white mass of growlers, real icebergs, and sudden pressure ridges.

For six days, Franklin tried every trick in his arctic inventory — spreading black coal powder on the ice ahead of them to melt it more quickly, backing sail, sending out fatigue parties day and night with their giant ice saws to remove the ice in front of them block by block, shifting ballast, having a hundred men at a time hack away with chisels, shovels, picks, and poles, setting kedge anchors far ahead of them in the thickening ice and winching *Erebus* — which had resumed the lead ahead of *Terror* on the last day before the ice had suddenly thickened — a yard at a time. Finally Franklin ordered every able man onto the ice, rigged lines for everyone and sledge harnesses for the largest men among them, and tried hauling the ships forward a sweating, cursing, shouting, spirit-killing, gut-wrenching, backbreaking inch at a time. Always, promised Sir John, was the reality of open coastal water just another twenty or thirty or fifty miles ahead of them.

The open water might as well have been on the surface of the moon.

During the lengthening night of 15 September, 1846, the temperature plummeted to below zero and the ice began moaning and scraping against both ships' hulls. In the morning, everyone who came on deck could see for themselves that in each direction the sea had become a white solid stretching to the horizon. Between sudden snow squalls, both Crozier and Fitzjames were able to get adequate sun sightings to fix their positions. Each captain figured that they were beset at roughly 70 degrees 5 minutes north latitude, 98 degrees, 23 minutes west longitude, some twenty-five miles off the northwest shore of King William Island, or King William Land, whichever the case might be. It was a moot point now.

They were in open sea ice — moving pack ice — and stranded directly in front of the full onslaught of Ice Master Blanky's "moving glacier," bearing down on them from polar regions to the northwest from all the way to the unimaginable North Pole. There was not a sheltering harbour, to their knowledge, within one hundred miles and no way to get there if there were one.

At two o'clock that afternoon, Captain Sir John Franklin ordered the boiler fires to be drawn on both *Erebus* and *Terror*. Steam was let down in both boilers. Just enough pressure would be kept up to move warmed water through the pipes heating the lower decks of each ship.

Sir John made no announcement to the men. None was required. That night as the men settled into their hammocks on *Erebus* and as Hartnell whispered his usual prayer for his dead brother, thirty-five-year-old Seaman Abraham Seeley, in the hammock next to him, hissed, "We're in a world of shit now, Tommy, and not your prayers nor neither Sir John's is going to get us out of it . . . not for another ten months at least."

8

CROZIER

It has been one year, two months, and eight days since Sir John's eventful conference aboard *Erebus,* and both ships are frozen in the ice roughly where they were that September day in 1846. Although the current from the northwest moves the entire mass of ice, over the past year it has rotated ice, icebergs, pressure ridges, and both trapped Royal Navy ships in slow circles so that their position has remained about the same, stranded some twenty-five miles north-northwest of King William Land and slowly revolving like a blotch of rust on one of the metal music disks in the officers' Great Room.

Captain Crozier has spent this November day — or rather those hours of darkness which once included daylight as a component — searching for his missing crewmen William Strong and Thomas Evans. There is no hope for either man, of course, and there is great risk that others will be taken by the thing on the ice, but they search nonetheless. Neither captain nor crew would have it any other way.

Four teams of five men each, one man to carry two lanterns and four ready with shotguns or muskets, search in four-hour shifts. As one team comes in frozen and shaking, a replacement team waits on deck in cold-weather slops, guns cleaned, loaded, and ready, lanterns filled with oil, and they resume the search in the quadrant the other team has just quit. The four teams are moving out from the ship in ever-widening circles through the ice jumbles, their lanterns now visible to the lookouts on deck through the icy mist and darkness, now obscured by growlers, ice boulders, pressure ridges, or distance. Captain Crozier and a seaman with a red lamp move from quadrant to quadrant, checking with each team and then returning to *Terror* to look in on the men and conditions there.

This goes on for twelve hours.

At two bells in the first dogwatch — 6:00 p.m. — the last search parties all come in, none having found the missing men but several seamen shamefaced at having fired their weapons at wind shrieking among the jagged ice or at the ice itself, thinking some serac a looming white bear. Crozier is the last one in and follows them down to the lower deck.

Most of the crewmen have stored their wet slops and boots and gone forward to their mess at tables that have all been cranked down on chains and the officers gone aft for their meal by the time Crozier comes down the ladder. His steward, Jopson, and first lieutenant, Little, hurry over to help him out of his ice-rimmed outer layers.

"You're frozen, Captain," says Jopson. "Your skin is white with frostbite. Come back aft to the officers' mess for supper, sir."

Crozier shakes his head. "I need to go talk to Commander Fitzjames. Edward, has there been a messenger from his ship while I was out?"

"No, sir," says Lieutenant Little.

"Please eat, Captain," persists Jopson. For a steward he's a large man, and his deep voice becomes more of a growl than a whine when he's imploring his captain.

Crozier shakes his head. "Be so kind as to wrap up a couple of biscuits for me, Thomas. I'll chew on them as I walk to *Erebus*."

Jopson shows his displeasure at this foolish decision but hurries forward to where Mr. Diggle is busy at his huge stove. Just now, at dinnertime, the lower deck is as toasty warm as it's going to be in any twenty-four-hour period — the temperature rising as high as the mid-forties. Very little coal is being burned for heat these days.

"How many men do you want to go with you, Captain?" asks Little.

"None, Edward. After the men have eaten, I want you to get at least eight parties on the ice for a final four hours of searching."

"But, sir, is it advisable for you to . . . ," begins Little but then stops.

Crozier knows what he was going to say. The distance between *Terror* and *Erebus* is only a little more than a mile, but it is a lonely, dangerous mile and sometimes takes several hours to cross. If a storm comes up or the wind simply starts blowing the snow, men can become lost or no longer make progress into the gale. Crozier himself has forbidden men to make the crossing alone and when messages have to be sent, he dispatches at least two men along with orders to turn back at the first bad weather. Besides the two-hundred-foot-high iceberg now rising between the two ships, often blocking views even of flares and fires, the pathway — although worked at being kept shoveled open and relatively flat almost every day — is really a maze of constantly shifting seracs, ice-stepped pressure ridges, upturned growlers, and ice jumble mazes.

"It's all right, Edward," says Crozier. "I'll take my compass."

Lieutenant Little smiles even though the joke is wearing thin after three years in the area. The ships are beset, as far as their instruments can measure, almost directly over the north magnetic pole. A compass is about as useful here as a divining rod.

Lieutenant Irving sidles up. The young man's cheeks glisten from applied salve where frostbite has left white patches and caused the skin to die and peel back. "Captain," begins Irving in a rush, "have you seen Silence out on the ice?"

Crozier has taken his cap and muffler off and is rubbing the ice out of his sweat- and mist-dampened hair. "You mean she's not in her little hidey-hole behind the sick bay?"

"No, sir."

"Did you look elsewhere on the lower deck?" Crozier is mostly worried that with most of the men gone on watch and out in search parties, the Esquimaux witch has gotten into something she shouldn't have.

"Aye, sir. No sign of her. I've asked around and no one remembers seeing her since yesterday evening. Since before . . . the attack."

"Was she on deck when the thing attacked Private Heather and Seaman Strong?"

"No one knows, Captain. She might have been. Only Heather and Strong were on deck then."

Crozier lets out a breath. It would be ironic, he thinks, if their mystery guest, who first appeared on the day this nightmare began six months ago, has finally been carried off by the creature so linked with her appearance.

"Search the whole ship, Lieutenant Irving," he says. "Every nook, cranny, cupboard, and cable locker. We'll use Occam's razor and assume that if she isn't on board that she's . . . been taken."

"Very well, sir. Shall I choose three or four men to help me in the search?"

Crozier shakes his head. "Just you, John. I want everyone else back out on the ice searching for Strong and Evans in the hours before lamps-out, and if you don't find Silence, assign yourself to a party and join them."

"Aye, aye, sir."

Reminded of his casualty, Crozier goes forward through the men's mess to the sick bay. Usually at supper time, even in these dark days, there is the morale-lifting sound of conversation and laughter from the men at their mess tables, but tonight there is silence broken only by the scrape of spoons on metal and the occasional belch. The men are exhausted, slumped on their sea chests they use as chairs, and only tired, slack faces look up at their captain as he squeezes past.

Crozier knocks on the wooden post to the right of the sick bay curtain and passes through.

Surgeon Peddie looks up from some sewing he is doing on Able Seaman George Cann's left forearm at a table in the centre of the space. "Good evening, Captain," says the surgeon. Cann knuckles his forehead with his good hand.

"What happened, Cann?"

The young sailor grunts. "Fucking shotgun barrel slides up me sleeve and touches me fucking bare arm when I was climbing a fucking ice ridge, Captain, pardon the language. I pull the shotgun out and six inches o' fucking flesh comes with it."

Crozier nods and looks around. The sick bay is small, but six cots are crammed into it now. One is empty. Three men, down with what Peddie and McDonald tell him is probably scurvy, are sleeping.

A fourth man, Davey Leys, is staring at the ceiling — he has been conscious but strangely unresponsive for almost a week now. The fifth cot holds Marine Private William Heather.

Crozier lifts a second lamp from its hook on the starboard partition and holds the light over Heather. The man's eyes glisten but he does not blink as Crozier brings the lamp closer. His pupils seem permanently dilated. His skull has been wrapped with a bandage but blood and grey matter are already seeping through.

"Is he alive?" Crozier asks softly.

Peddie comes over, wiping his bloody hands with a rag. "He is, strangely enough."

"But we could see his brains on deck. I can see them now."

Peddie nods tiredly. "That happens. In other circumstances, he might even recover. He would be an idiot, of course, but I could screw in a metal covering where his skull is missing and his family, if he has any, could take care of him. Keep him as a sort of pet. But here . . ." Peddie shrugs. "Pneumonia or scurvy or starvation will carry him away."

"How soon?" asks Crozier. Seaman Cann has gone out through the curtain.

"Only God knows," says Peddie. "Is there to be more searching for Evans and Strong, Captain?"

"Yes." Crozier sets the lantern back in place on the partition near the entrance. Shadows flow back over Marine Private Heather.

"You are aware, I am sure," says the exhausted surgeon, "that there is no chance for young Evans or Strong but every probability that each search will bring more wounds, more frostbite, a greater chance of amputation — many men have already lost one or more toes — and the inevitability that someone will shoot someone else in their panic."

Crozier looks steadily at the surgeon. If one of his officers or men had spoken to Crozier like this, he would have the man flogged. The captain makes allowance for the man's civilian status and exhausted state. Dr. McDonald has been in his hammock with the influenza for three days and nights and Peddie has been very busy. "Please let me worry about the risks of continued searching, Mr. Peddie. You worry about stitching up the men stupid enough to set bare metal against their skin when it's sixty below zero. Besides, if that thing out there carried you off into the night, wouldn't you want us to search for you?"

Peddie laughs hollowly. "If this particular specimen of *Ursus maritimus* carries me off, Captain, I can only hope that I have my scalpel with me. So I can put it through my own eye."

"Then keep your scalpel close, Mr. Peddie," says Crozier and goes out through the curtain into the odd silence of the crewmen's mess area.

Jopson is waiting in the galley glow with a kerchief of hot biscuits.

Crozier enjoys his walk in spite of the creeping cold that has made his face, fingers, legs, and feet feel like they are on fire. He knows that this is preferable to them being numb. And he enjoys the walk in spite of the fact that between the slow moanings and sudden shrieks of the ice moving under and around him in the dark and the constant moan of the wind, he is certain that he is being stalked.

Twenty minutes into his two-hour walk — more a climb, scuttle, and ass-sliding descent, up, over, and down pressure ridges for much of the way tonight than a walk — the clouds part and a three-quarters moon appears and illuminates the phantasmagoric landscape. The moon is bright enough to have an ice-crystalled lunar halo around it, actually two concentric halos, he notices, the diameter of the larger one sufficient to cover a third of the eastern night sky. There are no stars. Crozier dims his lamp to save oil and walks on, using the boat pike he's brought along to test every fold of black ahead of him to make sure it's a shadow and not a crack or crevasse. He has reached the area on the east side of the iceberg now where the moon is blocked, the berg throwing a black and twisted shadow for a quarter of a mile of ice. Jopson and Little insisted he take a shotgun, but he told them he did not want to carry the weight on the walk. More to the point, he doesn't really believe a shotgun will be of any use against the foe they had in mind.

In a particular moment of rare calm, everything strangely quiet except for his laboured breathing, Crozier suddenly recalls a resonant instance from when he was a young boy returning home late one winter evening from an afternoon in the wintry hills with his friends. At first he rushed headlong alone across the frost-rimed heather, but then he paused half a mile or so from his house. He remembers standing there watching the lighted windows in the village as the last of the winter twilight faded from the sky and the surrounding hills became vague, black, featureless shapes, unfamiliar to a boy so young, until even his own house, visible at the edge of town, lost all definition and three-dimensionality in the dying light. Crozier remembers the snow beginning to fall and himself standing there alone in the darkness beyond the stone sheep pens, knowing that he would be cuffed for his tardiness, knowing that arriving later would only make the cuffing worse, but having no will nor want to walk toward the light of home yet. He enjoyed the soft sound of night wind and the knowledge that he was the only boy — perhaps the only human being — out there in the dark on the windy, frozen-grass meadows on this night that smelled of coming snow, alienated from the lighted windows and the warm hearths, very aware that he was of the village but not *part* of it at that moment. It was a thrilling, almost erotic feeling — an illicit discovery of self separated from everyone and everything else in the cold and dark — and he feels it again now, as he has more than a few times during his years of arctic service at opposite poles of the earth.

Something is coming down the high ridge behind him.

Crozier turns the oil lantern up and sets it on the ice. The circle of golden light reaches barely fifteen feet and makes the darkness beyond all the worse. Using his teeth, he pulls off his heavy mitten, lets it drop to the ice, leaving only a thin glove on that hand, shifts the boat pike to his left hand, and pulls his pistol from his coat pocket. Crozier cocks the weapon as the rustle of sliding ice and snow on the pressure ridge becomes louder. The line of shadow from the iceberg blocks the moonlight here and the captain can make out only the huge shapes of ice blocks seeming to move and shift in the flickering light.

Then something furry and indistinct moves along the ice ledge he has just descended, some ten feet above him and less than fifteen feet to the west, well within leaping distance.

"Halt," Crozier says, extending the heavy pistol. "Identify yourself."

The shape makes no sound. It moves again.

Crozier holds his fire. Dropping the long boat pike, he grabs up the lantern and thrusts it forward.

He sees the rippling fur moving and almost fires, but checks himself at the last instant. The shape slides lower, moving quickly and surely down onto the ice. Crozier lowers the hammer on his pistol and sets it back in his pocket, crouching to retrieve his mitten even while keeping the lantern extended.

Lady Silence walks into the light, her fur parka and sealskin pants making her look like some short, rounded beast. The hood is pulled forward against the wind and Crozier cannot see her face.

"God-damn it, woman," he says softly. "You came a horny seaman's second from being shot. Where the hell have you been, anyway?"

She steps closer, almost within reaching distance, but her face remains veiled by darkness within the hood.

Feeling a sudden chill along the back of his neck and down his spine — Crozier is remembering his grandmother Moira's description of a banshee's transparent skull face within the folds of its black hood — he raises the lantern between them.

The young woman's face is human, not banshee, the dark eyes wide as they reflect the light. She has no expression. Crozier realizes that he has never seen an expression on her face, other than perhaps a mildly inquisitive look. Not even on the day they shot and killed her husband or brother or father and she watched the man choke to death on his own blood.

"No wonder the men think you're a witch and a Jonah," says Crozier. On the ship, in front of the men, he is always polite and formal to this Esquimaux wench, but he is not on the ship or in front of the men now. It is the first and only time he and the damned woman have been away from the ship at the same time. And he is very cold and very tired.

Lady Silence stares at him. Then she extends a mittened hand, Crozier lowers the lamp toward it, and he sees that she is offering him something — a limp grey offering, like a fish that has been gutted and boned, leaving only the skin.

He realizes that it is a crewman's woolen stocking.

Crozier takes it, feels the lump at the toe of the sock, and for a second is sure that the lump will be part of a man's foot, probably the ball of the foot and the toes, still pink and warm.

Crozier has been to France and known men posted to India. He has heard the story of werewolves and were-tigers. In Van Diemen's Land, where he met Sophia Cracroft, she told him of the locals' tales of natives who could turn into a monstrous creature there they called the Tasmanian devil — a creature capable of tearing a man limb from limb.

Shaking the stocking, Crozier looks into Lady Silence's eyes. They are as black as the holes in the ice through which the Terrors lowered their dead until even those holes froze solid.

It is a lump of ice, not part of a foot. But the stocking itself is not frozen hard. The wool has not been out here for long in −60-degree cold. Logic suggests that this woman has brought it with her from the ship, but for some reason Crozier does not think so.

"Strong?" says the captain. "Evans?"

Silence shows no reaction to the names.

Crozier sighs, stuffs the stocking in his coat pocket, and lifts the boat pike. "We're closer to *Erebus* than *Terror*," he says. "You'll just have to come with me."

Crozier turns his back on her, feeling the chill along his neck and spine again in doing so, and crunches off through the rising wind toward the now-visible outline of the *Terror*'s sister ship. A minute later he can hear her soft footsteps on the ice behind him.

They clamber over a final pressure ridge, and Crozier can see that *Erebus* is more brightly lit than he's seen before. A dozen or more lanterns hang from spars just on this visible port side of the icebound, absurdly lifted, and steeply canting vessel. It's a prodigious waste of lamp oil.

The *Erebus*, Crozier knows, has suffered more than his *Terror*. Besides bending the long propeller shaft last summer — the shaft that had been built to be retracted but hadn't done so in time to avoid damage from the underwater ice during their ice-breaking in July — and losing the screw itself, the flagship had been mauled more than her sister ship during the past two winters. The ice in the comparative shelter of the Beechey Island harbour had warped, splintered, and loosened hull timbers to a greater degree on *Erebus* than on *Terror;* the flagship's rudder was damaged in their past summer's mad dash for the Passage; the cold has popped more bolts, rivets, and metal brackets in Sir John's ship; much more of the iron icebreaker cladding on *Erebus* has been torn free or buckled. And while *Terror* has also been raised and squeezed by the ice, the last two months of this third winter have seen HMS *Erebus* lifted on a virtual pedestal of ice even while the pressure from the sea pack splintered a long section of the starboard bow, port stern, and bottom hull amidships.

Sir John Franklin's flagship, Crozier knows — and its current captain, James Fitzjames, and his crew also know — will never sail again.

Before stepping into the area lit by the ship's hanging lanterns, Crozier steps behind a ten-foot-tall serac and pulls Silence in behind him.

"Ahoy the ship!" he bellows in his loudest dockyard-commanding voice.

A shotgun roars and a serac five feet from Crozier splinters into a shower of ice chips catching the lantern's dim glow.

"Avast that, God-damn your blind eyes, you fucking lubbing idle-brained shit-for-wits idiot!" roars Crozier.

There is a commotion on *Erebus*'s deck as some officer wrestles the shotgun away from the shit-for-wits idiot sentinel.

"All right," Crozier says to the cowering Esquimaux girl. "We can go now."

He stops, and not just because Lady Silence is not following him out into the light. He can see her face by the reflected glow, and she is smiling. Those full lips that never move are curling up ever so slightly. Smiling. As if she had understood and enjoyed his outburst.

But before Crozier can confirm that the smile is real, Silence backs into the shadows of the ice jumble and is gone.

Crozier shakes his head. If the crazy woman wants to freeze out here, let her. He has business with Captain Fitzjames and then a long walk home in the dark before he can sleep.

Tiredly, realizing that he's not felt his feet for the past half hour at least, Crozier stumps his way up the ramp of dirty ice and snow toward the deck of the dead Sir John's broken flagship.

9

FRANKLIN

Lat. 70°-05' N., Long. 98°-23' W.
May, 1847

Captain Sir John Franklin may have been the only man aboard either ship who remained outwardly serene when spring and summer simply did not arrive in April, May, and June of 1847.

At first, Sir John had not formally announced that they were stuck for at least another year; he didn't have to. The previous spring, up at Beechey Island, the crew and officers had watched with eager anticipation not only as the sun returned but as the close pack broke up into discrete floes and slushy brash ice, open leads appeared, and the ice gave up its grip. By late May of 1846 they had been sailing again. Not so this year.

The previous spring crew and officers had observed the return of the many birds, whales, fish, foxes, seals, walruses, and other animals, not to mention the greening of the lichen and low heather on the islands they were sailing toward by early June. Not this year. No open water meant no whales, no walruses, almost no seals — the few ring seals they spied were as hard to catch or shoot now as they had been in early winter — and nothing but dirty snow and grey ice as far as the eye could see.

The temperature stayed cold despite the longer hours of sun each day. Although Franklin had the masts fully stepped, the spars reset, the rigging redone, and fresh canvas on both ships brought up by mid-April, there was no purpose to it. The steam boilers remained unfired except to move warm water through the heating pipes. Lookouts reported a solid table of white extending in all directions. Icebergs stayed in place where they had been frozen in place the previous September. Fitzjames and Lieutenant Gore, working with Captain Crozier from *Terror,* had confirmed from their star sightings that the current was pushing the ice flow south at a pitiful one and a half miles per *month,* but this mass of ice on which they were pinned had rotated counterclockwise all winter, returning them to where they had begun. Pressure ridges continued to pop up like white gopher burrows. The ice was thinning — fire-hole teams could saw through it now — but it was still more than ten feet thick.

Captain Sir John Franklin remained serene through all of this because of two things: his faith and his wife. Sir John's devout Christianity buoyed him up even when the press of responsibility and frustration collaborated to press him down. Everything that happened was, he knew and fervently believed, God's will. What seemed inevitable to the others need not be in a universe administered by an interested and merciful God. The ice might suddenly break up in midsummer, now less than six weeks away, and even a few weeks of sailing and steaming time would bring them triumphantly to the North-West Passage. They would steam west along the coast as long as they had coal, then sail the rest of the way to the Pacific, escaping the far northern latitudes sometime in mid-September just before the pack ice solidified again. Franklin had experienced greater miracles in his lifetime. Just being appointed commander of this expedition — at age sixty, after the humiliation of Van Diemen's Land — had been a greater miracle.

As deep and sincere as Sir John's faith in God was, his faith in his wife was even deeper and sometimes more frightening. Lady Jane Franklin was an indomitable woman . . . *indomitable* was the only word for her. Her will knew no bounds and in almost every instance, Lady Jane Franklin would bend the errant and arbitrary ways of the world to the iron command of her will. Already, he imagined, after being out of touch for two full winters, his wife had mobilized her very impressive private fortune, public contacts, and apparently limitless force of will to cajole the Admiralty, the Parliament, and God alone knew what other agencies into searching for him.

This last fact bothered Sir John somewhat. Above all else, he did not want to be "rescued" — approached either overland or by sea during the brief summer thaw by hastily assembled expeditions under the command of whiskey-breath Sir John Ross or the young Sir James Ross (who would be forced out of his arctic retirement, Sir John was sure, by Lady Jane's demands). That way lay shame and ignominy.

But Sir John remained serene because he knew that the Admiralty was not moved *quickly* on any matter, not even by such a forceful fulcrum and lever as his wife Jane. Sir John Barrow and the other members of the mythical Arctic Council, not to mention Sir John's official superiors in the Royal Navy Discovery Service, knew quite well that HMS *Erebus* and HMS *Terror* had provisions for three years, longer if severe rations were imposed, not to mention the capability of fishing and hunting game should they ever come in sight of any. Sir John knew that his wife — his *indomitable* wife — would force a rescue should it come to that, but the terrible and wonderful inertia of the Royal Navy would almost certainly ensure that such a rescue attempt would not be outfitted until the spring and summer of 1848, if not later.

Accordingly, in late May of 1847, Sir John prepared five sledge parties to look over the horizons in each direction, including one instructed to sledge back the way they had come, searching for any open water. They departed on May 21, 23, and 24, with Lieutenant Gore's party — the crucial one — departing last and sledging toward King William Land to the southeast.

Besides reconnoitering, First Lieutenant Graham Gore had a second important responsibility — leaving Sir John's first written message cached ashore since the beginning of the expedition.

Here Captain Sir John Franklin had come as close to disobeying orders as he ever had in his Naval lifetime. His instructions from the Admiralty had been to erect cairns and to leave messages in caches for the length of his exploration — should the ships not appear beyond the Bering Strait on schedule, this would be the only way for Royal Navy rescue ships to know in which direction Franklin had headed and what might have caused their delay. But Sir John had not left such a message at Beechey Island, even though he had almost nine months to prepare one. In truth, Sir John had hated that first cold anchorage — had been ashamed of the deaths of the three crewmen by consumption and pneumonia that winter — so he had privately decided to leave the graves behind as the only message he needed to send. With any luck, no one would find the graves for years after his victory of forcing the North-West Passage had been bannered everywhere in the world.

But it had now been almost two years since his last dispatch to his superiors, so Franklin dictated an update to Gore and set it in an air-tight brass cylinder — one of two hundred he'd been supplied with.

He personally instructed Lieutenant Gore and Second Mate Charles Des Voeux on where to put the message — into the six-foot-high cairn left on King William Land by Sir James Ross some seventeen years earlier at the westernmost point of his own explorations. It would be, Franklin knew, the first place the Navy would look for word of his expedition, since it was the last landmark on everyone's maps.

Looking at the lone squiggle of that last landmark on his own map in the privacy of his cabin on the morning before Gore, Des Voeux, and six crewmen set out, Sir John had to smile. In an act of respect seventeen years ago — not to mention an act now generating some minor irony — Ross had named the westernmost promontory along the shore Victory Point and then named the nearby highlands Cape Jane Franklin and Franklin Point. It was as if, Sir John thought, look-ing down at the weathered sepia map with its black lines and large unfilled spaces to the west of the carefully marked Victory Point, Destiny or God had brought him and these men here.

His dictated message — it was in Gore's handwriting — was, Sir John thought, succinct and businesslike:

_____ *of May 1847. HM Ships Erebus and Terror . . . Wintered in the Ice in Lat. 70°05′ N. Long. 98°23′ W. Having wintered in 1846–7 at Beechey Island in Lat. 74°43′28″ N Long. 90°39′15″ W after having ascended Wellington Channel to Lat. 77° — and returned by the*

*west side of Cornwallis Island. Sir John Franklin commanding the
Expedition. All well. Party consisting of 2 officers and 6 Men left the
ships on Monday 24ᵗʰ· May 1847. Gm. Gore, Lieut. Chas. F. Des
Voeux, mate.*

Franklin instructed Gore and Des Voeux to sign the note and fill
in the date before sealing the canister and setting it deep inside James
Ross's cairn.

What Franklin hadn't noticed during his dictation — nor Lieutenant Gore corrected — was that he had given the wrong dates for
their winter at Beechey Island. It had been the first winter of 1845–46
in their sheltered ice harbour at Beechey; this year's terrible time in the
open pack ice had been the winter of 1846–47.

No matter. Sir John was convinced that he was leaving a minor message to posterity — possibly to some Royal Navy historian who wished
to add an artifact to Sir John's future report on the expedition (Sir John
fully planned to write another book, the proceeds of which would
bring his private fortune almost up to that of his wife's) — and not dictating a report that would be read by anyone in the immediate future.

On the morning that Gore's sledge party set out, Sir John bundled
up and went down onto the ice to wish them Godspeed.

"Do you have everything you need, gentlemen?" asked Sir John.

First Lieutenant Gore — fourth in overall command behind Sir
John, Captain Crozier, and Commander Fitzjames — nodded, as did
his subordinate, Second Mate Des Voeux, the mate flashing a smile.
The sun was very bright and the men were already wearing the wire-
mesh goggles that Mr. Osmer, *Erebus*'s purser, had issued them to
prevent blindness from the sun's glare.

"Yes, Sir John. Thank you, sir," said Gore.

"Plenty of woollies?" joked Sir John.

"Aye, sir," said Gore. "Eight layers of well-woven good Northum-
berland sheep shearings, Sir John, nine if one counts the woolen
drawers."

The five crewmen laughed to hear their officers banter so. The
men, Sir John knew, loved him.

"Prepared for camping out on the ice?" Sir John asked one of the men, Charles Best.

"Oh, aye, Sir John," said the short but stocky young seaman. "We have the Holland tent, sir, and them eight wolfskin blanket robes what we sleep on and under. And twenty-four sleeping bags, Sir John, which purser sewn up for us from the fine Hudson's Bay blankets. We'll be toastier on the ice than aboard the ship, m'lord."

"Good, good," Sir John said absently. He looked to the southeast where King William Land — or Island, if Francis Crozier's wild theory was to be believed — was visible only as a slight darkening of the sky over the horizon. Sir John prayed to God, quite literally, that Gore and his men would find open water near the coast, either before or after caching the expedition's message. Sir John was prepared to do everything in his power — and beyond — to force the two ships, as beaten up as *Erebus* was, across and through the softening ice, if only it would soften, and into the comparative protection of coastal waters and the potential salvation of land. There they might find a calm harbour or gravel spit where the carpenters and engineers could make repairs enough to *Erebus* — straightening the propeller shaft, replacing the screw, shoring up the twisted internal iron reinforcements and perhaps replacing some of the missing iron cladding — to allow them to press on. If not, Sir John thought — but had not yet shared the thought with any of his officers — they would follow Crozier's distressing plan from the previous year and anchor *Erebus,* transfer its diminishing coal reserves and crew to *Terror,* and sail west along the coast in that crowded (but jubilant, Sir John was sure, jubilant) remaining ship.

At the last moment, the assistant surgeon on *Erebus,* Goodsir, had implored Sir John to allow him to accompany the Gore party, and although neither Lieutenant Gore nor Second Mate Des Voeux were enthusiastic about the idea — Goodsir was not popular with the officers or men — Sir John had allowed it. The assistant surgeon's argument for going was that he needed to gain more information on edible forms of wildlife to use against the scurvy that was the primary fear of all arctic expeditions. He was particularly interested in the behavior of the only animal present this odd non-summer arctic summer, the white bear.

Now, as Sir John watched the men finish lashing their gear to the heavy sledge, the diminutive surgeon — he was a small man, pale, weak-looking, with a receding chin, absurd side whiskers, and a strangely effeminate gaze that put off even the usually universally affable Sir John — sidled up to start a conversation.

"Thank you again for allowing me to accompany Lieutenant Gore's party, Sir John," said the little medico. "The outing could be of inestimable importance in our medical evaluation of the antiscorbutic properties of a wide variety of flora and fauna, including the lichens invariably present on the terra firma of King William Land."

Sir John involuntarily made a face. The surgeon could not have known that his commander had once survived on thin soup made from such lichen for several months. "You're very welcome, Mr. Goodsir," he said coolly.

Sir John knew that the slouching young popinjay preferred the title of "Doctor" to "Mister," a dubious distinction since, although from a good family, Goodsir had trained as a mere anatomist. Technically on par with the warrant officers on board both ships, the civilian assistant surgeon was entitled, in Sir John's eyes, only to be called *Mr.* Goodsir.

The young surgeon blushed at his commander's coolness after the easy banter with the crewmen, tugged at his cap, and took three awkward steps backward on the ice.

"Oh, Mr. Goodsir," added Franklin.

"Yes, Sir John?" The young upstart was actually red-faced, almost stammering with embarrassment.

"You must accept my apologies that in our formal communiqué to be cached at Sir James Ross's cairn on King William Land, we referred only to two officers and six *men* in Lieutenant Gore's party," said Sir John. "I had dictated the message prior to your request to accompany the party. I would have written *an officer, a warrant officer, an assistant surgeon, and five men* had I but known you would be included."

Goodsir looked confused for a moment, not quite sure of what Sir

John was trying to tell him, but then he bowed, tugged at his cap again, mumbled, "Very good, there is no problem, I understand, thank you, Sir John," and backed away again.

A few minutes later, as he watched Lieutenant Gore, Des Voeux, Goodsir, Morfin, Ferrier, Best, Hartnell, and Private Pilkington diminish across the ice to the southeast, Sir John, under his beaming countenance and outward serenity, actually contemplated failure.

Another winter — another full year — in the ice could undo them. The expedition would be out of food, coal, oil, pyroligneous ether for lamp fuel, and rum. This last item's disappearance might well mean mutiny.

More than that, if the summer of 1848 were as cold and unyielding as this summer of 1847 fully promised to be, another full winter or year in the ice would destroy one or both of their ships. Like so many failed expeditions before them, Sir John and his men would be fleeing for their lives, dragging longboats and whalers and hastily clabbered-together sledges across the rotten ice, praying for open leads and then cursing them when the sledges fell through the ice and the contrary winds blew the heavy boats back on the pack ice, leads that meant days and nights of rowing for the starving men. Then, Sir John knew, there would be the overland part of any escape attempt — eight hundred miles and more of featureless rock and ice, rivers of constant rapids strewn with boulders each capable of smashing their smaller boats (the larger boats could not get down northern Canada's rivers, he knew from experience), and native Esquimaux who were hostile more often than not and thieving liars even when they seemed to be friendly.

Sir John continued watching as Gore, Des Voeux, Goodsir, and the five crewmen and single sledge disappeared in the ice glare to the southeast and wondered idly if he should have brought dogs on this trip.

Sir John had never liked the idea of dogs on arctic expeditions. The animals were sometimes good for the men's morale — at least right up to the point when the animals had to be shot and eaten — but they were, in the final analysis, dirty, loud, and aggressive creatures. The deck of a ship carrying enough dogs to do any good, that is to harness to sledges the way the Greenland Esquimaux liked to do, was a deck filled with incessant barking, crowded kennels, and the constant stench of excrement.

He shook his head and smiled. They'd only brought one dog along on this expedition — the mutt named Neptune — not to mention a small monkey named Jocko — and that, Sir John was sure, was quite enough of a menagerie for this particular ark.

The week after Gore's departure seemed to crawl for Sir John. One by one the other sledge parties reported in, their men exhausted and frozen and their woolen layers soaked with sweat from the exertion of hauling their sledge across or around countless ridges. Their reports were the same.

From the east toward the Boothia Peninsula — no open water. Not even the smallest lead.

From the northeast toward Prince of Wales Island and the path of their approach to this frozen desert — no open water. Not even the hint of dark sky beyond the horizon which sometimes suggested open water. In eight days of hard sledging the men had not been able to reach Prince of Wales Island, nor even catch a glimpse of it. The ice was more tortured with ridges and icebergs than the men had ever seen.

From the northwest toward the unnamed strait that led the ice stream south toward them around the west coast and southern tip of Prince of Wales Island — nothing seen except white bears and frozen sea.

From the southwest toward the presumed landmass of Victoria Land and the theoretical passage between the islands and the mainland — no open water, no animals except the confounded white bears, hundreds of pressure ridges, so many frozen-in-place icebergs that Lieutenant Little — the officer from HMS *Terror* whom Franklin had put in command of this particular sledging party, made up of Terrors — reported that it was like trying to struggle west through a mountain range of ice where the ocean should be. The weather had been so bad on the last part of the trip that three of the eight men had seriously frostbitten toes and all eight of them were snow-blind to some extent, Lieutenant Little himself completely blind for the last five days and sick with terrible headaches. Little, an old arctic hand, Sir John understood, a man who had gone south with Crozier and James Ross eight years earlier, had to be loaded onto the sledge and hauled back by the few men who could still see well enough to pull.

No open water anywhere in the twenty-five straight-line miles or so they had explored — twenty-five straight-line miles gained in perhaps a hundred miles of marching around and over obstacles. No arctic foxes or hares or caribou or walruses or seals. Obviously no whales. The men had been prepared to haul their sledge around cracks and small leads in search of real open water, but the surface of the sea, Little reported, his sunburned skin peeling away from his nose and temples below and above the white bandages over his eyes, was a white solid. At the outermost point on their western odyssey, perhaps twenty-eight miles from the ships, Little had ordered the man with the best remaining eyesight, a bosun's mate named Johnson, to climb the tallest iceberg in their vicinity. Johnson had taken hours to do so, hacking out narrow steps for his feet with his pickaxe and then digging in the cleats the purser had driven through the soles of his leather boots. Once on the top, the seaman had used Lieutenant Little's telescope to look northwest, west, southwest, and south.

The report was dismal. No open water. No land. Jangles of seracs, ridges, and bergs to the distant white horizon. A few white bears, two of which they later shot for fresh meat — but the livers and heart were unhealthy to humans they'd discovered. The men's strength was already depleted from hauling the heavy sledge over so many ridges, and in the end they cut out less than a hundred pounds of the gamy, muscular meat to fold in tarps and haul back to the ship. Then they skinned the larger bear for its white fur, leaving the rest of the bears to rot on the ice.

Four of the five scouting expeditions returned with bad news and frostbitten feet, but Sir John waited most anxiously for Graham Gore's return. Their last, best hope had always been to the southeast, toward King William Land.

Finally, on the third of June, ten days after Gore's departure, lookouts from high in the masts called down that a sledge party was approaching from the southeast. Sir John finished his tea, dressed appropriately, and then joined the mob of men who'd rushed on deck to see what they could see.

The surface party was visible even by men on deck now, and when Sir John lifted his beautiful brass telescope — a gift from the officers and men of a twenty-six-gun frigate Franklin had commanded in the Mediterranean more than fifteen years earlier — one glance explained the lookouts' audible confusion.

At first glance all seemed well. Five men were pulling the sledge, just as during Gore's departure. Three figures were running alongside or behind the sledge, just as on the day Gore left. All eight accounted for then.

And yet . . .

One of the running figures did not appear to be human. At a distance of more than a mile and glimpsed between the seracs and ice-rubble upthrusts that had once been the placid sea here, it looked as if a small, round, headless but very furry animal was running behind the sledge.

And worse, Sir John could not make out Graham Gore's distinctive tall figure in the lead nor the dashing red comforter he sported. All of the other figures hauling or running — and certainly the lieutenant would not have been *hauling* the sledge while his subordinates were fit — seemed too short, too bent, and too *inferior.*

Worst of all, the sledge seemed far too heavily packed for the return trip — the rations had included a week's extra canned goods, but they were already three days over the estimated maximum round-trip time. For a minute Sir John's hopes soared as he considered the possibility that the men had killed some caribou or other large land animals and were bringing in fresh meat, but then the distant forms emerged from behind the last large pressure ridge, still more than half a mile away across the ice, and Sir John's telescope revealed something horrible.

Not caribou meat on the sledge, but what appeared to be two dead human bodies lashed atop the gear, one man stacked atop the other in a callous fashion that could only mean death. Sir John could now plainly make out two exposed heads, one at each end of the stack, with the head belonging to the body on top showing long white hair the likes of which no man aboard either ship possessed.

They were rigging ropes down the side of the canted *Erebus* to aid their portly captain's descent onto the steep ice there. Sir John went belowdecks only long enough to add his ceremonial sword to his uniform. Then, pulling his cold-weather slops on over uniform, medals, and sword, he went up on deck and then over the side — puffing and wheezing, allowing his steward to help him down the slope — to greet whoever or whatever was approaching his ship.

10

GOODSIR

Lat. 69° 37′ 42″ Long. 98° 41′
King William Land, 24 May–3 June, 1847

O ne reason that Dr. Harry D. S. Goodsir had insisted on coming along on this exploration party was to prove that he was as strong and able a man as most of his crewmates. He soon realized that he wasn't.

On the first day, he had insisted — over the quiet objections of Lieutenant Gore and Mr. Des Voeux — on taking his turn at man-hauling the sledge, allowing one of the five crewmen so assigned to take a break and walk alongside.

Goodsir almost could not do it. The leather-and-cotton harness the sailmakers and pursers had constructed, cleverly attached to the pull ropes by a knot the sailors could tie or undo in a second and which Goodsir could not figure out for the life of him, was too large for his narrow shoulders and sunken chest. Even by cinching the front girth of the harness as tight as it would go, it slipped on him. And he, in turn, slipped on the ice, falling repeatedly, forcing the other men off their stride of pull, pause, gasp, pull. Dr. Goodsir had not worn such issued ice boots before and the nails driven through the soles caused him to trip over his own feet.

He had trouble seeing out of the heavy wire-mesh goggles, but when he raised them to his forehead, the glare of arctic sun on arctic ice half-blinded him within minutes. He'd put on too many layers, and now several of those layers of wool were so soaked with his own sweat that he was shivering even while being overheated by the extraordinary exertion. The harness pinched on nerves and cut off circulation to his thin arms and cold hands. He kept dropping his outer mittens. His panting and gasping grew so loud and constant that he was ashamed.

After an hour of such absurdity, Bobby Ferrier, Tommy Hartnell, John Morfin, and Marine Private Bill Pilkington — the other men in harness, Charles Best walking alongside now — each pausing to brush the snow off his anorak, looking at one another but saying nothing, of him never finding the rhythm of literally working in harness with others, he accepted the offer of relief from Best and, during one of the brief stops, slipped out of the harness and let the true men pull the heavy, high-mounted sledge with its wooden runners that constantly wanted to freeze to the ice.

Goodsir was exhausted. It was still morning of the first day on the ice, and he was so tired out from the hour of pulling that he could have happily unfurled his sleeping bag, set it on one of the wolfskin blanket robes, and gone to sleep until the next day.

And this was before they reached the first real pressure ridge.

The ridges to the southeast of the ship were the lowest in sight for the first two miles or so, almost as if the beset *Terror* herself had somehow kept the ice smoother in her lee, forcing the ridges farther away. But by late afternoon of the first day, the real pressure ridges rose up to block them. These were taller than those that had separated the two ships during their winter in the ice here, as if the pressures under the ice closer to King William Land were more terrible.

For the first three ridges, Gore led them southwest to find low spots, dips in the ridges where they could clamber over without too much difficulty. It added miles and hours to their travel but was still an easier solution than unpacking the sledge. There was no going around the fourth ridge.

Every pause of more than a few minutes meant that one of the men — usually young Hartnell — had to remove one of the many bottles of pyroligneous fuel from the carefully lashed mass on the sled, fire up a small spirit stove, and melt some snow in a pan into hot water, not to drink — to quench their thirst they had flasks they kept under their outer garments to keep from freezing — but to pour the warm water the length of the wooden runners so as to free them from the self-freezing ruts they dug in the scrim of icy snow.

Nor did the sledge move across the ice like the sleds and sleighs Goodsir had known from his moderately privileged childhood. He'd discovered on his first forays onto the pack ice almost two years ago that one could not — even in regular boots — take a run across the ice and slide the way one did at home on a frozen river or lake. Some property of the sea ice — almost certainly the high salt content — increased the friction, reducing the ease of sliding to almost nil. A mild disappointment for a running man wishing to slide like a boy, but a huge increase in effort for a team of men trying to pull, push, and generally man-haul many hundreds of pounds of gear piled high on more hundreds of pounds of sledge across such ice.

It was like hauling a cumbersome thousand pounds of lumber and goods across moderately rough rock. And the pressure ridges could have been four-storey-high heaps of boulders and gravel for all the ease of crossing one.

This first serious one — just one of many stretching across their path to the southeast as far as they could see — must have been sixty feet high.

Unlashing the carefully secured top foods, boxes of fuel bottles, robes, sleeping bags, and heavy tent, they lightened the load, ending up with fifty- to hundred-pound bundles and boxes that they had to pull up the steep, tumbled, jagged ridge before even attempting to move the sledge.

Goodsir realized quickly that if the pressure ridges had been discrete things — that is, mere ridges rising out of relatively smooth sea ice — climbing them would not have been the soul-destroying exertion that it proved to be. None of the frozen sea was smooth, but for fifty to a hundred yards around each pressure ridge the sea ice became a truly insane maze of rough snow, tumbled seracs, and giant ice blocks — a maze that had to be solved and traversed before the real climbing could begin.

The climbing itself was never linear but always a tortuous back-and-forth, a constant search for footholds on treacherous ice or handholds on a block that might break away at any moment. The eight men zigzagged upward in ridiculous diagonals as they climbed, handed heavy loads up to one another, hacked away at clumps of ice with their pickaxes to create steps and shelves, and generally tried not to fall or be fallen upon. Parcels slipped out of icy mittens and crashed below, bringing up short but impressive clouds of curses from the five seamen below before Gore or Des Voeux shouted them into silence. Everything had to be unpacked and repacked ten times.

Finally the heavy sledge itself, with perhaps half its load still lashed to it, had to be pulled, shoved, lifted, braced, dislodged from entrapping seracs, angled, lifted again, and tugged to the summit of each uneven pressure ridge. There was no rest for the men even atop these ridges since to relax for a minute meant that eight layers of sweat-sodden outer clothing and underlayers would begin to freeze.

After tying new lines to the vertical posts and cross braces at the rear of the sledge, some of the men would get ahead of it to brace its descent — usually the large Marine, Pilkington, and Morfin and Ferrier had this duty — while others dug in their cleats and lowered it to a syncopated chorus of gasps, calls, warnings, and more curses.

Then they would carefully reload the sledge, double-check the lashings, boil snow to pour on the frozen-in runners, and be off again, forcing their way through the tumble-labyrinth on this side of the pressure ridge.

Thirty minutes later they would come to the next ridge.

Their first night out on the ice was terrifyingly memorable for Harry D. S. Goodsir.

The surgeon had never done any camping in his life, but he knew that Graham Gore was telling the truth when the lieutenant said, laughingly, that everything took five times longer on the ice: unpacking the materials, firing up the spirit lamps and stoves, laying out the brown Holland tent and securing screws as anchor stakes in the ice, unrolling the many blanket rolls and sleeping bags, and especially heating up the tinned soup and pork they'd brought along.

And all the while, one had to keep moving — waving arms and shaking legs and stamping feet — or extremities would freeze.

On a normal arctic summer, Mr. Des Voeux reminded Goodsir, citing their previous summer of ice-breaking southward from Beechey Island as an example, temperatures at this latitude on a sunny June day with no wind might rise as high as 30 degrees Fahrenheit. Not this summer. Lieutenant Gore had taken measurements of the air temperature at 10:00 p.m. — the time they stopped to make camp with the sun still on the southern horizon and the sky quite bright — and the thermometer read only −2 degrees Fahrenheit. The temperature at their midday tea and biscuit break had been +6 degrees.

The Holland tent was small. In a storm it would save their lives but this first night out on the ice was clear with almost no wind, so Des Voeux and the five sailors decided to sleep outside on their wolfskins and tarps with only their Hudson's Bay Company blanket sleeping bags for shelter — they would retreat to a very crowded tent if bad weather blew in — and after debating with himself for a moment, Goodsir decided to sleep outside with the men rather than inside with just Lieutenant Gore, as capable and affable a fellow as Gore was.

The daylight was maddening. It grew dim around midnight, but the sky was as light as an 8:00 p.m. London evening in midsummer, and Goodsir was damned if he could fall asleep. Here he was more physically tired than ever before in his life and he couldn't sleep. The aches and pains from the day's exertions also impeded sleep, he realized. He wished he'd brought some laudanum with him. A small draught of that would moderate the discomfort and allow him to sleep. Unlike some surgeons with a doctor's certificate to administer drugs, Goodsir was not an addict — he used the various opiates only to allow himself to sleep or to concentrate when he had to. No more than once or twice a week.

And it was *cold*. After eating the heated soup and beef from the tins and walking through the ice jumble to find a private place to relieve himself — also an outdoor lifetime first for him and one, he realized, that must be accomplished quickly if frostbite of very important areas was to be avoided — Goodsir settled in on one of the large six-foot-by-five-foot wolfskin-blanket sleeping robes, unrolled his personal sleeping bag, and crawled deep into it.

But not deep enough to get warm. Des Voeux had explained to him that he had to remove his boots and slide them down into the bag with him so that the leather would not freeze solid — at one point Goodsir had pricked the bottom of his foot on the nails hammered through the sole of one of the boots — but all the men left on all their other clothes. The wool — all the wool, Goodsir realized not for the first time that day — was soaked through with his sweat and exhalations from the long day. The endless day.

For a while around midnight, the light deepened toward twilight enough that a few stars — planets, Goodsir now knew from a private lecture at the ad hoc observatory atop the iceberg two years ago — became visible. But the light never disappeared.

Nor did the cold. No longer moving or exerting itself, Goodsir's thin body was defenseless against the cold that came in through the sleeping bag's too-wide opening and that crept up from the ice through the hair-out wolfskin pad beneath him, crawling through the thick Hudson's Bay Company blankets like some cold-fingered predator. Goodsir began to shake. His teeth chattered.

Around him, the four sleeping men — there were two on guard duty — snored so loudly that the surgeon wondered if the men on both ships miles northwest of them on the ice, beyond the countless pressure ridges — *dear God, we have to cross those again going back* — could hear the rasping and sawing and snorting.

Goodsir was shaking. At this rate he was sure he would not survive until morning. They would try to roust him out of his blanket and bag and find only a frozen, curled corpse.

He crawled as far down into the sewn-blankets sleeping bag as he could, pulling the ice-ridged opening closed above him, inhaling his own sour-sweat smell and exhalations rather than be exposed to that freezing air again.

In addition to the insidious light and the even more insidious creeping cold, the cold of death, Goodsir realized, the cold of the grave and of the black cliff wall above the Beechey Island headstones, there was the noise; the surgeon had thought himself accustomed to the groan of ship's timbers, occasional creakings and snappings of supercold ship's metal in the dark of two winters, and the constant noise antics of the ice holding the ship in its vise, but out here, with nothing separating his body from the ice except a few layers of wool and wolfskin, the groaning and movement of the ice beneath him was terrible. It was like trying to sleep on the belly of a living beast. The sense of the ice moving beneath him, however exaggerated, was real enough to give him vertigo as he curled more tightly into a fetal position.

Sometime around 2:00 a.m. — he had actually checked his pocket watch by the light filtering in through the bag opening — Harry D. S. Goodsir had begun drifting off into a state of semiconsciousness vaguely resembling sleep when he was pounded awake by two deafening explosions.

Struggling with his sweat-frozen bag like a newborn trying to chew through its caul, Goodsir managed to free his head and shoulders. The freezing night air hit his face with enough cold force to make his heart stutter. The sky was already brighter with sunlight.

"What?" he cried. "What has happened?"

Second Mate Des Voeux and three of the seamen were standing on their sleeping bags, long knives they must have slept with in their gloved hands. Lieutenant Gore had burst from the Holland tent. He was fully dressed with a pistol in his bare — *bare!* — hand.

"Report!" Gore snapped at one of the two sentries, Charlie Best.

"It was the bears, Lieutenant," said Best. "Two of them. Big bastards. They've been snooping around all night — you remember we saw them about half a mile out before we stopped to make camp — but they kept coming closer and closer, circling like, until finally John and me had to shoot at them to drive them away."

"John" was twenty-seven-year-old John Morfin, Goodsir knew, the other sentry this night.

"You both fired?" asked Gore. The lieutenant had climbed to the highest point of nearby heaped snow and ice and was searching the area with his brass telescope. Goodsir wondered why the man's bare hands hadn't already frozen to the metal.

"Aye, sir," said Morfin. He was reloading his breech-loading shotgun, his wool gloves fumbling with the shells.

"Did you hit them?" asked Des Voeux.

"Aye," said Best.

"Didn't do no good," said Morfin. "Just with shotguns over about thirty paces. Them bears have thick hides and thicker skulls. Hurt 'em enough though that they went away."

"I don't see them," said Lieutenant Gore from ten feet up on his ice hill above the tent.

"We think they come out of those little open holes in the ice," said Best. "The bigger one was running that way when John fired. We thought it went down, but we went out on the ice far enough to see there weren't no carcass there. It's gone."

The sledge-hauling team had noticed those soft areas in the ice — not quite round, about four feet across, too large for the tiny breathing holes ring seals made, seemingly too small and too far separated for the white bears, and always crusted over with several inches of soft ice. At first, the holes had raised hopes for open water, but in the end they were so few and far between that they were only treacherous. Seaman Ferrier, walking ahead of the sledge late in the afternoon, had almost fallen through one, his left leg going in to above the knee, and they'd all had to stop long enough for the shivering sailor to change into different boots, woollies, socks, and trousers.

"It's time for Ferrier and Pilkington to take the watch anyway," said Lieutenant Gore. "Bobby, fetch the musket from my tent."

"I'm better with shotgun, sir," said Ferrier.

"I'm comfortable with the musket, Lieutenant," said the big Marine.

"Get the musket then, Pilkington. Peppering those things with shotgun pellets is just going to get them angry."

"Aye, sir."

Best and Morfin, obviously shaking from their cold two hours on watch rather than from any tension, sleepily pulled off their boots and crawled into their waiting bags. Private Pilkington and Bobby Ferrier forced their swollen feet into boots retrieved from their bags and slouched off to the nearby ice ridges to keep watch.

Shaking worse than ever, his nose and cheeks now joining his fingers and toes in feeling numb, Goodsir curled up deep in his bag and prayed for sleep.

It did not come. A little more than two hours later, Second Mate Des Voeux began ordering everyone up and out of their bags.

"We have a long day ahead of us, boys," cried the mate in jovial tones.

They were still more than twenty-two miles from the shore of King William Land.

11

CROZIER

Y ou're frozen through, Francis," says Commander Fitzjames. "Come aft to the Common Room for brandy."

Crozier would prefer whiskey, but brandy will have to serve. He precedes *Erebus*'s captain down the long, narrow companionway toward what had been Captain Sir John Franklin's personal cabin and which is now the equivalent of *Terror*'s Great Room — a library and off-duty gathering place for officers and a meeting room when necessary. Crozier thinks that it says good things about Fitzjames that the commander kept his own tiny cubicle after Sir John's death, refitting the spacious aft chamber into a common area and sometimes sick bay for surgery.

The companionway is totally dark except for the glow from the Common Room and the deck is canted more steeply in the opposite direction from *Terror,* listing to port rather than starboard, down by the stern rather than bow. And although the ships are almost identical in design, Crozier always notices other differences as well. HMS *Erebus smells* different somehow — beyond the identical stench of lamp oil, dirty men, filthy clothes, months of cooking, coal dust, pails of urine, and the men's breath hanging in the cold, dank air, there is something else. For some reason, *Erebus* stinks more of fear and hopelessness.

There are two officers smoking their pipes in the Common Room, Lieutenant Le Vesconte and Lieutenant Fairholme, but both stand, nod toward the two captains, and withdraw, pulling the sliding door shut behind them.

Fitzjames unlocks a heavy cabinet and pulls out a bottle of brandy, pouring a large measure into one of Sir John's crystal water glasses for Crozier, a smaller amount for himself. For all of the fine china and crystal their late expedition leader loaded aboard for his and his officers' own use, there are no brandy snifters. Franklin was a devout teetotaler.

Crozier does no snifting. He drinks the brandy down in three gulps and allows Fitzjames to replenish it.

"Thank you for responding so quickly," says Fitzjames. "I expected a message in response, not for you to come in person."

Crozier frowns. "Message? I haven't received a message from you in over a week, James."

Fitzjames stares a moment. "You didn't receive a message this evening? I sent Private Reed to your ship with one about five hours ago. I presumed he was spending the night there."

Crozier shakes his head slowly.

"Oh . . . damn," says Fitzjames.

Crozier pulls the woolen stocking from his pocket and sets it on the table. In the brighter light from the bulkhead lamp here there are still no signs of violence. "I found it during my walk over. Closer to your ship than mine."

Fitzjames takes the stocking and studies it sadly. "I'll ask the men if they recognize it," he says.

"It could belong to one of mine," Crozier says softly. He succinctly tells Fitzjames about the attack, the mortal wounding of Private Heather, and the disappearance of William Strong and young Tom Evans.

"Four in one day," says Fitzjames. He pours more brandy for both of them.

"Yes. What is it you were sending me a message about?"

Fitzjames explains there had been sightings of something large moving through the ice jumbles, just beyond the lanterns' glow, all that day. The men had fired repeatedly but parties going onto the ice had found no blood nor other sign. "So I apologize, Francis, for that idiot Bobby Johns firing at you a few minutes ago. The men's nerves are stretched very tightly."

"Not so tightly that they think that thing on the ice has learned how to shout at them in English, I hope," Crozier says sardonically. He takes another sip of the brandy.

"No, no. Of course not. It was pure idiocy. Johns will be off his rum ration for two weeks. I apologize again."

Crozier sighs. "Don't do that. Rip him a new arsehole if you like, but don't take his rum away. This ship feels surly enough already. Lady Silence was with me and wearing her God-damned hairy parka. Johns may have got a glimpse of that. It would have served me right if he'd blown my head off."

"Silence was with you?" Fitzjames allowed his eyebrows to ask the questions.

"I don't know what in hell she was doing out on the ice," rasps Crozier. His throat is very sore from the day's cold and his shouting. "I almost shot her myself a quarter mile from your ship when she crept up on me. Young Irving is probably turning *Terror* upside down as we speak. I made a huge mistake when I put that boy in charge of looking out for that Esquimaux bitch."

"The men think she is a Jonah." Fitzjames's voice is very, very soft. Sounds travel easily through the partitions in such a crowded lower deck.

"Well why the hell shouldn't they?" Crozier feels the alcohol now. He hasn't had a drink since last night. It feels good in his belly and tired brain. "The woman shows up on the day this horror begins with that witch doctor father or husband of hers. Something has chewed her tongue out at the roots. Why the hell *shouldn't* the men think she's the cause of all this trouble?"

"But you've kept her aboard *Terror* for more than five months," says Fitzjames. There is no reproach in the younger captain's voice, only curiosity.

Crozier shrugs. "I don't believe in witches, James. Nor Jonahs much, for that matter. But I do believe that if we put her out on the ice, the thing will be eating her guts the way it's devouring Evans's and Strong's right now. And maybe your Private Reed's as well. Wasn't that Billy Reed, the redheaded Marine who always wanted to talk about that writer — Dickens?"

"William Reed, yes," says Fitzjames. "He was very fast when the men did footraces back on Disko Island two years ago. I thought that perhaps one man, with speed . . ." He stops and chews his lip. "I should have waited for morning."

"Why?" says Crozier. "It's no lighter then. Or not much lighter at noon, for that matter. Day or night doesn't mean anything anymore, and it won't for another four months. And it's not as if that damned thing out there only hunts at night . . . or even just in the dark, as far as that goes. Maybe your Reed will show up. Our messengers have gotten lost before out there in the ice and come in after five or six hours, shaking and cursing."

"Perhaps." Fitzjames's tone echoes his doubt. "I'll send out search parties in the morning."

"That's just what that thing wants us to do." Crozier's voice is very weary.

"Perhaps," Fitzjames says again, "but you just told me that you've had men out on the ice last night and all day today looking for Strong and Evans."

"If I hadn't brought Evans with me when I was looking for Strong, the boy would still be alive."

"Thomas Evans," says Fitzjames. "I remember him. Big chap. He was not really a boy, was he, Francis? He must be . . . have been . . . what? Twenty-two or twenty-three years old?"

"Tommy turned twenty this May," says Crozier. "His first birthday aboard was on the day after our departure. The men were in good spirits and celebrated his eighteenth birthday by shaving his head. He didn't seem to mind. Those who knew him say he was always big for his age. He served on HMS *Lynx* and before that on an East Indian merchantman. He went to sea when he was thirteen."

"As you did, I believe."

Crozier laughs a little ruefully. "As I did. For all the good it did me."

Fitzjames locks the brandy away in the cabinet and returns to the long table. "Tell me, Francis, did you actually dress up as a black footman to old Hoppner's lady of rank when you were frozen in up here in . . . what was it, '24?"

Crozier laughs again but more easily this time. "I did. I was a midshipman on the *Hecla* with Parry when he sailed north with Hoppner's *Fury* in '24, trying to find this same God-damned Passage. Parry's plan was to sail the two ships through Lancaster Sound and down the Prince Regent Inlet — we didn't know then, not until John and James Ross in '33, that the Boothia was a peninsula. Parry thought he could sail south around Boothia and go hell-bent for leather until he reached the coastline that Franklin had explored from land six, seven years earlier. But Parry left too late — why do these God-damned expedition commanders always start off too late? — and we were lucky to get to Lancaster Sound on ten September, a month late. But the ice was on us by thirteen September, and there was no chance of getting through the Sound, so Parry in our *Hecla* and Lieutenant Hoppner in *Fury* ran south, our tails between our legs.

"A gale blew us back into Baffin Bay and we were lucky sods to find an anchorage in a tiny, pretty little bay off Prince Regent Inlet. We were there ten months. Froze our tits off."

"But," says Fitzjames, smiling slightly, "you as a little black boy?"

Crozier nods and sips his drink. "Both Parry and Hoppner were fanatics for fancy dress-up galas during winters in the ice. It was Hoppner who planned this masque he called the Grand Venetian Carnivale, set for the first day in November, right when morale dips as the sun disappears for months. Parry came down *Hecla*'s side in this huge cloak that he didn't throw off even when all the men were assembled — most in costume, we had this huge trunk of costumes on each ship — and when he did throw down the cloak, we saw Parry as that old Marine — you remember the one with the peg leg what played the fiddle for ha'pennies near Chatham? No, you wouldn't, you're too young.

"But Parry — I think the old bastard always wanted to be an actor more than a ship's captain — he does the whole thing up right, scratching away at his fiddle, hopping on that fake peg leg, and shouting out,

'Give a copper to the poor Joe, your honour, who's lost his timbers in defence of his King and country!'

"Well, the men laughed their arses off. But Hoppner, who loved that make-believe rubbish even more than Parry, I think, he comes into the ball dressed as a noble lady, wearing the latest Parisian fashions from that year — low bustline, big crinoline dress bunched up over his ass, everything — and since I was full of piss and vinegar in those days, not to mention too stupid to know better, in other words still in my twenties, I was dressed as Hoppner's black footman — wearing this real footman's livery that old Henry Parkyns Hoppner had bought in some dandy's London livery store and brought along just for me."

"Did the men laugh?" asks Fitzjames.

"Oh, the men laughed their arses off again — Parry and his peg weren't in it after old Henry appeared in drag with me lifting his silk train behind him. Why wouldn't they laugh? All those chimney sweeps and ribbon girls, ragmen and hook-nosed Jews, bricklayers and Highland warriors, Turkish dancers and London match girls? Look! There's young Crozier, aging midshipman not even lieutenant yet who thinks he's going to be an admiral someday, forgetting that he's just another black Irish nigger."

Fitzjames says nothing for a minute. Crozier can hear the snores and farts from the creaking hammocks toward the bow of the dark ship. Somewhere on deck just above them, a lookout stamps his feet to keep them from freezing. Crozier is sorry he's ended the story this way — he speaks to no one like this when he is sober — but he also wishes that Fitzjames would get the brandy out again. Or the whiskey.

"When did *Fury* and *Hecla* escape from the ice?" asks Fitzjames.

"Twenty July the next summer," says Crozier. "But you probably know the rest of the story."

"I know that *Fury* was lost."

"Aye," says Crozier. "Five days after the ice relents — we'd been creeping along the shore of Somerset Island, trying to stay out of the pack ice, trying to avoid that God-damned limestone always falling from the cliffs — another gale grounds *Fury* on a spit of gravel. We man-hauled her free — using ice screws and sweat — but then both ships get frozen in, and a God-damned iceberg almost as big as that bastard squatting between *Erebus* and *Terror* shoves *Fury* against the shore ice, tears her rudder away, smashes her timbers to splinters, springs her hull plates, and the crew worked the four pumps in shifts day and night just trying to keep her afloat."

"And you did for a while," prompts Fitzjames.

"A fortnight. We even tried cabling her to a berg, but the fucking cable snapped. Then Hoppner tried raising her to get at her keel — just as Sir John wanted to do with your *Erebus* — but the blizzard put an end to that idea and both ships were in danger of being forced onto the lee shore of the headland. Finally the men just fell over where they were pumping — they were too exhausted to understand our orders — and on the twenty-first of August, Parry ordered everyone aboard *Hecla* and cast her off to save her from being driven aground and poor *Fury* got shoved right up onto the beach by a bunch of bergs that slammed her hard ashore there and blocked her way out. There wasn't even a chance of a tow. The ice was smashing her to bits as we watched. We barely got *Hecla* free, and that only with every man working the pumps day and night and the carpenter laboring round the clock to shore her up.

"So we never got close to the Passage — or even to sighting new land, really — and lost a ship, and Hoppner was court-martialed and Parry considered that *his* court-martial as well since Hoppner was under his command the whole time."

"Everyone was acquitted," says Fitzjames. "Even praised, as I recall."

"Praised but not promoted," says Crozier.

"But you all survived."

"Yes."

"I want to survive *this* expedition, Francis," says Fitzjames. His tone is soft but very determined.

Crozier nods.

"We should have done what Parry did and put both crews aboard *Terror* a year ago and sailed east around King William Land," says Fitzjames.

It is Crozier's turn to raise his brows. Not at Fitzjames agreeing that it is an island — their later-summer sledge reconnaissance had all but settled that — but in agreeing that they should have made a run for it last autumn, abandoning Sir John's ship. Crozier knows that there is no harder thing for a captain in anyone's navy to do than to give up his ship, but especially so in the Royal Navy. And while *Erebus* had been under the overall command of Sir John Franklin, Commander James Fitzjames had been its true captain.

"It is too late now." Crozier is in pain. Because the Common Room shares several outer bulkheads and has three overhead Preston Patent Illuminators, it is cold — the two men can see their breath in the air — but it's still sixty or seventy degrees warmer than it had been out on the ice and Crozier's feet, especially his toes, are thawing in a rush of jagged pin pokes and red-hot needle stabs.

"Yes," agrees Fitzjames, "but you were wise to have the gear and provisions sledged to King William Land in August."

"It wasn't a fraction of what we'll need to ferry there if that is to be our survival camp," Crozier says brusquely. He had ordered about two tons of clothing, tents, survival gear, and tinned food to be removed from the ships and stored on the northwest shore of the island should they have to abandon ships quickly during the winter, but the ferrying had been absurdly slow and extremely dangerous. Weeks of laborious sledging had left only a ton or so of cache there — tents, extra slops, tools, and a few weeks of canned food. Nothing more.

"That thing wouldn't let us stay there," he adds softly. "We all could have moved to tents in September — I had the ground prepared for two dozen of the big tents, you remember — but the campsite would not have been as defensible as the ships are."

"No," says Fitzjames.

"If the ships last the winter."

"Yes," says Fitzjames. "Have you heard, Francis, that some of the men — on both ships — are calling that creature the Terror?"

"No!" Crozier is offended. He does not want the name of his ship used to evil purposes such as that, even if the men are jesting. But he looks at Commander James Fitzjames's hazel-green eyes and realizes that the other captain is serious and so must be the men. "The Terror," says Crozier, and tastes bile.

"They think it is no animal," says Fitzjames. "They believe its cunning is something else, is preternatural . . . supernatural . . . that there is a demon out there on the ice in the dark."

Crozier almost spits he is so disgusted. "Demon," he says in contempt. "These are the very seamen who believe in ghosts, faeries, Jonahs, mermaids, curses, and sea monsters."

"I've seen you scratch the sail to summon wind," Fitzjames says with a smile.

Crozier says nothing.

"You've lived long enough and traveled far enough to see things that no man knew existed," Fitzjames adds, obviously trying to lighten the mood.

"Aye," says Crozier with a bark of a laugh. "Penguins! I wish they were the largest beastie up here, as they seem to be down south."

"There are no white bears there in the south arctic?"

"None that we saw. None that any south-sailing whaler or explorer has seen in seventy years of sailing toward and around that white, volcanic, frozen land."

"And you and James Ross were the first men ever to see the continent. And the volcanoes."

"Aye, we were. And it did Sir James much good. He's married to a beautiful young thing, knighted, happy, retired from the cold. And me . . . I am . . . here."

Fitzjames clears his throat as if to change the subject. "Do you know, Francis, until this voyage, I honestly believed in the Open Polar Sea. I was quite sure Parliament was correct when it listened to predictions from the so-called polar experts — in the winter before we sailed, do you remember? It was in the *Times* — all about the thermobaric barrier, about the Gulf Stream flowing up under this ice to warm the Open Polar Sea, and the invisible continent that must be up here. They were so convinced it existed that they were proposing and passing laws to send inmates of Southgate and other prisons up here to shovel the coal that must be in such plentitude just a few hundred miles from here on the North Polar Continent."

Crozier laughs with real humour this time. "Yes, to shovel coal to heat the hotels and supply the refueling stations for the steamships that will be making regular trips across the Open Polar Sea by the 1860s at the latest. Oh, God, that I were one of those prisoners in Southgate. Their cells are, required by law and for humanity's sake, twice the size of our cabins, James, and our future would be warm and secure if we only had to sit in such luxury and wait for word of that North Pole continent being discovered and colonized."

Both men are laughing now.

There comes a thumping from the deck above — running footsteps rather than mere feet stamping — and then voices and a sliding of cold air around their feet as someone opens the main hatch above the far end of the companionway and the sound of several pairs of feet clattering down the steps.

Both captains are silent and waiting when the soft knock comes on the Common Room's thin door.

"Enter," says Commander Fitzjames.

An *Erebus* crewman leads in two Terrors — Third Lieutenant John Irving and a seaman named Shanks.

"I'm sorry to disturb you, Commander Fitzjames, Captain Crozier," says Irving through only slightly chattering teeth. His long nose is white from the cold. Shanks is still carrying a musket. "Lieutenant Little sent me to report to Captain Crozier as soon as I could."

"Go ahead, John," says Crozier. "You're not still hunting for Lady Silence, are you?"

Irving looks blank for a second. Then, "We saw her out on the ice when the last search parties were coming in. No, sir, Lieutenant Little asked me to fetch you right away because . . ." The young lieutenant pauses as if forgetting the reason Little had sent him to report.

"Mr. Couch," says Fitzjames to the *Erebus* mate on duty who had led the two Terrors to the Common Room, "be so kind as to step out into the companionway and to close the door please, thank you."

Crozier has also heard the odd silence as the snoring and hammock creaking has all but ceased. Too many ears in the crew's forward berthing space were awake and listening.

When the door is shut, Irving says, "It's William Strong and Tommy Evans, sir. They're back."

Crozier blinks. "What the devil do you mean, *back?* Alive?" He feels the first surge of hope he's had for months.

"Oh, no sir," says Irving. "Just . . . one body . . . really. But it was propped against the stern rail when someone saw it as all the search parties were coming in for the day . . . about an hour ago. The guards on duty hadn't seen anything. But it was there, sir. On Lieutenant Little's orders, Shanks and I made the crossing as quickly as we could to inform you, Captain. Shanks Mare as it were."

"It?" snaps Crozier. "One body? *Back on the ship?*" This makes no sense at all to the *Terror*'s captain. "I thought you said both Strong and Evans were back."

Third Lieutenant Irving's entire face is frostbite white now. "They are, Captain. Or at least half of them. When we went to look at the body propped there at the stern, it fell over and . . . well . . . came apart. As best we can tell, it's Billy Strong from the waist up. Tommy Evans from the waist down."

Crozier and Fitzjames can only look at each other.

12

GOODSIR

Lieutenant Gore's cache party arrived at Sir James Ross's cairn on King William Land late on the evening of 28 May, after five hard days of travel across the ice.

The good news as they approached the island — invisible to them until the last minutes — was that there were pools of salt-free drinking water as they neared the shore. The bad news was that most of these pools had been leached from the base of an almost unbroken series of icebergs — some of them a hundred feet tall and more — that had been swept up against the shallows and shore and now stretched like a parapeted white castle wall as far as the eye could see around the curve of land. It took the men a full day to cross this barrier and even then they had to leave some of the robes, fuel, and provisions cached on the sea ice to lighten the sledge load. To add to their difficulties and discomfort, several of the cans of soup and pork they had opened on the ice had gone putrid and had to be thrown away, leaving them less than five days' rations for the return — assuming that more of the cans were not bad. On top of all that, they found that even here, at what must be the sea's edge, the ice was still seven feet thick.

Worst of all — for Goodsir, at least — King William Land, or King William Island as they later learned, was the greatest disappointment of his life.

Devon Island and Beechey Island to the north had been windswept, inhospitable to life at the best of times, and barren except for lichen and low plants, but that was a veritable Garden of Eden compared to what the men now found on King William Land. Beechey had boasted bare ground, some sand and soil, imposing cliffs, and a sort of beach. None of that was to be found on King William Land.

For half an hour after crossing the iceberg barrier, Goodsir did not know if he was on solid ground or not. He had been prepared to celebrate with the others since this would be the first time any of them had set foot on terra firma in more than a year, but the sea ice gave way beyond the bergs to great tumbles of shore ice and it had been impossible to tell where the shore ice left off and the shore began. Everything was ice, dirty snow, more ice, more snow.

Finally they reached a windswept area free of snow and Goodsir and several of the seamen threw themselves forward onto the gravel, going to hands and knees on the solid ground as if in thanksgiving, but even here the small round stones were frozen solid, as firm as London cobblestones in winter and ten times as cold, and this chill traveled up through their trousers and other layers covering their knees, then into their bones and up through their mittens to their palms and fingers like a silent invitation to the frozen infernal circles of the dead far below.

It took them four more hours to find Ross's cairn. A heap of rocks promised to be six feet high on or near Victory Point should be easy enough to find — Lieutenant Gore had said this to all of them earlier — but on this exposed point the heaps of ice were often at least six feet high and high winds had long since blown off the smaller top stones of the cairn. The late-May sky never darkened into night, but the dim, constant glow made it exceedingly difficult to see anything in three dimensions or to judge distances. The only things that stood out were the bears, and only because of their movement. Half a dozen of the hungry, curious things had been following them off and on all day. Beyond that occasional awkward waddle of movement, everything was lost in a grey-white glow. A serac that looked to be half a mile away and fifty feet high was really only twenty yards away and two feet tall. A bare patch of gravel and stone that seemed a hundred feet away turned out to be a mile away far out on the featureless wind-scoured point.

But they found the cairn finally, at almost 10:00 p.m. by Goodsir's still-ticking watch, all of the men so exhausted that their arms were hanging like those in sailors' tales of apes, all speech abandoned in their tiredness, the sledge left half a mile north of where they had first come ashore.

Gore retrieved the first of two messages — he had made a copy of this first one to cache somewhere farther south along the coast as per Sir John's instructions — filled in the date, and scribbled his name. So did Second Mate Charles des Voeux. They rolled the note, slid it into one of the two airtight brass cylinders they'd hauled with them, and, after dropping the cylinder into the centre of the empty cairn, replaced the rocks they'd removed to gain access.

"Well," said Gore. "That's that then, isn't it?"

The lightning storm began not long after they had trudged back to the sledge for a midnight supper.

To save weight during the iceberg crossing, they had left their heavy wolfskin blanket-robes, ground tarps, and most of the tinned food cached out on the ice. They assumed that since the food was in sealed and soldered tins, it would not attract the white bears that were always sniffing around and that even if it did the bears wouldn't be able to get into the tins. The plan was to get along on two days' reduced rations here on land — plus any game they might see and shoot, of course, but that dream was fading with the dismal reality of the place — and to have everyone sleep in the Holland tent.

Des Voeux supervised the preparation of dinner, removing the patented cook kit from its series of cleverly nested wicker baskets. But three of the four cans they had chosen for their first evening's meal on land were spoiled. That left only their Wednesday half-ration portion of salt pork — always the men's favorite since it was so rich with fat, but not nearly enough to assuage their hunger after such a day of heavy work — and the last good can, which was labeled "Superior Clear Turtle Soup," which the men hated, knowing from experience that it was neither superior nor clear and most likely not turtle at all.

Dr. McDonald on *Terror* had been obsessed for the last year and a half, ever since Torrington's death at Beechey Island, with the quality of their preserved foodstuffs and was constantly busy experimenting, with the other surgeons' help, to find the best diet by which to avoid scurvy. Goodsir had learned from the older doctor that a certain Stephan Goldner, the expedition's provisioner from Houndsditch who had won the contract through extraordinarily low bids, had almost certainly cheated Her Majesty's government and Her Majesty's Royal Navy Discovery Service by providing inadequate — and possibly frequently poisonous — victuals.

The men filled the freezing air with obscenities upon learning that the cans were filled with rotten stuff.

"Calm down, lads," said Lieutenant Gore after allowing the barrage of best sailor obscenity for a minute or two. "What say you that we open tomorrow's rations of cans until we find enough for a good meal and simply plan to get back to our ice cache by supper time tomorrow, even if that means midnight?"

There was a chorus of assent.

Two of the next four cans they opened were not spoiled — that included a strangely meatless "Irish Stew" that was only barely edible at the best of times and the deliciously advertised "Ox Cheeks and Vegetables." The men had decided that the oxen parts had come from a tannery and the vegetables from an abandoned root cellar, but it was better than nothing.

No sooner was the tent up with the sleeping bags unrolled for a floor inside and the food heated on their spirit stove and the hot metal bowls and dishes distributed than the lightning began to strike.

The first blast of electricity struck less than fifty feet from them and led to every man spilling his ox cheeks and vegetables and stew. The second crash was closer.

They ran for the tent. Lightning crashed and struck around them like an artillery barrage. It wasn't until they were quite literally piled inside the brown canvas tent — eight men in a shelter designed for four men and light gear — that Seaman Bobby Ferrier looked at the wood-and-metal poles holding the tent upright and said, "Well, fuck this," and scrambled for the opening.

Outside, cricket-ball-sized hail was crashing down, sending splinters of ice chips thirty feet into the air. The midnight arctic twilight was being shattered by explosions of lightning so contiguous that they overlapped, setting the sky ablaze in flashes that left blinding retinal echoes.

"No, no!" cried Gore, shouting over the thunder and grabbing Ferrier back from the entrance and throwing him down into the crowded tent. "Anywhere we go on this island, we're the tallest things around. Throw those metal-cored tent poles as far away as you can but stay under the canvas. Get in your bags and lie flat."

The men scrambled to do so, their long hair writhing like snakes under the edges of their Welsh wigs or caps and above their many-wrapped comforters. The storm increased in ferocity and the noise was deafening. The hail pounding them in the backs through canvas and blankets felt like huge fists battering them black and blue. Goodsir actually moaned aloud during the pummeling, more from fear than from pain, although the constant blows constituted the most painful beating he had suffered since his public school days.

"Holy fucking Christ!" cried Thomas Hartnell as both hail and lightning grew worse. The men with any brains were under their Hudson's Bay Company blankets now rather than in them, trying to use them as a buffer against the hail. The tent canvas threatened to suffocate all of them, and the thin canvas beneath them did nothing to keep the cold from flowing up and into them, taking their collective breath away.

"How can there be a lightning storm when it is so *cold?*" shouted Goodsir to Gore, who was lying next to him in the huddle of terrified men.

"It happens," the lieutenant shouted back. "If we decide to move from the ships to land camp, we'll have to bring one God-awful heap of lightning rods with us."

This was the first time that Goodsir had heard any hint of abandoning the ships.

Lightning struck the boulder they'd been huddled near during their abbreviated supper not ten feet from the tent, ricocheted over their canvas-covered heads to a second boulder no more than three feet from them, and every man huddled lower, trying to claw through the canvas beneath himself in an attempt to burrow into the rock.

"Good God, Lieutenant Gore," cried John Morfin, whose head was closest to the collapsed opening of the tent, "there's something moving around out there in the middle of all this."

All the men were accounted for. Gore shouted, "A bear? Walking around in this?"

"Too large to be a bear, Lieutenant," shouted Morfin. "It's . . ." Then the lightning struck the boulder again, another blast struck close enough to cause the tent fabric to leap in the air from the static discharge, and everyone cowered flatter, pressed their faces to cold canvas, and abandoned speech in favor of prayer.

The attack — Goodsir could only think of it as an attack, as if from Greek gods furious at their hubris for wintering in Boreas's realm — went on for almost an hour, until the last of the thunder moved past and the flashes became intermittent and then moved on to the southeast.

Gore was the first to emerge, but even the lieutenant whom Goodsir knew to be almost without fear did not rise to his feet for a full minute or more after the barrage ceased. Others crawled out on their knees and stayed there, staring around as if in stupefaction or supplication. The sky to the east was a latticework of air-to-air and air-to-ground discharges, the thunder still rolled across the flat island with enough violence to exert a physical pressure on their skins and to make them cover their ears, but the hail had ceased. The smashed white spheres were piled two feet high all around them as far as they could see. After a minute Gore got to his feet and began looking around. The others then also rose, stiffly, moving slowly, testing their limbs, heavily bruised, Goodsir judged, if his own pain was any measure of their common abuse by the heavens. The midnight twilight was dimmed enough by the thick clouds to the south that it almost seemed as if real darkness was falling.

"Look at this," called Charles Best.

Goodsir and the others gathered near the sledge. The tins of food and other matériel had been unpacked and stacked near the cooking area before their aborted supper, and somehow the lightning had contrived to strike the low pyramid of stacked cans while missing the sledge itself. All of Goldner's canned food had been blasted apart as surely as if a cannonball had struck the stack — a perfect roll in a game of cosmic ninepins. Charred metal and still-steaming inedible vegetables and rotten meat were scattered in a twenty-yard radius. Near the surgeon's left foot was a charred, twisted, and blackened receptacle with the legend COOKING APPARATUS (1) visible on its side. It was part of their travel mess kit and had been sitting on one of their spirit stoves when they had run for shelter. The metal bottle holding a pint of pyroligneous ether fuel next to it had exploded, sending shrapnel flying in all directions but evidently just barely passing over their heads as they huddled in the tent. If the lightning had ignited the stack of fuel bottles sitting in their wooden box next to the two shot-guns and shells a few feet away on the sledge, the explosion and flames would have consumed them all.

Goodsir had the urge to laugh but didn't do so out of fear he might weep at the same time. None of the men spoke for a moment.

Finally John Morfin, who had climbed the low ridge of hail-pummeled ice above their campsite, cried, "Lieutenant, you need to see this."

They climbed up to look toward where he was staring.

Along the backside of this low ice ridge, coming from the ice jumble south of them and disappearing toward the sea northwest of them, were absolutely impossible tracks. Impossible because they were larger than any tracks of any living animal on earth. For five days now, the men had seen the paw prints of the white bears in the snow, and some of those tracks were absurdly large — some twelve inches long — but these indistinct tracks were more than half again larger than that. Some appeared to be as long as a man's arm. And they were new — there was no doubt whatsoever of that — because the indentations were not in the old snow but pressed into the thick layer of fresh hailstones.

Whatever had walked past their camp had done so during the height of the lightning and hail storm, just as Morfin had reported.

"What is this?" said Lieutenant Gore. "This can't be. Mr. Des Voeux, be so kind as to fetch one of the shotguns and some shells from the sledge, please."

"Aye, sir."

Even before the mate came back with the shotgun, Morfin, Marine Private Pilkington, Best, Ferrier, and Goodsir began trudging after Gore as the lieutenant followed the impossible tracks northwest.

"These are too large, sir," said the Marine. He had been included in the party, Goodsir knew, because he was one of the few men aboard either ship who had ever hunted game larger than a grouse.

"I know that, Private," said Gore. He accepted the shotgun from Second Mate Des Voeux and calmly loaded a shell as the seven men strode through the heaps of hail toward the dark clouds beyond the iceberg-guarded shoreline.

"Maybe they're not paw prints, but something . . . an arctic hare or something hopping through the slush, making the prints with its entire body," said Des Voeux.

"Yes," said Gore absently. "Perhaps so, Charles."

But they *were* paw prints of some kind. Dr. Harry D. S. Goodsir knew that. Every man walking near him knew that. Goodsir, who had never hunted anything larger than a rabbit or partridge, could tell that this wasn't the track of some small thing throwing its body left, then right but rather the footprints of something walking first on four legs and then — if the tracks were to be believed — almost a hundred yards on two legs. At that point they were the tracks of a walking man, if a man had feet the length of his forearms and could cover almost five feet between strides while leaving no impressions of toes but rather the striations of claws.

They reached the windswept area of stones where Goodsir had thrown himself down on his knees so many hours before — the hail-stones here had shattered into countless icy shards so the area remained almost bare — and here the tracks stopped.

"Spread out," said Gore, still holding the shotgun casually under his arm as if he were taking a walk through his family's estate in Essex. He pointed to each man and then pointed to the edge of the open area he wanted that man to check. The rocky space was not much larger than a cricket pitch.

There were no tracks leading away from the stones. The men shuf-fled back and forth for several minutes, checking and double-checking, not wanting to pollute the unbroken snow beyond the rocks with their own footprints, and then all stood still, staring at one another. They were standing in an almost perfect circle. No tracks led away from the rocky space.

"Lieutenant . . . ," began Best.

"Quiet a minute," said Gore sharply but not unkindly. "I am thinking." He was the only man moving now, striding past the men and looking out onto the snow, ice, and hail around them as if there were some schoolboy prank being pulled. The light was stronger now as the storm passed farther east — it was almost two o'clock in the morning and the snow and layer of hail remained untouched beyond the stones.

"Lieutenant," persisted Best. "It's Tom Hartnell."

"What about him?" snapped Gore. He was beginning his third circuit of the loop.

"He's not here. I just realized — he hasn't been with us since we got out of the tent."

Goodsir's head snapped up and turned at the same second the others' did. Three hundred yards behind them, the low ice ridge hid the view of their collapsed tent and sledge. Nothing else moved on the vast expanse of white and grey.

They all began running at once.

———

Hartnell was alive but unconscious and still lying under the tent canvas. There was a huge welt on the side of his head — the thick canvas had torn where the fist-sized ball of hail had ripped through — and he was bleeding from his left ear, but Goodsir soon found a slow pulse. They pulled the unconscious man from the fallen tent, retrieved two sleeping bags, and made him as warm and comfortable as they could. Dark clouds were streaming overhead again.

"How serious is it?" asked Lieutenant Gore.

Goodsir shook his head. "We won't know until he wakes . . . *if* he wakes. I'm surprised more of us weren't knocked unconscious. It was a terrible downpour of solid objects."

Gore nodded. "I'd hate to lose Tommy after the death of his brother, John, last year. That would be too much for the family to bear."

Goodsir remembered preparing John Hartnell for burial in his brother Thomas's best flannel shirt. He thought of that shirt under the frozen soil and snow-covered gravel so many hundreds of miles to the north, the cold wind below that black cliff blowing between the wooden head markers. Goodsir shivered.

"We're all getting too chilled," said Gore. "We need to get some sleep. Private Pilkington, find the staves for the tent poles and help Best and Ferrier get the tent erected again."

"Aye, aye, sir."

While those two men were hunting for the tent staves, Morfin held up the canvas. Their tent had been so riddled by hailstones that it looked like a battle flag.

"Dear God," said Des Voeux.

"The sleeping bags are all sodden," reported Morfin. "The inside of the tent is soaked."

Gore sighed.

Pilkington and Best returned with two charred, bent stubs of wood and iron.

"The poles were struck, Lieutenant," reported the Marine private. "Looks like the iron core in them attracted the lightning, sir. Not much good as a centre pole now."

Gore just nodded. "We have the axe still on the sledge. Break it out and bring the extra shotgun to use as double poles. Melt some ice to use as an anchor for them if you have to."

"The spirit stove's busted," Ferrier reminded them. "We won't be melting no more ice for a while."

"We have two more stoves on the sledge," said Gore. "And we have some drinking water in the bottles. It's frozen now, but put the bottles inside your clothing until some melts. Pour that into a hole you chip in the ice. It will freeze soon enough. Mr. Best?"

"Aye, sir?" said the stocky young seaman, trying to stifle a yawn.

"Sweep out the tent as best you can, take your knife and cut the stitchings on two of the sleeping bags. We'll use those as over-and-under blankets while we all huddle together for warmth tonight. We have to get some sleep."

Goodsir was watching the unconscious Hartnell for any indications of consciousness, but the young man was as still as a corpse. The surgeon had to check his breathing to make sure he was still alive.

"Are we going back in the morning, sir?" asked John Morfin. "To fetch our cache on the ice and then back to the ships, I mean? We don't have enough food now to get back with anything like sensible rations."

Gore smiled and shook his head. "A couple of days of fasting won't harm us, man. But with Hartnell hurt, I'll send four of you back to the ice cache with him on the sledge. You make the best camp you can there while I take one man to head south as per Sir John's orders. I need to cache the second letter to the Admiralty, but more important, we need to press as far south as possible to see if there's any sign of open water. This whole trip will have been for nothing if we don't do that."

"I volunteer to go with you, Lieutenant Gore," said Goodsir and was astonished at the sound of his own voice. For some reason, pressing on with the officer was very important to him.

Gore also looked surprised. "Thank you, Doctor," he said softly, "but it would make more sense if you stayed with our wounded messmate, would it not?"

Goodsir blushed deeply.

"Best will go with me," said the lieutenant. "Second Mate Des Voeux will be in command of the ice party until I return."

"Yes, sir," both men said in unison.

"Best and I will leave in about three hours and we'll press as far south as we can, carrying only some salt pork, the message canister, one water bottle apiece, some blankets if we have to bivouac, and one of the shotguns. We'll turn back sometime around midnight and try to rendezvous with you on the ice by eight bells tomorrow morning. We'll have a lighter sledge load heading back to the ships — except for Hartnell, I mean — and we know the best places to cross the ridges, so I'll wager we get home in three days or less, rather than five.

"If Best and I aren't back to sea camp by midnight of the day after tomorrow, Mr. Des Voeux, take Hartnell and return to the ship."

"Aye, sir."

"Private Pilkington, are you especially tired?"

"Yes, sir," said the thirty-year-old Marine. "I mean no, sir. I'm ready for any duty you ask of me, Lieutenant."

Gore smiled. "Good. You get the next three hours' watch. All I can promise you is that you'll be the first man allowed to sleep when your sledge party reaches the cache camp later in the day. Take the musket there that's not doing tent pole duty but stay inside the tent — just poke your head out from time to time."

"Very good, sir."

"Dr. Goodsir?"

The surgeon's head came up.

"Would you and Mr. Morfin be so kind as to carry Mr. Hartnell into the tent and get him comfortable? We'll put Tommy in the centre of our little huddle to try to keep him warm."

Goodsir nodded and moved to lift his patient by the shoulders without removing him from the sleeping bag. The welt on the unconscious Hartnell's head was now as large as the surgeon's small, pale fist.

"All right," said Gore through chattering teeth, looking at the tattered tent that was going up, "let's the rest of us get those blankets spread and huddle together like the orphans we are and try to get an hour or two's sleep."

13

FRANKLIN

Lat. 70°-05′ N., Long. 98°-23′ W.
3 June, 1846

S ir John could not quite believe what he was seeing. There were eight figures, just as he had anticipated, but they were . . . *wrong.*

Four of the five exhausted, bearded, and goggled men in the sledge harness made sense — seamen Morfin, Ferrier, and Best, with the huge Private Pilkington leading — but the fifth man in harness was Second Mate Des Voeux, whose expression suggested he had been to Hell and back. Seaman Hartnell walked beside the sledge. The thin sailor's head was heavily bandaged and he was staggering along as if he were part of Napoleon's retreat from Moscow. The surgeon, Goodsir, was also walking alongside the sledge and administering to someone — or something — on the sledge itself. Franklin looked for Lieutenant Gore's distinctive red wool scarf — the comforter was almost six feet long and impossible to miss — but, bizarrely, it seemed that most of the dark, staggering figures were wearing shorter versions of it.

Finally, walking behind the sledge, there came a short, fur-parka-wrapped creature whose face was invisible under a hood but who could only be an Esquimaux.

But it was the sledge itself that made Captain Sir John Franklin cry out, "Dear God!"

This sledge was too narrow for two men to lie on side by side, and Sir John's telescope had not lied to him. Two bodies lay atop each other. The one on top was another Esquimaux — a sleeping or unconscious old man with a brown, lined face and streaming white hair flowing back on the wolfskin hood that someone had pulled back and propped under his head like a pillow. It was to this figure that Goodsir was attending as the sledge approached *Erebus*. Beneath the Esquimaux man's supine body was the blackened, distorted, and too-obviously dead face and form of Lieutenant Graham Gore.

Franklin, Commander Fitzjames, Lieutenant Le Vesconte, First Mate Robert Sergeant, Ice Master Reid, Chief Surgeon Stanley, and such petty officers as Brown, the bosun's mate; John Sullivan, captain of the maintop; and Mr. Hoar, Sir John's steward, all rushed to the sledge, as did forty or more of the seamen who had come up on deck upon the sound of the lookout's hail.

Franklin and the others stopped in their tracks before closing with the sledge party. What had looked through Franklin's telescope like a grey spattering of red wool comforters on the men turned out to be great smears of red on their dark greatcoats. The men were smeared with blood.

There was an explosion of babble. Some of the men in harness hugged friends who ran to them. Thomas Hartnell collapsed on the ice and was surrounded by men trying to help. Everyone was talking and shouting at once.

Sir John had eyes only for the corpse of Lieutenant Graham Gore. The body had been covered by a sleeping robe, but this had partially fallen away so that Sir John could see Gore's handsome face, now absolutely white in places from drained blood, burned black by the arctic sun in other areas. His features were distorted, the eyelids partially raised and the whites visible and glinting with ice, the jaw sagging open, tongue protruding, and the lips already pulling back away from the teeth in what looked to be a snarl or expression of pure horror.

"Get that . . . savage . . . off Lieutenant Gore," commanded Sir John. "*Immediately!*"

Several men hurried to comply, lifting the Esquimaux man by his shoulders and feet. The old man moaned and Dr. Goodsir exclaimed, "Careful! Easy with him! He has a musket ball near his heart. Carry him to the sick bay, please."

The other Esquimaux's parka hood was thrown back now and Sir John noted with shock that it was a young woman. She moved closer to the wounded old man.

"Wait!" cried Sir John, waving at his ship's assistant surgeon. "The sick bay? You are seriously suggesting that we allow that . . . native person . . . into the sick bay of our ship?"

"This man is my patient," Goodsir said with a brazen stubbornness that Sir John Franklin never would have guessed could reside in the short little surgeon. "I need to get him to a place where I may be able to operate — remove the ball from his body if that is possible. Stem the bleeding if it is not. Carry him in, please, gentlemen."

The crewmen holding the Esquimaux looked to their expedition commander for a decision. Sir John was so flummoxed that he could not speak.

"Hurry along now," commanded Goodsir in a confident voice.

Obviously taking Sir John's silence as tacit assent, the men carried the grey-haired Esquimaux man up the ramp of snow and onto the ship. Goodsir, the Esquimaux wench, and several crewmen followed, some helping young Hartnell along.

Franklin, almost unable to hide his shock and horror, stood where he was, still looking down at the corpse of Lieutenant Gore. Private Pilkington and Seaman Morfin were unlashing the lines holding Gore in place on the sledge. "For God's sake," said Franklin, "cover his face."

"Aye, sir," said Morfin. The sailor pulled up the Hudson's Bay Company blanket that had slipped away from the lieutenant's face during their rough day and a half on the ice and pressure ridges.

Sir John could still see the concavity of his handsome lieutenant's gaping mouth through the dry sag of the red blanket. "Mr. Des Voeux," snapped Franklin.

"Yes, sir." Second Mate Des Voeux, who had been overseeing the unlashing of the lieutenant's body, shuffled over and knuckled his forehead. Franklin could see that the whisker-stubbled man, his face sunburned a raw red and sandblasted by the wind, was so exhausted that he could only just raise his arm to salute.

"See to it that Lieutenant Gore's body is brought to his quarters, where you and Mr. Sergeant will see that the body is prepared for burial under the supervision of Lieutenant Fairholme here."

"Aye, sir," said Des Voeux and Fairholme in unison.

Ferrier and Pilkington, exhausted as they were, shook off efforts at assistance and lifted the body of their dead lieutenant. The corpse seemed as stiff as a piece of firewood. One of Gore's arms was bent and his bare hand, turned black from the sun or decomposition, was raised in a sort of frozen clawing gesture.

"Wait," said Franklin. He realized that if he sent Mr. Des Voeux off on this errand, it would be hours before he could receive an official report from the man who had been second in command on this party. Even the confounded surgeon was out of sight, taking the two Esquimaux with him. "Mr. Des Voeux," said Franklin, "after you've seen to Lieutenant Gore's initial preparation, report to me in my cabin."

"Aye, Captain," the mate said tiredly.

"In the meantime, who was with Lieutenant Gore at the end?"

"We all were, sir," said Des Voeux. "But Seaman Best was there with him — just the two of them — for most of the last two days we were on and near King William Land. Charlie saw everything there that Lieutenant Gore did."

"Very well," said Sir John. "Go on about your duties, Mr. Des Voeux. I will hear your report soon. Best, come with me and Commander Fitzjames now."

"Aye, aye, sir," said the sailor, cutting away the last of his leather harness because he was too exhausted to untie the knots. He did *not* have the strength to raise his arm in a salute.

———

The three Preston Patent Illuminators were milky overhead with the never-setting sunlight as Seaman Charles Best stood to make his report to a seated Sir John Franklin, Commander Fitzjames, and Captain Crozier — the captain of HMS *Terror* had arrived for a visit by convenient accident just minutes after the sledge party had come aboard. Edmund Hoar, Sir John's steward and sometime secretary, sat behind the officers, taking notes. Best stood, of course, but Crozier had suggested that the exhausted man could do with some medicinal brandy, and while Sir John's expression showed his disapproval, he had agreed to ask Commander Fitzjames to provide some out of his private stock. The liquor seemed to have revived Best somewhat.

The three officers interrupted from time to time with questions while the teetering Best made his report. When his description of the team's laborious sledge trip to King William Land threatened to stretch on too long, Sir John hurried the man to the events of the last two days.

"Yes, sir. Well, after that first night of lightning and thunder at the cairn and then finding them . . . tracks, marks . . . in the snow, we tried to sleep a couple of hours but didn't really succeed, and then Lieutenant Gore and I set off to the south with light rations while Mr. Des Voeux took the sledge and what was left of the tent and poor Hartnell, who was still out cold then, and we said our 'until tomorrows' and the lieutenant and I headed south and Mr. Des Voeux and his people headed out to the sea ice again."

"You were armed," said Sir John.

"Aye, Sir John," said Best. "Lieutenant Gore had a pistol. I had one of the two shotguns. Mr. Des Voeux kept the other shotgun with his party and Private Pilkington carried the musket."

"Tell us why Lieutenant Gore divided the party," commanded Sir John.

Best seemed confused by the question for a moment but then brightened. "Oh, he told us he was following your orders, sir. With the food at the cairn camp destroyed by lightning and the tent damaged, most of the party needed to get back to sea camp. Lieutenant Gore and me went on to cache that second message container somewhere south along the coast and to see if there was any open water. There wasn't any, sir. Open water, I mean. Not a hint. Not a fu— . . . not a single reflection of dark sky to suggest water."

"How far did the two of you go, Best?" asked Fitzjames.

"Lieutenant Gore figured we'd traveled about four miles south across that snow and frozen gravel when we reached a big inlet, sir . . . rather like the bay at Beechey where we wintered a year ago. But you know what four miles is like in the fog and wind and with ice, sirs, even on land around here. We probably hiked ten miles at least to cover the four. The inlet was frozen solid. Solid as the pack ice here. Not even that usual bit of open water you get between shore and ice in any inlet during the summer up here. So we crossed the mouth of her, sirs, and then went another quarter of a mile or so out along a promontory there where Lieutenant Gore and me built another cairn — not as tall or fancy as Captain Ross's, I'm sure, but solid, and high enough that anyone would see it right away. That land is so flat that a man is always the tallest thing on it. So we piled the rocks about eye-high and set in that second message, same as the first the lieutenant told me, in its fancy brass cylinder."

"Did you turn back then?" asked Captain Crozier.

"No, sir," said Best. "I admit I was worn out. So was Lieutenant Gore. The walking had been hard all that day, even the sastrugi were hard to kick our way through, but it'd been foggy so we only got glimpses of the coast along there from time to time when the fog lifted, so even though it was already afternoon by the time we finished building the cairn and leaving the message, Lieutenant Gore, he had us walk about six or seven more miles south along the coast. Sometimes we could see, most of the time we couldn't. But we could *hear*."

"Hear what, man?" asked Franklin.

"Something following us, Sir John. Something big. And breathing. Sometimes woofin' a bit . . . you know, sirs, like them white bears do, like they're coughing?"

"You identified it as a bear?" asked Fitzjames. "You said that you were the largest things visible on land. Certainly if a bear was following you, you could see it when the fog lifted."

"Aye, sir," said Best, frowning so deeply that it appeared he might start crying. "I mean, no, sir. We couldn't identify it as no bear, sir. We could have, normal like. We should have. But we didn't and couldn't. Sometimes we'd hear it coughin' right behind us — fifteen feet away in the fog — and I'd level the shotgun and Lieutenant Gore would prime his pistol, and we'd wait, sort of holding our breath, but when the fog lifted we could see a hundred feet and nothing was there."

"It must have been an aural phenomenon," said Sir John.

"Aye, sir," agreed Best, his tone suggesting that he did not understand Sir John's comment.

"The shore ice making noise," said Sir John. "Perhaps the wind."

"Oh, aye, yes, sir, Sir John," said Best. "Only there weren't no wind. But the ice . . . could've been that, m'lord. Always could be that." His tone explained that it could not have been.

Shifting as if he was feeling irritation, Sir John said, "You said at the outlet that Lieutenant Gore died . . . was killed . . . after you rejoined the other six men on the ice. Please proceed to that point in the narrative."

"Yes, sir. Well, it must've been close to midnight when we reached as far south as we could go. The sun was gone from the sky ahead of us but the sky had that gold glow . . . you know how it is around midnight up here, Sir John. The fog had lifted well enough for a short while that when we climbed a little rocky nub of a hill . . . not a hill, really, but a high spit maybe fifteen feet above the rest of the flat, frozen gravel there . . . we could see the shore twisting away farther to the south to the blurry horizon with glimpses of bergs poking up from over the horizon from where they'd piled up along the shoreline. No water. Everything frozen solid all the way down. So we turned around and started walking back. We didn't have no tent, no sleeping bags, just cold food to chew on. I broke a good tooth on it. We were both very thirsty, Sir John. We didn't have a stove to melt snow or ice, and we'd started with only a little bit of water in a bottle that Lieutenant Gore kept under his coats and waistcoat.

"So we walked through the night — through the hour or two of sort of twilight that passes for night here, sirs, and then on for more hours — and I fell asleep walking half a dozen times and would've walked in circles until I dropped, but Lieutenant Gore would grab me by the arm and shake me a bit and lead me the right way. We passed the new cairn and then crossed the inlet, and sometime around six bells, when the sun was full up high again, we reached the spot where we'd camped the night before near the first cairn, Sir James Ross's cairn I mean — actually it'd been two nights before, during the first lightning storm — and we just kept trudging on, following the sledge tracks out to the heaped shore bergs and then out onto the sea ice."

"You said 'during the first lightning storm,'" interrupted Crozier. "Were there more? We had several here while you were gone, but the worst seemed to be to the south."

"Oh, yes, sir," said Best. "Every few hours, even with the fog so heavy, the thunder would start rumblin' again and then our hair would start flying about, trying to lift off our heads, and anything metal we had — belt buckles, the shotgun, Lieutenant Gore's pistol — would start glowing blue, and we'd find a place to hunker down in the gravel and we'd just lie there trying to disappear into the ground while the world exploded around us like cannon fire at Trafalgar, sirs."

"Were you *at* Trafalgar, Seaman Best?" Sir John asked icily.

Best blinked. "No, sir. Of course not, sir. I'm only twenty-five, m'lord."

"*I* was at Trafalgar, Seaman Best," Sir John said stiffly. "As signals officer on HMS *Bellerophon,* where thirty-three of the forty officers were killed in that single engagement. Please restrain from using metaphors or similes from beyond your experience for the remainder of your report."

"Aye, aye, s-sir," stammered Best, weaving now not only from exhaustion and grief but with terror at making such a faux pas. "I apologize, Sir John. I didn't mean . . . I mean . . . I shouldn't . . . that is . . ."

"Continue with your narrative, seaman," said Sir John. "But tell us about the last hours of Lieutenant Gore."

"Yes, sir. Well . . . I couldn't've climbed the iceberg barrier without Lieutenant Gore helping me — God bless him — but we did, eventually, and then got out onto the ice itself to where it was just a mile or two to sea camp, where Mr. Des Voeux and the others were waiting for us, but then we got lost."

"How could you possibly get lost," asked Commander Fitzjames, "if you were following the sledge tracks?"

"I don't know, sir," said Best, his voice flattened by exhaustion and grief. "It was foggy. It was *very* foggy. Mostly we couldn't see ten feet in any direction. The sunlight made everything glow and made everything flat. I think we climbed the same ice ridge three or four times, and every time we did our sense of direction got more distorted. And out on the sea ice, there were long patches where the snow had blown away and the sledge's runners hadn't left no marks. But the truth is, sirs, I think we were both, Lieutenant Gore and me, marching along while asleep and just lost the tracks without knowing it."

"Very well," said Sir John. "Continue."

"Well, then we heard the shots . . . ," began Best.

"Shots?" said Commander Fitzjames.

"Aye, sir. Both musket and shotgun they were. In the fog, with the sound bouncin' back from the bergs and ice ridges all around, it sounded like the shots were coming from everywhere at once, but they were close. We started hallooing into the fog and pretty soon we hear Mr. Des Voeux hallooing back and thirty minutes later — it took that long for the fog to lift a bit — we stumbled into the sea camp. The boys had got the tent patched in the thirty-six hours or so we were gone — more or less patched — and it was set up next to the sledge."

"Were the shots to guide you in?" asked Crozier.

"No, sir," said Best. "They was shooting bears. And the old Esquimaux man."

"Explain," said Sir John.

Charles Best licked his torn and ragged lips. "Mr. Des Voeux can explain better than me, sirs, but basically they got back to sea camp the day before to find the tins of food all broken into and scattered and spoiled — by the bears, they reckoned — so Mr. Des Voeux and Dr. Goodsir decided to shoot some of the white bears that kept sniffing around the camp. They'd shot a sow and her two cubs just before we got there and had been dressing the meat. But they heard movement around them — more of that coughin', breathin' in the fog I described, sirs — and then, I guess, the two Esquimaux — the old man and his woman — came over a pressure ridge in the fog, just all more white fur, and Private Pilkington fired his musket and Bobby Ferrier fired his shotgun. Ferrier missed both targets, but Pilkington brought down the man with a ball to the chest.

"When we got there, they'd brought the shot Esquimaux and the woman and some of the white bear meat back to the sea camp — leaving bloody swaths on the ice, sirs, which is what we followed in for the last hundred yards or so — and Dr. Goodsir was trying to save the life of the old Esquimaux man."

"Why?" asked Sir John.

Best had no answer to that. No one else spoke.

"Very well," said Sir John at last. "How long was it after you were reunited with Second Mate Des Voeux and the others at this sea camp when Lieutenant Gore was attacked?"

"No more than thirty minutes, Sir John. Probably less."

"And what provoked the attack?"

"Provoked it?" repeated Best. His eyes no longer seemed focused. "You mean, like shooting them white bears?"

"I mean, what were the exact circumstances of the attack, Seaman Best?" said Sir John.

Best rubbed his forehead. His mouth was open for a long moment before he spoke.

"Nothing provoked it. I was talking to Tommy Hartnell — he was in the tent with his head all bandaged, but awake again — he couldn't remember nothing from until sometime before the first lightning storm — and Mr. Des Voeux was supervising Morfin and Ferrier getting two of the spirit stoves working so we could heat some of that bear meat, and Dr. Goodsir had the old Esquimaux's parka off and was probing a nasty hole in the old man's chest. The woman had been standing there watching, but I didn't see where she was right then because the fog had gotten thicker, and Private Pilkington was standing guard with the musket, when suddenly Lieutenant Gore, he shouts — 'Quiet, everyone! Quiet!' — and we all hushed up and quit what we were saying and doing. The only sound was the hiss of the two spirit stoves and the bubbling of the snow we'd melted to water in the big pans — we were going to make some sort of white bear stew, I guess — and then Lieutenant Gore took out his pistol and primed it and cocked it and took a few steps away from the tent and. . . ."

Best stopped. His eyes were completely unfocused, mouth still open, a glisten of saliva on his chin. He was looking at something not in Sir John's cabin.

"Go on," said Sir John.

Best's mouth worked but no sound came out.

"Continue, seaman," said Captain Crozier in a kinder voice.

Best turned his head in Crozier's direction but his eyes were still focused on something far away.

"Then . . . ," began Best. "Then . . . the ice just rose up, Captain. It just rose up and surrounded Lieutenant Gore."

"What are you talking about?" snapped Sir John after another interval of silence. "The ice can't just rise up. What did you *see?*"

Best did not turn his head in Sir John's direction. "The ice just rose up. Like when you can see the pressure ridges building all of a sudden. Only this was no ridge — no ice — it just rose up and took on a . . . *shape.* A white shape. A form. I remember there were . . . claws. No arms, not at first, but claws. Very large. And teeth. I remember the teeth."

"A bear," Sir John said. "An arctic white bear."

Best only shook his head. "Tall. The thing just seemed to rise up *under* Lieutenant Gore . . . *around* Lieutenant Gore. It was . . . *too tall.* Over twice as tall as Lieutenant Gore, and you know that he was a tall man. It was at least twelve feet tall, taller than that, I think, and too large. Much too large. And then Lieutenant Gore sort of disappeared as the thing . . . surrounded him . . . and all we could see was the lieutenant's head and shoulders and boots, and his pistol went off — he didn't aim, I think he fired into the ice — and then we were all screaming, and Morfin was scrambling for the shotgun and Private Pilkington was running and aiming the musket but was afraid to fire because the thing and the lieutenant were all one thing now, and then . . . then we heard the crunching and snapping."

"The bear was biting the lieutenant?" asked Commander Fitzjames.

Best blinked and looked at the ruddy commander. "Biting him? No, sir. The thing didn't bite. I couldn't even see its head . . . not really. Just two black spots floating twelve, thirteen feet in the air . . . black but also red, you know, like when a wolf turns toward you and the sun catches its eyes? The snapping and crunching was from Lieutenant Gore's ribs and chest and arms and bones breaking."

"Did Lieutenant Gore cry out?" asked Sir John.

"No, sir. He didn't make a noise."

"Did Morfin and Pilkington fire their weapons?" asked Crozier.

"No, sir."

"Why not?"

Best — strangely — smiled. "Why, there was nothing to shoot at, Captain. One second the *thing* was there, rising up over Lieutenant Gore and crushing him like you or me would crush a rat in our palm, and the next second it was *gone*."

"What do you mean, *gone?*" demanded Sir John. "Couldn't Morfin and the Marine private have fired at it while it was retreating into the fog?"

"Retreating?" repeated Best, and his absurd and disturbing smile grew broader. "The shape didn't retreat. It just went back down into the ice — like a shadow going away when the sun goes behind a cloud — and by the time we got to Lieutenant Gore he was dead. Mouth wide open. Didn't even have time to scream. The fog lifted then. There were no holes in the ice. No cracks. Not even a little breathing hole like the harp seals use. Just Lieutenant Gore lying there broken — his chest was all caved in, both arms was broke, and he was bleeding from his ears, eyes, and mouth. Dr. Goodsir pushed us away, but there was nothing that he could do. Gore was dead and already growing as cold as the ice under him."

Best's insane and irritating grin wavered — the man's torn lips were quivering but still drawn back over his teeth — and his eyes became less focused than ever.

"Did . . . ," began Sir John, but stopped as Charles Best collapsed in a heap to the deck.

14

GOODSIR

Lat. 70°-05′ N., Long. 98°-23′ W.
June, 1847

From the private diary of Dr. Harry D. S. Goodsir:

4 June, 1847 —

When Stanley and I stripped the wounded Esquimaux man naked, I was reminded that he was wearing an Amulet made up of a flat, smooth Stone, smaller than my fist, in the shape of a White Bear — the stone did not seem to have been carved but in its natural, thumb-smoothed state perfectly captured the long neck, small head, and powerful extended legs and forward motion of the living animal. I had seen the Amulet when I'd inspected the man's wound on the ice but thought nothing of it.

The ball from Private Pilkington's musket had entered the native man's Chest not an inch below that amulet, pierced flesh and muscle between the third and fourth ribs (deflected slightly by the higher of the two), passed through his Left Lung, and lodged in his Spine, severing numerous Nerves there.

There was no way that I could save him — I knew from earlier inspection that any Attempt to Remove the musket ball would have caused instant death, and I could not stem the internal Bleeding from Within the Lung — but I did my best, having the Esquimaux carried to the part of the Sick Bay which Surgeon Stanley and I have set up as a surgery. For Half an Hour yesterday after my return to the Ship, Stanley and I probed the wound front and back with our Cruelest Instruments and Cut with Energy until we found the location of the Ball in his Spine, and generally confirmed our prognosis of Imminent Death.

But the unusually tall, powerfully built grey-haired Savage had not yet agreed with our Prognosis. He continued to exist as a man. He continued to force breaths through his torn and bloodied lung, coughing blood repeatedly. He continued to stare at us through his disturbingly light-coloured — for an Esquimaux — eyes, watching our Every Movement.

Dr. McDonald arrived from Terror and, at Stanley's suggestion, took the second Esquimaux — the girl — into the rear alcove of the Sick Bay, separated from us by a blanket serving as a curtain, for an Examination. I believe that Surgeon Stanley was less interested in having the girl examined than he was in getting her out of the sick bay during our bloody probing of her husband's or father's wounds . . . although neither the Subject nor the Girl appeared disturbed by either the Blood or Wound which would have made any London Lady — and no few surgeons in training — faint dead away.

And speaking of fainting, Stanley and I had just finished our examination of the dying Esquimaux when Captain Sir John Franklin came in with two crewmen half-carrying Charles Best, who, they informed us, had passed out in Sir John's cabin. We had the men put Best on the nearest cot and it took only a minute's Cursory examination for me to list the reasons why the man had fainted: the same extreme Exhaustion which all of us on Lieutenant Gore's party were suffering after ten days of Constant Toil, hunger (we had had virtually nothing to eat except raw Bear Meat for our last two days and nights on the ice), a drying up of all moisture in our bodies (we could not afford the time to stop and melt snow on the spirit stoves, so we resorted to the Bad Idea of chewing on snow and ice — a process which depletes the body's water rather than adds to it), and, a reason most Obvious to me but strangely Obscure to the officers who had been Interviewing him — poor Best had been made to stand and report to the Captains while still wearing seven of his eight Layers of Wool, allowed time only to remove his bloodied Greatcoat. After ten days and nights on the ice at an average temperature near zero degrees, the warmth of Erebus was almost too much for me, and I had shed all but two layers upon reaching the Sick Bay. It had quickly proved too much for Best.

After being assured that Best would recover — a dose of Smelling Salts had already all but brought him around — Sir John looked with visible distaste at our Esquimaux patient, now lying on his bloodied chest and belly since

*Stanley and I had been probing his back for the ball, and our commander said,
Is he going to live?*

Not for long, Sir John, *reported Stephen Samuel Stanley.*

*I winced at speaking such in front of the patient — we doctors usually
deliver our direst prognoses to each other in neutral-toned Latin in the
presence of our dying clients — but realized at once that it was most unlikely
that the Esquimaux could understand English.*

Roll him over on his back, *commanded Sir John.*

*We did so, carefully, and while the pain must still have been beyond
excruciating for the grey-haired native, who had remained conscious during all
our probing and continued to do so now, he made no sound. His gaze was
fixed on our expedition Leader's face.*

*Sir John leaned over him and, raising his Voice and speaking slowly as if
to a Deaf Child or Idiot, cried,* Who . . . ARE . . . you?

The Esquimaux looked up at Sir John.

What . . . your . . . name? *shouted Sir John.* What . . . your . . . tribe?

The dying man made no response.

*Sir John shook his head and showed an expression of disgust, although
whether because of the Gaping Wound in the Esquimaux's chest or due to his
aboriginal obdurance, I know not.*

Where is the other native? *Sir John asked of Stanley.*

*My chief surgeon, both hands busy pressing against the wound and
applying the bloody bandages with which he hoped to slow, if not stem, the
constant pulse of lifeblood from the savage's lung, nodded in the direction of
the alcove curtain.* Dr. McDonald is with her, Sir John.

*Sir John brusquely passed through the blanket-curtain. I heard several
stammers, a few disjointed words, and then the Leader of our Expedition
reappeared, backing out, his face such a bright, solid red that I had fears that
our sixty-one-year-old commander was having a stroke.*

Then Sir John's red face went quite white with shock.

*I realized belatedly that the young woman must have been naked. A few
minutes earlier I had glanced through the partially opened curtain and noticed
that when McDonald gestured for her to take off her outer clothing — her
bearskin parka — the girl nodded, removed the heavy outer garment, and
was wearing nothing under it from the waist up. I'd been busy with the dying*

man on the table at the time, but I noted that this was a sensible way to stay warm under the loose layer of heavy fur — much better than the multiple layers of Wool which all of us in poor Lieutenant Gore's sledge party had worn. Naked under fur or animal hair, the body can warm itself when chilled, adequately cool itself when needed, as during exertion, since perspiration would quickly wick away from the body into the hairs of the wolfskin or bearskin hide. The wool we Englishmen had worn had soaked through with Sweat almost immediately, never really dried, quickly froze when we quit marching or pulling the sledge and lost much of its Insulating Quality. By the time we had Returned to the ship, I had no doubt that we were carrying almost twice the Weight on our backs than that with which we had departed.

I sh-shall return at a more suitable time, *stammered Sir John, and backed past us.*

Captain Sir John Franklin looked shaken, but whether it was because of the young woman's sensible Edenic Nakedness or something else he saw in the Sick Bay alcove, I could not say. He left the Surgery without another word.

A moment later McDonald called me into the rear alcove. The girl — young woman, I had noticed, although it has been scientifically shown that females from savage tribes reach puberty long before young ladies in civilized societies — had put her bulky parka and sealskin pants back on. Dr. McDonald himself looked agitated, almost upset, and when I queried him as to the problem, he gestured for the Esquimaux wench to open her mouth. Then he raised a lantern and a convex mirror to focus the light and I saw for myself.

Her tongue had been amputated near the roots. Enough was left, I saw — and McDonald concurred — to allow her to swallow and to eat most foods after a fashion, but certainly the articulation of complex sounds, if one might call any Esquimaux language complex in any form, would be beyond her ability. The scars were old. This had not happened recently.

I confess that I pulled away in Horror. Who would do this to a mere child — and why? But when I used the word "amputation," Dr. McDonald softly corrected me.

Look again, Dr. Goodsir, *he all but whispered.* It is not a neat surgical circular amputation, not even by so crude an instrument as a stone knife. The poor lass's tongue was chewed off when she was very small — and so close to the root of the member that there is no possibility she did this to herself.

I took a step away from the woman. Is she mutilated elsewhere? *I asked, speaking in Latin out of old habit. I had read of barbaric customs in the Dark Continent and among the Mohammedan in which their women were cruelly circumcised in a parody of the Hebrew custom for males.*

Nowhere else, *responded McDonald.*

Then I thought I understood the source of Sir John's sudden paleness and obvious shock, but when I asked McDonald whether he had shared this information with our commander, the surgeon assured me that he had not. Sir John had entered the alcove, seen the Esquimaux girl without her clothes, and left in some agitation. McDonald then began to give me the results of his quick physical inspection of our captive, or guest, when we were interrupted by Surgeon Stanley.

My first thought was that the Esquimaux man had died, but that did not turn out to be the Case. A crewman had come calling me to give my report before Sir John and the other Captains.

———

I could tell that Sir John, Commander Fitzjames, and Captain Crozier were disappointed in my Report of what I had observed of Lieutenant Gore's death, and while this ordinarily would have Distressed me, this day — perhaps due to my great Fatigue and to the Psychological Changes which may have taken place during my time with Lieutenant Gore's Ice Party — the disappointment of my Superiors did not Affect me.

I first reported again on the condition of our dying Esquimaux man and on the curious fact about the girl's missing tongue. The three captains murmured among themselves about this fact, but the only questions came from Captain Crozier.

Do you know why someone may have done this to her, Dr. Goodsir?

I have no idea, sir.

Could it have been done by an animal? *he persisted.*

I paused. The idea had not occurred to me. It could have been, *I said at last, although it was very hard to Picture some Arctic Carnivore chewing off a child's tongue yet leaving her alive. Then again, it was well known that these Esquimaux tended to live with Savage Dogs. I had seen this myself at Disko Bay.*

There were no more questions about the two Esquimaux.

They asked for the details of Lieutenant Gore's death and about the Creature who killed him, and I told the truth — that I had been working to save the life of the Esquimaux man who had come out of the fog and been shot by Private Pilkington and that I had looked up only in the final instant of Graham Gore's death. I explained that between the shifting fog, the screams, the distracting blast of the musket, and the report of the lieutenant's pistol going off, my limited vision from the side of the sledge where I knelt, the rapidly shifting movement of both men and light, I was not sure what I had seen: only that large white shape enveloping the hapless officer, the flash of his pistol, more shots, then the fog enfolding everything again.

But you are certain it was a white bear? *asked Commander Fitzjames.*

I hesitated. If it was, *I said at last,* it was an uncommonly large specimen of *Ursus maritimus.* I had the impression of a bearlike carnivore — a huge body, giant arms, small head, obsidian eyes — but the details were not as clear as that description makes them sound. Mostly what I remember is that the thing seemed to come out of nowhere — just rise up around the man — and that it towered twice as tall as Lieutenant Gore. That was very unnerving.

I am sure it was, *Sir John said drily, almost sarcastically, I thought.* But what else could it have been, Mr. Goodsir, were it not a bear?

It was not the first time that I had noticed that Sir John never complimented me with my proper Rank as Doctor. He used the "Mr." as he might with any mate or untutored warrant officer. It had taken me two years to realize that the aging expedition commander whom I held in such high esteem had no degree of reciprocal esteem for any mere ship's surgeon.

I don't know, Sir John, *I said. I wanted to get back to my patient.*

I understand you've shown an interest in the white bears, Mr. Goodsir, *continued Sir John.* Why is that?

I trained as an anatomist, Sir John. And before the expedition sailed, I had dreams of becoming a naturalist.

No longer? *asked Captain Crozier in that soft brogue of his.*

I shrugged. I find that fieldwork is not my forte, Captain.

Yet you've dissected some of the white bears we've shot here and at Beechey Island, *persisted Sir John*. Studied their skeletons and musculature. Observed them on the ice as we all have.

Yes, Sir John.

Do you find Lieutenant Gore's wounds consistent with the damage such an animal would produce?

I hesitated only a second. I had examined poor Graham Gore's corpse before we had loaded it onto the sledge for the nightmare journey back across the pack ice.

Yes, Sir John, *I said*. The white polar bear of this region is — as far as we know — the largest single predator on Earth. It can weigh half again as much and stand three feet taller on its hind legs than the Grizzly Bear, the largest and most ferocious bear in North America. It is a very powerful predator, fully capable of crushing a man's chest and severing his spine, as was the case with poor Lieutenant Gore. More than that, the white arctic bear is the only predator that commonly stalks human beings as its prey.

Commander Fitzjames cleared his throat. I say, Dr. Goodsir, *he said softly*, I did see a rather ferocious tiger in India once which — according to the villagers — had eaten twelve people.

I nodded, realizing at that second how terribly weary I was. The exhaustion worked on me like Powerful Drink. Sir . . . Commander . . . Gentle-men . . . , you have all seen more of the world than have I. However, from my rather extensive reading on the subject, it would seem that all other land carnivores — wolves, lions, tigers, other bears — may kill human beings if provoked, and some of them, such as your tiger, Commander Fitzjames, will become man-eaters if forced to due to disease or injury which precludes them from seeking out their natural prey, but only the white arctic bear — *Ursus maritimus* — actively stalks human beings as prey on a common basis.

Crozier was nodding. Where have you learned that, Doctor Goodsir? Your books?

To some extent, sir. But I spent most of our time at Disko Bay speaking to the locals there about the behaviour of the bears and also inquired of Captain Martin on his *Enterprise* and Captain Dannert on his *Prince of Wales* when we were anchored near them in Baffin Bay.

Those two gentlemen answered my questions about the white bears and put me in touch with several of their crewmen — including two elderly American whalers who had spent more than a dozen years apiece in the ice. They had many anecdotes about the white bears stalking the Esquimaux natives of the region and even taking men from their own ships when they were trapped in the ice. One old man — I believe his name was Connors — said that their ship in '28 had lost not one but two cooks to bears . . . one of them snatched from the lower deck where he was working near the stove while the men slept.

Captain Crozier smiled at that. Perhaps we should not believe every tale an old sailor has to tell, Doctor Goodsir.

No, sir. Of course not, sir.

That will be all, Mr. Goodsir, *said Sir John.* We shall call you back if we have more questions.

Yes, sir, *I said and turned tiredly to return forward to the sick bay.*

Oh, Dr. Goodsir, *called Commander Fitzjames before I stepped out the door of Sir John's cabin.* I have a question, although I am deucedly ashamed to admit that I do not know the answer. Why is the white bear called *Ursus maritimus?* Not out of its fondness for eating sailors, I trust.

No, sir, *I said.* I believe the name was bestowed on the arctic bear because it is more a sea mammal than land animal. I've read reports of the white arctic bear being sighted hundreds of miles at sea, and Captain Martin of the *Enterprise* told me himself that while the bear is fast on the attack on land or ice — coming at one at speeds of more than twenty-five miles per hour — that at sea it is one of the most powerful swimmers in the ocean, capable of swimming sixty or seventy miles without rest. Captain Dannert said that once his ship was doing eight knots with a fair wind, far out of sight of land, and that two white bears kept pace with the ship for ten nautical miles or so and then simply left it behind, swimming toward distant ice floes with the speed and ease of a beluga whale. Thus the nomenclature . . . *Ursus maritimus* . . . a mammal, yes, but mostly a creature of the sea.

Thank you, Mr. Goodsir, *said Sir John.*

You are most welcome, sir, *I said and left.*

4 June, 1847, continued . . .

The Esquimaux man died just a few minutes after midnight. But he spoke first.

I was asleep at the time, sitting up with my back against the Sick Bay bulkhead, but Stanley woke me.

The grey-haired man was struggling as he lay on the Surgical Bench, his arms moving almost as if he were trying to swim up into the air. His punctured lung was hemorrhaging and blood was pouring down his chin and onto his bandaged chest.

As I raised the light of the lantern, the Esquimaux girl rose up from the corner where she had been sleeping and all three of us leaned in toward the dying man.

The old Esquimaux hooked a powerful finger and poked at his chest, very near the bullet hole. Each gasp of his pumped out more bright red arterial blood, but he coughed out what could only be words. I used a piece of chalk to scribble them on the slate Stanley and I used to communicate when patients were sleeping nearby.

"Angatkut tuquruq! Quarubvitchuq . . . angatkut turquq. . . . Paniga . . . tuunbaq! Tanik . . . naluabmiu tuqutauyasiruq . . . umiaq-pak tuqutauyasiruq . . . nanuq tuqutkaa! Paniga . . . tunbaq nanuq . . . angatkut ququruq!"

And then the hemorrhaging grew so extreme he could talk no more. The blood geysered and fountained out of him, choking him until — even with Stanley and me propping him up, trying to help clear his breathing passages — he was inhaling only blood. After a terrible final moment of this his chest quit heaving, he fell back into our arms, and his stare became fixed and glassy. Stanley and I lowered him to the table.

Look out! *cried Stanley.*

For a second I did not understand the other surgeon's warning — the old man was dead and still, I could find no pulse or breath as I hovered over him — but then I turned and saw the Esquimaux woman.

She had seized one of the bloody scalpels from our worktable and was stepping closer, lifting the weapon. It was obvious to me at once that she was paying no attention to me — her fixed gaze was on the Dead Face and chest of the man who might have been her husband or father or brother. In those *few seconds, not knowing anything of the customs of her Heathen tribe, a Myriad of wild images came to my mind — the girl cutting out the man's heart, perhaps devouring it in some terrible ritual, or removing the dead man's eyes or slicing off one of his fingers or perhaps adding to the webwork of old scars that covered his body like a sailor's tattoos.*

She did none of that. Before Stanley could seize her and while I could think of nothing but to cower protectively over the dead man, the Esquimaux girl flicked the scalpel forward with a surgeon's dexterity — she obviously had used razor-sharp knives for most of her life — and she severed the rawhide cord that held the old man's amulet in place.

Catching up the flat, white, blood-spattered bear-shaped stone and its severed cord, she secreted it somewhere on her person under her parka and returned the scalpel to its table.

Stanley and I stared at each other. Then Erebus's chief surgeon went to wake the young sailor who served as the Sick Bay mate, sending him to inform the officer on watch and thence the Captain that the old Esquimaux was dead.

4 June, continued . . .

We buried the Esquimaux man sometime around one-thirty in the morning — three bells — shoving his canvas-wrapped body down the narrow fire hole in the ice only twenty yards from the ship. This single fire hole giving access to open water fifteen feet below the ice was the only one the men have managed to keep open this cold summer — as I have mentioned before, sailors are afraid of nothing so much as fire — and Sir John's instructions were to dispose of the body there. Even as Stanley and I struggled to press the body down the narrow funnel, using boat pikes, we could hear the chopping and occasional swearing from several hundred yards east on the ice where a party of twenty men was working through the night to hack out a more decorous hole for Lieutenant Gore's burial service the next day — or later the same day, actually.

Here, in the middle of the night, it was still light enough to read a Bible verse by — if anyone had brought a Bible out here on the ice to read a verse from, which no one had — and the dim light aided us, the two surgeons and two crewmen ordered to help us, as we poked, prodded, shoved, slid, and

finally slammed the Esquimaux man's body deeper and deeper into the blue
ice and thence into the Black Water beneath.

The Esquimaux woman stood silently, watching, still showing no expression.
There was a wind from the west-northwest and her black hair lifted from her
stained parka hood and moved across her face like a ruffle of raven feathers.

We were the only members of the Burial Party — Surgeon Stanley, the
two panting, softly cursing crewmen, the native woman, and me — until
Captain Crozier and a tall, lanky lieutenant appeared in the blowing snow
and watched the final moment or two of struggle. Finally the Esquimaux
man's body slid the last five feet and disappeared into the black currents
fifteen feet below the ice.

Sir John ordered that the woman not spend the night aboard
Erebus, Captain Crozier said softly. We've come to take her back to
Terror. To the tall lieutenant whose name I now remembered as Irving, Crozier
said, John, she will be in your charge. Find a place for her out of sight
of the men — probably forward of the sick bay in the stacks — and
make sure no harm comes to her.

Aye, sir.

Excuse me, Captain, *I said.* But why not let her go back to her
people?

Crozier smiled at this. Normally I would agree with that course of
action, Doctor. But there are no known Esquimaux settlements —
not the smallest village — within three hundred miles of here. They
are a nomadic people — especially those we call the Northern
Highlanders — but what brought this old man and young girl out
onto the pack ice so far north in a summer where there are no
whales, no walruses, no seals, no caribou, no animals of any sort
abroad except our white bears and the murderous things on the ice?

I had no answer to this, but it hardly seemed pertinent to my question.

It may come to the point, *continued Crozier,* where our lives might
depend upon finding and befriending these native Esquimaux. Shall
we let her go then before we've befriended her?

We shot her husband or father, *said Surgeon Stanley, glancing at the*
mute young woman who still stared at the now empty fire hole. Our Lady
Silence here might not have the most charitable of feelings toward us.

Precisely, *said Captain Crozier.* And we have enough problems right now without this lass leading a war party of angry Esquimaux back to our ships to murder us as we sleep. No, I think Captain Sir John is right . . . she should stay with us until we decide what to do . . . not only with her, but with ourselves. *Crozier smiled at Stanley. In two years, this was the first time that I could remember seeing Captain Crozier smile.* Lady Silence. That is good, Stanley. Very good. Come, John. Come, m'lady.

They walked west through the blowing snow toward the first pressure ridge. I went back up the ramp of snow to Erebus, *to my tiny little cabin which seemed like pure heaven to me now, and to the first solid night's sleep I had had since Lieutenant Gore led us south-southeast onto the ice more than ten days earlier.*

15

FRANKLIN

By the day that he was to die, Sir John had almost recovered from the shock of seeing the Esquimaux wench naked. It was the same young woman, the same teenaged harlot Copper squaw whom the Devil had sent to tempt him during his first ill-fated expedition in 1819, the wanton Robert Hood's fifteen-year-old bedmate named Greenstockings. Sir John was sure of that. This temptress had the same coffee-brown skin that seemed to glow even in the dark, the same high, round girl's breasts, the same brown areolae, and the same raven-feather slash of dark escutcheon above her sex.

It was the same succubus.

The shock to Captain Sir John Franklin of seeing her naked on surgeon McDonald's table in the sick bay — *on his ship* — had been profound, but Sir John was sure that he had been able to hide his reaction from the surgeons and from the other captains during the rest of that endless, disconcerting day.

Lieutenant Gore's burial service took place late on Friday, the fourth of June. It had taken a large work party more than twenty-four hours to get through the ice to allow for the burial at sea, and before they were done they had to use black powder to blow away the top ten feet of rock-hard ice, then use picks and shovels to excavate a broad crater to open the last five feet or so. When they were finished around midday, Mr. Weekes, the carpenter from *Erebus,* and Mr. Honey, the carpenter from *Terror,* had constructed a clever and elegant wooden scaffolding over the ten-foot-long and five-foot-wide opening into the dark sea. Work parties with long pikes were stationed at the crater to keep the ice from congealing beneath the platform.

Lieutenant Gore's body had begun to decay quickly in the relative heat of the ship, so the carpenters first constructed a most solid coffin of mahogany lined with an inner box of sweet-smelling cedar. Between the two enclosures of wood was set a layer of lead in lieu of the traditional two rounds of shot set in the usual canvas burial bag to ensure that the body would sink. Mr. Smith, the blacksmith, had forged, hammered, and engraved a beautiful memorial plate in copper, which was affixed to the top of the mahogany coffin by screws. Because the burial service was a mixture of shoreside burial and the more common burial at sea, Sir John had specified that the coffin be made heavy enough to sink at once.

At eight bells at the beginning of the first dogwatch — 4:00 p.m. — the two ships' companies assembled at the burial site a quarter of a mile across the ice from *Erebus*. Sir John had ordered everyone except the smallest possible ship's watches to be present for the service and furthermore had ordered them to wear no layer over their dress uniforms, so at the appointed time more than one hundred shivering but formally dressed officers and men had gathered on the ice.

Lieutenant Gore's coffin was lowered over the side of *Erebus* and lashed to an oversized sledge reinforced for this day's sad purpose. Sir John's own Union Jack was draped over the coffin. Then thirty-two seamen, twenty from *Erebus* and a dozen from *Terror,* slowly pulled the coffin-sledge the quarter mile to the burial site, while four of the youngest seamen, still on the roster as ship's boys — George Chambers and David Young from *Erebus,* Robert Golding and Thomas Evans from *Terror*— beat a slow march on drums muffled in black cloth. The solemn procession was escorted by twenty men, including Captain Sir John Franklin, Commander Fitzjames, Captain Crozier, and the majority of all the other officers and mates in full dress, excluding only those left in command in each near-vacant ship.

At the burial site, a firing party of red-coated Royal Marines stood waiting at attention. Led by *Erebus*'s thirty-three-year-old sergeant,

David Bryant, the party consisted of Corporal Pearson, Private Hopcraft, Private Pilkington, Private Healey, and Private Reed from *Erebus* — only Private Braine was missing from the flagship's contingent of Marines, since the man had died last winter and been buried on Beechey Island — as well as Sergeant Tozer, Corporal Hedges, Private Wilkes, Private Hammond, Private Heather, and Private Daly from HMS *Terror*.

Lieutenant Gore's cocked hat and sword were carried behind the burial sledge by Lieutenant H. T. D. Le Vesconte, who had assumed Gore's command duties. Alongside Le Vesconte walked Lieutenant James W. Fairholme, carrying a blue velvet cushion on which were displayed the six medals young Gore had earned during his years in the Royal Navy.

As the sledge party approached the burial crater, the line of twelve Royal Marines parted, opening to form a lane. The Marines turned inward and stood at reverse arms as the procession of sledge-pullers, funeral sledge, honor guard, and other mourners passed between their ranks.

As the hundred and ten men shuffled to their places amid the mass of officers' uniforms around the crater — some seamen standing on pressure ridges to get a better look — Sir John led the captains to their place on a temporary scaffolding at the east end of the crater in the ice. Slowly, carefully, the thirty-two sledge-pullers worked together to unlash the heavy coffin and lower it down precisely angled boards to its temporary resting place on the wooden superstructure just above the rectangle of black water. When the coffin was in place, it rested not only on the final planks but on three sturdy hawsers now manned on either side by the same men who had been chosen to pull the sledge.

When the muffled drums quit beating, all hats came off. The cold wind ruffled the men's long hair, all washed, parted, and tied back with ribbons for this service. The day was chilly — no more than five degrees at the last measuring at six bells — but the arctic sky, filled with ice crystals, was a solid dome of golden light. As if in honour of Lieutenant Gore, the single circle of the ice-occluded sun had been joined by three more suns — sun dogs floating above and to either side of the south-hanging true sun — all connected by a halo-band of rainbow-prismed light. Many men present bowed their heads at the aptness of the sight.

Sir John conducted the Service for the Dead, his strong voice easily audible to the hundred and ten men gathered round. The ritual was familiar to all there. The words were reassuring. The responses were known. By the end, the cold wind was ignored by most as the familiar phrases echoed across the ice.

"We therefore commit his body to the deep, to be turned into corruption, looking for the resurrection of the body, when the Sea shall give up her dead, and the life of the world to come, through our Lord Jesus Christ, who at his coming shall change our vile body, that it may be like his glorious body, according to the mighty working, whereby he is able to subdue all things to himself."

"Amen," said the assembled men.

The twelve men of the Royal Marine firing party raised their muskets and fired three volleys, the last one having only three shots rather than the four in the two volleys that had preceded it.

At the sound of the first volley, Lieutenant Le Vesconte nodded and Samuel Brown, John Weekes, and James Rigden slid the planks out from under the heavy casket, which now hung suspended only by the three hawsers. At the sound of the second volley, the coffin was lowered until it touched the black water. At the sound of the final volley, the hawsers were slowly let slip until the heavy casket with its copper plaque — Lieutenant Gore's medals and sword also now perched atop the mahogany — disappeared beneath the water's surface.

There was a slight roiling of icy water, the hawsers were pulled up and tossed aside, and the rectangle of black water was empty. To the south, the sun dogs and halo had disappeared and only a sullen red sun glowed under the dome of sky.

The men dispersed silently to their ships. It was only two bells into the first dogwatch. For most of the men it was time for their evening meal and their second portion of grog.

The next day, Saturday the fifth of June, saw both crews huddling in the lower decks of their ships as another arctic summer lightning storm exploded above them. Lookouts were called down from the topmains and those few who kept watch on deck kept away from all metal and masts as lightning crashed through fog, thunder rolled, great bolts of electricity struck and then restruck the lightning rods set on the masts and cabin roofs, and blue fingers of Saint Elmo's fire crept along the spars and slithered through the rigging. Haggard lookouts coming below after their watch told their wide-eyed mates of spheres of ball-lightning rolling and leaping across the ice. Later in the day — with the lightning and airborne electrical displays growing even more violent — the dogwatch lookouts reported something large, much too large to be a mere white bear, prowling and pacing along the ridges in the fog, now concealed, now made visible by lightning flash for only a second or two. Sometimes, they said, the shape walked on four legs like a bear. Other times, they swore, it walked easily on two legs, like a man. The thing, they said, was circling the ship.

Although the mercury was falling, Sunday dawned clear and thirty degrees colder — the temperature at noon was nine below zero — and Sir John sent out word that Divine Service would be compulsory that day on *Erebus.*

Divine Service was compulsory each week for the men and officers of Sir John's ship — he held it on the lower deck all during the dark winter months — but only the most devout Terrors made the ice crossing to join in the service. Since it was mandatory in the Royal Navy, by tradition as much as by regulation, Captain Crozier also held Divine Service on Sunday, but with no chaplain aboard it was an abbreviated effort — sometimes amounting to little more than reading the Ship's Articles — and ran twenty minutes of a morning rather than Sir John's enthusiastic ninety minutes or two hours.

This Sunday there was no option.

Captain Crozier led his officers, mates, and men across the ice for the second time in three days, this time with their greatcoats and mufflers over any dress uniforms, and they were surprised upon their arrival at *Erebus* to see that the service was to take place on deck, with Sir John preaching from the quarterdeck. Despite the pale blue sky above — no gold dome of ice crystals or symbolic sun dogs this day — the wind was *very* cold, and the mass of seamen huddled together for at least the illusion of warmth in the area below the quarterdeck, while the officers from both ships stood behind Sir John on the weather side of the deck like a solid mass of greatcoated acolytes. Once again, the twelve Marines were drawn up in rank, this time on the lee side of the main deck with Sergeant Bryant in front, while the petty officers massed before the mainmast.

Sir John stood at the binnacle, which had been covered with the same Union Jack that had been draped over Gore's casket "to answer the purpose of a pulpit," as per regulation.

He preached for only about an hour and no toes or fingers were lost as a result.

Being an Old Testament man by nature and inclination, Sir John led the way through several of the prophets, focusing awhile on Isaiah's judgement upon the earth — "Behold, the Lord maketh the earth empty and maketh it waste, and turneth it upside down, and scattereth abroad the inhabitants thereof" — and slowly through the barrage of words, it became apparent to even the most dimwitted seaman in the mass of greatcoats, mufflers, and mittens on the main deck that their commander was really talking about their expedition to find the North-West Passage and their current condition frozen in the icy wastes at latitude 70°- 05' N., longitude 98°- 23' W.

"The land shall be utterly emptied, and utterly spoiled: for the LORD hath spoken this word," continued Sir John. "Fear, and the pit, and the snare, *are* upon thee, O inhabitant of the earth . . . And it shall come to pass *that* he who fleeth from the noise of the fear shall fall into the pit; and he that cometh up out of the midst of the pit shall be taken in the snare: for the windows from on high are open, and the foundations of the earth do shake . . . The earth is utterly broken down, the earth is clean dissolved, the earth is moved exceedingly. They shall reel to and fro like a drunkard . . ."

As if in proof of this dire prophecy, a great groaning came up from the ice all around HMS *Erebus* and the deck shifted under the standing men. The ice-rimmed masts and spars above them seemed to vibrate and then make small circles against the weak blue sky. No man broke formation or made a noise.

Sir John shifted from Isaiah to Revelation and gave them even more dire images of what awaited those who abandoned their Lord.

"But of what of he . . . of we . . . who do not break covenant with our Lord?" asked Sir John. "I commend you to JONAH."

Some of the seamen sighed in relief. They were familiar with Jonah.

"Jonah was given a commission by God to go to Nineveh and to cry against it because of its wickedness," cried Sir John, his often weak voice now rising in volume as strongly and well as any inspired Anglican preacher's, "but Jonah — you all know this, shipmates — Jonah fled from his commission and from the presence of the Lord, going down to Joppa there to take a berth on the first ship leaving, which happened to be destined for Tarshish — a city beyond the edge of the world then. Jonah foolishly thought that he could sail beyond the limits of the Kingdom of the Lord.

" 'But the LORD sent out a great wind into the sea, and there was a mighty tempest in the sea, so that the ship was like to be broken.' And you know the rest . . . you know how the sailors cried out asking why this evil had fallen upon them, and they cast lots, and the lot fell upon Jonah. 'And they said unto him, What shall we do unto thee, that the sea may be calm unto us? And he said unto them, Take me up and cast me forth into the sea; so shall the sea be calm unto you: for I know that for my sake this great tempest *is* upon you.'

"But at first the sailors did not cast Jonah overboard, did they, shipmates? No — they were brave men and good sailors and professionals and rowed hard to bring their foundering ship to land. But finally they weakened, cried unto the Lord, and then did make a sacrifice of Jonah, casting him overboard.

"And the Bible says — 'Now the LORD had prepared a great fish to swallow up Jonah. And Jonah was in the belly of the fish three days and three nights.'

"Notice, shipmates, that the Bible does not say that Jonah was swallowed by a *whale*. No! This was no beluga nor right nor baleen nor sperm nor killer nor fin such as we would see in these high waters or in Baffin Bay on a normal arctic summer. No, Jonah was swallowed up by a 'great fish' which the Lord had prepared for him — which means a monster of the deep that Lord God Jehovah had made at the Creation for just this purpose, to swallow Jonah someday, and in the Bible this monster of a great fish is sometimes called Leviathan.

"And just so have we been sent on our mission beyond the farthest known edge of the world, shipmates, farther than the Tarshish — which was only in Spain, after all — we have been sent out to where the elements themselves seem to rebel, where lightning crashes from frozen skies, where the cold never relents, where white beasts walk the frozen surface of the sea, and where no man, civilized or otherwise, could ever call such a place home.

"But we are not beyond the Kingdom of God, shipmates! As Jonah did not protest his fate nor curse his punishment but rather prayed unto the Lord out of the fish's belly for three days and three nights, so we must not protest, but accept God's will of this exile of three long nights of winter in the belly of this ice, and like Jonah we must pray unto the Lord, saying, 'I am cast out of thy sight; yet I will look again toward thy holy temple. The waters compassed me about, *even* to the soul: the depth closed me round about, the weeds were wrapped about my head. I went down to the bottoms of the mountains: the earth with her bars *was* about me for ever: yet hast thou brought up my life from corruption, O Lord my God.'

" 'When my soul fainted within me I remembered the LORD: and my prayer came in unto thee, into thine holy temple. They that observe lying vanities foresake their own mercy. But I will sacrifice unto thee with the voice of thanksgiving; I will pay *that* that I have vowed. Salvation *is* of the Lord.

" 'And the LORD spake unto the fish, and it vomited out Jonah upon the dry *land*.'

"And, beloved shipmates, know in your hearts that we have given and must continue giving sacrifice unto the Lord with the voice of thanksgiving. We must pay that that we have vowed to pay. Our friend and brother in Christ, Lieutenant Graham Gore, may he sleep in the bosom of the Lord, saw that there would be no release from this belly of the Leviathan winter this summer. No escape from the cold belly of this ice this year. And this is the message he would have brought back had he survived.

"But we have our ships intact, shipmates. We have food for this winter and longer if need be . . . much longer. We have coal to burn for warmth and the deeper warmth of our companionship and the deepest warmth of knowing that our Lord *has not abandoned us.*

"One more summer and then winter here in the belly of this Leviathan, shipmates, and I swear to you that God's divine mercy shall see us out of this terrible place. The North-West Passage is real; it is only miles over that horizon to the southwest — Lieutenant Gore could almost see it with his own eyes a mere week ago — and we shall sail out to it and through it and out of it and away from it in a very few months, when this uncommon extended winter ends, for we shall cry by reason of our affliction unto the Lord, and he shall hear us out of the belly of Hell itself, for he has heardest my voice and yours.

"In the meantime, shipmates, we are afflicted by the dark spirit of that Leviathan in the form of some malevolent white bear — but only a bear, only a dumb beast, however the thing seeks to serve the Enemy, but like Jonah we shall pray unto the Lord that this terror too shall pass from us. And in the certainty that the Lord shall hear our voices.

"Kill this mere animal, shipmates, and on the day we do, by the hand of whichever man among us, I vow to pay each and every one of you ten gold sovereigns out of my own purse."

There came a murmuring among the men crowded into the waist of the ship.

"Ten gold sovereigns a man," repeated Sir John. "Not merely a bounty to the man who slays this beast the way David slew Goliath, but a bonus for everyone — share and share alike. And on top of that, you will continue to receive your Discovery Service pay and the equal of your advance pay in bonuses I promise this day — in exchange only for another winter spent eating good food, staying warm, and waiting for the thaw!"

If laughter had been thinkable during Divine Service, there would have been laughter then. Instead, the men stared at one another with pale, near-frostbitten faces. *Ten gold sovereigns a man.* And Sir John had promised a bonus equal to the advance pay that had persuaded so many of these seamen to enlist in the first place — twenty-three pounds for most of them! At a time when a man could purchase lodgings for sixty pence a week . . . twelve pounds for a whole year. And this on top of the common seaman's Discovery Service pay of sixty pounds per year — more than three times what any labourer ashore could earn! Seventy-five pounds for the carpenters, seventy for the boatswains, a full eighty-four pounds for the engineers.

The men were smiling even as they surreptitiously stamped their boots on the deck to keep from losing toes.

"I have ordered Mr. Diggle on *Terror* and Mr. Wall here on *Erebus* to make us a holiday dinner today in anticipation of our triumph over this temporary adversity and the sure certainty of the success of our mission of exploration," called down Sir John from his place at the flag-bedecked binnacle. "On both ships, I have allowed extra rations of rum for this day."

The Erebuses could only stare slack-jawed at one another. *Sir John Franklin* allowing grog to be served on Sunday — and extra rations of it at that?

"Join me in this prayer, shipmates," said Sir John. "Dear God, turn thy face in our direction again, O Lord, and be gracious unto thy servants. O satisfy us with thy mercy, and that soon: so shall we rejoice and be glad all the days of our lives.

"Comfort us again now after the time that thou has plagued us: and for the years wherein we have suffered adversity.

"Shew thy servants thy work: and their children thy glory.

"And the glorious Majesty of the Lord our God be upon us: prosper thou the work of our hands upon us, O prosper thou our handy-work.

"Glory be to the Father, and to the Son, and to the Holy Ghost.

"As it was in the beginning, is now, and ever shall be: world without end. Amen."

"Amen," came back a hundred and fifteen voices.

———

For four days and nights after Sir John's sermon, despite a June snow-storm that blew in from the northwest and made visibility poor and life miserable, the frozen sea echoed day and night to the blast of shot-guns and the rattle of musketry. Every man who could find any reason to be out on the ice — a hunting party, the fire-hole party, messengers passing between the ships, carpenters testing their new sledges, sea-men given permission to walk Neptune the dog — brought a weapon and fired at anything that moved or gave the impression through blow-ing snow or fog that it might be capable of movement. No men were killed, but three had to report to Dr. McDonald or Dr. Goodsir to have shotgun pellets removed from their thighs, calves, and buttocks.

On Wednesday a hunting party who had failed to find seals did bring in — strapped across two connected sledges — the carcass of a white bear and a living white bear cub about the size of a small calf.

There was some hue and cry for the ten gold sovereigns to be paid to each man, but even the men who had killed the beast a mile north of the ship — it had taken more than twelve shots from two muskets and three shotguns to bring the bear down — had to admit that it was too small, less than eight feet long when stretched out on the bloody ice, and too thin and female. They had killed the bear sow but left the mewling cub alive and dragged it back behind the sledge with them.

Sir John came down to inspect the dead animal, praised the men for finding meat — although everyone hated boiled bear meat and this thin animal looked more stringy and tough than most — but pointed out that it was not the monster of the Leviathan that had killed Lieutenant Gore. All the witnesses to the lieutenant's death were sure, Sir John explained, that even as he died, the brave officer had fired his pistol into the breast of the true beast. This bear sow had been riddled with shot, but there was no old pistol wound in her breast, nor pistol ball to be found. Thus, said Sir John, would the real white bear monster be identified.

Some of the men wanted to make a pet of the cub since the thing had been weaned and would eat thawed beef, while others wanted to butcher it then and there on the ice. On the advice of Marine Sergeant Bryant, Sir John ordered that the animal be kept alive, attached by collar and chain to a stake in the ice. It was that Wednesday evening, the ninth of June, that Sergeants Bryant and Tozer, along with the mate Edward Couch and old John Murray, the only sailmaker left on the voyage, asked to speak to Sir John in his cabin.

"We are going at this the wrong way, Sir John," said Sergeant Bryant, spokesman for the little group. "The hunting of the beast, I mean."

"How so?" asked Sir John.

Bryant gestured as if referring to the dead bear sow now being butchered out on the bloody ice. "Our men aren't hunters, Sir John. There's not a serious hunter aboard either ship. Those of us who do hunt shoot birds in our life ashore, not large game. Oh, a deer we could bring down, or an arctic caribou should we ever see one again, but this white bear is a formidable foe, Sir John. Those we've killed in the past we've killed more by luck than by skill. Its skull is thick enough to stop a musket ball. Its body has so much fat and muscle ringed about it that it might as well be armoured like some ancient knight. It's such a powerful animal, even the smaller bears — well, you have seen them, Sir John — even a shotgun blast to the belly or a rifle shot to the lungs does not bring them down. Their hearts seem hard to find. This scrawny female required a dozen shots by both shotgun and musket, all at short range, and even then she would have escaped had she not stayed behind to protect her cub."

"What are you suggesting, Sergeant?"

"A blind, Sir John."

"A blind?"

"As if we were hunting ducks, Sir John," said Sergeant Tozer, a Marine with a purple birthmark across his pale face. "Mr. Murray has an idea how to make it."

Sir John turned toward *Erebus*'s old sailmaker.

"We use extra iron rods meant for shaft replacements, Sir John, and bend them into the support shapes we want," said Murray. "That gives us a light frame for the blind, which'll be like a tent, you see.

"Only not a pyramid like our tents," continued John Murray, "but long and low with an overhanging awning, almost like a canvas booth at a country fair, m'lord."

Sir John smiled. "Wouldn't our bear notice a country fair canvas booth out there on the ice, gentlemen?"

"Nay, sir," said the sailmaker. "I'll have the canvas cut and sewn and painted snow white before nightfall — or this gloom we call night up here. We'll set the blind against a low pressure ridge where it will blend in. Only the slightest long firing slit will be visible. Mr. Weekes will use the wood from the burial service scaffolding to set benches inside so the shooters will be warm and snug up off the ice."

"How many shooters do you envision in this . . . bear blind?" asked Sir John.

"Six, sir," answered Sergeant Bryant. "It's volley fire that will bring this beast down, sir. Just as it brought down Napoleon's minions by the thousands at Waterloo."

"But what if the bear has a better sense of smell than Napoleon did at Waterloo?" asked Sir John.

The men chuckled but Sergeant Tozer said, "We thought of that, Sir John. Mostly these days the wind is out of the nor'-nor'west. If we built the blind against the low pressure ridge near where poor Lieutenant Gore was laid to rest, sir, well, we'd have that nice great expanse of open ice to the nor'west as a killing zone. Almost a hunded yards of open space. Odds are great that it would come down off the higher ridges from upwind, Sir John. And when it gets where we want it, quick volleys of Minié balls into its heart and lungs, sir."

Sir John thought about this.

"But we'll have to call off the men, sir," said Edward Couch, the mate. "With all the men crashing around out there on the ice, them and lookouts firing off their shotguns at every ice serac and gust of wind, no self-respecting bear would come within five miles o' the ship, sir."

Sir John nodded. "And what is going to lure our bear into this killing zone, gentlemen? Have you thought about bait?"

"Aye, sir," said Sergeant Bryant, smiling now. "It's fresh meat that draws these killers in."

"We have no fresh meat," said Sir John. "Not so much as a ring seal."

"No, sir," said the craggy Marine sergeant. "But we have that little bear. Once the blind is built and set in place, we'll butcher that little thing, not sparing the blood, sir, and leave the meat out there on the ice not twenty-five yards from our shooting position."

Sir John said, "So you think our animal is a cannibal?"

"Oh, aye, sir," said Sergeant Tozer, his face flushing under the purple birthmark. "We think this thing will eat anything that bleeds or smells of meat. And when it does, we'll pour the volleys of fire into it, sir, and then it's ten sovereigns per man and then winter and then triumph and then home."

Sir John nodded judiciously. "Make it so," he said.

———

On Friday afternoon, the eleventh of June, Sir John went out with Lieutenant Le Vesconte to inspect the bear blind.

The two officers had to admit that even from thirty feet away the blind was all but invisible, its floor and back built into the low ridge of snow and ice where Sir John had given the eulogy. The white sails blended almost perfectly and the firing slit had tatters of canvas hanging at irregular intervals to break up the solid horizontal line. The sailmaker and armourer had attached the canvas so cleverly to the iron rods and ribs that even in the rising wind now blowing snow across the open ice, there was not the slightest flap of canvas.

Le Vesconte led Sir John down the icy path behind the pressure ridge — out of sight of the shooting zone — and then over the low wall of ice and in through a slit at the back of the tent. Sergeant Bryant was there with the *Erebus* Marines — Corporal Pearson and Privates Healey, Reed, Hopcraft, and Pilkington — and the men started to rise as their expedition commander entered.

"Oh, no, no, gentlemen, keep your seats," whispered Sir John. Aromatic wooden planks had been set in high iron stirrups curled into the iron support bars at either side of the long, narrow tent, allowing the Marines to sit at shooting height when not standing by the narrow firing slit. Another layer of planking kept their feet off the ice. Their muskets were at the ready in front of them. The crowded space smelled of fresh wood, wet wool, and gun oil.

"How long have you been waiting?" whispered Sir John.

"Not quite five hours, Sir John," whispered Sergeant Bryant.

"You must be cold."

"Not a bit, sir," said Bryant in low tones. "The blind is large enough to allow us to move around from time to time and the planks keep our feet from freezing. The *Terror* Marines under Sergeant Tozer will relieve us at two bells."

"Have you seen anything?" whispered Lieutenant Le Vesconte.

"Not yet, sir," answered Bryant. The sergeant and the two officers leaned forward until their faces were in the cold air of the firing slit.

Sir John could see the carcass of the bear cub, its muscles a shocking red against the ice. They had skinned everything except the small white head, bled it out, captured the blood in pails, and spread the blood all around the carcass. The wind was blowing snow across the wide expanse of ice, and the red blood against all the white, grey, and pale blue was disconcerting.

"We have still to see whether our foe is a cannibal," whispered Sir John.

"Aye, sir," said Sergeant Bryant. "Would Sir John join us on the bench, sir? There's ample room."

There wasn't ample room, especially with Sir John's broad beam added to those beefy posteriors already lined up along the plank. But with Lieutenant Le Vesconte remaining standing and all the Marines scooted down as far as they could go, it was just manageable to have the seven men crowded onto the piece of timber. Sir John realized that he could see out onto the ice quite well from this raised position.

At this moment, Captain Sir John Franklin was as happy as he had ever been in the company of other men. It had taken Sir John years to realize that he was far more comfortable in the presence of women — including artistic, high-strung women such as his first wife, Eleanor, and powerful, indomitable women such as his current wife, Jane — than in the company of men. But since his Divine Service the previous Sunday, he had received more smiles, nods, and sincere looks of approbation from his officers and seamen than at any time in his forty-year career.

It was true that the promise of ten gold sovereigns per man — not to mention the doubling of the advance pay, equal to five months' regular salary for a sailor — had been made in a most unusual burst of good feeling and improvisation. But Sir John had ample financial resources, and should those suffer during his three years and more away, he was quite certain that Lady Jane's private fortune would be available to cover these new debts of honor.

All in all, Sir John reasoned, the financial offers and his surprise allowance of grog rations aboard his teetotaling ship had been strokes of brilliance. Like all others, Sir John had been deeply cast down by the sudden death of Graham Gore, one of the most promising young officers in the fleet. The bad news of no open ways in the ice and the terrible certainty of another dark winter here had weighed heavily upon everyone, but with a promise of ten gold sovereigns per man and a single feast day aboard two ships, he had surmounted that problem for the time being.

Of course, there was the other problem, brought to him by the four medicos only last week: the fact that more and more of the canned foodstuffs were being found to be putrid, possibly as a result of improper soldering of the cans. But Sir John had set that aside for now.

The wind blew snow across the wide expanse of ice, obscuring then revealing the tiny carcass in its congealing and freezing X of blood on the blue ice. Nothing moved from the surrounding pressure ridges and ice pinnacles. The men to Sir John's right sat easily, one chewing tobacco, the others resting their mittened hands on the upraised muzzles of their muskets. Sir John knew that those mittens would be off in a flash should their nemesis appear on the ice.

He smiled to himself as he realized that he was memorizing this scene, this moment, as a future anecdote for Jane and his daughter, Eleanor, and his lovely niece Sophia. He did that a lot these days, observing their predicament on the ice as a series of anecdotes and even setting them into words — not too many words, just enough to hold rapt attention — for future use with his lovely ladies and during evenings dining out. This day — the absurd shooting blind, the men crowded in, the good feeling, the smell of gun oil and wool and tobacco, even the lowering grey clouds and blowing snow and mild tension as they awaited their prey — should stand him in good stead in the years to come.

Suddenly Sir John's gaze turned far to the left, past Lieutenant Le Vesconte's shoulder, to the burial pit not twenty feet from the south end of the blind. The opening to the black sea had long frozen over and much of the crater itself had filled with blowing snow since the burial day, but even the sight of the depression in the ice made Sir John's now-sentimental heart hurt in memory of young Gore. But it had been a fine burial service. He had conducted it with dignity and proud military bearing.

Sir John noticed two black objects lying close together in the lowest part of the icy depression — dark stones perhaps? Buttons or coins left behind as remembrance of Lieutenant Gore by some seaman filing by the burial site precisely a week ago? And in the dim, shifting light of the snowstorm the tiny black circles, all but invisible unless one knew exactly where to look, seemed to stare back at Sir John with something like sad reproach. He wondered if by some fluke of climate two tiny openings to the sea itself had remained open during all the intervening freeze and snow, thus revealing these two tiny circles of black water against the grey ice.

The black circles blinked.

"Ah . . . Sergeant . . . ," began Sir John.

The entire floor of the burial crater seemed to erupt into motion. Something huge, white and grey and powerful exploded toward them, rising and rushing at the blind and then disappearing on the south side of the canvas, out of sight of the firing slit.

The Marines, obviously not sure of what they had just seen, had no time to react.

A powerful force struck the south side of the blind not three feet from Le Vesconte and Sir John, collapsing the iron and rending the canvas.

The Marines and Sir John leapt to their feet as the canvas ripped above them and behind them and to the side of them, black claws the length of Bowie knives tearing through thick sail. Everyone was shouting at once. There came a terrible carrion reek.

Sergeant Bryant raised his musket — the thing was inside, it was *inside,* with them, among them, surrounding them with the circumference of inhuman arms — but before he could fire there was a rush of air through the reek of predator breath. The sergeant's head flew off his shoulders and out through the firing slit and skittered across the ice.

Le Vesconte screamed, someone fired a musket — the ball striking only the Marine next to him. The top of the canvas blind was gone, something huge blocked the opening where the sky should be, and just as Sir John turned to throw himself forward out of the ripping sail canvas, he was struck by a terrible pain just below both knees.

Then things became blurred and absurd. He seemed to be upside down, watching men being scattered like tenpins across the ice, men being thrown from the destroyed blind. Another musket fired but only as the Marine threw the weapon down and tried to scramble away across the ice on all fours. Sir John saw all this — impossibly, absurdly — from an inverted and swinging position. The pain in his legs grew intolerable, there came the sound of saplings snapping, and then he was thrown forward, down into the burial crater, toward the new circle of black awaiting. His head smashed through the thin scrim of ice like a cricket ball through a windowpane.

The water's cold temporarily stopped Sir John's wildly pumping heart. He tried to scream but inhaled salt water.

I am in the sea. For the first time in my life, I am in the sea itself. How extraordinary.

Then he was flailing, turning over and over, feeling the torn fragments and rags of his shredded greatcoat peeling away, feeling nothing from his legs now and getting no purchase against the freezing water with his feet. Sir John used his arms and hands to pull and paddle, not knowing in the terrible darkness if he was fighting toward the surface or merely propelling himself deeper into the black water.

I am drowning. Jane, I am drowning. Of all the fates I had considered these long years in the Service, never once, my darling, did I contemplate drowning.

Sir John's head struck something solid, almost knocking him unconscious, forcing his face beneath the water again, filling his mouth and lungs with salt water again.

And then, my Dears, Providence led me to the surface — or at least to the thin inch of breathable air between the sea and fifteen feet of ice above.

Sir John's arms flailed wildly as he rotated onto his back, his legs still not working, fingers scrabbling at ice above. He forced himself to calm his heart and limbs, forced discipline so that his nose could find that tiniest fraction of air between ice and freezing cold water. He breathed. Raising his chin, he coughed out seawater and breathed through his mouth.

Thank you, dear Jesus, Lord. . . .

Fighting down the temptation to scream, Sir John scrabbled along the underside of the ice as if he were climbing a wall. The bottom of the pack ice here was irregular, sometimes protruding down into the water and giving him no fraction of an inch of air to breathe, sometimes rising five or six inches or more and almost allowing him to lift his full face out of the water.

Despite the fifteen feet of ice above him, there was a dim glow of light — blue light, the Lord's light — refracted through the rough facets of ice just inches from his eyes. Some daylight was coming in via the hole — Gore's burial hole — through which he had just been thrown.

All I had to do, my dear ladies, my darling Jane, was to find my way back to that narrow hole in the ice — get my bearings, as it were — but I knew that I had only minutes. . . .

Not minutes, seconds. Sir John could feel the cold water freezing the life out of him. And there was something terribly wrong with his legs. Not only could he not *feel* them, but he could feel an absolute *absence* there. And the seawater tasted of his own blood.

And then, ladies, the Lord God Almighty shewed me the light. . . .

To his left. The opening was some ten yards or less to his left. The ice was high enough above the black water here that Sir John could raise his head, set the top of his bald and freezing pate against rough ice, gasp in air, blink water and blood out of his eyes, and actually *see* the glow of the Saviour's light not ten yards away. . . .

Something huge and wet rose between him and the light. The darkness was absolute. His inches of breathable air were suddenly taken away, filled with the rankest of carrion breath against his face.

"Please . . . ," began Sir John, sputtering and coughing.

Then the moist reek enveloped him and huge teeth closed on either side of his face, crunching through bone and skull just forward of his ears on both sides of his head.

16

CROZIER

I t was five bells, 2:30 a.m., and Captain Crozier was back from *Erebus*, had inspected the corpses — or half-corpses — of William Strong and Thomas Evans where the thing on the ice had left them propped up near the stern rail on the quarterdeck, had seen to their stowage in the Dead Room below, and now he sat in his cabin contemplating the two objects on his desk — a new bottle of whiskey and a pistol.

Almost half Crozier's small cabin was taken up by the built-in bunk set against the starboard hull. The bunk looked like a child's cradle with carved, raised sides, built-in cupboards below, and a lumpy horsehair mattress set almost chest-high. Crozier had never slept well on real beds and often wished for the swinging hammocks he'd spent so many years in as a midshipman, young officer, and when he served before the mast as a boy. Set against the outer hull as this bunk was, it was one of the coldest sleeping places aboard the ship — chillier than the bunks of the warrant officers with their cubbies in the centre of the lower deck aft, and *much* colder than the sleeping hammocks of the lucky seamen forward, strung as they were on the mess deck near the still-glowing Frazer's Patent Stove that Mr. Diggle cooked on twenty hours out of the day.

Books set into built-in shelves along the rising, inward-sloping hull helped insulate Crozier's sleeping area a little but not much. More books ran under the ceiling for the five-foot width of the cabin, filling a shelf that hung under curving ship's timbers three feet above the foldout desk connecting Crozier's bunk to the hall partition. Directly overhead was the black circle of the Preston Patent Illuminator, its convex opaque glass piercing a deck now dark beneath three feet of snow and protective canvas. Cold air constantly flowed down from the Illuminator like the freezing exhalations of something long dead but still labouring to breathe.

Opposite Crozier's desk was a narrow shelf holding his bathing basin. No water was kept in the basin since it would freeze; Crozier's steward, Jopson, brought his captain hot water from the stove each morning. The space between desk and basin left just enough room in the tiny cabin for Crozier to stand, or — as now — sit at his desk on a backless stool that slid under the basin shelf when not in use.

He continued staring at the pistol and bottle of whiskey.

The captain of HMS *Terror* often thought that he knew nothing about the future — other than that his ship and *Erebus* would never again steam or sail — but then he reminded himself of one certainty: when his store of whiskey was gone, Francis Rawdon Moira Crozier was going to blow his brains out.

The late Sir John Franklin had filled his storeroom with expensive china — all bearing Sir John's initials and family crest, of course — as well as cut crystal, forty-eight beef tongues, fancy silver also engraved with his crest, barrels of smoked Westphalia hams, towers of double Gloucestershire cheeses, bag upon bag of specially imported tea from a relative's plantation in Darjeeling, and crocks of his favorite raspberry jam.

And while Crozier had packed some special foods for the occasional officers' dinners he had to host, most of his money and allocated hold space had been dedicated to three hundred and twenty-four bottles of whiskey. It was not fine Scotch whiskey, but it would suffice. Crozier knew that he had long since reached that point of being the kind of drunkard where quantity always trumped quality. Sometimes here, as in the summer when he was especially busy, a bottle might last him two weeks or more. Other times — as during this past week — he might go through a bottle a night. The truth was, he had quit counting the empty bottles when he passed two hundred the previous winter, but he knew that he must be nearing the end of his supply. On the night he drinks the last of the last and his steward tells him there are no more — Crozier knew it would be at night — he firmly planned to cock the pistol, set the muzzle to his temple, and pull the trigger.

A more practical captain, he knew, might remind himself that there were the not-insignificant liquid remnants of four thousand five hundred gallons — *gallons* — of concentrated West Indian rum in the Spirit Room below, and that each jug was rated between 130 and 140 proof. The rum was doled out each day to the men in units of gills, one fourth of a pint cut with three-quarters pint of water, and there were enough gills and gallons left to swim in. A less finicky and more predatory drunkard-captain might consider the men's rum his reserve. But Francis Crozier did not like rum. He never had. Whiskey was his drink, and when it was gone, so would be he.

Seeing young Tommy Evans's body severed at the waist, the trousered legs sticking out in an almost comical Y, the boots still firmly laced over the dead feet, had reminded Crozier of the day he'd been summoned to the shattered bear blind a quarter of a mile from *Erebus.* In less than twenty-four hours, he realized, it would be the fifth-month anniversary of that eleventh of June debacle. At first Crozier and the other officers who had come running could make little sense of the havoc at the blind. The structure itself had been torn to shreds, the very iron bars of its frame bent and battered. The plank seat had been smashed to splinters and amid those splinters lay the headless body of Marine Sergeant Bryant, the ranking Marine on the expedition. His head — not yet recovered when Crozier arrived — had been batted almost thirty yards across the ice until it stopped next to a skinned bear cub's carcass.

Lieutenant Le Vesconte had suffered a broken arm — not from the bear-monster, it turned out, but from falling out onto the ice — and Private William Pilkington had been shot through the upper left shoulder by the Marine next to him, Private Robert Hopcraft. The private had received eight broken ribs, a pulverized collarbone, and a dislocated left arm from what he later described as a glancing blow from a monster's huge paw. Privates Healey and Reed had survived without serious injury but with the ignominy of having fled the melee in panic, tumbling and screaming and scrambling on all fours across the ice. Reed had broken three fingers in his flight.

But it had been the two trousered and boot-buckled legs and feet of Sir John Franklin — intact below the knees but separated, one lying in the blind, another having been dropped somewhere near the hole through the ice in the burial crater — which had commanded Francis Crozier's attention.

What kind of malevolent intelligence, he wondered while drinking whiskey from his glass, severs a man at the knees and then carries the still-living prey to a hole in the ice and drops him in, to follow a second later? Crozier had tried not to imagine what may have happened next under the ice, although some nights after a few drinks and while trying to fall asleep, he could see the horror there. He also thought for a certainty that Lieutenant Graham Gore's burial service one week earlier to the hour had been nothing more than an elaborate banquet unwittingly offered up to a creature already waiting and watching from beneath the ice.

Crozier had not been overly devastated by Lieutenant Graham Gore's death. Gore was precisely that kind of well-bred, well-educated, C of E, public school, war-hero Royal Navy officer, come natural to command, at ease with superiors and inferiors, modest in all things but destined for great things, well-mannered British kind-even-to-Irishmen, upper-class fucking toff twit whom Francis Crozier had watched being promoted over him for more than forty years.

He took another drink.

What kind of malevolent intelligence kills but does not eat all its prey in such a winter of no game as this but rather returns the upper half of the corpse of Able-Bodied Seaman William Strong and the lower part of the corpse of young Tom Evans? Evans had been one of the "ship's boys" who had beat muffled drums in Gore's funeral procession five months earlier. What kind of creature plucks that young man from Crozier's side in the dark but leaves the captain standing three yards away . . . then returns half the corpse?

The men knew. Crozier knew what they knew. They knew it was the Devil out there on the ice, not some overgrown arctic bear.

Captain Francis Crozier did not disagree with the men's assessment — for all his pish-posh talk earlier that night over brandy with Captain Fitzjames — but he knew something that the men did not; namely that the Devil trying to kill them up here in the Devil's Kingdom was not just the white-furred thing killing and eating them one by one, but *everything* here — the unrelenting cold, the squeezing ice, the electrical storms, the uncanny lack of seals and whales and birds and walruses and land animals, the endless encroachment of the pack ice, the bergs that plowed their way through the solid white sea not even leaving a single ship's length lee of open water behind them, the sudden white-earthquake up-eruption of pressure ridges, the dancing stars, the shoddily tinned cans of food now turned to poison, the summers that did not come, the leads that did not open — *everything*. The monster on the ice was just another manifestation of a Devil that wanted them dead. And that wanted them to suffer.

Crozier took another drink.

He understood the arctic's motivation better than his own. The ancient Greeks had been right, thought Crozier, when they stated that there were five bands of climate on this disk of an earth, four of them equal, opposite, and symmetrical like so many things Greek, wrapped around the world like bands on a snake. Two were temperate and made for human beings. The central band, the equatorial region, was not meant for intelligent life — although the Greeks had been wrong in assuming that no humans could live there. Just no civilized humans, thought Crozier, who'd had his glimpse of Africa and the other equatorial areas and was sure nothing of value would ever come from any of them. The two polar regions, the Greeks had reasoned long before the arctic and antarctic wastes were reached by explorers, were inhuman in every sense — unfit even to travel through, much less to reside in for any length of time.

So why, wondered Crozier, did a nation like England, blessed to be placed by God in one of the most gentle and verdant of the two temperate bands where mankind was meant to live, keep throwing its ships and its men into the ice of the northern and southern polar extremes where even fur-wearing savages refuse to go?

And more pertinent to the central question, why did one Francis Crozier keep returning to these terrible places time after time, serving a nation and its officers that have never recognized his abilities and worth as a man, even while he knew in his heart that someday he would die in the arctic cold and dark?

The captain remembered that even when he was a small boy — before he went to sea at age thirteen — he had carried his deep mood of melancholy within him like a cold secret. This melancholic nature had manifested itself in his pleasure at standing outside the village on a winter night watching the lamplights fade, by finding small places in which to hide — claustrophobia had never been a problem for Francis Crozier — and by being so afraid of the dark, seeing it as the avatar of the death that had claimed his mother and grandmother in such a stealthy way, that he had perversely sought it out, hiding in the root cellar while other boys played in the sunlight. Crozier remembered that cellar — the grave chill of it, the smell of cold and mold, the darkness and inward-pressing which left one alone with dark thoughts.

He filled his small glass and took another drink. Suddenly the ice groaned louder, and the ship groaned back in response — trying to shift its place in the frozen sea but having no place to go. In recompense it squeezed itself tighter and moaned. Metal brackets in the hold deck contracted, the sudden cracks sounding like pistol shots. The seamen forward and the officers aft snored on, used to the night noises of the ice trying to crush them. On deck above, the officer on watch in the seventy-below night stomped his feet to renew circulation, the four sharp stamps sounding to the captain like a weary parent telling the ship to hush its protestations.

It was hard for Crozier to believe that Sophia Cracroft had visited this ship, stood in this very cabin, exclaimed how neat it was, how tidy, how cozy, how very learned with its row of books, and how pleasant the austral light pouring down from the Illuminator.

It had been seven years ago almost to the week, the Southern-Hemispheric spring month of November of 1840, when Crozier had

arrived in Van Diemen's Land south of Australia in these very ships —
Erebus and *Terror* — on the way to Antarctica. The expedition had
been under the command of Crozier's friend, although always his
social superior, Captain James Ross. They had stopped at Hobart
Town to finish their provisioning before heading into antarctic waters,
and the governor of that penal island, Sir John Franklin, insisted that
the two younger officers — Captain Ross and Commander Crozier —
stay at Government House during their visit.

It had been an enchanting time and — to Crozier — a romanti-
cally fatal one.

The inspection of the expedition's ships had occurred on the second day of the visit — the ships were clean, refitted, almost fully provisioned, their young crews not yet bearded or made haggard by the
two winters in the antarctic ice to come — and while Captain Ross
personally hosted Governor Sir John and Lady Jane Franklin, Crozier
had found himself escorting the governor's niece, the dark-haired and
bright-eyed young Sophia Cracroft. He had fallen in love on that day
and had carried that blossoming love into the darkness of the next
two southern winters, where it had bloomed into an obsession.

The long dinners under the servant-turned fans of the governor's
house were filled with lively conversation. Governor Franklin was a
worn-out man in his midfifties, dispirited by the lack of recognition
of his accomplishments and dispirited further by the opposition of
the local press, wealthy landowners, and bureaucrats during his third
year in Van Diemen's Land, but both he and his wife, Lady Jane, had
come alive during this visit by their Discovery Service countrymen
and, as Sir John liked to address them, his "fellow explorers."

Sophia Cracroft, on the other hand, showed no signs of unhappi-
ness. She was witty, alive, vivacious, sometimes shocking in her comments and boldness — even more so than her controversial aunt, the
Lady Jane — and young and beautiful and seemingly interested in
every aspect of the forty-four-year-old bachelor Commander Francis
Crozier's opinions, life, and sundry thoughts. She laughed at all of
Crozier's initially hesitant jokes — he was not used to this level of
society and strived to be on his best behaviour, drinking less than he

had in years and that only wine — and she always answered his tentative bon mots with increasingly higher levels of wit. To Crozier, it was like learning tennis from a far better player. By the eighth and final day of their extended visit, Crozier felt the equal of any proper Englishman — a gentleman born in Ireland, yes, but one who had made his own way and had also lived an interesting and exciting life, the equal of any man — and the superior of most men in Miss Cracroft's amazing blue eyes.

When HMSs *Erebus* and *Terror* left the Hobart Town harbour, Crozier was still calling Sophia "Miss Cracroft," but there was no denying the secret connections they had made: the secret glances, the companionable silences, the shared jokes and private moments alone. Crozier knew that he was in love for the first time in a life whose "romance" had consisted of dockyard doxies' cribs, back-alley knee-wobblers, some native girls doing the deed for trinkets, and a few overpriced nights out in gentlemen's whorehouses in London. All that was behind him now.

Francis Crozier now understood that the most desirable and erotic thing a woman could wear were the many modest layers such as Sophia Cracroft wore to dinner in the governor's house, enough silken fabric to conceal the lines of her body, allowing a man to concentrate on the exciting loveliness of her wit.

Then followed almost two years of pack ice, glimpsing Antarctica, the stink of penguin rookeries, naming two distant, smoking volcanoes after their tired ships, darkness, spring, the threat of being frozen in, finding and fighting their way out by sail only through a sea now named after James Ross, and finally the rough Southern Sea passage and the return to Hobart Town on the island of eighteen thousand prisoners and one very unhappy governor. This time there was no inspection of *Erebus* and *Terror;* they stank too much of grease and cooking and sweat and fatigue. The boys who had sailed south were now mostly hollow-eyed and bearded men who would not sign up for future Discovery Service expeditions. Everyone except HMS *Terror's* commander was eager to return to England.

Francis Crozier was eager only to see Sophia Cracroft again.

He took another drink of whiskey. Above him, barely audible through the deck and snow, the ship's bell rang six bells. Three a.m.

The men were sorry when Sir John had been killed five months ago — most of them because they knew that the promise of ten sovereigns per man and a second advance-pay bonus had died with the paunchy, bald old man — but little actually changed after Franklin's death. Commander Fitzjames was now acknowledged as the captain of *Erebus* that he'd always been in reality. Lieutenant Le Vesconte, gold tooth flashing when he smiled, his arm in a sling, took Graham Gore's place in the hierarchy of command with no visible ripple of disruption. Captain Francis Crozier now assumed the rank of expedition commander, but with the expedition frozen in the ice, there was little he could do differently now from what Franklin would have done.

One thing Crozier did almost immediately was ship more than five tons of supplies across the ice to a point not far from the Ross cairn on King William Land. They were now fairly certain it was an island because Crozier had sent out sledge parties — monster bear be damned — to scout the area. Crozier himself went along on half a dozen of these early sledge parties, helping to smash easier, or at least less impossible, paths through the pressure ridges and iceberg barrier along the shore. They brought extra winter slops, tents, lumber for future cabins, casks of dried foods and hundreds of cans of the tinned foods, as well as lightning rods — even brass bed rods from Sir John's appropriated cabin to be fashioned into lightning rods — and the essentials of what both crews would need if the ships had to be abandoned suddenly in the midst of the next winter.

Four men had been lost to the creature on the ice before winter returned, two from one tent during one of Crozier's trips, but what stopped the transfer sledge trips in mid-August was a return of the severe lightning and thick fog. For more than three weeks both ships sat in the midst of the fog, suffered the lightning to strike them, and only the briefest ice outings — hunting parties mostly, a few fire-hole teams — were allowed. By the time the freakish fog and lightning had passed, it was early September, and the cold and snow had begun again.

Crozier then resumed sending cache-supply sledge parties to King William Land despite the terrible weather, but when Second Master Giles MacBean and a seaman were killed just a few yards ahead of the three sledges — the deaths unseen because of the blowing snow but their last screams all too audible to the other men and to their officer, Second Lieutenant Hodgson — Crozier "temporarily" suspended the supply trips. The suspension had now lasted two months, and by the first of November no sane crewman wanted to volunteer for an eight- to ten-day sledge trip in the dark.

The captain knew that he should have cached at least ten tons of supplies on the shore rather than the five tons he'd hauled there. The problem was — as he and a sledge party had learned the night the crea-ture had ripped through a tent near the captain's and would have carried off seaman George Kinnaird and John Bates if they had not run for their lives — any campsite on that low, windswept gravel-and-ice spit of land was not defensible. Aboard the ships, as long as they lasted, the hulls and raised deck acted as a wall of sorts, turning each ship into a kind of fort. Out on the gravel and in tents, no matter how tightly clus-tered, it would take at least twenty armed men watching day and night to guard the perimeter, and even then the thing could be among them before guards could react. Everyone who had sledged to King William Land and camped out there on the ice knew this. And as the nights grew longer, the fear of those unprotected hours in the tents — like the arctic cold itself — seeped deeper into the men.

Crozier drank some more whiskey.

It had been April of 1843 — early autumn in the Southern Hemi-sphere, although the days were still long and warm — when *Erebus* and *Terror* returned to Van Diemen's Land.

Ross and Crozier were once again guests at the governor's house — officially called Government House by the old-time inhabitants of Hobart Town — but this time it was obvious that a shadow lay over both Franklins. Crozier was willing to be oblivious to this, his joy at being near Sophia Cracroft was so great, but even the irrepressible Sophia had been subdued by the mood, events, conspiracies, betrayals, revelations, and crises that had been brooding in Hobart during the two years *Erebus* and *Terror* had been in the southern ice, so in the course of his first two days in Government House, he'd heard enough to piece together the reasons for the Franklins' depression.

It seemed that local and venial landed interests, personified in one undercutting, backstabbing Judas of a colonial secretary named Captain John Montagu, had decided early on in Sir John's six years as governor that he simply would not do, nor would his wife, the outspoken and unorthodox Lady Jane. All Crozier heard from Sir John himself — overheard, actually, as the despondent Sir John spoke to Captain Ross while the three men took brandy and cigars in the booklined study in the mansion — was that the locals had "a certain lack of neighbourly feelings and a deplorable deficiency in public spirit."

From Sophia, Crozier learned that Sir John had gone, in the public eye at least, from being "the man who ate his shoes" to his self-styled description of "a man who wouldn't hurt a fly" then quickly to a description widespread on the Tasmanian Peninsula of "a man in pet-ticoats." This last calumny, Sophia assured him, came from the colony's dislike of Lady Jane as much as it had from Sir John's and his wife's attempts to improve things for the natives and prisoners who laboured there in inhuman conditions.

"You understand that the previous governors simply loaned out prisoners for the local plantation owners' and city business tycoons' insane projects, took their cut of the profits, and kept their mouths shut," explained Sophia Cracroft as they walked in the shadows of the Government House gardens. "Uncle John has not played that game."

"Insane projects?" said Crozier. He was very aware of Sophia's hand on his arm as they walked and spoke in hushed whispers, alone, in the warm near-dark.

"If a plantation manager wants a new road on his land," said Sophia, "the governor is expected to loan him six hundred starving prisoners — or a thousand — who work from dawn until after dark, chains on their legs and manacles on their wrists, through this tropical heat, without water or food, being flogged if they fall or falter."

"Good Lord," said Crozier.

Sophia nodded. Her eyes remained fixed on the white stones of the garden path. "The colonial secretary, Montagu, decided that the prisoners should excavate a pit mine — although no gold has been found on the island — and the prisoners were set to digging it. It was more than four hundred feet deep before the project was abandoned — it flooded constantly, the water table here is very shallow, of course — and it was said that two to three prisoners died for every foot excavated of that abhorred mine."

Crozier restrained himself before he could say *Good Lord* again, but in truth that was all that came to his mind.

"A year after you left," continued Sophia, "Montagu — that weasel, that viper — persuaded Uncle John to dismiss a local surgeon, a man very popular with the decent people here, on trumped-up charges of dereliction of duty. It divided the colony. Uncle John and Aunt Jane became the lightning rod for all criticism, even though Aunt Jane had disapproved of the surgeon's dismissal. Uncle John — you know, Francis, how very much he hates controversy, much less to administer pain of any sort, why he's often said he would not hurt a fly. . . ."

"Yes," said Crozier, "I have seen him carefully remove a fly from a dining room and release it."

"Uncle John, listening to Aunt Jane, eventually reinstated the surgeon, but that made a lifelong enemy out of this Montagu. The private bickerings and accusations became public, and Montagu — in essence — called Uncle John a liar and a weakling."

"Good Lord," said Crozier. What he was thinking was, *If I had been in John Franklin's place, I would have called this Montagu fucker out to the field of honor and there put a bullet in each of his testicles before I placed a final one in his brain.* "I hope that Sir John sacked the man."

"Oh, he did," said Sophia with a sad little laugh, "but that only made things worse. Montagu returned to England last year on the same ship carrying Uncle John's letter announcing his dismissal, and it turns out, sadly, that Captain Montagu is a close friend of Lord Stanley, secretary of state for the Colonies."

Well, the Governor is well and truly buggered, Crozier thought as they reached the stone bench at the far end of the garden. He said, "How unfortunate."

"More than Uncle John or Aunt Jane could have imagined," said Sophia. "The Cornwall *Chronicle* ran a long article entitled 'The Imbecile Reign of the Polar Hero.' The *Colonial Times* blames Aunt Jane."

"Why attack Lady Jane?"

Sophia smiled without humour. "Aunt Jane is, rather like myself . . . unorthodox. You have seen her room here at Government House, I believe? When Uncle John gave you and Captain Ross a tour of the estate the last time you were here?"

"Oh, yes," said Crozier. "Her collection was wonderful." Lady Jane's boudoir, the parts they were allowed to see, had been crammed carpet to ceiling with animal skeletons, meteorites, stone fossils, Aborigine war clubs, native drums, carved wooden war masks, ten-foot paddles that looked capable of propelling HMS *Terror* along at fifteen knots, a plethora of stuffed birds, and at least one expertly taxidermied monkey. Crozier had never seen anything like it in a musuem or zoo, much less in a lady's bedroom. Of course, Francis Crozier had seen very few ladies' bedrooms.

"One visitor wrote to a Hobart newspaper that, and I quote verbatim, Francis, 'our governor's wife's private rooms at Government House look more like a museum or a menagerie than the boudoir of a lady.'"

Crozier made a clucking noise and felt guilty about his similar thoughts. He said, "So is this Montagu still making trouble?"

"More than ever. Lord Stanley — that viper's viper — backed Montagu, reinstated that worm in a position similar to the one Uncle John dismissed him from, and sent Uncle John a reprimand so terrible that Aunt Jane told me in private that it was the equivalent of a horsewhipping."

I'd shoot that bugger Montagu in the balls and then cut Lord Stanley's off and serve them to him only slightly warmed, thought Crozier. "That is terrible," he said.

"There is worse," said Sophia.

Crozier looked for tears in the dim light but saw none. Sophia was not a woman given to weeping.

"Stanley made public the rebuke?" guessed Crozier.

"The . . . bastard . . . gave a copy of the official rebuke to Montagu, *before he sent it to Uncle John,* and that weasel's weasel rushed it here by the fastest post ship. Copies were made and passed around here in Hobart Town to all of Uncle John's enemies months before Uncle John received the letter through official channels. The entire colony was sniggering every time Uncle John or Aunt Jane attended a concert or performed the governor's role in some official function. I apologize for my unlady-like language, Francis."

I'd feed Lord Stanley his balls cold in a fried dough of his own shit, thought Crozier. He said nothing but nodded that he forgave Sophia her choice of language.

"Just when Uncle John and Aunt Jane thought it could get no worse," continued Sophia, her voice trembling slightly, but with anger, Crozier was sure, not with weakness, "Montagu sent to his plantation friends here a three-hundred-page packet containing all the private letters, Government House documents, and official dispatches which he had used to make his case against the governor to Lord Stanley. That packet is in the Central Colonial Bank here in the capital, and Uncle John knows that two thirds of the old families and business leaders in town have made their pilgrimage to the bank to read and hear what it contains. Captain Montagu calls the governor a 'perfect imbecile' in those papers . . . and from what we hear, that is the most polite thing in the detestable document."

"Sir John's position here seems untenable," said Crozier.

"At times I fear for his sanity, if not his life," agreed Sophia. "Governor Sir John Franklin is a sensitive man."

He wouldn't hurt a fly, thought Crozier. "Will he resign?"

"He will be recalled," said Sophia. "The entire colony knows it. This is why Aunt Jane is almost beside herself . . . I have never seen her in such a state. Uncle John expects official word of his recall before the end of August, if not sooner."

Crozier sighed and pushed his walking stick along a furrow in the garden path gravel. He had looked forward to this reunion with

Sophia Cracroft for two years in the southern ice, but now that he was here he could see that their visit would be lost in the shadow of mere politics and personality. He stopped himself before he sighed again. He was forty-six years old and acting like a fool.

"Would you like to see the Platypus Pond tomorrow?" asked Sophia.

Crozier poured another glass of whiskey for himself. There came a scream of banshees from above, but it was only the arctic wind in what was left of the rigging. The captain pitied the men on watch.

The whiskey bottle was almost empty.

Crozier decided then and there that they would have to resume cache-hauling sledge trips to King William Land this winter, through the dark and storms and with the threat of the *thing* on the ice ever present. He had no choice. If they had to abandon the ships in the coming months — and *Erebus* was already showing signs of imminent collapse in the ice — it would not do merely to set up a sea camp here on the ice near where the ships would be destroyed. Normally that might make sense — more than one hapless polar expedition had set up camp on the ice and let the Baffin Bay current carry them hundreds of miles south to open sea — but this ice was going nowhere and a camp here on the ice would be even less defensible from the creature than would a camp on the frozen gravel on the shore — peninsula or island — twenty-five miles away in the dark. And he'd already cached more than five tons of gear there. The rest would have to follow before the sun returned.

Crozier sipped his whiskey and decided that he would lead the next sledge trip. Hot food was the greatest single morale builder cold men could have, short of sight of rescue or extra gills of rum, so his next sledge trips would consist of stripping the four whaler boats — serious craft rigged for serious sailing should the real ships be abandoned at sea — of their cookstoves. The Frazer's Patent Stove on *Terror* and its twin on *Erebus* were too massive to move to shore — and Mr. Diggle would be using his to bake biscuits right up to the minute Crozier gave the order to abandon ship — so it was best to use the boat stoves. The four stoves were iron and would be heavy as Satan's hooves, especially if the sledges were hauling more gear, food, and clothing to cache, but they'd be safe on shore and could be fired up quickly, although the coal itself would also have to be hauled across the cold hell of a pressure-ridged twenty-five miles of sea ice. There was no wood on King William Land nor any for hundreds of miles south of there. The stoves would go next, Crozier decided, and he would go with them. They would sledge through the absolute darkness and unbelievable cold and let the Devil take the hindmost.

Crozier and Sophia Cracroft had ridden out that next April morning in 1843 to see the Platypus Pond.

Crozier had expected they'd be taking a buggy as they did for sojourns into Hobart Town, but Sophia had two horses saddled for them and a pack mule loaded with picnic things. She rode like a man. Crozier realized that the dark "skirt" she'd appeared to be wearing was actually a pair of gaucho trousers. The white canvas blouse she wore with it was somehow both feminine and rugged. She wore a broad-brimmed hat to keep the sun off her skin. Her boots were high, polished, soft, and must have cost roughly a year of Francis Crozier's captain's salary.

They rode north, away from Government House and the capital, and followed a narrow road through plantation fields, past penal colony pens, and then through a patch of rain forest and out into open higher country again.

"I thought that platypuses were found only in Australia," said Crozier. He was having trouble finding a comfortable position in the saddle. He'd never had much opportunity or reason to ride. It was embarrassing when his voice vibrated as he jounced and bounced. Sophia seemed completely at home in the saddle; she and the horse moved as one.

"Oh, no, my dear," said Sophia. "The strange little things are found only in certain coastal areas on the continent to our north, but all across Van Diemen's Land. They're shy though. We see none around Hobart Town any longer."

Crozier's cheeks grew warm at the sound of the "my dear."

"Are they dangerous?" he asked.

Sophia laughed easily. "Actually the males are dangerous in mating season. They have a secret poisonous spur on their hind legs, and during the breeding season the spurs become quite venomous."

"Enough to kill a man?" asked Crozier. He'd been joking about the comical little creatures he'd seen only in illustrations being dangerous.

"A small man," said Sophia. "But survivors of the platypus's spur say that the pain is so terrible that they would have preferred death."

Crozier looked to his right at the young woman. Sometimes it was very difficult to tell when Sophia was joking and when she was serious. In this instance, he would assume that she was telling the truth.

"Is it breeding season?" he asked.

She smiled again. "No, my dear Francis. That is between August and October. We should be quite safe. Unless we encounter a devil."

"The Devil?"

"No, my dear. *A* devil. What you may have heard described as a Tasmanian devil."

"I have heard of those," said Crozier. "They're supposed to be terrible creatures with jaws that open as wide as the hatch on a ship's hold. And they're reputed to be ferocious — insatiable hunters — able to swallow and devour a horse or Tasmanian tiger whole."

Sophia nodded, her face serious. "All true. The devil is all fur and chest and appetite and fury. And if you had ever heard one's noise — one cannot really call it a bark or growl or roar, but rather the garbled gibbers and snarls one might expect out of a burning asylum — well, then I guarantee that not even so courageous an explorer as thee, Francis Crozier, would go into the forest or fields here alone at night."

"You've heard them?" asked Crozier, searching her serious face again to see if she was pulling his leg.

"Oh, yes. An indescribable noise — absolutely terrifying. It causes their prey to freeze just long enough for the devil to open those impossibly wide jaws and to swallow its victim whole. The only noise as frightening may be the screams of its prey. I've heard an entire flock of sheep bleating and crying as a single devil devoured them all, one at a time, leaving not so much as a hoof behind."

"You're joking," said Crozier, still staring at her intently to see if she was.

"I never joke about the devil, Francis," she said. They were riding into another patch of dark forest.

"Do your devils eat platypuses?" asked Crozier. The question was serious, but he was very glad that neither James Ross nor any of his crewmen had been around to hear him ask it. It sounded absurd.

"A Tasmanian devil will and does eat *anything*," said Sophia. "But once again, you are in luck, Francis. The devil hunts at night, and unless we get terribly lost, we should have seen the Platypus Pond — and the platypus — and had our lunch and returned to Government House before nightfall. God help us if we are out here in the forest come darkness."

"Because of the devil?" asked Crozier. He'd meant the question to be light and teasing, but he could hear the undercurrent of tension in his own tone.

Sophia reined her mare to a halt and smiled at him — truly, dazzlingly, completely smiled at him. Crozier managed, not gracefully, to get his own gelding stopped.

"No, my dear," said the young woman in a breathy whisper. "Not because of the devil. Because of my *reputation*."

Before Crozier could think of anything to say, Sophia laughed, spurred her horse, and galloped ahead down the road.

There was not enough whiskey left in the bottle for two last glassfuls. Crozier poured most of it, held the glass up between him and the flickering oil lamp set on the inner partition wall, and watched the light dance through the amber liquid. He drank slowly.

They never saw the platypus. Sophia assured him the platypus was almost always to be seen in this pond — a tiny circle of water not fifty yards across, a quarter mile off the road in a thick forest — and that the entrances to its burrow were behind some gnarled tree roots that ran down the bank, but he never saw the platypus.

He did, however, see Sophia Cracroft naked.

They'd had a pleasant picnic at the more shaded end of the Platypus Pond, an expensive cotton tablecloth spread on the grass to hold the picnic basket, glasses, food containers, and themselves. Sophia had ordered the servants to pack some waterproof cloth-wrapped parcels of roast beef in what was the most expensive of all commodities here but the cheapest from whence Crozier had come — ice — to keep it from going bad during the morning's ride. There were broiled potatoes and small bowls of a tasty salad. She'd also packed a very good bottle of Burgundy in with actual crystal glasses from Sir John's crest-etched collection, and she drank more of it than did the captain.

After the meal they'd reclined just a few feet apart and talked of this and that for an hour, all the while looking out at the dark surface of the pond.

"Are we waiting for the platypus, Miss Cracroft?" asked Crozier during a short gap in their discussion of the dangers and beauties of arctic travel.

"No, I think it would have shown itself by now if it wanted us to see it," said Sophia. "I've been waiting for an interval before we go bathing."

Crozier could only look at her quizzically. He certainly had not brought beach bathing attire. He did not *own* beach bathing attire. He knew it was another one of her jests, but she always spoke in such evident earnestness that he was never 100 percent sure. It made her puckish sense of humour all the more exciting to him.

Extending her rather titillating joke, she stood, brushed some dead leaves from her dark gaucho pants, and looked around. "I believe I shall undress behind those shrubs there and enter the water from that grassy shelf. You are invited to join me in the swim, of course, Francis, or not, according to your personal sense of decorum."

He smiled to show her he was a sophisticated gentleman, but his smile was unsteady.

She walked to the thick bushes without another glance back. Crozier remained on the tablecloth, lying half reclined and with an amused look on his carefully shaven face, but when he saw her white blouse suddenly lifted up by pale arms to be draped across the top of the tall shrub, his expression froze. But his prick did not. Beneath his corduroy trousers and too-short waistcoat, Crozier's private part went from parade rest to top of the mizzen in two seconds.

Sophia's dark gaucho pants and other white, frilly unnamed things joined the blouse atop the thick shrub a few seconds later.

Crozier could only stare. His easy smile became a dead man's rictus. He was sure that his eyes were bulging out of his head, but he could not turn away, nor avert his gaze.

Sophia Cracroft stepped out into the sunlight.

She was absolutely naked. Her arms hung easily at her sides; her hands were slightly curled. Her breasts were not large but were very high and very white and tipped with large nipples that were pink, not brown as had been the case with all the other women — crib doxies, gap-toothed prostitutes, native girls — whom Crozier had seen naked before this moment.

Had he *ever* seen another woman truly naked before? A white woman? At this instant he thought not. And if he had, he knew, it mattered not in the least.

The sunlight reflected off young Sophia's blindingly white skin. She did not cover herself. Still frozen in languid posture and vapid expression, only his penis reacting by becoming even more turgid and aching, Crozier realized that he was astonished that this goddess in his mind, this perfection of English womanhood, the woman he already mentally and emotionally had chosen to be his wife and the mother of his children, had thick, luxurious pubic hair that seemed intent, here and there, on leaping out of its proper black V of an inverted triangle. *Unruly* was the only word that came to his otherwise empty mind. She had unpinned her long hair and let it fall to her shoulders.

"Are you coming in, Francis?" she called softly from where she stood on the grassy shelf. Her tone was as neutral as if she were asking him if he would like a bit more tea. "Or are you just going to stare?"

Without another word she dived into the water in a perfect arc, her pale hands and white arms cleaving the mirrorlike surface an instant before the rest of her.

By this time Crozier had opened his mouth to speak, but articulate speech was obviously an impossibility. After a moment he closed his mouth.

Sophia swam easily back and forth. He could see her white buttocks rising behind her strong, white back, along which her wet hair lay separated like three brushstrokes of the blackest of India inks.

She raised her head, treading water easily while stopping at the far end of the pond near the large tree she'd pointed out upon her arrival. "The platypus's burrow is behind these roots," she called. "I don't think it wants to come out and play today. It's shy. Don't you be, Francis. *Please.*"

As if in a dream Crozier felt himself rising, walking to the thickest patch of shrubbery he could find close to the water on the opposite side of the pond from where Sophia was. His fingers shook violently as he worked to undo his buttons. He found himself folding his clothing in tight, proper little squares, setting the squares within a larger square on the grass at his feet. He was sure he was taking hours. His throbbing erection would not go away. Will it gone as he would, imagine it away as he might, it persisted in rising rigid to his navel and pitching back and forth there, the glans as red as a signal lantern and extended several taut inches free of its foreskin.

Crozier stood irresolute behind the bush, hearing the splashes as Sophia continued to swim. If he dithered another moment, he knew, she would be climbing out of the pond, be back behind her own curtain of a shrub drying herself off, and he would curse himself for a coward and a fool for the rest of his days.

Peeking through the branches of his shrub, Crozier waited until the lady's back was turned as she swam toward the far shore, and then, with much speed and clumsiness, he threw himself forward into the water, stumbling more than diving, abandoning all grace in his single-minded effort to get his treacherous prick beneath the water and out of sight before Miss Cracroft turned her face his way.

When he surfaced, spluttering and blowing, she was treading water twenty feet away and smiling at him.

"I'm delighted you decided to join me, Francis. Now if the male platypus emerges with his venomous spur, you can protect me. Shall we inspect the burrow entrance?" She pivoted gracefully and swam toward the huge tree where it overhung the water.

Vowing to keep at least ten — no, fifteen — feet of open water between them, like a foundering ship surrendering to a lee shore, Crozier dog-paddled after her.

The pond was surprisingly deep. As he stopped twelve feet from her and treaded water clumsily to keep his head above the surface, Crozier realized that even here at the edge, where roots from the large tree came down five feet of steep bank into the water and tall grasses hung over casting afternoon shadows, Crozier's flailing feet and seeking toes could not at first find purchase on the bottom.

Suddenly Sophia was coming toward him.

She must have seen the panic in his eyes; he did not know whether to back-paddle furiously or just somehow warn her away from his condition of *prick-rampant,* because she paused mid-breaststroke — and he could see her white breasts bobbing beneath the surface — nodded to her left, and swam easily toward the tree roots.

Crozier followed.

They hung on to the roots, only about four feet from each other, but the water was blessedly dark below chest level, and Sophia pointed to what might have been a burrow opening, or just a muddy indentation, in the bank between the tangle of tree roots.

"This is a camping or bachelor burrow, not a nesting burrow," said Sophia. She had beautiful shoulders and collarbones.

"What?" said Crozier. He was happy — and mildly amazed — that his power of speech had returned, but less than satisfied by the odd, strangled sound of the syllable and by the fact that his teeth were chattering. The water was not cold.

Sophia smiled. A strand of dark hair was plastered along one of her sharp cheeks. "Platypuses make two kinds of burrows," she said softly, "this kind — what some naturalists call a camping burrow — which both the male and female use except during breeding season. The bachelors live here. The nesting burrow is dug out by the female for the actual breeding, and after that deed is performed, she excavates another small chamber to act as a nursery."

"Oh," said Crozier, clinging to the root as tightly as he had ever clung to any ship's line while two hundred feet up in the rigging during a hurricane.

"Platypuses lay eggs, you know," continued Sophia, "like reptiles. But the mothers secrete milk, like mammals."

Through the water he could see the dark circles in the centres of the white globes of her breasts.

"Really?" he said.

"Aunt Jane, who is something of a naturalist herself, believes that the venomous spurs on the hind legs of the male are used not only to fight other male platypuses and intruders, but to hang on to the female while they are swimming and mating at the same time. Presumably he does not secrete the venom when clinging to his breeding partner."

"Yes?" said Crozier and wondered if he should have said *No?* He had no idea what they were talking about.

Using the tangle of roots, Sophia pulled herself closer, until her breasts were almost touching him. She laid her cool hand — a surprisingly large hand — flat against his chest.

"Miss Cracroft . . . ," he began.

"Shhhh," said Sophia. "Hush."

She shifted her left hand from the root to his shoulder, hanging from him as she had hung from the tree root. Her right hand slid lower, pressing across his belly, touching his right hip, then coming back to his centre and going lower again.

"Oh, my," she whispered by his ear. Her cheek was against his now, her wet hair in his eyes. "Is this a venomous spur I've found?"

"Miss Cra— . . . ," he began.

She squeezed. She floated gracefully so that suddenly her strong legs were on either side of his left leg, and then she lowered her weight and warmth, rubbing against him. He raised that leg slightly to buoy her up and keep her face above water. Her eyes were closed. Her hips ground, her breasts flattened against him, and her right hand began to stroke the length of him.

Crozier moaned, but it was only an anticipatory moan, not one of release. Sophia made a soft sound against his neck. He could feel the heat and wetness of her nether regions against his raised leg and thigh. *How can anything be wetter than water?* he wondered.

Then she moaned in earnest, and Crozier closed his eyes as well — sorry that he could not continue seeing her but having no choice — she pressed herself hard against him once, twice, a third downward-pressing time, and her stroking became hurried, urgent, expert, knowing, and demanding.

He buried his face against her wet hair as he throbbed and pulsed into the water. Crozier thought the pulsing ejaculation might never end, and — if he had been able — he would have apologized to her at once. Instead, he moaned again and almost lost his grip on the tree root. They both bobbled, their chins dripping beneath the waterline.

What confused Francis Crozier most at that moment — and everything in the universe confused him right then, while nothing in the universe bothered him — was the fact of the lady's downward-pressing, her thighs strong around him, her cheek pressed hard against his own while she closed her eyes so tightly, and her own moan. Certainly women could not feel the kind of intensity that men do? Some of the doxies had moaned, but certainly that had been only because they knew the men liked it — it had been obvious that they felt nothing.

And yet . . .

Sophia pulled back, looked into his eyes, smiled easily, kissed him full on the lips, raised her legs into an almost jackknife, kicked off from the roots, and swam for the shore where her clothes lay on the mildly quaking bush.

Incredibly, they dressed, picked up their picnic things, packed the mule, mounted, and rode all the way back to Government House in silence.

Incredibly, that evening during dinner, Sophia Cracroft laughed and chatted with her aunt, Sir John, and even with the unusually loquacious Captain James Clark Ross, while Crozier sat mostly silent and staring at the table. He could only admire her . . . what did the Frogs call it? — her *sangfroid,* while Crozier's attention and soul felt precisely as his body had at the moment of his endless orgasm in the Platypus Pond — atoms and essence scattered to every corner of the universe.

Yet Miss Cracroft did not act aloof toward him nor offer any sense of reproof. She smiled at him, made comments to him, and attempted to include him in the conversation just as she did every evening in Government House. And certainly her smile toward him was a little warmer? More affectionate? Even smitten? It had to be so.

After dinner that night, when Crozier suggested a walk in the garden, she begged off, pleading a previous engagement of cards with Captain Ross in the main parlour. Would Commander Crozier care to join them?

No, Commander Crozier begged off in return, understanding from the warm and easy undertones in her warm and easy surface banter that all must be kept normal in Government House that evening and until the two of them could meet to discuss their future. Commander Crozier announced loudly that he had a bit of a headache and would turn in early.

He was awake, dressed in his best uniform, and walking the halls of the mansion before dawn the next day, certain that Sophia would have the same impulse of meeting early.

She did not. Sir John was the first to come to breakfast, and he made endless, insufferable small talk with Crozier, who had never mastered the insipid art of small talk, much less been able to hold up his end of a conversation on what the proper tariff should be on renting prisoners for digging canals.

Lady Jane came down next, and even Ross appeared for breakfast before Sophia finally made an appearance. By this time Crozier was on his sixth cup of coffee, which he had learned to prefer over tea in the morning during his winters with Parry in the northern ice years earlier, but he stayed while the lady had her usual eggs, sausage, beans, toast, and tea.

Sir John disappeared somewhere. Lady Jane deliquesced. Captain Ross wandered off. Sophia finally finished her breakfast.

"Would you like to walk in the garden?" he asked.

"So early?" she said. "It's already very hot out there. This autumn shows no signs of cooling off."

"But . . . ," began Crozier and attempted to communicate the urgency of his invitation with his gaze.

Sophia smiled. "I would be delighted to walk in the garden with you, Francis."

They strolled slowly, interminably, waiting for a single prisoner-gardener to finish his task of unloading heavy bags of fresh fertilizer.

When the man was gone, Crozier steered her upwind to the stone bench at the far and shaded end of the long formal garden. He helped her take her seat and waited while she folded her parasol. She looked up at him — Crozier was too agitated to sit and loomed over her, shifting from foot to foot as he loomed — and he imagined that he could see the expectation in her eyes.

Finally he had the presence of mind to go to one knee.

"Miss Cracroft, I am aware that I am a mere commander in Her Majesty's Navy and that you deserve only the attentions of the full Admiral of the Fleet . . . no, I mean, of royalty, of one who would command a full Admiral . . . but you must be aware, I know you are aware, of the intensity of my feelings toward you, and if you could see yourself finding reciprocal feelings for . . ."

"Good God, Francis," interrupted Sophia, "you are not going to propose marriage, are you?"

Crozier had no answer to that. On one knee, both hands clasped and extended toward her as if in prayer, he waited.

She patted his arm. "Commander Crozier, you are a wonderful man. A *gentle* man despite all those rough edges which may never be rounded off. And you are a *wise* man — especially in understanding that I shall never be a commander's wife. That would not be fitting. That would never be . . . *acceptable.*"

Crozier tried to speak. No words came to mind. That part of his brain still working was trying to complete the endless sentence proposing marriage which he had lain awake all night composing. He had got through almost a third of it — after a fashion.

Sophia laughed softly and shook her head. Her eyes darted, making sure that no one — not even a prisoner — was within sight or hearing. "Please do not be concerned about yesterday, Commander Crozier. We had a wonderful day. The . . . interlude . . . at the pond was pleasant for both of us. It was a function of . . . my nature . . . as much as a result of mutual feelings of closeness we felt *for those few moments*. But please disabuse yourself, my dear Francis, that there remains upon you any burden or compulsion to act in any way on my behalf because of our brief indiscretion."

He looked at her.

She smiled, but not with as much warmth as he had become used to. "It is not," she said so softly that the words came through the hot air as slightly more than a firm whisper, "as if you compromised my honour, Commander."

"Miss Cracroft . . . ," Crozier began again and stopped. If his ship had been in the act of being forced against a lee shore with the pumps out of action and four feet of water in the hold and climbing, the rigging snarled and the sails in tatters, he would have known what orders to give. What to say next. At this moment not a single word came to mind. There was only a rising pain and astonishment in him that hurt all the worse for being a recognition of something old and all too well understood.

"If I were to marry," continued Sophia, opening her parasol again and spinning it above her, "it would be to our dashing Captain Ross. Although I am not destined to be a mere captain's wife either, Francis. He would have to be knighted . . . but I am sure he will be soon."

Crozier stared into her eyes, searching for some sign of jest. "Captain Ross is engaged," he said finally. His voice sounded like the croak of a man who has been stranded without water for many days on end. "They plan to marry immediately after James's return to England."

"Oh, pshaw," said Sophia, standing now and twirling the parasol more quickly. "I will be returning to England by swift packet boat myself this summer, even before Uncle John is recalled. Captain James Clark Ross has not seen the last of me."

She looked down at him where he remained, absurdly, still on one knee in the white gravel. "Besides," she said brightly, "even if Captain Ross marries that young pretendress waiting for him — he and I have spoken of her often, and I can assure you that she is a fool — marriage is the end of nothing. It is not death. It is not Hamlet's 'Unknown Country' from which no man returns. Men have been known to return from marriage and find the woman who has been right for them all along. Mark my words on this, Francis."

He stood then, finally. He stood and brushed the white gravel from the knee of his best dress uniform trousers.

"I must go now," said Sophia. "Aunt Jane, Captain Ross, and I are going into Hobart Town this morning to see some new stallions the Van Diemen Company have just imported for breeding services. Do feel free to come with us if you so choose, Francis, but for heaven's sake change your clothing and your expression before you do."

She touched his forearm lightly and walked back into Government House, twirling her parasol as she went.

Crozier heard the muffled bell on deck ring eight bells. It was 4:00 a.m. Usually, on a ship at sea, the men would be rousted from their hammocks in half an hour to begin holystoning the decks and cleaning everything in sight. But here in the darkness and the ice — and in the wind, Crozier could hear it still howling in the riggings, meaning another blizzard was probable, and this only the tenth of November of their third winter — the men were allowed to sleep late, lazing away until four bells in the morning watch. Six a.m. Then the cold ship would come alive with the mates' shouts and the men's finneskoed feet hitting the deck before the mates carried out their threats of cutting their hammocks down with the seamen still in them.

This was a lazy paradise compared to sea duty. The men not only slept late but were allowed to have their breakfast here on the lower deck at eight bells before having to get on with their morning duties.

Crozier looked at the whiskey bottle and glass. Both were empty. He raised the heavy pistol — extra heavy with its full charge of powder and ball. His hand could tell.

Then he set the pistol into the pocket of his captain's coat, removed the coat, and hung it on a hook. Crozier wiped out the whiskey glass with the clean cloth that Jopson left every evening for that purpose and set it away in his drawer. Then he carefully set the empty whiskey bottle in the covered wicker basket that Jopson left near the sliding door for just that purpose. A full bottle would be in the basket by the time Crozier returned from his dark day's duties.

For a moment he had considered getting more fully dressed and going up on deck — exchanging his finneskoes for real boots, pulling on his comforter, cap, and full slops, and going out into the night and storm to await the rousing of the men, coming down for breakfast with his officers and going the full day with no sleep.

He had done it many other mornings.

But not this morning. He was too weary. And it was too cold to stand here for even a minute with only four layers of wool and cotton on. Four a.m., Crozier knew, was the coldest belly of the night and the hour at which the most ill and wounded men gave up the ghost and were carried away into that true Unknown Country.

Crozier crawled under the blankets and sank his face into the freezing horsehair mattress. It would be fifteen minutes or more before his body heat would begin to warm the cradled space. With luck, he'd be asleep before that. With luck he'd get almost two hours of a drunkard's sleep before the next day of darkness and cold began. With luck, he thought as he drifted off, he wouldn't wake at all.

17

IRVING

Lat. 70°-05' N., Long. 98°-23' W.
13 November, 1847

S ilence was missing, and it was Third Lieutenant John Irving's job to find her.

The captain hadn't ordered him to do so . . . not exactly. But Captain Crozier *had* told Irving to watch over the Esquimaux woman when the captains decided to keep her aboard HMS *Terror* six months earlier in June and Captain Crozier never rescinded that order, so Irving felt responsible for her. Besides, the young man was in love with her. He knew it was foolish — insane even — to have fallen in love with a savage, a woman who was not even a Christian, and an uneducated native who couldn't speak a word of English, or any language for that matter with her tongue torn out as it was, but Irving was still in love with her. Something about her made the tall, strong John Irving weak in his knees.

And now she was gone.

They first noticed she wasn't in her assigned berth — that little den set back amid the crates in the cluttered part of the lower deck just forward of the sick bay — on Thursday, two days earlier, but the men were used to Lady Silence's odd comings and goings. She was off the ship as much as she was on it, even at night. Irving reported to Captain Crozier on Thursday afternoon, the eleventh of November, that Silence had gone missing, but the captain, Irving, and the others had seen her out on the ice two nights before. Then, after the remains of Strong and Evans had been found, she'd gone missing again. The captain said not to worry, that she'd show up.

But she hadn't.

The storm had blown in that Thursday morning, bringing heavy snow and high winds. Work teams labouring by lantern light to repair the trail cairns between *Terror* and *Erebus* — four-foot-high tapered columns of ice bricks every thirty paces — had been forced to return to the ships that afternoon and hadn't been able to work out on the ice since. The last messenger from *Erebus,* who had arrived late Thursday and been forced to stay on *Terror* because of the storm, confirmed that Silence was not aboard Commander Fitzjames's ship. By this Saturday morning, watch was being changed on deck every hour and the men still came below crusted with ice and shaking with cold. Work parties had to be sent topside into the gale with axes every three hours to hack the ice off the remaining spars and lines so that the ship would not tip over from the weight. Also, the falling ice was a hazard to those on watch and did damage to the deck itself. More men struggled to shovel snow off the icy deck of the forward-listing *Terror* before it built up to a depth where they couldn't get the hatches open.

When Lieutenant Irving reported again to Captain Crozier on this Saturday night after supper that Silence was still missing, the captain said, "If she's out in this, she may not be coming back, John. But you have permission to search the entire ship tonight after most of the men are in their hammocks, if only to make sure she's gone."

Even though Irving's officer-on-deck watch had ended hours earlier this evening, the lieutenant now got back into his cold-weather slops, lit an oil lantern, and climbed the ladderway to the deck again.

Conditions had not improved. If anything they were worse than when Irving had gone below for supper five hours earlier. The wind howled in from the northwest, blowing snow before it and reducing visibility to ten feet or less. Ice had recoated everything even though there was a five-man axe party hacking and shouting somewhere forward of the snow-laden canvas sagging above the hatchway. Irving struggled out through a foot of new spindrift under the canvas pyramid, lantern blowing back toward his face, as he searched for one of the men *not* swinging an axe in the darkness.

Reuben Male, captain of the fo'c'sle, had watch and work-party officer duty, and Irving found him by following the faint glow to the other man's lantern on the port side.

Male was a snow-encrusted mound of wool. Even his face was hidden under a makeshift hood wrapped about by layers of heavy wool comforters. The shotgun in the crook of his bulky arm was sheathed in ice. Both men had to shout to be heard.

"See anything, Mr. Male?" shouted Lieutenant Irving, leaning close to the thick turban of wool that was the fo'c'sle captain's head.

The shorter man tugged down the scarf a bit. His nose was icicle white. "You mean the ice parties, sir? I can't see 'em once they get above the first spars. I just listen, sir, while I fill in for young Kinnaird's port watch duty. He was on the third watch shoveling party, sir, and still ain't thawed out."

"No, I mean on the ice!" shouted Irving.

Male laughed. It was, quite literally, a muffled sound. "None of us have seen as far as the ice for forty-eight hours, Lieutenant. You know that, sir. You was out here earlier."

Irving nodded and wrapped his own comforter tighter around his forehead and lower face. "No one's seen Silence . . . Lady Silence?"

"What, sir?" Mr. Male leaned closer, the shotgun a column of ice-rimmed metal and wood between them.

"Lady Silence?" shouted Irving.

"No, sir. I understand that no one's seen the Esquimaux woman for days. She must be gone, Lieutenant. Dead out there somewhere, and good riddance, I say."

Irving nodded, patted Male on his bulky shoulder with his own bulky mitten, and made his way around by the stern — staying away from the mainmast, where giant chunks of ice were falling out of the blowing snow and crashing like artillery shells onto the deck — to speak to John Bates where the man stood watch on the starboard side.

Bates had seen nothing. He hadn't even been able to see the five men of the axe party as they set to work.

"Beggin' your pardon, sir, but I don't have no watch and I'm afraid I won't hear the bell what with all this choppin' and fallin' and the wind blowin' and crashin' of ice, sir. Is there much time left on this watch?"

"You'll hear the bell when Mr. Male rings it," shouted Irving, leaning close to the ice-shrouded globe of wool that was the twenty-six-year-old's head. "And he'll come around to check on you before going below. As you were, Bates."

"Aye, sir."

The wind tried to knock Irving off his feet as he went around to the front of the canvas cover, waited for a break in the falling ice — hearing the men curse and shout in the main-trees and thrumming rigging above — and then he hurried as quickly as he could through the two feet of new snow on deck, ducked under the frozen canvas, and clambered through the hatch and down the ladderway.

He'd searched the lower decks multiple times, of course — especially behind the remaining crates forward of the sick bay where the woman had previously had her little den — but now Irving walked aft. The ship was quiet this late at night except for the stamping and crash of ice on the deck above, the snores from the exhausted men in their hammocks forward, Mr. Diggle's usual bangs and curses from the direction of the stove, and the ever-present howl of wind and grind of ice.

Irving felt his way along the dark and narrow companionway. Except for Mr. Male's room, none of the sleeping cubicles here in officers' country were empty. HMS *Terror* had been lucky in that respect. While *Erebus* had lost several officers to that thing on the ice, including Sir John and Lieutenant Gore, none of *Terror*'s officers, warrant officers, or petty officers had died yet except for young John Torrington, the lead stoker, who'd died of natural causes a year and a half earlier back at Beechey Island.

No one was in the Great Cabin. It was rarely warm enough to tarry long there now and even the leatherbound books looked cold on their shelves; the wooden instrument that played metal musical disks when cranked was silent these days. Irving had time to notice that Captain Crozier's lamp was still lit behind his partition before the lieutenant pushed forward through the officers' and mates' empty mess rooms and back to the ladderway.

The orlop deck below was, as it always was, very cold and very dark. With fewer provision-carrying parties coming down here because of the severe rationing due to the many spoiled cans of food the surgeons had discovered, and with fewer coal-sack hauling parties because of the dwindling coal supplies and reduced hours of heating for the ship, Irving found himself alone in the frigid space. The black wood beams and frost-covered metal brackets groaned around him as he made his way forward before working his way back toward the stern. The lamplight seemed to be swallowed up by the thick darkness, and Irving had trouble seeing the faint glow through the fog of ice crystals created by his own breathing.

Lady Silence was not in the bow area — not in the carpenter's storeroom or the bosun's storeroom nor in the almost-empty Bread Room aft of these closed compartments. The midship section of the orlop deck had been crammed deck to ceiling with crates, barrels, and other packages of supplies when *Terror* had sailed, but now much of the deck-space was clear. Lady Silence was nowhere amidships.

Lieutenant Irving let himself into the Spirit Room, using the key Captain Crozier had loaned him. There were brandy and wine bottles left, he could see by the glow of the dimming lantern, but he knew that the level of rum was low in the huge main cask. When the rum ran out — when the men's daily noon supply of grog disappeared — then, Lieutenant Irving knew, as all officers in the Royal Navy knew, mutiny would become a much more serious concern. Mr. Helpman, the captain's clerk, and Mr. Goddard, the captain of the hold, had reported recently that they estimated another six weeks or so of rum remained, and that much only if the standard one-fourth pint of rum in the gill, diluted with three-fourths pint of water, was reduced by half. The men would grumble even then.

Irving did not think Lady Silence could have sneaked into the locked Spirit Room despite all the whispering of the men about her witchlike powers, but he searched the space carefully, peering under tabletops and counters. The row upon row of cutlasses, sword bayonets, and muskets on the shelves above him glittered coldly in the lantern light.

He went aft to the Gunner's Storeroom, with its adequate remaining supplies of powder and shot, peered into the captain's private storeroom — only Crozier's few remaining whiskey bottles sat on the shelves, the food having been parceled out to the other officers in recent weeks. Then he searched the Sail Room, Slop Room, aft cable lockers, and mate's storeroom. If Lieutenant John Irving had been an Esquimaux woman attempting to hide aboard the ship, he thought he might have chosen the Sail Room, with its mostly untouched heaps and rolls of spare canvas, sheets, and long-unused sailing gear.

But she was not there. Irving had a start in the Slop Room when his lantern showed a tall, silent figure standing in the rear of the room, shoulders looming against a dark bulkhead, but it turned out to be only some wool greatcoats and a Welsh wig hanging on a peg.

Locking doors behind him, the lieutenant went down the ladder to the hold.

Third Lieutenant John Irving, although appearing younger than his years because of his boyish blond looks and quick blush, was not in love with the Esquimaux woman because he was a lovesick virgin. Actually, Irving had had more experience with the fairer sex than many of those braggarts on the ship who filled the fo'c'sle with tales of their sexual conquests. Irving's uncle had brought him down to the Bristol docks when the boy turned fourteen, introduced him to a clean and pleasant dockside whore named Mol, and paid for the experience — not merely a quick back-alley knee-wobbler, but a proper evening and night and morning in a clean room under the eaves of an old inn overlooking the quay. It had given young John Irving a taste for the physical which he had indulged many times since.

Nor had Irving had less luck with the ladies in polite society. He had courted the youngest daughter of Bristol's third most important family, the Dunwitt-Harrisons, and that lass, Emily, had allowed, even initiated, personal intimacies most young men would have sold their left bollock to have experienced at such an age. Upon arriving in London to complete his Naval education in artillery on the gunnery training vessel HMS *Excellent,* Irving had spent his weekends meeting, courting, and enjoying the company of several attractive upper-class young ladies, including the obliging Miss Sarah, the shy but ultimately surprising Miss Linda, and the truly shocking — in private — Miss Abigail Elisabeth Lindstrom Hyde-Berrie, with whom the fresh-faced third lieutenant soon found himself engaged to be married.

John Irving had no intention of being married. At least not while he was in his twenties — his father and uncle had both taught him that these were the years in which he should see the world and sow wild oats — and most probably not when he was in his thirties. He saw no compelling reason to marry while he would be in his forties. So although Irving had never once considered the Discovery Service — he had never enjoyed cold weather, and the thought of being frozen in at either of the poles was both absurd and appalling to him — the week after he awoke to find himself engaged, the third lieutenant followed the promptings of his older chums George Hodgson and Fred Hornby and went along to an interview on HMS *Terror* to apply for transfer.

Captain Crozier, obviously in foul spirits and hungover that beautiful spring Saturday morning, had glowered, harrumphed, scowled, and quizzed them carefully. He laughed at their gunnery training on a mastless ship and demanded to know just how they could be of service on an expedition sailing ship which carried only small arms. Then he asked them pointedly if they would "do their duty as Englishmen" (whatever on earth that meant, Irving remembered thinking, when said Englishmen were locked into a frozen sea a thousand miles from home) and promptly assured them of berths.

Miss Abigail Elisabeth Lindstrom Hyde-Berrie was distraught, of course, and shocked that their engagement should be extended over months or actual years, but Lieutenant Irving consoled her first with assurances that the extra money from the Discovery Service duty would be an absolute necessity for them, and then by explaining his need for the adventure and then fame and glory that might well come from writing a book upon his return. Her family understood these priorities even if Miss Abigail did not. Then, when they were alone, he coaxed her out of her tears and anger with hugs, kisses, and expert caresses. The consolation grew to interesting heights — Lieutenant Irving knew that he might well be a father by now, two and a half years after the consoling. But he had not been unhappy to wave good-bye to Miss Abigail some weeks later as *Terror* slipped her moorings and was pushed away by two steam tugs. The disconsolate young lady stood on the docks at Greenhithe in her green-and-pink silk dress under a pink parasol and waved her matching silk pink handkerchief, using another less-expensive cotton handkerchief to dry her copious tears.

He knew that Sir John fully expected to stop in both Russia and China after negotiating the North-West Passage, so Lieutenant Irving had already made plans to transfer to a Royal Navy ship assigned to one of those waters, or perhaps even resign from the Navy, write his adventure book, and look after his uncle's silk and millinery interests in Shanghai.

The hold was darker and colder than the orlop deck.

Irving hated the hold. It reminded him, even more than did his freezing berth or the dimly lit, freezing lower deck, of a grave. He only came down here when he had to, mostly to supervise the stowing of shrouded dead bodies — or the parts of dead bodies — in the locked Dead Room. Each time he wondered if someone soon would be supervising the stowing of his corpse down here. He lifted his lantern and headed aft through the slush-melt and thick air.

The boiler room appeared to be empty, but then Lieutenant Irving saw the body on the cot near the starboard bulkhead. No lantern glowed, only the low red flicker through the grate of one of the four closed boiler doors, and in the dim light, the long body stretched out on the cot looked dead. The man's open eyes stared up at the low ceiling and he did not blink. Nor did he turn his head when Irving came into the room and hung his lantern on a hook near the coal scuttle.

"What brings you down here, Lieutenant?" asked James Thompson. The engineer still neither moved his head nor blinked. Sometime in the past month he had quit shaving, and whiskers now sprouted everywhere on his thin, white face. The man's eyes lay deep in dark sockets. His hair was wild and spiky with soot and sweat. It was near freezing even here in the boiler room with the fires damped so low, but Thompson was lying only in his trousers, undershirt, and suspenders.

"I'm looking for Silence," said Irving.

The man on the cot continued to stare at the deck above him.

"Lady Silence," clarified the young lieutenant.

"The Esquimaux witch," said the engineer.

Irving cleared his throat. The coal dust was so thick here that it was hard to breathe. "Have you seen her, Mr. Thompson? Or heard anything unusual?"

Thompson, who still had not blinked or turned his head, laughed softly. The sound was disturbing — a rattle of small stones in a jar — and it ended in a cough. "Listen," said the engineer.

Irving turned his head. There were only the usual noises, although louder down here in the dark hold: the slow moan of ice pressing in, the louder groaning of the iron tanks and structural reinforcements fore and aft of the boiler room, the more distant moan of the blizzard winds far above, the crash of falling ice carried down as vibration through the ship's timbers, the thrum of the masts being shaken in their sockets, random scratching noises from the hull, and a constant hiss, screech, and claw-sliding noise from the boiler and pipes all around.

"There's someone or something else breathing on this deck," continued Thompson. "Do you hear it?"

Irving strained but heard no breathing, although the boiler sounded like something large panting hard. "Where are Smith and Johnson?" asked the lieutenant. These were the two stokers who worked round-the-clock here with Thompson.

The supine engineer shrugged. "With so little coal to shovel these days, I need them only a few hours a day. I spend most of my time alone, crawling among the pipes and valves, Lieutenant. Patching. Taping. Replacing. Trying to keep this . . . *thing* . . . working, moving hot water through the lower deck for a few hours each day. In two months, three at the most, it will all be academic. We already have no coal to steam. We'll soon have no coal to heat."

Irving had heard these reports in the officers' mess but had little interest in the subject. Three months seemed a lifetime away. Right now he had to make sure Silence was not on board and report to the captain. Then he had to try to find her if she was not aboard *Terror.*

Then he had to survive another three months. He would worry about shortages of coal later.

"Have you heard the rumors, Lieutenant?" asked the engineer. The long form on the couch still had neither blinked nor turned his head to look at Irving.

"No, Mr. Thompson, which rumor?"

"That the . . . *thing* on the ice, the apparition, the Devil . . . comes into the ship whenever it wants to and walks the hold deck late at night," said Thompson.

"No," said Lieutenant Irving. "I've not heard that."

"Stay down here alone on the hold deck through enough watches," said the man on the cot, "and you'll hear and see everything."

"Good night, Mr. Thompson." Irving took his sputtering lantern and went back out into the companionway and forward.

There were few places left to search on the hold deck and Irving had every intention of making a fast job of it. The Dead Room was locked; the lieutenant had not asked his captain for the key, and after inspecting that the heavy lock was solid and secured, he moved on. He didn't want to see what was causing the scrabbling and chewing sounds he could hear through the thick oak door.

The twenty-one huge iron water tanks along the hull offered no place for an Esquimaux to hide, so Irving went into the coal bunkers, his lantern dimming in the thick, coal-dust-blackened air. The remaining sacks of coal, once filling each bin and stacked from hull bottom to the deck beams above, merely lined the edge of each sooty room like low barriers of sandbags now. He couldn't imagine Lady Silence making a new shelter in one of these lightless, reeking, pestilential hellholes — the decks were awash in sewage and rats scuttled everywhere — but he had to look.

When he was finished searching the coal storage lockers and the stores amidships, Lieutenant Irving moved out into the remaining crates and barrels in the forepeak, directly below the crew's berthing area and Mr. Diggle's huge stove two decks above. A narrower ladder came down through the orlop deck to this stores area and tons of lumber were hanging from the heavy beams overhead, turning the space into a maze and requiring the lieutenant to proceed in a half crouch, but there were far fewer crates, barrels, and heaps of goods than there had been two and a half years earlier.

But more rats. Many more.

Searching between and in some of the larger crates, glancing to make sure that the barrels awash in the slush were either empty or sealed, Irving had just stepped around the vertical forward ladder when he saw a flash of white and heard harsh breathing, gasps and caught a rustle of frenzied movement just beyond the dim circle of the lantern light. It was large, moving, and was not the woman.

Irving had no weapon. For the briefest instant he considered dropping the lantern and running back through the darkness toward the midship ladderway. He did not, of course, and the thought was gone almost before it was formed. He took a step forward and, in a voice stronger and more authoritative than he thought he might be capable of right then, shouted, "Who goes there? Identify yourself!"

Then he saw them in the lantern light. The idiot, Magnus Manson, the largest man on the expedition, struggling back into his trousers, his huge, grimy fingers fumbling with buttons. A few feet away Cornelius Hickey, the caulker's mate, barely five feet tall, beady-eyed and ferret-faced, was pulling his suspenders into place.

John Irving's mouth hung open. It took several seconds for the reality of what he was looking at to filter through his mind toward acceptance — *sodomites*. He had heard of such goings-on, of course, had joked with his mates about such things, had once witnessed a flogging around the fleet when an ensign on the *Excellent* had confessed to such doings, but Irving had never thought that he would be on a ship where . . . to serve with men who . . .

Manson, the giant, was taking an ominous step toward him. The man was so large that everywhere belowdecks he had to walk in a stooped crouch to avoid the beams, giving him an habitual hunchbacked shuffle that he used even in the open air. Now, his huge hands glowing in the lamplight, he looked like an executioner advancing on a condemned man.

"Magnus," said Hickey. "No."

Irving's jaw dropped farther. Were these . . . *sodomites* . . . threatening him? The prescribed sentence for sodomy on a ship of Her Majesty's Navy was hanging, with two hundred lashes from the cat while being flogged around the fleet — literally from ship to ship in harbour — being considered great leniency.

"How dare you?" said Irving, although whether he was talking about Manson's threatening attitude or their unnatural act, even he did not know.

"Lieutenant," said Hickey, words rushing in that flute-high rush of the caulker's mate's Liverpool accent, "begging your pardon, sir, Mr. Diggle sent us down for some flour, sir. One of them damn rats rushed up Seaman Manson's trouser leg, sir, and we was trying to set it right. Filthy buggers, them rats."

Irving knew that Mr. Diggle had not yet started the late-night baking of biscuits and that there was ample flour in the cook's stores up on the lower deck. Hickey was not even trying to make his lie convincing. The little man's beady, evaluating eyes reminded Irving of the rats scurrying in the darkness around them.

"We'd appreciate it if you wouldn't tell no one, sir," continued the caulker's mate. "Magnus here would hate to be made fun of for bein' afraid of a little rat runnin' up his leg."

The words were a challenge and a defiance. Almost a command. Insolence came off the little man in waves while Manson stood there empty-eyed, as dumb as a beast of burden, huge hands still flexed, passively awaiting the next command from his diminutive lover.

The silence between the men stretched. Ice moaned against the ship. Timbers creaked. Rats scurried close by.

"Get out of here," Irving said at last. *"Now."*

"Aye, sir. Thank you, sir," said Hickey. He unshielded a small lantern that had been on the deck near him. "Come, Magnus."

The two men scrambled up the narrow forward ladder into the darkness of the orlop deck.

Lieutenant Irving stood where he was for several long minutes, listening to but not hearing the groans and snaps of the ship. The blizzard howl was like a distant dirge.

If he reported this to Captain Crozier, there would be a trial. Manson, the village idiot of this expedition, was well liked by the crew, however much they teased him about his fear of ghosts and goblins. The man did the heavy work of any three of his comrades. Hickey, while not especially liked by any of the other warrant or regular officers, was respected by the regular seamen for his abilities to get his friends extra tobacco, an extra gill of rum, or an article of needed clothing.

Crozier wouldn't hang either man, thought John Irving, but the captain had been in an especially foul mood in recent weeks and the punishments could be dramatic. Everyone on the ship knew that just weeks ago the captain threatened to lock Manson into the Dead Room with his chum Walker's rat-chewed corpse if the huge idiot ever again refused an order to carry coal on the hold deck. No one would be surprised if he carried out that sentence now.

On the other hand, thought the lieutenant, what had he just seen? What could he testify to, his hand on the Holy Bible, if there were an actual court of inquiry? He hadn't *seen* any unnatural act. He'd not caught the two sodomites in the act of copulation or . . . any other unnatural posture. Irving had heard the breathing, the gasps, something that must have been whispered alarm at the approach of his lantern, and then seen the two struggling to raise their trousers and tuck in their shirts.

That would be enough to get one or both of them hanged under normal circumstances. But here, stuck in the ice, with months or years ahead of them before any chance of rescue?

For the first time in many years, John Irving felt like sitting down and weeping. His life had just become complex beyond all his imagining. If he did report the two sodomites, none of his crewmates — officers, friends, subordinates — would ever look at him quite the same way again.

If he did *not* report the two men, he would open himself to endless insolence from Hickey. His cowardice in not reporting the man would expose Irving to a form of blackmail for weeks and months to come. Nor would the lieutenant ever sleep well again or feel comfortable on watch in the darkness outside or in his cubicle — as comfortable as anyone could be with that monstrous white thing killing them all one by one — waiting, as he would be now, for Manson's white hands to close around his throat.

"Oh, bugger me," Irving said aloud into the creaking cold of the hold. Realizing exactly what he had said, he laughed aloud — the laugh sounding stranger, weaker, yet more ominous than the words.

Having looked everywhere except a few hogshead barrels and the forward cable locker, he was ready to give up his search, but he didn't want to go up to the lower deck until Hickey and Manson were out of sight.

Irving made his way past floating empty crates — the water was above his ankles here, this far toward the downward-tilting bow, and his soaked boots broke through the scrim of ice. Another few minutes and he'd have frostbitten toes for sure.

The cable locker was at the most forward part of the forepeak, right where the hull came together at the bow. It was not really a room — the two doors were only three feet tall and the space within not much more than four feet high — but rather a place to stow the heavy hawsers used for the bow anchors. The cable locker always stank to high heaven of river and estuary mud, even months or years after a ship's weighing anchor from that place. It never fully lost its stench, and the massive hawsers, coiled and overlapping, left little or no free room in the low, black, evil-smelling space.

Lieutenant Irving pried open the reluctant doors to the locker and held his lantern to the opening. The grinding of the ice was especially loud here where the bow and bowsprit were pressed into the shifting pack ice itself.

Lady Silence's head shot up and her dark eyes reflected the light like a cat's.

She was naked except for white-brown furs spread under her like a rug and another heavy fur — perhaps her parka — draped over her shoulders and naked body.

The floor of the cable locker was raised more than a foot above the flooded deck outside. She had moulded and shoved the massive hawsers aside until the space opened made a low, fur-lined cave within the overhanging tangle of huge hemp ropes. A small food can filled with oil or blubber provided light and heat from an open flame. The Esquimaux woman was in the process of eating a haunch of red, raw, bloody meat. She was slicing directly from the meat to her mouth with quick cuts from a short but obviously very sharp knife. The knife had a bone or antler handle with some sort of design on it. Lady Silence was on her knees, leaning forward over the flame and the meat, and her small breasts hung down in a way that reminded the literate Lieutenant Irving of pictures he had seen of the statue of a she-wolf nursing the infants Romulus and Remus.

"I'm terribly sorry, madam," said Irving. He touched his cap and shut the doors.

Staggering back a few steps in the slush, sending rats scurrying, the lieutenant tried to think through shock for the second time in five minutes.

The captain had to know about Silence's hiding place. The fire danger alone from the open flame there would have to be dealt with.

But where had she got the knife? It looked like something made by Esquimauxs, rather than a weapon or tool from the ship. Certainly they had searched her six months ago in June. Could she have hidden it all this time?

What else could she be hiding?

And the fresh meat.

There was no fresh meat on board, Irving was sure of that.

Could she have been hunting? In the winter and blizzard and dark? And hunting what?

The only things out there on the ice or under the ice were the white bears and the thing stalking the men of *Erebus* and *Terror.*

John Irving had a terrible thought. For a second he was tempted to go back and test the lock to the Dead Room.

Then he had an even more terrible thought.

Only half of William Strong and Thomas Evans had been found.

Lieutenant John Irving stumbled aft, feet sliding on the ice and slush as he fumbled and felt his way toward the central ladderway to fight his way up and out toward the light of the lower deck.

18

GOODSIR

From the private diary of Dr. Harry D. S. Goodsir:

Saturday, 20 November, 1847 —

We do not have enough food to survive another Winter and Summer here in the ice.

We should have had. Sir John had Provisioned the two ships for Three Years at extraordinarily full rations for all hands, Five Years for reduced but still adequate rations for men doing heavy work each day, and Seven Years with serious rationing but adequate for all men. By Sir John's Calculations — and those of his ships' captains, Crozier and Fitzjames — HMSs Erebus *and* Terror *should have been amply provisioned until the year 1852.*

Instead, we shall be running out of our last edible supplies sometime next spring. And should we all perish because of this, the Reason is Murder.

Dr. McDonald on Terror *had been suspicious of the canned food supplies for some Time, and he shared his concerns with me after the Death of Sir John. Then the problem with spoiled and Poisonous canned foods on our First Outing to King William Land last Summer — tins removed from a deeper part of Stores beneath Deck — confirmed the problem. In October, the four of us Surgeons petitioned Captain Crozier and Commander Fitzjames to allow us to take a Full Inventory. Then the Four of us — aided by crewmen assigned to help us move the hundreds upon hundreds of crates, barrels, and heavy cans in both lower decks, orlop decks, and holds, and to open and test selected samplings — had done the Inventory twice so as not to make a mistake.*

More than Half the canned Food aboard both ships *is worthless.*

We reported this three weeks ago to both captains in Sir John's large and freezing former cabin. Fitzjames, while nominally still a mere Commander, is called "Captain" by Crozier, the new Expedition Leader, and others follow suit. In the secret meeting were the four of us surgeons, Fitzjames, and Crozier.

Captain Crozier — I have to remember that he is Irish after all — flew into a rage the likes of which I have never seen. He demanded a full explanation, as if We Surgeons had been responsible for the Stores and Victuals on the Franklin Expedition. Fitzjames, on the other hand, had always had his doubts about the canned goods and the victualler who had canned them — the only member of the Expedition or the Admiralty who seems to have expressed such reservations — but Crozier remained incredulous that such an act of criminal fraud could have been carried out on ships of the Royal Navy.

John Peddie, Crozier's chief surgeon on Terror, *has seen the most Sea Duty of any of us four Medical Officers, but most of it had been aboard HMS* Mary *— along with Crozier's boatswain John Lane — and that was in the Mediterranean, where very little of the Ship's Stores had consisted of Canned Goods. Similarly, my nominal superior on* Erebus, *Chief Surgeon Stephen Stanley, had little experience with such Great Quantities of Canned Provisions aboard ship. Sensitive to the Various Diets thought Necessary to prevent scurvy, Dr. Stanley was shocked into speechlessness when our Inventory suggested via sampling that almost half the remaining tins of food, vegetables, meat, and soup may well be Contaminated or otherwise Ruined.*

Only Dr. McDonald, who had worked with Mr. Helpman — Captain Crozier's Clerk in Charge — during the provisioning, had his Theories.

As I recorded some Months ago in this Journal, besides the 10,000 cases of preserved cooked meats aboard Erebus, *our tinned rations include boiled and roast mutton, veal, a wide variety of vegetables including potatoes, carrots, and parsnips, various types of Soups, and 9,450 pounds of Chocolate.*

Alex McDonald had been our Expedition's medical liaison with the Captain Superintendent of the Deptford Victualling Yard and with a certain Mr. Stephan Goldner, our Expedition's Victualling Contractor. McDonald reminded Captain Crozier in October that four contractors had put in bids to provide Canned Ship's Stores for Sir John's expedition — the firms of Hogarth, Gamble, Cooper & Aves, and that of the aforementioned Mr. Goldner. Dr. McDonald reminded the

*Captain — and astonished the rest of us — by reporting that Goldner's bid was
only half that of the other three (Much Better Known) victuallers. In addition,
while the other contractors set a schedule of delivering the food in a month or
three weeks, Goldner had promised immediate delivery (with the crating and
drayage thrown in for no charge). Such immediate delivery was impossible, of
course, and Goldner's bid would have required him to lose a fortune if the food
had been the quality advertised and cooked and prepared in the ways advertised,
but no one except Captain Fitzjames appears to have taken notice of this.*

*The Admiralty and the three Commissioners of the Discovery Service —
everyone involved in the selection except for the experienced Comptroller of
the Deptford Victualling Yard — immediately recommended accepting
Goldner's offer at a full-payment value, or more than 3,800 pounds. (A
fortune for any man, but especially for the foreigner that McDonald explained
Goldner to be. The man's only canning factory, Alex said, was in Golatz,
Molavia.) Goldner was given one of the largest consignments in the history of
the Admiralty — 9,500 cans of meats and vegetables in sizes weighing one to
eight pounds, as well as 20,000 cans of soup.*

*McDonald had brought one of Goldner's handbills — Fitzjames recognized
it at once — and looking over it made my mouth water: seven kinds of mutton,
fourteen preparations of veal, thirteen kinds of beef, four varieties of lamb. There
were listings for jugged hare, ptarmigan, rabbit (in onion sauce or curried),
pheasant, and half a dozen other varieties of game. If the Discovery Service
wished to have seafood, Goldner had offered to provide canned lobsters in the
shell, cod, West Indian turtle, salmon steaks, and Yarmouth bloaters. For fine
dining — at only fifteen pence — Goldner's handbill offered truffled pheasant,
calf's tongue sauce piquant, and beef à la Flamande.*

In reality, *said Dr. McDonald,* we're used to receiving salt horse in a
harness cask.

*I had been at Sea long enough to recognize the terms — horse flesh
substituted for beef until the sailors called the barrels a harness cask. But they
ate the salted meat readily enough.*

Goldner cheated us much worse than that, *continued McDonald in
front of a livid Captain Crozier and an angrily nodding Commander
Fitzjames.* He substituted cheap foods under labels that sold for much
more on the handbill — regular "Stewed Beef" under a label reading

"Stewed Rump Steaks," for instance. The former is listed at nine pence, but he charged fourteen pence by changing the label.

Good God, man, *exploded Crozier, every* victualler does that to the Admiralty. Cheating the Navy is as old as Adam's foreskin. That can't explain why we're suddenly almost out of food.

No, Captain, *continued McDonald.* It's the cooking and soldering.

The what? *demanded the Irishman, obviously trying to keep his Temper in check. Crozier's face was crimson and white under his battered cap.*

The cooking and soldering, *said Alex.* As to the cooking, Mr. Goldner bragged of a patented process in which he adds a large dose of nitrate of soda — calcium chloride — into the huge vats of boiling water to increase the processing temperature . . . primarily to speed production.

What's wrong with that? *demanded Crozier.* The cans were overdue as it was. Something needed to be done to build a fire under Goldner's arse. His patented process hurried things up.

Yes, Captain, *said Dr. McDonald,* but the fire under Goldner's arse was hotter than the fire under these meats, vegetables, and other foods that were hurriedly cooked before canning. Many of us in the medical field believe that proper cooking of food rids it of Noxious Influences that can cause disease — but I myself witnessed Goldner's cooking processes and he simply did not cook the meat, vegetables, and soups long enough.

Why didn't you report this to the Discovery Service Commissioners? *snapped Crozier.*

He did, *Captain Fitzjames said tiredly.* So did I. But the only one who listened was the Comptroller of the Deptford Yard Victualling Service, and he had no vote on the final commission.

So you're saying that more than half our food has gone bad in the last three years because of poor cooking methods? *Crozier's Countenance continued to be a Mottle of crimson and white.*

Yes, *said Alex McDonald,* but equally to blame, we think, is the soldering.

The soldering of the cans? *asked Fitzjames. His doubts about Goldner evidently had not extended to this technicality.*

Yes, Commander, *said* Terror's *assistant surgeon*. Preserving food in tins is a recent innovation — an amazing part of our Modern Age — but we know enough in the past few years of its use to know that proper soldering the flange along the seams of the cylindrical body of the can is important if the foodstuffs within are not to turn Putrid.

And Goldner's people did not properly solder these tins? *asked Crozier. His voice was a low, menacing growl.*

Not in about sixty percent of the tins we've inspected, *said McDonald*. The gaps in the careless soldering have resulted in incomplete seams. The incomplete seams appear to have accelerated the putrefaction of our tinned beef, veal, vegetables, soups, and other foodstuffs.

How? *asked Captain Crozier. He was shaking his broad head like a man who has been stunned by a physical blow.* We've been in polar waters since shortly after the two ships left England. I thought it was cold enough up here to preserve anything until Judgement Day.

Apparently not, *said McDonald*. Many of Goldner's remaining twenty-nine thousand cans of food have ruptured. Others are already swelling from the gases caused by internal putrefaction. Perhaps some Noxious vapours entered the tins in England. Perhaps there is some microscopic animalcule of which Medicine and Science are not yet aware which invaded the tins during transit or even at Goldner's victualling factory.

Crozier frowned more deeply. Animalcule? Let's avoid the fantastic here, Mr. McDonald.

The assistant surgeon only shrugged. Perhaps it is fantastical, Captain. But you have not spent the hundreds of hours straining at the eyepiece of a microscope such as I have. We have little understanding of what any of these animalcules are, but I assure you that if you saw how many are present in a simple drop of drinking water, you would be deeply sobered.

Crozier's coloration had calmed somewhat, but he blushed again at the comment which might have been a reflection of his frequently less-than-sober state. All right. Some of the food is ruined, *he said brusquely.* What can we do to make sure the rest is safe for the men's consumption?

I cleared my throat. As you know, Captain, the men's summer diet included a daily ration of one and a quarter pounds of salt meat with vegetables consisting of only one pint of peas and three-quarters pound of barley a week. But they received their daily bread and biscuits. When we went into winter quarters, the flour ration was cut back twenty-five percent on the baking of bread so as to conserve coal. If we could just begin cooking the remaining canned food rations longer and renewing the baking of bread, it would help not only in preventing the fouled meats in the canned goods from threatening our health but also help in the prevention of scurvy.

Impossible, *snapped Crozier.* We barely have enough coal left to heat both ships until April as it is. If you doubt me, ask Engineer Gregory or Engineer Thompson here on *Terror.*

I don't doubt you, Captain, *I said sadly.* I've spoken to both engineers. But without a resumption of extended cooking of the remaining canned goods, our chances of being poisoned are very high. All we can do is throw out the obviously ruined canned foods and avoid the many poorly soldered cans. This cuts down on our remaining stores most dramatically.

What about the ether stoves? *asked Fitzjames, brightening a bit.* We could use the camping stoves to heat the tinned soups and other doubtful provisions.

It was McDonald who shook his head. We tested that, Commander. Dr. Goodsir and I experimented with heating some of the canned so-called Beef Stew on the patented Cooking Apparatus spirit stoves. The pint-sized bottles of ether do not last long enough to thoroughly heat the food and the temperatures are low. Also, our sledge parties — or all of us, should we be forced to Abandon Ship — will be dependent upon the spirit stoves to melt snow and ice for drinking water once we are on the ice. We should preserve the ether spirits.

I was with Lieutenant Gore on our first sledge party to King William Land — and we used the spirit stoves daily, *I added softly.* The men used just enough ether and flame to get the canned soups to bubble a bit before digging in ravenously. The food was barely tepid.

There was a long silence.

You report that over half the canned food we had been counting on to get through the next year or two — if necessary — is ruined, *Crozier said at last.* We don't have the coal to recook this food on either *Erebus*'s or *Terror's* large Frazer's Patent Stoves, nor on the smaller whaleboat iron stoves, and you tell me that there is insufficient fuel to use the ether spirit stoves. What *can* we do?

All five of us — the Four Surgeons and Captain Fitzjames — remained Silent. The only answer was to Abandon Ship and seek out a more hospitable clime, preferably Ashore somewhere south, where we might shoot fresh game.

As if reading our collective minds, Crozier smiled — it was a uniquely mad Irish smile, I thought at the time — and said, The problem, gentlemen, is that there's not a man aboard either ship, not even one of our venerable Marines, who knows how to catch or kill a seal or walrus — should those creatures ever grace us with their presence again — nor with the experience of shooting large game such as caribou, of which we have seen none.

The Rest of Us remained silent.

Thank you for your diligence, effort at doing the Inventory, and excellent report, Mr. Peddie, Mr. Goodsir, Mr. McDonald, and Mr. Stanley. We shall continue separating the cans you consider fully soldered and safe from those insufficiently soldered or bloated, distended, or otherwise visibly Putrid. We shall stay on the current Two-Thirds Rations until after Christmas Day, at which time I shall instigate a more draconian rationing plan.

Dr. Stanley and I pulled on our many layers of winter slops and went up to the deck to watch Dr. Peddie, Dr. McDonald, Captain Crozier, and an honor guard of four seamen armed with shotguns begin their long trek back to Terror *in the dark. As their lanterns and torches disappeared in the blowing snow and the wind howled in the rigging, the roar mixing with the constant grind and groan of the ice working against* Erebus's *hull, Stanley leaned close and shouted into my mufflered ear:* It would be a blessing if they missed the cairns and got lost on the way back. Or if the Thing on the ice got them tonight.

I could only turn and stare in horror at the chief surgeon.

Death by starvation is a terrible thing, Goodsir, *continued Stanley.*

Trust me. I've seen it in London and I've seen it with shipwreck. Death by scurvy is worse. It would be better if the Thing took us all tonight.

And with that we went below to the flame-flickering Darkness of the lower deck and to a cold almost the equal of the Dante-esque Ninth Circle Arctic Night without.

19

CROZIER

O n a Tuesday dogwatch in the third week of November, the thing from the ice came aboard *Erebus* and took the well-liked bosun, Mr. Thomas Terry, snatching him from his post near the stern, leaving only the man's head on the railing. There had been no blood at Terry's stern watch post: no blood on the ice-covered deck or on the hull. The conclusion was that the thing had taken Terry, carried him hundreds of yards out into the darkness where the seracs rose like trees of ice in a thick white forest, murdered and dismembered him — perhaps eaten him, although the men were growing increasingly doubtful that the white thing killing their crewmates and officers was actually doing so for food — and then it returned Mr. Terry's head before the starboard or port watchmen noticed that the bosun had gone missing.

The men who found the bosun's head at the end of that watch spent the week telling and retelling the others about poor Mr. Terry's visage — jaws open wide as if frozen in the middle of a scream, lips pulled back from his teeth, eyes protruding. There was not a tooth wound or claw mark on his face or head, only the ragged tearing at the neck, the thin pipe of his esophagus protruding like a rat's grey tail, and the stump of white spinal cord showing.

Suddenly the more than one hundred surviving seamen found religion. Most of the men aboard *Erebus* had grumbled for two years about Sir John Franklin's endless Divine Services, but now even the men who wouldn't have recognized a Bible if they'd wakened next to one after a three-day drunk found a deep need for some sort of spiritual reassurance. As word of Thomas Terry's beheading spread — Captain Fitzjames had put the sail-wrapped bundle in *Erebus*'s own sealed Dead Room down on the hold deck — the men began requesting a single Sunday service for both crews. It was ferret-faced Cornelius Hickey who came to Crozier late on Friday night with the request. Hickey had been on a torchlight work party repairing ice cairns between the ships and had spoken to the men from *Erebus*.

"It's unanimous, sir," said the caulker's mate as he stood in the doorway of Captain Crozier's tiny cabin. "All the men would like a combined Divine Service. Both ships, Captain."

"You speak for every man on both ships?" Crozier asked.

"Aye, sir, I do," said Hickey, flashing a once-winning smile that now showed only four of his remaining six teeth. The little caulker's mate was nothing if not confident.

"I doubt it," said Crozier. "But I'll talk to Captain Fitzjames and let you know about the service. Whatever we decide, you can be our appointed courier to tell *all* the men." Crozier had been drinking when Hickey rapped on his door. And he'd never liked the officious little man. Every ship had sea lawyers — like rats, they were a fact of Naval life — and Hickey, despite his bad grammar and total lack of formal education, struck Crozier as the kind of sea lawyer that, on a difficult voyage, soon began fomenting actual mutiny.

"One of the reasons we'd all of us like a service such as that what Sir John — God bless and rest his soul, Captain — used to provide is that all of us . . ."

"That will be *all*, Mr. Hickey."

———

Crozier drank heavily that week. The melancholia that usually hovered over him like a fog now lay on him like a heavy blanket. He'd known Terry and thought him a more-than-capable boatswain, and it was certainly a horrible enough way to die, but the Arctic — at either pole — offered a myriad of horrible enough ways to die. So did the Royal Navy during peacetime or war. Crozier had witnessed more than a few of these horrible ways to die during his long career, so while Mr. Terry's death was among the more uncanny he'd personally known and the recent plague of violent deaths more frightening than any real plague he'd seen aboard ships, what brought on Crozier's deeper melancholy was more the reaction of the surviving members of the expedition.

James Fitzjames, the hero of the Euphrates, seemed to be losing heart. He was made a hero by the press even before his first ship had left Liverpool when young Fitzjames had plunged overboard to rescue a drowning customs agent even though the handsome young officer was, as the *Times* said, "embarrassed by a greatcoat, hat, and very valuable watch." The merchants of Liverpool, knowing the value — as Crozier well knew — of a customs officer who was already bought and paid for, had rewarded young Fitzjames with an engraved silver plate. The Admiralty had taken notice first of the silver plate, then of Fitzjames's heroism — although in Crozier's experience, an officer rescuing a drowning man was an almost weekly occurrence since few sailors knew how to swim — and finally of the fact that Fitzjames was "the handsomest man in the Navy" as well as a well-bred young gentleman.

It hadn't hurt the rising young officer's reputation that he had twice volunteered to lead raiding parties against Bedouin bandits. Crozier noticed in the official reports that Fitzjames had broken his leg in one such foray and been captured by the bandits in the second adventure, but the handsomest man in the Navy had managed to escape, which made Fitzjames all the more the hero to the London press and the Admiralty.

Then came the Opium Wars and in 1841 Fitzjames showed himself to be a real hero, being commended by his captain and by the Admiralty no fewer than five times. The dashing lad — twenty-nine at the time — had used rockets to drive the Chinese off the hilltops of Tzekee and Segoan, used rockets again to drive them out of Chapoo, fought ashore at the Battle of Woosung, and returned to his expertise with rockets during the capture of Ching-Kiang-Fu. Seriously wounded, Lieutenant Fitzjames had managed, on crutches and in bandages, to attend the Chinese surrender at the signing of the Treaty of Nanking. Promoted to commander at the tender age of thirty, the handsomest man in the Navy had been given command of the sloop of war HMS *Clio,* and his bright future seemed assured.

But then in 1844 the Opium Wars ended, and — as always happened to rising prospects in the Royal Navy when treacherous peace suddenly broke out — Fitzjames found himself without a command, on shore, and on half pay. Francis Crozier knew that if the Discovery Service offer of command to Sir John Franklin had been a godsend to the largely discredited old man, the offer of effective command of HMS *Erebus* had been a shining second chance to Fitzjames.

But now "the handsomest man in the Navy" had lost his pink cheeks and usual ebullient humor. While most of the officers and men were maintaining their weight even on two-thirds rations — for members of the Discovery Service received a richer diet than 99 percent of Englishmen ashore — Commander, now Captain, James Fitzjames had lost more than two stone. His uniform hung loosely on him. His boyish curls now fell limp from under his cap or Welsh wig. Fitzjames's face, always a bit too chubby, now appeared drawn, wan, and hollow-cheeked in the light from the oil lamps or hanging lanterns.

The commander's public demeanor, which was always an easy mix of self-effacing humor and firm command, remained the same, but in private with only Crozier in attendance, Fitzjames spoke less, smiled less frequently, and too often looked distracted and miserable. For a melancholy man like Crozier, the signs were obvious. At times it was like staring into a looking glass, except for the fact that the melancholy countenance staring back was a proper lisping English gentleman rather than an Irish nobody.

On Friday the third of December, Crozier loaded a shotgun and made the long solo walk through the cold darkness between *Terror* and *Erebus.* If the thing on the ice wanted to take him, Crozier thought, a few more men with guns would make little difference in the outcome. It hadn't for Sir John.

Crozier arrived safely. He and Fitzjames discussed the situation — the men's morale, the requests for a religious service, the situation with the food tins, and the need to enforce strict rationing soon after

Christmas — and they agreed that a combined Divine Service on the following Sunday might be a good idea. Since there were no chaplains or self-appointed ministers aboard — Sir John had filled both those roles until the previous June — both captains would give a sermon. Crozier hated this task more than dockside dentistry but realized that it had to be done.

The men's moods were in a dangerous state. Lieutenant Edward Little, Crozier's executive officer, reported that men on *Terror* had begun to fashion necklaces and other fetishes from the claws and teeth of some of the white bears they had shot during the summer season. Lieutenant Irving reported weeks ago that Lady Silence had gone into hiding in the forward cable locker and the men had started leaving portions of their rum and food rations down there in the hold as if making offerings to a witch or saint in hopes of intercession.

"I've been thinking about your ball," said Fitzjames as Crozier began bundling up to leave.

"My ball?"

"The Grand Venetian Carnivale that Hoppner set up when you wintered over with Parry," continued Fitzjames. "When you went as a black footman."

"What about it?" asked Crozier as he bound his comforter around his neck and face.

"Sir John had three large trunks of masks, clothing, and costumes," said Fitzjames. "I found them among his personal stores."

"He did?" Crozier was surprised. The aging windbag who would have held Divine Service six times a week if he had been allowed and who, despite his frequent laughter, never seemed to understand anyone else's jokes, seemed like the last sort of expedition commander to load trunks of frivolous costumes the way the stagestruck Parry had.

"They're old," confirmed Fitzjames. "Some of them may have belonged to Parry and Hoppner — may have been the same costumes you chose from while frozen in Baffin Bay twenty-four years ago — but there are over a hundred tattered rags in there."

Crozier stood bundled in the doorway of Sir John's former cabin where the two captains had held their sotto voce meeting. He wished Fitzjames would get to the point.

"I thought we might hold a masque for the men soon," said Fitzjames. "Nothing as fancy as your Grand Venetian Carnivale, of course, not with the . . . unpleasantness . . . out on the ice, but a diversion nonetheless."

"Perhaps," said Crozier, allowing his tone to convey his lack of enthusiasm at the idea. "We shall discuss it after this accursed Divine Service on Sunday."

"Yes, of course," Fitzjames said hurriedly. His slight lisp became more pronounced when he was nervous. "Shall I send some men to escort you back to *Terror*, Captain Crozier?"

"No. And turn in early tonight, James. You look fagged out. We'll both need our energy if we're to properly sermonize the assembled crew on Sunday."

Fitzjames smiled dutifully. Crozier thought it a wan and strangely disturbing expression.

———

On Sunday the fifth of December, 1847, Crozier left behind a skeleton crew of six men commanded by First Lieutenant Edward Little — who, like Crozier, would rather have his kidney stones removed with a spoon than be forced to suffer sermons — as well as his assistant surgeon, McDonald, and the engineer, James Thompson. The other fifty-some surviving crewmen and officers trooped off across the ice following their captain, Second Lieutenant Hodgson, Third Lieutenant Irving, First Mate Hornby, and the other masters, clerks, and warrant officers. It was almost 10:00 a.m. but would have been absolutely dark under the shivering stars except for the return of the aurora which pulsed, danced, and shifted above them, throwing a long line of their shadows onto the fractured ice. Sergeant Soloman Tozer — the shocking birthmark on his face especially noticeable in the coloured light from the aurora — headed up the guard of Royal Marines with muskets marching points, flank, and behind the column, but the white thing in the ice left the men alone this Sabbath morning.

The last full gathering of both crews for Divine Service — presided over by Sir John shortly before the creature carried their devout leader down into the darkness under the ice — had been on the open deck under cold June sunlight, but since it was now at least 50 degrees below zero outside, when the wind was not blowing, Fitzjames had arranged the lower deck for the service. The huge cookstove could not be moved, but the men had cranked up the seamen's dining tables to their maximum height, taken down the removable bulkhead partitions that had delineated the forward sick bay, and removed other partitions that had created the warrant officers' sleeping area, the subordinate officers' stewards' cubicle, and the first and second mates' and second master's berths. They also removed the walls of the warrant officers' mess room and assistant surgeon's sleeping room. The space would be crowded still, but adequate.

In addition, Fitzjames's carpenter, Mr. Weekes, had created a low pulpit and platform. It was raised only six inches because of the lack of headroom under the beams, hanging tables, and stored lumber, but it would allow Crozier and Fitzjames to be seen by the men in the back of the jam of bundled bodies.

"At least we'll be warm," Crozier whispered to Fitzjames as Charles Hamilton Osmer, *Erebus*'s bald purser, led the men in opening hymns.

Indeed, the packed bodies had raised the temperature on the lower deck here higher than it had been since *Erebus* had been burning great heaps of coal and forcing hot water through its heating pipes six months earlier. Fitzjames had also tried to lighten up the usually dark and smoky place by burning ship's oil at a furious rate in no fewer than ten hanging lamps that lit the space more brightly than at any time since sunlight had poured through the overhead Preston Patent Illuminators more than two years earlier.

The crewmen rocked the dark oak beams with their singing. Sailors, Crozier knew from his forty-plus years of experience, loved to sing under almost any circumstance. Even, if all else failed, during Divine Service. Crozier could see the top of caulker's mate Cornelius Hickey's head in the crowd, while next to him, hunched over so that his head and shoulders would not hit the overhead beams, stood the idiot giant Magnus Manson, who bellowed out the hymn in a boom so off-key that it made the grinding of the ice outside sound like close harmony. The two were sharing one of the tattered hymnals that Purser Osmer had handed out.

Finally the hymns were finished and there came a low din of shuffling, coughing, and clearing of throats. The air smelled of fresh-baked bread since Mr. Diggle had come over hours earlier to aid *Erebus*'s cook, Richard Wall, in the baking of biscuits. Crozier and Fitzjames had decided that the extra coal, flour, and lamp oil were worth expending this special day if it helped the men's morale. The darkest two months of the arctic winter were still ahead.

Now it was time for the two sermons. Fitzjames had shaved and powdered carefully and allowed his personal steward, Mr. Hoar, to take in his baggy waistcoat, trousers, and jacket, so he looked calm and handsome in his uniform and shining epaulettes. Only Crozier, standing behind him, could see Fitzjames's pale hands clenching and unclenching as he set his personal Bible on the pulpit and opened it to Psalms.

"The reading today shall be from Pthalm Forty-six," said Captain Fitzjames. Crozier winced slightly at the upper-class lisp that had become more pronounced with tension.

> God *is* our refuge and strength,
>> and ever-prethent help in trouble.
> Therefore we will not fear, though the earth give way
>> and the mountainth fall into the heart
>>> of the sea,
> though its waterth roar and foam
>> and the mountains quake with their
>>> thurging.

> There is a river whose streams make glad
>> the city of God,
>> the holy place where the Most High dwellth.
> God is within her, she will not fall;
>> God will help her at break of day.
> Nations are in uproar, kingdomth fall;

he lifts his voice, the earth melts.
The Lord Almighty is with us;
the God of Jacob is our fortreth.

Come and see the workth of the LORD,
the desolations he has brought on the earth.
He makes wars cease to the endth of the spear,
he burns the shields with fire.
"Be still, and know that I am God; I will be
exalted among the nations,
I will be exalted in the earth."

The LORD Almighty is with us;
the God of Jacob is our fortress.

The men roared "Amen" and shuffled their warming feet in appreciation.

It was Francis Crozier's turn.

The men were hushed, as much out of curiosity as respect. The Terrors in the assembled mass knew that their captain's idea of a reading for Divine Service was a solemn recitation of the Ship's Articles — "If a man refuses to obey orders from an officer, that man shall be flogged or put to death, punishment to be determined by the captain. If a man commits sodomy with another member of the crew or a member of the ship's livestock, that man shall be put to death . . ." and so forth. The Articles had the proper biblical weight and resonance and served Crozier's purpose.

But not today. Crozier reached to the shelf under the pulpit and pulled out a heavy leather-bound book. He set it down with a reassuring thud of authority.

"Today," he intoned, "I shall read from the *Book of Leviathan,* Part One, Chapter Twelve."

There was a murmuring in the crowd of seamen. Crozier heard a toothless *Erebus* in the third row mutter, "I know the fucking Bible, and there ain't no fucking *Book of Leviathan.*"

Crozier waited for silence and began.

" 'And for that part of Religion, which consisteth in opinions concerning the nature of Powers Invisible, . . ."

Crozier's voice and Old Testament cadence left no doubt as to which words were celebrated with capital letters.

" '. . . there is almost nothing that has a name, that has not been esteemed amongst the Gentiles, in one place or another, a God, or Divell; or by their Poets feigned to be inanimated, inhabited, or possessed by some Spirit or other.

" 'The unformed matter of the World, was a God, by the name of *Chaos.*

" 'The Heaven, the Ocean, the Planets, the Fire, the Earth, the Winds, were so many Gods.

" 'Men, Women, a Bird, a Crocodile, a Calf, a Dogge, a Snake, an Onion, a Leeke, Deified. Besides, that they filled almost all places, with spirits called *Daemons:* the plains, with *Pan,* and *Panises,* or Satyres; the Woods, with Fawnes, and Nymphs; the Sea, with Tritons, and other Nymphs; every River and Fountayn, with a Ghost of his name, and with Nymphs; every house with its *Lares,* or Familiars; every man, with his *Genius;* Hell, with Ghosts, and spirituall Officers, as *Charon, Cerberus,* and the *Furies;* and in the night time, all places with *Larvae, Lemures,* Ghosts of men deceased, and a whole kingdome of Fayries, and Bugbears. They have also ascribed Divinity, and built Temples to meer Accidents, and Qualities; such as are Time, Night, Day, Peace, Concord, Love, Contention, Vertue, Honour, Health, Rust, Fever, and the like; which when they are prayed for, or against, they prayed to, as if there were Ghosts of those names hanging over their heads, and letting fall, or withholding that Good, or Evill, for, or against which they prayed. They invoked also their own Wit, by the name of *Muses;* their own Ignorance, by the name of *Fortune;* their own Lust, by the name of *Cupid;* their own Rage, by the name of *Furies;* their own privy members by the name of *Priapus;* and attributed their pollutions, to *Incubi* and *Succubae:* insomuch as there was nothing which a Poet could introduce as a person in his Poem, which they did not make either a *God* or a *Divel.*' "

Crozier paused and looked out at the staring white faces.

"And thus endeth Part One, Chapter Twelve, of the *Book of Leviathan*," he said and closed the heavy tome.

"Amen," chorused the happy seamen.

———

The men ate hot biscuits and full rations of their beloved salt pork at dinner that afternoon, the extra forty-some Terrors crowding around the lowered tables forward or using casks for surfaces and extra sea chests for chairs. The din was reassuring. All of the officers from both ships ate aft, sitting around the long table in Sir John's former cabin. Besides their required antiscorbutic lemon juice that day — Dr. McDonald was now fretting that the five-gallon kegs were losing their potency — the seamen each received an extra gill of grog before dinner. Captain Fitzjames had dipped into his reserve ship's stores and provided the officers and warrant officers with three fine bottles of Madeira and two of brandy.

At about 3:00 p.m. civilian time, the Terrors bundled up, wished their *Erebus* counterparts good-bye, and went up the main ladder, out under the frozen canvas, and then down the snow and ice embankment onto the dark ice for the long walk home under the still-shimmering aurora. There were whispers and muted comments in the ranks about the *Leviathan* sermon. The majority of men were certain that it was in the Bible somewhere, but wherever it had come from, no one was quite sure what their captain had been getting at, although opinions ran strong after the double ration of rum. Many of the men still fingered their good-luck fetishes of white-bear teeth, claws, and paws.

Crozier, who headed up the column, felt half certain that they would return to find Edward Little and the watch murdered, Dr. McDonald in pieces, and Mr. Thompson, the engineer, dismembered and strewn about the pipes and valves of his useless steam engine.

All was well. Lieutenants Hodgson and Irving handed out the parcels of biscuits and meat that had been warm when they'd left *Erebus* the better part of an hour earlier. The men who had remained on watch in the cold took their extra rations of grog first.

Although he was chilled through — the relative heat of *Erebus*'s crowded lower deck had made the outside cold worse somehow — Crozier stayed on deck until the watch was relieved. The officer on duty was now Thomas Blanky, the Ice Master. Crozier knew that the men below would be doing Sunday make-and-mend, many already looking forward to afternoon tea and then supper with its sad fare of Poor John — salted and boiled codfish with a biscuit — with the hopes that there might be an ounce of cheese to go with their half pint of Burton's ale.

The wind was coming up, blowing snow across the serac-strewn ice fields on this side of the huge berg blocking the view of *Erebus* to the northeast. Clouds were hiding the aurora and stars. The afternoon night became much darker. Eventually, thinking of the whiskey in his cabin, Crozier went below.

20

BLANKY

Lat. 70°-05′ N., Long. 98°-23′ W.
5 December, 1847

Half an hour after the captain and the other men returning from the Divine Service party on *Erebus* went below, Tom Blanky couldn't see the watch lanterns or the mainmast for all the blowing snow. The Ice Master was glad the blow had come up when it had; an hour earlier and their group trek back from *Erebus* would have been a buggering bitch.

On port watch under Mr. Blanky's command this black evening were thirty-five-year-old Alexander Berry — not an especially intelligent man, Blanky knew, but dependable and good in the rigging — as well as John Handford and David Leys. This last man, Leys, now on bow watch, had just turned forty in late November and the men had thrown quite a fo'c'sle party for him. But Leys wasn't the same man who had signed up for the Discovery Service two and a half years ago. Back in early November, just a few days before Marine Private Heather had his brains dashed out while on starboard watch and young Bill Strong and Tom Evans had disappeared, Davey Leys had simply gone to his hammock and quit talking. For almost three weeks Leys had simply *left* — his eyes stayed open, staring at nothing, but he hadn't responded to voice, flame, shaking, shouts, or pinching. For most of that time he was in the sick bay, lying next to poor Private Heather, who somehow drew breaths even with his skull scooped open and some of his brains missing. While Heather lay there gasping, Davey continued to lie there in silence, staring unblinkingly at the overhead as if already dead himself.

Then, as soon as the fit had come on, it was over, and Davey was his old self again. Or almost his old self again. His appetite had come back — he'd lost almost twenty pounds during his time away from his own body — but the old Davey Leys's sense of humour was gone, as was his easy, boyish smile and his willingness to enter into fo'c'sle conversations during make-and-mend or supper. Also, Davey's hair, which had been a rich reddish brown the first week in November, was pure white when he came out of his funk. Some of the men said that Lady Silence had put a hex on Leys.

Thomas Blanky, Ice Master for more than thirty years, did not believe in hexes. He was ashamed of the men who were wearing polar bear claws, paws, teeth, and tails as some sort of anti-hex amulets. He knew that some of the less-educated men — centered around the caulker's mate, Cornelius Hickey, whom Blanky had never liked nor respected — were spreading the word that the Thing on the Ice was some sort of demon or devil — or *Daemon* or *Divell* as their captain had later said the spelling ran in his odd *Book of Leviathan* — and some around Hickey were already making sacrifices to the monster, setting them outside the forward cable locker in the hold where everyone now knew Lady Silence, obviously an Esquimaux witch, was hiding. Hickey and his giant idiot friend, Magnus Manson, seemed to be the high priests of this cult — or rather, Hickey was the priest and Manson the acolyte who did whatever Hickey said — and they appeared to be the only ones allowed to bring the various offerings down to the hold. Blanky had gone down there into the sulfurous dark and stench and cold recently and was disgusted to see little pewter plates of food, burned-down candles, tiny tots of rum.

Thomas Blanky was no natural philosopher, but he had been a creature of the arctic as both man and boy, working as able-bodied seaman or ice master for American whalers when the Royal Navy had no use for him, and he knew these polar regions as few others on the expedition did. While this area was strange to him — as far as Blanky knew, no ship had ever sailed this far south of Lancaster Sound and so near to King William Land before, nor sailed so far west of

Boothia Peninsula — most of the terrible arctic conditions were as familiar to him as a summer in Kent where he was born.

More familiar, actually, Blanky realized. He'd not seen a Kent summer in almost twenty-eight years.

The howling snow this night was familiar, as was the solid surface of ice and seracs and grumbling pressure ridges which were pushing poor *Terror* higher on its capstan of rising ice even while squeezing the life out of her. Blanky's ice-master counterpart on *Erebus,* James Reid, a man Blanky highly respected, had informed him just today after the odd Divine Service that the old flagship hadn't much longer to last. Besides its coal scuttles being drawn down even farther than the failing *Terror*'s, the ice had seized Sir John's ship in a fiercer and less-forgiving grip more than a year ago when they'd first been locked fast into their current positions.

Reid had whispered that since *Erebus* was stern-down in the encroaching ice — the opposite of *Terror*'s bow-down position — the unrelenting pressure was squeezing Sir John's ship more tightly and growing more terrible as it pushed the creaking, groaning ship higher above the surface of the frozen sea. Already the rudder had been splintered and the keel damaged beyond repair outside of a dry dock. Already the stern plates were sprung — there were three feet of frozen water in the stern, which was down by ten degrees, and only sandbags and coffer dams kept the slushy sea out of the boiler room — and the mighty oak beams that had survived decades of war and service were splintering. Worse, the spiderwebs of iron bracings set in place in 1845 to make *Erebus* impervious to the ice moaned constantly now from the terrible pressure. From time to time, smaller stanchions gave way at the join with the sound of a small cannon being fired. This often happened late at night and the men would snap upright in the hammocks, identify the source of the explosion, and go back to sleep with soft curses. Captain Fitzjames usually went below with some of his officers to investigate. The heavier braces would hold, Reid said, but only by tearing through the contracting oak-and-iron-layered hulls. When that happened, the ship would sink, ice or no ice.

Erebus's ice master said that their ship's carpenter, John Weekes, spent every day and half of most nights with a work party of no fewer than ten men down in the hold and orlop deck, shoring everything with every stout plank the ship had brought along — and many quietly borrowed from *Terror* — but the resulting web of internal wooden structure was a temporary fix, at best. Unless *Erebus* escaped the ice by April or May, Reid quoted Weekes as saying, it would be crushed like an egg.

Thomas Blanky knew ice. In the early summer of 1846, all the time he was guiding Sir John and his captain south through the long sound and newly discovered strait south of the Barrow Strait — the new strait remained nameless in their logs but some were already calling it "Franklin Strait," as if naming the channel that had trapped the dead old fool would make his ghost feel better about being carried away by a monster — Blanky had been at his station atop the mainmast, shouting down advice to the helmsman as *Terror* and *Erebus* gingerly picked their way through more than 250 miles of changing ice and narrowing leads and dead-end channels.

Thomas Blanky was good at his job. He knew that he was one of the best ice masters and pilots in the world. From his precarious post high atop the mainmast — these old bombardment ships had no crow's nests like a mere whaler — Blanky could tell the difference of drift ice from brash ice at eight miles' distance. Asleep in his cubicle, he knew at once when the ship had moved from the *glug-glug-glug* passage through sludge ice into the metal-file rasp of pancake ice. He knew at a glance which bergy bits were a threat to the ship and which could be taken head-on. Somehow his aging eyes could make out the blue-white submerged growlers in a blue-white sea alive with sun sparkles and even tell which of the growlers would merely grind and groan as they slid along the ship's hull and which — like an actual berg — would put the ship at risk.

So Blanky was proud of the job he and Reid had done leading both ships more than 250 miles south and then west of their first wintering spot at Beechey and Devon Islands. But Thomas Blanky also cursed himself for a fool and a villain for helping lead the two ships and their 126 souls 250 miles south and then west of their wintering spot at Beechey and Devon.

The ships could have retreated from Devon Island, back through Lancaster Sound and then down Baffin Bay, even if they'd had to wait two cold summers, or even three, to escape the ice. The little bay there at Beechey would have protected the ships from this open-sea ice abuse. And sooner or later the ice along Lancaster Sound would have relented. Thomas Blanky *knew* that ice. It behaved the way arctic ice was meant to behave — treacherous, deadly, ready to destroy you after a single wrong decision or moment's lapse, but predictable.

But *this* ice, thought Blanky as he stomped about the dark stern to keep his feet from freezing, seeing the lanterns glowing port and starboard where Berry and Handford paced with their shotguns, *this* ice was like no ice in his experience.

He and Reid had *warned* Sir John and the two captains fifteen months ago, right before the ships became frozen in place. *Go for broke,* Blanky had advised, agreeing with Captain Crozier that they needed to turn tail while there were still the slightest open leads, needed to seek out open water as close to the Boothia Peninsula as fast as they could steam that long-ago September. The water there close to a known coast — at least the east side of it was known to old Discovery Service and whaler veterans such as Blanky — almost certainly would have stayed liquid for another week, perhaps two, into that lost-opportunity September. Even if they hadn't been able to steam north along the coast again because of hummocky floes and old pack ice — Reid called it *screw pack ice* — they would have been infinitely safer behind the shelter of what they now were certain, after the dead Lieutenant Gore's sledge expedition last summer, was James Ross's King William Land. That landmass, as low, frozen, windswept, and lightning-ravaged as they now knew it to be, would have sheltered the ships from this Devil-sent constant northwest blast of arctic wind, blizzards, cold, and endless assaulting sea ice.

Blanky had never seen ice like this. One of the few advantages of pack ice, even when your ship was frozen in like a musket ball blasted into an iceberg, was that the pack ice *drifted.* The ships, while seemingly motionless, *moved.* When Blanky had been ice master on the American whaler *Pluribus* in '36, winter had roared in on the twenty-seventh of

August, taking everyone including the experienced one-eyed American captain by surprise and freezing them into Baffin Bay hundreds of miles north of Disko Bay.

The next arctic summer had been bad — almost as cold as this last summer, 1847, during which there had been no summer ice melt, air warmth, or return of birds or other wildlife here — but the whaler *Pluribus* was in more predictable pack ice and drifted more than seven hundred miles south until, late that next summer, they'd reached the ice line and been able to sail their way south through sludge-ice seas and narrow leads and what the Russians called *polynyas,* cracks in the ice that opened up as you watched, until the American whaler reached open water and could sail southeast to a Greenland port for refitting.

But not here, Blanky knew. Not in this truly godforsaken white hell. This pack ice was, as he'd described to the captains a year and three months ago, more like an endless glacier being pushed down from the north pole. And with the mostly uncharted bulk of arctic Canada to their south, King William Land to their southwest, and Boothia Peninsula beyond their reach to the east and nor'east, there was no real ice drift here — as Crozier's and Fitzjames's and Reid's and Blanky's repeated sun and star sextant readings kept telling them — just a sickening pivot around a fifteen-mile circumference. It was as if they were flies pinned to one of the metal music disks no longer used by the men in the Great Room below. Going nowhere. Always returning to the same spot again and again.

And this open pack ice was more like the coastal fast ice of Blanky's experience, only here at sea the ice was twenty to twenty-five feet thick around the ships rather than the three-foot depth of regular fast ice. So thick that the captains couldn't keep open the usual fire holes that *all* ships locked in the ice kept free all winter.

This ice didn't even allow them to bury their dead.

Thomas Blanky wondered if he had been an instrument of evil — or perhaps just of folly — when he had used his more than three decades of ice-master skills to get 126 men the impossible 250 miles through ice to this place where all they could do was die.

Suddenly there came a shout. Then a shotgun blast. Another shout.

21

BLANKY

Lat. 70°-05' N., Long. 98°-23' W.
5 December, 1847

Blanky tugged his right overmitten off with his teeth, let it drop to the deck, and raised his own shotgun. Tradition was for the officers on watch not to be armed, but Captain Crozier had ended that tradition with a single order. Every man on deck was to be armed at all times. Now, with his mitten off, Blanky's thin wool underglove allowed his finger to crook through the trigger guard of the shotgun, but his hand immediately felt the biting cold of the wind.

It was Seaman Berry's lantern — the port watch — whose glow had disappeared. The shotgun blast had sounded as if it had come from the left of the midship winter canvas rigging, but the Ice Master knew that wind and snow distorted sounds. Blanky could still see the glow of the starboard-side lantern, but it was bobbing and moving.

"Berry?" he shouted toward the dark port side. He could almost feel the two syllables hurled astern by the howling wind. "Handford?"

The starboard lantern glow disappeared. At the bow, Davey Leys's lantern would have been visible beyond the midship tent on a clear night, but this was no longer a clear night.

"Handford?" Mr. Blanky began moving forward to the port side of the long tent covering, carrying his shotgun in his right hand and the lantern he'd lifted off the sternpost in his left. He had three more shotgun shells in his right greatcoat pocket, but he knew from experience how long it took to fumble them out and load them in this cold.

"Berry!" he bellowed. "Handford! Leys!" One of the dangers now was that the three men would shoot each other in the dark and storm on the tilted, icy deck, although it had sounded as if Alex Berry had already discharged his weapon. There had not been a second blast. But Blanky knew that if he moved to the port side of the frozen tent pyramid and Handford or Leys suddenly came around to investigate, the nervous men might fire at anything, even a moving lantern.

He moved forward anyway.

"Berry?" he shouted, coming within ten yards of the port watch station.

He caught a blur of movement amid the driving snow, something far too large to be Alex Berry, and then there came a crash louder than any shotgun. A second explosion. Blanky staggered back ten paces toward the stern as casks, wooden kegs, boxes, and other ship's stores flew through the air. It took him a few seconds to realize what had happened; the permanent pyramid of frozen canvas running fore and aft along the centre of the deck had suddenly collapsed, throwing thousands of pounds of accumulated snow and ice in each direction even while flinging wide the deck stores beneath — mostly flammable pitch, caulkers' materials, and sand to put down for traction atop the snow deliberately shoveled onto the deck — and also sending the mainmast's lower spars, which had been rotated fore and aft more than a year ago to act as ridgepoles for the tent, crashing down onto the main hatch and ladderway.

There was no way for Blanky and the other three men on watch to get to the lower deck now, and no way that the men down there could get up to investigate the explosions on deck, not with the main spars and all that weight of canvas and snow blocking the hatch. The Ice Master knew that the men below would soon run to the forward hatch and begin unbattening its nailed-down winter seals, but that would take time.

Will we be alive when they get up here? wondered Blanky.

Moving as carefully as he could on the sand-covered packed snow of the tilted deck, Blanky made his way around the debris pile at the rear of the collapsed tent area and started down the narrow aisle on the starboard side of the heap.

A shape rose before him.

Still holding the lantern high in his left hand, Blanky lifted the shotgun, finger on the trigger, ready to fire. "Handford!" he said when he saw the pale blob of a face amid the black mass of coats and comforters. The man's Welsh wig was in disarray. "Where's your lantern?"

"I dropped it," said the seaman. The man was shaking violently, his hands bare. He huddled close to Thomas Blanky as if the Ice Master were a source of heat. "I dropped it when the thing knocked the spar down. The flame went out in the snow."

"What do you mean, 'when the thing knocked the spar down'?" demanded Blanky. "No living thing could knock the mainmast spar down."

"*It* did!" said Handford. "I heard Berry's shotgun fire. Then he shouted something. Then his lantern went out. Then I saw something . . . large, something very large . . . leap up on the spar and that's when everything collapsed. I tried to fire at the thing on the spar, but my shotgun misfired. I left it at the rail."

Leap up onto the spar? thought Blanky. The swiveled mainmast spar was twelve feet above the deck. Nothing could leap onto it. With the mainmast sheathed in ice, nothing could climb to it either. Aloud, he said, "We have to find Berry."

"There is no way in God's universe that I'm going over there to the port side, Mr. Blanky. You can write me up and have Bosun's Mate Johnson give me fifty with the cat, but there's no way in God's universe that I'm going over there, Mr. Blanky." Handford's teeth were chattering so wildly that he was barely understandable.

"Calm down," snapped Blanky. "No one's being written up. Where's Leys?"

From this vantage point on the starboard-watch side, Blanky should have been able to see David Leys's lantern glowing at the bow. The bow was dark.

"His went out the same time I dropped mine," said Handford through his clattering teeth.

"Get your shotgun."

"I can't go back there where . . . ," began Handford.

"God-*damn* your eyes!" roared Thomas Blanky. "If you don't retrieve that weapon *this gob-fucking minute,* a flogging of fifty from the cat will be the *least bugger-fucking thing* you have to worry about, John Handford. Now *move!*"

Handford moved. Blanky followed him, never turning his back on the collapsed heap of canvas at the centre of the ship. Because of the driving snow, the lantern created a sphere of light ten feet or less across. The Ice Master kept both the lantern and the shotgun raised. His arms were very tired.

Handford was attempting to retrieve his weapon in the snow with fingers that had obviously gone numb with cold.

"Where the hell are your mittens and gloves, man?" snapped Blanky.

Handford's teeth were chattering too wildly for him to respond.

Blanky set his own weapon down, brushed the seaman's arms aside, and lifted the man's shotgun. He made sure the single barrel was not blocked with snow, then broke the breech and handed the weapon back to Handford. Blanky finally had to tuck it under the other man's arm so he could cradle it with his two frozen hands. Setting his own shotgun under his left arm where he could shift it quickly, Blanky fumbled a shell out of his greatcoat pocket, loaded Handford's shotgun, and clicked it shut for the man. "If anything larger than Leys or me comes out of that pile," he said, almost shouting into Handford's ear because of the wind roar, "aim and pull that trigger if you have to use your fucking teeth to do it."

Handford managed a nod.

"I'm going forward to find Leys and help him open the forward hatch," said Blanky. Nothing seemed to be moving downhill toward the bow amid the dark jumble of frozen canvas, dislodged snow, broken spars, and tumbled crates.

"I can't . . . ," began Handford.

"Just stay where you are," snapped Blanky. He set the lantern down next to the terrified man. "Don't shoot me when I come back with

Leys or I swear to God my ghost will haunt you 'til you die, John Handford."

Handford's pale blob of a face nodded again.

Blanky started toward the bow. After a dozen steps, he was beyond the glow of the lantern but his night vision did not return. The hard particles of snow struck his face like pellets. Above him, the rising wind howled in what little rigging and shrouds they'd left in place during the endless winter. It was so dark here that Blanky had to carry the shotgun in his left hand — his still-mittened hand — while feeling along the ice-encrusted railing with his right hand. As far as he could tell, the main-mast spar here on the forward side of the mast had also collapsed.

"Leys!" he shouted.

Something very large and vaguely white in the hurtling snow lumbered out of the heap of debris and stopped him in his tracks. The Ice Master couldn't tell if the thing was a white bear or a tattooed demon or if it was ten feet in front of him or thirty feet away in the dark, but he knew that it had completely blocked his progress toward the bow.

Then the thing reared up on its hind legs.

Blanky could see only the mass of it — he sensed the dark bulk of it mostly through the amount of blowing snow it blocked — but he knew it was huge. The tiny triangular head, if that *was* a head up there in the darkness, rose higher than the space where the spars had been. There seemed to be two holes punched into that pale triangle of a head — eyes? — but they were at least fourteen feet above the deck.

Impossible, thought Thomas Blanky.

It moved toward him.

Blanky shifted the shotgun to his right hand, jammed the stock against his shoulder, steadied it with his mittened left hand, and fired.

The flash and explosion of sparks from the barrel gave the Ice Master a half-second's glimpse of the black, dead, emotionless eyes of a shark staring into him — no, not a shark's eyes at all, he realized a second later as the retinal afterimage of the blast blinded him, but two ebony circles far more frighteningly malevolent and intelligent than even a shark's black-circle gaze — but also the pitiless stare of a pred-ator that sees you only as food. And these bottomless black-hole eyes were far above him, set on shoulders wider than Blanky's arms could spread, and were coming closer as the looming shape surged forward.

Blanky threw the useless shotgun at the thing — there was no time at all to reload — and leapt for the man lines.

Only four decades of experience at sea allowed the Ice Master to know, in the dark and storm and without even attempting to look, exactly where the icy man lines would be. He caught them with the crooked fingers of his mittenless right hand, flung his legs up, found the cross ropes with his flailing boots, pulled off his left mitten with his teeth, and began clambering upward while hanging almost upside down on the inside of the inward-slanting lines.

Six inches beneath his arse and legs, something cleaved the air with the power of a two-ton battering ram swinging at full extension. Blanky heard three thick vertical ropes of the man lines rip, tear . . . impossible! . . . and swing inward, almost throwing Blanky down to the deck.

He hung on. Flinging his left leg around the outside of those lines remaining taut, he found purchase on the icy rope and began climbing higher without pausing for a second. Thomas Blanky moved like the monkey he'd been as an unrated boy of twelve who thought the masts, sails, lines, and upperworks' rigging of the three-masted warship on which he shipped had all been constructed by Her Majesty solely for his enjoyment.

He was twenty feet up now, approaching the level of the second spar — this one still set at the proper right angle to the length of the ship — when the thing below hit the base of the man-line rigging again, tearing wood and dowels and pins and ice and iron blocks completely free of the railing.

The web of climbing rope swung inward toward the mainmast. Blanky knew that the impact would knock him off and send him hurtling down into the thing's arms and jaws. Still not able to see anything more than five feet away in the blowing dark, the Ice Master leapt for the shrouds.

His freezing fingers found the spar and its lines under them at the same instant one of his flailing feet caught a foot line. This shroud-line scuttle was best done barefoot, Blanky knew, but not tonight.

He heaved himself up over the second spar, more than twenty-five feet above the deck, and clung to the icy oak with legs and arms both, the way a terrified rider would cling to the body of a horse, wildly sliding his feet along the ice-hard shroud to find more purchase on the slippery shroud lines.

Normally, even in the darkness, wind, snow, and hail, any decent sailor could scramble another sixty feet higher into the upperworks and rigging here until he reached the mainmast crosstrees, from which point he could hurl down insults at his stymied pursuer like a chimpanzee in a tall tree throwing down fruit or feces from a point of perfect safety. But there were no upperworks or high rigging on HMS *Terror* this December night. There was no point of perfect safety up here when fleeing from something so powerful it could smash a main spar. And there was no upperworks rigging to which a man could flee.

A year ago September, Blanky had helped Crozier and Harry Peglar, Captain of the Foretop, as they prepared *Terror* for her wintering-over for the second time this expedition. It was not an easy job, nor one without danger. The yards and running rigging were struck down and stored below. Then the topgallant masts and topmasts were carefully struck down — carefully because a slip with winch or block or sudden tangle of tackle could have sent the heavy masts hurtling down through the top deck, lower deck, orlop deck, and hull bottom like a massive spear piercing wicker armour. Ships had sunk from such missteps while striking down upper masts. But if they'd remained up, too many tons of ice would accumulate during the endless winter. The ice would have provided a constant barrage of missiles for the men on watch or other duty on the deck and rigging below, but the weight of it also could capsize a ship.

With only the three stumps of the lower masts remaining — a sight as ugly to a seaman as a triple-amputee human being might be to a painter of pictures — Blanky had helped supervise the loosening of all remaining shrouds and standing rigging; overly taut canvas and ropes simply could not bear the weight of so much snow and ice. Even *Terror*'s boats — the two large whaleboats and two smaller cutters, as well as the captain's skiff, pinnaces, jolly boats, and dinghies, ten in all — had been taken down, inverted, lashed, covered, and stored on the ice.

Now Thomas Blanky was on the mainmast's second-spar shrouds twenty-five feet above the deck and had only one level higher to go, and any man lines leading up to that third and last level would be more ice than rope or wood. The mainmast itself was a column of ice with an extra coating of snow on its forward curve. The ice master straddled the second spar and tried to peer down through the darkness and snow. It was pitch black below. Either Handford had extinguished the lantern Blanky had given him or it had been extinguished for him. Blanky assumed that the man was either cowering in the dark or dead; either way he would be no help. Spread-eagled over the spar shrouds, Blanky looked to his left and saw that there still was no light forward in the bow where David Leys had been on watch.

Blanky strained to see the thing directly below him but there was too much movement — the torn canvas flapping in the dark, kegs rolling on the tilted deck, loose crates sliding — and all he could make out was a dark mass shuffling toward the mainmast, batting aside two- and three-hundred-pound kegs of sand as if they were so many china vases.

It can't climb the mainmast, thought Blanky. He could feel the cold of the spar through his straddling legs and chest and crotch. His fingers were beginning to freeze through the thin undergloves. Somewhere he had lost his Welsh wig and wool-scarf comforter. He strained to hear the sound of the forward hatch being unbattened and flung free, to hear shouts and to see lanterns as the rescue party came up in force, but the bow of the ship remained a silent darkness hidden by hurtling snow. *Has it somehow blocked the forward hatch as well? At least it can't climb the mainmast. Nothing that size can climb. No white bear — if it is a white bear — has experience climbing.*

The thing began climbing the attenuated mainmast.

Blanky felt the vibration as it slammed claws into the wood. He heard the smack and scrape and grunting . . . a thick, bass grunting . . . as it climbed.

It climbed.

The thing had most probably reached the snapped-off stubs of the first spar just by raising its forearms over its head. Blanky strained to see in the darkness and was sure he could make out the haired and muscled mass hauling itself up headfirst, gigantic forelegs — or arms — as big as a man already flung over the first spar and clawing higher for leverage even while powerful rear legs and more claws there found support on the splintered oak of the spars.

Blanky inched out farther along the icy second spar, his arms and legs wrapped around the wind-thrummed ten-inch-round horizontal spar in a sort of frenzied lover's embrace. There were two inches of new snow lining the bow-facing outer curve of the ever-thinning spar and then ice under that. He used the shroud lines for purchase when he could.

The huge thing on the mainmast had reached the level of Blanky's spar. The Ice Master could see the bulk of it only by craning to look over his own shoulder and arse and even then could make it out only as a giant, pale *absence* where the subliminal vertical slash of the main-mast should be.

Something struck the spar with so much force that Blanky flew up into the air, dropping two feet back onto the spar to land hard on his balls and belly, the impact on the spar and folds of frozen shroud knocking the wind out of him. He would have fallen then if both freezing hands and his right boot hadn't been firmly entangled in the shroud lines just below the icy underside of the spar. As it was, it felt like a horse made of cold iron had bucked him two feet into the air.

The blow came again and would have launched Blanky out into the darkness thirty feet above the deck, but he was prepared for this second smash and clung with all his might. Even ready as he was, the vibration was so forceful that Blanky slipped off and swung helplessly *under* the icy spar, numb fingers and kicking boot still mixed in with the shroud lines there. He managed to leverage himself back on top of the spar just as the third and most violent blow struck. The Ice Master heard the cracking, felt the solid spar begin to sag, and realized that he had only seconds before he and the spar, the shroud, the shroud lines, the ratlines, and the wildly swinging man lines all fell more than twenty-five feet to the pitched deck and tumbled debris below.

Blanky did the impossible. On the pitching, cracking, tilted and icy spar, he got to his knees, then to his feet, standing with both arms waving comically and absurdly for balance in the howling wind, boots slipping on the snow and ice, and then he hurled himself into space with arms and hands extended, seeking one of the invisible hanging ratlines that should be — might be — *could be* — somewhere there, allowing for the ship's down-at-the-bow attitude, for the howling wind, for the impact of the blowing snow on the thin lines, and for the possible effects of the vibration from the thing's ongoing shattering of the mainmast's second level of spars.

His hands missed the single hanging line in the dark. His freezing face hit it, and as he fell, Thomas Blanky grabbed the line with both hands, slid only six feet lower along its icy length, and then began frantically to hook and haul himself up toward the third and final height of spar on the foreshortened mainmast, less than fifty feet above the deck.

The thing roared beneath him. Then came another roar as the second spar, shrouds, tackle, and lines let go and crashed to the deck. The louder of the two roars had been from the monster clinging to the mainmast.

This ratline was a simple rope which usually hung about eight yards out from the mainmast. It was meant for descending quickly from the crosstrees or upper spars, not for climbing. But Blanky climbed it. Despite the fact that the line was ice-covered and blowing in the snow and despite the fact that Thomas Blanky could no longer feel the fingers on his right hand, he climbed the ratline like a fourteen-year-old midshipman larking in the upperworks with the other ship's boys after supper on a tropical evening.

He couldn't pull himself onto the top spar — it was simply too coated with ice — but he found the shroud lines there and shifted from the ratline to the loosened, folded shroud beneath the spar. Ice broke away and hurtled to the deck below. Blanky imagined — or hoped — that he heard a tearing and banging forward, as if Crozier and the crewmen were hacking their way out of the forward battened hatch with axes.

Clinging like a spider to the frozen shrouds, Blanky looked down and to his left. Either the driving snow had let up or his night vision had improved, or both. He could see the mass of the monster. It was climbing steadily to his third and final spar level. The shape was so big on the mainmast that Blanky thought it looked like a large cat climbing a very thin tree trunk. Except, of course, thought Blanky, it looked nothing at all like a cat save for the fact that it was climbing by slamming claws deep into ice and royal oak and iron bands that a midweight cannonball could not have penetrated.

Blanky continued edging outward along the shroud, dislodging ice as he went and causing the frozen shroud lines and canvas to creak like overly starched muslin.

The giant shape behind him had reached the level of the third spar. Blanky felt the spar and shrouds vibrate and then sag as a portion of that massive weight on the mast was shifted to the spars on either side. Imagining the thing's huge forelegs thrown over the spars, imagining a paw the size of his chest freeing itself to slam into the thinner spar up here, Blanky crawled and crabbed faster, almost forty feet out from the mast now, already beyond the edge of the deck fifty feet below. A seaman falling from this far out on the spar or shrouds when working the sails would fall into the sea. If Blanky fell, it would be onto the ice more than sixty feet below.

Something snagged Blanky's face and shoulders — a net, a spiderweb, he was trapped — and for a second he came close to screaming. Then he realized what it was — the man lines, the threaded squares of primary climbing rope from the railing to the second crosstrees, rerigged for winter to the top of the stump of the mainmast so that work parties could dislodge ice up here. This was the starboard manline rigging that had been, impossibly, smashed free of its multiple moorings along the rail and deck by two blows of the thing's giant claws. Thick enough with ice now that the squares of interlaced rope acted like small sails, the loosened man lines had blown far out to the starboard side of the ship.

Once again, Blanky acted before allowing himself time to think about the action. To think about this next move, sixty feet and more above the ice, was to decide not to do it.

He threw himself from the crackling shrouds onto the swinging man-line rigging.

As he'd known it would, his sudden weight swung the lines back toward the mainmast. He passed within a foot of the huge, hairy mass at the T of spars. It was too dark to see much more than the terrible general shape of it, but a triangular head as large as Thomas Blanky's torso whipped around on a neck too long and serpentine to be of this world and there was a loud *SNAP* as teeth longer than Blanky's frozen fingers clamped shut on the air he'd just swung through. The Ice Master inhaled the breath of the thing — a carnivore and predator's hot rotten-meat exhalation, not the fishy stink Blanky had noticed coming from the open maws of the polar bears they'd shot and skinned on the ice. This was the hot stench of decaying human flesh mixed with sulfur, as warm as the blast from a steam boiler's open hearth.

At that instant Thomas Blanky realized that the seamen whom he'd silently cursed as being superstitious fools had been right; this thing from the ice was as much demon or god as it was animal flesh and white fur. It was a force to be *appeased* or worshipped or simply fled.

He'd half-expected the manrope rigging swinging below him to become stuck in the stub of the spars down there, or to snag in the port-side spar or shrouds as he swung past the centreline — then all the creature had to do was reel him in like a big fish in a net — but the momentum of his weight and twisting swung him out fifteen feet or more past and to the port side of the mainmast.

Now the man-line rigging was preparing to swing him back into the huge left forearm that he could see extending through the blowing snow and darkness.

Blanky twisted, threw his weight forward toward the bow, felt the clumsy torn rigging follow his inertia, and then he was swinging both legs free, flailing and kicking for the third-level spar on this side.

His left boot found it as he swung above it. The lug soles slipped on ice and the boot went past, but when the man line swung back toward the stern, both boots found the ice-coated spar and he pushed with all the energy in his legs.

The tangled web of man line swung back past the mainmast, but now in a curving arc toward the stern. Blanky's legs were hanging free, still kicking against empty air fifty feet above the ruined tent and stores below, and he arched his back in close to the ropes as he swung toward the mainmast and the thing waiting for him there.

Claws sliced the air not five inches from his back. Even in his terror, Blanky marveled — he knew that the arc of his kick had put almost ten feet of air between him and the mainmast as he swung past. The thing must have sunk the claws of its right paw — or hand, or talon, or Devil's nails — into the mast itself while hanging almost free and swinging six feet or more of massive left arm at him.

But it had missed.

It would not miss again when Blanky swung back to the centre.

Blanky grabbed the edge of the man-line rigging and slid down it as quickly he would a free line or ratline, his numbed fingers tearing against the cross ropes, each impact threatening to throw him off the rigging and out into darkness.

The man line had reached the apogee of its outer arc, somewhere beyond the starboard railing, and was starting to swing back.

Still too high, thought Blanky as the tangle of rope rigging above him swung back to the mainmast.

The creature easily caught the rigging as it reached the midline of the ship, but Blanky was twenty feet below that level now, using his frozen hands on the crossropes to scramble lower.

The thing began dragging the entire mass of rigging up to it.

This is God-fucking wondrous awful, Thomas Blanky had time to think as the entire ton or ton and a half of ice-encrusted manrope and human being began being pulled upward as easily and surely as if a fisherman were hauling up his net after a casting.

The Ice Master did what he had planned in the last ten seconds of inward swing, sliding lower on the rigging at the same time he shifted his weight back and forward — picturing himself a boy on a rope swing — increasing his lateral arc even as the thing above pulled him higher. As fast as he clambered down while he swung, the thing hauled him an equal distance closer. He would reach the bottom of the manrope rigging about the time the creature hauled him in and still be fifty feet in the air.

But there was still enough slack that he could arc twenty feet to starboard, both hands on the vertical lines, legs straightening against the cross-rigging. He closed his eyes and regained the image of a boy on a rope swing.

There was an anticipatory cough from less than twenty feet above him. Then came a strong jerk and the entire rigging rose another five or eight feet with Blanky on it.

Not knowing whether he was twenty feet above the deck now or forty-five, caring only about the timing of his outward swing, Blanky twisted the rigging around as he swung outward over the starboard darkness, kicked his boots free, and launched himself into the air.

The fall seemed interminable.

His first job was to twist again in midair so as not to land on his head or back or belly. There would be no give to the ice — less, of course, if he struck the railing or deck — but there was no longer anything he could do about that. The Ice Master knew as he fell that his life now depended upon simple Newtonian arithmetic; Thomas Blanky had become a minor problem in ballistics.

He sensed the starboard rail going past six feet from his head and only just had time to curl and ready his legs and extended arms before his lower body slammed into the slope of snow and ice that dropped away from the pressure-raised *Terror* like a ramp. The Ice Master had done the best dead reckoning he could on his blind outward swing, trying to place the end of his falling arc just forward of the cement-hard path of ice the men used in climbing to and from the ship, but also to place his point of impact just aft of the snowy heaps where the whaleboats were shrouded and tied down under frozen canvas and three feet of snow.

He landed on the snowy incline just forward of the ice ramp and just astern the snow-shrouded boats. The impact knocked the wind out of him. Some muscle tore or bone snapped in his left leg — Blanky had time for a prayer to whatever gods were awake this night that it was a muscle and not a bone — and then he was rolling down the long, steep slope, cursing and exclaiming as he went, kicking up his own small flurry of snow and epithets within the larger blizzard blowing around the ship.

Thirty feet beyond the ship, somewhere out on the snow-covered sea ice, Blanky rolled to a stop on his back.

He took stock as quickly as he could. His arms were unbroken, although he'd hurt his right wrist. His head seemed intact. His ribs hurt and he was having trouble taking a breath, but he thought this was probably more the result of fear and excitement than of broken ribs. But his left leg hurt like the very Devil.

Blanky knew that he had to be up and running . . . *now* . . . but he couldn't obey his own command. He was completely satisfied lying there on his back, spread-eagled on the dark ice, bleeding heat into the ice beneath him and into the air above him, trying to get his breath and wits back.

Now there were definite human cries and shouts on the foredeck. Spheres of lantern light, none wider than ten feet or so, appeared near the bow, illuminating the hurtling horizontal lines of wind-driven snow. Then Blanky heard the heavy thump and crash as the demon-thing slid down the mainmast to the deck. There came more men's shouts — alarmed now, although they wouldn't be able to see the creature clearly since it was farther astern within the tumble and jumble of broken spars, fallen rigging, and scattered casks amidships. A shotgun roared.

Aching, hurting, Thomas Blanky got to all fours on the ice. His undergloves were completely gone now. Both hands were bare. He was also bareheaded, his long grey-streaked hair blowing in the wind, its queue having come unknotted during his contortions. He could not feel his fingers, face, or extremities, but everything in between was giving him one sort of pain or another.

The creature came hurtling over the starboard railing toward him, the mass of it backlit by lantern-glow, clearing the low barrier with all four huge legs in the air.

In an instant Blanky was on his feet and running out into the sea ice and serac darkness.

Only after he'd gotten fifty yards or so from the ship, slipping and falling and rising and running again, did he realize that he may well have just signed his own death warrant.

He should have stayed close to the ship. He should have run around the snow-heaped boats along the forward starboard length of the hull, clambered over the bowsprit now pressed down deep into the ice, and made for the port side, shouting to the men above for help as he did so.

No, he realized, he would have been dead before he got through the tangle of bow rigging. The thing would have caught him in ten seconds.

Why did I run in this direction?

He'd had a plan before the deliberate fall from the rigging. What the hell had it been?

Blanky could hear scraping and thudding on the sea ice behind him.

Someone, perhaps the assistant surgeon from *Erebus,* Goodsir, had once told him and some other seamen how fast a white bear could charge across sea ice toward its prey — twenty-five miles per hour? Yes, at least that. Blanky had never been a fast runner. And now he had to dodge seracs and ice ridges and cracks in the ice that he couldn't see until he was a few feet from them.

That's why I ran this way. That was the plan.

The creature was loping along behind him, dodging the same jagged seracs and pressure-ridge slabs that Blanky was clumsily slaloming around in the dark. But the Ice Master was panting and wheezing like a torn bellows, while the huge shape behind him was grunting only slightly — with amusement? anticipation? — as its forepaws thudded down onto the ice with each stride that was the equal to four or five of Blanky's.

Blanky was in the ice field about two hundred yards from the ship now. Bouncing off an ice boulder he hadn't seen until it was too late to dodge, taking the impact on his right shoulder and feeling that shoulder instantly go numb to join other numb parts of him, the Ice Master realized that he'd been blind as a bat the entire time he'd been running for his life. The lanterns on *Terror*'s deck were far, far behind him now — an impossible distance away — and he didn't have time or reason to turn and look for them. They could give no illumination this far away from the ship, and they could only distract him from what he was doing.

What he was doing, Blanky realized, was running and dodging and swerving through his mental map of the ice fields and crevasses and small bergs that surrounded HMS *Terror* to the horizon. Blanky had had more than a year to stare out at this frozen sea with all its disturbances and ridges and bergs and upthrustings, and for a few months of that time he'd had the thin arctic daylight to see by. Even in winter, there were hours on watch in moonlight and starlight and in the glow of the dancing aurora when he'd studied this circle of ice around the trapped ship with an Ice Master's professional eye.

About two hundred yards out here in the ice jumble, beyond a last pressure ridge he'd just stumbled and clambered over — he could hear the thing leaping it less than ten yards behind him — he remembered a maze of former bergy bits, small icebergs calved from their larger brethren, upended into a tiny mountain range of cottage-sized ice boulders.

As if realizing where its doomed prey was headed, the unseen shape behind him grunted and picked up speed.

Too late. Dodging the last of the tall seracs, Blanky was into the bergy labyrinth. Here his mental map failed him — he'd only seen the miniature berg field from afar or through a telescope — and he bounced off one ice wall in the dark, fell on his arse, and was scrambling forward on all fours in the snow with the creature closing to within a few yards before Blanky regained his breath and wits.

The crevice between two carriage-sized bergs was less than three feet wide. Blanky scurried into this — still on all fours, his bare hands as unfeeling and remote as the black ice under them — just as the thing reached the crack and swept a giant forepaw in after him.

The Ice Master rejected all images of mice and cats as impossibly huge claws tossed up ice chips not ten inches from his boot soles. He stood in the narrow gap, fell, got to his feet again, and stumbled forward in near absolute blackness.

This was no good. The ice alley was too short — less than eight feet — and it had dumped Blanky into an open gap beyond it. He could already hear the thing loping and grunting its way around the block of ice to his right. He might as well be on a clear cricket pitch as try to stay here — and even the crevice, its walls more snow than ice, would be only a temporary hiding place. It was a place to wait for only a minute or so in the darkness until the thing enlarged the opening and clawed its way in. It was only a place in which to die.

The wind-sculpted little bergs he remembered from looking through his glass were . . . which way? To his left, he thought.

He staggered left, bounced off ice pinnacles and seracs that would do him no good, stumbled over a crevasse that dropped only two feet or so, scrambled up a low ridge of serrated ice, slid back, scrambled up again, and heard the thing hurtle around the ice block and slide to a stop not ten feet behind him.

The larger bergs began just beyond this ice boulder. The one with the hole he'd observed through the glass would be . . .

. . . these things move every day, every night of every day . . .

. . . they collapse, regrow, and reshape themselves as pressure shoves them willy-nilly . . .

. . . the thing is clawing its way up the ice slope behind him onto this flat but dead-end plateau of ice where Blanky now teeters . . .

Shadows. Crevices. Cracks. Dead-end alleys of ice. None large enough for him to slide into. Wait.

There was a single hole about four feet high on the face of a little upended berg on his right. The clouds parted ever so slightly and five seconds of starlight gave Blanky just enough illumination to see the irregular circle in the wall of dark ice.

He lunged forward and threw himself into it, not knowing if the ice tunnel was ten yards or ten inches deep. He didn't fit.

The outer layers of his clothing — cold-weather slops and great-coat — made him too bulky.

Blanky ripped at his clothing. The thing had clawed its way up the final slope and was behind him, rearing onto its hind legs. The Ice Master could not see it — he did not take time even to turn to look — but he could *feel* it rearing.

Without turning, the Ice Master flung his greatcoat and other layers of outer wool backward at the thing, hurling the heavy garments as quickly as he could.

There was a *woof* of surprise — a gust of sulfurous stench — and then the tearing noise of Blanky's clothing being ripped apart and tossed far out into the ice maze. But the distraction had bought him five seconds or more.

Again he threw himself forward into the ice hole.

His shoulders only just fit. The toes of his boots flailed, slid, finally found grip. His knees and fingers clawed for purchase.

Blanky was only four feet into the hole when the thing reached in after him. First it tore off his right boot and part of his foot. The Ice Master felt the shocking impact of claws into his flesh and thought — hoped — that it was only his heel that had been torn away. He had no way of knowing. Gasping, fighting a sudden stab of pain that even cut through the numbness of his injured leg, he clawed and wriggled and forced himself deeper into the hole.

The ice tunnel was tightening, growing narrower.

Claws raked ice and tore down his left leg, ripping flesh exactly where Blanky had already injured himself in the fall from the rigging. He smelled his own blood and the thing must also have smelled it because it quit clawing for a second. Then it roared.

The roar was deafening in the ice tunnel. Blanky's shoulders were jammed, he could go no farther forward, and he knew the rear half of his body was still within reach of the monster. It roared again.

Blanky's heart and testicles froze at the sound, but it did not frighten him into immobility. Using his few seconds of reprieve, the Ice Master wriggled backward into the less-restrictive space through which he'd just crawled, forced his arms forward, and kicked and kneed ice with the last of his remaining strength, ripping clothing and skin from his shoulders and sides as he tore through an ice aperture never meant for a man of even his moderate size.

Beyond this narrowest point, the ice tunnel widened and dropped lower. Blanky let himself slide forward on his belly, the slide lubricated by his own blood. His remaining clothing was in tatters. He could feel the encroaching cold of the ice against his clenched belly muscles and tightened scrotum.

The thing roared a third time but the horrible noise seemed to be a few feet farther away.

At the last instant, just before he dropped over the edge of the tunnel into an open space, Blanky was sure that all this had been for nothing. The tunnel — most likely made by melting so many months ago — had cut through the edge of the little berg but now had dropped him outside again. Suddenly, he was lying on his back under the stars. He could smell and feel his blood soaking into fresh-fallen snow. He could also hear the thing loping around the berg, first to the left, then to the right, eager to get at him, confident, certain now that it could follow the maddening smell of the human's blood to its prey. The Ice Master was too injured and too exhausted to crawl any farther. Let whatever was going to happen to him happen now and may a Sailor's God fuck to Hell this fucking thing that was going to eat him. Blanky's last prayer was that one of his bones would lodge in the thing's throat.

It was a full minute more and half a dozen more roars — each growing in volume and frustration, each coming from another point on the dark compass of night around him — before Blanky realized that the thing couldn't get to him.

He was lying in the open and under the stars here, but in a box of ice no larger than five feet by eight — an enclosure created by at least three of the thick bergs being jostled and tumbled together by the pressure of sea ice. One of the tilted bergs hung over him like a falling wall, but Blanky could still see the stars. He could also see starlight coming from two vertical apertures on opposite sides of his ice coffin — he could *see* the great mass of the predator blocking the starlight at the end of these cracks, less than fifteen feet from him — but the gaps between bergs were no more than six inches wide. The melt tunnel he'd crawled through was the only real way into this space.

The monster roared and paced for another ten minutes.

Thomas Blanky forced himself to a sitting position and set his lacerated back and shoulders against the ice. His coats and slops were gone, and his trousers, two sweaters, wool and cotton shirts, and wool undershirt were just bloody tatters, so he prepared to freeze to death.

The thing was not leaving. It paced round and round the three-berg box like some restless carnivore in one of London's trendy new zoological gardens. But it was Blanky who was in a cage.

He knew that even if the thing miraculously left, he had neither energy nor will to crawl out through the narrow tunnel. And if he could somehow make his way through the tunnel, he still might as well be on the moon — the moon which was now coming out from behind the roiling clouds and illuminating the bergs round about in a soft explosion of blue glow. And even if he miraculously crawled out of the bergy field, the three hundred yards to the ship was an impossible distance. He could no longer feel his body or move his legs.

Blanky settled his cold behind and bare feet deeper into the snow — the accumulation was greater here where the wind did not reach — and wondered if his fellow Terrors would ever find him. Why should they even look? He was just another of their party who had been carried off by the thing on the ice. At least his disappearance would not require the captain to haul another corpse — or part of a corpse wastefully wrapped in good ship's sailcloth — down to the Dead Room.

There came more roars and noises from the far end of the cracks and tunnel, but Blanky ignored them. "Fuck you and the sow or devil who spawned you," mumbled the Ice Master through numb, frozen lips. Perhaps he did not speak at all. He realized that freezing to death — even while bleeding to death, although some of the blood from his various wounds and lacerations already seemed to have frozen — was not painful at all. In truth, it was peaceful . . . quite restful. A wonderful way to . . .

Blanky realized that there was light coming through the cracks and tunnel. The thing was using torches and lanterns to fool him into coming out. But he wouldn't fall for that old ruse. He would stay silent until the light went away, until he slipped that last small bit into soft, eternal sleep. He would not give the thing the satisfaction of hearing him speak now after their long, silent duel.

"God-*damn* it, Mr. Blanky!" boomed Captain Crozier's bass bellow down the ice tunnel. "If you're in there, *answer,* God-damn it, or we'll just leave you there."

Blanky blinked. Or rather, he *tried* to blink. His lashes and eyelids were frozen. Was this some other ruse and stratagem of the demon-thing?

"Here," he croaked. And again, aloud this time, "Here!"

A minute later, the head and shoulders of the caulker's mate, Cornelius Hickey, one of the smallest men on *Terror,* poked easily through the hole. He was carrying a lantern. Blanky thought dully that it was like watching a gimlet-faced gnome being born.

In the end, all four surgeons had a go at him.

Blanky came in and out of his pleasant fog from time to time to see how things were progressing. Sometimes it was his own ship's surgeons working on him — Peddie and McDonald — and sometimes it was *Erebus*'s sawbones, Stanley and Goodsir. Sometimes it was just one of the four cutting or sawing or packing or stitching away. Blanky had the urge to tell Goodsir that polar white bears could run much faster than twenty-five miles per hour when they put their mind to it. But then again — had it been a polar white bear? Blanky did not think so. Polar white bears were creatures of this earth, and this thing had come from somewhere else. Ice Master Thomas Blanky had no doubt of that.

In the end, the butcher's bill was not so bad. Not bad at all, really.

John Handford, it turned out, had not been touched. After Blanky had left him with the lantern, the man on starboard watch had doused this light and fled the ship, running around to the port side to hide while the creature was climbing up to get to the Ice Master.

Alexander Berry, whom Blanky had presumed dead, had been found under the fallen canvas and scattered kegs right where he'd been standing port watch when the thing had first appeared there and then shattered the fore and aft ridgepole spar. Berry had hit his head seriously enough to have no memory of anything that happened that night, but Crozier told Blanky that they'd found the man's shotgun and it had been fired. The Ice Master also had fired his, of course, from point-blank range at a shape that was looming over him like a pub wall, but there had been no trace of the thing's blood anywhere on the deck at either site.

Crozier asked Blanky how this could be — how could two men fire shotguns at an animal at point-blank range and draw no blood? — but the Ice Master ventured no opinion. Inside, of course, he *knew*.

Davey Leys was also alive and unharmed. The forty-year-old on bow watch must have seen and heard much — including quite possibly the thing on the ice's first appearance on deck — but Leys was not talking about it. Once again David Leys could only stare silently. He was taken first to *Terror*'s sick bay, but since all of the surgeons needed that bloodstained space to work on Blanky, Leys was transported by litter to *Erebus*'s more spacious sick quarters. There Leys lay, according to the Ice Master's talkative visitors, once again staring unblinkingly at the overhead beams.

Blanky himself had not come through unscathed. The thing had clawed off half of his right foot at the heel, but McDonald and Goodsir had cut and cauterized what was left and assured the Ice Master that — with the help of the carpenter or ship's armourer — they would rig a leather or wood prosthesis held on by straps so that he could walk again.

His left leg had taken the worst of the creature's abuse — flesh raked away to the bone in several places and then the long leg bone itself striated with claws — and Dr. Peddie later confessed that all four of the surgeons had been sure they would have to amputate it at the knee. But slowness of infection and gangrene in a wound was one of the few blessings of the arctic, and after resetting the bone itself and receiving more than four hundred stitches, Blanky's leg — although twisted and wildly scarred and lacking entire tracts of muscle here and there — was healing slowly. "Your grandkids will love them scars," said James Reid when the other Ice Master made a courtesy call.

The cold had also taken its toll. Blanky managed to keep all of his toes — he would need them for balance on the ruined foot, the surgeons told him — but had lost all fingers save for his thumb on his right hand and the two smallest fingers and his thumb on his left hand. Goodsir, who evidently knew something about such things, assured him that someday he would be able to write and eat gracefully with just the remaining adjoining two fingers on his left hand, and be able to button his trousers and shirts again with those two fingers and the thumb on his right hand.

Thomas Blanky did not give a good gob fart about buttoning his trousers and shirts. Not yet. He was alive. The thing on the ice had done its best to make him otherwise, but he was still alive. He could taste food, chat with his mates, drink his daily gill of rum — already his bandaged hands were capable of holding his pewter mug — and read a book if someone propped it up for him. He was determined to read *The Vicar of Wakefield* before he shuffled off what was left of his mortal coil.

Blanky was alive and he planned to stay that way for as long as he could. In the meantime, he was strangely happy. He was looking forward to getting back to his own cubicle aft — between Third Lieutenant Irving's and Jopson's, the captain's steward's, equally tiny berths — and that would happen any day now, whenever the surgeons were absolutely sure they were done snipping and stitching and sniffing at his wounds.

In the meantime, Thomas Blanky was happy. Lying on his sick bay bunk late at night, the men grousing and whispering and farting and laughing in the darkened berthing space just a few feet beyond the partition, hearing Mr. Diggle growl out his commands at his lackeys as the cook baked biscuits deep into the night, Thomas Blanky listened to the grind and growl of the sea ice as it tried to crush HMS *Terror* and allowed it to put him to sleep as surely as would a lullaby from his long-sainted mother's lips.

22

IRVING

Third Lieutenant John Irving needed to know how Silence got on and off the ship without being seen. Tonight, one month to the day since he'd first found the Esquimaux woman in her lair, he would solve the puzzle if it cost him his toes and fingers.

The day after he first found her, Irving reported to his captain that the Esquimaux woman had moved her den to the forward cable locker on the hold deck. He did not report that she appeared to be eating fresh meat in there, mostly because he doubted what he had seen in that terrifying second of staring into the small flame-lit space. Nor had he reported the apparent sodomy he'd interrupted in the hold between Caulker's Mate Hickey and Seaman Manson. Irving knew that he was abrogating his professional duty as an officer in the Royal Navy's Discovery Service by not informing his captain of this shocking and important fact, but . . .

But what? All John Irving could think of as a reason for his serious breach of duty was that HMS *Terror* had enough rats aboard it already.

But Lady Silence's apparently magical appearances and disappearances — although accepted by the superstitious crew as final evidence of her witchcraft and ignored by Captain Crozier and the other officers as a myth — seemed far more important to young Irving than whether a caulker's mate and shipboard idiot were pleasuring each other in the stinking darkness of the hold.

And it *was* a stinking darkness, thought Irving, in the third hour of his watch crouched on a crate above the slush and behind a pillar near the forward cable locker. The stench in the freezing, dark hold was getting worse by the day.

At least there were no more half-eaten plates of food, tots of rum, or pagan fetishes on the low platform outside the cable locker. One of the other officers had brought this practice to Crozier's attention shortly after Mr. Blanky's amazing escape from the thing on the ice, and the captain had flown into a fury, threatening to cut off the rum ration — *forever* — of the next man stupid enough, superstitious enough, addle-brained enough, and generally *un-Christian* enough to offer up scraps of food or mugs of perfectly good watered-down Indian rum to a *native woman. A heathen child.* (Although those sailors who had gained a peek of Lady Silence naked, or heard the surgeons discussing her, knew that she was no child and muttered as much to one another.)

Captain Crozier had also made it completely clear that he would tolerate no show of white-bear fetishes. He announced at the previous day's Divine Service — actually a reading of Ship's Articles, although many of the men were eager for more words from the *Book of Leviathan* — that he would add one extra late-night watch or two seats-of-ease thunder-jar disposal duties to each man for every single bear tooth, bear claw, bear tail, new tattoo, or other fetish item he saw on that hapless sailor. Suddenly the enthusiasm for pagan fetishes became invisible on HMS *Terror* — although Lieutenant Irving heard from his friends on *Erebus* that it was still thriving there.

Several times Irving had tried to follow the Esquimaux in her furtive movements around the ship at night, but — not wanting her to know that he was following her — he had lost her. Tonight he knew that Lady Silence was in her locker. He had followed her down the main ladder more than three hours ago, after the men's supper and then after she had quietly and almost invisibly received her portion of "Poor John" cod and a biscuit and glass of water from Mr. Diggle and gone below with it. Irving posted a man at the forward hatch just forward of the huge stove and another curious sailor to watch the main ladderway. He arranged for these watches to trade off every four hours. If the Esquimaux woman climbed either ladder tonight — it was already past 10:00 p.m. — Irving would know where she went and when.

But for three hours now the cable locker doors had been tightly shut. The only illumination in this forward part of the hold had been the slightest leakage of light around the edges of those low, wide locker doors. The woman still had some source of illumination in there — either a candle or other open flame. This fact alone would cause Captain Crozier to have her plucked out of the cable locker in a minute and returned to her little den in the storage area forward of the lower-deck sick bay . . . or thrown out onto the ice. The captain feared fire in the ship as much as any other veteran sailor and he seemed to harbour no sentimental feelings toward their Esquimaux guest.

Suddenly the dim rectangle of light around the ill-fitted locker doors disappeared.

She's gone to sleep, thought Irving. He could imagine her — naked, just as he'd seen her, pulling her cocoon of furs around her in there. Irving also could imagine one of the other officers hunting for him in the morning and finding his lifeless body curled here on a crate above the slush-flooded hull, obviously an ungentlemanly cad who had frozen to death while trying to sneak a peek at the only woman on board. It would not be an heroic death report for Lieutenant John Irving's poor parents to read.

At that moment a veritable breeze of icy air moved through the already frigid hold. It was as if a malevolent spirit had brushed past him in the darkness. For a second, Irving felt the hairs on the back of his neck rise up, but then a simple thought struck him — *it's just a draft. As if someone has opened a door or window.*

He knew then how Lady Silence magically came and went from the *Terror.*

Irving lit his own lantern, jumped off the crate, splashed through the sludge-slush, and tugged at the doors of the cable locker. They were secured from the inside. Irving knew that there was no lock *inside* the forward cable locker — there wasn't even a lock on the outside since no one had any reason to attempt to steal cable hawsers — so therefore the native woman herself had found a way to secure it.

Irving had prepared for this contingency. He carried a thirty-inch pry bar in his right hand. Knowing that he would have to explain any damage to Lieutenant Little and possibly to Captain Crozier, he jammed the narrow end of the bar in the crack between the three-foot-high doors and leveraged hard. There came a creaking and groaning but the doors opened only an inch or two. Still holding the pry bar in place with one hand, Irving reached under his slops, great-coat, undercoat, and waistcoat and pulled his boat knife from his belt.

Lady Silence had somehow driven nails into the backsides of the cable locker doors and run some sort of elastic rawhide material — gut? sinew? — back and forth until the doors were secured as if by a white spiderweb. There was no way that Irving could enter now without leaving a clear trace that he'd been there — the pry bar had already seen to that — so he used the knife to slash through the cat's cradle of sinew. It was not easy. The strands of sinew were more resistant to the sharp blade than rawhide or ship's rope.

When the strands finally fell away, Irving extended the hissing lantern into the low space.

The little cave-den he'd seen four weeks earlier was, except for the absence of any flame now other than his lantern's, just as he remembered — the coiled hawsers pushed back and pulled almost overhead to create a sort of cave within the raised locker area — and there were the same signs that she'd been eating meals there: one of *Terror's* pewter plates with only a few crumbs of Poor John remaining on it, a pewter grog mug, and some sort of storage bag that looked as if Silence had stitched it together from scraps of discarded sail canvas. Also on the locker deck was one of the ship's small oil lanterns — the kind with just enough oil in it for the men to use when going above to one of the seats of ease at night. Its flue was still very warm to the touch when Irving removed his mitten and glove.

But no Lady Silence.

Irving could have tugged and jerked the heavy hawsers this way and that to look behind them, but he knew from experience that the rest of the triangular cable-locker space was crammed tight with the anchor ropes. Two and a half years since they had sailed and they still carried the stink of the Thames on them.

But Lady Silence was gone. There was no way up through the deck and beams above or out through the hull. So were the superstitious seamen correct? Was she was an Esquimaux witch? A she-shaman? A pagan sorcerer?

Third Lieutenant John Irving did not believe it. He noticed that the active breeze was no longer flowing around him. Yet the flame of his lantern still danced to some smaller draft.

Irving moved the lantern around at arm's length — that was all the free space there was in the crowded and cramped hawser locker — and stopped when the lamp flame danced the most: forward just starboard of the apex of the bow.

He set the lantern down and began moving hawser aside. Immediately Irving saw how cleverly she had arranged the massive anchor line here — what appeared to be another huge coil of hawser was merely a curled section of another coil set into an empty space to simulate a stack of hawser, easy to pull aside into her den-space. Behind the faux hawser coil was the curve of wide hull timbers.

Once again she had chosen carefully. Above and beneath the cable locker ran a complex webbing of wood and iron beams set in place during HMS *Terror*'s refitting for ice service some months before the expedition sailed. Up here by the bow there were iron vertical beams, oak crossbeams, triple-thick support struts, iron triangular supports, and huge oak diagonal beams — many as thick as primary hull timbers — lacing back and forth as part of the ship's modern-design reinforcement for the polar ice. One London reporter, Lieutenant Irving knew, had described all the tons of iron and oak internal reinforcements, as well as the addition of African oak, Canadian elm, and more African oak to the English oak on the sides of the hull, as being enough to make "a mass of timber about eight feet thick."

That was almost literally true for the actual bow and for the sides of the hull, Irving knew, but here where the last five feet or so of hull timber met at the bow in and above the cable locker, there were only the original six inches of stout English oak for the hull boards rather than the ten inches of layered hardwoods found elsewhere along both sides of the hull. It was thought that the areas a few feet to the immediate port and starboard of the heavily reinforced bow stem would have to be of fewer layers in order to flex during the terrible stresses of ice-breaking.

And so they had. The five belts of lumber at the sides of the hull, combined with the iron-and-oak-reinforced bow and internal areas, had produced a marvel of modern ice-breaking technology that no other Navy or civilian expedition service in the world could match. *Terror* and *Erebus* had gone places where no other ice ship on earth could hope to survive.

This bow area was a marvel. But it was no longer secure.

It took Irving several minutes to find it, extending the lantern for drafts and feeling with his freezing bare fingers and probing with his knife blade to see where a three-foot section of the foot-and-a-half-wide hull timber had been loosened. There. The aft end of the single curved board was secured by two long nails that now worked as a sort of hinge. The forward end — only a few feet from the huge bow and keel timber that ran the length of the ship — had been only pressed into place.

Working the hull timber loose with the pry bar — wondering how on earth the young woman could have done this with only her fingers — and then letting it drop, Irving felt the blast of cold air and found himself looking into darkness through an eighteen-inch-by-three-foot gap in the hull.

This was impossible. The young lieutenant knew that *Terror*'s bows had been armoured for twenty feet back from their stems with inch-thick rolled and tempered plates of specially fitted sheet iron. Even if an internal timber were somehow dislodged, the ship's bow areas — for almost a third of the way aft — were armour-plated.

Not now. The cold blew in from ice-black cave darkness beyond the dislodged plank. This part of the bow had been forced under the ice by the ship's constant tilt forward as ice built under *Terror*'s stern.

Lieutenant Irving's heart pounded furiously. If *Terror* were to be refloated miraculously tomorrow, she would sink.

Could Lady Silence have done this to the ship? The thought terrified Irving more than any belief in her magical ability to appear and disappear at will. Could a young woman not yet twenty years old rip iron hull plates off a ship, dislodge heavy bow timbers that it had taken a shipyard to bend and nail into place, and know *exactly* where to do all this so sixty men aboard who knew the ship better than their mothers' faces would not notice?

Already on his knees in the low place, Irving found that he was breathing through his open mouth, his heart still pounding.

He had to believe that *Terror*'s two summers of wild battle with the ice — across Baffin Bay, through Lancaster Sound, all the way around Cornwallis Island before the winter at Beechey Island, the next summer crashing south down the sound and then through what the men were now calling Franklin's Strait — somewhere there toward the end, some of the iron bow armour below the waterline must have been dislodged and this thick hull timber displaced inward only *after* the ice had seized the ship in its grasp.

But could something other than the ice have loosened the oak hull timber? Was it something else — something trying to get in?

It didn't matter now. Lady Silence could not have been gone more than a few minutes and John Irving was dedicated to following her, not only to see where she went out there in the darkness but to see if — somehow, impossibly, miraculously, given the thickness of the ice and the terrible cold — she was finding and killing her own fresh fish or game.

If she was, Irving knew, this fact might save them all. Lieutenant Irving had heard what the others had heard about the spoilage in the Goldner canned stores. Everyone aboard both ships had heard the whispers that they would be out of provisions before next summer.

He couldn't fit through the hole.

Irving pried at the surrounding hull timbers, but everything save for this one hinged board was rock solid. This eighteen-inch-by-three-foot gap in the hull was the only way out. And he was too bulky.

He stripped off his oilskin slops, his heavy greatcoat, his comforter, cap, and Welsh wig and shoved them through the gap ahead of him . . . he was still too wide in the shoulders and upper body, although he was one of the thinnest officers aboard. Shaking from the cold, Irving unbuttoned his waistcoat and the wool sweater he wore under that, shoving them through the black aperture as well.

If he couldn't get out through the hull now, he'd have the Devil's own time explaining why he came back up from the hold minus all of his outer layers.

He did fit. Just barely. Grunting and cursing, Irving squeezed through the tight space, buttons tearing off his wool shirt.

I'm outside the ship, under the ice, he thought. The idea did not seem quite real.

He was in a narrow cave in the ice that had built up around the bow and bowsprit. There was no room for him to get back into his coats and clothes, so he pushed them on ahead of him. He considered reaching back into the cable locker for the lantern, but a full moon had been in the sky when he'd been officer on watch a few hours earlier. In the end, he took the metal pry bar instead.

The ice cave must have been at least as long as the bowsprit — more than eighteen feet — and indeed may have been created by the heavy bowsprit beam's working of the ice here during the brief thaw and freeze cycles of the previous summer. When Irving finally emerged from the tunnel it took him a few extra seconds of crawling before he realized that he was out — the thin bowsprit, its mass of lashed rigging, and curtains of frozen jib shrouds still loomed over him, blocking, he realized, not only his view of the sky but also any chance for the man on bow watch to see *him.* And out here beyond the bowsprit, with *Terror* only a huge black silhouette looming above, the ice illuminated only by a few thin lantern beams, the way forward continued into and through the jumble of ice blocks and seracs.

Shaking hard, Irving tugged on his various layers. His hands were shaking too fiercely for him to button his wool waistcoat, but that didn't matter. The greatcoat was hard to pull on but at least the buttons were much larger. By the time he had his oil slops on, the young lieutenant was frozen to the bone.

Which way?

The ice jumble here, fifty feet beyond the ship's bow, was a forest of ice boulders and wind-sculpted seracs — Silence could have gone in any direction — but the ice seemed worn down in a roughly straight line out from the ice tunnel into the ship. At the very least it offered the path of least resistance — and most concealment — away from the ship. Getting to his feet, lifting the pry bar in his right hand, Irving followed the slippery ice trough toward the west.

———

He would never have found her had it not been for the unearthly sound.

He was several hundred yards from the ship now, lost in the ice maze — the blue-ice trough underfoot had long since disappeared, or rather been joined by a score of other such grooves — and although the light from the full moon and stars illuminated everything as if it were day, he had seen no movement, nor footprints in the snow.

Then came the unearthly wailing.

No, he realized, stopping in his tracks and trembling all over — he had been shaking from the cold for many minutes but now the trembling went deeper — this was not *wailing*. Not of the sort a human being can make. This was the amelodic playing of some infinitely strange musical instrument . . . part muffled bagpipe, part horn hoot, part oboe, part flute, part human chant. It was loud enough for him to hear dozens of yards away but almost certainly not audible on the deck of the ship — especially since the wind, most unusually, was blowing from the southeast this night. Yet all the tones were one blended sound from one instrument. Irving had never heard anything like it.

The playing — which seemed to begin suddenly, increase its rhythm almost sexually, and then stop abruptly, as if in physical climax and not in the least as if someone was following notes on a sheet of music — was coming from a serac field near a high pressure ridge less than thirty yards to the north of the torch-cairn path Captain Crozier insisted on maintaining between *Terror* and *Erebus*. No one was working on the cairns tonight; Irving had the frozen ocean to himself. To himself and to whoever or whatever was producing that music.

He crept through the blue-lit maze of ice boulders and tall seracs. Whenever he became disoriented, he would look up at the full moon. The yellow orb looked more like another full-sized planet suddenly looming in the starlit sky than like any moon Irving remembered from his years ashore or brief assignments at sea. The air around it seemed to quake with the cold, as if the atmosphere itself were on the verge of freezing solid. Ice crystals in the upper air had created a huge double halo encircling the moon, the lower bands of both circles invisible behind the pressure ridge and icebergs round about. Set around the outer halo, like diamonds on a silver ring, were three bright, glowing crosses.

The lieutenant had seen this phenomenon several times before this during their night-winters up here near the north pole. Ice Master Blanky had explained that it was just the moonlight refracting off ice crystals the way a light would through a diamond, but it added to Irving's sense of religious awe and wonder here in the blue-glowing ice field as that odd instrument began hooting and moaning again — just yards away behind the ice now — its tempo again hurrying to an almost ecstatic pace before suddenly breaking off.

Irving tried to imagine Lady Silence playing some hitherto unseen Esquimaux instrument — some caribou-antler variation on a Bavarian flügelhorn, say — but he rejected the idea as silly. First of all, she and the man who had died had arrived with no such instrument. And second, Irving had the strangest feeling that it was not Lady Silence who was playing this unseen instrument.

Crawling over the last low pressure ridge between him and the seracs from whence the sound was coming, Irving continued forward on all fours, not wanting the crunch of his lug-soled boots to be heard on the hard ice or soft snow.

The hooting — seemingly just behind the next blue-glowing serac, this one carved by wind into something like a thick flag — had begun again, rising quickly to the loudest, fastest, deepest, and most frenzied noise Irving had heard so far. To his amazement, he found that he had an erection. Something about this instrument's deep, booming, reed-fluttering sound was so . . . *primal* . . . that it quite literally stirred his loins even as he shivered.

He peered around the last serac.

Lady Silence was about twenty feet away across a smooth blue-ice space. Seracs and ice boulders circled the spot, making Irving feel as if he'd suddenly found himself amid a Stonehenge circle in the ice-haloed and star-crossed moonlight. Even the shadows here were blue.

She was naked, kneeling on thick furs that must be her parka. Her back was in three-quarters profile to Irving and while he could see the curve of her right breast, he could also see the bright moonlight illuminating her long, straight, black hair and setting silver highlights on the hillocked flesh of her firm backside. Irving's heart was pounding so hard that he was afraid she might hear it.

Silence was not alone. Something else filled the dark gap between Druidic ice boulders on the opposite side of the clearing, just beyond the Esquimaux woman.

Irving knew it was the thing from the ice. White bear or white demon, it was here with them — almost atop the young woman, looming over her. As much as the lieutenant strained his eyes, it was hard to make out the shape — white-blue fur against white-blue ice, heavy muscles against heavy ridges of snow and ice, black eyes that might or might not be separate from the absolute blackness behind the thing.

The triangular head on the strangely long bear neck was weaving and bobbing like a snake, he saw now, six feet above and beyond the kneeling woman. Irving tried to estimate the size of the creature's head — for future reference in terms of killing it — but it was impossible to isolate the precise shape or size of the triangular mass with its coal-black eyes because of its odd and constant movement.

But the thing was looming over the girl. Its head was almost directly above her now.

Irving knew that he should cry out — rush forward with the pry bar in his mittened hand since he had brought no other weapon except for his resheathed ship's knife — and try to save the woman, but his muscles would not have obeyed such a command at that moment. It was everything he could do to keep watching in a sort of sexually excited horror.

Lady Silence had extended her arms, palms up, like a popish priest saying Mass and inviting the miracle of the Eucharist. Irving had a cousin in Ireland who was popish, and he'd actually gone to a Catholic service with him once during a visit. The same sense of strange magical ceremony was being played out here in the blue moonlight. Silence, without a tongue, made no noise, but her arms were thrown wide, her eyes were closed, her head was thrown back — Irving had crawled far enough forward that he could see her face now — and her mouth was open and wide, like a supplicant awaiting Communion.

The creature's neck thrust forward and down as quickly as a cobra's strike and the thing's jaws opened wide and seemed to snap shut on Lady Silence's lower face, devouring half her head.

Irving almost screamed then. Only the ceremonial *heaviness* of the moment and his own incapacitating fear kept him silent.

The thing had not devoured her. Irving realized that he was looking at the top of the monster's blue-white head — a head at least three times larger than the woman's — as it had closed, but not snapped shut, its giant jaws fitting over her open mouth and upthrust jaw. Her arms were still flung wide to the night, almost as if ready to embrace the gigantic mass of hair and muscle enfolding her.

The music began then.

Irving saw the bobbing of both heads — creature's and Esquimaux's — but it took him half a minute before he realized that the orgiastic bass hootings and erotic bagpipe-flute notes were emanating from . . . *the woman.*

The monstrous thing looming as large as the ice boulders beside it, white bear or demon, was blowing down into her open mouth, playing her vocal cords as if her human throat were a reed instrument. The trills and low notes and bass resonances came louder, faster, more urgently — he saw Lady Silence raise her head and bend her neck one way while the serpentine-necked, triangular-headed bear-thing above her bent its head and neck in the opposite direction, the two looking like nothing so much as lovers straining to plunge deeper while seeking to find the best and deepest angle for a passionate open-mouthed kiss.

The musical notes pounded faster and faster — Irving was sure that the rhythm must be heard on the ship now, must be giving every man on the ship as powerful and permanent an erection as he was suffering at this second — and then suddenly, without warning, the noise cut off with the suddenness of the climax of wild lovemaking.

The thing's head reared up and back. The white neck bobbed and coiled.

Lady Silence's arms dropped to her naked sides as if she was too exhausted or transported to hold them out any longer. Her head lolled forward over her moon-silvered breasts.

It will devour her now, thought Irving through all the insulating layers of numbness and disbelief at what he had just seen. *It will rend and eat her now.*

It did not. For a second the bobbing white mass was gone, shuffled swiftly away on all fours through the blue Stonehenge of ice pillars, and then it was back, bowing its head low before Lady Silence, dropping something onto the ice in front of her. Irving could hear the noise of something organic hitting the ice and the smack had a familiar ring to it, but right now nothing was in context — Irving could make sense of nothing he saw or heard.

The white thing ambled away again; Irving could feel the impact of its huge feet through the solid sea ice. In a minute it was back, dropping something else in front of the Esquimaux girl. Then a third time.

And then it was simply gone . . . blended back into the darkness. The young woman was kneeling alone in the ice clearing with only the low heap of dark shapes in front of her.

She remained that way for another minute. Irving thought of his distant Irish cousin's popish church again and the old parishioners who stayed praying in their pews after the service had finished. Then she got to her feet, quickly slipping her bare feet into fur boots and pulling on her fur pants and parka.

Lieutenant Irving realized that he was shaking wildly. At least part of that was from the cold, he knew. He'd be lucky if he had enough warmth in him and strength in his legs to get back to the ship alive. He had no idea how the girl had survived her nakedness.

Silence swept up the objects the thing had dropped in front of her and was now carrying them carefully in her fur-parka arms, the way a woman would carry one or more infants still suckling at her breast. She seemed to be heading back to the ship, crossing the clearing to a point between the Stonehenge seracs about ten degrees to his left.

Suddenly she stopped, her hooded head turning in his direction, and although he could not see her black eyes, he could feel her gaze boring into him. Still on all fours, he realized that he was in full sight in the bright moonlight, three feet away from the concealment of any serac. In his absolute need to get a better view, he had forgotten to stay hidden.

For a long moment neither of them moved. Irving could not breathe. He waited for her motion, a slapping of ice perhaps, and then for the quick return of the thing from the ice. Her protector. Her avenger. His destroyer.

Her hooded gaze moved away and she walked on, disappearing between the ice pillars on the southeast side of the circle.

Irving waited another several minutes, still shaking as if from ague, and then he struggled to his feet. His body was frozen through, its only sensation coming from his now detumescing, burning erection and from his uncontrollable shaking, but instead of staggering toward the ship after the girl, he moved forward to where she had knelt in the moonlight.

There was blood on the ice. The stains were black in the bright blue moonlight. Lieutenant Irving knelt, tugged off his mitten and underglove, set some of the spreading stain to his finger, and tasted it. It was blood, but he did not think it was human blood.

The thing had brought her raw, warm, freshly killed meat. Some sort of flesh. The blood tasted coppery to Irving, the way his own blood or any human blood would, but he assumed that freshly killed animals also had such coppery-tasting blood. But what animal and from where? The men of the Franklin Expedition had seen no land animals for more than a year.

Blood freezes in a few fast minutes. This thing had killed its gift to Lady Silence only minutes ago, even as Irving had been stumbling around out here in the ice maze trying to find her.

Backing away from the black stain in the moonlit snow the way he might back away from a pagan stone altar where some innocent victim had just been sacrificed, Irving concentrated first on trying to breathe normally — the air was ripping at his lungs as he gasped — and then on urging his frozen legs and numbed mind to get him back to the ship.

He would not try going in through the ice tunnel and loose plank to the cable locker. He would hail the starboard lookout before he got in shotgun range and walk up the ice ramp like a man, answering no questions until he spoke to the captain.

Would he tell the captain about this?

Irving had no idea. He didn't even know if the thing on the ice — which must still be nearby — would let him return to the ship. He didn't know if he had the warmth and energy remaining for the long walk.

He only knew that he would never be the same again.

Irving turned to the southeast and reentered the forest of ice.

23

HICKEY

Hickey had decided that the tall, skinny lieutenant — Irving — had to die and that today was the day to do it.

The diminutive caulker's mate had nothing personal against the naive young toff, other than his poor timing in the hold more than a month earlier, but that was enough to swing the scales against Irving.

Work and watch schedules kept Hickey from his task. Twice he had rotated onto watch duties when Irving was officer on deck, but Magnus Manson had not been on duty abovedecks either time. Hickey would plan the timing and method of the deed, but he needed Magnus for the execution. It was not that Cornelius Hickey was afraid of killing a man; he'd cut a man's throat before he was old enough to go into a whorehouse without a sponsor. No, it was simply the means and method that this murder called for, which required his idiot disciple and arse-fuck buddy on this expedition, Magnus Manson.

Now all the conditions were perfect. It was a Friday morning work party — although "morning" meant little when it was as dark out as midnight — with more than thirty men out on the ice repairing and improving the torch-cairns between *Terror* and *Erebus*. Nine musket-armed Marines were, in theory, providing security for the work parties, but in truth the line of working men was spread out for almost a mile, with only five men or fewer under the command of each officer. The three officers here on the east half of the dark cairn trail were from *Terror* — Lieutenants Little, Hodgson, and Irving — and Hickey had helped sort the work parties so that he and Magnus were working on the farthest cairns under Irving.

The Marines were out of sight most of the time, supposedly prepared to come running should there be an alarm but really just doing their best to stay warm near the fire roaring in the iron brazier set up near the highest pressure ridge less than a quarter mile from the ship. John Bates and Bill Sinclair were also working under Lieutenant Irving this morning, but the two were chums — and lazy — and tended to stay out of the young officer's sight so they could work at the next ice cairn as slowly as they pleased.

The day, though dark as night, was not as cold as some recently — perhaps only forty-five below out — and almost windless. There was no moon or aurora, but the stars vibrated in the morning sky, shedding enough light that if a man had to walk out of the range of a lantern or torch, he could see well enough to make his way back. With the thing on the ice still out there in the darkness somewhere, not many men wandered far. Still, the very nature of finding and stacking the correctly sized ice chips and blocks to repair and enlarge a proper five-foot-tall cairn required the men to keep wandering in and out of the lantern light.

Irving was checking on both cairns while frequently giving the men a hand with the physical labour. Hickey only had to wait until Bates and Sinclair were out of sight beyond the curve in the trail through the ice blocks and Lieutenant Irving's guard was down.

The caulker's mate could have used a hundred iron or steel instruments from the ship — a Royal Navy vessel was a treasure trove of murder weapons, some of them quite ingenious — but he preferred that Magnus simply blindside the blond-haired dandy of an officer, haul him off twenty yards or so into the ice, break his neck, then — when he was well and truly dead — rip some of the toff's clothing off, smash in his ribs, kick in his pink-cheeked happy face and teeth, break an arm and two legs (or a leg and two arms), and leave the corpse there on the ice to be found. Hickey had already chosen the killing ground — an area of tall seracs and with no snow underfoot in which Manson would leave boot prints. He'd warned Magnus not to get the lieutenant's blood on him, not to leave any sign that he'd been there with him, and, most important, not to take time to rob the man.

The thing on the ice had killed men with about every variation of violence imaginable, and if the physical damage to poor Lieutenant Irving was vicious enough, no one on either ship would give a second thought as to what happened. Lieutenant John Irving would be just another canvas-wrapped corpse for *Terror*'s Dead Room.

Magnus Manson was not a born killer — just a born idiot — but he'd murdered men for his caulker's-mate lord and master before. It would not bother him to do so again. Cornelius Hickey doubted that Magnus would even ask himself why the lieutenant had to die — it was just another order from his master to be obeyed. So Hickey was surprised when the physical giant pulled him aside when Lieutenant Irving was out of earshot and whispered with some urgency, "His ghost won't haunt me, will it, Cornelius?"

Hickey patted his huge partner on the back. "Of course not, Magnus. I wouldn't tell you to do nothing that led to having a ghost haunt you, now would I, love?"

"No, no," rumbled Manson, shaking his head in agreement. His wild hair and beard seemed to leap out from under the wool comforter and Welsh wig. His heavy brow furrowed. "By *why* won't his ghost haunt me, Cornelius? Me killin' him while not having nothing against him and all?"

Hickey thought fast. Bates and Sinclair were walking farther on to where a work party from *Erebus* was erecting a snow-block fence along a twenty-yard stretch where the wind always blew. More than one man had gotten lost in whiteouts there, and the captains thought that a snow fence would improve the couriers' chances of finding the next cairns. Irving would make sure that Bates and Sinclair were busy on their task there, and then he'd walk back to where he and Magnus were working alone on the last cairn before the clearing.

"That's *why* the lieutenant's ghost won't haunt you, Magnus," he whispered to the stooping giant. "You kill a man in heat of temper, now *that's* a reason for that man's ghost to come back and try to get even with you. It resents what you did. But Mr. Irving's ghost now, it'll know there was nothing personal in what you had to do, Magnus. It won't have no reason to come back to bother you."

Manson nodded but did not look completely convinced.

"Besides," continued Hickey, "the ghost won't be able to find its soddin' way back to the ship now, will it? Everyone knows that when someone dies outside here, so far from the ship, the ghost goes straight up. It can't figure its way through all the ice ridges and bergs and such. Ghosts ain't the smartest blokes around, Magnus. Take my word on that, m'love."

The huge man brightened at hearing this. Hickey could see Irving returning through the torchlit gloom. The wind was coming up and causing the torch flames to dance wildly. *Better if there's wind,* thought Hickey. *If Magnus or Irving make some noise, no one'll hear.*

"Cornelius," whispered Manson. He looked worried again. "If *I* die out here, does that mean my ghost won't be able to find its way back to the ship? I'd hate to be out here in the cold so far away from you."

The caulker's mate patted the slop-shrouded wall of the giant's back. "You ain't going to die out here, love. You have my solemn promise as a Mason and a Christian on that. Now hush and get ready. When I take off my cap and scratch my head, you grab Irving from behind and drag him to where I showed you. Remember — don't leave no boot prints behind and don't get no blood on you."

"I won't, Cornelius."

"That's a good love."

The lieutenant came closer in the darkness, moving into the dim circle of light thrown by the lantern on the ice here near the cairn. "Almost finished with this cairn, Mr. Hickey?"

"Aye, sir. Just set these last blocks up here and it's done, Lieutenant. Solid as a lamppost in Mayfair."

Irving nodded. He seemed to be uncomfortable to be alone with the two seamen, even though Hickey was using his most affable and charming voice. *Well, fuck you,* thought the caulker's mate as he continued to show his gap-toothed smile. *You ain't going to be around much longer to put on such dandified airs, you blond-haired, apple-cheeked bastard. Five minutes and you'll be just another frozen side of beef to hang down in the hold, boyo. Too bad them rats are so hungry these days that they'll eat even a fucking lieutenant, but nothing I can do about that.*

"Very good," said Irving. "When you and Manson are finished, please join Mr. Sinclair and Mr. Bates on working on the wall. I'm going to walk back and bring up Corporal Hedges with his musket."

"Aye, sir," said Hickey. He caught Magnus's eye. They had to intercept Irving before he walked back along the dimly visible line of torches and lanterns. It would do no good to have Hedges or another Marine up here.

Irving walked to the east but paused at the edge of the light, obviously waiting for Hickey to set the last two blocks of ice in place at the top of the rebuilt cairn. As the caulker's mate bent to lift the penultimate square of ice, he nodded to Magnus. His partner had moved into position behind the lieutenant.

Suddenly there was an explosion of shouts from the darkness to the west. A man screamed. More voices joined in the shouting.

Magnus's huge hands were hovering just behind the lieutenant's neck — the big man had removed his mittens for a better grip, and his undergloves loomed black just beyond Irving's pale face in the lantern light.

More shouts. A musket fired.

"Magnus, *no!*" shouted Cornelius Hickey. His partner had been about to break Irving's neck despite the commotion.

Manson stepped back into the darkness. Irving, who had taken three steps toward the shouting in the west, whirled in confusion. Three men came running along the ice path from the direction of *Terror.* One of them was Hedges. The roly-poly Marine was wheezing as he ran, his musket held in front of his massive bulge of belly.

"Come!" said Irving and led the way toward the shouting. The lieutenant was carrying no weapon, but he'd grabbed up the lantern. The six of them ran across the sea ice, out of the seracs, into the starlit clearing where several men were milling. Hickey could make out the familiar Welsh wigs of Sinclair and Bates and recognized one of the three Erebuses already there as Francis Dunn, his caulker's-mate counterpart on the other ship. He saw that the musket that had fired belonged to Private Bill Pilkington, who'd been in the hunting blind when Sir John was killed last June and who had been shot in the shoulder by one of his fellow Marines during those moments of chaos. Now Pilkington was reloading and then aiming the long musket into the darkness beyond a fallen section of the snow fence wall.

"What has happened?" Irving demanded of the men.

Bates answered. He, Sinclair, and Dunn, as well as Abraham Seeley and Josephus Greater from *Erebus*, had been working on the wall under the command of *Erebus*'s first mate, Robert Orme Sergeant, when suddenly one of the larger blocks of ice just beyond the circle of lantern and torchlights had seemed to come alive.

"It lifted Mr. Sergeant ten feet into the air by his head," said Bates, his voice shaking.

"It's the God's truth," said Caulker's Mate Francis Dunn. "One minute 'e was standin' among us, next minute 'e's flying up into the air so alls we can see is the bottom of 'is boots. And the noise . . . the crunching . . ." Dunn broke off and continued breathing hard until his pale face was all but lost in a halo of ice crystals.

"I was coming up to the torches when I saw Mr. Sergeant just . . . disappear," said Private Pilkington, lowering the musket with shaking arms. "I fired once as the thing went back into the seracs. I think I hit it."

"You could've hit Robert Sergeant just as easily," said Cornelius Hickey. "Maybe he was still alive when you shot."

Pilkington gave *Terror*'s caulker's mate a look of pure venom.

"Mr. Sergeant wasn't alive," said Dunn, not even noticing the exchange of glares between the Marine and Hickey. " 'E screamed once and the thing crunched 'is skull like a walnut. I seen it. I *'eard* it."

Others came running up then, including Captain Crozier and Captain Fitzjames, looking wan and insubstantial even in his heavy layers of slops and greatcoat, and Dunn, Bates, and the others all rushed to explain what they had seen.

Corporal Hedges and two other Marines who had run to the commotion returned from the darkness to say there was no sign of

Mr. Sergeant, only a thick trail of blood and torn clothing that led off into the thicker ice jumble in the direction of the largest iceberg.

"It wants us to follow," muttered Bates. "It'll be waiting for us."

Crozier showed his teeth in something between a mad grin and a snarl. "Then we won't disappoint it," he said. "This is as good a time as any to go after the thing again. We have the men out on the ice already, we have enough lanterns, and the Marines can fetch more muskets and shotguns. And the trail is fresh."

"Too fresh," muttered Corporal Hedges.

Crozier barked orders. Some men went back to the two ships to bring the weapons. Others formed up in hunting parties around the Marines, who were already armed. Torches and lanterns were brought from the work sites and assigned to the killing parties. Dr. Stanley and Dr. McDonald were sent for in the low probability that Robert Orme Sergeant might still be alive or the higher probability that someone else might be injured.

After Hickey was handed a musket, he considered shooting Lieutenant Irving by "accident" once out in the dark, but the young officer now seemed wary of both Manson and the caulker's mate. Hickey caught several concerned glances the toff was throwing toward Magnus before Crozier assigned them to different search parties, and he knew that whether Irving had caught a glimpse of Magnus behind with his arms raised in that second before the shots and shouts were first heard or whether the officer simply sensed something wrong, it wouldn't be as easy to ambush him the next time.

But they would. Hickey was afraid that John Irving's suspicions would finally cause him to report to the captain what he'd seen in the hold, and the caulker's mate could not abide that. It wasn't so much the punishment for sodomy that bothered him — seamen were rarely hanged anymore, nor flogged around the fleet for that matter — but rather the ignominy. Caulker's Mate Cornelius Hickey was no mere idiot's bum-bugger.

He would wait until Irving lowered his guard again and then do the deed himself if he had to. Even if the ships' surgeons discovered that the man had been murdered, it wouldn't matter. Things had gone too far on this expedition. Irving would be just another corpse to deal with come the thaw.

In the end, Mr. Sergeant's body was not found — the blood and strewn clothing trail ended halfway to the towering iceberg — but no one else died in the search. A few men lost toes to the cold and everyone was shaking and frostbitten to some extent when they finally called off the hunt an hour after their supper should have been served. Hickey did not see Lieutenant Irving again that afternoon.

It was Magnus Manson who surprised him as they trudged back to *Terror* again. The wind was beginning to howl at their backs and the Marines slouched along with rifles and muskets at the ready.

Hickey realized that the idiot giant next to him was weeping. The tears instantly froze to Magnus's bearded cheeks.

"What is it, man?" demanded Hickey.

"It's sad, is all, Cornelius."

"What is sad?"

"Poor Mr. Sergeant."

Hickey shot a glance at his partner. "I didn't know you had such tender feelings for them damned officers, Magnus."

"I don't, Cornelius. They can all die and be damned for all I care. But Mr. Sergeant died out on the ice."

"So?"

"His ghost won't find his way back to the ship. And Captain Crozier passed the word when we was done searchin' that we're all having an extra tot o' rum this evenin'. Makes me sad his ghost won't be there, is all. Mr. Sergeant always liked his rum, Cornelius."

24

CROZIER

Lat. 70°-05' N., Long. 98°-23' W.
31 December, 1847

C hristmas Eve and Christmas Day about HMS *Terror* were low-key to the point of invisibility, but the Second Grand Venetian Carnivale on New Year's Eve would soon make up for that.

There had been four days of violent storms keeping the men inside in the days preceding Christmas — the blizzards were so fierce that the watches had to be shortened to one hour — and Christmas Eve and the sacred day itself became exercises in lower-deck gloom. Mr. Diggle had prepared special dinners — cooking up the last of the noncanned salt pork in half a dozen imaginative ways, along with the last of the jugged hares depickled from their briny casks. In addition, the cook had — with the recommendation of the quartermasters, Mr. Kenley, Mr. Rhodes, and Mr. David McDonald, as well as the careful supervision of surgeons Peddie and Alexander McDonald — chosen from some of the better-preserved Goldner tinned goods, including turtle soup, beef à la Flamande, truffled pheasant, and calf's tongue. For dessert both evenings, Mr. Diggle's galley slaves had cut and scraped the worst of the mold from the remaining cheeses, and Captain Crozier had contributed the last five bottles of brandy from the Spirit Room's stores set aside for special occasions.

The mood stayed sepulchral. There were a few attempts to sing by both the officers in the freezing Great Room astern and the common seamen in their slightly warmer berthing space forward — there was not enough coal left in the hold-deck scuttles for extra heating even if it was Christmas — but the songs died after a few rounds. Lamp oil had to be conserved, so the lower deck had all the visual cheer of a Welsh mine illuminated by a few flickering candles. Ice covered the timbers and beams and the men's blankets and wool clothing were always damp. Rats scuttled everywhere.

The brandy raised spirits some, but not enough to dispel the literal and emotional gloom. Crozier came forward to chat with the men, and a few handed him presents — a tiny pouch of hoarded tobacco, the carving of a white bear running, the exaggerated ursine cartoon face suggesting fear (given in jest, almost certainly, and probably with some trepidation lest the formidable captain punish the man for fetishism), a mended red-wool undershirt from a man's recently deceased friend, an entire carved chess set from Marine Corporal Robert Hopcraft (one of the quietest and least assuming men on the expedition and the one who had been promoted to corporal after receiving eight broken ribs, a fractured collarbone, and a dislocated arm during the thing's attack on Sir John's hunting blind in June). Crozier thanked everyone, pressed hands and shoulders, and went back to the officers' mess, where the mood was a little more lively thanks to First Lieutenant Little's surprise donation of two bottles of whiskey he'd kept hidden for almost three years.

The storm stopped on the morning of 26 December. Snow had drifted twelve feet above the level of the bow and six feet higher than the railing along the starboard forward quarter. After digging the ship out and excavating the cairn-lined path between the ships, the men got busy preparing for what they were calling the Second Grand Venetian Carnivale — the first one, Crozier assumed, being the one he'd taken part in as a midshipman on Parry's botch of a polar voyage in 1824.

On that midnight-black morning of 26 December, Crozier and First Lieutenant Edward Little left the supervision of the shoveling and surface parties to Hodgson, Hornby, and Irving and made the long walk through the drifts to *Erebus*. Crozier was mildly shocked to find that Fitzjames had continued to lose weight — his waistcoat and trousers were several sizes too large for him now despite more obvious attempts by his steward to take them in — but he was even more shocked during their conversation when he realized that *Erebus*'s commander was not fully paying attention most of the time. Fitzjames seemed distracted, rather like a man pretending to converse but whose actual attention was riveted on music being played in some adjoining room.

"Your men are dyeing sail canvas out on the ice," said Crozier. "I saw them preparing large vats of green, blue, and even black dye. For perfectly good spare sail. Is this acceptable to you, James?"

Fitzjames smiled distantly. "Do you really think we shall need that sail again, Francis?"

"I hope to Christ we will," grated Crozier.

The other captain's serene and maddening little smile remained. "You should see our hold deck, Francis. The destruction has proceeded and accelerated since our last inspection the week before Christmas. *Erebus* would not stay afloat an hour in open water. The rudder is in splinters. And it was our spare."

"New rudders can be jury-rigged," said Crozier, fighting the urge to grind his teeth and clench his fists. "Carpenters can shore up sprung timbers. I've been working on a plan for digging a pit in the ice around both ships, creating dry docks about eight feet deep in the ice itself before the spring thaw. We can get to the outer hulls that way."

"Spring thaw," repeated Fitzjames and smiled almost condescendingly.

Crozier decided to change the subject. "You're not worried about the men conducting this elaborate Venetian Carnivale?"

Fitzjames defied his gentleman's heritage by shrugging. "Why should I be? I can't speak for your ship, Francis, but Christmas on *Erebus* was an exercise in misery. The men need something to raise their morale."

Crozier couldn't argue the point about Christmas being an exercise in misery. "But a carnivale masque on the ice during another day of total darkness?" he said. "How many hands will we lose to the thing waiting out there?"

"How many will we lose if we hide in our ships?" asked Fitzjames. Both the small smile and the distracted air remained. "And it worked out all right when you had the first Venetian Carnivale under Hoppner and Parry in '24."

Crozier shook his head. "That was only two months after we were first frozen in," he said softly. "And both Parry and Hoppner were fanatics about discipline. Even with all the frivolity and both captains' love of theatrics, Edward Parry used to say, 'masquerades without licentiousness' and 'carnivals without excess!' Our discipline has not been so well maintained on this expedition, James."

Fitzjames finally lost his distracted air. "Captain Crozier," he said stiffly, "are you accusing me of allowing discipline to become lax aboard my ship?"

"No, no, no," said Crozier, not knowing if he was accusing the younger man of that yet or not. "I am just saying that this is our third *year* in the ice, not our third month as it was with Parry and Hoppner. There's bound to be some loss of discipline to go along with illness and sagging morale."

"Would that not be all the more reason for allowing the men to have this diversion?" asked Fitzjames, his voice still brittle. His pale cheeks had coloured at his superior's implied criticism.

Crozier sighed. It was too late to stop this God-damned masque now, he realized. The men had the bit in their teeth, and those on *Erebus* who were heading up the Carnivale preparations most enthusiastically were precisely those men who would be the first to foment mutiny should the time come. The trick as captain, Crozier knew, was never to allow that time to come. He honestly did not know whether this carnivale would help or hurt that cause.

"All right," he said at last. "But the men have to understand that they may not waste even a lump, drop, or drip of coal, lamp oil, pyroligneous fuel, or ether for the spirit stoves."

"They promise that it will be torches only," said Fitzjames.

"And there's no extra spirits or food for that day," added Crozier. "We've just gone on the severely reduced rations today. We're not changing that on the fifth day for a masque carnivale that neither of us fully endorsed."

Fitzjames nodded. "Lieutenant Le Vesconte, Lieutenant Fairholme, and some of the men who are better than average rifle shots will go on hunting parties this week before the carnivale in hopes of finding game, but the men understand that it is rations as usual — or rather, the new, reduced fare — should the hunters return empty-handed."

"As they have every other time in the past three months," muttered Crozier. In a friendlier voice, he said, "All right, James. I'll be getting back." He paused at the doorway of Fitzjames's tiny cabin. "By the way, why *are* they dyeing the sails green, black, and those other colours?"

Fitzjames smiled distractedly. "I have no idea, Francis."

———

The morning of Friday, 31 December, 1847, dawned cold but still — although of course there was no real dawn. *Terror*'s morning watch under Mr. Irving registered the temperature as −73 degrees. There was no measurable wind. Clouds had moved in during the night and now concealed the sky from horizon to horizon. It was very dark.

Most of the men seemed eager to head off to Carnivale as soon as breakfast was finished — a faster meal on the new rations, consisting of a single ship's biscuit with jam and a reduced scoop of Scotch barley mush with a dollop of sugar — but all ship's duties had to be attended to and Crozier had agreed to liberty for general attendance at the gala only after the day's work and supper were finished. Still, he'd agreed that those men without specific duties that day — holystoning the lower deck, the usual watches, deicing the rigging, deck shoveling, ship repair, cairn repair, tutoring — could go work on final preparations for the masque, and about a dozen men headed off into the darkness after breakfast, two Marines with muskets accompanying them.

By noon and the issuing of the further-diluted grog, the excitement of the remaining ship's company was a palpable thing. Crozier released six more men who'd finished their day's duties and sent Second Lieutenant Hodgson along with them.

That afternoon, while pacing the stern deck in the dark, Crozier could already see the bright glow of torches just beyond the largest iceberg rising between the two ships. There still was no wind or starlight.

By supper time, the remaining men were as fidgety as young children on Christmas Eve. They finished their meal in record time, although with the reduced rations — since this Friday was not a "flour day" with baking, they were eating little more than Poor John, some Goldner canned vegetables, and two fingers of Burton's ale — and Crozier didn't have the heart to hold them in the ship while the officers finished their more leisurely mess. Besides, the remaining officers on board were as eager as the seamen to go to Carnivale. Even the engineer, James Thompson, who rarely showed interest in anything outside the machinery in the hold and who had lost so much weight he resembled an ambulatory skeleton, was on the lower deck and dressed and ready to go.

So by 7:00 p.m., Captain Crozier found himself bundled in every layer he could add on, making the final inspection of the eight men left to watch the ship — First Mate Hornby had the duty but would be relieved before midnight by young Irving, who would return with three seamen so that Hornby and his watch could attend the gala — and then they were descending the ice ramp to the frozen sea and walking briskly through −80-degree air toward *Erebus*. The crowd of thirty-some men soon strung out into a long line in the dark, and Crozier found himself walking with Lieutenant Irving, Ice Master Blanky, and a few petty officers.

Blanky was moving slowly, using a well-padded crutch under his right arm since he'd lost the heel on his right foot and still hadn't quite mastered walking on its wood-and-leather replacement, but seemed in a fine mood.

"Good evenin' to you, Captain," said the ice master. "Don't let me slow you down, sir. My mates here — Fat Wilson and Kenley and Billy Gibson — will see me there."

"You seem to be moving as fast as we are, Mr. Blanky," said Crozier. As they passed the torches lit on every fifth cairn, he noticed that there still was no breath of wind; the flames flickered vertically. The path had been well trod out, the pressure ridge gaps shoveled and hacked out to provide an easy passage. The large iceberg still half a mile ahead of them seemed to be lit from within by all the torches burning on the other side of it and now resembled some phantasmagorical siege tower glowing in the night. Crozier recalled going to regional Irish fairs when he was a boy. The air tonight, while a good bit colder than an Irish summer night's, was filled with a similar excitement. He glanced behind them to make sure that Private Hammond, Private Daly, and Sergeant Tozer were bringing up the rear with their weapons at port arms and their outer mittens off.

"Strange how excited the men are about this Carnivale, ain't it, Captain?" said Mr. Blanky.

Crozier could only grunt at that. This afternoon he had drunk the last of his self-rationed whiskey. He dreaded the coming days and nights.

Blanky and his mates were moving so quickly — crutch or no — that Crozier let them get ahead. He touched Irving's arm, and the gangly lieutenant dropped back from where he was walking with Lieutenant Little, surgeons Peddie and McDonald, the carpenter, Honey, and others.

"John," Crozier said when they were out of earshot of the officers but still far enough ahead of the Marines so as not to be heard, "any news of Lady Silence?"

"No, Captain. I checked the forward locker myself less than an hour ago, but she'd already gone out her little back door."

When Irving had reported to Crozier on their Esquimaux guest's extracurricular excursions earlier in December, the captain's first instinct had been to collapse the narrow ice tunnel, seal and reinforce the ship's bows, and evict the wench onto the ice once and for all.

But he hadn't done that. Instead, Crozier had ordered Lieutenant Irving to assign three crewmen to watch Lady Silence whenever that was feasible and for him to follow her out onto the ice again if possible. So far, they'd not seen her go out her back door again, although Irving had spent hours hiding in the ice jumble beyond the ship's bow, waiting. It was as if the woman had seen the lieutenant during her witchly meeting with the creature on the ice, as if she had *wanted* him to see and hear her out there, and that had been enough. She appeared to be subsisting on ship's rations these days and using the forward cable locker only for sleeping.

Crozier's reason for not immediately evicting the native woman was simple: his men were beginning the slow process of starving to death, and they would not have adequate stores to get through the spring, much less the next year. If Lady Silence *was* getting fresh food from the ice in the middle of winter — trapping seals perhaps, walrus hopefully — it was a skill that Crozier knew his crews would have to learn in order to survive. There was not a serious hunter or ice fisherman among the hundred-some survivors.

Crozier had discounted Lieutenant Irving's embarrassed, heavily self-critical account of seeing something that seemed like the creature on the ice making some sort of music with the woman and bringing food offerings to her. The captain simply would never believe that Silence had trained a huge white bear — if such the thing was — to hunt and bring her fish or seal or walrus like a proper English bird dog fetching pheasant for its master. As for the music . . . well, that was absurd.

But she had chosen this day to go missing again.

"Well," said Crozier, his lungs aching from the cold air, even filtered as it was through his thick wool comforter, "when you return with the relief watch at eight bells, check her locker again, and if she's not there . . . what in the name of Christ Almighty?"

They had passed through the last line of pressure ridges and come out onto the flat sea ice on the last quarter mile to *Erebus.* The scene that met Crozier's eyes made his jaw sag under the wool scarf and high-pulled jacket collars.

The captain had assumed that the men would be having the Second Grand Venetian Carnivale on the flat sea ice immediately below *Erebus,* the way Hoppner and Parry had set their masque on the short stretch of ice between the frozen-in *Hecla* and *Fury* in 1824, but while *Erebus* sat bow up, dark and desolate-looking on its dirty pedestal of ice, all the light, torches, motion, and commotion came from an area a quarter of a mile away, immediately in front of the largest iceberg.

"Good heavens," said Lieutenant Irving.

While *Erebus* looked to be a dark hulk, a new mass of rigging — a veritable city of coloured canvas and flickering torches — had risen on the bare circle of sea ice, forest of seracs, and wide-open area beneath the towering, glowing iceberg. Crozier could only stand and stare.

The riggers had been busy. Some obviously had ascended the berg itself, sinking huge ice screws deep in the ice sixty feet high on its face, pounding in bolt rings and pulley stands, adding enough rigging, running lines, and blocks from the stores to outfit a three-masted man-of-war at full sail.

A spiderweb of a hundred ice-frosted lines ran down from the berg and back toward *Erebus,* supporting a city of lighted and coloured tent walls. These dyed walls of canvas — some of the mains'l sheets thirty feet high and taller — were staked to sea ice and serac and ice block but pulled taut on their vertical spars with stays running diagonally to the tall berg.

Crozier walked closer, still blinking. The ice in his eyelashes threatened to freeze his eyelids shut, but he continued blinking.

It was as if a series of gigantic coloured tents had been pitched on the ice, but these tents had no roofs. The vertical walls, lighted from within and without by scores of torches, snaked from the open sea ice into the serac forest and continued up to the vertical wall of the iceberg itself. As it was, giant rooms or coloured apartments had been erected almost overnight on the ice. Each chamber stood at an angle to the preceding chamber, a sharp turn in the rigging, staves, and canvas apparent every twenty yards or so.

The first chamber opened eastward onto the ice. The canvas here had been dyed a bright, rich blue — the blue of skies not seen in so many months that the colour made a knot rise in Captain Crozier's constricted throat — and torches and braziers of flame outside the canvas chamber's vertical sides made the blue walls glow and pulse.

Crozier walked past Mr. Blanky and his mates, who were staring in open wonder. "Christ," he heard the ice master mutter.

Crozier walked still closer, actually entering the space defined by the glowing blue walls.

Brightly clad and strangely garbed figures pranced and swooped around him — ragpickers with streaming comet tails of coloured cloth trailing behind them, tall chimney sweeps in death-black tails and sooty top hats doing jigs, exotic birds with long gold beaks stepping lightly, sheikhs of Araby with red turbans and pointed Persian slippers sliding along the dark ice, pirates with blue death masks pursuing a prancing unicorn, generals of Napoleon's army wearing white masks from some Greek Chorus filing by in solemn procession. Something dressed all in bulky green — a wood sprite? — ran up to Crozier on the unslippery ice and chirped in falsetto, "The trunk of costumes is to your left, Captain. Feel free to mix and match," and then the apparition was gone, blending back into the shifting crowds of bizarrely dressed figures.

Crozier continued walking deeper into the maze of coloured apartments.

Beyond the blue chamber, turning sharply to the right, was a long purple room. Crozier saw that it was not empty. The men realizing this Carnivale had placed rugs, tapestries, tables, or casks here and there in each apartment, their furnishings and fixtures dyed or painted the same hue as the glowing walls.

Beyond the purple room, bending back sharply to the left here but at such an odd angle that Crozier would have had to look at the stars — had there been any stars visible — to ascertain his exact bearings, was a long green chamber. This long room held the most revelers yet: more exotic birds, a princess with a long horse's face, creatures so segmented and oddly jointed that they appeared to be giant insects.

Francis Crozier recalled none of these costumes from Parry's trunks on the *Fury* and *Hecla,* but Fitzjames had insisted that Franklin had brought precisely those moldering old artifacts.

The fourth chamber was furnished and lighted with orange. The torchlight through the thin orange-dyed canvas here seemed rich enough to taste. More orange canvas, painted and dyed to resemble tapestries, had been laid out on the sea ice, and there was a huge punch bowl on the orange-sheeted table at the center of the interior space. At least thirty or more wildly costumed figures had converged on the punch bowl, some dipping their beaked or fanged visages to drink deeply.

Crozier realized with a shock that loud music was coming from the fifth segment of the apartment maze. Following another bend to the right, he came into a white chamber. Sheet-covered sea trunks and officers' mess-room chairs had been set along the white canvas walls here, and the almost forgotten mechanical music player from *Terror*'s Great Cabin was being cranked by a costumed fantastic at the far end of the chamber, the machine pouring out music hall favorites from its large rotating metal disks. The sound somehow seemed much louder out here on the ice.

Revelers were coming out of the sixth chamber and Crozier walked past the music player, took the sharp angle to the left, and entered a violet room.

The captain's seaman's eyes admired the rigging that rose from upended spare spars to a tethered spar hanging in midair — webs of rigging came in from the other six chambers there to be tied off — and the master cables that ran up from this center spar to anchors high on the wall of the iceberg. The riggers from *Erebus* and *Terror* who had conceived and executed this seven-chamber maze obviously had also exorcised some of the incredible frustration at not being able to pursue their trade due to being icebound and static for so many months, their ships' topmasts, spars, and rigging pulled down and stored on the ice. But this violet room had few costumed crewmen tarrying in it and the light was strangely oppressive. The only furniture here consisted of stacks of empty crates at the center of the room, all draped in violet sheets. The few birds, pirates, and ragmen in this room paused to drink from their crystal goblets carried from the white room, looked around, then quickly returned to the outer chambers again.

The final room beyond the violet room seemed to have no light at all coming from it.

Crozier followed the sharp angle to the right from the violet chamber and found himself in a chamber of almost absolute blackness.

No, that was not true, he realized. Torches burned outside the black-dyed sail walls here just as they did beyond all the other chambers, but the effect was only of a subdued glow through ebony air. Crozier had to stop to allow his eyes to adapt, and when they did, he took two startled steps backward.

The ice underfoot was gone. It was as if he were walking above the black water of the arctic sea.

It took only seconds for the captain to realize the trick. The seamen had taken soot from the boiler and coal sack holds and spread it across the sea ice here — an old seaman's trick when wanting to melt the sea ice more quickly in late spring or recalcitrant summer, but there was no melting tonight with the sunless days and temperatures dropping toward −100 degrees. Instead, the soot and carbon made the ice underfoot invisible in the ebony gloom of this final, terrible compartment.

As Crozier's eyes adapted further, he saw that there was only one piece of furniture in the long black compartment, but his jaws clenched with anger when he saw what it was.

Captain Sir John Franklin's tall ebony grandfather clock was set at the far end of this black compartment, its back to the rising iceberg that served as the far wall to the ebony room and the end of the seven-chamber maze. Crozier could hear the heavy ticking of the thing.

And above the ticking clock, extruding from the ice like something struggling to gain its freedom from the iceberg, was the white-furred head and ivory-yellow teeth of a monster.

No, he checked himself again, not a monster. The head and neck of a large white bear somehow had been mounted onto the ice. The creature's mouth was open. Its black eyes reflected the small amount of torchlight that made its way through the black-dyed canvas walls. The bear's fur and teeth were the brightest things in the ebony compartment. Its tongue was a shocking red. Beneath the head, the ebony clock ticked like a heartbeat.

Filled with a fury that he could not define, Crozier marched from the ebony compartment, paused in the white room, and bellowed for an officer — any officer.

A Satyr with a long papier-mâché face and a priapic cone rising from its red belt scuttled forward on black metal hooves set beneath heavy boots. "Yes, sir?"

"Take off that fucking mask!"

"Aye, aye, Captain," said the Satyr, sliding the mask up to reveal Thomas R. Farr, *Terror's* captain of the maintop. A Chinese woman with huge breasts next to him lowered her mask to show the round, fat face of John Diggle, the cook. Next to Diggle was a giant rat who lowered its snout enough to show the face of Lieutenant James Walter Fairholme of *Erebus.*

"What in hell is the meaning of all this?" roared Crozier.

Various fantastical creatures cringed back toward the white walls at the sound of Crozier's voice.

"Of which exactly, Captain?" asked Lieutenant Fairholme.

"This!" bellowed Crozier, raising both arms and hands to indicate the white walls, the rigging overhead, the torches . . . everything.

"No meaning, Captain," responded Mr. Farr. "It's simply . . . Carnivale." Crozier had always, until this moment, thought Farr a reliable and sensible hand and a fine maintop captain.

"Mr. Farr, did you help in the rigging?" he asked sharply.

"Yes, sir."

"And Lieutenant Fairholme, were you aware of the . . . animal's head . . . exhibited so bizarrely in that final chamber?"

"Aye, Captain," said Fairholme. The lieutenant's long, weathered face showed no sign of fear at his expedition commander's anger. "I shot it myself. Yesterday evening. Two of the bears, actually. A mother and its almost grown male cub. We're going to roast the meat toward midnight — have a sort of feast, sir."

Crozier stared at the men. He could feel his heart pounding in his chest, could feel the anger that — mixed with the whiskey he'd had that day and the certainty there would be no more in the days to come — had often led him to violence ashore.

He had to be careful here.

"Mr. Diggle," he said to the fat Chinese woman with the huge breasts, "you know the liver of the white bears has made us ill."

Diggle's jowls bobbled up and down as freely as the pillowed bosoms beneath them. "Oh, yes, Captain. There's something foul in the polar beast's liver that we haven't been able to heat out of it. There'll be neither liver nor lights in the feast I cook tonight, Captain, I assure thee. Only fresh meat — hundreds and hundreds of pounds of fresh meat, grilled and singed and fried to perfection, sir."

Lieutenant Fairholme spoke. "The men are taking it as a hopeful omen that we blundered across the two bears on the ice and were able to kill them, Captain. Everyone's looking forward to the feast at midnight."

"Why wasn't I told of the bears?" demanded Crozier.

The officer, maintop captain, and cook looked at one another. Birds and beasts and faeries nearby looked at one another.

"The sow and cub were only shot late last night, Captain," Fairholme said at last. "I guess all the traffic between the ships today has been Terrors coming over to the Carnivale to work and get ready, no messengers from *Erebus* making the return trip. My apologies for not informing you, sir."

Crozier knew that it was Fitzjames who had been negligent in this regard. And he knew the men around him knew it.

"Very well," he said at last. "Carry on." But as the men began setting their masks back in place, he added, "And God help you if Sir John's clock is damaged in any way."

"Aye, Captain," said all the masked shapes around him.

With a final, almost apprehensive glance back through the violet room toward the terrible black compartment — almost nothing in Francis Crozier's fifty-one years of frequent melancholy had oppressed him as much as that ebony compartment had — he walked from the white room to the orange room, thence from the orange room to the green room, then from the green room to the purple room, from the purple room to the blue room, and from the widening blue room out onto the darker open ice.

Only when he was out of the dyed-sail maze did Crozier feel that he could breathe properly.

Costumed shapes gave the glowering captain a wide berth as he made his way toward *Erebus* and the dark, heavily cloaked figure standing at the top of the ice ramp there.

Captain Fitzjames was alone near the ship's railing at the top of the ramp. He was smoking his pipe. "Good evening to you, Captain Crozier."

"Good evening, Captain Fitzjames. Have you been inside that . . . that . . ." Words failed him, and Crozier gestured toward the loud and lighted city of coloured walls and elaborate rigging behind him. The torches and braziers burned bright there.

"Aye, I have," said Fitzjames. "The men have shown incredible ingenuity, I would say."

Crozier had nothing to say to that.

"The question now," said Fitzjames, "is whether their many hours of labour and ingenuity have gone to serve the expedition . . . or the Devil."

Crozier tried to see the younger officer's eyes under the muffler-tied bill of his cap. He had no idea if Fitzjames was joking.

"I warned them," growled Crozier, "that they could waste not one pint of oil or one extra lump of coal on this damned Carnivale. Just look at those fires!"

"The men assured me," said Fitzjames, "that they are only using the oil and coal thay have saved by not heating *Erebus* these past weeks!"

"Whose idea was that . . . maze?" asked Crozier. "The coloured compartments? The ebony room?"

Fitzjames blew smoke, removed his pipe, and chuckled. "All the idea of young Richard Aylmore."

"Aylmore?" repeated Crozier. He remembered the name but hardly the man. "Your gunroom steward?"

"The same."

Crozier recalled a small man, quiet, with sunken, brooding eyes, a pedant's tone to his voice, and a wispy black mustache. "Where in the hell did he come up with this?"

"Aylmore lived in the United States for several years before return-ing home in 1844 and enlisting in the Discovery Service," said

Fitzjames. The stem of the pipe clattered slightly against his teeth. "He maintains that he read an absurd story five years ago, in 1842, describing a masqued ball just such as this with such coloured compartments, read it while he was living in Boston with his cousin. In a trashy little piece called *Graham's Magazine,* if I recall correctly. Aylmore can't remember the plot of the story exactly, but he remembers that it was about a strange masqued ball given by a certain Prince Prospero . . . and he says that he is quite certain of the sequence of the rooms, ending in that terrible ebony compartment. The men loved his idea."

Crozier could only shake his head.

"Francis," continued Fitzjames, "this was a teetotaling ship for two years and one month under Sir John. Despite that, I managed to smuggle aboard three bottles of fine whiskey my father gave me. I have one bottle left. I would be honoured if you would share it with me this evening. It will be another three hours until the men begin cooking up the two bears they shot. I authorized my Mr. Wall and your Mr. Diggle yesterday to set up two of the whaleboats' stoves on the ice for heating incidentals such as canned vegetables and to build a huge grill in what they are calling the White Room for the actual cooking of the bear meat. If nothing else, it will be our first fresh meat in more than three months. Would you care to be my guest over that bottle of whiskey down in Sir John's former cabin until it's time for the feast?"

Crozier nodded and followed Fitzjames into the ship.

25

CROZIER

C rozier and Fitzjames emerged from *Erebus* some time before midnight. The Great Cabin had been ferociously cold, but the deeper cold out here in the night was an assault on their bodies and senses. The wind had come up slightly in the last couple of hours and everywhere the torches and tripod braziers — Fitzjames had suggested, and after the first hour of whiskey Crozier had agreed, sending out extra sacks of coal and coal oil to fuel open-flame braziers to keep the revelers from freezing — were rippling and crackling in the hundred-below freezing night.

The two captains had talked very little, each lost in his own melancholic reverie. They'd been interrupted a dozen times. Lieutenant Irving came to report that he was taking the replacement watch back to *Terror;* Lieutenant Hodgson came to report that his watch had arrived at the Carnivale; other officers in absurd costumes came to report that all was well with Carnivale itself; various *Erebus* watches and officers came to report coming off duty and going on duty; Mr. Gregory the engineer came to report that they might as well use the coal for the braziers since there wasn't enough to fuel the steam engine for more than a few hours of steaming come the mythical thaw and then went off to make arrangements for several sacks to be hauled out to the increasingly wild ceremony on the ice; Mr. Murray, the old sailmaker — dressed as some sort of mortician with a skull under his high beaver hat, a skull not so different from his own wizened visage — begged their pardon and asked if he and his helpers could break out two spare jibs to rig a wind shield upwind of the new tripod braziers.

The captains had given their acknowledgments and permissions, passed along their commands and admonitions, never really rising out of their whiskey-induced thoughts.

Sometime between eleven and midnight, they bundled themselves back into their outer slops, came up on deck, and then went out onto the ice again after both Thomas Jopson and Edmund Hoar, Crozier's and Fitzjames's respective stewards, came down to the Great Cabin with Lieutenants Le Vesconte and Little — all four men in bizarre costumes squeezed over and under their many layers — to announce that the bear meat was being cooked up, that prime portions were being set aside for the captains, and could the captains please come to the feast now?

Crozier realized that he was very drunk. He was used to holding his liquor without letting it show, and the men were used to him smelling like whiskey while he was in complete command of situations, but he hadn't slept for several nights and this midnight, coming out into the chest-slamming cold and walking toward the lighted canvas and glowing iceberg and movement of strange forms, Crozier *felt* the whiskey burning in his belly and brain.

They'd set up the main grilling area in the white room. The two captains traversed the series of compartments without comment either to each other or to any of the dozens upon dozens of wildly costumed figures flitting about. From the open-ended blue room, they walked through the purple and green rooms, then through the orange room and into the white.

It was obvious to Crozier that most of the men were also drunk. How had they done that? Had they been hoarding their allotments of grog? Hiding away the ale usually served with their suppers? He knew that they hadn't broken into the Spirit Room aboard *Terror* because he'd had Lieutenant Little check to make sure the locks were secure both this morning and this afternoon. And *Erebus*'s Spirit Room was empty thanks to Sir John Franklin, and had been since they'd sailed.

But the men had gotten into hard spirits somehow. As a seaman of more than forty years who had served his time before the mast as a boy, Crozier knew that — at least in terms of fermenting, hoarding, or finding alcohol — a British sailor's ingenuity knew no bounds.

Huge haunches and racks of bear meat were being grilled over an open fire by Mr. Diggle and Mr. Wall, pewter plates of the steaming victuals being handed out to the queues of men by a grinning Lieutenant Le Vesconte, his gold tooth gleaming, and by other officers and stewards of both ships. The smell of grilling meat was incredible and Crozier found himself salivating despite all his private vows not to enjoy this Carnivale feast.

The queue gave way to the two captains. Ragmen, popish priests, French courtiers, faerie sprites, motley beggars, a shrouded corpse, and two Roman legionnaires in red capes, black masks, and gold chest armour gestured Fitzjames and Crozier to the front of the queue and bowed as the officers passed.

Mr. Diggle himself, his fat-Chinese-lady's pendulous bosoms now down around his waist and wobbling as he moved, cut a prime piece for Crozier and then another for Captain Fitzjames. Le Vesconte gave them proper officers' mess cutlery and white linen napkins. Lieutenant Fairholme poured ale into two cups for them.

"The trick out here, Captains," said Fairholme, "is to drink quickly, dipping like a bird, so that your lips don't freeze to the cup."

Fitzjames and Crozier found a place at the head of a white-shrouded table, sitting on white-shrouded chairs, pulled back for them on the protesting ice by Mr. Farr, the captain of the maintop whom Crozier had braced earlier in the evening. Mr. Blanky was sitting there with his ice-master counterpart, Mr. Reid, as were Edward Little and a half dozen of the *Erebus* officers. The surgeons clustered at the other end of the white table.

Crozier took his mittens off, flexed cold fingers under wool gloves, and tried the meat gingerly, careful not to let the metal fork touch his lips. The bear cutlet burned his tongue. He had the urge to laugh then — a hundred below zero out here in the New Year's night, his breath hanging in front of him in a cloud of ice crystals, his face hidden down the tunnel of his comforters, caps, and Welsh wig, and he'd just burned his tongue. He tried again, chewing and swallowing this time.

It was the most delicious steak he'd ever eaten. This surprised the captain. Many months ago, the last time they'd tried fresh bear meat, the cooked flesh seemed gamy and rancid. The liver and possibly some of the other commonly prized organs made the men actively ill. It had been decided that the meat of the white arctic bear would be eaten only if survival demanded it.

And now this feast . . . this sumptuous feast. All around him in the white room, and obviously at canvas-covered casks, chests, and tables in the adjoining orange and violet rooms, crewmen were wolfing down the steaks. The noise and chatter of happy men easily rose over the roar of the grill flames or the flapping of canvas as the wind came up again. A few of the men here in the white room were using knives and forks — many just spearing the steaming bear steaks and chewing on them that way — but most were using their mittened hands. It was as if more than a hundred predators were reveling in their kill.

The more Crozier ate, the more ravenous he became. Fitzjames, Reid, Blanky, Farr, Little, Hodgson, and the others around him — even Jopson, his steward, at a nearby table with the other stewards — appeared to be wolfing down the meat with equal gusto. One of Mr. Diggle's helpers, dressed as a baby Chinaman, came around the tables, dishing out steaming vegetables from a pan heated on one of the whaleboat's iron stoves, but the canned vegetables, however wonderfully hot, simply had no taste next to the delicious fresh bear meat. Only Crozier's position as expedition commander stopped him from muscling his way to the front of the queue and demanding another helping when he finished his heavy slab of bear steak. Fitzjames's expression was anything but distracted now; the younger commander looked as if he was about to weep from happiness.

Suddenly, just as most of the men had finished the steaks and were drinking down their ale before the alcohol-rich liquid froze solid, a Persian king near the entrance to the violet room began cranking the musical disk player.

The applause — thick mittens pounding thunderously — began almost as soon as the first notes tinkled and thunked out of the crude

machine. Many of the musical men aboard both ships had complained about the mechanical music player — its range of sounds
emanating from the turning metal disks was almost precisely that of a
corner organ grinder's instrument — but these notes were unmistakable. Dozens of men rose to their feet. Others began singing at once,
the vapour from their breaths rising in the torchlight shining through
the white canvas walls. Even Crozier had to grin like an idiot as the
familiar words of the first stanza echoed off the iceberg towering
above them in the freezing night.

> When Britain first at Heav'n's command, Arose from
> out the azure main;
> This was the charter of the land, And guardian
> angels sang this strain;

Captains Crozier and Fitzjames rose to their feet and joined in the
first bellowing chorus.

> Rule, Britannia! Britannia, rule the waves; Britons never
> shall be slaves!

Young Hodgson's pure tenor led the men in six of the seven
coloured compartments as they sang the second stanza.

> The nations not so blest as thee, Shall in their turns
> to tyrants fall;
> While thou shalt flourish great and free, The dread
> and envy of them all.

Vaguely aware that there was a commotion two rooms to the east,
in the entrance to the blue room, Crozier threw his head back and,
warm with whiskey and bear steak, bellowed with his men:

> Rule, Britannia! Britannia, rule the waves; Britons never,
> *never* shall be slaves!

The men in the outer rooms of the seven compartments were singing, but they were also laughing now. The commotion grew. The mechanical music player cranked louder. The men sang louder still. Even while standing and singing the third stanza between Fitzjames and Little, Crozier stared in shock as a procession entered the white room.

> Still more majestic shalt thou rise, More dreadful from each
>   foreign stroke;
> As the loud blast that tears the skies, Serves but to
>   root thy native oak.

Someone led the procession in the theatrical costume version of an admiral's uniform. The epaulettes were so absurdly broad that they hung out eight inches beyond the little man's shoulders. He was very fat. The gold buttons on his old-fashioned Naval jacket would never have buttoned. He was also headless. The figure carried its papier-mâché head under the crook of his left arm, his moldering plumed admiral's hat under his right.

Crozier quit singing. The other men did not.

> Rule, Britannia! Britannia, rule the waves! Britons
>   never, never, *never* shall be slaves!

Behind the headless admiral, who obviously was meant to be the late Sir John Franklin even though it had not been Sir John decapitated that day at the bear blind, ambled a monster ten or twelve feet tall.

It had the body and fur and black paws and long claws and triangular head and black eyes of a white arctic bear, but it was walking on its hind legs and was twice the height of a bear and with twice the arms' length. It walked stiffly, almost blindly, swinging its upper body to and fro, the small black eyes staring at each man it approached. The swinging paws — the arms hanging loose as bell pulls — were larger than the costumed crewmen's heads.

"That's your giant, Manson, on the bottom," laughed *Erebus*'s second mate, Charles Frederick Des Voeux, next to Crozier, raising his voice to be heard over the next stanza. "It's your little caulker's mate — Hickey? — riding on his shoulders. It took the men all night to sew up the two hides into a single costume."

> Thee haughty tyrants ne'er shall tame, All their attempts
>   to bend thee down
> Will but arouse thy generous flame, But work
>   their woe, and thy renown.

As the giant bear ambled past, dozens of men from the blue, green, and orange rooms followed it in procession through the white room and into the violet room. Crozier stood as if literally frozen to his spot near the white banquet table. Finally he turned his head to look at Fitzjames.

"I swear I did not know, Francis," said Fitzjames. The other captain's lips were pale and very thin.

The white room began emptying of costumed figures as the scores there followed the headless admiral and the swinging, towering, slowly ambling bipedal bear-giant into and through the relative gloom of the long violet room. The drunken singing roared around Crozier.

> RULE, BRITANNIA! BRITANNIA, RULE THE WAVES!
> BRITONS NEVER, NEVER, NEVER, *NEVER*
> SHALL BE SLAVES!

Crozier began following the procession into the violet chamber and Fitzjames followed him. The captain of HMS *Terror* had never felt this way in all of his years of command; he knew that he had to stop this travesty of a lampoon — no Naval discipline could tolerate a farce in which the death of the expedition's former commander became a source of humour. But at the same time he knew that it had already proceeded to a point where simply shouting down the singing, ordering Manson and Hickey out of their obscene monster suit, ordering *everyone* out of their costumes and back to their berths on the ships would be almost as absurd and useless as the pagan ritual Crozier was watching with growing anger.

TO THEE BELONGS THE RURAL REIGN, THY CITIES
SHALL WITH COMMERCE SHINE;
ALL THINE SHALL BE THE SUBJECT MAIN, AND
EVERY SHORE IT CIRCLES THINE!

The headless admiral, ambling bear-thing, and the following procession of a hundred costumed men or more had not paused long in the violet room. As Crozier entered the violet-coloured space — the torches and outside tripod fires were whipping on the north side of the violet-dyed canvas wall and the sails themselves were rippling and cracking in the rising wind — he arrived just in time to see Manson and Hickey and their singing mob pause at the entrance to the ebony room.

Crozier resisted the impulse to shout out "No!" It was an obscenity for the effigy of Sir John and the towering bear-thing to play this out in any forum, but unthinkably vile in that black, oppressive ebony room with its polar bear head and ticking clock. Whatever final dumb show the men had in mind, at least it would soon be finished. This had to be the finale of this ill-thought-out mistake of a Second Grand Venetian Carnivale. He would let the singing end of its own, the pagan mime close to drunken cheers from the men, and then he would order the mobs out of their costumes, send the frozen and drunken seamen back to their ships, but order the riggers and organizers to strike the canvas and rigging immediately — tonight — whether that meant frostbite or no. He would then deal with Hickey, Manson, Aylmore, and his officers.

The swaying, much-cheered headless admiral and swaying bear-monster entered the ebony compartment.

Sir John's black clock within began striking midnight.

The mob of bizarrely costumed sailors at the rear of the procession began pressing forward, the rear ranks eager to get into the ebony compartment to see the fun, even while the ragmen, rats, uni-

corns, dustmen, one-legged pirates, Arab princes and Egyptian princesses, gladiators, faeries, and other creatures at the front of the mob,
already making the turn and crossing the threshold into the black
room, began resisting the advance, pushing back, no longer sure
they wanted to be in that soot-floored and black-walled darkness.

Crozier elbowed his way forward through the mob — the mass
surging forward and then back as those in the front thought twice
about actually entering the ebony gloom — certain now that if he
couldn't end this farce before the finale, at least he could shorten this
final act.

He'd no sooner entered the darkness with twenty or thirty men at
the front of the procession who'd also halted upon stepping in —
his eyes had to adapt in here, and the black soot on the ice gave him
a terrible sense of falling into a black void — when he felt the blast
of cold air against his face. It was as if someone had opened a door
in the wall of the iceberg that loomed over everything. Even the
costumed figures here in the dark were still singing, but the real volume came from the pushing mobs still back in the violet room.

> RULE, BRITANNIA! BRITANNIA, RULE THE WAVES;
> BRITONS NEVER, NEVER, NEVER, NEVER,
> *NEVER*
> SHALL BE SLAVES!

Crozier could only just make out the white of the disembodied
bear's head emerging from the ice over the ebony clock —
the chimes had struck six now and seemed terribly loud in the darkened space — and he could see that under the taller, swaying, white
bear-monster's form, Manson and Hickey were finding it difficult to
keep their balance on the sooty ice, in the icy blackness with the north
canvas walls flapping and rippling wildly with the wind.

Crozier saw that there was a *second* large white shape in the room. It
also stood on its hind legs. It was farther back in the darkness than
Manson and Hickey's bearhide-white glow. And it was much larger.
And taller.

As the men fell silent and the clock was striking its last four chimes, something in the room roared.

THE MUSES, STILL WITH FREEDOM FOUND, SHALL
TO THY HAPPY COAST REPAIR;
BLEST ISLE! WITH MATCHLESS BEAUTY CROWNED,
AND MANLY HEARTS TO GUIDE THE FAIR!

Suddenly the men in the ebony room were shoving backward against the still-pushing throng of seamen trying to get in.

"What in God's name?"asked Dr. McDonald. The four surgeons, all in Harlequin costumes but with their masks hanging down now, were recognizable to Crozier in the brighter violet glow coming around the canvased curve between the rooms.

A man in the ebony room screamed in terror. There came a second roar, unlike anything that Francis Rawdon Moira Crozier had ever heard; it was something more at home in a thick jungle of some previous Hyborian Age than in the Arctic of the nineteenth century. The sound ground so low into the bass regions, grew so reverberating, and emerged so ferocious that it made the captain of HMS *Terror* want to piss his pants right there in front of his men.

The larger of the two white shapes in the gloom charged forward.

Costumed men screamed, tried to push backward against the wave of the forward-pushing curious, and then ran to the left and right in the darkness, colliding with the nearly invisible black-dyed canvas walls.

Crozier, unarmed, stood where he was. He *felt* the mass of the thing brush past him in the darkness. He sensed it with his *mind* . . . felt it in his *head*. There was a sudden stench as of old blood, then the reek of a carrion pit.

Princesses and faeries were throwing off costumes and cold-weather slops in the darkness, clawing at the black walls and fumbling for their boat knives on their buried belts.

Crozier heard a meaty, sickening *slap* as huge plate-sized paws or knife-sized claws slammed into a man's body. Something crunched sickeningly as teeth longer than bayonet blades bit through skull or bone. In the outer rooms, men still sang.

RULE, BRITANNIA! BRITANNIA, RULE THE
WAVES!
   BRITONS NEVER, NEVER, NEVER, NEVER,
   NEVER
      SHALL BE SLAVES!!

The ebony clock concluded its striking. It was midnight. It was 1848.

Men used their knives to slash through the black-dyed walls and strips of wind-tormented canvas were immediately whipped into the flames of torches and tripods out on the ice. Flames leapt skyward and almost immediately engaged the rigging.

The white shape had moved out into the violet room. Men there were screaming and scattering, cursing and shoving, some already slashing at the walls there rather than trying to make the long run out through the compartment maze, and Crozier shoved seamen aside as he tried to follow. Both walls of the ebony room were ablaze now. More men screamed and one man ran past Crozier, his Harlequin costume, Welsh wig, and hair shooting flames behind him like yellow silk streamers.

By the time Crozier shoved himself free of the surging mob of fleeing, costumed forms, the violet compartment was also burning and the thing from the ice had moved on to the white room. The captain could hear the shouts from scores of men as they ran ahead of the white apparition in a wave of waving arms and shed costumes. The web of beautifully rigged ropes attaching the canvas and spar struts to the overhanging iceberg was burning now, the patterns of flame slashing like scribbled runes of fire against the black slate of sky. The hundred-foot wall of ice reflected the flames in its thousand facets.

The spars themselves that rose like exposed ribs along the burning walls of the ebony room, the violet room, and now the white room, were also on fire. Years of storage in the virtual desert of the arctic dryness had leached all moisture from the wood. They fed the flames like thousand-pound pieces of tinder.

Crozier gave up all hope of mastering the situation and ran with the others. He had to get out of the burning maze.

The white room was fully engaged. Flames shot up from the white walls, from the canvas carpets on the ice, from the former sheet-draped banquet tables and casks and chairs and from Mr. Diggle's metal cooking grill. Someone had knocked over the mechanical disk player in their panicked flight and the oak-and-bronze instrument reflected the flames from all of its beautifully crafted faces and curves.

Crozier saw Captain Fitzjames standing in the white room, the only figure not costumed and not running. He grabbed the motionless man by his slops' sleeve. "Come, James! We have to *go.*"

The commander of HMS *Erebus* slowly turned his head and looked at his superior officer as if they had never met. Fitzjames had that small, absent, maddening smile on his face again.

Crozier slapped him. "Come *on!*"

Pulling and tugging the sleepwalking Fitzjames, Crozier stumbled through the burning white room, out through the fourth room, whose walls were more orange with flames than with dye now, and into the burning green room. The maze seemed to go on and on. Costumed figures lay on the ice here and there — some moaning and with ripped and mauled vestments, one man naked and burned — but other seamen were stopping to help them up, shoving them onward and outward. The sea ice underfoot, where there were no burning canvas carpets, was littered with shreds of costumes and abandoned cold-weather gear. Most of these tatters and fabrics were either ablaze or the about to burn.

"Come *on!*" repeated Crozier, still tugging a stumbling Fitzjames in his wake. A seaman lay unconscious on the ice — young George Chambers from *Erebus,* Crozier saw, one of the ship's boys, although twenty-one now, one of the drummers in their early burials on the ice — and no one seemed to be taking notice of him. Crozier released Fitzjames just long enough to lift Chambers over his shoulder, and then he grabbed the other captain's sleeve again and began running just as flames on either side exploded to the rigging above.

Crozier heard a monstrous *hissing* behind him.

Certain that the thing had circled behind him in the confusion, perhaps crashing up through the impenetrable ice, he swung to confront it with only his one mittened fist free.

The entire iceberg was steaming and popping from the heat. Huge chunks and heavy overhangs were breaking off and crashing down to the ice, hissing like snakes as they fell into the cauldron of flame that had been the tent maze. The sight held Crozier in motionless rapture for a minute — the berg's countless facets reflecting the flames made him think of a hundred-storey fairy-tale castle tower ablaze with light. He knew at that instant that as long as he lived he would never again see anything like this.

"Francis," lisped Captain James Fitzjames. "We have to go."

The green room's walls were falling away but there were only more flames on the ice beyond. The rapidly advancing fissures and tendrils and fingers of fire had spread to the final two compartments.

Shielding his face with his free hand, Crozier charged forward through the flames, herding the last of the fleeing revelers on ahead of him.

Out through the burning purple room staggered the survivors as Crozier led them into the blazing blue room. The wind from the northwest was howling now, joining with screams and roars and hisses that might have been only in Francis Crozier's head for all he knew at that moment, and the flames were blowing across the blue compartment's wide opening, creating a barrier of fire.

A cluster of about a dozen men, some still wearing shreds of their costume finery, had slid to a stop before those flames.

"MOVE!" roared Crozier, bellowing in his most commanding typhoon voice. A lookout in the crosstrees at the top of a mainmast two hundred feet above the deck could have heard the command clearly in an eighty-knot wind with forty-foot waves crashing around them. And he would have obeyed. These men also obeyed, jumping, screaming, and running through the flames with Crozier right behind them, still carrying Chambers along on his right shoulder and tugging Fitzjames along with his left hand.

Once outside, his slops steaming, Crozier continued running, catching and passing some of the dozens of men who were spreading out in every direction in the night. The captain did not immediately see the white creature among the men, but everything was very confused out here — even with the flames throwing light and shadows five hundred feet in every direction — and then he was busy shouting for his officers and trying to find an ice boulder on which to lay the still-unconscious George Chambers.

Suddenly there came the *pop-pop-pop* of musket fire.

Incredibly, unbelievably, obscenely, a line of four Marines just outside the circle of light from the flames had taken their knees on the ice and were firing into the clumps and mobs of running men. Here and there a figure — still sadly and absurdly in costume — fell to the ice.

Releasing Fitzjames, Crozier ran forward, stepping into the line of volley fire and waving his arms. Musket balls whizzed past his ears.

"CEASE FIRE! GOD-DAMN YOUR EYES, SERGEANT TOZER, I'LL BREAK YOU TO A PRIVATE FOR THIS AND HAVE YOU HANGED IF YOU DON'T *CEASE THAT FUCKING FIRE IMMEDIATELY!*"

The firing popped and stopped.

The Marines snapped to a standing salute, Sergeant Tozer shouting that the white thing was out there among the men. They'd seen it backlit by the flames. It was carrying a man in its jaws.

Crozier ignored him. Shouting and shoving both Terrors and Erebuses into clumps around him on the ice, sending obviously mauled or burned men back to Fitzjames's nearby ship, the captain was hunting for his officers — or *Erebus* officers — or anyone he could give an order to and have it relayed to the clusters of terrified men still running out through seracs and across pressure ridges into the howling arctic darkness.

If those men didn't come back, they'd freeze to death out there. Or the thing would find them. Crozier decided that no one was going the mile back to *Terror* until they had warmed up on the lower deck of *Erebus*.

But first Crozier had to get his men calmed, organized, and busy pulling the wounded and the bodies of the dead from what was left of the burning Carnivale compartments.

In the first moments he found only the *Erebus* mate Couch and Second Lieutenant Hodgson, but then Lieutenant Little came up

through the smoke and steam — the top few inches of ice were melting in an irregular radius around the flames and sending a thick fog
out across the sea ice and into the serac forest — saluted clumsily, his
right arm was burned, and reported for duty.

With Little at his side, Crozier found it easier to gain control of the
men, get them back toward *Erebus,* and start taking roll. He ordered
the Marines to reload and set them in a defensive skirmish line
between the accumulating mass of staggering men near *Erebus*'s ice
ramp and the still roaring inferno.

"My God," said Dr. Harry D. S. Goodsir, who had just come out
of *Erebus* and was standing nearby, tugging off his slops and greatcoat. "It's actually *warm* out here with the flames."

"So it is," said Crozier, feeling the sweat on his face and body. The
fire had brought the temperature up a hundred degrees or more. He
wondered idly if the ice would melt and they'd all drown. To Goodsir
he barked, "Go over there to Lieutenant Hodgson and tell him to
begin to assess the numbers of dead and wounded and to get them to
you. Find the other surgeons and get *Erebus*'s sick bay fitted out in Sir
John's Great Room — set it up as they trained you surgeons to do for
a combat engagement at sea. I don't want the dead laid out on the ice
— that thing is still out here somewhere — so tell your seamen to
carry them to the forepeak on the lower deck. I'll check in on you in
forty minutes — have a complete butcher's bill ready for me."

"Aye, Captain," said Goodsir. Grabbing up his outer clothes, the
surgeon rushed toward Lieutenant Hodgson and the ice ramp to
Erebus.

The canvas and rigging and ice-set masts and costumes and tables
and casks and other furniture in the inferno that had been the seven
coloured compartments continued to burn all through that night and
deep into the darkness of the next morning.

26

GOODSIR

Lat. 70°-05' N., Long. 98°-23' W.
4 January, 1848

From the private diary of Dr. Harry D. S. Goodsir:

Tuesday, 4 January, 1848 —

I am the only one left.

Of the Expedition's Surgeons, I am the only one left. All agree that we were incredibly Lucky to have lost only Five in Death to the Grand Venetian Carnivale's Horror and Conflagration, but the fact that Three of those Five were my Fellow Surgeons is, at the very least, Extraordinary.

The two Chief Surgeons, Drs. Peddie and Stanley, died of Burns. My Assistant Surgeon counterpart on HMS Terror, Dr. McDonald, survived the flames and Raging Beast only to be Struck Down by a Marine's Musket Ball upon fleeing the burning tents.

Both of the other two Fatal Casualties were also Officers. First Lieutenant James Walter Fairholme of Erebus had his chest crushed in the Ebony Room, presumably by the creature there. Although Lt. Fairholme's Body was found Burned in the ice-melted wreckage of that Loathsome Tent Maze, my postmortem examination showed that he had Died Instantly when his collapsing Rib Cage had pulverized his Heart.

The final fatality of the New Year's Eve Fire and Mayhem was Terror's First Mate Frederick John Hornby, who had been Eviscerated in that Canvas Enclosure in what the men had called the White Room. The sad irony of Mr. Hornby's death was that the gentleman had been on Watch Duty aboard Terror through most of the evening and had been relieved by Lieutenant Irving not an hour before the Violence broke out.

Captain Crozier and Captain Fitzjames now find themselves without three of their Four Surgeons and without the Advice and Services of two of their most trusted officers.

Eighteen other men were injured — six seriously — during the Venetian Carnivale Nightmare. Of those six — Ice Master Mr. Blanky from Terror; *Carpenter's Mate Wilson, also from that ship (the men affectionately call him "Fat Wilson"); Seaman John Morfin, with whom I Traveled to King William Land some months ago;* Erebus's *purser's steward, Mr. William Fowler; Seaman Thomas Work, also from* Erebus; *and* Terror *boatswain Mr. John Lane — I am pleased to report that all should survive. (Although it is another irony that Mr. Blanky, who had suffered less serious injuries from the Same Creature only less than a Month Ago — injuries to which all four of us Surgeons applied our time and expertise — had not been burned at the Carnivale Mayhem but was injured yet again in the right leg — mauled or bitten by the thing from the ice, he believes, although he says that he was cutting his way through burning Canvas and Rigging at the time. This time I had to amputate his right leg just below the knee. Mr. Blanky remains remarkably Chipper for a man who has sustained so much damage in so Short a Time.)*

Yesterday, Monday, all of us Survivors witnessed Floggings. It was the first such Naval Corporal Punishment I have ever seen and I Pray God that I shall never see more.

Captain Crozier — who has been visibly consumed by an Anger Beyond Words since the Fire last Friday night — assembled every Surviving Crew Member of both ships on the lower deck of Erebus *at 10:00 a.m. yesterday. The Royal Marines made a line with muskets at the vertical. Drums were beaten.*

Erebus *gunroom steward Mr. Richard Aylmore and* Terror *caulker's mate Cornelius Hickey, as well as a truly huge common Seaman named Magnus Manson, were marched bareheaded and wearing only their trousers and undershirts to a place in front of the ship's Stove, where a wooden Hatch Cover had been rigged vertically. One by one, starting with Mr. Aylmore, they were Tied to this Hatch.*

But before this, the men were made to stand there, Aylmore's and Manson's heads bowed, Hickey's upright and defiant, as Captain Crozier read the charges.

For Aylmore, it was fifty lashes for Insubordination and Reckless Behavior endangering his ship. If the quiet gunroom steward had simply come up with the idea for the coloured tents — an Idea he acknowledged had come from some Fantastical American Magazine Story — the Punishment would have been certain but less Severe. But in addition to being a Primary Planner of the Grand Venetian Carnivale, Aylmore had made the Mistake of costuming himself as the Headless Admiral — a Major Impropriety, given the circumstances surrounding Sir John's death, and one we all understood could have resulted in Aylmore's hanging. We had each heard tales of Aylmore's private Testimony before the Captains in which he had described how he had Screamed and then Fainted in the Ebony Room upon Realizing that the Thing from the Ice was there in the Darkness with the mummers.

For Manson and Hickey, it was fifty lashes for Sewing and Wearing the Dead Bears' animal skins — a violation of all of Captain Crozier's previous Orders about not wearing such Heathen Fetishes.

It was understood that fifty or more other men were Complicit in the Planning, Rigging, Dyeing of Sails, and Staging of the Grand Carnivale, and that Crozier could have handed out an Equal Number of Lashes to all. In a sense, this Sad Trinity of Aylmore, Manson, and Hickey was receiving Punishment for the Entire Crew's bad judgement.

As the drums stopped beating and the Men stood in a line before the Assembled Crews, Captain Crozier spoke. I hope that I remember his words exactly here:

These men are about to Receive the Lash for Violations of Ship's Articles and for the Unwise Behavior in which every man here participated. Including myself.

Let it be known and remembered by All here Assembled, that the Ultimate Responsibility for the folly that claimed the lives of Five of Our Crewmates, the Leg of Another, and which will leave Scars on almost a Score More, was mine. A captain is responsible for everything that happens on his Ship. The leader of an Expedition is doubly responsible. The fact that I allowed these plans to proceed without my Attention or Intervention was Criminal Negligence, and I will admit as much during my Inevitable Court-Martial . . . inevitable, that is, *if* we Survive and escape from the ice that Binds

Us. These lashes — and more — should be mine and *will* be mine when falls the inevitable Punishment meted out by *my* superiors.

I glanced then at Captain Fitzjames. Certainly any Self-Blame that Captain Crozier would cast upon himself would also apply to the commander of Erebus, since it was he, not Crozier, who had overseen most of the Carnivale's arrangements. Fitzjames's face was impassive and Pale. His gaze seemed unfocused. His thoughts seemed elsewhere.

Until such a day of my own reckoning for Responsibility, *Crozier concluded,* we proceed with the Punishment of These Men, duly tried by Officers of HMSs *Erebus* and *Terror* and Found Guilty of Violation of the Ship's Articles and of the Additional Crime of Endangering the lives of their Comrades. Boatswain Mate Johnson . . .

And here Thomas Johnson, large and Capable boatswain mate of HMS Terror, *old Shipmate of Captain Crozier — having served five years in the South Polar Ice on* Terror *with him — stepped forward and nodded for the first man, Aylmore, to be tied to the Grate.*

Bosun Johnson then laid out on a cask a leather-bound Box and unlatched its ornate brass snaps. Incongruously, the interior lining was of Red Velvet. Set into its Proper Receptacle in this Red Velvet Lining was the palm-darkened leather grip and folded Tails of the Cat.

While two Seamen bound Aylmore securely, Bosun's Mate Johnson lifted out the Cat and tested it with a preparatory Flick of his thick Wrist. It was not a Motion done for Show but a true preparation for the Hideous Punishment to come. The nine leather tails — of which I had heard so many Shipboard Jokes — flicked out with distinct and Audible and terrible cracks. There were small Knots at the end of each tail.

Part of me could not believe that this was happening. It seemed impossible in this crowded, sweat-stinking Gloom of the Lower Deck, with the low Overhead Beams and Lumber and Gear hanging lower, that Johnson could possibly manage the Cat so as to effect any Punishment. I had heard the phrase "not Enough Room to Swing a Cat In" since I was a boy, but never had I Understood it until this Moment.

Execute the punishment for Mr. Aylmore, *said Captain Crozier. The drums beat again briefly and stopped abruptly.*

Johnson took a broad sideways stance, setting his feet like a Boxer in the

Ring, then swung the Cat back, and then Forward in a Violent, Sudden but Smooth Sidearm Motion, the knotted Tails passing less than a Foot from the Front Ranks of Assembled Men.

The sound of the Cat's tails striking Flesh is something I shall never Forget.

Aylmore screamed — a more Inhuman Sound, some said later, than the roar they had heard from the creature in the Ebony Room.

Crimson Stripes appeared immediately upon the man's thin, pale back, and droplets of Blood spattered the faces of those men standing nearest the Grate, myself included.

ONE, counted Charles Frederick Des Voeux, who had assumed the duties of Erebus's First Mate upon the death of Mate Robert Orme Sergeant in December. It was the Duty of both first mates to administer this punishment.

Aylmore screamed again even as the Cat was pulled back for another blow, almost certainly in horrid anticipation of Forty-nine More Lashes. I confess that I swayed on my feet . . . the Press of Unwashed Bodies, the Stink of Blood, the sense of Confinement in the Dim, Stinking Gloom of the Lower Deck, all making my head swim. Surely this was Hell. Nor was I out of it.

The Gunroom Steward passed out on the Ninth Lash. Captain Crozier gestured to me to ascertain that the flogged man was still breathing. He was. Normally, as I was made to understand later, a Second Mate would have thrown a Bucket of Water on the victim of punishment to revive him so that he must Fully Suffer the remaining lashes. But there was no Liquid Water on the Lower Deck of HMS Erebus that morning. All was frozen. Even the droplets of Bright Blood on Aylmore's back appeared to be freezing into crimson pellets.

Aylmore stayed unconscious but the Punishment continued.

After Fifty Lashes, Aylmore was untied and carried Aft to Sir John's former cabin, since the Great Cabin was still being used as the Sick Bay in the aftermath of the Carnivale injuries. There were Eight Men on cots in there, including David Leys, still unresponsive since the Thing's attack on Mr. Blanky early in December.

I started to go aft to attend to Aylmore, but Captain Crozier silently gestured me back into the ranks. Evidently it was protocol for all crew members to witness the complete series of Floggings, even should Aylmore bleed to death due to my absence.

Magnus Manson was next. The huge man dwarfed the second mates

tying him to the Grate. If the Giant had decided to Resist at that moment,
I have Little Doubt that the ensuing Chaos and Carnage would have
resembled New Year's Eve's mayhem in the Seven Coloured Compartments.

He did not resist. As far as I could tell, Boatswain's Mate Johnson
administered the endless Flogging with the same force and Severity as he had
for Aylmore — no more, no less. Blood flew from the first Impact. Manson
did not scream. He did something Infinitely Worse. From the first touch of the
Lash, he wept like a child. He sobbed. But afterward he was able to walk
between the two Seamen escorting him back to the Sick Bay, although — as
always — Manson had to hunch over so that his head did not strike the
Beams overhead. As he passed me, I noticed Strips of Flesh hanging loose on
his back between the crisscrossed Scourging wounds of the Cat.

Hickey, the smallest of the three men being punished, barely made a
sound during the long Administration of the Lashes. His narrow Back tore
open more freely than had the flesh of the other two, but he did not cry out.
Nor did he pass out. The diminutive Caulker's Mate seemed to remove his
mind to something beyond the Grate and Overhead Deck upon which his
obviously angry glare was firmly fixed and his only reaction to the Terrible
Flogging was a gasp for breath between each of the fifty lashes of the Cat.

He walked aft to the provisional Sick Bay without accepting help from the
seamen on either side of him.

Captain Crozier announced that punishment had been duly meted out
according to the Ship's Articles and Dismissed the Company. Before going aft,
I ran up on deck very briefly to watch the departure of the men from Terror.
They went down the ice ramp from the ship and began their long walk back to
the other ship in the dark — passing the scorched and partially melted area
where the Carnivale Conflagration had taken place. Crozier and his primary
officer, Lieutenant Little, brought up the rear. None of the more than forty men
had said a word by the time they had disappeared beyond the small circle of light
radiating from Erebus's deck lanterns. Eight men remained as a sort of
companion Guard to walk with Hickey and Manson when they were ready to be
returned to Terror.

I hurried down and aft to the new Sick Bay to take care of my new
charges. Beyond Washing and Bandaging their wounds — the Cat had left a
Sickening array of welts and gouges on each man and some Permanent Scars,

I would think — there was little else I could do. Manson had ceased his Weeping, and when Hickey abruptly ordered him to stop his Snuffling, the giant did so at once. Hickey suffered my Ministrations in silence and gruffly ordered Manson to get fully dressed and to follow him out of the Sick Bay.

Aylmore, the gunroom steward, had been unmanned by the punishment. From the minute he had regained consciousness, according to young Henry Lloyd, my current Surgeon's Assistant, Aylmore had moaned and cried aloud. He continued doing so as I Washed and Bandaged him. He was still moaning piteously and seemed unable to walk by himself when some of the other warrant officers — the elderly John Bridgens, the Subordinate Officer's Steward, Mr. Hoar, the Captain's Steward, Mr. Bell the Quartermaster, and Samuel Brown, the Boatswain's Mate — arrived to help him back to his quarters.

I could hear Aylmore moaning and crying out all the way down the Companionway and around the Main Ladderway as the other men half-carried him to the gunroom steward's cubicle on the starboard side between William Fowler's empty berth and my own, and I knew that I would probably be listening to Aylmore's cries through the thin wall all through the night.

Mr. Aylmore reads a lot, *said William Fowler from his place on his cot in the Sick Bay. The Purser's Steward had received serious burns and a Terrible Mauling during the night of the Carnivale Conflagration, but never once during the last four days of stitchings or skin removals had Fowler cried out. With wounds and burns on both his Back and Stomach, Fowler attempted to sleep on his side, but not once had he complained to Lloyd or me.*

Men who read a lot have a more sensitive disposition, *added Fowler.* And if the poor bloke hadn't read that stupid story by that American, he wouldn't have suggested the different-coloured compartments for Carnivale — an idea we all thought was Wonderful at the time — and none of this would have happened.

I did not know what to say to this.

Maybe reading is a sort of curse is all I mean, *concluded Fowler.* Maybe it's better for a man to stay inside his own mind.

Amen, *I felt like saying, although I do not know why.*

As I write this, I am in Dr. Peddie's former surgeon's berth on HMS Terror *since Captain Crozier has instructed me to spend each Tuesday through*

Thursday aboard his ship and the Remaining Days of the Week aboard Erebus.
Lloyd is watching my six recovering charges in the Erebus sick bay and I was
Distressed to discover almost as many seriously ill men here aboard Terror.

For many of them, it is the disease we Arctic Doctors first called Nostalgia
and then Debility. The early severe stages of this disease — besides bleeding
gums, Confusion of Thought, weakness in the Extremities, bruises
everywhere, and bleeding from the Colon — often include a tremendous
Sentimental Wish to go home. From Nostalgia the weakness, confusion,
Impaired Judgement, bleeding from Anus and Gums, open Sores, and other
symptoms worsen until the patient is unable to stand or work.

Another name for Nostalgia and Debility — one which all Surgeons
hesitate to say aloud and which I have not yet done — is Scurvy.

Meanwhile, Captain Crozier took to his Private Cabin yesterday and is
terribly sick. I can hear his stifled moans since the late Peddie's compartment
borders the captain's here on the starboard stern side of the ship. I think
Captain Crozier is biting down on something hard — perhaps a Strip of
Leather — to keep those moans from being heard. But I have always been
Blessed (or Cursed) with good hearing.

The Captain turned over the handling of the Ship's and Expedition's
affairs to Lieutenant Little yesterday — thus quietly but Firmly giving
Command to Little rather than to Captain Fitzjames — and explained to
me that he, Captain Crozier, was battling a recurrence of Malaria.

This is a lie.

It is not just the symptoms of Malaria which I hear Captain Crozier
suffering — and almost certainly will continue to hear through the walls until
I head back to Erebus on Friday morning.

Because of my uncle's and my father's weaknesses, I know the Demons
the Captain is battling tonight.

Captain Crozier is a man addicted to Hard Spirits, and either those
Spirits on board have been used up or he has decided to go off them of his
own Volition during this Crisis. Either way, he is suffering the Torments of
Hell and shall continue to do so for many days more. His sanity may not
survive. In the meantime, this ship and this Expedition are without their
True Leader. His stifled moans, in a ship descending into Sickness and
Despair, are Pitiable to the extreme.

*I wish I could help him. I wish I could help the dozens of other Sufferers —
all the victims of wounds, maulings, burns, diseases, incipient malnutrition, and
melancholic despair — aboard this entrapped ship and her sister ship. I wish
I could help myself, for already I am showing the early signs of Nostalgia and
Debility.*

*But there is little that I — or any surgeon in this Year of Our Lord 1848 —
can do.*

God help us all.

27

CROZIER

Lat. 70°-05′ N., Long. 98°-23′ W.
11 January, 1848

I t will not end.

The pain will not end. The nausea will not end. The chills will not end. The terror will not end.

Crozier writhes in the frozen blankets of his bunk and wants to die.

During his lucid moments this week, which are few, Crozier laments the most sane act he had performed before retreating to his demons; he had given his pistol to Lieutenant Little with no explanation other than to tell Edward not to return it unless and until he, the captain, asks for it while on deck and in full uniform again.

Crozier would pay anything now for that charged and loaded weapon. This level of pain is unsupportable. These *thoughts* are unsupportable.

His grandmother on his late, unlamented father's side, Memo Moira, had been the outcast, the unmentioned and unmentionable Crozier. In her eighties, when Crozier was not yet a teenager, Memo lived two villages away — an immense, inestimable, and unbridgeable distance for a boy — and his mother's family neither included her in family events nor mentioned her existence.

She was a Papist. She was a witch.

Crozier began sneaking over to her village, cadging rides on pony carts, when he was ten. Within a year he was going with the old woman to that strange village's Papist church. His mother and aunt and maternal grandmother would have died if they had known. He would have been renounced and exiled and held in as much scorn by that proper Irish-English Presbyterian side of his family as the Naval Board and Arctic Council had held him in for all these years just for being an Irishman. And a commoner.

Memo Moira had thought him special. She told him that he had the Second Sight.

The thought did not frighten young Francis Rawdon Moira Crozier. He loved the darkness and the mystery of the Catholic service — the tall priest strutting like a carrion crow and pronouncing magic in a dead language, the immediate magic of the Eucharist bringing the dead back to life so that the faithful could devour Him and become of Him, the smell of incense and the mystical chanting. Once, when he was twelve, shortly before he ran away to sea, he told Memo that he wanted to become a priest, and the old woman laughed that wild, husky laugh of hers and told him to put such nonsense out of his mind. "Being a priest is as common and useless as being an Irish drunkard. Use your Gift instead, Young Francis," she'd said. "Use the Second Sight that has been in my family for a score of generations. It will help you go places and see things that no person on this sad earth has ever seen."

Young Francis did not believe in Second Sight. It was about that same time that he realized that he also did not believe in God. He went to sea. He believed in everything he learned and saw there, and some of these sights and lessons were strange indeed.

Crozier rides on crests of pain rolling in on waves of nausea. He awakens only to vomit into the bucket that Jopson, his steward, has left there and replaces each hour. Crozier hurts to the cavity in the center of his self where he is sure his soul had resided until it floated away on a sea of whiskey over the decades. All through these days and nights of cold sweat on frozen sheets, he knows he would give up his rank, his honours, his mother, his sisters, his father's name, and the memory of Memo Moira herself for one more glass of whiskey.

The ship groans as it continues to be squeezed inexorably to fragments by the never-ceasing ice. Crozier groans as his demons continue to squeeze him inexorably to fragments through chills, fever, pain, nausea, and regret. He has cut a six-inch strap from an old belt, and to keep from moaning aloud he bites down on that in the darkness. He moans anyway.

He imagines it all. He *sees* it all.

Lady Jane Franklin is in her element. Now, with two and a half years of no word from her husband, she is in her element. Lady Franklin the Indomitable. Lady Franklin the Widow Who Refused to Be a Widow. Lady Franklin the Patroness and Saint of the Arctic that has killed her husband . . . Lady Franklin who will never accept such a fact.

Crozier can see her as clearly as if he does have Second Sight. Lady Franklin has never looked more beautiful than now in her resolve, in her refusal to grieve, in her determination that her husband is alive and that Sir John's expedition must be found and rescued.

More than two and a half years have passed. The Navy knows that Sir John had provisioned *Erebus* and *Terror* for three years at normal rations but had expected to emerge beyond Alaska in the summer of 1846, certainly no later than August of 1847.

Lady Jane will have bullied the lethargic Navy and Parliament into action by now. Crozier can see her writing letters to the Admiralty, letters to the Arctic Council, letters to her friends and former suitors in Parliament, letters to the queen, and, of course, letters to her dead husband every day, writing in her perfect, no-nonsense script and telling the dead Sir John that she knows that her darling is still alive and that she looks forward to her inevitable reunion with him. He can see her telling the world that she does this. She will be sending sheaves and folios of letters to him off with the first rescue ships about now . . . Naval ships, to be sure, but also quite probably private ships hired with either the dwindling money of Lady Jane's own fortune or by subscriptions from worried and rich friends.

Crozier, rising from his visions, tries to sit up in his bunk and smile. The chills make him shake like a topgallant in a gale. He vomits into the almost full pail. He falls back onto his sweat-soaked, bile-smelling pillow and closes his eyes to ride the waves of his seeing.

Whom would they send to save *Erebus* and *Terror?* Whom had they already sent?

Crozier knew that Sir John Ross would be champing at the bit to lead any rescue parties into the ice, but he also sees that Lady Jane Franklin will ignore the old man — she thinks him vulgar — and will choose his nephew, James Clark Ross, with whom Crozier had explored the seas around Antarctica.

The younger Ross had promised his young bride that he would never go on a sea exploration again, but Crozier sees that he could not refuse this request from Lady Franklin. Ross would choose to go with two ships. Crozier saw them sailing this coming summer of 1848. Crozier saw the two ships sailing north of Baffin Island, west through Lancaster Sound, where Sir John had sailed *Terror* and *Erebus* three years ago — he could almost make out the names on the bows of Ross's ships — but Sir James would encounter the same relentless pack ice beyond Prince Regent Inlet, perhaps beyond Devon Island, that holds Crozier's ships in thrall now. Next summer there will be no full thaw of the sounds and inlets Ice Masters Reid and Blanky had sailed them south through. Sir James Clark Ross will never get within three hundred miles of *Terror* and *Erebus*.

Crozier saw them turning back to England in the freezing early autumn of 1848.

He weeps as he moans and bites down hard on his leather strap. His bones are freezing. His flesh is on fire. Ants crawl everywhere on and under his skin.

His Second Sight sees there would be other ships sent, other rescue expeditions this year of our Lord 1848, some most likely launched at the same time or earlier than Ross's search party. The Royal Navy was slow to act — a maritime sloth — but once in motion, Crozier knows, it tended to overdo everything it undertook. Wretched excess after interminable stalling was standard procedure for the Navy Francis Crozier has known for four decades.

In his aching mind, Crozier saw at least one other Naval expedition setting sail for Baffin Bay in search of the lost Franklins this coming summer and most probably even a third Naval squadron sent all the way around Cape Horn to rendezvous, theoretically, with the other search-party ships near the Bering Strait, searching for them in the western arctic, to which *Erebus* and *Terror* had never come within a thousand miles. Such ponderous operations would stretch into 1849 and beyond.

And this is only the beginning of the second week of 1848. Crozier doubts if his men will live to see the summer.

Would there be an overland party sent up from Canada to follow the Mackenzie River to the arctic coastline, then east to Wollaston Land and Victoria Land in search of their ships stranded somewhere along the elusive North-West Passage? Crozier is sure there will be. The chances of such an overland expedition finding them twenty-five miles out at sea to the northwest of King William Island are nil. Such a party would not even know that King William Island *was* an island.

Would the First Lord of the Admiralty announce in the House of Commons a reward for the rescue of Sir John and his men? Crozier thinks he will. But how much? A thousand pounds? Five thousand pounds? Ten thousand? Crozier closes tight his eyes and sees, as if on parchment hanging before him, the sum of twenty thousand pounds offered for anyone who "might render efficient assistance in saving the lives of Sir John Franklin and his squadron."

Crozier laughs again, which brings on the vomiting again. He is shaking with cold and pain and the clear absurdity of the images in his head. All around him the ship groans as the ice crushes it. The captain can no longer tell the groaning of the ship from his own moans.

He sees an image of eight ships — six British, two American — clustered within a few miles of one another in mostly frozen anchorages that look to Crozier like Devon Island, near Beechey, or perhaps Cornwallis Island. It is obviously a late arctic-summer day, perhaps late August, mere days before the sudden freeze that may capture all of them. Crozier has the sense that this image is two or three years in the future of his terrible reality this moment in 1848. Why eight ships sent out for rescue would end up clumped together like this in one location rather than fanning out throughout thousands of square miles of the arctic to hunt for signs of Franklin's passing makes no sense to Crozier whatsoever. It is the delusion of toxic madness.

The craft range in size from a small schooner and a yacht-sized craft far too flimsy for such serious ice work to 144-ton and 81-ton American ships strange to Crozier's eye to an odd little 90-ton English pilot boat crudely fitted out for arctic sailing. There are also several proper British Naval vessels and steam cruisers. In his aching mind's eye he can see the names of the ships — *Advance* and *Rescue,* these under the American flag, and *Prince Albert* for the former pilot boat, as well as the *Lady Franklin* at the head of the anchored British squadron. There are also two ships Crozier associates with old John Ross — the undersized schooner *Felix* and the totally inappropriate little yacht *Mary*. Finally there are two true Royal Navy vessels, *Assistance* and *Intrepid*.

As if viewing them through the eyes of a high-soaring arctic tern, Crozier can see that all eight of these ships are clustered within forty miles of one another — four of the smaller British craft at Griffith Island above the Barrow Strait, four of the remaining English ships at Assistance Bay on the south tip of Cornwallis, and the two American ships farther north, just around the eastern curve of Cornwallis Island, just across Wellington Channel from Sir John's first winter anchorage at Beechey Island. None are within two hundred and fifty miles of the spot far to the southwest where *Erebus* and *Terror* lie trapped.

A minute later, a mist or cloud clears, and Crozier sees six of these vessels anchored within a quarter of a mile of one another just off the curve of a small island's shoreline.

Crozier sees men running across frozen gravel under a vertical black cliff wall. The men are excited. He can almost hear their voices in the freezing air.

It is Beechey Island, he is sure. They have found the weathered wooden headboards and graves of Stoker John Torrington, Seaman John Hartnell, and Marine Private William Braine.

However far in the future this fever-dream discovery is, Crozier knows, it will do him and the other men of *Erebus* and *Terror* no good whatsoever. Sir John had left Beechey Island in a mindless hurry, sailing and steaming the first day the ice relented enough to allow the ships to leave their anchorage. After nine months frozen there, the Franklin Expedition had left not so much as a note saying which direction they were sailing.

Crozier had understood at the time that Sir John did not feel it necessary to inform the Admiralty that he was obeying their orders by sailing south. Sir John Franklin always obeyed orders. Sir John assumed that the Admiralty would trust that he had done so again. But after nine months on the island — and after building the proper cairn and even leaving a cairn of pebble-filled Goldner food cans behind as a sort of joke — the fact remained that the message cairn at Beechey Island was left empty contrary to Franklin's orders.

The Admiralty and Discovery Service had outfitted the Franklin Expedition with two hundred airtight brass cylinders for the express purpose of leaving behind messages of their whereabouts and destination along the entire course of their search for the North-West Passage, and Sir John had used . . . one: the useless one sent to King William Land twenty-five miles to the southeast of their present position, cached a few days before Sir John was killed in 1847.

On Beechey Island, nothing.

On Devon Island, which they had passed and explored, nothing.

On Griffith Island, where they had searched for harbours, nothing.

On Cornwallis Island, which they had circumnavigated, nothing.

Down the entire length of Somerset Island and Prince of Wales Island and Victoria Island along which they had sailed south for the entire summer of 1846, nothing.

And now, in his dream, the rescuers in the six ships — now all on the verge of being frozen in themselves — were looking north to what open sea remained up the Wellington Channel toward the North Pole. Beechey Island revealed no clues whatsoever. And Crozier could see from his magical arctic tern's high viewpoint that Peel Sound to the south — down which *Erebus* and *Terror* had found their way a year and a half ago during that brief summer thaw — was now, in this future summer, a solid sheet of white as far as the men on Beechey Island and sailing Barrow Strait could see.

They never even consider that Franklin could have gone that way . . . that he could have obeyed orders. Their attention — for the coming years, since Crozier sees that they are frozen in solid now in Lancaster Sound — is to search to the north. Sir John's secondary orders had been that if he could not continue his way south to force the Passage, he should turn north to sail through the theoretical rim of ice into the even more theoretical Open Polar Sea.

Crozier knows in his sinking heart that the captains and men of these eight rescue ships have all come to the conclusion that Franklin had gone north — precisely the opposite direction he had in fact sailed.

He wakes in the night. His own moaning has awakened him. There is light, but his eyes cannot stand the light so he tries to understand what is happening just through the burning of touch and the crash of sound. Two men — his steward, Jopson, and the surgeon, Goodsir — are stripping him of his filthy and sweat-soaked nightshirt, bathing him with miraculously warm water, and carefully dressing him in a clean nightshirt and socks. One of them tries to feed him soup with a spoon. Crozier vomits up the thin gruel, but the contents of his full-to-the-brim vomit pail are frozen solid and he is vaguely aware of the two men cleaning the deck. They make him drink some water and he falls back into his cold sheets. One of them spreads a warm blanket over him — *a warm, dry, unfrozen blanket* — and he wants to weep with gratitude. He also wants to speak but is slipping back into the maelstrom of his visions and cannot find or frame the words before all words are lost to him again.

He sees a boy with black hair and greenish skin curled in a fetal position against a brick-tile wall the colour of urine. Crozier knows that the boy is an epileptic in an asylum, in some bedlam somewhere. The boy shows no movement except for his dark eyes, which constantly flicker back and forth like a reptile's. *That shape am I.*

As soon as he thinks this, Crozier knows that this is not *his* fear. It is some other man's nightmare. He was briefly in some other mind.

Sophia Cracroft enters him. Crozier moans around the biting strap.

He sees her naked and straining against him at the Platypus Pond. He sees her distant and dismissive on the stone bench at Government House. He sees her standing and waving — not at him — in her blue silk dress on the dock at Greenhithe on the May day that *Erebus* and *Terror* sailed. Now he sees her as he has never seen her before — a future-present Sophia Cracroft, proud, grieving, secretly happy to be grieving, renewed and reborn as her aunt Lady Jane Franklin's full-time assistant and companion and amanuensis. She travels everywhere with Lady Jane — two indomitable women, the press will call them — Sophia, almost as much as her aunt, always visibly earnest and hopeful and strident and feminine and eccentric and bent to the task of cajoling the world to rescue Sir John Franklin. She will never mention Francis Crozier, not even in private. It is, he sees at once, a perfect role for Sophia: brave, imperious, entitled, able to play the coquette for decades with the perfect excuse for avoiding commitment or real love. She will never marry. She will travel the world with Lady Jane, Crozier sees, never publicly giving up hope that the missing Sir John will be found, but — long after real hope is surrendered — still enjoying the entitlement, sympathy, power, and position that this once-removed widowhood affords her.

Crozier tries to vomit, but his stomach has been empty now for hours or days. He can only curl up and suffer the cramps.

He is in a darkened parlour in a cramped, fussily furnished American farm home in Hydesdale, New York, some twenty miles west of Rochester. Crozier has never heard of either Hydesdale or Rochester, New York. He knows that it is spring of this year, 1848, perhaps only a few weeks in his future. Just visible through a crack in the drawn, thick drapes, a lightning storm surges and flashes. Thunder shakes the house.

"Come, Mother!" cries one of two girls at the table. "We promise you will find this edifying."

"I will find it terrifying," says the mother, a drab middle-aged woman with a perpetual frown line bisecting her forehead from her tightly pulled, greying bun to her heavy, frowning eyebrows. "I don't know why I allow you to talk me into this."

Crozier can only marvel at the flat ugliness of the American rural dialect. Most of the Americans he has known have been defecting sailors, U.S. Navy captains, or whalers.

"Hurry, Mother!" The girl commanding her mother in such a bossy tone is 15-year-old Margaret Fox. She is modestly dressed and attractive in a simpering and not especially intelligent way that Crozier has noticed is often the case with the few American women he has met socially. The other girl at the table is Margaret's 11-year-old sister Catherine. The younger girl, her pale face only just visible in the flickering candlelight, more resembles her mother, down to the dark eyebrows, too-tight bun, and incipient frown line.

The lightning flashes in the gap between dusty drapes.

The mother and two girls join hands around the circular oak table. Crozier notices that the lace doily on the table has yellowed with age. All three females have their eyes closed. Thunder shakes the single candle's flame.

"Is someone there?" asks 15-year-old Margaret.

A crashingly loud rap. Not thunder, but a *crack,* as if someone has struck wood with a small mallet. Everyone's hands are in sight.

"Oh my!" cries the mother, obviously ready to throw her hands up over her mouth in fear. Her two daughters hold tight and keep her from breaking the circle. The table rocks from their tugging.

"Are you our Guide tonight?" asks Margaret.

A loud *RAP.*

"Have you come to hurt us in any way?" asks Katy.

Two even louder *RAP*s.

"See, Mother?" whispers Maggie. Closing her eyes again, she says in a theatrical whisper, "Guide, are you the gentle Mr. Splitfoot who communicated with us last night?"

RAP.

"Thank you for convincing us last evening that you were real, Mr. Splitfoot," continues Maggie, speaking almost as if she were in a trance. "Thank you for telling Mother the details about her children, telling all our ages, and for reminding her of the sixth child who died. Will you answer our questions tonight?"

RAP.

"Where is the Franklin Expedition?" asks little Katy.

RAP RAP RAP rap rap rap rap RAP RAP rap RAP RAP . . . the percusssions go on for half a minute.

"Is this the Spiritual Telegraph you spoke of?" whispers their mother.

Maggie shushes her. The rapping breaks off. Crozier sees, as if he can float through wood and see through wool and cotton, that both girls are double-jointed and are taking turns snapping and popping their big toes against their second toes. It was an amazingly loud rapping sound from such small toes.

"Mr. Splitfoot says that the Sir John Franklin whom the papers say everyone is seeking is well and with his men, who are also all well but very frightened, on their ships and in the ice near an island five days' sail south of the cold place where they stopped their first year out," intones Maggie.

"It is very dark where they are," adds Katy.

There come more rappings.

"Sir John tells his wife, Jane, not to worry," interprets Maggie. "He says that he shall see her soon — in the next world, if not in this one."

"Oh my!" Mrs. Fox says again. "We have to call for Mary Redfield and Mr. Redfield, and Leah, of course, and Mr. and Mrs. Duesler, and Mrs. Hyde, and Mr. and Mrs. Jewell . . ."

"Ssshhhh!" hisses Katy.

RAP, RAP, RAP, raprapraprap, RAP.

"The Guide does not want you to speak when He is leading us," whispers Katy.

Crozier moans and bites his leather strap. The cramps that had begun in his gut now rack his entire body. He shakes from the chill one moment and throws off the blankets the next.

There is a man dressed like an Esquimaux — animal-fur parka, high furry boots, a fur hood like Lady Silence's. But this man is standing on a wooden stage in front of footlights. It is very hot. Behind the man, a painted backdrop shows ice, icebergs, a wintry sky. Fake white snow litters the stage. There are four overheated dogs of the type used by the Greenland Esquimaux lying on the stage, their tongues lolling.

The bearded man in the heavy parka is talking from the white-speckled podium. "I speak to you today for humanity, not for money," says the little man. His American accent grates on Crozier's aching ear as fiercely as had the teenaged girls'. "And I have traveled to England to speak to Lady Franklin herself. She wishes me Godspeed on our next expedition — contingent, of course, on whether we raise the money here in Philadelphia and in New York and in Boston to mount the expedition — and says that she would be honoured if the sons of the United States were to bring home her husband. So today I ask for your generosity, but only for the sake of humanity. I ask for this in Lady Franklin's name, in her lost husband's name, and in the secure hopes of bringing glory to the United States of America. . . ."

Crozier sees the man again. The bearded fellow is out of his parka and naked and in bed in the Union Hotel in New York with a very young naked woman. It is a hot night and the bedclothes have been thrown back. There is no sign of the sledge dogs.

"Whatever may be my faults," the man is saying, speaking softly because the window and transom are open to the New York night, "I have at least loved you. Were you an empress, darling Maggie, instead of a little nameless girl following an obscure and *ambiguous* profession, it would be the same."

Crozier realizes that the young naked woman is Maggie Fox — only a few years older. She is still attractive in that simpering American way, even without her clothes on.

Maggie says in a tone much more throaty than the teenager's imperious command Crozier heard earlier, "Dr. Kane, you know I love you."

The man shakes his head. He has lifted a pipe from the bedside table and now frees his left arm from behind the girl to tamp in the tobacco and light it. "Maggie, my dear, I hear those words from your little deceitful mouth, feel your hair tumbling onto my chest, and would love to believe them. But you cannot rise above your station, my dear. You have many traits which lift you above your calling, Maggie . . . you are refined and lovable and, with a different education, would have been innocent and artless. But you are not worthy of a permanent regard from me, Miss Fox."

"Not worthy," repeats Maggie. Her eyes, perhaps her prettiest feature now that her plump breasts are covered from Crozier's view, appear to be brimming with tears.

"I am sold to different destinies, my child," says Dr. Kane. "Remember that I have my own sad vanities to pursue, even as you and your venial sisters and mother pursue your own. I am as devoted to my calling as you, poor child, can be to yours, if such theatrical spiritualist poppycock can be *called* a calling. Remember then, as a sort of a dream, that Dr. Kane of the Arctic Seas loved Maggie Fox of the Spirit Rappings."

Crozier comes awake in the dark. He does not know where or when he is. His cubicle is dark. The ship seems dark. The timbers moan — or is that an echo of his own moans of the last hours and days? It is very cold. The warm blanket he seems to remember Jopson and Goodsir setting on him is now as damp and frozen as the other bedsheets. The ice moans against the ship. The ship continues its answering groans from pressured oak and cold-strained iron.

Crozier wants to get up but finds that he is too weak and hollow to stir. He can barely move his arms. The pain and visions roll over him like a breaking wave.

Faces of men he has known or met or seen in the Service.

There is Robert McClure, one of the most guileful and ambitious men Francis Crozier has ever known — another Irishman intent on making good in an English world. McClure is on the deck of a ship in the ice. Cliffs of ice and rock rise all around, some six or seven hundred feet high. Crozier has never seen anything like it.

There is old John Ross on the stern deck of a little ship — a sort of yacht — heading eastward. Heading home.

There is James Clark Ross, older and fatter and less happy than Crozier has ever seen him. The rising sun shines through ice-rimmed jib lines as his ship leaves the ice for the open sea. He is heading home.

There is Francis Leopold M'Clintock — someone Crozier somehow knows has searched for Franklin under James Ross and then come back on his own again in later years. What later years? How long from now? How far in our future?

Crozier can see images flit by as if from a magic lantern, but he does not hear answers to his questions.

There is M'Clintock sledging, man-hauling, moving more quickly and efficiently than Lieutenant Gore or any of Sir John's or Crozier's men ever have.

There is M'Clintock standing at a cairn and reading a note just pulled from a brass cylinder. Is it the note that Gore left on King William Land seven months ago? Crozier wonders. The frozen gravel and grey skies behind M'Clintock look the same.

Suddenly there is M'Clintock, alone on the ice and gravel, his sledging party visible coming up several hundred yards behind him in the blowing snow. He is standing in front of a horror — a large boat tied and lashed atop of a huge cobbled-together sledge made of iron and oak.

The sledge looks like something Crozier's carpenter, Mr. Honey, would build. It has been assembled as if it was meant to last for a century. Every join shows care. The thing is massive — it must weigh at least 650 pounds. Atop it is a boat that weighs another 800 pounds.

Crozier recognizes the boat. It is one of *Terror*'s 28-footers — one of the pinnaces. He sees that it has been extensively rigged for river travel. The sails are furled and tied and shrouded and iced over.

Climbing onto a rock and looking into the open boat as if over M'Clintock's shoulder, Crozier sees two skeletons. The teeth in the two skulls seem to gleam at M'Clintock and Crozier. One skeleton is little more than a heap of visibly chewed and heavily gnawed and partially devoured bones tumbled into a rough pile in the bow. Snow has drifted over the bones.

The other skeleton is intact, undisturbed, and still clothed in the tatters of what looks to be an officer's greatcoat and layers of other warm clothing. The skull still has remnants of a cap on it. This corpse is sprawled on the after-thwarts, its skeletal hands extended along the gunwales toward two double-barreled shotguns propped there. At the body's booted feet lie stacks of wool blankets and canvas clothing and a partially snow-covered burlap bag filled with powder-shot cartridges. Set on the bottom of the pinnace midway between the dead man's boots, like a pirate's booty about to be counted and gloated over, are five gold watches and what looks to be thirty or forty pounds of individually wrapped chunks of chocolate. Also nearby are 26 pieces of silverware — Crozier can see, and knows that M'Clintock can see, the personal crests of Sir John Franklin's, Captain Fitzjames's, six other officers', and his — Crozier's — on the various knives, spoons, and forks. He sees similarly engraved dishes and two silver serving plates sticking up out of the ice and snow.

Along the 25 feet of pinnace bottom separating the two skeletons lies a dizzying array of bric-a-brac protruding from the few inches of snow that have accumulated: two rolls of sheet metal, a full canvas boat cover, eight pairs of boots, two saws, four files, a stack of nails, and two boat knives next to the bag of powder-shot cartridges near the skeleton in the stern.

Crozier also sees paddles, folded sails, and rolls of twine near the clothed skeleton. Closer to the pile of partially devoured bones in the bow are a stack of towels, bars of soap, several combs and a toothbrush, a pair of handworked slippers just inches from scattered white toe bones and metatarsals, and six books — five Bibles and *The Vicar of Wakefield,* which now sits on a shelf in the Great Cabin of HMS *Terror.*

Crozier wants to close his eyes but cannot. He wants to fly away from this vision — all these visions — but has no control over them.

Suddenly Francis Leopold M'Clintock's vaguely familiar face seems to melt, sag, then reform itself into the visage of a younger man, someone Francis Crozier does not know. Everything else stays the same. The younger man — a certain Lieutenant William Hobson, whom Crozier now knows without knowing how he knows — is standing in the same spot that M'Clintock had and is peering into the open boat with the same expression of sickened incredulity that Crozier had seen on M'Clintock's face a moment earlier.

Without warning, the open boat and the skeletons are gone and Crozier is lying in a cave of ice next to a naked Sophia Cracroft.

No, it is not Sophia. Crozier blinks, feeling Memo Moira's Second Sight burning through and from his aching brain like a fist of fever, and now he sees that he is lying naked next to a naked Lady Silence. They are surrounded by furs, and they are lying on some sort of snow or ice shelf. Their space is illuminated by a flickering oil lamp. The curved ceiling is made from blocks of ice. Silence's breasts are brown, and her hair is long and very black. She is leaning on one elbow amid the furs and looking at Crozier with some earnestness.

Do you dream my dreams? she asks without moving her lips or opening her mouth. She has not spoken in English. *Am I dreaming yours?*

Crozier *feels* her inside his mind and heart. It feels like a jolt of the best whiskey he has ever swallowed.

And then the most terrible nightmare of all comes.

This stranger, this blend of M'Clintock and someone named Hobson, is not looking down at the open boat with two skeletons in it but is watching young Francis Rawdon Moira Crozier secretly attending Catholic Mass with his witch-Papist Memo Moira.

It was one of the deepest secrets of Crozier's life that he had done this thing — not only gone to the forbidden service with Memo Moira but partaken of the heresy of the Catholic Eucharist, the much-derided and forbidden Holy Communion.

But this form of M'Clintock-Hobson stands like an altar boy as a trembling Crozier — now a child, now a scarred man in his fifties — approaches the altar rail, kneels, puts his head back, opens his mouth, and extends his tongue for the Forbidden Wafer — the Body of Christ — pure transubstantiated cannibalism to all the other adults in Crozier's village and family and life.

But something is strange. The grey-haired priest looming over him in his white robes is dripping water on the floor and altar rail and onto Crozier himself. And the priest is too large even for a child's point of view — huge, wet, muscled, lumbering, throwing a shadow over the kneeling communicant. He is not human.

And Crozier is naked as he kneels, sets his head back, closes his eyes, and extends his tongue for the Sacrament.

The priest looming and dripping over him has no Wafer in his hand. He has no hands. Instead, the dripping apparition leans over the altar rail, leans far too close, and opens its own inhuman maw as if Crozier is the Bread to be devoured.

"Dear Jesus Christ God Almighty," whispers this watching M'Clintock-Hobson form.

"Dear Jesus Christ God Almighty," whispers Captain Francis Crozier.

"He's back with us," Dr. Goodsir says to Mr. Jopson.

Crozier moans.

"Sir," the surgeon says to Crozier, "can you sit up? Are you able to open your eyes and sit up? That's a good captain."

"What day is it?" croaks Crozier. The dull light from the open door and the even duller light from his oil lamp turned low are like explosions of painful sunshine against his sensitive eyes.

"It's Tuesday, the eleventh day of January, Captain," says his steward. And then Jopson adds, "The year of our Lord eighteen hundred and forty-eight."

"You were very ill for a week," says the surgeon. "Several times in the last few days I was sure that we had lost you." Goodsir gives him some water to sip.

"I was dreaming," manages Crozier after drinking the ice-cold water. He can smell his own stink in the nest of frozen bedclothes around him.

"You were moaning very loudly the last few hours," says Goodsir. "Do you remember any of your malarial dreams?"

Crozier remembers only the sense-of-flying weightlessness of his dreams, yet at the same time the weight and horror and humour of visions that had already fled like wisps of fog before a strong wind.

"No," he says. "Mr. Jopson, please be so kind as to fetch me hot water for my toilet. You may have to help me shave. Dr. Goodsir . . ."

"Yes, Captain?"

"Would you be so kind as to go forward and tell Mr. Diggle that his captain wants a very large breakfast this morning."

"It is six bells in the evening, Captain," says the surgeon.

"Nonetheless, I want a very large breakfast. Biscuits. What's left of our potatoes. Coffee. Pork of some sort — bacon if he has it."

"Aye, sir."

"And, Dr. Goodsir," Crozier says to the departing surgeon. "Would you also be so kind as to ask Lieutenant Little to come aft with a report on the week I have missed and also ask him to bring my . . . property."

28

PEGLAR

Lat. 70°-05' N., Long. 98°-23' W.
29 January, 1848

arry Peglar had planned it so that he received the duty to carry a message to *Erebus* on the day the sun returned. He wanted to celebrate it — as much as anything could be celebrated these days — with someone he loved. And somebody he'd once been in love with.

Chief Petty Officer Harry Peglar was captain of the foretop on *Terror,* chosen leader of the carefully picked topmen who worked the highest rigging, topsail, and topgallant yards in blaze of day or dark of night as well as in the highest seas and worst weather the world could throw at a wooden ship. This was a position that required strength, experience, leadership, and, most of all, courage, and Harry Peglar was respected for all of these traits. Now almost forty-one years old, he had proved himself hundreds of times not only in front of the crew of HMS *Terror* but on a dozen other ships on which he'd served over his long career.

It had been only mildly ironic then that Harry Peglar had been illiterate until he was a twenty-five-year-old midshipman. Reading was now his secret pleasure, and he had already devoured more than half of the 1,000 volumes in *Terror*'s Great Cabin on this voyage. It had been a mere officers' steward on the survey bark HMS *Beagle* who had transformed Peglar into a literate man, and it was the same steward who had made Harry Peglar ponder what it meant to be a man.

John Bridgens was that steward. He was now the oldest man on the expedition, by far. When they had sailed from England, the joke in both *Erebus*'s and *Terror*'s fo'c'sles had been that John Bridgens, lowly subordinate officers' steward, was the same age as the elderly Sir John Franklin but twenty times as wise. Harry Peglar, for one, knew that this was true.

Old men below the rank of captain or admiral rarely were allowed on Discovery Service expeditions, so it was with some good humour that both crews learned that John Bridgens's age on the official ship's muster had been reversed — either by accident or by a purser with a sense of irony — and listed as "26." There had been many jokes made to the grey-haired Bridgens about his youth and callowness and presumed sexual prowess. The quiet steward had smiled and said nothing.

It had been Harry Peglar who had sought out a younger steward Bridgens on the HMS *Beagle* during their five-year round-the-world scientific survey voyage under Captain FitzRoy from December of 1831 to October of 1836. Peglar had followed an officer he'd served under on HMS *Prince Regent,* a lieutenant named John Lort Stokes, from the first-rate 120-gun ship of the line to the lowly *Beagle.* The *Beagle* was only a *Cherokee* class 10-gun brig adapted as a survey bark — hardly the kind of ship that an ambitious topman like young Peglar would normally pick — but even then Harry had been interested in scientific survey work and exploration, and the voyage of the little *Beagle* under FitzRoy had been an education for him in more ways than one.

Steward Bridgens had been about eight years older then than Peglar was now — in his late forties — but already known as the wisest and most widely read warrant officer in the fleet. He was also known as a sodomite, a fact that hadn't bothered twenty-five-year-old Peglar much at the time. There were two types of sodomites in the Royal Navy: those who sought their satisfaction only on shore and never brought their activities to sea, and those who continued their habits at sea, often by seducing the young boys almost always present on Royal Navy ships. Bridgens, everyone in the *Beagle* fo'c'sle and in the Navy knew, was the former — a man who liked men when ashore but who never bragged of it nor brought his inclinations to sea. And, unlike the caulker's mate on Peglar's current ship, Bridgens was no pederast. Most of his crewmates thought that a boy at sea was safer with subordinate officers' steward John Bridgens than he would have been with his village vicar at home.

Besides that, Harry Peglar was living with Rose Murray when he sailed in 1831. Although never formally married — she was a Catholic and would not marry Harry unless he converted, which he could not bring himself to do — they were a happy couple when Peglar was ashore, although Rose's own illiteracy and lack of curiosity about the world reflected the younger Peglar's life and not the man he would later become. Perhaps they would have married if Rose could have had children, but she could not — a condition she referred to as "God's punishment." Rose died while Peglar was at sea on the long *Beagle* voyage. He had loved her, in his way.

But he had also loved John Bridgens.

Before the five-year mission of the survey ship HMS *Beagle* had ended, Bridgens — at first accepting his role of mentor with reluctance but finally bending under the young topsail midshipman's eager insistence — had taught Harry to read and write not only in English but also in Greek and Latin and German. He had taught him philosophy and history and natural history. More than that, Bridgens had taught the intelligent young man to think.

It had been two years after that voyage that Peglar had looked up the older man in London — Bridgens had been on extended shore leave with most of the rest of the fleet in 1838 — and requested more tutoring. By then, Peglar was already captain of the foretop on the HMS *Wanderer.*

It was during those months of shorebound discussion and further tutoring that the close friendship between the two men had moved into something more resembling lovers' interactions. The revelation that he was capable of doing such a thing astounded Peglar — dismaying him at first but then causing him to reconsider every aspect of his life, morals, faith, and sense of self. What he discovered confused him but, to his astonishment, did not change his basic sense of who Harry Peglar was. What was even more astounding to him was that he had been the one to instigate intimate physical contact — not the older man.

The intimate aspect of their friendship lasted only a few months and ended by mutual choice as much as by Peglar's long absences at sea on *Wanderer* until 1844. Their friendship survived intact. Peglar began writing long philosophical letters to the former steward and would spell all words backward, the last letter of the last word in each sentence now first and capitalized. Mostly because the formerly illiterate foretop captain's spelling was so atrocious, Bridgens suggested in one responding letter that "your childlike idea of Leonardo's backward-writing encryption, Harry, is almost unbreakable." Peglar now kept his journals in the same crude code.

Neither man had told the other that he was applying for Discovery Service duty on Sir John Franklin's North-West Passage expedition. Both were astonished a few weeks before sailing time when they saw the other's name on the official roster. Peglar, who had not been in communication with Bridgens for more than a year, traveled from the Woolwich barracks up to the steward's North London rooms to ask if he should drop out of the expedition. Bridgens insisted that *he* should be the one to remove his name from the list. In the end, they agreed that neither of them should lose the opportunity for such adventure — certainly Bridgens' last opportunity because of his advanced age (*Erebus*'s purser, Charles Hamilton Osmer, had been a longtime friend of Bridgens and had smoothed his enlistment with Sir John and the officers, even going so far as to hide the subordinate officers' steward's real age by being the one to write it as "26" on the official rolls). Neither Peglar nor Bridgens said it aloud, but both knew that the older man's long-standing vow never to bring his sexual desires to sea would be honoured by both of them. That part of their history, they both knew, was closed.

As it turned out, Peglar had seen almost nothing of his old friend during the voyage, and in three and a half years, they rarely had a minute alone.

———

It was still dark, of course, when Peglar arrived at *Erebus* sometime around eleven on this Saturday morning two days before the end of January, but there was a glow in the south that promised to be, for the first time in more than eighty days, a predawn glow. The slight glow did not dispel the bite from the −65-degree temperatures, so he did not dawdle as the lanterns of the ship came into sight.

The view of *Erebus*'s truncated masts would have dismayed any topman, but it hurt Harry Peglar more than most since he had, with his *Erebus* captain of the foretop counterpart, Robert Sinclair, helped supervise the dismantling and storage of both ships' upper masts for the endless winters. It was an ugly sight at any time and was made no prettier by *Erebus*'s bizarre stern-down, bow-up posture in the encroaching ice.

Peglar was hailed by the watch, invited aboard, and he carried his message from Captain Crozier down to Captain Fitzjames, who was sitting and smoking his pipe in the aft officers' mess since the Great Cabin was still being used as an ad hoc sick bay.

The captains had begun using the brass canisters meant for cached reports to send their written messages back and forth — the couriers hated this change since the cold metal burned fingers even through heavy gloves — and Fitzjames had to order Peglar to open the canister with his mittens, since the tube was still too cold for the captain to touch. Fitzjames did not dismiss him, so Peglar stood in the doorway to the officers' mess while the captain read the note from Crozier.

"No return message, Mr. Peglar," said Fitzjames.

The foretop captain knuckled his forehead and went up onto the deck again. About a dozen Erebuses had come up to watch the sunrise and more had been getting into their slops below to do so. Peglar had noticed that the Great Cabin sick bay had about a dozen men in it on cots — about the same number as *Terror*. Scurvy was setting in on both ships.

Peglar saw the small, familiar figure of John Bridgens standing at the rail on the stern's port side. He came up behind him and tapped the man on the shoulder.

"Ah, a little touch of Harry in the night," said Bridgens even before he turned.

"Not night for long," said Peglar. "And how did you know it was me, John?"

Bridgens had no comforter over his face, and Peglar could see his smile and watery blue eyes. "Word of visitors travels quickly on a small ship frozen in the ice. Do you have to hurry back to *Terror?*"

"No. Captain Fitzjames had no response."

"Would you care to take a stroll?"

"By all means," said Peglar.

They went down the starboard side ice ramp and walked toward the iceberg and high pressure ridge to the southeast so as to get a better view of the glowing south. For the first time in months, HMS *Erebus* was backlit by something other than the aurora or lantern or torchlight.

Before they reached the pressure ridge, they passed the scuffed, sooted, and partially melted area where the Carnivale fire had burned. The area had been well cleaned up on Captain Crozier's orders in the week after the disaster, but post holes where the staves had served as tent poles remained, as did shreds of rope or canvas that had melted into the ice and then been frozen in place. The rectangle of the ebony room still showed even after repeated efforts to remove the black soot and several snowfalls.

"I've read the American writer," said Bridgens.

"American writer?"

"The chap who caused little Dickie Aylmore to receive fifty lashes for his inventive set decorations for our late, unlamented carnivale. A strange little fellow by the name of Poe, if memory serves. Very melancholy and morbid stuff with a touch of the truly unhealthy macabre. Not very good, overall, but very *American* in some undefinable sense. I did not, however, read the fateful story that brought on the lashes."

Peglar nodded. His foot struck something in the snow, and he bent to pry it out of the ice.

It was the bear's skull that had been hanging above Sir John's ebony clock, which had not survived the flames — the skull's flesh, hide, and hair gone and bone blackened by the fire, eye sockets empty, but the teeth still ivory-coloured.

"Oh, my, Mr. Poe would love that, I think," said Bridgens.

Peglar dropped it back into the snow. The thing must have been hidden beneath chunks of fallen ice when the clean-up parties worked here. He and Bridgens walked another fifty yards to the tallest pressure ridge in the area and clambered up it, Peglar repeatedly giving his hand to help the older man up.

On a flat slab of ice atop the ridge, Bridgens was panting heavily. Even Peglar, normally as fit as one of the ancient Olympic athletes he'd read about, found himself breathing harder than usual. Too many months of no real physical duty, he thought.

The southern horizon was glowing a subdued, washed-out yellow, and most of the stars in that half of the sky had paled.

"I almost can't believe it's returning," said Peglar.

Bridgens nodded.

Suddenly there it was, the disk of red-gold rising hesitantly above dark masses that looked like hills but must be low clouds far to the south. Peglar heard the forty or so men on the deck of *Erebus* give three cheers, and — because the air was very cold and very still — he could hear a duplicate but fainter cheer coming from *Terror,* just visible almost a mile to the east across the ice.

"Dawn stretches forth her rosy fingertips," Bridgens said in Greek.

Peglar smiled, mildly amused that he remembered the phrase. It had been several years since he'd read the *Iliad* or anything else in Greek. He remembered the excitement of his first encounter with this language and with Troy and its heroes as *Beagle* had been anchored off São Tiago, a volcanic island in the Cape Verde Islands, almost seventeen years earlier.

As if reading his mind, Bridgens said, "Do you remember Mr. Darwin?"

"The young naturalist?" said Peglar. "Captain FitzRoy's favorite interlocutor? Of course I do. Five years on a small bark with a man leaves an impression, even if he was a gentleman and I wasn't."

"And what was your impression, Harry?" Bridgens' pale blue eyes were watering more heavily, either out of emotion at seeing the sun again or just in reaction to the unaccustomed light, as pale as it was.

The red disk had not completely cleared the dark clouds before it started descending again.

"Of Mr. Darwin?" Peglar was also squinting — more to bring back memory of the thin young naturalist than because of the sun's wonderful illumination. "I found him pleasant, as such gentlemen go. Very enthusiastic. He certainly kept the men busy transporting and crating up all those damned dead animals — at one point I thought the finches alone were going to fill the hold — but he wasn't above getting his own hands dirty. Remember the time he joined in the rowing to help tow old *Beagle* upstream in the river? And he saved a boat from the tidal wave that other time. And once, when whales were alongside us — off the coast of Chile, I believe — I was amazed to find that he'd climbed all the way up to the crosstrees on his own to get a better view. I had to help him down, but not before he looked through the glass at the whales for over an hour, the tails of his coat flapping in the breeze."

Bridgens smiled. "I was almost jealous when he lent you that book. What was it? Lyell?"

"*Principles of Geology,*" said Peglar. "I didn't really understand it. Or rather, I did just enough to realize how dangerous it was."

"Because of Lyell's contention about the age of things," said Bridgens. "About the very un-Christian idea that things change slowly over immense aeons of time rather than very quickly due to very violent events."

"Yes," said Peglar. "But Mr. Darwin was very keen on it. He sounded like a man who had experienced a religious conversion."

"I believe he had, in a manner of speaking," said Bridgens. Only the top third of the sun was visible now. "I mention Mr. Darwin because mutual friends told me before we sailed that he is writing a book."

"He published several already," said Peglar. "Do you remember, John, we discussed his *Journal of Researches into the Geology and Natural History of the Various Countries Visited by H.M.S. Beagle* in the year I came to study with you . . . 1839. I couldn't afford to buy it, but you said you'd read it. And I believe he published several volumes on the plant and animal life he saw."

"*The Zoology of the Voyage of H.M.S.* Beagle," said Bridgens. "Yes, I purchased that as well. No, I meant he has been working on a much more important book according to my dear friend Mr. Babbage."

"Charles Babbage?" said Peglar. "The fellow who tinkers up so many odd things including some sort of computing engine?"

"The same," said Bridgens. "Charles tells me that all these years, Mr. Darwin has been working on a quite interesting volume discussing the mechanisms of organic evolution. Apparently it draws in information from comparative anatomy, embryology, and paleontology . . . all great interests of our former shipboard naturalist's, you may remember. But for whatever reasons, Mr. Darwin is loath to publish and the book may not see print, according to Charles, in anyone's lifetime."

"Organic evolution?" repeated Peglar.

"Yes, Harry. That's the idea that species, despite all civilized Christian agreement to the contrary, are not fixed since creation, but may change and adapt over time . . . much time. Mr. Lyell's amounts of time."

"I know what organic evolution is," said Peglar, trying not to show his irritation at being talked down to. The problem with a student-teacher relationship was, he realized not for the first time, that it never changes while everything around it does. "I've read Lamarck on the concept. Also Diderot. And Buffon, I believe."

"Yes, it's an old theory," said Bridgens, his tone sounding amused but also slightly apologetic. "Montesquieu has written about it, as has Maupertuis and the others you mentioned. Even Erasmus Darwin, our former shipmate's grandfather, had proposed it."

"Then why would Mr. Charles Darwin's book be important?" asked Peglar. "Organic evolution is an old idea. It's been rejected by the Church and other naturalists for generations."

"If Charles Babbage and other friends Mr. Darwin and I have in common are to be believed," said Bridgens, "this new book — should it ever be published — offers proof of an actual mechanism for organic evolution. And it should give a thousand — perhaps ten thousand — solid examples of this mechanism in action."

"And the mechanism is what?" asked Peglar. The sun had disappeared. Rose shadows faded into the pale yellow gloom that had preceded its rising. Now that the sun was gone, Peglar hardly believed he had seen it.

"Natural selection arising from competition *within* the countless species," said the elderly subordinate officers' steward. "A selection passing along advantageous traits and weeding out disadvantageous traits — that is, ones which add to the probability of neither survival nor reproduction — over vast amounts of time. Lyellian amounts of time."

Peglar thought about this for a minute. "Why did you bring this up, John?"

"Because of our predatory friend out here on the ice, Harry. Because of the blackened skull you left back where the ebony room had once echoed to the ticking of Sir John's ebony clock."

"I don't quite understand," said Peglar. He used to say that very frequently when he was John Bridgens's student during the five years of *Beagle*'s seemingly endless wanderings. The voyage had been planned as a two-year venture, and Peglar had promised Rose he would be back in two years or less. She had died of consumption during *Beagle*'s fourth year at sea. "Do you think the thing on the ice is some form of species evolutionary adaptation from the more common white bear we've encountered so frequently up here?"

"Quite the contrary," said Bridgens. "I find myself wondering if we might have encountered one of the last members of some ancient species — something larger, smarter, faster, and infinitely more violent than its descendant, the smaller north polar bear we see in such abundance."

Peglar thought about this. "Something from an antediluvian age," he said at last.

Bridgens chuckled. "In a metaphorical sense, at least, Harry. You may remember that I was no advocate of any literal belief in the Flood."

Peglar smiled. "You were dangerous to be around, John." He stood in the cold thinking for another few minutes. The light was fading. The stars were filling in the southern sky once again. "Do you think this . . . thing . . . this last of its breed . . . walked the earth when the huge lizards were around? If so, why haven't we found fossils of it?"

Bridgens chuckled again. "No, somehow I do not believe our predator on the ice contested with the giant lizards. Perhaps mammals such as *Ursus maritimus* did not coexist with the giant reptiles at all. As Lyell showed and our Mr. Darwin seems to understand, Time . . . with a capital *T*, Harry . . . may be much vaster than we have the ability to comprehend."

The two men were silent for a few moments. The wind had started up a little and Peglar realized that it was too cold to stay out here like this much longer. He could see the older man shivering slightly. "John," he said. "Do you think that understanding the origin of the beast . . . or *thing*, it sometimes seems too intelligent to be a beast . . . will help us kill it?"

Bridgens laughed aloud this time. "Not in the least, Harry. Just between you and me, dear friend, I think the creature already has the better of us. I think our bones will be fossils before its will . . . although, when one thinks about it, a huge creature which lives almost completely on the polar ice, not breeding or living on dry land as the more common white bears evidently do, perhaps even *preying* on the more common polar bear as its primary source of food, may well leave no bones, no trace, no fossils . . . at least ones we are able to find beneath the frozen polar seas at our current state of scientific technology."

They began walking back toward *Erebus*.

"Tell me, Harry, what is happening on *Terror?*"

"You heard about the near mutiny three days ago?" asked Peglar.

"Was it really so close a thing?"

Peglar shrugged. "It was ugly. Any officer's nightmare. The caulker's mate, Hickey, and two or three other agitators, had the men all worked up. It was a mob mentality. Crozier defused it brilliantly. I don't think I've ever seen a captain handle a mob with more finesse and certainty than Crozier did on Wednesday."

"And it was all over the Esquimaux woman?"

Peglar nodded, then pulled his Welsh wig and comforter tighter. The wind was very biting now. "Hickey and a majority of the men had learned that the wench had tunneled a way out through the hull before

Christmas. Until the day of Carnivale, she'd been coming and going at will from her den in the forward cable locker. Mr. Honey and his carpenter mates had fixed the breech in the hull, and Mr. Irving had collapsed the outside tunnel route the day after the Carnivale fire — and word leaked out."

"And Hickey and the others thought that she had something to do with the fire?"

Peglar shrugged again. If nothing else, the motion helped keep him warm. "For all I know, they thought she *was* the thing on the ice. Or at least its consort. Most of the men have been convinced for months that she's a heathen witch."

"Most of the crew on *Erebus* agree," said Bridgens. His teeth were chattering. The two men picked up their pace back toward the canting ship.

"Hickey's mob had made plans to waylay the girl when she came up for her evening biscuit and cod," said Peglar. "And to cut her throat. Perhaps with some formal ceremony."

"Why didn't it happen that way, Harry?"

"There's always someone who informs," said Peglar. "When Captain Crozier got wind of it — possibly only hours before the murder was supposed to happen — he dragged the girl up to the lower deck and called a meeting of all officers and men. He even called the watch below, which is unheard of."

Bridgens turned his pale square of a face toward Peglar as they walked. It was getting darker quickly now and the wind was holding out of the nor'west.

"It was just at supper time," continued Peglar, "but the captain had all the men's tables winched up again and made the men sit on the deck. No casks or chests — just on the bare deck — and had the officers, armed with sidearms, stand behind him. He held the Esquimaux girl by the arm, as if she was an offering he was going to throw to the men. Like a piece of meat to jackals. In a sense that's what he did."

"How do you mean?"

"He told the crew that if they were going to do murder, that they had to do it right then . . . at that moment. With their boat knives.

Right there on the lower deck where they ate and slept. Captain Crozier said that they would all have to do it together — seamen and officers alike — because murder on a ship is like a canker and spreads unless everyone is already inoculated by being an accomplice."

"Very strange," said Bridgens. "But I am surprised that it worked to deter the men's bloodthirst. A mob is a brainless thing."

Peglar nodded again. "Then Crozier called Mr. Diggle forward from his place by the stove."

"The cook?" said Bridgens.

"The cook. Crozier asked Mr. Diggle what was for supper that night . . . and for every night in the coming month. 'Poor John,' said Diggle. 'Plus whatever canned things haven't gone rotten or poisonous.'"

"Interesting," said Bridgens.

"Crozier then asked Dr. Goodsir — who happened to be on *Terror* that day — how many men had shown up for sick call in the last three days. 'Twenty-one,' says Goodsir. 'With fourteen sleeping nights in sick bay until you called them forward for this meeting, sir.'"

It was Bridgens' turn to nod now, as if he could see where Crozier had been headed.

"And then the captain said, 'It's scurvy, boys.' The first time any officer — surgeon, captain, even mates — had said the word aloud to the crew in three years," continued Peglar. 'We're coming down with scurvy, Terrors,' the captain said. 'And you know the symptoms. Or if you don't . . . or if you don't have the balls to think about it . . . you need to listen.' And then Crozier called Dr. Goodsir up front, next to the girl, and made him list the symptoms of scurvy.

" 'Ulcers,' said Goodsir," continued Peglar as they approached *Erebus.* " 'Ulcers and haemorrhages everywhere on your body. That's pools of blood,' he said, 'under the skin. Flowing from the skin. Flowing from every orifice before the disease runs it course — your mouth, your ears, your eyes, your arse. Rictus of limbs,' he said, 'which means first your arms and legs hurt, then they become stiff. They won't work. You'll be clumsy as a blind ox. Then your teeth will fall out,' said Goodsir and paused. It was so silent, John, that you couldn't even hear the fifty men breathing, only the creaking and groaning of the ship in the ice. 'And while your teeth are falling out,' the surgeon went on, 'your lips will turn black and pull back from any remaining teeth you might have. Like a dead man's lips,' he said. 'And your gum tissue will bloom . . . that means swell. And stink. That's the source of the terrible stench that comes from scurvy,' he said, 'your gums rotting and festering from the inside out.'

" 'But that's not all,' Goodsir went on," continued Peglar. " 'Your vision and hearing will be impaired . . . compromised . . . as will your judgement. You'll suddenly see no problem walking out in fifty-below-zero weather with no gloves and no hat. You'll forget which way is north or how to drive a nail. And your senses will not only fail, they'll turn on you,' he says. 'If we had a fresh orange to give you, when you have scurvy, the smell of the orange might make you writhe in agony or literally drive you mad. The sound of a sledge's runner on ice might drop you to your knees in pain; the report of a musket could be fatal.'

" " 'Ere now!' shouts one of Hickey's legion into the silence," continued Peglar. " 'We got our lemon juice!'

"Goodsir just shook his head sadly. 'We won't have it for much longer,' he said, 'and what we have is not worth much. For some reason no one understands, the simple antiscorbutics like the lemon juice lose their potency after months. It's almost gone now after more than three years.'

"There was this second terrible silence then, John. You *could* hear the breathing then, and it was ragged. And there was a smell rising from the mob — fear and something worse. Most of the men there, including a majority of the officers, had seen Dr. Goodsir in the past two weeks with early symptoms of scurvy. Suddenly one of Hickey's compatriots shouts out, 'What's all this got to do with getting rid of a Jonah of a witch?'

"Crozier stepped forward then, still holding the girl like a captive, still seeming to offer her to the mob. 'Different captains and surgeons try different things to ward off or cure scurvy,' Crozier said to the men. 'Violent exercise. Prayer. Canned foods. But none of these things work in the long run. What is the only thing that works, Dr. Goodsir?'

"Every head on the lower deck turned to look at Goodsir then, John. Even the Esquimaux girl's.

" 'Fresh food,' said the surgeon. 'Especially fresh meat. Whatever deficiency in our food brings on scurvy, only fresh meat can cure it.'

"Everyone looked back at Crozier," said Peglar. "The captain all but thrust the girl at them. 'There's one person on these two dying ships who has been able to find fresh meat this autumn and winter,' he says. 'And she's standing right in front of you. This Esquimaux girl . . . merely a girl . . . but one who somehow knows how to find and trap and kill seals and walruses and foxes when the rest of us can't even find a track in the ice. What will it be like if we have to abandon ship . . . once we're out on the ice with no food stores left? There is one person out of the hundred and nine of us remaining alive who knows how to get us fresh meat to survive . . . *and you want to kill her.*' "

Bridgens showed bleeding gums of his own when he smiled. They were at the ice ramp to *Erebus*. "Our successor to Sir John may be a common man," he said softly, "with little formal education, but no one ever accused Captain Crozier — within my earshot at least — of being a stupid man. And I understand he has changed since his serious illness a few weeks ago."

"A sea change," said Peglar, enjoying both the pun and using a phrase Bridgens had introduced him to sixteen years earlier.

"How so?"

Peglar scratched his frozen cheek above the comforter. The mitten rasped on his stubble. "It's hard to describe. My own guess is that Captain Crozier is completely sober now for the first time in thirty years or more. The whiskey never seemed to compromise the man's competence — he's a fine sailor and officer — but it put a . . . buffer . . . a barrier . . . between him and the world. Now he's *there* more. Missing nothing. I don't know how else to describe it."

Bridgens nodded. "I presume there's been no more talk of killing the witch."

"None," said Peglar. "The men gave her extra biscuits for a while, but then she left — moved out onto the ice somewhere."

Bridgens started up the ramp and then turned back. When he spoke, his voice was very low so that none of the men on watch above could hear. "What do you think of Cornelius Hickey, Harry?"

"I think he's a treacherous little shit," said Peglar, not caring who heard him.

Bridgens nodded again. "He is that. I've known *of* him for years before I sailed on this expedition with him. He used to prey on boys during long voyages — turning them into little more than slaves for his needs. In recent years, I've heard, he's chosen to bend older men to his service, like the idiot . . ."

"Magnus Manson," said Peglar.

"Yes, like Manson," said Bridgens. "If it were just for Hickey's pleasure, we need not worry. But the little homunculus is worse than that, Harry . . . worse than your average would-be mutineer or conniving sea lawyer. Be careful of him. Watch him, Harry. I fear he could do great harm to us all." Bridgens laughed then. "Listen to me. 'Do great harm.' As if we weren't all doomed anyway. When I see you next, we may all be abandoning the ships and taking to the ice on our last long, cold walk. Take care of yourself, Harry Peglar."

Peglar did not speak. The captain of the foretop took off his mitten and then his glove, and lifted his frozen fingers until they touched the frozen cheek and brow of subordinate officers' steward John Bridgens. The touch was very light and neither man could feel it through the incipient frostbite, but it would have to serve.

Bridgens went back up the ramp. Without looking back, Peglar tugged on his glove and started the cold walk back through the rising dark to HMS *Terror*.

29

IRVING

It was Sunday, and Lieutenant Irving had served two straight watches up on deck in the cold and dark, one of them covering for his friend George Hodgson, who was ill with the symptoms of dysentery, missing his own warm supper in the officers' mess as a consequence and having only a small ice-hard slab of salt pork and a weevil-filled biscuit instead. But now he had eight blessed straight hours off before he had to go on duty again. He could drag himself belowdecks, crawl under the frozen blankets in the cot in his berth, thaw them some with his body heat, and sleep for the full eight hours.

Instead, Irving told Robert Thomas, the first mate who was taking his place as the officer on deck, that he was going for a walk and would be back presently.

Then Irving went over the side and down the ice ramp and onto the dark pack ice.

He was searching for Lady Silence.

Irving had been shocked weeks ago when Captain Crozier had appeared to be ready to toss the woman to the mob that was building, after crewmen listening to the mutinous whispers of Caulker's Mate Hickey and others started shouting that the woman was a Jonah and should be killed or cast out. When Crozier had stood there with Lady Silence's arm gripped in his hand, thrusting her toward the angry men much like an ancient Roman emperor might have tossed a Christian to the lions, Lieutenant Irving had not been sure what to do. As a junior lieutenant, he could only watch his captain, even if it meant Silence's death. As a young man in love, Irving was ready to step forward and save her even if it cost him his own life.

When Crozier won the majority of the men over with his argument that Silence might be the only soul on board who would know how to hunt and fish on the ice should they have to abandon ship, Irving had let out a silent sigh of relief.

But the Esquimaux woman moved off the ship completely the day after that showdown, coming back at supper time every second or third day for biscuits or the occasional gift of a candle, then disappearing back onto the dark ice. Where she was living or what she was doing out there was a mystery.

The ice was not too dark this night; the aurora danced brightly overhead, and there was enough moonlight to throw ink-black shadows behind the seracs. Third Lieutenant John Irving was not, unlike the first time he had followed Silence, carrying out this search on his own initiative. The captain had again suggested that Irving discover — if he could do so without endangering himself too much — the Esquimaux wench's secret hiding place on the ice.

"I was serious when I told the men that she might have skills that would keep us alive on the ice," Crozier had said softly in the privacy of his cabin as Irving leaned closer to hear. "But we can't wait until we're on the ice to find out where and how she gets the fresh meat she seems to be finding. Dr. Goodsir tells me that scurvy will take us all if we do not find some source of fresh game before summer."

"But unless I actually spy her hunting, sir," Irving had whispered, "how can I get the secret from her? She cannot speak."

"Use your initiative, Lieutenant Irving," was all that Crozier had said in response.

This was the first opportunity that Irving had had since that conversation in which he might be able to use his initiative.

In the leather shoulder bag, Irving carried a few enticements should he find Silence and work out a way to communicate with her. There were biscuits far fresher than the weevil-filled one he'd chewed for dinner. Those were wrapped in a napkin, but Irving had also brought a beautiful Oriental silk handkerchief that his rich London girlfriend had given to him as a present shortly before their . . . unpleasant parting. And his pièce de résistance was wrapped in that attractive handkerchief: a small crock of peach marmalade.

Surgeon Goodsir was hoarding and doling out the marmalade as an antiscorbutic, but Lieutenant Irving knew that the treat was one of the few things the Esquimaux girl had ever shown enthusiasm about when accepting Mr. Diggle's offerings of food. Irving had seen her dark eyes glint when she got a daub of marmalade on her biscuit. He'd scraped off his own jam treats a dozen times over the past month to get the precious amount he now carried in the tiny porcelain crock that had once been his mother's.

Irving had come completely around to the port side of the ship and now advanced from the ice plain there into a maze of seracs and minibergs that rose like an icy version of Birnam's wood come to Dunsinane about two hundred yards south of the ship. He knew that he was running a great risk of becoming the next victim of the thing on the ice, but for the last five weeks there had been no sign of the creature, not even a clear sighting from a distance. No crewmen had been lost to it since the night of Carnivale.

Then again, thought Irving, *no one but me has come out here alone, without even a lantern, and gone wandering into the serac forest.*

He was very aware that the only weapon he carried was the pistol sunk deep in the pocket of his greatcoat.

Forty minutes of searching through seracs in the dark and −45-degree wind and Irving was close to deciding that he would exercise his initiative another day, preferably in a few weeks, when the sun stayed above the southern horizon for more than a few minutes each day.

And then he saw the light.

It was an eerie sight — an entire snowdrift in an ice gully between several seracs seemed to be glowing goldly from within, as if from some inner faerie light.

Or witch's light.

Irving walked closer, pausing at each serac shadow to make sure that it was actually not another narrow crevasse in the ice. The wind made a soft whistling sound through the tortured-ice tops of the seracs and ice-boulder columns. Violet light from the aurora danced everywhere.

The snowdrift had been heaped — either by wind or by Silence's hands — into a low dome thin enough to show a flickering yellow light shining through it.

Irving dropped down into the small ice gully, actually just a depression between two pressure-pushed plates of pack ice rounded over with snow, and approached a small black hole that seemed too low to be associated with the dome set higher in the drift to one side of the gully.

The entrance — if an entrance it was — was barely as wide as Irving's heavily layered shoulders.

Before crawling in, he wondered if he should extract and cock his pistol. *Not a very friendly gesture of greeting,* he thought.

Irving wriggled into the hole.

The narrow passage went down for half the length of his body and then angled up for eight feet or more. When Irving's head and shoulders popped out of the far end of the tunnel and into the light, he blinked, looked around, and his jaw fell slack.

The first thing he noticed was that Lady Silence was naked under her open robes. She was lying on a platform carved out of the snow about four feet from Lieutenant Irving and almost three feet higher. Her bosoms were quite visible and quite bare — he could see the small stone talisman of the white bear she had taken from her dead companion dangling on a thong between her breasts — and she made no effort to cover them as she stared unblinkingly at him. She had not been startled. Obviously she had heard him coming long before he squeezed himself into the snow-dome's entry passage. In her hand was that short but very sharp stone knife he had first seen in the forward cable locker.

"I beg your pardon, miss," said Irving. He was at a loss of what to do next. Good manners demanded that he wriggle backward out of this lady's boudoir, as awkward and ungainly as that motion must be, but he reminded himself that he was here on a mission.

It did not escape Irving's attention that wedged in the opening to the snow-house as he was, Silence could easily lean over and cut his throat with that knife while there would be very little he could do about it.

Irving finished extricating himself from the entry passage, pulled his leather bag in behind him, got to his knees, and then to his feet. Because the floor of the snow-house had been dug out lower than the surface of the snow and ice outside, Irving had enough room to stand in the center of the dome with several inches to spare. He realized that while the snow-house had seemed like nothing more than a glowing snowdrift from the outside, it had actually been constructed of carved blocks or slabs of snow angling and arching inward in a most clever design.

Irving, trained at the Royal Navy's best gunnery school and always good at mathematics, immediately noticed the upward spiral of the blocks and how each block leaned in just slightly more than the previous one until a final capping key block had been pushed down through the apex of the dome and then tugged into position. He saw the tiny smoke hole, or chimney — no more than two inches across — just to one side of the key block.

The mathematician in Irving knew at once that the dome was not a true hemisphere — a dome built upon the principle of a circle would collapse — but rather was a catenary: that is, the shape of a chain held in both hands. The gentleman in John Irving knew that he was studying the ceiling, the blocks, and the geometric structure of this clever dwelling so as not to stare at Lady Silence's naked breasts and bare shoulders. He assumed he had given her enough time to draw the fur robes up over herself, and he looked back in her direction.

Her bosoms were still bared. The polar white bear amulet made her brown skin look all the more brown. Her dark eyes, intent and curious but not necessarily hostile, still watched him unblinkingly. The knife was still in her hand.

Irving let out a breath and sat on the robe-covered platform across the small central space from her sleeping platform.

For the first time he realized that it was warm in the snow-house. Not just warmer than the freezing night outside, nor just warmer than the freezing lower deck of HMS *Terror,* but *warm.* He had actually started to sweat under his many stiff and filthy layers. He saw perspiration on the soft brown bosom of the woman only a few feet from him.

Tearing his gaze away again, Irving unbuttoned his outer slops and realized that the light and heat were coming from one small paraffin tin that she must have stolen from the ship. As soon as he had this thought of her thieving, he felt sorry for it. It was a *Terror* paraffin tin all right, but one empty of paraffin, one of hundreds they had thrown overboard in the huge garbage area they had excavated out of the ice only thirty yards from the ship. The flame was not burning from paraffin but from some sort of oil — not whale oil, he could tell from the scent — seal oil? A cord made out of animal gut or sinew hung down from the ceiling, suspending a strip of blubber over the paraffin lamp and dripping oil into it. Irving saw at once how, when the oil level would grow lower, the candlewick, which seemed to be made of twined strands of anchor-cable hemp, would become longer and the flame would burn higher, melting more blubber and dripping more oil into the lamp. It was an ingenious system.

The paraffin container was not the only interesting artifact in the snow-house. Above and to one side of the lamp was an elaborate frame consisting of what appeared to be four ribs from what might have been seals — *how had Lady Silence caught and killed those seals?* wondered Irving — thrust upright in the snow of the shelf and connected by a complex web of sinew. Hanging from the bone frame was one of the larger rectangular Goldner food cans — also obviously scavenged from *Terror*'s garbage dump — with holes punched in the four corners. Irving saw at once that it would make a perfect cooking pot or teakettle hanging low over the seal-oil flame.

Lady Silence's bosoms were still uncovered. The white bear amulet moved up and down with her breathing. Her gaze never left his face.

Lieutenant Irving cleared his throat.

"Good evening, Miss . . . ah . . . Silence. I apologize for bursting in on you this way . . . uninvited as it were." He stopped.

Didn't the woman ever blink?

"Captain Crozier sends his compliments. He asked me to look in on you to see . . . ah . . . how you were getting along."

Irving had rarely felt more the fool. He was sure that despite her months on the ship, the girl understood not one word of English. Her nipples, he could not help noticing, had risen in the brief blast of cold air that he had brought into the snow-house with him.

The lieutenant rubbed the sweat off his forehead. Then he removed his mittens and undergloves, bobbing his head as if to ask permission of the lady of the house as he did so. Then he mopped his forehead again. It was incredible how warm this little space under a cantenary dome made out of snow could get just from the heat of a single lamp burning dripping blubber.

"The captain would like . . . ," he began, and stopped. "Oh, bugger it." Irving reached into his leather valise and brought out the biscuits wrapped in an old napkin and the crock of marmalade wrapped in his finest Oriental silk handkerchief.

He offered the two bundles across the central space to her with hands that were slightly trembling.

The Esquimaux woman made no attempt to take the bundles.

"Please," said Irving.

Silence blinked twice, slipped the knife under her robe, and took the small, lumpy packages, setting them next to her where she reclined on the platform. As she lay on her side, the tip of her right bosom was almost touching his Chinese handkerchief.

Irving looked down and realized that he was also sitting on a thick animal fur set onto this narrow platform. *Where did she get this second animal skin?* he wondered before remembering that more than seven months earlier she had been given the outer parka of the old Esquimaux man. The grey-haired old one who had died on the ship after being shot by one of Graham Gore's men.

She untied the old galley napkin first, showing no response to the five ship's biscuits wrapped in it. Irving had spent a serious bit of time finding the least weevil-infested biscuits possible. He felt a little piqued at her lack of recognition of his labours. When she unwrapped his mother's little porcelain crock, sealed with wax on top, she paused to lift the Chinese silk handkerchief — its elaborate designs were in bright red, green, and blue — and to set it against her cheek for a moment. Then she laid it aside.

Women are the same everywhere was John Irving's giddy thought. He realized that while he had enjoyed sexual congress with more than one young woman, he had never felt such a strong sense of . . . *intimacy* . . . as he did at this moment sitting chastely in the seal-oil lamplight with this half-naked young native woman.

When she pried open the wax and saw the marmalade, Lady Silence's gaze snapped up to Irving's face again. She seemed to be studying him.

He made a rough pantomime of her spreading the marmalade on the biscuits and eating them.

She did not move. Her gaze did not shift.

Finally she leaned out and extended her right arm as if reaching for him across the blubber fire, and Irving flinched a bit before realizing that she was reaching to a niche — just a small recess in the ice block — at the head of his robe-covered platform. He feigned not noticing that her own robe had slipped lower and that both her bosoms were bobbing free as she reached.

She offered him something white and red and reeking like a dead and decaying fish. He realized that it was another slab of seal or other-animal blubber that had been stored in the snowy niche to be kept cold.

He accepted it, nodded, and held it in his hands above his knees. He had no clue what to do with it. Was he supposed to bring it home to serve as part of his own seal-oil blubber lamp?

Silence's lips twitched then, and for an instant, Irving almost thought she had smiled. She took out her short, sharp knife and gestured, drawing the blade quickly and repeatedly right up to and against her lower lip as if she were going to cut that full, pink lip off.

Irving stared and continued holding the soft mass of blubber and skin.

Sighing, Silence reached over, took the blubber from him, held it to her own mouth, and cut several slices off with her knife, pulling the short blade actually into her mouth between her white teeth with each morsel. She paused to chew a moment and then handed the blubber and rubbery sealskin — he was almost certain it was seal now — back to him.

Irving had to fumble down through six layers of slops, greatcoat, jacket, sweaters, and waistcoat to get to his boat knife that was sheathed on his belt. He held the blade up to show her, feeling like a child seeking approbation during a lesson.

She nodded ever so slightly.

Irving set the reeking, stinking, dripping blubber next to his open mouth and pulled the sharp edge of his knife back quickly the way she had.

He almost cut his nose off. He *would* have sliced his lower lip off if the knife had not caught in the sealskin — if sealskin it was — and soft meat and white blubber and jerked upward slightly. As it was, a single drop of blood dripped from his sliced septum.

Silence ignored the blood, shook her head ever so slightly, and handed him her knife.

He tried it again, feeling the strange weight of her knife in his palm, slicing confidently toward his lip even as a drop of blood dripped from his nose onto the blubber.

The blade went through effortlessly. Her little stone knife was — somehow, incredibly — many times sharper than his own.

The strip of blubber filled his mouth. He chewed, trying to idiot-mime and nod his appreciation toward the woman from behind his upraised strip of blubber and poised knife.

It tasted like a ten-week-dead carp dredged from the floor of the Thames beneath the Woolwich sewer outlets.

Irving felt a great urge to vomit, started to spit the wad of half-chewed blubber on the floor of the snow-house instead, decided that this would not further the goals of his delicate diplomatic mission, and swallowed.

Grinning his appreciation for the delicacy while trying to force down his continued nausea — all the while surreptitiously mopping at his barely sliced but vigorously bleeding nose with a bunched-up frozen mitten serving as handkerchief — Irving was horrified to see the Esquimaux woman clearly gesture for him to cut and eat more of the blubber.

Still smiling, he sliced and swallowed another piece. It was, he thought, precisely what it must feel like to be filling one's mouth with a giant glob of some other creature's nasal mucus.

Amazingly, his empty stomach rumbled, cramped, and demanded more. Something in the reeking blubber seemed to be satisfying some deep craving he had not even known he felt. His body, if not his mind, wanted more of it.

The next few minutes were quite the domestic scene, thought Lieutenant Irving, with him sitting on his white bear robe on his little snow shelf, quickly if not enthusiastically cutting and swallowing strips of seal blubber, while Lady Silence crumbled strips of ship's biscuit, dunked them in his mother's crock as quickly as a sailor mopping up gravy with his bread, and devoured the marmalade with satisfied grunts that seemed to come from deep in her throat.

And all this time her bosoms remained bare and visible for Third Lieutenant John Irving's constant and appreciative, if not relaxed, perusal over his diminishing strip of seal blubber.

What would Mother think if she could see her boy and her crock now? wondered Irving.

When the two were finished, after Silence had eaten all the biscuits and emptied the marmalade crock and Irving had made a serious dent in the blubber, he tried to mop his chin and lips with his mitten, but the Esquimaux woman reached to the niche once again and presented him with a handful of loose snow. Since the high temperature in the little snow-house felt as if it were actually above freezing, Irving self-consciously mopped the blubber grease off his face, dried his face with his sleeve, and started to hand the remaining strip of sealskin and fat back to the girl. She gestured to the storage niche and he stuffed the piece of blubber as far back into the niche as he could reach.

Now comes the hard part, thought the lieutenant.

How does one communicate just by the use of hands and dumb show that there are more than a hundred hungry men threatened by scurvy who need someone else's hunting and fishing secrets?

Irving made a game try at it. With Lady Silence's deep, dark eyes watching unblinkingly, he acted out men walking, rubbing his stomach to show that they were hungry, the three masts of each ship, men getting sick — he stuck his tongue out, crossed his eyes in a way that used to upset his mother, and mimed falling over onto the bearskin robe — and then pointed to Silence and energetically acted out her casting a spear, holding a fishing pole, pulling in a catch. Irving pointed to the blubber he'd just stuffed away, in more ways than one, and pointed vaguely beyond the snow-house, again rubbing his stomach, crossing his eyes and falling, then rubbing his stomach again. He pointed to Lady Silence, floundered a moment on the sign language for "show us how to do it ourselves," and then repeated the spear-throwing and fish-catching mimes while pausing to point to her, shoot splay-fingered rays out his eyes, and rub his stomach to specify the recipients of her teaching.

When he was finished, sweat dripped from his brow.

Lady Silence looked at him. If she had blinked again, he'd missed it during his antics.

"Oh, well, bloody hell," said Third Lieutenant Irving.

In the end, he just buttoned up his layers and slops again, stuffed the ship's napkin and his mother's crock back in his leather valise, and called it a day. Perhaps he had got his message across after all. He might never know. Perhaps if he returned often enough to the snow-house . . .

Irving's speculation veered into the highly personal at that point, and he reined himself in as if he were a coachman with a matched set of willful Arabians.

Perhaps if he returned often . . . he would be able to go with her during one of her nocturnal seal-hunting expeditions.

But what if the thing on the ice is still giving her these things? he wondered. After seeing what he had seen so many weeks ago, he had half-convinced himself that he had not seen what he had seen. But the more honest half of Irving's memory and mind knew that he *had* seen it. The creature on the ice had brought her chunks of seal or arctic foxes or other game. Lady Silence had left that place among the ice boulders and seracs that night with fresh meat.

And then there was *Erebus*'s mate, Charles Frederick Des Voeux, with his stories of men and women in France who transformed themselves into wolves. If that was possible — and many of the officers and all of the crewmen seemed to think it was — why could not a native woman with a talisman of the white bear around her neck turn herself into something like a giant bear with the cunning and evil of a human being?

No, he had seen the two together on the ice. Hadn't he?

Irving shivered as he finished buttoning his slops. It was *very* warm in this little snow-house. Ironically, it was giving him the chills. He felt the blubber working at his bowels and decided it was time to go. He would be lucky if he made it back to *Terror*'s seat of ease in time as it was and he had no wish to stop out on the ice to see to such functions. It was bad enough when his *nose* became frostbitten.

Lady Silence had watched while he packed away the old napkin and his mother's crock — items that he realized much later she might very much have wanted — but now she touched her cheek with the silk handkerchief a final time and tried to hand that back to him.

"No," said Irving, "that is a gift from me. A token of my friendship and deep esteem. You must keep it. I would be offended if you do not."

Then he tried to sign and act out what he had just said. The muscles along either side of the young Esquimaux woman's mouth almost twitched as she watched him.

He pushed her hand holding the handkerchief back, taking care not to touch her naked bosom as he did so. The white stone of the bear amulet between her breasts seemed to glow from its own illumination.

Irving realized that he was much, much too hot. The room seemed to swim a bit in his vision. His insides lurched, calmed, then lurched again.

"Toodaloo," he said — three syllables he would agonize over for weeks to come, cringing in his bunk out of embarrassment even though she could not have understood the inanity and absurdity and inappropriateness of it. But still . . .

Irving touched his cap, wrapped his comforter around his face and head, tugged on his gloves and mittens, clutched his valise to his chest, and dove for the exit passageway.

He did not whistle during his walk back to the ship, but he was tempted to. He had all but forgotten about the possibility of some huge man-eater lurking in the moon shadows of the seracs out here so far from the ship, but if there was such a thing watching and listening that night, it would have heard Third Lieutenant John Irving talking to himself and occasionally slapping himself on the head with his mitten.

30

CROZIER

Lat. 70°-05' N., Long. 98°-23' W.
15 February, 1848

Gentlemen, it is time we looked at our possible courses of action in the coming months," said Captain Crozier. "I have decisions to make."

The officers and some warrant officers and other specialists, such as the two civilian engineers, foretop captains, and ice masters, as well as the last surviving surgeon, had been called to this meeting in *Terror*'s Great Cabin. *Terror* had been chosen by Crozier not to inconvenience Captain Fitzjames and his officers — who had to make the crossing during the brief hour of sunlight and hoped to be back before it grew dark again — nor to emphasize the change of flagship, but only because fewer men on Crozier's ship were confined to sick bay. It had been easier to move those few to a temporary sick bay in the bow to free up the Great Cabin for the meeting of officers; *Erebus* had twice the number of men down with symptoms of scurvy, and Dr. Goodsir had indicated that a few of them were too sick to be moved.

Now fifteen of the expedition's leaders were crowded around the long table that in January had been cut into shorter lengths to serve as operating tables for the surgeon but now was set to rights by Mr. Honey, *Terror*'s carpenter. The officers and civilians had left their rainproof slops, mittens, Welsh wigs, and comforters at the base of the main ladder, but they still wore all their other layers. The room smelled of wet wool and unwashed bodies.

The long cabin was cold and no light came through the Preston Patent Illuminators overhead since the deck remained under three feet of snow and its winter canvas cover. The whale-oil lamps on the bulkheads flickered dutifully but did little to dispel the gloom.

The gathering at the table resembled a gloomier version of the summer war council Sir John Franklin had called almost eighteen months earlier on *Erebus,* but now instead of Sir John at the head of the table on the starboard side, Francis Crozier sat there. On the aft side of the table, to Crozier's left, were the seven officers and warrant officers from *Terror* whom he had asked to be present. His executive officer, First Lieutenant Edward Little, was at Crozier's immediate left. Next was Second Lieutenant George Hodgson, with Third Lieutenant John Irving to his left. Then the civilian engineer — given warrant officer status on the expedition but looking thinner, paler, and more cadaverous than ever — James Thompson. On Thompson's left were Ice Master Thomas Blanky, who appeared to be stumping along very nicely on his wooden peg leg these days, and Captain of the Foretop Harry Peglar, the only petty officer Crozier had invited. Also present was *Terror*'s Sergeant Tozer — who had been out of both captains' graces since the night of the Carnivale when his men had fired on survivors of the fire but who was still the highest-ranked survivor of his heavily thinned group of lobsterbacks — speaking for the Marines.

At the port end of the long table sat Captain Fitzjames. Crozier knew that Fitzjames had not bothered to shave for several weeks, growing a reddish beard surprisingly flecked with grey, but he had made the effort today — or had ordered Mr. Hoar, his steward, to shave him. The effect only made his face look thinner and more pale, and now it was covered with countless small scrapes and cuts. Even with multiple layers of clothes on, it was obvious that Fitzjames's garments hung on a much frailer frame these days.

To Captain Fitzjames's left, along the forward side of the long table, sat six Erebuses. Immediately to his left was his only other surviving Naval officer — Sir John Franklin, First Lieutenant Gore, and Lieutenant James Walter Fairholme had all been killed by the thing on the ice — Lieutenant H. T. D. Le Vesconte, the man's gold tooth gleaming the few times he smiled. Next to Le Vesconte was Charles Frederick Des Voeux, who had taken over the duties of first mate from Robert Orme Sergeant, who had been killed by the thing while overseeing torch-cairn repair in December.

Next to Des Voeux sat the only surviving surgeon, Dr. Harry D. S. Goodsir. While technically the expedition's and Crozier's surgeon now, both the commanding officers and the surgeon had thought it appropriate for him to sit with his former *Erebus* crewmates.

To Goodsir's left sat Ice Master James Reid, and to his left the only *Erebus* petty officer present, Captain of the Foretop Robert Sinclair. And sitting on the forward side of the table was *Erebus*'s engineer, John Gregory, looking much healthier than his *Terror* counterpart.

Tea and weevil-rich biscuits were being served by Mr. Gibson of *Terror* and Mr. Bridgens of *Erebus* since the captains' stewards were both in sick bay with signs of scurvy.

"Let's discuss things in order," said Crozier. "First, can we stay in the ships until a possible summer thaw? And part of that answer has to be, can the ships sail in June or July or August if there *is* a thaw? Captain Fitzjames?"

Fitzjames's voice was a hollow husk of its once-confident firmness. Men on both sides of the table leaned closer to hear him.

"I don't think *Erebus* will last until summer, and it's my opinion — and the opinion of Mr. Weekes and Mr. Watson, my carpenters, and Mr. Brown, my bosun's mate, Mr. Rigden, my coxswain, and of Lieutenant Le Vesconte and First Mate Des Voeux here — that she will sink when the ice melts."

The cold air in the Great Cabin seemed to grow colder and to press more heavily on everyone. No one spoke for half a minute.

"The pressure from the ice these past two winters has squeezed the oakum right out from between the hull boards," continued Fitzjames in his small, hoarse voice. "The main shaft to the screw has been twisted beyond all repair — all of you know that it was designed to be retracted into an iron well all the way up to the orlop deck to be kept out of harm's way, but it will no longer retract any higher than the hull bottom — and we have no more replacement shafts. The screw itself has been shattered by the ice, as has been our rudder. We can jury-rig another rudder, but the ice has torn our hull bottom to splinters all along the length of the keel. We're missing almost half of our iron plating along the bow and sides.

"Worse," said Fitzjames, "the ice has squeezed the hull until the iron crossbeams added for reinforcement and the cast-iron replacements for her knees have either snapped or punctured the hull in more than a dozen places. If she were to float, even if we patched every breach and managed somehow to repair the problem with the screw-shaft well leaking, she would have no internal bracing against the ice. Also, while the wooden channels added to her side for this expedition have largely succeeded in keeping the ice from climbing over the raised gunwales, the downward pressure on these channels resulting from her raised position in the encroaching ice has caused splitting of the hull timbers along every channel seam."

Fitzjames seemed to notice their rapt attention for the first time. His unfocused stare went away and he looked down as if embarrassed. When he looked up again, his voice sounded almost apologetic. "Worst of all," he said, "is that the twisting pressure of the ice has so corkscrewed the sternpost and started the heads and ends of planking that *Erebus* has been bent far out of true by the stress. The decks break upward now . . . the only thing holding them in place is the weight of the snow . . . and none of us believe that our pumps could equal the leaks should she be floated again. I will let Mr. Gregory speak to the condition of the boiler, coal supplies, and propulsion system."

All eyes shifted to John Gregory.

The engineer cleared his throat and licked his chapped and bleeding lips. "There is no steam propulsion system left on HMS *Erebus*," he said. "With the main shaft twisted and jammed in the retraction well, we'd need a Bristol dry dock to set her right. Nor do we have enough coal left for a day's steaming. By the end of April, we'll be out of coal to heat the ship, even at the rate of moving just forty-five minutes of hot water a day only to parts of the lower deck that we're trying to keep habitable now."

Crozier said, "Mr. Thompson. What is *Terror*'s status in terms of steam?"

The living skeleton looked at his captain for a long minute and said in a voice that was surprisingly strong, "We wouldn't be able to steam for more than an hour or two, sir, if *Terror* was floated this afternoon. Our shaft was retracted all right a year and a half ago, and the screw is workable — and we have a replacement for that — but we're almost out of coal. If we were to transfer what's left of *Erebus*'s coal stores here and just *heat* the ship, we'd keep the boiler going and the hot water running two hours a day until . . . I'd venture . . . early May. But that wouldn't leave any coal for steaming. With just *Terror*'s stores of fuel, we'll have to stop heating by mid- or late April."

"Thank you, Mr. Thompson," said Crozier. The captain's voice was soft and betrayed no emotion. "Lieutenant Little and Mr. Peglar, would both of you be so kind as to give your assessment of *Terror*'s seaworthiness?"

Little nodded and looked down the table before returning his gaze to his captain. "We're not as knocked up as *Erebus,* but there's been ice-pressure damage to the hull, knees, outer plating, rudder, and inner bracings. Some of you know that before Christmas, Lieutenant Irving discovered not only that we had lost most of our iron plating along the starboard side back from the bow, but that the ten inches of oak and elm in the bow area had actually sprung the timbers in the forward cable locker on the hull deck, and we've found since that the thirteen inches of solid oak along her bottom has been sprung or compromised in twenty or thirty places. The bow boards've been replaced and reinforced, but we can't get to all her bottom because of the frozen slush down there.

"I think she'll float and steer, Captain," concluded Lieutenant Little, "but I can't promise that the pumps will be able to keep up with the leaks. Especially after the ice has another four or five months to work at her. Mr. Peglar can speak to that better than I can."

Harry Peglar cleared his throat. He obviously wasn't used to speaking in front of so many officers.

"If she'll float, sirs, then the foretop crew will get the masts reset and the rigging, shrouds, and canvas up within forty-eight hours of the time you give the word. I can't guarantee that sailing will get us through the thick ice of the sort we saw coming south, but if we have open water under us and ahead of us, we'll be a sailing ship again. And if you don't mind me making a recommendation, sirs ... I'd suggest we steep the masts sooner rather than later."

"You're not worried about ice building up and capsizing the ship?" asked Crozier. "Or ice falling on us when we're working on deck? We have months of blizzards ahead of us still, Harry."

"Aye, sir," said Peglar. "And capsizing's always a worry, even if we were just to tumble over onto the ice here, the ship being all catty-wampus the way she is. But I still think it'd be better to have the top-masts up and the rigging in place in case there's a sudden thaw. We might have to sail with ten minutes' warning. And the topmen need the exercise and work, sir. As for the ice falling ... well, it'll just be another thing to keep us alert and on our toes out there. That and the beastie on the ice."

Several men around the table chuckled. Little's and Peglar's mostly positive reports had helped ease some of the tension. The thought of even one of the two ships being able to float and sail raised morale. It felt to Crozier as if the temperature in the Great Cabin had actually risen — and perhaps it had, since many of the men seemed to be exhaling again.

"Thank you, Mr. Peglar," said Crozier. "It looks like if we want to sail out of here, we'll all have to do it — both crews — aboard *Terror*."

None of the surviving officers present mentioned that this had been precisely what Crozier had suggested doing almost eighteen months earlier. Every officer present appeared to be thinking it.

"Let's take a minute to talk about that thing on the ice," said Crozier. "It hasn't seemed to have made an appearance recently."

"I've not had to treat anyone for wounds since the first of January," said Dr. Goodsir. "And no one has died or disappeared since Carnivale."

"But there have been sightings," said Lieutenant Le Vesconte. "Something large moving among the seracs. And men on watch hear things in the dark."

"Men on watch at sea have always heard things in the dark," said Lieutenant Little. "Going back to the Greeks."

"Perhaps it has gone away," said Lieutenant Irving. "Migrated. Moved south. Or north."

Everyone fell silent again at this thought.

"Perhaps it's eaten enough of us to know we're not very tasty," said Ice Master Blanky.

Some of the men smiled at this. No one else could have said it and been excused the gallows humour, but Mr. Blanky, with his peg leg, had earned some prerogatives.

"My Marines have been searching, as per Captain Crozier's and Captain Fitzjames's orders," said Sergeant Tozer. "We've shot at a few bears, but none of them seemed to be the big one . . . the thing."

"I hope your men have been better shots than they were on the night of the Carnivale," said Sinclair, *Erebus*'s foretop captain.

Tozer turned to his right and squinted down the table at him.

"There'll be no more of that," said Crozier. "For the time being, we'll have to assume that the thing on the ice is still alive and will be back. Any activities we have to do off the ships will have to include some plan of defense against it. We don't have enough Marines to accompany every possible sledge party — especially if they're armed and not man-hauling — so perhaps the answer is to arm all ice parties and have the extra men, the ones not hauling, take turns serving as sentries and guards. Even if the ice doesn't open again this summer, it will be easier to travel in the constant daylight."

"You'll pardon my phrasing it this bluntly, Captain," said Dr. Goodsir, "but the real question is, can we afford to wait until summer before deciding whether to abandon the ships?"

"Can we, Doctor?" asked Crozier.

"I do not believe so," said the surgeon. "More of the canned food is contaminated or putrefied than we had thought. We're running low on all other stores. The men's diet is already below what they need for the work they're doing every day on the ship or out on the ice. Everyone is losing weight and energy. Add to that the sudden rise in scurvy cases and . . . well, gentlemen, I simply do not believe that many of us on *Erebus* or *Terror* — if the ships themselves last that long — will have the energy or concentration abilities to make *any* sledge trip if we wait until June or July to see if the ice breaks up."

The room was silent again.

Into the silence, Goodsir added, "Or rather, a few men may well have the energy to haul sledges and boats in a bid for rescue or to reach civilization, but they will have to leave the vast majority of others behind to starve."

"The strong could go for help to bring rescue parties back to the ships," said Lieutenant Le Vesconte.

It was Ice Master Thomas Blanky who spoke up. "Anyone heading south — say by hauling our boats south to the mouth of the Great Fish River and then upstream 850 miles farther south to Great Slave Lake where there's an outpost — wouldn't get there until late autumn or winter at the best and couldn't return with an overland rescue party until late summer of 1849. Everyone left behind on the ships would be dead of scurvy and starvation by then."

"We could load sledges and all head east to Baffin Bay," said First Mate Des Voeux. "There might be whalers there. Or even rescue ships and sledge parties already searching for us."

"Aye," said Blanky. "That's a possibility. But we'd have to man-haul sledges across hundreds of miles of open ice, what with all its pressure ridges and maybe open leads. Or follow the coast — and that would be more than twelve *hundred* miles. And then we'd have to cross the whole Boothia Peninsula with all its mountains and obstacles to get to the east coast where the whalers might be. We could haul the boats with us to cross leads, but that would triple our effort. One thing is sure — if the ice ain't opening here, it won't be open if we head northeast toward Baffin Bay."

"There would be far less weight if we only take sledges with provisions and tents to the northeast across Boothia," said Lieutenant Hodgson from the *Terror* side of the table. "One of the pinnaces must weigh at least six hundred pounds."

"More like eight hundred pounds," Captain Crozier said softly. "Without stores in it."

"Add to that more than six hundred pounds for a sledge that could carry a boat," said Thomas Blanky, "and we'd be man-hauling between fourteen and fifteen hundred pounds for each party — just the weight of the boat and sledge — not counting food, tents, weapons, clothes, and other things we'd have to haul with us. No one has ever man-hauled that much weight for more than a thousand miles — and much of it would be across open sea ice if we head for Baffin Bay."

"But a sledge with runners on the ice and possibly a sail — especially if we leave in March or April before the ice gets runny and sticky — would be easier going than man-hauling gear overland or through summer slush," said Lieutenant Le Vesconte.

"I say we leave the boats behind and travel light to Baffin Bay with just sledges and survival stores," said Charles Des Voeux. "If we arrive on the east coast of Somerset Island to the north before the whaling season ends, we're bound to be picked up by a ship. And I would wager that there will be Navy rescue ships and sledge parties there looking for us."

"If we leave the boats behind," said Ice Master Blanky, "one open stretch of water will stop us for good. We die out there on the ice."

"Why would rescuers be on the east side of Somerset Island and the Boothia Peninsula in the first place?" asked Lieutenant Little. "If they're searching for us, won't they follow our path through Lancaster Sound to Devon and Beechey and Cornwallis Islands? They know Sir John's sailing orders. They will presume we made it through Lancaster Sound since it's open most summers. There's no chance at all of any of us making it *that* far north."

"Perhaps the ice is as bad up at Lancaster Sound this year as it is down here," said Ice Master Reid. "That would keep the search parties farther south, out on the east side of Somerset Island and the Boothia."

"Maybe they'll find the messages what we left in the cairns way up at Beechey if they do get through," said Sergeant Tozer. "And send sledges or ships south the way we come."

Silence descended like a shroud.

"There were no messages left at Beechey," Captain Fitzjames said into that silence.

In the embarrassed vacuum that followed this statement, Francis Rawdon Moira Crozier found a strange, hot, pure flame burning in his chest. It was a sensation rather like a first sip of whiskey after days without it, but also nothing at all like that.

Crozier wanted to live. It was that simple. He was *determined* to live. He was going to survive this bad patch in the face of all odds and gods dictating that he would not and could not. This fire in his chest had been there even in the shaky, sick hours and painful days after he had emerged from the pit of his malaria-and-withdrawal brush with death in early January. The flame grew stronger every day.

Perhaps more than any other man around the long table in the Great Cabin this day, Francis Crozier understood the near impossibility of the courses of action being discussed. It was folly to head south across the ice toward Great Fish River. Folly to head for Somerset Island across twelve hundred miles of coastal ice, pressure ridges, open leads, and an unknown peninsula. Folly to think that the ice would open up this summer and allow *Terror* — overcrowded with two crews and almost empty of provisions — to sail out of the hopeless trap that Sir John had led them into.

Nonetheless, Francis Crozier was determined to live. The flame burned in him like strong Irish whiskey.

"Have we given up on the idea of sailing out?" Robert Sinclair was saying.

James Reid, *Erebus*'s Ice Master, answered. "We would have to sail almost three hundred miles north up the unnamed strait and sound that Sir John discovered, then through Barrow Strait and Lancaster Sound, then get south through Baffin Bay before the ice closed on us again. We had the steam engine and armour plating to help us bash through the ice heading south. Even if the ice relents to levels it was two summers ago, we would have great difficulty traversing that distance just with sail. And with our weakened wooden hull."

"The ice may be considerably less than in 1846," said Sinclair.

"Angels may fly out my arse," said Thomas Blanky.

Because of his missing leg, none of the officers at the table reprimanded the ice master. A few smiled.

"There might be another option . . . for sailing, I mean," said Lieutenant Edward Little.

Eyes turned in his direction. Enough men had saved some rations of tobacco — stretched out by adding unspeakable things to it — that half a dozen were now smoking pipes around the table. The smoke haze made the gloom even thicker in the dim flicker of the whale-oil lamps.

"Lieutenant Gore last summer thought that he spied land to the south of King William Land," continued Little. "If he did, that has to be the Adelaide Peninsula — known territory — which quite often has a channel of open water between the coast ice and the pack ice. If enough leads open to allow *Terror* to sail south — just a little over one hundred miles, perhaps, rather than the three hundred miles back through Lancaster Sound — we could follow open channels along the coast west until we reach the Bering Strait. Everything beyond here would be known territory."

"The North-West Passage," said Third Lieutenant John Irving. The words sounded like a mournful incantation.

"But would we have enough able-bodied men to crew the ship by late summer?" asked Dr. Goodsir, his voice very soft. "By May, the scurvy may have all of us in its grip. And what would we do for food during the weeks or months of our passage west?"

"Hunting might be good farther west," said Marine Sergeant Tozer. "Musk oxen. Them big deer. Walruses. White foxes. Maybe we'd be eating like pashas before we got to Alaska."

Crozier half-expected Ice Master Thomas Blanky to say, "And musk oxen might fly out my arse," but the sometimes-giddy ice master seemed to be lost in his own reveries.

Lieutenant Little answered instead. "Sergeant, our problem is that even if the game were to miraculously return after two summers' absence, none of us aboard seems able to hit anything with muskets . . . your men excluded, of course. We'd need more than your few surviving Marines to hunt. And it appears that none of us has any experience hunting anything much larger than birds. Will the shotguns bring down the game you're talking about?"

"If you gets close enough," Tozer said sullenly.

Crozier interrupted this line of discussion. "Dr. Goodsir made an excellent point earlier ... if we wait until midsummer, or perhaps even until June to see if the pack ice breaks up, we may be too ill and hungry to crew the ship. We'd *certainly* be too low on provisions to start a sledge trip. And we have to assume three or four months of travel across the ice or up Fish River, so if we're going to abandon the ships and take to the ice with the hopes of arriving at either Great Slave Lake or the east coast of Somerset Island or Boothia before winter sets in again, our departure obviously has to be before June. But how early?"

There was another thick bout of silence.

"I would suggest no later than the first of May," Lieutenant Little said at last.

"Earlier, I would think," said Dr. Goodsir, "unless we find sources of fresh meat soon and if the illness continues to spread as quickly as it currently is."

"How much earlier?" asked Captain Fitzjames.

"No later than mid-April?" Goodsir said hesitantly.

The men looked at one another through the tobacco smoke and cold air. That was less than two months away.

"Perhaps," said the surgeon, his voice sounding both firm and tentative to Crozier, "if conditions continue to worsen."

"How could they get worse?" asked Second Lieutenant Hodgson.

The young man obviously had meant it as a joke to lessen the tension but was rewarded with baleful and angry stares.

Crozier did not want the council of war to end on that note. The officers, warrant officers, petty officers, and civilian at the table had looked at their choices and seen that they were as bleak as Crozier had known they would be, but he did not want his ships' leaders' morale to get any lower than it already was.

"By the way," Crozier said in a conversational tone, "Captain Fitzjames has decided to conduct Divine Service next Sunday on *Erebus*— he'll be giving a special sermon that I'm interested in hearing, although I have it on good authority that it will *not* be a reading from the *Book of*

Leviathan — and I thought that since the ships' companies will be assembled anyway, we should have full rations of grog and dinner that one day."

The men smiled and bantered. None of them had expected to bring back good news to their specialized portions of the crews from this meeting.

Fitzjames raised one eyebrow very slightly. His "special sermon" and this Divine Service five days away, Crozier knew, were news to him, but Crozier thought it would probably do the thinning captain good to be preoccupied with something and to be the center of attention for a change. Fitzjames nodded ever so slightly.

"Very well then, gentlemen," Crozier said a bit more formally. "This exchange of thoughts and information has been very helpful. Captain Fitzjames and I will consult and perhaps talk to several of you again, one to one, before we make up our minds on a course of action. I will let you Erebuses get back to your ship before our midday sunset. Godspeed, gentlemen. I shall see you all on Sunday."

The men filed out. Fitzjames came around, leaned close, and whispered, "I may want to borrow that *Book of Leviathan* from you, Francis," and followed his men forward to where they were struggling into their frozen slops.

Terror's officers went back to their duties. Captain Crozier sat for a few minutes in his chair at the head of the table, thinking about what had been discussed. The fire for survival burned hotter than ever in his aching chest.

"Captain?"

Crozier looked up. It was the old steward from *Erebus*, Bridgens, who had filled in on the serving because of both captains' stewards' illnesses. The man had been helping Gibson clean up the pewter plates and teacups.

"Oh, you can go, Bridgens," said Crozier. "Go on with the others. Gibson will attend to all this. We don't want you walking back to *Erebus* on your own."

"Yes, sir," said the old subordinate officers' steward. "But I wonder if I might have a word with you, Captain."

Crozier nodded. He did not invite the steward to sit down. He'd never felt comfortable around this old man — far too old for Discovery Service. If Crozier had been the one to make the decision three years earlier, Bridgens never would have been included on the roster — certainly not listed with an age of "26" to fool the Navy — but Sir John had been amused by having a steward aboard even older than himself and that had been that.

"I couldn't help but hear the discussion, Captain Crozier — the three options of staying with the ships and hoping for a thaw, heading south to Fish River, or crossing the ice to Boothia. If the captain doesn't mind, I'd like to suggest a fourth option."

The captain did mind. Even an egalitarian Irishman like Francis Crozier bridled a bit at having a subordinate officers' steward give advice on life-and-death command problems. But he said, "Go ahead."

The steward went to the wall of books set into the stern bulkhead and pulled two large volumes, bringing them over to the table and setting them down with a thud. "I know you're aware, Captain, that in 1829, Sir John Ross and his nephew James sailed their ship *Victory* down the east coast of Boothia Felix — the peninsula they discovered and which we now call Boothia Peninsula."

"I am *very* aware of this, Mr. Bridgens," Crozier said coldly. "I know Sir John and his nephew Sir James very well." After five years in the ice of Antarctica with James Clark Ross, Crozier thought he was understating the acquaintance.

"Yes, sir," said Bridgens, nodding but not seeming abashed. "Then I'm sure you know the details of their expedition, Captain Crozier. They spent *four winters* in the ice. That first winter, Sir John anchored *Victory* in what he named Felix Harbour on the east coast of Boothia . . . almost due east of our position here."

"Were you *on* this expedition, Mr. Bridgens?" asked Crozier, willing the old man to get on with it.

"I did not have that honor, Captain. But I have read these two large volumes written by Sir John detailing his expedition. I wondered if you have had the time to do the same, sir."

Crozier felt his Irish anger building. This old steward's brashness was skirting on impertinence. "I have looked at the books, of course," he said coolly. "I have not had the time to read them carefully. Is there a point to this, Mr. Bridgens?"

Any other officer, warrant officer, petty officer, seaman, or Marine under Crozier's command would have received the message and been backing out of the Great Cabin while bowing low by now, but Bridgens seemed oblivious of his expedition commander's irritation.

"Yes, Captain," said the old man. "The point is that John Ross . . ."

"*Sir* John," interrupted Crozier.

"Of course. Sir John Ross had much the same problem we do now, Captain."

"Nonsense. He and James and *Victory* were frozen in on the *east* side of Boothia, Bridgens, precisely where we'd like to sledge to if we have the time and wherewithal. Hundreds of miles east of here."

"Yes, sir, but at the same latitude, although *Victory* didn't have to face this God-cursed pack ice coming down from the northwest all the time, thanks to Boothia. But she spent *three winters* in the ice there, Captain. James Ross sledged more than six hundred miles west across Boothia and the ice to King William Land just twenty-five miles sou'-southeast of us, Captain. He named Victory Point . . . the same point and cairn site that poor Lieutenant Gore sledged to last summer before his unfortunate accident."

"Do you think I don't know that Sir James discovered King William Land and named Victory Point?" demanded Crozier. His voice was taut with irritation. "He also discovered the God-damned north magnetic pole during that expedition, Bridgens. Sir James is . . . was . . . the most outstanding long-distance sledger of our era."

"Yes, sir," said Bridgens. His small steward's smile made Crozier want to strike him. The captain knew — had known before sailing — that this old man was a well-known sodomite, at least on shore. After the caulker mate's near mutiny, Captain Crozier was sick of sodomites. "My point is, Captain Crozier, that after *three winters* in the ice, with his men as sick with scurvy as ours will be by this summer, Sir John decided that they would never get out of the ice and sank *Victory* in ten fathoms of water there off the east coast of Boothia, due east of us, and they headed north to Fury Beach, where Captain Parry had left supplies and boats."

Crozier realized that he could hang this man, but he could not shut him up. He frowned and listened.

"You remember, Captain, that Parry's supplies of food and boats were there at Fury Beach. Ross took the boats and sailed north along the coast to Cape Clarence, where from the cliffs there they could see north across Barrow Strait and Lancaster Sound to where they hoped to find whaling ships . . . but the sound was solid ice, sir. That summer was as bad as our last two summers have been and as this coming one may be."

Crozier waited. For the first time since his deathly illness in January, he wished he had a glass of whiskey.

"They went back to Fury Beach and spent a fourth winter there, Captain. Men were close to dying of scurvy. The next July . . . 1833, four years after they had entered the ice up there . . . they set out in the small boats north and then east down Lancaster Sound past Admiralty Inlet and Navy Board Inlet, when on the morning of twenty-five August, James Ross . . . Sir James now . . . saw a sail. They waved, hallooed, and fired rockets. The sail disappeared east over the horizon."

"I remember Sir James mentioning something about that," Crozier said drily.

"Yes, Captain, I imagine he would," said Bridgens with his maddening little pedant's smile. "But the wind calmed, and the men rowed like smoke and oakum, sir, and they caught up to the whaler. She was the *Isabella,* Captain, the same ship that Sir John had commanded way back in 1818.

"Sir John and Sir James and the crew of *Victory* spent four years in the ice at our latitude, Captain," continued Bridgens. "And only one man died — the carpenter, a Mr. Thomas, who had a dyspeptic and disagreeable disposition."

"Your point?" asked Crozier again. His voice was very flat. He was too aware that more than a dozen men had died under his command on this expedition.

"*There are still boats and stores at Fury Beach,*" said Bridgens. "And my

guess is that any rescue party sent out for us — last year or this coming summer — will leave more boats and stores there. It's the first
place the Admiralty will think of to leave caches for us and for future
rescue parties. Sir John's survival assured that."

Crozier sighed. "Are you in the habit of thinking like the Admiralty,
Subordinate Officers' Steward Bridgens?"

"Sometimes, yes," said the old man. "It's a habit of decades, Captain Crozier. After a while, proximity to fools forces one to think like
a fool."

"That will be all, Steward Bridgens," snapped Crozier.

"Aye, sir. But read the two volumes, Captain. Sir John lays it all out —
how to survive on the ice. How to fight the scurvy. How to find and use
Esquimaux natives to help in the hunting. How to build little houses out
of blocks of snow . . ."

"That will be *all*, Steward!"

"Aye, sir." Bridgens knuckled his forehead and turned toward the
companionway, but not before sliding the two thick volumes closer to
Crozier.

The captain sat alone in the freezing Great Cabin for another ten
minutes. He listened to the Erebuses clatter up the main ladderway
and stomp across the deck above. He heard shouts as *Terror* officers
on deck bid their comrades farewell and wished them a safe crossing
of the ice. The ship quieted except for the bustle of men settling
down after their supper and grog forward. Crozier heard the tables
ratcheted up in the crewmen's berthing area. He heard his officers
clump down the ladderway, hang their slops, and come aft for their
own supper. They sounded more chipper than they had at breakfast.

Crozier finally stood — stiff with cold and body aches — lifted
the two heavy volumes, and carefully set them back in their place on
the shelf set into the aft bulkhead.

31

GOODSIR

The surgeon woke to shouts and screaming.

For a minute he did not know where he was and then he remembered — Sir John's Great Cabin, now the sick bay on *Erebus*. It was the middle of the night. All the whale-oil lamps had been extinguished and the only light came through the open door to the companionway. Goodsir had fallen asleep on an extra cot — seven men seriously ill with scurvy and one man with stones in his kidney were sleeping in the other cots. The man with stones had been dosed with opium.

Goodsir had been dreaming that his men were screaming as they were dying. They were dying, in his dream, because he did not know how to save them. Trained as an anatomist, Goodsir was less skilled than the three dead expedition surgeons had been at a Naval surgeon's primary responsibility — dispensing pills, potions, emetics, herbs, and boluses. Dr. Peddie had once explained to Goodsir that the vast majority of the medicines were useless for the specific sailor's ailments — most merely served to clean out the bowels and belly in an explosive manner — but the more powerful the purgative, the more effective the seamen thought the treatment was. It was the *idea* of medicinal help that helped the sailors heal, according to the late Peddie. In most cases not involving actual surgery, the body either healed itself or the patient died.

Goodsir had been dreaming that they were all dying — screaming as they died.

But these screams were real. They seemed to be coming up through the deck.

Henry Lloyd, Goodsir's assistant, ran into the sick bay with his shirttails hanging out from under his sweaters. Lloyd was carrying a lantern and Goodsir could see that he had no shoes on. He must have run straight from his hammock.

"What's going on?" whispered Goodsir. The sick men had not been roused from sleep by the screams from below.

"The captain wants you forward by the main ladder," said Lloyd. He made no attempt to lower his voice. The young man sounded shrill and terrified.

"Shhh," said Goodsir. "What's happening, Henry?"

"The thing's inside, Doctor," Lloyd cried through chattering teeth. "It's below. It's killing men below."

"Watch the men here," ordered Goodsir. "Fetch me if any of them wakes or takes a turn for the worse. And go put your boots and outer layers on."

Goodsir went forward through a milling of warrant officers and petty officers coming out of their cubicles and struggling into their clothes. Captain Fitzjames was standing with Le Vesconte at the head of the hatchway open to the lower decks. The captain had a pistol in his hand.

"Surgeon, there have been men injured below. You'll come with us when we go down to fetch them. You will need your slops."

Goodsir nodded dumbly.

First Mate Des Voeux came down the ladder from the deck above. Cold air rolled down with him, taking Goodsir's breath away. For the past week *Erebus* had been rocked and battered by a blizzard and staggeringly low temperatures, some reaching down to −100 degrees. The surgeon had not been able to spend his allotted time on *Terror.* There had been no communication between the ships while the blizzard raged.

Des Voeux brushed snow off his slops. "The three men on watch haven't seen anything outside, Captain. I told them to stand by."

Fitzjames nodded. "We need weapons, Charles."

"The three shotguns up on deck are all we've issued tonight," said Des Voeux.

Another scream came up from the darkness below. Goodsir could not tell if it came from the orlop deck or deeper, from the lower hold deck. Both hatches seemed to be open below.

"Lieutenant Le Vesconte," barked Fitzjames, "take three men down through the scuttle in the officers' mess to the Spirit Room and hand up as many muskets and shotguns — and bags of cartridges, powder, and shot — as you can. I want every man on the lower deck here armed."

"Aye, sir." Le Vesconte pointed to three seamen, and the four shoved their way aft through the darkness.

"Charles," Fitzjames said to First Mate Des Voeux. "Light lanterns. We're going down. Collins, you're coming. Mr. Dunn, Mr. Brown — you're with us."

"Yes, sir," chorused the caulker and his mate.

Henry Collins, the second master, said, "Without guns, Captain? You want us to go down there without weapons?"

"Bring your knife," said Fitzjames. "I have this." He held up the single-shot pistol. "Stay behind me. Lieutenant Le Vesconte will follow us with an armed party and bring extra weapons. Surgeon, you stay by me as well."

Goodsir nodded numbly. He'd been pulling on his slops — or someone's — and seemed to be having a child's difficulty in getting his left arm through the sleeve.

Fitzjames, his hands bare and wearing only a tattered jacket over his shirt, took a lantern from Des Voeux and plunged down the ladder. From somewhere below rose a series of terrible crashes, as if something was breaking timbers or bulkheads. There were no more screams.

Goodsir remembered the captain's command to "stay by me" and fumbled his way down the dark ladder after the two men, forgetting to take a lantern. He did not have his bag of medical instruments and bandages with him. Brown and Dunn clattered after him, with a cursing Collins bringing up the rear.

The orlop deck was only seven feet below the lower deck but it seemed like another world. Goodsir almost never came down here. Fitzjames and the first mate were standing away from the ladder, swinging their lanterns. The surgeon realized that the temperature down here must be forty degrees below that of the lower deck where they ate and slept — and the lower deck's average temperature these days was below freezing.

The crashing had stopped. Fitzjames ordered Collins to stop his cursing and the six men stood in a silent circle around the hatch open-ing to the hold deck below them. Everyone except Goodsir had a lantern and now extended it, although the small spheres of light seemed to penetrate only a few feet of the misted, freezing air. The men's breath glowed in front of them like golden ornaments. The hurried footsteps banging on the lower deck above them seemed to Goodsir to be coming from miles away.

"Who was on duty down here tonight?" whispered Fitzjames.

"Mr. Gregory and one stoker," replied Des Voeux. "Cowie, I think. Or maybe it was Plater."

"And Carpenter Weekes and his mate Watson," hissed Collins in an urgent whisper. "They were working through the night to shore up that stove-in part of the hull in the starboard for'ard coal-storage bin."

Something roared beneath them. The sound was a hundred times louder and more bestial than any animal sound Goodsir had ever heard — worse even than the roar from the ebony room at midnight during Carnivale. The force of it echoed off every timber, iron brace, and bulkhead on the orlop deck. Goodsir was sure that the men on watch two decks above in the howling night could hear it as if the thing were on deck with them. His testicles tried to crawl back up into his body.

The roar had come from down in the hold deck.

"Brown, Dunn, Collins," snapped Fitzjames. "Go forward past the Bread Room and secure the forward hatch. Des Voeux, Goodsir, come with me."

Fitzjames stuck his pistol in his belt, held the lantern in his right hand, and clambered down the ladder into the blackness.

Goodsir had to use all his will just to avoid pissing himself. Des Voeux hurried down the ladder next and only an overwhelming sense of shame at the thought of *not* following the other men combined with a fear of being left alone in the dark set the trembling surgeon into motion after the first mate. His arms, hands, and legs felt as insensate as if they were made of wood, but he knew it was fear, not the cold, that caused this.

At the bottom of the ladder — in a black cold somehow more thick and terrible than the hostile outside arctic had ever felt to Harry Goodsir — the captain and first mate were holding their lanterns out as far as they could reach. Fitzjames had his pistol extended and fully cocked. Des Voeux was holding a standard boat knife. The mate's hand was shaking. No one moved or breathed.

Silence. The crashing, thudding, and screams had all stopped.

Goodsir wanted to scream. He could *feel* the presence of something down on this dark hold deck with them. Something huge and not human. It could be twelve feet away, just beyond the puny circles of the lantern glow.

Along with the press of certainty that they were not alone came a strong copperish smell. Goodsir had smelled that many times before. Fresh blood.

"This way," whispered the captain and led the way aft down the narrow starboard companionway.

Toward the boiler room.

The oil lamp that always burned in there had been extinguished. The only glow that came through the open door was a dim red-and-orange flickering from the few bits of coal burning in the boiler hearth.

"Mr. Gregory?" called the captain. Fitzjames's shout was loud enough and sudden enough that Goodsir again came close to wetting himself. "Mr. Gregory?" the captain called a second time.

There was no answer. From their position in the corridor, the surgeon could see only a few square feet of the floor of the boiler room and some spilled coal. There was a smell in the air as if someone was grilling beef. Goodsir found himself salivating despite the sense of horror rising in him.

"Stay here," Fitzjames said to Des Voeux and Goodsir. The first mate was looking first forward and then astern, swinging his lantern in a circle, keeping his knife high, obviously straining to see down the dark corridor past the narrow circle of light. Goodsir could do nothing but stand there and bunch his freezing hands into fists. His mouth filled with saliva at the almost forgotten smell of grilling meat and his belly rumbled in spite of his fear.

Fitzjames stepped around the door frame and into the boiler room, out of sight.

For an eternity of five to ten seconds there was no sound. Then the captain's soft voice literally echoed from the metal-walled room. "Mr. Goodsir. Come in here, please."

There were two human bodies in the room. One was recognizable as the engineer, John Gregory. He had been disemboweled. His body lay in the corner against the aft bulkhead, but grey strings and strands of his intestines had been thrown around the boiler room like party streamers. Goodsir had to watch carefully where he stepped. The other body, a thickset man in a dark blue sweater, lay on his stomach with his arms by his sides, palms upward, his head and shoulders in the boiler's furnace.

"Help me pull him out," said Fitzjames.

The surgeon grabbed the man's left leg and his smoldering sweater, the captain took the other leg and right arm, and together they pulled the man back out of the flames. The man's open mouth stuck against the lower flange of the furnace hearth's metal grate for a second but then came free with a brittle snapping of teeth.

Goodsir rolled the corpse over while Fitzjames removed his jacket and beat out the flames rising from the dead man's face and hair.

Harry Goodsir felt as if he were watching all this from a great distance. The professional part of his mind noticed with cool detachment that the furnace, as poorly banked as the low coal flames had been, had melted the man's eyes, burned away his nose and ears, and turned his face into the texture of an overbaked, bubbling raspberry flan.

"Do you recognize him, Mr. Goodsir?" asked Fitzjames.

"No."

"It's Tommy Plater," gasped Des Voeux from where he stood just within the doorway. "I recognize him by the sweater and by the earring melted into his jaw where his ear used to be."

"God-damn it, Mate," snapped Fitzjames. "Stand guard out in the corridor."

"Aye, sir," said Des Voeux and stepped out. Goodsir heard the sound of retching from the companionway.

"I will need you to note . . . ," began the captain, speaking to Goodsir.

There came a crashing, a tearing, and then a resounding thud from the direction of the bow so loud that Goodsir was sure that the ship had broken in half.

Fitzjames grabbed up his lantern and was out the door in a second, leaving his smoldering jacket behind in the boiler room. Goodsir and Des Voeux followed him as they ran forward past scattered casks and smashed crates and then squeezed between the black iron bulkheads that held what was left of *Erebus*'s fresh water supply and the few remaining sacks of its coal.

They passed a black opening to a coal bin and Goodsir glanced to his right and saw a shirtless human arm protruding over the iron rim of the door frame. He paused and bent to see who lay there, but the light had moved away as the captain and mate continued to run forward with the lanterns. Goodsir was left in the absolute darkness with what was almost certainly another corpse. He stood and ran to catch up.

More crashes. Shouts now from the deck above. A musket or pistol shot. Another shot. Screams. Several men screaming.

Goodsir, outside the bobbing circles of lantern light, came out of the narrow corridor into an open, dark area and ran headfirst into a thick oak post. He fell on his back into eight inches of ice and sludgy meltwater. He couldn't focus his eyes — the lanterns above him were only swinging orange blurs as he struggled to stay conscious — and everything at that moment stank and tasted of sewage and coal dust and blood.

"The ladder's gone!" cried Des Voeux.

Sitting arse-deep in vile slush, Goodsir could see better as the lanterns steadied. The forward ladderway, made of thick oak and easily able to support several large men hauling hundred-pound sacks of coal up and down, had been smashed into splinters. Fragments hung from the open scuttle frame above.

The screaming was coming from up on the orlop deck.

"Boost me up," cried Fitzjames, who had tucked his pistol into his belt and set down the lantern and was now reaching up, trying to get a handhold on the splintered frame of the scuttle. He started pulling himself up. Des Voeux bent to boost him.

Flames suddenly exploded above and through the square opening.

Fitzjames cursed and fell onto his back in the icy water only a few yards from Goodsir. It looked as if the entire forward scuttle and everything above it on the orlop deck was on fire.

Fire, thought Goodsir. Acrid smoke filled his nostrils.

There's nowhere to run. It was a hundred degrees below zero outside and a blizzard was raging. If the ship burned now, they would all die.

"The main ladderway," said Fitzjames and got to his feet, found the lantern, and began running aft. Des Voeux followed.

Goodsir crawled on all fours through the ice and water, got to his feet, fell again, crawled, then ran after the receding lanterns.

Something on the orlop deck roared. There came a rattle of muskets and the distinct blast of shotguns.

Goodsir wanted to stop in the coal bunker to see if the man belonging to the arm was dead or alive — or even attached to the out-flung arm — but there was no light when he got there. He ran on in the dark, ricocheting off the iron, coal, and water bunker bulkheads.

The lanterns were already disappearing up the ladderway to the orlop deck. Smoke billowed down.

Goodsir clambered upward, was kicked in the face by a boot belonging to the captain or mate, and then he was on the orlop deck.

He couldn't breathe. He couldn't see. Lanterns bobbed around him but the air was so thick with smoke that there was no illumination.

Goodsir's impulse was to find the ladderway up to the lower deck and keep climbing, then keep climbing again until he was outside into the clean air, but there were men shouting to his right — toward the bow — so he dropped to all fours. The air was breathable here. Just. Toward the bow was a bright orange glow, far too bright to be lanterns.

Goodsir crawled forward, found the port companionway to the left of the Bread Room, crawled farther. Ahead of him somewhere in the smoke, men were beating at flames with blankets. The blankets were catching fire.

"Get a bucket brigade," shouted Fitzjames from somewhere ahead of him in the smoke. "Get water down here!"

"There's no water, Captain," shouted a voice so agitated that Goodsir could not recognize it.

"Use the piss buckets." The captain's voice cut like a blade through the smoke and shouting.

"They're frozen!" shouted a voice that Goodsir did recognize. John Sullivan, captain of the maintop.

"Use them anyway," shouted Fitzjames. "And snow. Sullivan, Sinclair, Reddington, Seeley, Pocock, Greater — get the men to form a bucket line from the deck down here to the orlop deck. Scoop up as much snow as you can. Throw it on the flames." Fitzjames had to stop to cough violently.

Goodsir stood. Smoke swirled around him as if someone had opened a door or window. One second he could see fifteen or twenty feet forward toward the carpenter's and bosun's storerooms, clearly see the flames licking the walls and timbers, and the next second he could not see two feet in front of him. Everyone was coughing and Goodsir joined them.

Men shoved against him in their rush to get up the ladderway and Goodsir pressed himself to the bulkhead, wondering if he should go up to the lower deck. He was no use here.

He remembered the bare arm flung out of the coal bunker below in the hold deck. The thought of going down there again made him want to vomit.

But the thing is on this deck.

As if to confirm that thought, four or five muskets not ten feet in front of the surgeon fired at once. The explosions were deafening. Goodsir flung his palms over his ears and fell to his knees, remembering how he had told the crew of *Terror* that scurvy victims could die from the mere sound of a musket shot. He knew that he had the early symptoms of scurvy.

"Belay that firing!" shouted Fitzjames. "Hold off! There are men up there."

"But, Captain . . ." came the voice of Corporal Alexander Pearson, the highest ranking of the four surviving *Erebus* Royal Marines.

"Hold off, I tell you!"

Goodsir could now see Lieutenant Le Vesconte and the Marines there silhouetted against the flames, Le Vesconte standing and the Marines each on one knee, reloading their muskets as if they were in the midst of a battle. The surgeon thought that the walls, timbers, and loose casks and cartons toward the bow were all on fire. Sailors batted at the flames with blankets and rolls of canvas. Sparks flew everywhere.

The burning silhouette of a man staggered out of the flames toward the Marines and clustered seamen.

"Hold your fire!" shouted Fitzjames.

"Hold your fire!" repeated Le Vesconte.

The burning man collapsed into Fitzjames's arms. "Mr. Goodsir!" called the captain. John Downing, the quartermaster, ceased beating a blanket against the fire in the corridor and stamped out the flames emanating from the wounded man's smoldering clothes.

Goodsir ran forward and took the weight of the collapsing man from Fitzjames. The right side of the man's face was almost gone — not burned but clawed away, the skin and eye hanging loose — and parallel marks ran down the right side of his chest, the claw marks cutting deep through eight layers of fabric and flesh. Blood soaked his waistcoat. The man's right arm was missing.

Goodsir realized that he was holding Henry Foster Collins, the second master whom Fitzjames earlier had ordered to go toward the bow with Brown and Dunn, the caulker and his mate, to secure the forward hatch.

"I need help getting him up to the surgery," gasped Goodsir. Collins was a big man, even without his arm, and his legs had finally given way. The surgeon was able to hold him upright only because he was braced against the Bread Room bulkhead.

"Downing!" Fitzjames called to the silhouette of the tall quarter-master who had returned to fighting flames with his burning blanket.

Downing tossed the blanket away and ran back through the smoke. Without asking a question, the quartermaster hooked Collins's remaining arm over his own shoulder and said, "After you, Mr. Goodsir."

Goodsir started up the ladderway but a dozen men with buckets were trying to come down through the smoke.

"Make way!" bellowed Goodsir. "Wounded man coming up."

The boots and knees pressed back.

As Downing carried the now unconscious Collins up the almost vertical ladder, Goodsir came up onto the lower deck where they all lived. Seamen gathered around and stared back at him. The surgeon realized that he must look like a casualty himself — his hands and clothes and face were bloody from crashing into the post, and he knew that they were also black with soot.

"Aft to the sick bay," ordered Goodsir as Downing lifted the burned and mauled man in his arms. The quartermaster had to twist sideways to carry Collins down the narrow companionway. Behind Goodsir, two dozen men were handing buckets down the ladder from the deck while others poured snow onto the steaming, hissing deck boards in the seamen's berthing area around the stove and forward scuttle. If the deck there caught fire, Goodsir knew, the ship was lost.

Henry Lloyd came out of the sick bay, his face pale and eyes wide.

"Are my instruments laid out?" demanded Goodsir.

"Yes, sir."

"Bone saw?"

"Yes."

"Good."

Downing laid the unconscious Collins on the bare surgical table in the middle of the sick bay.

"Thank you, Mr. Downing," said Goodsir. "Would you be so kind as to get a seaman or two and help these other sick men to a bed in a cubicle somewhere? Any empty berth will do."

"Aye, Doctor."

"Lloyd, get forward to Mr. Wall and tell the cook and his mates that we need as much hot water from the Frazer's stove as he can give us. But first, turn up those oil lamps. Then get back here. I'll need your hands and a lantern."

For the next hour, Dr. Harry D. S. Goodsir was so busy that the sick bay could have caught fire and he would not have noticed except to be glad for the extra light.

He stripped Collins's upper body naked — the open wounds steamed in the freezing air — threw the first pan of hot water over them to cleanse them as best he could, not for hygiene but to briefly clear away the blood in order to see how deep they were, decided that the claw wounds themselves were not immediately life threatening, and went to work on the second master's shoulder, neck, and face.

The arm had come off cleanly. It was as if a huge guillotine had severed Collins's arm with one drop. Used to industrial and shipboard accidents that mauled and twisted and tore flesh to shreds, Goodsir studied the wound with something like admiration, if not awe.

Collins was bleeding to death, but the flames he'd been caught in had cauterized the gaping shoulder wound to some extent. It had saved his life. So far.

Goodsir could see the shoulder bone — a glistening white knob — but there was no remaining arm bone that he had to cut away. With Lloyd shakily holding a lantern close and sometimes putting his finger where Goodsir ordered — often on a spurting artery — Goodsir deftly tied off the severed veins and arteries. He had always been good at this sort of thing — his fingers worked almost by themselves.

Amazingly, there seemed to be little or no fabric or foreign material in the wound. This lowered the chance of fatal sepsis, although that was still a probability. Goodsir cleansed what he could see with the second and final pan of hot water brought aft by Downing. Then he cut away any loose shards of flesh and sutured where he could. Luckily there were flaps of skin long enough that the surgeon could fold them back over the wound and sew them with broad stitches.

Collins moaned and stirred.

Goodsir worked as quickly as he could now, wanting to finish the worst of it before the man came fully awake.

The right side of Collins's face hung down on his shoulder like a loosened Carnivale mask. It reminded Goodsir of the many autopsies he had performed, cutting away the face and folding it up over the top of the skull like a tight wet cloth.

He had Lloyd pull the long flap of facial skin as far up and as tight as he could — his assistant turned away to vomit on the deck but then immediately returned, wiping his sticky fingers on his wool waistcoat — and Goodsir quickly stitched the loose part of Collins's face to a thick flap of skin and flesh just below the man's receding hairline.

He could not save the second master's eye. He tried pressing it back into place, but the man's suborbital ridge had been shattered. Bone splinters were in the way. Goodsir snapped off the splinters, but the eyeball itself was too damaged.

He took shears out of Lloyd's shaking hands and cut away the retinal nerve, throwing the eye into the bucket already filled with bloody rags and shreds of Collins's flesh.

"Hold that lantern closer," ordered Goodsir. "Quit shaking."

Amazingly, there was some eyelid left. Goodsir pulled it down as far as he could and deftly stitched it to a flap of loose skin below the eye. These stitches he made closer together since they would have to serve for years.

If Collins survived.

Having done the best he could on the second master's face for the time being, Goodsir turned his attention to the burns and claw wounds. The burns were superficial. The claw wounds ran deep enough that Goodsir could see the always shocking whiteness of exposed ribs here and there.

Directing Lloyd to apply salve to the burns with his left hand while holding the lantern close with his right, Goodsir cleaned and closed the torn muscles and sewed the surface flesh and skin back in place where he could. Blood continued to flow from the shoulder wound and Collins's neck, but at a much reduced rate. If the flames had cauterized the flesh and veins enough, the second mate might have enough blood left in him to allow for his survival.

Other men were being carried in, but they were suffering only from burns — some serious but none life threatening — and now that the most urgent part of his work on Collins was finished, Goodsir hung the lantern on the brass hook above the table and ordered Lloyd to help the others with salve, water, and dressings.

He was just finishing with Collins — administering opium so the waking, screaming man would sleep — when he turned to find Captain Fitzjames standing next to him.

The captain was as sooty and bloody as the surgeon.

"Will he live?" asked Fitzjames.

Goodsir set down a scalpel and opened and then closed his bloody hands as if to say *only God knows.*

Fitzjames nodded. "The fire is contained," said the captain. "I thought you'd want to know."

Goodsir nodded. He'd not thought about the fire at all in the past hour. "Lloyd, Mr. Downing," he said. "Would you be so kind as to carry Mr. Collins to that cot nearest the forward bulkhead. It's the warmest there."

"We lost all of the carpenter's stores on the orlop deck," continued Fitzjames, "and many of our remaining food stores that were in crates near the forward scuttle and bow area, and a good part of the Bread Room stores as well. I'd say a third of our remaining supply of canned and casked food is gone. And we're sure there is damage on the hold deck, but we haven't been back down there yet."

"How did the fire begin?" asked the surgeon.

"Collins or one of his men threw a lantern at the thing when it came up out of the scuttle at them," said the captain.

"What happened to the . . . thing?" asked Goodsir. Suddenly, he was so exhausted that he had to reach for the edge of the bloody surgical table to keep from falling.

"It must have gone out the way it came in," said Fitzjames. "Back down the forward scuttle and out somewhere down on the hold deck. Unless it's waiting down there still. I have armed men at each of the scuttles. It's so cold and smoky down there on the orlop deck that we'll have to change the guard every half hour.

"Collins saw it best. That's why I came up . . . to see if I could talk to him. The others just saw the shape across the flames — eyes, teeth, claws, a white mass or black silhouette. Lieutenant Le Vesconte had the Marines fire at it, but no one saw if it was hit. There is blood all forward of the burned-out carpenter's storeroom, but we don't know if any of it is from the beast. Can I speak to Collins?"

Goodsir shook his head. "I've just doused the second master with an opiate. He'll sleep for hours. I have no idea if he will ever awaken. The odds are against it."

Fitzjames nodded again. The captain looked as exhausted as the surgeon felt.

"What about Dunn and Brown?" asked Goodsir. "They went forward with Collins. Have you found them?"

"Yes," Fitzjames said dully. "They're alive. They escaped to the starboard side of the Bread Room when the fire started and the thing went after poor Collins." The captain took a breath. "The smoke below is dissipating, so I need to lead some men down to the hold to retrieve the bodies of Engineer Gregory and Stoker Tommy Plater."

"Oh my God," said Goodsir. He told Fitzjames about the bare arm he'd seen protruding from the coal bunker.

"I didn't see that," said the captain. "I was so eager to get to the forward scuttle that I did not look down, just ahead."

"I should have looked ahead," the surgeon said ruefully. "I banged into a pillar or post."

Fitzjames smiled. "So I see. Physician, heal thyself. You have a deep laceration from your hairline to your brow and a blue swelling the size of Magnus Manson's fist."

"Really?" said Goodsir. He gingerly touched his forehead. His bloody fingers came away bloodier even though he could feel the thick crust of dried blood on the huge contusion up there. "I'll sew it up with a mirror or have Lloyd do it later," he said tiredly. "I'm ready to go, Captain."

"Go where, Mr. Goodsir?"

"Down to the hold," said the surgeon, feeling his guts twist with nausea at the thought of it. "To see who's lying in the coal bunker. He might be alive."

Fitzjames looked him in the eye. "Our carpenter, Mr. Weekes, and his mate, Watson, are missing, Dr. Goodsir. They were working in a starboard coal bunker, shoring up a breach in the hull. But they must be dead."

Goodsir had heard the "doctor." Franklin and his commander had almost never called the surgeons that, not even Stanley and Peddie, the chief surgeons. They — and Goodsir — had almost always been the lower "Mister" to Sir John and the aristocratic Fitzjames.

But not this time.

"We have to go down to see," said Goodsir. "*I* have to go down to see. One or the other might still be alive."

"The thing from the ice might be alive and waiting down there as well," Fitzjames said softly. "No one saw or heard it leave."

Goodsir nodded tiredly and lifted his medical bag. "May I have Mr. Downing to come with me?" he asked. "I may need someone to hold the lantern."

"I'll come with you, Dr. Goodsir," said Captain Fitzjames. He held up an extra lamp that Downing had carried in. "Lead on, sir."

32

CROZIER

L ieutenant Little," said Captain Crozier, "please pass the order to abandon ship."

"Yes, Captain." Little turned and shouted the order down the crowded deck. The other officers and surviving second mate were absent, so John Lane, the bosun, picked up the order and bellowed it toward the bow. Thomas Johnson, the bosun's mate and the man who had administered the lashes to Hickey and the other two men in January, shouted the order down the open hatchway before finally closing and battening down the scuttle.

There was no one left belowdecks, of course. Crozier and Lieutenant Little had walked the ship stern to bow on each deck, looking into every compartment — from the cold boiler room with its banked furnaces to the hold deck's empty coal scuttles to the cramped but empty forward cable locker and then up through the decks. On the orlop deck they had checked that the Spirit Room and Gunner's Storeroom were empty of all muskets, shotguns, powder, and shot — only rows of cutlasses and bayonets remained in the racks overhead, gleaming coldly in the lantern light. Two officers had checked that all necessary clothing had been removed from the Slop Room over the past month and a half and then gone on to the empty Captain's Storeroom and equally empty Bread Room. On the foredeck, Little and Crozier had looked into every cabin and berth, noticing how neat the officers had left their bunks and shelves and remaining possessions, then seeing the seamen's hammocks tucked up for the final time, their sea chests lightened but still in place as if awaiting the call to supper, going aft then to notice the missing books in the Great Room where men had made their choices from the volumes and carried scores of them onto the ice with them. Finally, standing next to the huge stove that was absolutely cold for the first time in almost three years, Lieutenant Little and Captain Crozier had called again down the forward scuttle, making sure that no one had remained behind. They would do a head count above, but this was part of the protocol of abandoning ship.

Then they had gone up on deck and left the scuttle open behind them.

The men standing on deck now were not surprised by the order to abandon ship. They had been called up and assembled for it. There were only about twenty-five Terrors present this morning; the rest were at Terror Camp two miles south of Victory Point or sledging materials to the camp or out hunting or reconnoitering near Terror Camp. An equal number of Erebuses waited below on the ice, standing near sledges and piles of gear where the *Erebus* gear-and-supply tents had been pitched since the first of April when that ship had been abandoned.

Crozier watched his men file down the ice ramp, leaving the ship forever. Finally only he and Little were left standing on the canted deck. The fifty-some men on the ice below looked up at them with eyes almost made invisible under low-pulled Welsh wigs and above wool comforters, all squinting in the cold morning light.

"Go ahead, Edward," Crozier said softly. "Over the side with you."

The lieutenant saluted, lifted his heavy pack of personal possessions, and went down first the ladder and then the ice ramp to join the men below.

Crozier looked around. The thin April sunlight illuminated a world of tortured ice, looming pressure ridges, countless seracs, and blowing snow. Tugging the bill of his cap lower and squinting toward the east, he tried to record his feelings at the moment.

Abandoning ship was the lowest point in any captain's life. It was an admission of total failure. It was, in most cases, the end of a long

Naval career. To most captains, many of Francis Crozier's personal acquaintance, it was a blow from which they would never recover.

Crozier felt none of that despair. Not yet. More important to him at the moment was the blue flame of determination that still burned small but hot in his breast — *I will live.*

He wanted his men to survive — or at least as many as possibly could. If there was the slightest hope of any man from HMS *Erebus* or HMS *Terror* surviving and going home to England, Francis Rawdon Moira Crozier was going to follow that hope and not look back.

He had to get the men off the ship. And then off the ice.

Realizing that almost fifty sets of eyes were looking up at him, Crozier patted the gunwale a final time, scrambled down the ladder they'd set on the starboard side as the ship had begun to cant more steeply to port in recent weeks, and then walked down the well-worn ice ramp to the waiting men.

Hoisting his own pack and stepping into line near the men in harness at the rearmost sledge, he looked up a final time at the ship and said, "She looks fine, doesn't she, Harry?"

"She does that, Captain," said Captain of the Foretop Harry Peglar. As good as his word, he and the topmen had managed to steep all of the stored masts and restore the yards and rigging in the past two weeks, despite blizzards, low temperatures, lightning storms, surging ice pressures, and high winds. Ice gleamed everywhere on the now top-heavy ship's restored topmasts, spars, and rigging. She looked to Crozier as if she were bedecked in jewels.

After the sinking of HMS *Erebus* on the last day of March, Crozier and Fitzjames had decided that even though *Terror* had to be abandoned soon if they were to have any chance of walking or taking the boats to safety before winter, the ship should be restored to sailing shape. Should they be stuck at Terror Camp on King William Land for months into summer and the ice miraculously open, they could, theoretically, take the boats back to *Terror* and try sailing to freedom.

Theoretically.

"Mr. Thomas," he called to Robert Thomas, the Second Mate and lead hauler on the first of the five sledges, "lead off when you're ready."

"Aye, aye, sir," called back Thomas and leaned into the harness. Even with seven men straining in harness, the sledge did not budge. The runners had frozen to the ice.

"Hearty does it, Bob!" said Edwin Lawrence, laughing, one of the seamen in harness with him. The sledge groaned, men groaned, leather creaked, ice tore, and the high-packed sledge moved forward.

Lieutenant Little gave the order for the second sledge, headed up by Magnus Manson, to start off. With the giant in the lead of the men, the second sledge — although more heavily laden than Thomas's — immediately started off with only the slightest rasp of ice under the wooden runners.

And so it went for the forty-six men, thirty-five of them man-hauling for the first stretch, five walking in reserve with shotguns or muskets, waiting to pull, four of the mates from both ships and the two officers — Lieutenant Little and Captain Crozier — walking alongside and occasionally pushing and less frequently slipping into harness themselves.

The captain remembered that several days earlier, when Second Lieutenant Hodgson and Third Lieutenant Irving were preparing to leave for yet another boat-sledge trip to Camp Terror — both officers then ordered to take men from that camp to hunt and reconnoiter over the next few days — Irving had surprised his captain by requesting that one or the other of two men assigned to his team be left back at *Terror*. Crozier had been initially surprised because his estimate of young John Irving had been that the junior lieutenant was capable of dealing with seamen and carrying out and enforcing any orders given to him, but then Crozier heard the names involved and understood. Lieutenant Little had put the names of both Magnus Manson and Cornelius Hickey on Irving's sledge and scouting team rosters, and Irving was respectfully requesting, without giving any reasons, that one or the other man be assigned to another team. Crozier had acceded to the request immediately, reassigning Manson to the last day's sledge pulls and allowing the small caulker's mate to go ahead with Lieutenant Irving's sledge team. Crozier did not trust Hickey either, especially after the near mutiny weeks ago, and he knew that the little man was much more treacherous with the huge idiot Manson by his side.

Now, walking away from the ship, seeing Manson pulling fifty feet ahead of him, Crozier deliberately kept his face directed forward. He had resolved that he would not look back at *Terror* for at least the first two hours of the pulling.

Looking at the men leaning and straining ahead of him, the captain was very aware of those who were absent.

Fitzjames was absent this day, serving as commanding officer at Camp Terror on King William Land, but the real reason for his absence was tact. No captain wanted to abandon his ship in full view of another captain if at all possible, and all captains were sensitive to this. Crozier, who had visited *Erebus* almost every day from the beginning of its breakup from ice pressure two days after the fire and invasion of the thing from the ice in early March, had made a point of not being there midday on 31 March when Fitzjames had to abandon ship. Fitzjames had returned the favour this week by volunteering for command duties far from *Terror*.

Most of the other men's absences were for a far more tragic and depressing reason. Crozier brought up their faces as he marched alongside the last sledge.

Terror had been much luckier than *Erebus* when it came to loss of its officers and leaders. Of his primary officers, Crozier had lost his first mate, Fred Hornby, to the beast during the Carnivale debacle, Second Master Giles MacBean to the thing during a sledge trip the previous September, and both his surgeons, Peddie and McDonald, also during the New Year's Eve Carnivale. But his first, second, and third lieutenants were alive and reasonably well, as was his second mate, Thomas; Blanky, his ice master; and the indispensable Mr. Helpman, his primary clerk.

Fitzjames had lost his commanding officer — Sir John — and his first lieutenant, Graham Gore, as well as Lieutenant James Walter Fairholme and First Mate Robert Orme Sergeant, all killed by the creature. He'd also lost his primary surgeon, Mr. Stanley, and Henry Foster Collins, his second master. That left only Lieutenant H. T. D. Le Vesconte, Second Mate Charles Des Voeux, Ice Master Reid,

Surgeon Goodsir, and his purser, Charles Hamilton Osmer, as his remaining complement of officers. Instead of the crowded officers' mess of the first two years — Sir John, Fitzjames, Gore, Le Vesconte, Fairholme, Stanley, Goodsir, and clerk Osmer all dining together — the final weeks had seen only the captain and his sole surviving lieutenant, the surgeon, and clerk dining in the cold of the officers' wardrooom. And even that in the last days, Crozier knew, had been an absurd sight once the ice had tilted *Erebus* almost thirty degrees to starboard. The four men had been forced to sit on the deck, their plates on their knees and their feet braced hard against a batten.

Hoar, Fitzjames's steward, was still sick with scurvy, so poor old Bridgens had been the steward scurrying like a crab to serve the officers braced on the wildly tilted deck.

Terror had also been luckier in keeping her warrant officers intact. Crozier's engineer, chief boatswain, and carpenter were still alive and functioning. *Erebus* had seen her engineer, John Gregory, and her carpenter, John Weekes, both eviscerated in March when the thing on the ice had come aboard in the night. The ship's other warrant officer, Boatswain Thomas Terry, had been beheaded by the creature the previous November. Fitzjames had no warrant officers left alive.

Of *Terror*'s twenty-one petty officers — mates, quartermasters, fo'c'sle, hold, maintop, and foretop captains, coxswains, stewards, caulkers, and stokers — Crozier had lost only one man: Stoker John Torrington, the first man on the expedition to die, so long ago on 1 January 1846, way back at Beechey Island. And that, Crozier remembered, had been from consumption that young Torrington had brought aboard with him in England.

Fitzjames had lost another of his petty officers, Stoker Tommy Plater, on the day in March when the thing had gone on its murderous rampage on the lower decks. Only Thomas Watson, the carpenter's mate, had survived the thing's attack down on the hold deck that night, and he had lost his left hand.

Since Thomas Burt, the armourer, had been sent back to England from Greenland even before they'd encountered real ice, that left *Erebus* with twenty surviving petty officers. Some of these men, such as the ancient sailmaker, John Murray, and Fitzjames's own steward, Edmund Hoar, were too sick with scurvy to be useful, while others, such as Thomas Watson, were too mauled to be of help, while still others, such as the flogged gunroom steward Richard Aylmore, were too sullen to be of much use.

Crozier told one of the men who was obviously fagged out to take a break and to walk with the armed guard while he, the captain, took a turn in the harness. Even with six other men pulling, the terrible exertion of hauling more than fifteen hundred pounds of canned food, weapons, and tents was a strain on his weakened system. Even after Crozier fell into the rhythm — he'd joined sledging parties since March, when he first began dispatching boats and gear to King William Land, and well knew the drill of man-hauling — the pain of the straps across his aching chest, the weight of the mass being pulled, and the discomfort from sweat that froze, thawed, and refroze in his clothes were all a shock.

Crozier wished they had more able-bodied seamen and Marines.

Terror had lost two of its rated sailors — Billy Strong, torn in half by the creature, and James Walker, the idiot Magnus Manson's good friend before the giant fell completely under the sway of the little rat-faced caulker's mate. It had been fear of Jimmy Walker's ghost in the hold, Crozier remembered, that had brought the hulking Manson to his first point of mutiny so many months ago.

For once HMS *Erebus* had been luckier than its counterpart. The only able seaman Fitzjames had lost during this expedition had been John Hartnell, also dead of consumption and buried in the winter of '46 on Beechey Island.

Crozier leaned into the straps and thought about the faces and names — so many officers dead, so few regular sailors — and grunted as he pulled, thinking that the thing on the ice seemed to be deliberately coming after the leaders of this expedition.

Don't think that way, Crozier ordered himself. *You're giving the beast powers of reasoning it doesn't have.*

Doesn't it? asked another, more fearful part of Crozier's mind.

One of the Royal Marines walked by, carrying a musket rather than shotgun in the crook of his arm. The man's face was completely hidden by caps and wraps, but from the slouched way the man walked, Crozier knew that it was Robert Hopcraft. The Marine private had been seriously injured by the creature on the day a year ago in June when Sir John was killed, but while Hopcraft's other injuries had healed, his shattered collarbone left him always slouching to his left as if he had trouble maintaining a straight line. Another Marine walking with them was William Pilkington, the private who had been shot through his shoulder in the blind that same day. Crozier noticed that Pilkington didn't seem to be favouring that shoulder or arm today.

Sergeant David Bryant, *Erebus*'s ranking Marine, was decapitated just seconds before Sir John had been carried off under the ice by the beast. With Private William Braine dead on Beechey Island in 1846 and Private William Reed disappeared on the ice on 9 November of last fall while sent to deliver a message to *Terror* — Crozier remembered the date well since he had walked to *Erebus* from *Terror* in the dark himself that first full day of winter darkness — the beast had reduced Fitzjames's Marine guard to only four: Corporal Alexander Pearson in command, Private Hopcraft with his ruined shoulder, Private Pilkington with his bullet wound, and Private Joseph Healey.

Crozier's own Marine detachment had lost only Private William Heather to the thing on the ice, on the night the previous November when the creature had come aboard and bashed the man's brains out while the private was on watch. But amazingly, shockingly, Heather had refused to die. After lying comatose in the sick bay for weeks, obscenely hovering between life and death, Private Heather had been carried by his Marine mates to his hammock forward in the crew berthing area and they had fed him and cleaned him and carried him to the seat of ease and dressed him every day since. It was as if the staring, drooling man was their pet. He'd been evacuated to Terror Camp just last week, bundled up warmly by the other Marines and set carefully, almost royally, into a special one-man toboggan made for him by Alex "Fat" Wilson, the carpenter's mate. The seamen had not objected to the extra load and had volunteered to take turns pulling the living corpse's little sled across the ice and over the pressure ridges to Terror Camp.

That left Crozier five Marines — Daly, Hammond, Wilkes, Hedges, and thirty-seven-year-old Sergeant Soloman Tozer, an unschooled fool but now commanding officer among the total of nine functional surviving Royal Marines on the Sir John Franklin Expedition.

After the first hour in harness, the sledge seemed to slide more easily and Crozier had fallen into the rhythm of panting that passed for breathing while hauling such dead weight across such nonslippery ice.

That was all the categories of men lost that Crozier could think of. Except for the boys, of course, those young volunteers who had signed on to the expedition at the last minute and had been listed on the roster as "Boys" even though three of the four were a full-grown eighteen years old. Robert Golding was nineteen when they sailed.

Three of the four "boys" survived, although Crozier himself had been forced to carry the unconscious George Chambers from the burning Carnivale compartments on the night of the fire. The only fatality among the boys had been Tom Evans, the youngest in demeanor as well as in age; the thing on the ice had plucked the lad literally from beneath Captain Crozier's nose as they were out on the ice in the dark hunting for the missing William Strong.

George Chambers, although recovering consciousness two days after Carnivale, had never been the same. A bright lad before his violent encounter with the thing, the concussion he received reduced him to a level of intelligence even below that of Magnus Manson. George was no living corpse like Private Heather — he could obey simple orders according to *Erebus*'s bosun's mate — but he hardly ever spoke after that terrible New Year's Eve.

Davey Leys, one of the more experienced men on the expedition, was another man who had physically survived two encounters with the white thing on the ice but who was as useless as the literally brainless Private Heather these days. After the night the white thing encountered Leys and John Handford on watch and then chased Ice Master Thomas Blanky into the darkness, Leys had slipped back into his earlier state of unresponsive staring and had never returned from it. He had been transported to Terror Camp — along with the seriously injured or those too ill to walk, such as Fitzjames's steward,

Hoar — bundled in coats and tucked into one of the boats being dragged atop a sledge. There were too many men now sick with scurvy, wounds, or low morale who were of little use to Crozier or Fitzjames. More mouths to feed and bodies to haul with them when the men were hungry and sick and barely able to walk.

Weary, realizing that he had not really slept the past two nights, Crozier tried counting the dead.

Six officers from *Erebus*. Four dead from *Terror*.

All three warrant officers from *Erebus*. Zero from *Terror*.

One petty officer from *Erebus*. One from *Terror*.

Just one seaman from *Erebus*. Four from *Terror*.

That was twenty dead, not counting the three Marines and the boy Evans. Twenty-four men lost on the expedition already. A frightful loss — greater than Crozier could remember from any arctic expedition in Naval history.

But there was a more important number, and one that Francis Rawdon Moira Crozier tried to focus on: 105 living souls remaining under his care.

One hundred and five men alive, including himself, on this day he had been forced to abandon HMS *Terror* and cross the ice.

Crozier put his head down and leaned more into the harness. The wind had come up and was blowing snow around them, obscuring the sledge ahead, hiding the walking Marines from sight.

Was he sure in the count? Twenty dead not counting the three Marines and one boy? Yes, he was certain that he and Lieutenant Little had checked the muster that morning and confirmed 105 men spread out between the sledging parties, Terror Camp, and HMS *Terror* that morning . . . but *was* he certain? Had he forgotten anyone? Was his addition and subtraction correct? Crozier was very, very tired.

Francis Crozier might get muddled in the count for a short while — he had not slept at all in two, no, three nights — but he had not forgotten a single man's face or name. Nor would he ever.

———

"Captain!"

Crozier came out of the trance that he fell into when he was man-hauling sledges. He could not have told anyone at this moment whether he had been in harness an hour or six hours. The world had become the glare of the cold sun in the southeastern sky, the blowing ice crystals, the rack of his breath, the pain of his body, the shared weight behind him, the resistance of the sea ice and new snow, and most of all the oddly blue sky with wisps of white clouds curling around on all sides as if they were all walking in a blue-and-white-rimmed bowl.

"Captain!" It was Lieutenant Little shouting.

Crozier realized that his fellow pullers had come to a halt. All of the sledges were stopped on the ice.

Ahead of them to the southeast, perhaps a mile beyond the next heaped-ice pressure ridge, a three-masted ship was moving north to south. Its sails were furled and shrouded, its yards rigged for anchorage, but it moved anyway, as if on a strong current, gliding slowly and majestically on what must be a wide avenue of open water just beyond the next high ridge.

Rescue. Salvation.

The steady blue flame of hope in Crozier's aching chest flared brighter for a few exhilarating seconds.

Ice Master Thomas Blanky, his peg leg set into something rather like a wooden boot that Carpenter Honey had devised, stepped up to Crozier and said, "A mirage."

"Of course," said the captain.

He'd recognized the distinctive bomb-ship masts and rigging of HMS *Terror* almost immediately, even through the shimmering, shifting air, and for a few seconds of confusion bordering on vertigo, Crozier had wondered if somehow they had managed to get lost, turned around, and were actually heading back to the northwest toward the ship they'd abandoned hours earlier.

No. There were the old sledge tracks, drifted over in spots but deeply worn into the ice by more than a month's repeated passage back and forth, heading straight for the tall pressure ridge with its narrow passes hacked out with picks and shovels. And the sun was still ahead of them and to their right, deep in the south. Beyond the pressure ridge, the three masts shimmered, dissolved briefly, and then returned more solidly than ever, only upside down, with the hull of the ice-entombed *Terror* blending into a white-cirrus sky.

Crozier and Blanky and so many of the others had seen this phenomenon many times before — false things in the sky. Years ago, on a fine winter morning frozen in off the coast of the landmass they were calling Antarctica, Crozier had seen a smoking volcano — the very one named after this ship — rising upside down from solid sea to the north. Another time on this very expedition, in the spring of 1847, Crozier had come on deck to find black spheres floating in the southern sky. The spheres turned into solid figure eights, then divided again into what looked like a symmetrical progression of ebony balloons and then, within the course of a quarter hour, evaporated completely.

Two seamen on the third sledge had literally dropped in their traces and were on their knees in the rutted snow. One man was weeping loudly and the other had unleashed a string of the most imaginative sailor curses Crozier had ever heard — and the captain had heard his fill over the decades.

"God-damn it!" shouted Crozier. "You've seen arctic mirages before. Belay that sniveling and cursing or you'll be man-hauling that God-damn sledge by yourselves and I'll be sitting on it with one boot up each of your arses. Get on your feet, by God! You're men, not weak sisters. Fucking act like it!"

The two seamen got to their feet and clumsily brushed off ice crystals and snow. Crozier couldn't immediately identify them by their slops and Welsh wigs and he did not want to.

The line of sledges started up again with much grunting but no cursing. Everyone knew that the high pressure ridge ahead of them, carved out as it had been by countless previous trips in the past weeks, was still going to be a Christ-fucking cob. They would have to lift and wrestle the heavy sledges up at least fifteen feet of steep incline between the perilous sixty-foot ice cliffs on either side. The threat of tumbling ice boulders would be very real then.

"It's as if there's some dark God who wants to torment us," Thomas Blanky said almost cheerily. The ice master had no pulling duties and was still stumping alongside Crozier.

The captain did not respond to this, and after a minute Blanky fell back to stump along beside one of the outriding Marines.

Crozier called for one of the extra men to take his place in harness — something they had rehearsed doing without stopping the forward motion of the sledges — and when the extra hand took over, he stepped aside out of the ruts and checked his watch. They had been pulling about five hours. Looking behind, Crozier saw that the real *Terror* had been out of sight for some time, at least five miles and several low pressure ridges behind them. The mirage image had been a final offering from some evil arctic god that seemed intent on tormenting them all.

Still leader of this ill-fated expedition, Francis Rawdon Moira Crozier realized for the first time that he was no longer captain of a ship in Her Majesty's Royal Navy Discovery Service. That part of his life — and being a seaman and Naval officer had *been* his life since he was a boy — was over forever. After being responsible for losing so many men and both his ships, he knew the Admiralty would never give him another command. In terms of his long Naval career, Crozier knew, he was now a dead man walking.

They were still two hard days of man-hauling away from Terror Camp. Crozier fixed his gaze on the tall pressure ridge ahead and trudged forward.

33

GOODSIR

From the private diary of Dr. Harry D. S. Goodsir:

22 April, 1848 —

I have been four Days at this place we are calling Terror Camp. I believe it lives up to its name.

Captain Fitzjames is in Charge of sixty men here, including Myself.

I confess that when I first sledged within sight of the place last week, the first Image that came to mind was something out of Homer's Iliad. The camp is set along the edge of a wide Inlet about two Miles south of a cairn raised almost two Decades ago at Victory Point by James Clark Ross. It is somewhat more Sheltered from the Wind and Snow blowing off the ice pack here.

Perhaps scenes from the Iliad were evoked by the 18 long boats pulled up in a row by the edge of the sea ice — 4 boats lying on their sides in the gravel, the other 14 Boats tied upright on Sledges.

Behind the Boats are 20 tents, ranging in Size from the small Holland tents of the Design we used almost a Year Ago when I accompanied the late Lieutenant Gore to Victory Point — each Holland tent is large enough for six men to sleep in, three per bag in the 5-foot-wide Wolfskin Blanket-Robe sleeping bags — to the somewhat larger tents made by the sailmaker, Murray, including tents meant for Captain Fitzjames and Captain Crozier and their personal stewards, and the largest two tents, each roughly the size of the Great Cabins on Erebus and Terror, one serving as Sick Bay, the other as the Seamen's Mess Tent. There are other mess tents for warrant officers, petty

*officers, and the officers and their Civilian Counterparts, such as Engineer
Thompson and Myself.*

Or perhaps the Iliad *was evoked because when one approaches Terror
Camp at Night — and all of the Sledging Parties coming from HMS* Terror
*to the Camp arrived after dark on their Third Day — one is first struck by
the number of bonfires and campfires. There is no wood to burn, of course,
except for some spare Oak brought from the crushed* Erebus *precisely for that
Purpose, but many of the Last Remaining sacks of Coal had been ferried
across the ice from the Ships over the past month, and many of these coal
Fires were burning when I first saw Terror Camp. Some were in Fire Rings
made from rocks; some were in four of the tall Braziers salvaged from the
Carnivale Fire.*

*The effect was flames and light, added to by the occasional torch and
lantern.*

*After spending several days in Terror Camp, I have decided that the place
more resembles a Pirate Encampment than any camp of Akilleus, Odysseus,
Agamemnon, and the other Homeric Heroes. The Men's clothes are ragged,
frayed, and many times repaired. Most are Ill or Limping or both. Their faces
are Pale under sometimes Thick beards. Their eyes stare out of Sunken
Sockets.*

*They swagger or stagger around with their Boat Knives dangling from
crude belts set around their outer Slops in clanking Sheaths made from cut-
down Bayonet Scabbards. It was Captain Crozier's idea, as were the Goggles
improvised from Wire Mesh that the men wear on sunny days to safeguard
them from Sun blindness. The overall effect is one of a ragtag group of
Ruffians.*

And most now show signs of Scurvy.

*I have been very busy in the Sick Bay Tent. The sledge teams had spent
the Extra Energy to haul a Dozen Cots with them across the ice and over the
Frightful Pressure Ridges (plus two more cots for their Captains' tents), but
at the moment I have 20 men in Sick Bay, so 8 are on Blanket Pallets set
onto the cold ground itself. Three oil lamps provide us with Illumination
during the long nights.*

*Most of the men sleeping in the Sick Bay have collapsed from Scurvy, but
not all. Sergeant Heather is back in my care, complete with the gold sovereign*

Dr. Peddie had screwed into his skull to replace the bone Dashed Out with some of his brains by the Thing from the Ice. The Marines have been taking care of Heather for months and planned to continue to do so here at Terror Camp — the Sergeant was transported here on his Own Little Sled designed by Mr. Honey — but a possible Chill during the three days and nights of the Crossing has brought on a Pneumonia. This time, I do not expect the Marine Sergeant, who has been a disturbing Miracle of Survival, to Survive much longer.

Also here is David Leys, whom his crewmates call Davey. His catatonic condition has not changed in Months, but after the Crossing this week — he came Across with my group — he has not been able to keep down even the Thinnest Gruel or water. Today is Saturday. I do not expect Leys to be alive by this time Wednesday.

Due to the Great Exertion of hauling the boats and so much Matériel from the Ship to the Island — over pressure ridges I had Trouble climbing even when not in man-hauling harness — there were the usual complement of bruises and Broken Bones for me to deal with. These included one serious compound fracture of seaman Bill Shanks's arm. I have kept the man here after setting the bones for fear of sepsis. (The flesh and skin were punctured by sharp bone fragments in two places.)

But Scurvy remains the Primary Killer lurking in this tent.

Mr. Hoar, Captain Fitzjames's Personal Steward, may well be the first Man to Die of it Here. He is no longer Conscious for much of the day. As with Leys and Heather, he had to be man-hauled across the 25 Miles separating our doomed Ship from this Terror Camp.

Edmund Hoar is an early but Typical example of the progression of this disease. The Captain's Steward is a Young Man — he will turn 27 in a little more than two weeks, on May 9. If he survives that long.

For a Steward, Hoar is a large man — six feet tall — and to all appearances to Chief Surgeon Stanley and myself, he was in fine health when the Expedition sailed. He was quick, smart, alert, energetic in his Duties, and unusually athletic for a steward. During the running and man-hauling Games held so frequently on the ice at Beechey Island in the winter of 1845–46, Hoar was frequently a winner and leader of his various teams.

He has had slight symptoms of the Scurvy since last autumn — the weariness, lassitude, increasingly frequent Confusion — but the disease became most Pronounced after the Debacle of the Venetian Carnivale. He continued serving Captain Fitzjames sixteen hours a day and more into February, but finally his health broke down.

The first Symptom to make itself known with Mr. Hoar is what the men in the fo'c'sle are calling the Crown of Thorns.

Blood began weeping from Edmund Hoar's hair. And not just from the hair on his head. First his Caps and then his Undershirts and then his Underthings became stained with Blood each day.

I have observed this carefully, and the blood on the Scalp does come from the follicles themselves. Some of the Seamen attempted to avoid this Early Symptom by shaving their heads, but of course that does no good. With Welsh wigs, caps, scarves, and now pillows being soaked with blood by the Majority of the men, the sailors and officers have begun wearing Towels under their headgear and laying their head on them at night.

This does not, of course, Alleviate the Embarrassment and Discomfort of bleeding from all Points that have body hair.

Hemorrhages began appearing under Steward Hoar's skin in January. Although the Outside Games were a distant Memory by then and Mr. Hoar's duties rarely took him far from the Ship or into Great Physical Exertion, the slightest Bump or Bruise would show on his Body as a massive red-and-blue blotch. It would not heal. A Scratch from peeling potatoes or carving Beef would stay open and continue to bleed for weeks.

By late January, Mr. Hoar's legs had swollen to Twice their Normal Size. He had to borrow filthy Trousers from larger crewmen just to stay dressed while serving his captain. He could not sleep because of the ever-increasing Pain in his Joints. By early March, any movement at all was Agony for Edmund Hoar.

All through March, Hoar insisted that he could not stay in Erebus's Sick Bay — that he had to return to his berth and to serving and caring for Captain Fitzjames. His blond hair was constantly soaked with caked blood. His swollen arms, legs, and face began to look like pasty Dough. Every day that I tested his skin, it had Lost more Elasticity; by the week before Erebus was crushed, I could push deep into Edmund Hoar's flesh and the dimple would stay there permanently, the new Bruise spreading and spilling into a patchwork of earlier Hemorrhages.

By mid-April, Hoar's entire body had become a Bloated, Misshapened mass. His face and hands were Yellow from jaundice. His eyes were a Bright Yellow, made all the more shocking due to the bleeding from his eyebrows.

Despite my assistant's and my own efforts to turn and move the patient several times a Day, by the day we carried him from the dying Erebus, Hoar was covered with bedsores that had become brownish-purple ulcers that never ceased Suppurating. His face, especially on either side of his Nose and Mouth, was also ulcerated, constantly oozing Pus and Blood.

Pus from a Scurvy victim has an extraordinarily foul stench.

By the day we moved Mr. Hoar to Terror Camp, he had lost all but two of his teeth. And this was a man who — on Christmas Day — had boasted the healthiest smile of any young man on the Expedition.

Hoar's gums have blackened and receded. He is conscious only a few hours each day and is in Terrible Pain during every second of that time. When we open his mouth to feed him, the Stench is close to unbearable. Since we cannot wash Towels, we have lined his Cot with sailcloth which is now Black with Blood. His frozen and filthy clothing is also Brittle with dried Blood and Crusted Pus.

As terrible as his Appearance and Suffering are, the more Terrible Fact is that Edmund Hoar may linger on like this — getting Worse each Day — for more Weeks or even Months. Scurvy is an Insidious killer. It Tortures for a long time before it grants its victim a final peace. By the time one dies of Scurvy, one's closest Relative often will not be able to recognize the Sufferer and not enough of the Sufferer's mind will be left to recognize the relative.

But that is not a problem here. With the Exception of brothers serving together on this Expedition — and Thomas Hartnell lost his older brother on Beechey Island — there are no relatives who will ever come out here on the ice or onto this Terrible Island of wind, snow, ice, lightning, and fog. There is no one to identify us when we fall, much less Bury us.

Twelve of the men in the Sick Bay are dying of Scurvy, and more than Two thirds of the 105 survivors, including myself, have one or more symptoms of it.

*We will be out of the lemon juice — our most successful antiscorbutic,
although its Efficacy has been Declining steadily the past year — in less than a
week. The only Defense I will have then is Vinegar. A week ago — in the Stores
Tent on the ice outside HMS* Terror *— I personally presided over the decanting
of our remaining volumes of Vinegar from casks to be proportioned out into 18
Smaller Kegs — one for each boat that had been sledged to Terror Camp.*

*The men hate Vinegar. Unlike the lemon juice, whose Tartness can be
somewhat disguised with dollops of Sugar Water or even Rum, Vinegar tastes
like poison to men whose palates have already been damaged by the Scurvy
growing in their systems.*

*Officers who have dined more on Goldner's Canned Foods than the
seamen have — they ate their beloved (although rancid) Salted Pork and Beef
until those casks were empty — appear to be more prone to coming down
with the advanced symptoms of Scurvy than the regular sailors.*

*This confirms Dr. McDonald's theory that there is some vital Element
lacking — or some Poison present — in the purely canned meats and
vegetables and soups as opposed to spoiled but once-fresh victuals. If there was
some miraculous way I could discover that Element — poison or life-saver —
I would not only have a good Chance of saving these men, possibly even Mr.
Hoar, but would run an excellent Chance of being Knighted when we are
rescued or reach safe harbour by ourselves.*

*But there is no way to do it, given our current Conditions and my lack of
any Scientific Apparatus. The best I can do is insist that the men eat any
fresh meat that our hunters shoot and bring in — even the Blubber and
sweetmeats, I feel, against all logic, may strengthen us against Scurvy.*

*But our hunters have found no living things to shoot. And the ice is too
thick to chop through for fishing.*

*Last night Captain Fitzjames stopped by as he does at the beginning and
end of each of his long, long Days, and after he had his usual Rounds of the
sleeping men, asking me the Changes in Condition of each, I was Forward
enough to ask him the question I had been wondering about for so many
weeks now.*

Captain, *I said,* I understand if you are too busy to answer this or
if you prefer not to, since it is a Lubber's question, there is no doubt
of it, but I've been wondering for some time — why 18 Boats?

We seem to have brought Every Boat from *Erebus* and *Terror*, yet we have only 105 men.

Captain Fitzjames said, Come outside with me if you will, Dr. Goodsir.

I told Henry Lloyd, my Weary Assistant, to watch over the men, and followed Captain Fitzjames outside. I had noticed in the Sick Bay Tent that his Beard, which I had thought was coming in Red, was actually mostly Grey, only rimmed in dried Blood.

The captain had brought an extra Lantern from the Sick Bay and he led the way with it down to the graveled Beach.

There was no Wine-Dark Sea lapping at the Shingle of this Beach, of course. Instead, the heap of coastal Tall Bergs that formed a Barrier between us and the Ice Pack still lined the Shore.

Captain Fitzjames raised his lantern along the long line of boats. What do you see, Doctor? *he asked.*

Boats, *I ventured, feeling every Inch the Lubber I had accused myself of being.*

Can you tell the difference between them, Dr. Goodsir?

I looked more carefully in the lantern light.

These first four are not on Sledges, *I said. I had been quick to notice that even the first night I was here. I had no idea why this was the case, when Mr. Honey had gone to such Care to make special Sledges for all the Rest. It seemed like Rank Carelessness to me.*

Aye, you are correct, *said Captain Fitzjames.* These Four are our Whaleboats from *Erebus* and *Terror*. Thirty feet long. Lighter than the Others. Very strong. Six oars each. Double-ended like canoes . . . d'ye see now?

I did now. I had never noticed that the whaleboats seemed to have two bows, like a canoe.

If we had ten whaleboats, *continued the Captain,* everything would have been perfect.

Why is that? *I asked.*

They're strong, Doctor. Very strong. And light, as I said. And we could pile Supplies in them and drag them across the Ice without having had the need to build Sledges as we did for the Others. If we find Open Water, we could launch them straight from the ice.

I shook my head. Knowing that Captain Fitzjames would think me a Total Fool as soon as I asked the question — I asked it anyway: But why can the whaleboats be dragged on the ice when the others cannot, Captain?

Captain Fitzjames's voice showed no impatience when he said, Do you see the rudder, Doctor?

I looked at each end, but I did not. I confessed that to the captain.

Exactly, *he said.* Whaleboats have a Shallow Keel and no fixed Rudder. An oarsman at the stern steers her.

Is that good? *I asked.*

It is if you want a light, tough boat with a shallow Keel and no tender Rudder to be broken off when you're dragging her, *said Captain Fitzjames.* Perfect for man-hauling across the ice, even though she's 30 Feet long and can carry up to a Dozen Men with room for Supplies.

I nodded as if I understood. I almost did — but I was very tired.

Do you see her mast, Doctor?

Again I looked. Again I failed to find that which had been requested of me to find. I admitted as much.

That's because the whaleboats have a single *collapsible* mast, *said the Captain.* It's there folded under the Canvas the men have Rigged over her gunwales.

I have noticed that canvas and wood covering all the boats, *I said, to show that I was not totally unobservant.* Is that to keep the snow out?

Fitzjames was lighting his pipe. He had run out of Tobacco long ago. I did not want to Know what he was burning in it. The Boat Covers were put on to shield the Crews of all 18 Boats, even though we may only take 10 boats with us, *he said softly. Most of the men in camp were sleeping. Guards paced coldly just at the edge of the lantern light.*

We'll be *under* that canvas when we cross Open Water to the mouth of the Back's Great Fish River? *I asked. I had never pictured us hunkered down under Canvas and wood. I had always imagined us rowing happily in Sunlight.*

We may not use the Boats on the River, *he said, puffing out aromatic clouds of what smelled like dried human excrement.* If the Waters along the Coast open up this Summer, Captain Crozier would prefer to Sail us to Safety.

All the way to Alaska and St. Petersburg? *I asked.*

To Alaska at least, *said the Captain.* Or perhaps Baffin Bay if the Coastal Leads open to the North. *He took several steps and swung the lantern closer to the Boats on Sledges.* Do you know these Boats, Doctor?

Are they different, Captain? *I found that such terrible Fatigue was a great Inducement to Honesty without Embarrassment.*

Aye, *said Fitzjames.* These next two lashed to Mr. Honey's special Sledges here are our Cutters. Surely you noticed them when they were Lashed on Deck or on the ice next to the Ships these past Three Winters?

Yes, of course, *I said.* But are you saying these are different from the first, the whaleboats?

Quite different, *said Captain Fitzjames, taking the time to relight his pipe.* Do you notice any masts on these boats, Doctor?

Even in the dim light from the lantern I could see two masts rising from each of these craft. The Canvas had been Artfully shaped and cut and Stitched around them. I told the Captain my observation.

Aye, very good, *he said. He did not sound Condescending.*

Are these collapsible masts not collapsed for a purpose? *I asked, as much to show that I had been listening earlier as for any better reason.*

They're not collapsible, Dr. Goodsir. These masts are Lug Rigged . . . or you may know them as Gaff Rigged. Quite permanent. And do you see fixed rudders on these? And the deeper keels?

I could. I did. The Rudders and Keels are the reason they could not be Dragged like the whaleboats? *I ventured.*

Exactly. You have Diagnosed the Problem, Doctor.

Could not the Rudders be removed, Captain?

Possibly, Dr. Goodsir, but the deep Keels . . . they would have been Stuck or Ripped out by the first Pressure Ridge, now wouldn't they?

I nodded again and laid my mittened hand on the gunwale. Is it my imagination, or are these four boats slightly shorter than the whaleboats?

You have a very good Eye indeed, Doctor. 28 feet long as

opposed to 30 feet for the whaleboats. And heavier . . . the Cutters
are Heavier. And square-sterned.

*For the first time I noticed that these 2 Boats, unlike the whalers,
definitely had a Bow and a squared-off stern. No Canoes here.* How many
men will the Cutters carry? *I asked.*

Ten. And they pull 8 Oars. They have Room for quite a few
Stores, and there will be Room for us all to Huddle down out of the
Storm, even on the Open Sea, and with the two masts the Cutters
will offer twice the Canvas to the wind that the whaleboats do, but
the Cutters will not be as good as the Whalers if we have to go up
Back's Great Fish River.

*Why is that? I asked, feeling that I should already know, that he had
already told me.*

The deeper draft, sir. Let us look at the next two . . . the jolly
boats.

I found nothing jolly-looking about either of the next two boats. They
seem longer than the Cutters, *I said.*

They are, Doctor. 30 feet Long apiece . . . the same Length as our
whaleboats. But Heavier, Doctor, Heavier even than the Cutters.
A great Trial, with their 900-lb. Sledges to haul across the Ice . . .
even this far . . . I assure you. Captain Crozier may choose to leave
them here.

I asked, Then should we not have left them behind at the ships?

He shook his head. No. We need to choose which boats will best
serve to allow 100 men to survive for several weeks or months at
sea, or even on the river. Did you know that Boats . . . all of these
Boats . . . have to be Rigged differently for sailing on the sea or
catching the Wind going upriver, Doctor?

It was my turn to shake my head.

No matter, *said Captain Fitzjames.* We'll get into the niceties of
river rigging versus sea rigging some other time, preferably on a
Sunny, Warm day far South of here. These last 8 Boats . . . the first
Two are Pinnaces, the next Four are Ship's Boats, and the final Two
are Dinghies.

The Dinghies seem much shorter, *I said.*

Captain Fitzjames puffed on his literally execrable pipe and nodded as if I had revealed Some Pearl of Wisdom from Holy Scripture. Aye, he said sadly. The Dinghies are only 12 feet Long, as opposed to the Pinnaces' 28-foot Length and the Ship's Boats 22 feet. But none of them can be rigged for masts and sailing and they're all lightly Oared. The men in these Boats would be in for some Hard Times if we went to the Open Sea, I am afraid. I would not be surprised if Captain Crozier chooses to Leave them Behind.

I thought, Open Sea? The idea of actually sailing any of these craft on anything more expansive than Back's Great Fish River, which I imagined rather like the Thames, had never occurred to me before tonight, even though I had been present at various war councils discussing such possibilities. It seemed to me, looking at the smaller and rather delicate-looking Dinghies and Ship's Boats lashed on their Sledges, that the men going to sea in these would be doomed to watch the Pinnaces with their Two Masts and the Whaleboats with their single Tall Masts simply sail away over the horizon.

The men in these Smaller Boats would be Doomed. How would the crews be chosen? Had they been chosen already, in secret, by the Two Captains?

And which boat — and which Fate — had I been assigned?

If we take the Smaller Boats, we'll draw lots for them, *said the Captain.* The places in the pinnaces, jolly boats, and whaleboats would be assigned according to man-hauling teams.

I must have looked at him in alarm.

Captain Fitzjames laughed — a laugh that turned into a racking cough — and knocked out the ashes from his pipe against his Boot. The wind was coming up, and it was very cold. I had no idea of the time — sometime after Midnight. It had been dark for at least seven hours.

Don't worry, Doctor, *he said softly.* I wasn't reading your mind. Only your expression. As I say, we'll Draw Lots for the smaller boats, but we may not take the Smaller Boats. In either case, we won't leave anyone behind. We'll tie the ships together on the Open Water.

I smiled at this, hoping that the Captain could see my smile in the lantern light but not my Bleeding Gums. I didn't know that ships under sail could be tied to other ships not under sail, *I said, showing my ignorance again.*

Most of the time, they cannot, *said Captain Fitzjames. He touched me lightly on the back — a touch I could hardly feel through my outer Slops.* Now that you've learned the Nautical Secrets of all 18 Boats that might end up in our little Fleet, Doctor, shall we get back? It's rather cold, and I have to get some Sleep before I rise at Four Bells to check on the Watch.

I bit my lip, tasting blood. I do have one last question, Captain, if you don't mind.

Not at all.

When will Captain Crozier choose the boat we take and when will he put those boats in the water? *I said. My voice was very hoarse.*

The Captain moved slightly and was silhouetted against the light from the bonfire near the Seamen's Mess Tent. I could not see his face.

I don't know, Dr. Goodsir, *he said at last.* I doubt if Captain Crozier could tell you. Lady Luck may be with us and the Ice may break up in a few Weeks . . . if it does, I'll sail you to Baffin Island myself. Or we could be launching some of these craft against the current at the Mouth of the Great Fish River in three months . . . conceivably there could still be time to get to Great Slave Lake and the outpost there before Winter fully sets in, even if it takes until July to reach the River.

He patted the curved side of the Pinnace closest to him. I felt a strange, quiet pride in being able to identify it as a Pinnace.

Or perhaps it was one of the 2 Jolly Boats.

I tried not to think of the condition of Edmund Hoar and what it forecast for all the rest of us if we did not begin the 850-mile Venture up Back's River . . . the river they also call the Great Fish River . . . for another Three Months. Who could possibly be left Alive if a boat made it to Great Slave Lake months later than that?

Or, *he said softly,* if Lady Luck is not with us, these hulls and keels may never feel water under them again.

There was nothing to say to that. It was our Death Sentence. I turned from the light to walk back to the Sick Bay Tent. I respected

Captain James Fitzjames and I did not want him to see my face at that Moment.

Captain Fitzjames's hand fell on my shoulder, stopping me.

Should that be the case, *he said, his voice fierce,* we'll just have to bloody well *walk* home, shan't we?

34

CROZIER

Lat. 69° 37' 42" N., Long. 98° 41' W.
22 April, 1848

Pulling toward the arctic sunset, Captain Crozier knew the mathematics of this purgatory. Eight miles this first day on the ice to Sea Camp One. Nine miles the next, if all went well, ending in a midnight arrival at Sea Camp Two. Eight miles — including some of the hardest going near the coast where the sledges had to be hauled up over the barrier where pack ice met coastal ice — the third and final day. And there the tentative safe haven of Terror Camp.

Both crews would be together for the first time. If Crozier's sledge teams survived this ice crossing — and kept ahead of the thing following them on the ice — all 105 men would be together on the wind-scoured northwestern coast of the island.

The early sledge trips to King William Land in March — most of them in darkness — had made such slow going that often the men with their sledges had camped the first night on the ice within sight of the ship. One day, with a storm blowing in their faces out of the southeast, Lieutenant Le Vesconte had made less than a mile after twelve hours of constant effort.

But it was much easier in the sunlight with the sledge trail laid down and the path through pressure ridges reduced in difficulty, if not actually leveled.

Crozier had not wanted to end up on King William Land. His visits to Victory Point had not convinced him, despite the huge dump of food and gear there and the preparation of tent circles, that the men could survive there for long. The weather blowing almost always out of the northwest was murderous in winter, atrocious in the spring and brief autumn, and life threatening during the summer. The late Lieutenant Gore's experience of wild lightning storms during the first visit to the landmass in the summer of 1847 had been repeated again and again that summer and early autumn. One of the first things Crozier authorized hauling to land the previous summer had been the ship's extra lightning rods along with brass curtain rods from Sir John's quarters to jury-rig more.

Right up until the crushing of *Erebus* on the last day of March, Crozier had hopes that they could set off for the east coast of the Boothia Peninsula, the possible stores there at Fury Beach, and the probable sighting by whalers coming in from Baffin Bay. Like old John Ross, they could hike or boat north along the east coast of Boothia up to Somerset Island or even Devon Island again if they had to. Sooner or later they would spy a ship in Lancaster Sound.

And there were Esquimaux villages in that direction. Crozier knew this for a fact — he'd seen them on his first voyage to the arctic with William Edward Parry in 1819 when he was twenty-two. He'd returned to the area again with Parry two years later in a quest to find the Passage and again two years after that, still searching for the North-West Passage — a search that would kill Sir John Franklin twenty-six years later.

And might yet kill us all, thought Crozier and shook his head to get the defeatist thought out of it.

The sun was very close to the southern horizon. Just before it set, they would stop and eat a cold dinner. Then they would harness up again and walk another six to eight hours through the deep afternoon, evening, and nighttime darkness to reach Sea Camp One a little more than a third of the way to King William Land and Terror Camp.

There was no sound now except for the panting of the men, the creak of leather, and the rasp of runners. The wind had died completely but the air was even colder with the dimming of the twilight afternoon sun. Ice crystals of breath hung above the procession of men and sledges like slowly collapsing spheres of gold.

Walking near the front of the line now as they approached the tall pressure ridge, ready to help with the initial pulling and lifting and shoving and soft cursing, Crozier looked toward the setting sun and thought of how hard he had tried to find a way to Boothia and the whalers from Baffin Bay.

At age 31 Crozier had accompanied Captain Parry into those arctic waters a fourth and final time, this time to reach the North Pole. They'd accomplished a "farthest north" record that easily stood until this day but had eventually been stopped by solid pack ice that stretched to the northern limits of the world. Francis Crozier no longer believed in the Open Polar Sea: when someone finally reached the Pole, he was sure they'd be doing it by sledge.

Perhaps by sleds pulled by dogs, the way the Esquimaux preferred to travel.

Crozier had seen the natives and their light sleds — not real sledges at all by Royal Navy standards, but only flimsy little sleds — sliding along behind those strange dogs of theirs in Greenland and along the east side of Somerset Island. They moved much faster than Crozier's team ever could with this man-hauling. But most central to his plan to head east if at all possible was the fact that the Esquimaux were out there to the east somewhere at Boothia or beyond. And, like Lady Silence, whom they had seen going ahead to Terror Camp following Lieutenants Hodgson's and Irving's sledge teams earlier that week, these natives knew how to hunt and fish for themselves in this godforsaken white world.

After Irving reported to him way back in early February about the young lieutenant's difficulties in following Lady Silence or communicating with her about where and how she got the seal meat and fish Irving swore he had seen her with, Crozier contemplated threatening the girl's life with pistol or boat knife to make her show them how she found the fresh food. But in his heart he'd known how such a threat would end up — the Esquimaux wench's tongueless mouth would stay firmly shut and her huge dark eyes would stare unblinkingly at Crozier and his men until he had to back down or make good on his threat. Nothing would be accomplished.

So he'd left her out in her little snow-house Irving had described to him and allowed Mr. Diggle to give her the occasional biscuit or scrap. The captain had tried to put her out of his mind. That he had been shocked to be reminded she was still alive when the lookout reported her following a few hundred yards behind Hodgson's and Irving's relay trip to Terror Camp last week showed Crozier that he had succeeded in not thinking about the wench. But he knew he still dreamed about her.

If Crozier were not so very, very tired, he might have taken some small pride in the design and durability of the various sledges that the men were now man-hauling southeast across the ice.

In mid-March, even before it was certain that *Erebus* would break up from the rising pressure, he had Mr. Honey, the expedition's surviving carpenter, and his mates, Wilson and Watson, working day and night to design and build sledges that could haul the ships' boats as well as gear.

As soon as the first prototype larger oak-and-brass sledges were finished that spring, Crozier had the men out on the ice testing them and learning the best ways to haul them. He had the riggers and quartermasters and even the foretopmen constantly fiddling with the design of the harnesses to give the men the best pulling leverage with the least interruption of their movement and breathing. By mid-March, the sledge designs were set, more were being built, and it seemed that a design of harnesses for eleven men for the large sledges carrying boats and seven men for the smaller supply sledges would be best.

This was for the initial supply crossings to Terror Camp on King William Land. If they took to the ice after that, Crozier knew, with some of the men too sick to pull and perhaps others dead by then, eighteen boats and sledges, each loaded to the gunwales with survival rations and gear, requiring man-hauling by one hundred men — or fewer — it would mean fewer than eleven men pulling each burden. More work and even heavier loads for men who presumably would be deeper in the pit of scurvy and exhaustion by then.

By the last week in March, even as *Erebus* was in her death throes, both crews were out on the ice in darkness and the brief sunlight, competing in man-hauling contests with the different sledges, finding the right match of men to sledge, learning the right techniques, and putting together the best teams composed of men from both ships and all ranks. They were competing for cash — silver and gold — and even though Sir John had planned to buy many souvenirs in Alaska, Russia, the Orient, and the Sandwich Islands and there were chests of shillings and guineas in the dead man's private storeroom, these coins came out of Francis Crozier's pocket.

Crozier wanted badly to head toward Baffin Bay as soon as the days grew long enough to support long-distance sledging. He knew instinctively and from listening to Sir John's tales and from reading George Back's history of ascending more than 650 miles of the Back's Great Fish River to Great Slave Lake fourteen years ago — the volume was in *Terror*'s library and now in Crozier's personal pack on one of the sledges — that the odds of any of them finishing or surviving the trip were low.

The 160-some miles between *Terror*'s position off King William Land and the mouth of Great Fish River might not be traversable, even as a prelude to the arduous voyage up the river. It combined the worst of coastal ice with threats of open leads that could make them abandon the sledges and — even if there were no leads — the assured agony of hauling sledges and boats across the frozen gravel of the island itself, all while exposed to the worst of the pack-ice storms.

Once on the river, if they ever reached the river, they would be confronted with what Back had described as "a violent and tortuous course of 530 geographical miles, running through an iron-ribbed country without a single tree on the whole of its banks" and then "no fewer than 83 falls, cascades, and rapids." Crozier had trouble imagining his men, after another month or more of man-hauling, being fit enough or well enough to confront 83 falls, cascades, and rapids in even the sturdiest boats. The portages alone would kill them.

A week earlier, before heading out with the boat-sledge teams to Terror Camp, Surgeon Goodsir told Crozier that the lemon-juice antiscorbutic, their only defense against scurvy now — as weak as it had become — would run out in three weeks or less, depending upon how many men died between now and then.

Crozier knew how quickly the full onslaught of scurvy would weaken all of them. For this 25 miles to King William Land with light sledges and full teams, on full half rations for the crossing, on a runners path that had been beaten into the ice for more than a month, they had to cover a little more than eight miles a day. On the rough terrain or coastal ice of King William Land and south, that distance might be cut in half or worse. Once the scurvy began having its way with them, they might only cover a mile a day and, if the wind died, might well not be able to pole or paddle the heavy boats upstream against the current of Back's River. A portage of any distance in the weeks or months to come might soon become impossible.

The only things working in their favor in heading south were the very long-shot chance that a rescue party was already heading north from Great Slave Lake, searching for them, and the simple fact that it would be getting warmer as they traveled farther south. They would be following the thaw, at the very least.

Still, Crozier would have preferred staying in the northern latitudes and going the longer distance east and north to Boothia Peninsula and then across it. He knew there was only one even relatively safe way to attempt that: take the men to King William Land, cross it, then make the relatively short traverse across open ice, sheltered from the worst of the northwest wind and weather by the island itself, to the southwestern coast of the Boothia, then slowly north along the edge of the ice or on the coastal plain itself, and finally across the mountains toward Fury Bay, hoping every step of the way to meet Esquimaux.

It was the safe way. But it was the long way. 1,200 miles, almost half again longer than the alternate route south around King William Land and then further south up Back's River.

Unless they met friendly Esquimaux soon after crossing to the Boothia, they would all be dead weeks or months before such a twelve-hundred-mile trip could be completed.

Even so, Francis Crozier would have preferred to have wagered everything on a dash straight across the ice — northeast over the worst of the pack ice in a mad attempt to replicate the astounding 600-mile small-group sledge trip made by his friend James Clark Ross eighteen years earlier when the *Fury* was frozen in on the opposite side of the Boothia Peninsula. The old steward — Bridgens — had been absolutely correct. John Ross had taken the best bet on survival, forcing his way north by foot and sledge and then in boats left behind up to Lancaster Sound and waiting for whalers. And his nephew James Ross showed that it was possible — just possible — to sledge from King William Land back to Fury Beach.

————

Erebus was still in its final ten days of agony when Crozier had detached the best man-haulers from each ship — the winners of the biggest prizes and the last money Francis Crozier had in the world — given them the best-designed sledge, and ordered Mr. Helpman and Mr. Osmer, the purser, to fit this superteam of man-haulers out with everything they might need for six weeks on the ice.

It was an eleven-man sledge headed by *Erebus* second mate Charles Frederick Des Vouex, its lead puller the giant Manson. Each of the other nine men were asked to volunteer. Each man did.

Crozier had to know if it was possible to man-haul a fully loaded boat sledge across the open ice in such a straight dash toward rescue. The eleven men left at six bells on 23 March, in the dark, with the temperature at thirty-eight below zero, to three rousing cheers from every ambulatory crewman assembled from both ships.

Des Voeux and his men were back in three weeks. No one had died, but they were all exhausted and four of the men had serious frostbite. Magnus Manson was the only one of the eleven-man team, including the apparently indefatigable Des Voeux, who did not seem close to death from exhaustion and hardship.

In three weeks they had been able to travel less than twenty-eight miles in a straight line from *Terror* and *Erebus*. Des Voeux later estimated that they had man-hauled more than a hundred and fifty miles to gain those twenty-eight, but there was no possibility of traveling in a straight line that far out on the pack ice. The weather northeast of their current position was more terrible than the Ninth Circle of Hell where they had been trapped for two years. Pressure ridges were Legion.

Some rose to heights greater than eighty feet. Even steering their course was close to impossible when clouds hid the southerly sun and the stars were hidden for several eighteen-hour nights on end. Compasses, of course, were useless this close to the north magnetic pole.

The team had brought five tents for safety's sake, although they had planned to sleep in only two of them. The nights were so cold out on the exposed ice that the eleven men slept the last nine nights, when they were able to sleep at all, in a single tent. But in the end they'd had no choice in the matter, since four of the sturdy tents had blown away or been ripped to shreds by the twelfth night on the ice.

Somehow Des Voeux had kept them moving to the northeast, but every day the weather worsened, the pressure ridges grew closer together, the necessary deviations from their course became longer and more treacherous, and the sledge sustained serious damage in their Herculean struggle to haul and shove it over the jagged ice ridges. Two days were lost just repairing the sledge in the howl of wind and blowing snow.

The mate had decided to turn around on their fourteenth morning on the ice. With only one tent left, he gauged their chances of survival as low. They then tried to follow their own thirteen days of ruts back to the ships, but the ice was too active — shifting slabs, moving bergs within the pack ice, and new pressure ridges rising in front of them had obliterated their track. Des Voeux, the finest navigator on the Franklin Expedition except for Crozier, took theodolite and sextant readings in the few clear moments he found in the days and nights but ended up setting his course based mostly on dead reckoning. He told the men that he knew precisely where they were. He was sure, he later admitted to Fitzjames and Crozier, that he would miss the ships by twenty miles.

On their last night on the ice, the final tent ripped and they abandoned their sleeping bags and pressed on to the southwest blindly, man-hauling just to stay alive. They jettisoned their extra food and clothing, continuing to man-haul the sledge only because they needed their water, shotguns, cartridges, and powder. Something large had been following them for their entire voyage. They could see it through the spindrift and fog and pelting hail. They could hear it circling them each endless night in the darkness.

Des Voeux and his men were sighted on the northern horizon, still headed due west and oblivious of *Terror* three miles south of them, on the morning of their twenty-first day on the ice. An *Erebus* lookout had spotted them, but the ship itself was gone by then — crushed and splintered and sunk. It was Des Voeux's and his men's good fortune that the lookout, Ice Master James Reid, had climbed the huge iceberg that had been part of the Grand Venetian Carnivale before dawn that day and spotted the men through his glass just at first light.

Reid, Lieutenant Le Vesconte, Surgeon Goodsir, and Harry Peglar led the party that went out to fetch the Des Voeux team, bringing them back past the crushed timbers, tumbled masts, and tangled rigging that was all that remained of the sunken ship. Five of the Des Voeux champion team were not able to walk the last mile to *Terror* but had to be sledged there by their mates. The six Erebuses among the superteam of sledgers, including Des Voeux, wept at the sight of their destroyed home as they were led past it.

So . . . the short way northeast to Boothia was no longer an option. After debriefing Des Voeux and the other shattered men, both Fitzjames and Crozier agreed that a few of the 105 survivors might make it to Boothia, but the vast majority were certain to perish on the ice under such conditions, even with the longer days, slightly rising temperatures, and added sunlight. The possibility of open leads would only add to the hazard.

The choices now were either stay on the ships or set up a camp on King William Land with the option of making a run south to Back's River.

Crozier began the planning for the evacuation the next day.

———

Just before sunset and their dinner stop, the procession of sledges came across a hole in the ice. They stopped, the five sledges and harnessed men making a ring around the pit. The black circle far below them was the first open water the men had seen in twenty months.

"This weren't here last week when we brung the pinnaces to Terror Camp, Captain," said Seaman Thomas Tadman. "You can see how close them runner tracks come to it. We would've seen it, sure like. There was nothing here."

Crozier nodded. This was no ordinary *polynya* — the Russian word for one of those rare holes in pack ice that remained open all year long. The ice was more than ten feet thick here — less thick than the congealed pack ice around *Terror* but still solid enough to erect a London building on — but there was no sign of pressure slabs or cracking around this hole. It was as if someone or something had taken a gigantic ice saw of the sort both ships packed and cut a perfectly round hole through the ice.

But the ships' ice saws would not cut so cleanly through ten feet of ice.

"We could take our dinner here," said Thomas Blanky. "Enjoy our victuals by the seaside, as it were."

The men shook their heads. Crozier agreed — he wondered if the others felt the same unease he did about the uncannily perfect circle, deep pit, and black water. "We'll keep moving for another hour or so," he said. "Lieutenant Little, have your sledge take the lead, please."

It was perhaps twenty minutes later, the sun had set with an almost tropical suddenness and stars were shaking and twitching in the cold sky, when Privates Hopcraft and Pilkington, who had been serving as rear guard, crunched up to Crozier where he was walking beside the rearmost sledge. Hopcraft whispered, "Captain, there's something following us."

Crozier pulled his brass telescope from the top-lashed box on the sled and stood stationary on the ice with the two men for a minute while the sledges rasped their way past them into the gathering gloom.

"There, sir," said Pilkington, pointing with his good arm. "Maybe it come up out of that hole in the ice, Captain. Do you think it did? Bobby and I think it probably did. Maybe it was just down there in the black water under the ice waiting for us to pass and then come up for us. Or hoping for us to tarry there. Do you think, sir?"

Crozier did not answer. He could see it through the glass, just visible in the failing light. It looked white but only because it was briefly silhouetted against storm clouds building in the night-black sky to the northwest. As the thing passed seracs and ice boulders the sledge procession had grunted its way past only twenty minutes earlier, it was easier to get a sense of its enormous size. At the shoulder, even when it was moving on all fours as it was now, it was taller than Magnus Manson. It moved lithely for something so massive — the movement looked to be more foxlike than bear-heavy. As Crozier struggled to steady the glass in the rising wind, he saw the thing rise up and begin walking on two legs. It moved a little less rapidly that way, but still more quickly than men attached to 2,000-lb. sledges. It now towered over seracs whose tops Crozier could not have reached with his fully raised arm and extended telescope.

Then it was dark and he could no longer make it out against the background of pressure ridges and seracs. He led the Marines back to the sledge procession and set his glass into the storage box as the men ahead leaned steeply into their harnesses and grunted and panted and pulled.

"Stay close to the sledges but keep looking rearward and keep your weapons primed," he said softly to Pilkington and Hopcraft. "No lanterns. You'll need whatever vision you have in the dark." The bulky shapes of the Marines nodded and moved rearward. Crozier noted that the guards ahead of the first sledge had lit their lanterns. He could no longer see the men, just the ice-crystal-haloed circles of light.

The captain called Thomas Blanky over. The man's peg leg and wooden foot exempted him from man-hauling even though the foot had been thoughtfully studded with nails and cleats for the ice. The half-leg simply didn't give Blanky the leverage and pulling power he needed. But the men knew that the ice master might soon figuratively, if not literally, pull his weight and more; knowledge of ice conditions would be crucial if they encountered leads and had to launch their boats from Terror Camp in the coming weeks or months.

Now Crozier used Blanky as a messenger. "Mr. Blanky, would you be so good as to go forward and pass the word to the men not hauling that we will not be stopping for supper? They should retrieve the cold beef and biscuits from the appropriate sledge boxes and pass them out to the Marines and men in harness along with the word that everyone should eat on the march and drink from the water bottles they carry under their outer clothing. And also please ask our guards to make sure that their weapons are ready. They might wish to remove their outer mittens."

"Yes, Captain," said Blanky and disappeared ahead into the gloom. Crozier could hear the crunch of his hobnailed wooden foot.

The captain knew that within ten minutes, every man on the march would understand that the thing on the ice was following them and closing the gap.

35

IRVING

Except for the fact that John Irving was sick and half-starving and his gums were bleeding and he feared that two of his side teeth were loose and he was so tired that he was afraid he would collapse in his tracks at any moment, this was one of the happiest days of his life.

All this day and the previous day, he and George Henry Hodgson, old friends from the gunnery training ship *Excellent* before this expedition, had been in charge of teams of men doing some hunting and honest-to-God exploring. For the first time in this accursed expedition's three years of sitting around and freezing, Third Lieutenant John Irving was a true *explorer.*

It was true that the island he was exploring eastward across, the same King William Land to which he'd come with Lieutenant Graham Gore a little more than eleven months ago, wasn't worth a drop of Chinaman's piss what with it being all frozen gravel and low hills, none rising more than twenty or so feet above sea level, inhabited only by howling winds and pockets of deep snow and then more frozen gravel, but Irving was *exploring.* Already this morning he had seen things that no other white man — and perhaps no other human being on the planet — had ever seen. Of course, it was just more low hills of frozen gravel and more windswept pockets of ice and snow, not so much as an arctic fox track or a mummified ring seal to be found, but it was *his* discovery: Sir James Ross had sledged around the northern coast to reach Victory Point two decades or so ago, but it was John Irving — originally from Bristol and then the young master of London Town — who was the first explorer of the interior of King William Land.

Irving had half a mind to name the interior *Irving Land*. Why not? The point not far from Terror Camp was named after Sir John's wife, Lady Jane Franklin, and what had *she* ever done to deserve the honour except marry an old, fat, bald man?

The various man-hauling teams were beginning to think of themselves as distinct groups. So yesterday, Irving led this same band of six men on a hunting party while George Hodgson took his men out to reconnoiter the island, as per Captain Crozier's instructions. Irving's hunters had found not so much as an animal track in the snow.

The lieutenant had to admit that since all of his men had been armed with shotguns or muskets yesterday (Irving himself had carried only a pistol in his coat pocket, as he was doing today), there had been moments when he had felt some concern about the caulker's mate, Hickey, being behind him and carrying a gun. But, of course, nothing had happened. With Magnus Manson more than twenty-five miles away at the ship, Hickey was not only polite but actually deferential to Irving, Hodgson, and the other officers.

It reminded John Irving of how their tutor used to separate his brothers and him during classes at their Bristol home when the boys had become too rowdy during the long, dreary days of lessons. The tutor would actually set the boys in separate rooms in the old manor and conduct their lessons separately for hours, moving from one part of the second floor of the old wing to the next, his high-heeled buckled shoes echoing on the ancient oak floors. John and his brothers, David and William, such a handful around Mr. Candrieau when the three were together, became almost timid in front of the pale-faced, knobby-kneed beanpole of a white-wigged tutor when alone with him. Originally very reluctant to approach Captain Crozier about leaving Manson behind, Irving was now glad he had spoken up. He was even gladder that the captain had not pressed him for a reason; Irving had never told the captain about what he had seen going on between the caulker's mate and big seaman that night on the hold deck and never would.

But today there was no tension about Hickey or anything else. The only member of the scouting party to carry a weapon, other than Irving himself with his pistol, was Edwin Lawrence, who was armed with a musket. Shooting practice near the line of sledge-mounted boats at Terror Camp had shown that Lawrence was the only man in this group who could shoot a musket worth a damn, so he was their guard and protector today. The rest carried only canvas packs slung over their shoulders, jury-rigged bags hanging from one strap. Reuben Male, the captain of the fo'c'sle and an inventive type, had worked with Old Murray the sailmaker to make up these packs for all the men, so naturally the seamen called them Male Bags. In the Male Bags they kept their lead or pewter water bottles, some biscuits and dried pork, a tin of Goldner's canned goods for emergency rations, some extra layers of clothing, the wire goggles that Crozier had ordered made up to protect them from sun blindness, extra powder and shot for when they were hunting, and their blanket sleeping bags just in case something should prevent them from returning to camp and they had to bivouac that night.

This morning they had hiked inland for more than five hours. The group stayed on the slight gravel rises when they could; the wind was stronger and colder there, but the walking was easier than in the snow- and ice-filled swales. They had seen nothing that might enhance everyone's chance of survival — not even green lichen or orange moss growing on rock. Irving knew from reading books in *Terror's* Great Cabin library — including two books by Sir John Franklin himself — that hungry men could make a sort of soup from the scrapings of moss and lichen. *Very* hungry men.

When his reconnoitering team had stopped for their cold dinner and water and some much-needed rest while huddled down out of the wind, Irving had handed over temporary command to Captain of the Maintop Thomas Farr and gone on for a while by himself. He told himself that the men were exhausted by their extraordinary sledge pulls of the past few weeks and needed the rest, but the truth was, he needed the solitude.

Irving had told Farr that he would be back in an hour and that to make sure he did not get lost he would frequently dip down across snowy patches out of the wind, leaving his boot tracks for himself to follow back or for the others to use to find him if he was late returning. As he walked farther east, blissfully alone, he had chewed on a hard biscuit, feeling how loose his two teeth were. When he pulled the biscuit away from his mouth, there was blood on it.

As hungry as he was, Irving had little appetite these days.

He waded up through another snow field onto frozen gravel and trudged up the rise to yet another windswept low ridge, then stopped suddenly.

Black specks were moving in the broad snow-swept valley ahead of him.

Irving used his teeth to tug off his mittens and fumbled in his Male Bag for his prized possession, the beautiful brass telescope his uncle had given him upon entering the Navy. The brass eyepiece would freeze to his cheek and brow if he allowed it to touch, so it was harder getting a steady image while holding it away from his face, even holding the long glass in both hands. His arms and hands were shaking.

What he had thought to be a small herd of woolly animals turned out to be human beings.

Hodgson's hunting party.

No. These forms were dressed in heavy fur parkas of the sort Lady Silence wore. And there were ten figures laboriously crossing the snowy valley, walking close together but not in a single-file line; George only had six men with him. And Hodgson had taken his hunting party south along the coast today, not inland.

This group had a small sledge with them. Hodgson's hunting party had no sledge with them. There was not a sledge this small at Terror Camp.

Irving fiddled with the focus of his beloved telescope and held his breath to keep the instrument from shaking.

This sledge was being pulled by a team of at least six dogs.

These were either white rescuers wearing Esquimaux garb or actual Esquimaux.

Irving had to lower the telescope and then go to one knee on the cold gravel and lower his head for a moment. The horizon seemed to be spinning. The physical weakness he'd been holding back for weeks through sheer force of will welled up through him like concentric circles of nausea.

This changes everything, he thought.

The figures below — they still did not appear to have seen him, probably because he had crossed over the rise and would not be very visible here with his dark coat blending into the dark rock — could be hunters out from some unknown farther-north Esquimaux village that was not far away. If so, the 105 survivors of *Erebus* and *Terror* were almost certainly saved. The natives would either feed them or show them how to feed themselves up here in this lifeless land.

Or there was a chance that the Esquimaux were a war party and that the crude spears Irving had caught a glimpse of in the glass were meant for the white men they'd somehow heard had invaded their lands.

Either way, Third Lieutenant John Irving knew that it was his job to go down, encounter them, and find out.

He closed the telescope, set it carefully amid extra sweaters in his shoulder bag, and — throwing one arm high in what he hoped the savages would see as a gesture of greeting and peace — started down the long hill toward the ten humans who had suddenly stopped in their tracks.

36

CROZIER

Lat. 69° 37' 42" N., Long. 98° 41' W.
24 April, 1848

T he third and last day on the ice was by far the hardest. Crozier had made this crossing at least twice before in the last six weeks with some of the earliest and larger sledge parties, but even with the trail less established, it had been much easier then. He'd been healthier. And he'd been infinitely less tired.

Francis Crozier was not truly aware of it, but since his recovery from his near-fatal withdrawal illness in January, his severe melancholia had made him an insomniac. As a sailor and then a captain, Crozier had always prided himself — as most captains did — on needing very little sleep and waking from the deepest sleep at any change in the ship's condition: a slight change in the ship's direction, the rising of wind in the sails, the sound of too many feet running on deck above him during any specific watch, any alteration in the sound of the water moving against the ship's hull . . . anything.

But in recent weeks, Crozier slept less and less each night, until he'd fallen into the habit of only half dozing for an hour or two in the middle of the night, perhaps catching a nap of thirty minutes or less during the day. He told himself it was just the result of so many details to watch over and commands to give in the last days and weeks before taking to the ice, but in truth it was melancholia trying to destroy him again.

His mind was sodden much of the time. He was a smart man whose mind was stupid with the chemical by-products of constant fatigue.

Sleeping at Sea Camps One and Two had been damned near impossible for any of the men the past two nights, no matter how tired they were. There had been no need to erect tents at either camp since eight Holland tents there had been left up permanently over the past weeks, any wind or snow damage being repaired by the next party that came through.

The three-person reindeer-skin sleeping bags were many times warmer than the sewn-together Hudson's Bay blanket bags, and these good bags had been drawn by lottery. Crozier had not even taken part in the lottery, but when, the first time he'd been on the ice, he'd come into the tent he shared with two other officers, he found that his steward, Jopson, had laid out a reindeer-skin bag tailored for him. Neither the ailing Jopson nor the men thought it right that their captain would have to share a bag with two other snoring, farting, shoving men — even other officers — and Crozier had been too tired and grateful to argue.

Nor had he told Jopson or the others that sleeping in a bag by one's self was much chillier than his experience sleeping in three-man bags. The other men's body heat was the only thing that kept them warm enough to sleep through the night.

But Crozier hadn't tried to sleep through the night at either sea camp.

Every two hours he was up and walking the perimeter to make sure that the watch had changed on time. The wind came up during the night, and the men on watch huddled behind hastily erected low snow walls. Because the biting wind and blowing snow kept the men curled low behind their snow-block barriers, the thing on the ice would have been visible to them only if it actually stepped on one of the men.

It did not make its appearance that night.

During the fitful minutes of sleep he did find, Crozier was revisited by the nightmares he'd had during his January illness. Some of the dreams returned so many times — and startled the captain out of sleep so many times — that he remembered fragments of them. Teenaged girls carrying out a séance. M'Clintock and another man staring down into an open boat at two skeletons, one sitting up and fully clothed in peacoat and slops, the other just a mass of tumbled and gnawed bones.

Crozier walked through his days wondering if he was one of those skeletons.

But the worst dream, by far, was the Communion dream in which he was a boy or a sicker, older version of himself and was kneeling naked at the altar rail in Memo Moira's forbidden church while the huge, inhuman priest — dripping water in shredded white vestments through which showed the raw, red flesh of a badly burned man — loomed over him and leaned closer, breathing carrion breath into Crozier's uplifted face.

The men all rose in the dark a little after 5:00 a.m. on the morning of 23 April. The sun would not rise until almost 10:00 a.m. The wind continued to blow, flapping the brown canvas of the Holland tents and stinging their eyes as they huddled to eat breakfast.

On the ice, the men were supposed to heat their food thoroughly in small tins labeled "Cooking Apparatus (1)," using their small spirit stoves fueled by pints of ether carried in bottles. Even without wind, it was often difficult or nearly impossible to get the spirit stoves primed and started; in a wind like that morning's, it was simply not possible, even when taking the risk of firing up the spirit stoves inside the tents. So — reassuring themselves that Goldner's canned meats and vegetables and soups had already been cooked — the men just spooned the frozen or near-frozen masses of congealed glop straight out of the cans. They were starving and had an endless day of man-hauling ahead of them.

Goodsir — and the three dead surgeons before Goodsir — had talked to Crozier and Fitzjames about the importance of heating Goldner's tinned foodstuffs, especially the soup. The vegetables and meats, Goodsir had pointed out, had indeed been precooked, but the soups — mostly cheap parsnips and carrots and other root vegetables — were "concentrated," meant to be diluted with water and brought to a boil.

The surgeon could not name the poisons that could be lurking in unboiled Goldner soups — and perhaps even in the meats and vegetables — but he kept reiterating the need for full heating of the tinned foods, even while on the march on the ice. These warnings were one of the main reasons Crozier and Fitzjames had ordered the heavy iron whaleboat stoves transported to Terror Camp over the ice and pressure ridges.

But there were no stoves here at Sea Camp One or at Sea Camp Two the next night. The men ate all the tinned foods cold from the can when the spirit stoves failed — and even when the ether of the little stoves lighted, there was just enough fuel to *melt* the frozen soups, not bring them to a boil.

That would have to suffice, thought Crozier.

As soon as breakfast was finished, the captain's belly began rumbling with hunger again.

The plan had been to fold up the eight Holland tents at both sea camps and haul them to Terror Camp on the sledges, to serve as backup should the groups have to go out on the ice again soon. But the wind was too high and the men were too weary even after just one day and night on the ice this trip. Crozier conferred with Lieutenant Little and they decided that three tents would be enough to bring along from this camp. Perhaps they would do better the next morning after Sea Camp Two.

Three men in harness broke down that second day on the ice on 23 April 1848. One began vomiting blood onto the ice. The other two simply fell in their tracks and were unable to pull for the rest of that day. One of those two had to be set onto a sledge and hauled.

Not wanting to reduce the number of armed pickets walking behind, ahead, and to the sides of the procession of sledges, Crozier and Little tied on harnesses and man-hauled for most of that endless day.

The pressure ridges weren't as high during this middle day of the crossing and the previous sledge tracks had left a virtual highway on this stretch of open sea ice, but the wind and blowing snow eliminated almost all of these advantages. Men pulling a sledge could not see the next sledge fifteen feet in front of them. The Marines or sailors carrying weapons and walking along as guards could see no one else when they were twenty feet or more from the sledges and had to walk within a yard or two of the sledge parties so as not to get lost. Their usefulness as lookouts was nil.

Several times during the day, the lead sledge — usually Crozier's or Lieutenant Little's — would lose the worn sledge track, and everyone would then have to stop for up to half an hour while some men unharnessed themselves, tied on a rope so as not to get lost in the howling snow, and walked left and right of the false route, seeking out the faint depressions of the actual track on a surface quickly being covered by inches of blowing snow.

To lose the route midway like this would cost not only time, it might well cost all of them their lives.

Some of the sledge teams hauling heavier loads this spring had done this nine miles of flat sea ice in under twelve hours, arriving at Sea Camp Two only hours after the sun had set. Crozier's group arrived long after midnight and almost missed the camp completely. If Magnus Manson — whose keen hearing seemed as unusual as his size and low intelligence — had not heard the flapping of tents in the wind far to their port side, they would have marched past their shelter and food cache.

As it was, Sea Camp Two had been largely destroyed by the day's incessant and rising winds. Five of the eight tents had been blown away into the darkness — even though they had been secured by deep ice screws — or simply torn to tatters. The exhausted and starving men managed to pitch two of the three tents they'd man-hauled from Sea Camp One, and forty-six men who would have been comfortable but crowded in eight tents squeezed into five.

For the men taking turns on watch that night — sixteen of the forty-six — the wind, snow, and cold were a living hell. Crozier stood one of the 2:00 a.m. to 4:00 a.m. watches. He preferred being able to move since his one-man sleeping bag would not allow him to get warm enough to sleep anyway, even with men stacked like cordwood around him in the flapping tent.

The final day on the ice was the worst.

The wind had stopped shortly before the men roused themselves at 5:00 a.m., but as in evil compensation for the gift of the blue skies to come, the temperature dropped at least thirty degrees. Lieutenant Little took the measurements that morning: the temperature at 6:00 a.m. was −64 degrees.

It's only eight miles, Crozier kept telling himself that day as he pulled in harness. He knew that the other men were thinking the same thing. *Only eight miles today, a full mile less than yesterday's terrible haul.* With more men dropping from sickness or exhaustion, Crozier ordered the accompanying guards to stow their rifles, muskets, and shotguns on the sledges and to tie on to the harnesses as soon as the sun rose. Every man who could walk would pull.

Lacking guards, they trusted in the clarity of the day. The brown blur of King William Land was visible as soon as the sun rose — the wall of high bergs and jostled coastal ice along its rim distressingly more visible, distantly gleaming in the thin, cold sunlight like a barrier of broken glass — but the clear light ensured they would not lose the old sledge tracks and that the thing on the ice could not sneak up on them.

But the thing was out there. They could see it — a small dot loping along to the southwest of them, moving much faster than they could haul. Or run, should it come to that.

Several times during the day, Crozier or Little would unstrap from harness, retrieve their telescopes from the sledges or their Male Bags, and look across the miles of ice at the creature.

It was at least two miles away and moving on all fours. From this distance, it might be just another white arctic bear of the kind they had shot and killed in such plentitude in the last three years. Until, that is, the thing took to its hind legs, rose up above the surrounding ice blocks and minibergs, and sniffed the air as it stared in their direction.

It knows we've abandoned the ships, thought Crozier, staring through his brass telescope that had become scuffed and scarred from so many years' use at both poles. *It knows where we're going. It's planning to get there first.*

They pulled on through the day, stopping only at the midafternoon sunset to eat frozen chunks out of cold cans. Their rations of salt pork and stale biscuits had been used up. The ice walls separating King William Land from the pack ice glowed like a city with ten thousand burning gas lamps in the minutes before darkness spread across the sky like spilled ink.

They still had four miles to go. Eight men were on sledges now, three of the seamen unconscious.

They crossed the Great Ice Barrier separating the pack ice from land sometime after 1:00 a.m. The wind stayed low but the temperature continued to drop. During one pause to rerig ropes for the lifting of the sledges over a thirty-foot wall of ice, made not at all easier by the passage of sledges in weeks past since the movement of the ice had tumbled a thousand new ice blocks into their path from the towering bergs on either side, Lieutenant Little took another temperature reading. It was −82 degrees.

Crozier had been working and giving commands from within a deep trench of exhaustion for many hours. At sunset, when he'd last looked to the south at the distant creature loping ahead of them now — it was already crossing the sea ice barrier in easy leaps — he had made the mistake of taking his mittens and gloves off for a moment so as to write some position notes in his log. He had forgotten to don the gloves before lifting the telescope again and his fingertips and one palm had instantly frozen to the metal. In pulling his hands away quickly, he had ripped a layer of skin and some flesh off his right thumb and three fingers on that hand, and lifted a swath off his left palm.

Such wounds did not heal up here in the arctic, especially not after the early symptoms of scurvy had set in. Crozier had turned away from the others and vomited from the pain. The sickening burning in his ravaged fingers and left palm only grew worse through the long night of hauling, tugging, lifting, and pushing. His arm and shoulder muscles bruised and bled internally under the pressure of the harness straps.

For a while on the last barrier, around one thirty in the morning, with the stars and planets shimmering and shifting in the endless clear but murderously cold sky overhead, Crozier stupidly considered leaving all the sledges behind and making a dash for Terror Camp, still a full mile away across the frozen gravel and drifted snow. Other men could come back with them tomorrow and help fetch these impossibly heavy burdens the last mile or so.

Enough of Francis Crozier's mind and command instincts remained for him to reject this thought at once. He could do just that, of course, abandon the sledges — the first party in weeks to do so — and ensure their survival by staggering across the ice to the safety of Terror Camp without their burdens, but he would lose all leadership forever in the eyes of his 104 surviving men and officers.

Even though the pain from his torn hands caused him to vomit frequently and silently onto the ice wall as they pulled and pushed the sledges over — a distant part of Crozier's mind noticed that the vomitus was liquid and red in the lantern light — he continued giving orders and lending a hand as the thirty-eight men well enough to continue the struggle managed to get the sledges and themselves over the Barrier and onto the ice and runner-scraping gravel of the shoreline.

If he hadn't been sure that the cold would rip the skin of his lips off, Crozier might have fallen to his knees in the dark and kissed the solid ground as they heard that new sound of gravel and stone protesting under the sledge runners for the final mile.

There were torches burning at Terror Camp. Crozier was in the lead harness of the lead sledge as they approached. Everyone tried to stand tall — or at least stagger in an upright position — as they pulled the dead-weight sledges and the unconscious men on them the last hundred yards into camp.

There were men fully dressed in slops and outside the tents waiting for them. At first Crozier was touched by their concern, sure that the two dozen or so men he saw in the torchlight had been on the verge of sending out a rescue party in search of their overdue captain and comrades.

As Crozier leaned into the harness, pulling the last sixty feet or so into the light from the torches, his hands and bruises aflame with pain, he prepared a little joke for their arrival — something along the lines of declaring it Christmas again and announcing that everyone would sleep the next week through — but then Captain Fitzjames and some of the other officers stepped closer to greet them.

Crozier saw their eyes then: Fitzjames's eyes and Le Vesconte's and Des Voeux's and Couch's and Hodgson's and Goodsir's and the others' there. And he knew — through Memo Moira's Second Sight or his demonstrated captain's sense or just through the clear, unfiltered-by-thought perception of a completely exhausted man — he *knew* that something had happened and that nothing would now be as he had planned or hoped and might never be again.

37

IRVING

T here were ten Esquimaux standing there: six men of inde-
terminate age, one very old man with no teeth, one boy, and
two women. One woman was old, with a collapsed mouth
and a face that was a mass of wrinkles, and one was very young.
Perhaps, Irving thought, *they are mother and daughter.*

The men were uniformly short; the top of the tallest man's head
barely came up to the tall third lieutenant's chin. Two had their hoods
back, showing wild thatches of black hair and unlined faces, but the
other men stared at him from the depths of their hoods, some with
their faces shrouded and surrounded by a luxuriant white fur that Irving believed might be from the arctic fox. Other hood ruffs were
darker and more bristly and Irving guessed that the fur might be from
wolverines.

Every male except the boy carried a weapon, either a harpoon or
short spear with a bone or stone point, but after Irving had
approached and shown his empty hands, none of the spears were
now raised or pointed at him. The Esquimaux men — hunters, Irving
assumed — stood easily, legs apart, hands on their weapons, with
their sled being held back by the oldest man, who kept the boy close.
There were six dogs harnessed to the sled, a vehicle much shorter and
lighter than even the smallest folding sledges on *Terror.* The dogs
barked and snarled, showing vicious canines, until the old man beat
them into silence with a carved stick he carried.

Even while trying to think of a way to communicate with these strange people, Irving continued to marvel at their dress. The men's parkas were shorter and darker than Lady Silence's or her deceased male companion's, but just as furry. Irving thought that the dark hair or fur might be from caribou or foxes, but the knee-length white trousers were definitely from the white bears. Some of the long, hairy boots seemed to be from caribou skins, but others were more supple and pliable. Sealskin? Or some sort of caribou hide turned inside out?

The mittens were visibly sealskin and looked both warmer and more supple than Irving's own.

The lieutenant had looked to the six younger men to see who was the leader, but it wasn't clear. Other than the old man and the boy, only one of the males stood out, and that was one of the older bare-headed men who wore a complicated white caribou fur headband, a thin belt from which many odd things dangled, and some sort of pouch around his neck. It was not, however, a simple talisman such as Lady Silence's white stone bear amulet.

Silence, how I wish you were here, thought John Irving.

"Greetings," he said. He touched his chest with his mittened thumb. "Third Lieutenant John Irving of Her Majesty's Ship *Terror.*"

The men mumbled among themselves. He heard words that sounded like *kabloona* and *qavac* and *miagortok,* but had no clue whatsoever as to what they might mean.

The older bareheaded man with the pouch and belt pointed at Irving and said, "*Piifixaaq!*"

Some of the younger men shook their head at this. If it was a pejorative term, Irving hoped that the others were rejecting it.

"John Irving," he said, touching his chest again.

"*Sixam ieua?*" said the man opposite him. "*Suingne!*"

Irving could only nod at this. He touched his chest again. "Irving." He pointed toward the other man's chest in a questioning manner.

The man stared at Irving from between the fringes of his hood.

In desperation, the lieutenant pointed to the lead dog that was still barking and growling while being held back and beaten wildly by the old man next to the sled.

"Dog," said Irving. "Dog."

The Esquimaux man closest to Irving laughed. "*Qimmiq,*" he said clearly, also pointing to the dog. "*Tunok.*" The man shook his head and chuckled.

Although he was freezing, Irving felt a warm glow. He'd gotten somewhere. The Esquimaux word for the hairy dog they used was either *qimmiq* or *tunok,* or both. He pointed at their sled.

"Sled," he stated firmly.

The ten Esquimaux stared at him. The young woman was holding her mittens in front of her face. The old woman's jaw hung down and Irving could see that she had precisely one tooth in her mouth.

"Sled," he said again.

The six men in front looked at one another. Finally, Irving's interlouctor to this point said, "*Kamatik?*"

Irving nodded happily even though he had no idea if they had really begun communicating. For all he knew, the man had just asked him if he wanted to be harpooned. Nonetheless, the junior lieutenant could not stop grinning. Most of the Esquimaux men — with the exception of the boy, the old man who was still beating the dog, and the bareheaded older man with the pouch and belt — were grinning back.

"Do you speak English by any chance?" asked Irving, realizing that he was a bit tardy with the question.

The Esquimaux men stared and grinned and scowled and remained silent.

Irving repeated the query in his schoolboy French and atrocious German.

The Esquimaux continued to smile and scowl and stare.

Irving crouched and squatted and the six men closest to him squatted. They did not sit on the freezing gravel, even if a larger rock or boulder was near. After so many months up here in the cold, Irving understood. He still wanted to know someone's name.

"Irving," he said, touching his chest again. He pointed at the closest man.

"*Inuk*," said the man, touching his chest. He tugged off his mitten with a flash of white teeth and held up his right hand. It was missing the two smaller fingers. "*Tikerqat.*" He grinned again.

"Pleased to make your acquaintance, Mr. Inuk," said Irving. "Or Mr. Tikerqat. *Very* pleased to make your acquaintance."

He decided that any real communication would have to be through sign language and pointed back the way he had come, toward the northwest. "I have many friends," he said confidently, as if saying this would make him safer with these savage people. "Two large ships. Two . . . ships."

Most of the Esquimaux looked the way Irving pointed. Mr. Inuk was frowning slightly. "*Nanuq*," the man said softly, and then seemed to correct himself with a shake of his head. "*Tôrnârssuk.*" The others looked away or lowered their heads at this last word, almost, it seemed, as if in reverence or fear. But the lieutenant was sure that it was not at the thought of two ships or a group of white men.

Irving licked his bleeding lips. Better to begin trading with these people than to engage in a long conversation. Moving slowly, so as not to startle any of them, he reached into his leather shoulder valise to see if there was any food or bauble he could give them as a gift.

Nothing. He had eaten the only salted pork and old biscuit he'd brought for his day's rations. Something shiny and interesting then . . .

There were only his ragged sweaters, two stinking extra socks, and a disposable rag he had brought along for his alfresco privy purposes. At that moment Irving bitterly regretted giving his prized Oriental silk handkerchief to Lady Silence — wherever the wench was. She had slipped away from Terror Camp their second day there and not been seen again since. He knew that these natives would have loved the red-and-green silk handkerchief.

Then his cold fingers touched the curved brass of his telescope.

Irving's heart leapt and then wrenched itself with pain. The telescope was perhaps his most prized possession, the last thing his uncle had given him before that good man had died suddenly of heart trouble.

Smiling wanly at the waiting Esquimaux, he slowly pulled the instrument from his bag. He could see the brown-faced men tightening their grips on their spears and harpoons.

———

Ten minutes later Irving had the entire family or clan or tribe of Esquimaux close around him like schoolchildren grouped around an especially beloved teacher. Everyone, even the suspicious, squinty-eyed older man with the headband, pouch, and belt, had taken a turn looking through the glass. Even the two females had their turn — Irving allowed Mr. Inuk Tikerqat, his new fellow ambassador, to hand the brass instrument to the giggling young woman and the old woman. The ancient man who had been holding down the sled came over for a look and a shouted exclamation with the women chanting along:

> *ai yei yai ya na*
> *ye he ye ye yi yan e ya qana*
> *ai ye yi yat yana*

The group enjoyed looking at one another through the glass, staggering back in shock and laughter when huge faces loomed. Then the men, quickly learning how to focus the glass, zoomed in on distant rocks, clouds, and ridgelines. When Irving showed them that they could reverse the glass and make things and each other tiny, the men's laughs and exclamations echoed in the small valley.

He used his hands and body language — finally refusing to take the telescope back and pressing it into Mr. Inuk Tikerqat's hands — to let them know that it was a present.

The laughter stopped and they stared at him with serious faces. For a minute Irving wondered if he had violated some taboo, offended them somehow, but then he had a strong hunch that he had presented them with a problem in protocol; he had given them a wonderful gift and they'd brought nothing in return.

Inuk Tikerqat conferred with the other hunters and then turned to Irving and began making unmistakable pantomimes, lifting his hand to his mouth, then rubbing his belly.

For a terrible second Irving thought his interlocutor was asking for food — of which Irving had none — but when he tried to convey this fact, the Esquimaux shook his head and repeated the gestures. Irving suddenly realized that they were asking him if *he* was hungry.

Eyes filling with tears from a gust of wind or sheer relief, Irving repeated the gestures and nodded enthusiastically. Inuk Tikerqat grabbed him by his slop's frozen shoulder and led him back to the sled. *What had been their word for this?* thought Irving. "*Kamatik?*" he said aloud, remembering it at last.

"*Ee!*" cried Mr. Tikerqat approvingly. Kicking the growling dogs aside, he swept back a thick fur atop the sled. Stack upon stack of frozen and fresh meat and fish were piled atop the *kamatik*.

His host was pointing toward different delicacies. Pointing at the fish, Inuk Tikerqat said, "*Eqaluk,*" in the slow, patient tones an adult uses with a child. Toward slabs of seal meat and blubber, "*Nat-suk.*" Toward larger and more solidly frozen slabs of a darker meat, "*Oo ming-mite.*"

Irving nodded. He was embarrassed that his mouth had suddenly filled with saliva. Not sure if he was just supposed to admire the cache of food or choose from it, he pointed diffidently at the seal meat.

"*Ee!*" Mr. Tikerqat said again. He lifted a strip of soft meat and blubber, reached under his short parka, pulled a very sharp bone knife from his waistband, and cut a strip for Irving and another for himself. He handed the lieutenant his piece before cutting into his own.

The old woman standing nearby made a sort of wailing sound. "*Kaaktunga!*" she cried. And when none of the men paid any attention to her, she shouted again, "*Kaaktunga!*"

He made a face toward Irving, the kind one man makes to another when a woman demands something in their presence, and said, "*Orssunguvoq!*" But he cut the old woman a strip of seal blubber and tossed it to her as one would to a dog.

The toothless old crone laughed and began gumming the blubber.

Immediately the group gathered around the sled, men with their knives out, and everyone began cutting and eating.

"*Aipalingiagpoq,*" said Mr. Tikerqat, pointing to the old woman and laughing. The other hunters, old man, and boy — everyone except the older man with the headband and pouch — joined in the laughter.

Irving smiled broadly, although he had no idea what the joke was.

The older man in the headband pointed to Irving and said, "*Qavac . . . suingne! Kangunartuliorpoq!*"

The lieutenant did not need a translator to know that whatever the man had said, it had not been laudatory or kind. Mr. Tikerqat and several of the other hunters just shook their heads while eating.

Everyone, even the young woman, was using his or her knife the way Lady Silence had in her snow-house more than two months earlier — cutting the skin, meat, and blubber *toward* their mouths so the sharp blades came within a hairsbreadth of their greasy lips and tongues.

Irving cut his the same way — as best he could — but his knife was duller and he made a clumsy mess of it. But he did not cut his nose as he had the first time with Silence. The group ate in a companionable silence interrupted only by polite belches and the occasional fart. The men occasionally drank from some sort of pouch or skin, but Irving had already taken out the bottle he kept close to his body so the water would not freeze.

"*Kee-nah-oo-veet?*" Inuk Tikerqat said suddenly. He pounded his chest. "*Tikerqat.*" Again the young man removed his mitten and showed his two remaining fingers.

"Irving," said the lieutenant, again tapping his own chest.

"*Eh-vunq,*" repeated the Esquimaux.

Irving smiled over the blubber. He pointed at his new friend. "Inuk Tikerqat, *ee?*"

The Esquimaux shook his head. "*Ah-ka.*" The man made a wide sweep with his arms and hands, encompassing all the other Esquimaux as well as himself. "*Inuk,*" he said firmly. Holding up his mutilated hand and waggling his two remaining fingers while hiding his thumb, he said again, "*Tikerqat.*"

Irving interpreted all this to mean that "Inuk" was not the man's name but a description of all ten Esquimaux there — perhaps their tribal name or racial name or clan name. He guessed "Tikerqat" to be not a last name now but the entirety of his interlocutor's name, and probably one meaning "Two Fingers."

"*Tikerqat*," said Irving, trying to pronounce it properly while still cutting and chewing blubber for himself. The fact that the meat and greasy fat were old, smelly, and raw meant almost nothing. It was as if his body craved this fat above all other things. "*Tikerqat*," he said again.

There followed, in the midst of the squatting, cutting, and chewing, a general introduction. Tikerqat began both the introductions and the explanations by acting things out to explain the meaning of the name — if the names had a meaning — but then the other men picked up on it and acted out their own names. The moment had the feeling of a joyous child's game.

"*Taliriktug*," said Tikerqat slowly, pushing forward the barrel-chested young man next to him. Two Fingers grabbed his companion's upper arm and squeezed it, making *ah-yeh-I* noises, then flexing his own muscle and comparing it to the other man's thicker biceps.

"*Taliriktug*," repeated Irving, wondering if it meant "Big Muscle" or "Strong Arm" or something similar.

The next man, a shorter one, was named *Tuluqaq*. Tikerqat tugged the man's parka hood back, pointed to his black hair, and made flapping noises with his hand, miming a bird flying.

"*Tuluqaq*," repeated Irving, nodding politely toward the man as he chewed. He wondered if the word meant "Raven."

The fourth man thumped himself on the chest, grunted, "*Amaruq*," and threw back his head and howled.

"*Amaruq*," repeated Irving and nodded. "Wolf," he said aloud.

The fifth hunter was named *Mamarut* and acted out some pantomime involving waving his arms and dancing. Irving repeated the name and nodded but had no idea what the name might mean.

The sixth hunter, a younger man of very serious demeanor, was introduced by Tikerqat as *Ituksuk*. This man stared at Irving with deep black eyes and said and acted out nothing. Irving nodded politely and chewed his blubber.

The older man with the headband and the pouch was introduced by Tikerqat as *Asiajuk,* but the man neither blinked nor showed recognition of the introduction. It was obvious he did not like or trust Third Lieutenant John Irving.

"A pleasure to meet you, Mr. Asiajuk," said Irving.

"*Afatkuq,*" Tikerqat said softly, nodding slightly in the direction of the unsmiling older man in the headband.

Some sort of medicine man? wondered Irving. As long as Asiajuk's hostility remained only on the level of silent suspicion, the lieutenant thought that things would be all right.

The old man at the sled was introduced as *Kringmuluardjuk* to the young lieutenant. Tikerqat pointed to the still-snarling dogs, brought his hands together in some sort of diminutive gesture, and laughed.

Then Irving's laughing interlocutor pointed to the shy boy, who appeared to be about ten or eleven years old, pointed to his own chest again, and said, "*Irniq,*" followed by "*Qajorânguaq.*"

Irving guessed that *Irniq* might mean "son" or "brother." Probably the former, he thought. Or perhaps the boy's name was *Irniq* and *Qajorânguaq* meant son or brother. The lieutenant nodded respectfully, just as he had with the older hunters.

Tikerqat shoved the old woman forward. Her name appeared to be *Nauja,* and Tikerqat again made a bird-flying motion. Irving repeated the name as best he could — there was a certain glottal sound that the Esquimaux made that he could not approximate — and nodded respectfully. He wondered if *Nauja* was an arctic tern, a seagull, or something more exotic.

The old woman giggled and stuffed more blubber in her mouth.

Tikerqat put his arm around the young woman, not much more than a girl really, and said, "*Qaumaniq.*" Then the hunter grinned broadly and said, "*Amooq!*"

The girl wriggled in his grasp while smiling, and all the men except the possible medicine man laughed loudly.

"*Amooq?*" said Irving, and the laughter rose in volume. Tuluqag and Amaruq spit out blubber they were laughing so hard.

"*Qaumaniq . . . amooq!*" said Tikerqat and made a two-handed, open-fingered grabbing gesture in front of his own chest that was universal.

But to make sure he got the point across, the hunter grabbed his wriggling woman — Irving had to think she was his wife — and quickly lifted her short, dark parka top.

The girl was naked under the animal skin, and her breasts were, indeed, very large . . . very large indeed for a woman so young.

John Irving felt himself blush from his blond hairline down to his chest. He lowered his gaze to the blubber he was still chewing. At that moment he would have laid fifty quid that *Amooq* was the Esquimaux language equivalent of "Big Tits."

The men around him howled with laughter. The *Qimmiq* — the wolflike sled dogs around the wooden *kamatik* — howled and leapt against their tethers. The old man behind the sled, Kringmuluardjuk, actually fell onto the snow and ice he was laughing so hard.

Suddenly Amaruq — Wolf? — who had been playing with the telescope, pointed to the bare ridge from which Irving had descended into the valley and snapped what sounded like *"Takuva-a . . . kabloona qukiuttina!"*

The group fell silent immediately.

The wolfish dogs began barking wildly.

Irving stood from where he had been crouching and shielded his eyes from the sun. He did not want to ask for the telescope back. There was the quickest motion of a human form in greatcoat silhouetted against the top of the ridge.

Wonderful! thought Irving. All through the blubber feast and introductions, he'd been trying to decide how to get Tikerqat and the others to come back to Terror Camp with him. He'd been afraid that he would not be able to communicate well enough with just his hands and motions to persuade the eight Esquimaux males and two women and their dogs and sled to make the three-hour trip back to the coast with him, so he'd been trying to think of a way to get just Tikerqat to come along with him.

It was certain that the lieutenant could not just let these natives hike back to wherever they had come from. Captain Crozier would be at the camp tomorrow, and Irving knew from several conversations with the captain that contact with the local peoples was precisely what the tired and beleaguered captain most hoped might happen. *The northern tribes, what Ross called northern highland tribes, are rarely warlike,* Crozier had told his third lieutenant one night. *If we come across a village of theirs on our way south, they may feed us well enough to get us provisioned properly for the long upstream haul to Great Slave Lake. At the very least, they could show us how to live off the land.*

And now Thomas Farr and the others had come looking for him, following his footprints through the snow to this valley. The figure on the ridgeline had gone back over the ridge and out of sight — out of shock at seeing ten strangers in the valley or concern that he might frighten them? — but Irving had caught a glimpse of the greatcoat blowing in silhouette and the Welsh wig and comforter and knew that one of his problems had been solved.

If he could not persuade Tikerqat and the others to come back with them — and old Asiajuk the shaman might be a problem convincing — Irving and a few of his party would stay with the Esquimaux here in the valley, convince them to stay there with conversation and other presents from some of the other men's packs, while he sent the fastest seamen running back to the coast to bring Captain Fitzjames and many more men to this place.

I can't let them get away. These Esquimaux could be the answer to our problems. They may be our salvation.

Irving felt his heart pounding against his ribs.

"It's all right," he said to Tikerqat and the others, speaking in the calmest and most confident tones he could summon. "It's just my friends. A few friends. Good men. They won't harm you. We only have one rifle with us, and we won't bring that down here. It's all right. Just friends of mine whom you will enjoy meeting."

Irving knew that they couldn't understand a word he was saying, but he kept talking, using the same soft, reassuring voice he would have used at his family's stables in Bristol to calm a skittish colt.

Several of the hunters had pulled their spears or harpoons from the snow and were holding them casually, but Amaruq, Tulugaq, Taliriktug, Ituksuk, the boy Qajorânguaq, the old man Kringmuluard-juk, and even the scowling shaman Asiajuk were looking to Tikerqat for guidance. The two women quit chewing blubber and quietly found their place behind the line of men.

Tikerqat looked at Irving. The Esquimaux's eyes were suddenly very dark and very alien-looking to the young lieutenant. The man seemed to be waiting for some explanation. "*Khat-seet?*" he said softly.

Irving showed open palms in a calming gesture and smiled as easily as he could. "Just friends," he said, matching the softness of Tikerqat's tone. "A few friends."

The lieutenant glanced up at the ridgeline. It was still empty against the blue sky. He was afraid that whoever had come looking for him had been alarmed by the congregation in the valley and might be headed back. Irving was not sure how long he could wait here . . . how long he could keep Tikerqat and his people calm before they took flight.

He took a deep breath and realized that he would have to go after the man up there, call him back, tell him what had happened and send him to bring back Farr and the others as quickly as possible. Irving couldn't wait.

"Please stay here," said Irving. He set his leather valise in the snow near Tikerqat in an attempt to show that he was coming right back. "Please wait. I shan't be a moment. I won't even get out of your sight. Please stay." He realized that he was gesturing with his hands as if asking the Esquimaux to sit, the way he would talk to a dog.

Tikerqat did not sit, nor did he reply, but he remained where he was standing while Irving backed away slowly.

"I'll be right back," called the lieutenant. He turned and jogged quickly up the steep scree and ice, onto the dark gravel at the top of the ridgeline.

Barely able to breathe with the tension, he turned back at the top and looked down.

The ten figures, barking dogs, and sled were exactly where he had left them.

Irving waved, made gestures to show that he would be right back, and hurried over the ridge, ready to shout at any retreating sailor.

Twenty feet down the northeast side of the ridge, Irving saw something that made him stop in his tracks.

A tiny man was dancing naked except for his boots around a tall heap of discarded clothing on a boulder.

Leprechaun, thought Irving, remembering some of Captain Crozier's tales. The image made no sense to the third lieutenant. It had been a day of strange sightings.

He stepped closer and saw that it was no leprechaun dancing but rather the caulker's mate. The man was humming some sailor's ditty as he danced and pirouetted. Irving could not help noticing the grub-white paleness of the little man's skin, how his ribs pushed out so visibly, the goose bumps everywhere rising on his flesh, the fact that he was circumcised, and how absurd the pale white buttocks were when he pirouetted.

Walking up to him, shaking his head in disbelief, not in the mood to laugh but his heart still pounding with the excitement of finding Tikerqat and the others, Irving said, "Mr. Hickey. What on *earth* do you think you're doing?"

The caulker's mate quit pirouetting. He raised one bony finger to his lips as if to shush the lieutenant. Then he bowed and showed Irving his arse as he bent over his pile of coats and clothing on the boulder.

The man's gone mad, thought Irving. *I can't let Tikerqat and the others see him like this.* He wondered if he could slap some sense into the little man and still use him as a messenger to bring Farr and the others here quickly. Irving had a few sheets of paper and a stub of graphite with which he could write a note, but they were in his valise down in the valley.

"See here, Mr. Hickey . . . ," he began sternly.

The caulker's mate swung up and around so quickly with his arm fully extended that for a second or two Irving thought he was resuming his dance.

But there had been a sharp boat knife in that extended hand.

Irving felt a sudden sharp pain in his throat. He started to speak again, found that he couldn't, raised both hands to his throat, and looked down.

Blood was cascading over Irving's hands and down onto his chest, dripping onto his boots.

Hickey swung the blade again in a wide, vicious arc.

This blow severed the lieutenant's windpipe. He fell to his knees and raised his right arm, pointing at Hickey through vision that had suddenly been narrowed by a dark tunnel. John Irving was too surprised even to feel anger.

Hickey took a step closer, still naked, all sharp knees and thin thighs and tendons, crouching now like some pale, bony gnome. But Irving had fallen to his side on the cold gravel, vomited an impossible amount of blood, and was dead before Cornelius Hickey ripped away the lieutenant's clothing and began wielding the knife in earnest.

38

CROZIER

His men collapsed into tents and slept the sleep of the dead as soon as they reached Terror Camp, but Crozier did not sleep at all the night of 24 April.

First he went to a special medical tent that had been erected so that Dr. Goodsir could do the postmortem and prepare the body for burial. Lieutenant Irving's corpse, white and frozen after its long voyage back to camp on the savages' requisitioned sledge, did not look quite human. Besides the gaping wound on the throat — so deep that it exposed the white vertebrae of his spine from the front and made the head yaw back as if on a loose hinge — the young man had been emasculated and disemboweled.

Goodsir was still awake and working on the body when Crozier came into the tent. The surgeon was inspecting several organs removed from the corpse, poking at them with some sharp instrument. He glanced up and gave Crozier a strange, thoughtful, almost guilty look. Neither man said anything for a long moment as the captain stood over the body. Finally Crozier brushed back a strand of blond hair that had fallen over John Irving's forehead. The lock had been almost touching Irving's open, clouded but still staring blue eyes.

"Have his body ready for burial at noon tomorrow," said Crozier.

"Yes, sir."

Crozier went to his tent, where Fitzjames was waiting.

When Crozier's steward, the thirty-year-old Thomas Jopson, had supervised the loading and transport of "the captain's tent" to Terror Camp some weeks ago, Crozier had been furious to learn that Jopson had not only had a double-sized tent sewn for the purpose — the captain had anticipated just a regular brown Holland tent — but had also had the men haul an oversized cot and several solid oak and mahogany chairs from the Great Room, as well as an ornate desk that had belonged to Sir John.

Now Crozier was glad for the furniture. He arranged the heavy desk between the tent entrance and the private bunking area with the two chairs behind the desk and none in front. The lantern hanging from the tall tent's peak harshly illuminated the empty space in front of the desk while leaving the area for Fitzjames and Crozier in semi-darkness. The space had the feel of a court-martial room.

That's exactly what Francis Crozier wanted.

"You should go to bed, Captain Crozier," said Fitzjames.

Crozier looked at the younger captain. He did not look young any longer. Fitzjames looked like a walking corpse — pale to the point of his skin becoming transparent, bearded with whiskers and dried blood from leaking follicles, with hollow cheeks and sunken eyes. Crozier had not looked at himself in a mirror for several days and had avoided the one hanging at the rear of this tent of his, but he hoped to Christ he did not look as bad as the former wunderkind of the Royal Navy, Commander James Fitzjames.

"You need some sleep yourself, James," said Crozier. "I can interrogate these men myself."

Fitzjames shook his head tiredly. "I questioned them, of course," he said, his voice a dead monotone, "but haven't visited the site or really interrogated them. I knew you would want to."

Crozier nodded. "I want to be at the site by first light."

"It's about two hours' brisk walk to the southwest," said Fitzjames.

Crozier nodded again.

Fitzjames pulled his cap off and combed back his long, greasy hair with dirty fingers. They had used the boat stoves that had been transported here to melt water for drinking and just enough to shave by should an officer want to shave, but there was none left for bathing. Fitzjames smiled. "Caulker's Mate Hickey asked if he could sleep until it was his time to report."

"Caulker's Mate Hickey can fucking well stay awake like the rest of us," said Crozier.

Fitzjames said softly, "That's more or less what I told him. I put him on guard duty. The cold should keep him awake."

"Or kill him," said Crozier. His tone suggested that this would not be the worst turn of events. In a loud voice, shouting to Private Daly who stood guard at the tent's door, Crozier said, "Send in Sergeant Tozer."

———

Somehow the large, stupid Marine managed to stay beefy even when all the men were starving on one-third rations. He stood at attention, minus his musket, as Crozier conducted the interrogation.

"What was your impression of today's events, Sergeant?"

"Very pretty, sir."

"Pretty?" Crozier remembered the condition of Third Lieutenant Irving's throat and body as he lay in the postmortem tent immediately behind Crozier's own tent.

"Aye, sir. The attack, sir. Went off like clockwork. Like clockwork. We come walking down that big hill, sir, muskets and rifles and shot-guns lowered as if we had no harsh feelings in the world, sir, and them savages watched us come. We opened fire at less than twenty yards and raised pure holy Cain amongst their motley God-be-damned ranks, sir, that I can tell you. Raised pure holy Cain."

"Were they in ranks, Sergeant?"

"Well, no, Captain, not as you might say on a Bible, sir. More like standing around like the savages they was, sir."

"And your opening salvos cut them down?"

"Oh, aye, sir. Even the shotguns at that range. It was a sight to behold, sir."

"Like shooting fish in a rain barrel?"

"Aye, sir," said Sergeant Tozer with a huge grin on his red face.

"Did they put up any resistance, Sergeant?"

"Resistance, sir? Not really. Not any you might speak of, sir."

"Yet they were armed with knives and spears and harpoons."

"Oh, aye, sir. A couple of the godless savages threw their harpoons and one got a spear off, but them what flung them was already wounded and it done them no good but a little nick in the leg of young Sammy Crispe, who took his shotgun and blew the savage who nicked him straight to Hell, sir. Straight to Hell."

"Yet two of the Esquimaux got away," said Crozier.

Tozer frowned. "Aye, sir. I apologize about that. They was a lot of confusion, sir. And two of 'em who went down got up when we was shooting those pox-besotted dogs, sir."

"Why did you shoot their dogs, Sergeant?" It was Fitzjames who asked this question.

Tozer looked surprised. "Why, they was barking and snarling and lunging at us, Captain. They was more wolves than dogs."

"Did you consider, Sergeant, that they might have been useful to us?" asked Fitzjames.

"Yes, sir. As *meat*."

Crozier said, "Describe the two Esquimaux that got away."

"A little one, Captain. Mr. Farr said that he thought it might have been a woman. Or a girl. She had blood on her hood but obviously she wasn't dead."

"Obviously," Crozier said drily. "What about the other one who escaped?"

Tozer shrugged. "A little man with a headband is all I know, Captain. He'd fallen behind the sledge there, and we all thought he was a deader. But he got up and run with the girl when we was busy shooting the dogs, sir."

"Did you pursue them?"

"Pursue them, sir? Oh, yes, absolutely. We run our ar— . . . we run after them hard, Captain. And we was reloading and firing as we went, sir. I think I hit that little Esquimaux bitch again, but she didn't slow down one whit, sir. They was just too fast for us. But they won't be coming back this way no time soon, sir. We saw to that."

"How about their friends?" Crozier said drily.

"Pardon, sir?" Tozer was grinning again.

"Their tribe. Village. Clan. Other hunters and warriors. These people came from somewhere. They haven't been out on the ice all winter. Presumably they'll return to that village, if they're not there already. Did you consider that the other Esquimaux hunters — men who kill every day — might take it personally that we killed eight of their kindred, Sergeant?"

Tozer looked confused.

Crozier said, "You're dismissed, Sergeant. Send in Second Lieutenant Hodgson."

———

Hodgson looked as miserable as Tozer had complacent. The young lieutenant was obviously distraught over the death of his closest friend on the expedition and sickened by the attack he had ordered after he had come across Irving's reconnaissance group and been led to Irving's body.

"At ease, Lieutenant Hodgson," said Crozier. "Do you need a chair?"

"No, sir."

"Tell us how you came to join up with Lieutenant Irving's group. Your orders from Captain Fitzjames were to go on a hunting expedition *south* of Terror Camp."

"Yes, Captain. And we did that much of the morning. There was not so much as a rabbit track in the snow along the coast, sir, and we couldn't get out onto the sea ice because of the height of the bergs piled up along the shore ice. So around ten a.m. we turned inland, thinking maybe there'd be sign of some caribou or foxes or musk oxen or something."

"But there wasn't?"

"No, sir. We came across the tracks of about ten people wearing soft-soled Esquimaux-type boots instead. That and their sledge and dog tracks."

"And you followed those tracks back northwest instead of continuing hunting?"

"Yes."

"Who made that decision, Second Lieutenant Hodgson? You or Sergeant Tozer, who was second in your party?"

"Me, sir. I was the only officer there. I made that and all the other decisions."

"Including the final decision of attacking the Esquimaux?"

"Yes, sir. We spied on them a minute from the ridge where poor John had been murdered and gutted, and . . . well, you know what they did to him, Captain. The savages looked like they were preparing to leave, heading back to the southwest. That's when we decided to attack them in force."

"You had how many weapons, Lieutenant?"

"Our group had three rifles, two shotguns, and two muskets, sir. Lieutenant Irving's group just had the one musket. Oh, and a pistol we fetched from John's . . . from Lieutenant Irving's greatcoat pocket."

"The Esquimaux left the weapon in his pocket?" asked Crozier.

Hodgson paused a moment as if he had not considered this before. "Yes, sir."

"Was there any other sign of theft of his personal possessions?"

"Yes, sir. Mr. Hickey had reported to us as to how he'd seen the Esquimaux rob John . . . Lieutenant Irving . . . of his telescope and valise before they killed him up on the ridge, sir. When we got to that ridge, I could see through our own glass that the natives were going through his valise and passing his telescope around down there in the valley where I guess they'd stopped after murdering and . . . mutilating . . . him."

"Were there tracks?"

"Pardon me, sir?"

"Tracks . . . of the Esquimaux . . . going down from the bare ridgeline where you found the lieutenant's body to where the natives were going through his possessions."

"Uh . . . yes, sir. I think so, Captain. I mean, I can remember a thin line of tracks that I thought were just John's at the time but must have been the rest of theirs as well. They must have gone up and down in a line, sort of, Captain. Mr. Hickey said that they were all around him up on the bare ridge there as they cut his throat and . . . did the other things, sir. He said that it wasn't all of them . . . not the women and the boy, maybe . . . but it was six or seven of the heathens. The hunters, sir. The younger men."

"And the old man?" asked Crozier. "I understand that there was a toothless old man among the bodies when you were done."

Hodgson nodded. "He had one tooth left, Captain. I can't remember if Mr. Hickey said the old man was part of the group that killed John."

"How was it that you first came upon Mr. Farr's group — Lieutenant Irving's reconnaissance party — if you had been following the Esquimaux's tracks north, Lieutenant?"

Hodgson nodded briskly as if relieved to be asked a question he could answer with certainty. "We lost the natives' footprints and sledge tracks about a mile south of where Lieutenant Irving was attacked, sir. They must have been moving more east then, across the low ridgetops where there was ice, but mostly rock, sir . . . you know, that frozen gravel. We couldn't find their sledge or dog tracks or footprints anywhere in the valleys, so we continued due north, the way they'd been going. We came down off a hill and found Thomas Farr's group — John's reconnaissance party — just finishing their dinner. Mr. Hickey had come back to report on what he'd seen just a minute or two earlier, and I guess we frightened Thomas and his men . . . they thought we were the Esquimaux coming for them."

"Did you observe anything odd about Mr. Hickey?" asked Crozier.

"Odd, sir?"

Crozier waited in silence.

"Well," continued Hodgson, "he was shaking very hard. As if palsied. And his voice was very agitated, almost shrill. And he . . . well, sir . . . he was laughing some. Giggling, like. But all that's to be expected from a man who'd just seen what he'd just seen, isn't it, Captain?"

"And what did he see, George?"

"Well . . ." Hodgson looked down to regain his composure. "Mr. Hickey had told Captain of the Maintop Farr, and he repeated to me, that he'd been out to check on Lieutenant Irving and came over a ridge just in time to see these six or seven or eight Esquimaux stealing the lieutenant's belongings and stabbing and mutilating him. Mr. Hickey said — he was still shaking hard, sir, very upset — that he'd seen them cut off John's private parts."

"You saw Lieutenant Irving's body just a few minutes later, didn't you, Lieutenant?"

"Aye, sir. It was about a twenty-five-minute walk from where Farr's group had been eating dinner."

"But you didn't start shaking uncontrollably after you saw Irving's body, did you, Lieutenant? Shaking for twenty-five minutes or more?"

"No, sir," said Hodgson, obviously not understanding the reason for Crozier's question. "But I threw up, sir."

"And when did you decide to attack the Esquimaux group and kill all of them?"

Hodgson swallowed audibly. "After I spied them from the ridge through my glass going through John's valise and playing with his telescope, Captain. As soon as we all took a look — Mr. Farr, Sergeant Tozer, and myself — and realized that the Esquimaux had turned their sledge around and were getting ready to leave."

"And you gave the order to take no prisoners?"

Hodgson looked down again. "No, sir. I didn't really think about it one way or the other. I was just so . . . angry."

Crozier said nothing.

"I did tell Sergeant Tozer that we had to ask one of the Esquimaux about what happened, Captain," the lieutenant continued. "So I guess I thought before the action that some would be alive after. I was just so . . . *angry.*"

"Who gave the actual order to fire, Lieutenant? You or Sergeant Tozer or Mr. Farr or someone else?"

Hodgson blinked several times, very rapidly. "I don't remember, sir. I'm not sure there *was* an order given. I just remember that we got to within about thirty yards, perhaps less, and I saw several of the Esquimaux men grab their harpoons or spears or whatever they were, and then everyone along our line was firing and reloading and firing. And the natives were running and the women were screaming . . . the older woman kept screaming like, well, like the banshees you've told us about, Captain . . . a high, warbling, constant scream . . . even after several balls had hit her, she kept up that God-awful screaming. Then Sergeant Tozer walked up and stood over her with John's pistol and . . . it all happened very fast, Captain. I've never been involved in anything like that."

"Nor have I," said Crozier.

Fitzjames said nothing. He'd been the hero of several wild land campaigns during the Opium Wars. His gaze now was downcast and seemed to be turned inward.

"If mistakes were made, sirs," said Hodgson, "I take full responsibility. I was the ranking officer of the two groups with Jo— . . . with Lieutenant Irving dead. It's all my responsibility, sirs."

Crozier looked at him. The captain could feel the dead flatness of his own gaze. "You *were* the only officer present, Lieutenant Hodgson. For good or ill, it *was* and *is* your responsibility. In about four hours, I want to lead a party to the site of the murder and shootings. We'll leave by lantern light and follow your sledge tracks back to the place, but I want to be there by the time the sun rises. You and Mr. Farr will be the only men from today's actions that I want along with us. Get some sleep and be fed and ready to go by six bells."

"Aye, sir."

"And send in Caulker's Mate Hickey."

39

GOODSIR

From the private diary of Dr. Harry D. S. Goodsir:

Tuesday, 25 April, 1848 —

I liked Lieutenant Irving very much. My Impression of him was that he was a Decent and Caring young man. I did not know him Well, but through all these Hard Months — especially during the many Weeks that I spent time on Terror *as well as* Erebus *— I never once saw the Lieutenant shirk a duty or speak harshly to the Men or deal with them or me with anything other than gentleness and Professional Courtesy.*

I know that Captain Crozier is especially Devastated by the Loss. His face was so Pale when He came into camp this morning sometime after 2:00 a.m. that I would have staked my Professional Reputation on the opinion that it could not grow any paler. But it did upon his hearing the News. Even his lips became as white as the ice-pack snow we have been staring at now for the better part of three years.

But however much I liked and respected Lieutenant Irving, I had to perform my Professional Duties and put all memories of Friendly Acquaintance aside.

I removed the remnants of Lieutenant Irving's clothing — buttons had been ripped off all layers from his Waistcoat to his Long Underwear, and the Caked Blood had frozen the clumped Fabric into iron-hard wrinkled masses — and had my assistant, Henry Lloyd, help me in bathing Lieutenant Irving's body. The water — from ice and snow Mr. Diggle's mates melted using some of the

Coal we brought over from the Ships — was precious, but it was necessary that we honour young Irving this way.

I did not, of course, have to make my usual inverted-Y incision from hip bones to umbilicus — the base of the upside-down Y running up to the sternum — since Lieutenant Irving's Murderers had already done so.

I made my usual Notes and Sketches as I proceeded, my Fingers aching from the Cold. The Cause of Death holds no Mysteries. The Wound to Lieutenant Irving's Neck had been caused by at least two savage slashes by a nonserrated blade, and he Bled to Death. I seriously doubt if there is a Pint of blood left in the hapless young Officer's body.

The Trachea and Larynx have been severed and there are blade gouges on the exposed cervical vertebrae.

His abdominal cavity has been opened by repeated sawing of a Short Blade through skin, flesh, and connecting Tissue, and the majority of his Upper and Lower intestines have been cut out and removed. Lieutenant Irving's spleen and kidneys have also been slashed and opened by a Sharp Object or Objects. His liver is missing.

The lieutenant's penis has been amputated approximately one Inch above its Base and is missing. His Scrotum has been cut open along its Central Axis and the testes cut out. Repeated Applications of the Blade were required to cut through the scrotal sac, the epididymis, and the tunica vaginalis. It is possible that the Assailant's Blade was growing Dull by this point.

While the testes are absent, remnants of the vas deferens and the urethra and major portions of connecting tissue from the base of the penis into the body cavity remain.

While there are signs of multiple Bruisings on Lieutenant Irving's body — many of them Consistent with a diagnosis of growing Scurvy — there are no other Serious Wounds visible anywhere. It is interesting that there are no Defensive Cuts on his hands, forearms, or palms.

It seems apparent that Lieutenant Irving was taken completely by Surprise. His Assailant or Assailants cut his throat before he had the Least Opportunity to defend himself. They then took some time Disemboweling him and Removing his Private Parts through repeated Incisions and Sawing Motions.

In preparing the lieutenant's body for burial later today, I sewed up his Neck and Throat as best I could and — after setting some Nonoriginal but decomposing fibrous substances (a folded sweater from the lieutenant's own pack of personal belongings) in his Abdominal Cavity so that the aforementioned Cavity would not look so visibly vacant and shrunken under his uniform when viewed by the men — I prepared to sew the abdominal Cavity back up as best I could (there was much tissue destroyed or missing).

But first I hesitated and Decided to do something unusual.

I opened Lieutenant Irving's stomach.

There was no real Postmortem Examinatory Reason to do this. There was no doubt of the Cause of the young lieutenant's death. There was no reason to check for Disease or Chronic Conditions — we are all suffering from Scurvy to one extent or the other, and we are all slowly Starving to Death.

But I opened his Stomach anyway. It looked strangely Distended — more so than bacterial action and the resulting Decomposition would suggest in this extreme cold — and no postmortem examination would be complete without an Inspection of this Anomaly.

His stomach was full.

Very shortly before Lieutenant Irving's death, he had ingested Large Quantities of Seal Meat, some Sealskin, and much Fatty Blubber. The Digestive Process had barely begun working on it.

The Esquimaux had Fed him before they Murdered Him.

Or perhaps Lieutenant Irving had Bartered his Telescope, valise, and few personal possessions in the Valise in exchange for this Seal Meat and Blubber.

But that is not possible, since Caulker's Mate Hickey reported that he saw the Esquimaux Murder and Rob the Lieutenant.

Seal Meat and Fish were on the Esquimaux Sled that Mr. Farr brought back, using it to transport Lieutenant Irving's body. Farr reported that they had thrown other objects off the Sled — baskets, Cooking Pots of some sort, things Lashed above the Seal Meat and Fish — so as to better situate the Lieutenant's corpse on the light sled. We wanted to make Lieutenant Irving as comfortable as possible, was what Sergeant Tozer had said.

So the Esquimaux must have first offered him their food, allowed him time to Eat it — if not Digest it — and then repacked their sled before Falling Upon him with such Savagery.

To approach someone as a Friend and then to Murder and Mutilate him so — can we Believe that there is a Race so Treacherous and so Malevolent and so Barbarous?

What could have Prompted this sudden and Violent change of attitude on the part of the Natives? Could the Lieutenant have said or done something that violated their Sacred Taboos? Or did they simply want to Rob him? Was the brass Telescope the reason for Lieutenant Irving's terrible Death?

There is another possibility, but one so Heinous and so Unlikely that I hardly wish to Record it here.

The Esquimaux did not kill Lieutenant Irving.

But this makes no sense either. Caulker's Mate Hickey clearly stated that he SAW six to eight of the Natives assailing the Lieutenant. He SAW them steal the Lieutenant's valise, telescope, and other possessions — while strangely they did not find his Pistol or go through his other pockets. Caulker's Mate Hickey told Captain Fitzjames today — I was present during the discussion — that he, Hickey, WATCHED from a distance as the Savages disemboweled our friend.

Hickey Hid and Watched as all this went on.

It is still pitch-dark and very Cold, but Captain Crozier is leaving in twenty Minutes to take a few men the Several Miles to the Site of the Murder and of today's Deadly Skirmish with the Esquimaux. Presumably their bodies are still Lying in the Valley there.

I have just completed Stitching Lieutenant Irving. As tired as I am — I have not slept for more than 24 Hours — I will have Lloyd finish the dressing of the Lieutenant and make final preparations for his burial later Today. As Providence would have it, Irving brought his Dress Uniform in his bag of personal possessions from Terror. He will be dressed in that.

I am going now to ask Captain Crozier if I may accompany him, Lieutenant Little, Mr. Farr, and the others to the Murder Site.

40

PEGLAR

When the fog shifted, something that looked like an over-sized human brain seemed to be rising out of the frozen ground: grey, convoluted, coiled upon itself, glistening with ice.

Harry Peglar realized that he was looking at John Irving's entrails.

"This is the spot," Thomas Farr said needlessly.

Peglar had been somewhat surprised that the captain had ordered him to come along on this trip to the murder site. The captain of the foretop had not been in either party — Irving's or Hodgson's — involved in yesterday's incidents. But then Peglar had looked at the other men chosen to go on this predawn investigatory expedition — First Lieutenant Edward Little, Tom Johnson (Crozier's bosun's mate and old crewman from the south polar expedition), Captain of the Maintop Farr who *had* been here yesterday, Dr. Goodsir, Lieutenant Le Vesconte from *Erebus,* First Mate Robert Thomas, and a guard of four Marines with weapons — Hopcraft, Healey, and Pilkington under the command of Corporal Pearson.

Harry Peglar hoped he was not flattering himself to think that, for whatever reason, Captain Crozier had chosen people he trusted for this outing. Malcontents and incompetents had been left behind at Terror Camp; the sea lawyer Hickey heading up a detail to dig Lieutenant Irving's grave for this afternoon's burial service.

Crozier's party had left camp long before dawn, following the footprints from yesterday and the tracks of the Esquimaux sledge that had borne the body to the camp southeast by lantern light. When the tracks disappeared on the stony ridgelines, they were easily found in the snowy vales beyond. The temperature had risen at least fifty-five degrees during the night, bringing the air up to zero degrees or higher, and a thick fog had rolled in. Harry Peglar, a veteran of weather on most of the earth's seas and oceans, had no idea how it could be so foggy when there was no unfrozen liquid water within hundreds and hundreds of miles. Perhaps these were low clouds skimming across the surface of the pack ice and colliding with this godforsaken island that rose only a few yards above sea level at its highest point. The sunrise, when it came, was no sunrise at all but only a vague yellow glow in the swirling fog-cloud around them, seeming to come from all directions.

The dozen men stood in silence at the murder site for a few minutes. There was little to see. John Irving's cap had blown against a nearby boulder, and Farr retrieved it. There was frozen blood on the frozen stones, the heap of human guts next to that dark stain. A few tatters of ripped clothing.

"Lieutenant Hodgson, Mr. Farr," said Crozier, "did you see any sign of the Esquimaux up here when Mr. Hickey led you to this scene?"

Hodgson seemed confused by the question. Farr said, "Other than their bloody handiwork, no, sir. We approached the ridgeline on our bellies and peered down into the valley using Mr. Hodgson's glass, and there they were. Still fighting over John's telescope and other spoils."

"Did you see them fight amongst themselves?" snapped Crozier.

Peglar never remembered seeing his captain — or any captain he had ever served under — look so tired. Crozier's eyes had visibly sunken in their sockets over the past days and weeks. Crozier's voice, always a bass bark of command, was now little more than a croak. It looked as if his eyes were ready to bleed.

Peglar knew something about bleeding these days. He hadn't told his friend John Bridgens yet, but he was feeling the scurvy badly. His once-proud muscles were atrophying. His flesh was mottled with bruises. He'd lost two teeth in the past ten days. Every time he brushed his remaining teeth, the brush came away red. And every time he squatted to relieve himself, he shat blood.

"Did I actually *see* the Esquimaux fighting amongst themselves?" repeated Farr. "Not really, sir. They were jostling and laughing, though. And two of the bucks were tugging at John's fine brass telescope."

Crozier nodded. "Let us go down in the valley, gentlemen."

Peglar was shocked by the blood. He'd never seen the site of a land battle before, not even a small skirmish such as this, and while he had prepared himself to see the dead bodies, he'd not imagined how red the spilled blood would be on the snow.

"Someone's been here," said Lieutenant Hodgson.

"What do you mean?" asked Crozier.

"Some of the bodies have been moved," said the young lieutenant, pointing to a man and then to another man and then to an old woman. "And their outer coats — the fur coats, such as Lady Silence wears — and even some of their mittens and boots are gone. So are several of the weapons . . . harpoons and spears. See, you can see the imprint in the snow where they were lying yesterday. They're gone."

"Souvenirs?" rasped Crozier. "Did our men . . ."

"No, sir," Farr said quickly and firmly. "We threw some baskets and cooking pots and other things off the sled to make room and took that sled up the hill to load Lieutenant Irving's body. We were all together from then until we reached Terror Camp. No one lagged behind."

"Some of those pots and baskets have gone missing as well," said Hodgson.

"There seem to be some newer tracks here, but it's hard to tell since the wind was blowing last night," said Bosun's Mate Johnson.

The captain was going from corpse to corpse, rolling them over when they were facedown. He seemed to be studying each dead man's face. Peglar noticed that they were not all dead men — one was a boy. One was an old lady whose open mouth — as if frozen by Death into an eternal silent scream — looked like a black pit. There was much blood. One of the natives had received the full force of a shotgun blast at what must have been very short range, perhaps after he had already been hit by musket or rifle fire. The back of his head was gone.

After inspecting each face as if hoping to find answers there, Crozier stood. The surgeon, Goodsir, who had also been looking carefully at the dead, said something softly into the captain's ear, pulling down his comforter scarf and the captain's as well while whispering. Crozier took a step back, looked at Goodsir as if in surprise, but then nodded.

The surgeon went to one knee by a dead Esquimaux and removed several surgical instruments from his bag, including one very long, curved, and serrated knife that reminded Peglar of the ice saws they used to cut chunks from the iron tanks of frozen water on the hold deck of *Terror*.

"Dr. Goodsir needs to examine several of the savages' stomachs," Crozier said.

Peglar imagined that nine others besides himself were wondering why. No one asked the question. The squeamish — including three of the Marines — looked away as the small surgeon tore open fur or animal-skin garments and began sawing on the first corpse's abdomen. The sound of the saw cutting into hard-frozen flesh reminded Peglar of someone sawing wood.

"Captain, who do you think might've fetched up the weapons and clothing?" asked First Mate Thomas. "One of the two who got away?"

Crozier nodded distractedly. "Or others from their village, although it's hard to imagine a village on this godforsaken island. Perhaps these were part of a larger hunting group camped nearby."

"This group had so much food with them," said Lieutenant Le Vesconte. "Imagine how much the main hunting party might have with them. We might be able to feed all one hundred and five of us."

Lieutenant Little smiled over his breath-rimed coat collars. "Would you like to be the one to walk into their village or larger hunting party and politely ask them for some food or hunting advice? Now? After this?" Little gestured toward the sprawled, frozen bodies and patches of red on the snow.

"I think we have to get away from Terror Camp and this island *now*," said Second Lieutenant Hodgson. The young man's voice was quavering. "They're going to kill us in our sleep. Look what they did to John." He stopped, visibly abashed.

Peglar studied the lieutenant. Hodgson showed all the signs of starvation and exhaustion that the rest of them did, but not as many signs of scurvy. Peglar wondered if he would become unmanned like this if and when he saw a spectacle similar to what Hodgson had seen less than twenty-four hours earlier.

"Thomas," Crozier said softly to his bosun's mate, "would you be so kind as to go over that next ridge and see if you can see anything? Specifically tracks leading away from here . . . and if so, how many and what kind?"

"Aye, sir." The large mate jogged uphill through deep snow and onto the dark-gravel ridge.

Peglar found himself watching Goodsir. The surgeon had cut open the greyish pink, distended stomach of the first Esquimaux man and then had gone on to the old woman and next the young boy. It was a terrible thing to watch. In each case, Goodsir — his hands bare — used a smaller surgical instrument to slit the stomach open and lifted out the contents, kneading through the frozen chunks and gobbets as if searching for a prize. Sometimes Goodsir snapped the frozen stomach contents into smaller bits with an audible crack. When he was finished with the first three corpses, Goodsir idly wiped his bare hands in the snow, tugged on his mittens, and whispered in Crozier's ear again.

"You can tell everyone," Crozier said loudly. "I want everyone to hear this."

The little surgeon licked his cracked and bleeding lips. "This morning I opened Lieutenant Irving's stomach . . ."

"Why?" shouted Hodgson. "That was one of the few parts of John that the fucking savages did not mutilate! How could you?"

"Silence!" barked Crozier. Peglar noticed that the captain's old authoritative voice had returned for that command. Crozier nodded to the surgeon. "Please continue, Dr. Goodsir."

"Lieutenant Irving had eaten so much seal meat and blubber that he was literally full," said the surgeon. "He'd had a larger meal than any of us have had in months. Obviously it came from the Esquimaux's cache on their sledge. I was curious if the Esquimaux had eaten with him — if the contents of their stomachs would show they also had eaten seal blubber shortly before they died. With these three, it is obvious they did."

"They broke bread with him . . . ate their meat with him . . . and then killed him as he was leaving?" said First Mate Thomas, obviously confused by this information.

Peglar was also confused. It made no sense . . . unless these savages were as mercurial and treacherous in their temperament as some natives he had come across in the South Seas during the five-year voyage of the old *Beagle*. The foretop captain wished that John Bridgens were here to give his opinion on all this.

"Gentlemen," said Crozier, obviously including even the Marines, "I wanted you all to hear this because I may require your knowledge of these facts at some future time, but I don't want anyone else to hear about it. Not until I say that it should be public knowledge. And I may never do so. If any of you tells anyone else — a single soul, your closest chum, if you so much as mumble this in your sleep — I swear to Christ I'll find out who disobeyed my order to silence and I'll leave that man behind on the ice without so much as an empty pan to shit in. Do I make myself clear, gentlemen?"

The other men grunted affirmation.

Thomas Johnson returned then, puffing and wheezing his way down the hill. He paused and looked at the silent clump of men as if to ask what was wrong.

"What did you see, Mr. Johnson?" Crozier asked briskly.

"Tracks, Captain," said the bosun's mate, "but old ones. Heading southwest. The two who got away yesterday — and whoever came back to the valley to loot the parkas and weapons and pots and such — must have followed that track as they ran. I saw nothing new."

"Thank you, Thomas," said Crozier.

The fog whirled around them. Somewhere to the east, Peglar heard what sounded like big guns firing in a Naval engagement, but he'd heard that many times out here over the past two summers. It was distant thunder. In April. With the temperature still twenty degrees below freezing, at least.

"Gentlemen," said the captain, "we have a burial to attend. Shall we head back?"

On the long trek back, Harry Peglar mulled over what he had seen — the frozen entrails of an officer he liked, the bodies and still-bright blood in the snow, the missing parkas and weapons and tools, Dr. Goodsir's ghoulish examinations, Captain Crozier's odd statement that he might "require your knowledge of these facts at some future time" as if he was preparing them to act as jurors at some future court-martial or court of inquiry.

Peglar anticipated writing all this down in the commonplace book he had been keeping for so long. And he hoped that he would find the opportunity to talk to John Bridgens after the burial service, before the groups of men from both boats went back to their own tents and mess circles and man-hauling teams. He wanted to hear what his dear wise Bridgens might have to say about all this.

41

CROZIER

O death, where is thy sting? O grave, where is thy victory?'"
Lieutenant Irving had been Crozier's officer, but Captain Fitzjames had a better voice — the lisp had all but disappeared — and a better way with Scripture, so Crozier was grateful that he was doing a majority of the burial-service reading.

All of the men in Terror Camp had turned out except those on watch, those in sick bay, or those performing essential services such as Lloyd in sick bay and Mr. Diggle and Mr. Wall and their mates labouring over the four whaleboat stoves cooking up some of the Esquimaux's fish and seal meat for dinner. At least eighty men were at this graveside about a hundred yards from camp, standing like dark wraiths in the still-swirling fog.

" 'The sting of death is sin; and the strength of sin is the law. But thanks be to God, which giveth us the victory through our Lord Jesus Christ. Therefore, my beloved brethren, be ye steadfast, unmovable, always abounding in the work of the Lord, forasmuch as ye know that your labour is not in vain in the Lord.'"

The other surviving officers and two mates were to carry Irving to the grave. There was not enough wood at Terror Camp to make a coffin, but Mr. Honey, the carpenter, had found enough wood to knock together a door-sized pallet on which Irving's body, now securely sewn into canvas, could be transported on and upon which the body could be lowered into the grave. Although the ropes were set across the grave in proper Naval fashion, as they would be for any land burial, there would not be much lowering to do. Hickey and his men had been unable to dig deeper than three feet — the ground below that level was as hard-frozen as solid stone — so the men had gathered scores of large stones to lay over the body before piling on the frozen topsoil and gravel, then more stones to lay over that. No one had real hopes that it would keep the white bears or the other summer predators out, but the labour was a sign of most of the men's affection for John Irving.

Most of the men.

Crozier glanced over at Hickey, standing next to Magnus Manson and the *Erebus* gunroom steward who had been flogged after Carnivale, Richard Aylmore. There was a cluster of other malcontents around these men — several of the *Terror* seamen who had been eager to kill Lady Silence even if it took a mutiny to do so back in January — but, like all the others standing around the pathetic hole in the ground, they had their Welsh wigs and caps off and their comforters pulled up to their noses and ears.

———

Crozier's middle-of-the-night interrogation of Cornelius Hickey in the captain's command tent had been tense and terse.

"Good morning to you, Captain. Would you like me to tell you what I told Captain Fitzjames and . . ."

"Take off your slops, Mr. Hickey."

"Pardon me, sir?"

"You heard me."

"Aye, sir, but if you want to hear how it was when I saw the savages murderin' poor Mr. Irving . . ."

"It's *Lieutenant* Irving, Caulker's Mate. I heard your story from Captain Fitzjames. Do you have anything to add or retract from it? Anything to amend?"

"Ah . . . no, sir."

"Take those outer slops off. Mittens too."

"Aye, sir. There, sir, how's 'at? Shall I just set 'em over on the . . ."

"Drop them on the floor. Jackets off too."

"My jackets, sir? It's bloody cold in here . . . yes, sir."

"Mr. Hickey, why did you volunteer to go search for Lieutenant Irving when he hadn't yet been gone much more than an hour? No one else was worried about him."

"Oh, I don't think I volunteered it, Captain. My recollection is that Mr. Farr asked me to go look for . . ."

"Mr. Farr reported that you asked several times if Lieutenant Irving wasn't overdue and volunteered to go find him on your own while the others rested after their meal. Why did you do that, Mr. Hickey?"

"If Mr. Farr says that . . . well, we must've been worried about him, Captain. The lieutenant, I mean."

"Why?"

"May I put my jackets and slops back on, Captain? It's bloody freezing in . . ."

"No. Take off your waistcoat and sweaters. Why were you worried about Lieutenant Irving?"

"If you're concerned . . . that is, thinking I was wounded today, Captain, I wasn't. The savages never saw me. No wounds on me, sir, I assure you."

"Take that sweater off as well. Why were you worried about Lieutenant Irving?"

"Well, the lads and me . . . you know, Captain."

"No."

"We was just concerned, you know, that one of our party was missin', like. Also, sir, I was cold, sir. We'd been sittin' around to eat what little cold food we had. I thought that walkin', following the lieutenant's tracks to make sure he was all right, would warm me up, sir."

"Show me your hands."

"Pardon me, Captain?"

"Your hands."

"Aye, sir. Pardon my shaking, sir. I ain't been warm all day and with all my layers off but this shirt and . . ."

"Turn them over. Palms up."

"Aye, sir."

"Is that blood under your nails, Mr. Hickey?"

"Could be, Captain. You know how it is."

"No. Tell me."

"Well, we ain't had real water what to bath ourselves in for months, sir. And what with the scurvy and dysentery-like, there's a certain amount of bleedin' when we see to the necessaries . . ."

"Are you saying that a Royal Navy petty officer on my ship wipes his arse with his fingers, Mr. Hickey?"

"No, sir . . . I mean . . . may I put my layers back on now, Captain? You can see I ain't wounded or anything. This cold is enough to shrink a man's . . ."

"Take your shirts and undershirts off."

"Are you serious, sir?"

"Don't make me ask a second time, Mr. Hickey. We don't have a brig. Any man I send to the brig will spend time chained to one of the whaleboats."

"Here, sir. How's this. Just me flesh, freezing as it is. If my poor missus could see me now . . ."

"It didn't say on your muster papers that you were married, Mr. Hickey."

"Oh, my Louisa's been dead going on seven years now, Captain. Of the pox. God rest her soul."

"Why did you tell some of the other men before the mast that when it came time to kill officers, Lieutenant Irving should be the first?"

"I never said no such thing, sir."

"I have reports of you saying that and other mutinous statements going back to before the Carnivale on the ice, Mr. Hickey. Why did you single out Lieutenant Irving? What had that officer ever done to you?"

"Why, nothing, sir. And I never said no such thing. Bring in the man who said I did and I'll dispute it to his face and spit in his eye."

"What had Lieutenant Irving ever done to you, Mr. Hickey? Why did you tell other men from both *Erebus* and *Terror* that Irving was a whoremaster and a liar?"

"I swear to you, Captain . . . pardon my teeth chattering, Captain, but *Jesus Christ* the night is cold against the bare skin. I swear to you, I didn't say no such thing. A lot of us looked on poor Lieutenant Irving sorta like a son, Captain. A son. It was only my worry for him out there today that made me go check on him. Good thing I did, too, sir, or we would've never caught the murdering bastards who . . ."

"Put your layers on, Mr. Hickey."

"Aye, sir."

"No. Do it outside. Get out of my sight."

———

" 'Man that is born of a woman hath but a short time to live and is full of misery,' " intoned Fitzjames. " 'He cometh up and is cut down, like a flower; he fleeth as it were a shadow, and never continueth in one stay.' "

Hodgson and the other pallbearers were using great care in lowering the pallet with Irving's canvas-wrapped body to the ropes held in place above the shallow hole by some of the healthier seamen. Crozier knew that Hodgson and Irving's other friends had gone into the postmortem tent one at a time to pay their respects before the lieutenant had been sewn into his sail shroud by Old Murray. The visitors had set several tokens of their affection next to the lieutenant's body — the recovered brass telescope, its lenses shattered in the shooting, that the boy had so esteemed, a gold medal with his name engraved on it that he had won in competitions on the gunnery ship HMS *Excellent,* and at least one five-pound note, as if some old wager had been paid at last. For some reason — optimism? youthful naïveté? — Irving had packed his dress uniform in his small bag of personal belongings, and he was being buried in it now. Crozier wondered idly if the gilt buttons on the uniform — each bearing the image of an anchor surrounded by a crown — would be there when nothing else but the boy's bleached bones and the gold gunnery medal survived the long process of decay.

" 'In the midst of life we are in death,' " Fitzjames recited from memory, his voice sounding tired but properly resonant, " 'of whom may we seek for succour, but of thee, O Lord, who for our sin art justly displeased?' "

Captain Crozier knew that there was one other item sewn into the sail-shroud with Irving, one that no one else knew about. It lay under his head like a pillow.

It was a gold, green, red, and blue silk Oriental handkerchief, and Crozier had surprised the giver by coming into the postmortem tent after Goodsir, Lloyd, Hodgson, and the others had departed, just before Old Murray the sailmaker was to enter and sew up the shroud he had prepared and upon which Irving already lay in state.

Lady Silence had been there, bending over the corpse, setting something beneath Irving's head.

Crozier's first impulse had been to reach for his pistol in his great-coat pocket, but he'd frozen in place as he saw the Esquimaux girl's eyes and face. If there were no tears in those dark, hardly human eyes, there was something else luminous there with some emotion he could not identify. Grief? The captain did not think so. It was more some kind of complicit recognition at seeing Crozier. The captain felt the same strange stirring in his head that he had so often felt around his Memo Moira.

But the girl obviously had set the Oriental handkerchief carefully in place under the dead boy's head as some sort of gesture. Crozier knew the handkerchief had been Irving's — he'd seen it on special occasions as far back as the day they'd sailed in May of 1845.

Had the Esquimaux wench stolen it? Plundered it from his dead body just yesterday?

Silence had followed Irving's sledge party from *Terror* to Terror Camp more than a week ago and then had just disappeared, never joining the men in the camp. Almost everyone, excluding Crozier, who still held hopes she might lead them to food, had considered this good riddance. But all during this terrible morning, part of Crozier had wondered if somehow Silence had been responsible for his officer's murder out there on the windswept gravel ridge.

Had she led her Esquimaux hunter friends back here to raid the camp and run into Irving on the way, first giving a fete to the starving man with meat and then murdering him in cold blood to keep him from telling the others here of his encounter? Had Silence been the "possibly a young woman" that Farr and Hodgson and the others had caught a glimpse of, fleeing with an Esquimaux man with a headband? She could have changed her parka if she had returned to her village in the past week, and who could tell young Esquimaux wenches apart at a glance?

Crozier considered all of these things, but now in a time-stopped moment — both he and the young woman were startled into immobility for long seconds — the captain looked into her face and knew, whether in his heart or in what Memo Moira insisted was his second sight, that she wept inside for John Irving and was returning a gift of the silk handkerchief to the dead man.

Crozier guessed that the handkerchief had been presented to her during the February visit to the Esquimaux's snow-house that Irving had dutifully reported to the captain . . . but had reported with few details. Now Crozier wondered if the two had been lovers.

And then Lady Silence was gone. She'd slipped under the tent flap and was gone without a sound. When Crozier later queried the men in the camp and those on guard if they had seen anything, none had.

At that moment in the tent, the captain had gone over to Irving's body, looked down at the pale, dead face made even whiter with the small pillow of the brightly covered handkerchief behind it, and then he had pulled the canvas over the lieutenant's face and body, shouting for Old Murray to come in and do the sewing.

" 'Yet, O Lord God most holy, O Lord most mighty, O holy and most merciful Saviour,' " Fitzjames was saying, " 'deliver us not into the bitter pains of eternal death.'

" 'Thou knowest, Lord, the secrets of our hearts; shut not thy merciful ears to our prayer; but spare us, Lord most holy, O God most mighty, O holy and merciful Saviour, thou most worthy Judge eternal, suffer us not, at our last hour, for any pains of death, to fall from thee.' "

Fitzjames's voice fell silent. He stepped back from the grave.

Crozier, lost in reverie, stood for a long moment until a shuffling of feet made him realize that his part of the service had arrived.

He walked to the head of the grave.

" 'We therefore commit the body of our friend and officer John Irving to the deep,' " he rasped, also reciting from memory that remained all too clear from many repetitions despite the pall of fatigue in his mind, " 'to be turned into corruption, looking for the resurrection of the body, when the Sea and the Earth shall give up their dead.' " The body was lowered the three feet, and Crozier tossed a handful of frozen soil onto it. The gravel made a strangely moving rasping sound as it landed on the canvas above Irving's face and slid to the sides. " 'And the life of the world to come, through our Lord Jesus Christ, who at his coming shall change our vile body, that it may be like his glorious body, according to the mighty working, whereby he is able to subdue all things to himself.' "

The service was over. The ropes had been retrieved.

Men stamped cold feet, tugged on their Welsh wigs and caps, rewrapped their comforters, and filed back through the fog to Terror Camp for their hot dinner.

Hodgson, Little, Thomas, Des Voeux, Le Vesconte, Blanky, Peglar, and a few of the other officers stayed behind, dismissing the seamen's detail that had been waiting to bury the body. The officers shoveled soil and began setting in the first layer of stones together. They wanted Irving buried as best he could be under the circumstances.

When they finished, Crozier and Fitzjames walked away from the others. They would eat their dinners much later — for now they planned to walk the two miles up to Victory Point where Graham Gore had left his brass canister and optimistic message in James Ross's old cairn almost a year ago.

Crozier planned to leave word there today on what the fate of their expedition had been in the past ten and a half months since Gore's note had been written and on what they planned to do next.

Plodding tiredly through the fog, hearing one of the ship's bells ringing for dinner somewhere in the roiling fog behind them — they had, of course, brought both *Terror*'s and *Erebus*'s bells along in the whaleboats dragged across the frozen sea to camp when the ships were abandoned — Francis Crozier hoped to Christ that he would decide on their course of action by the time that he and Fitzjames reached the cairn. If he could not, he thought, he was afraid he might start weeping.

42

PEGLAR

Lat. 69° 37' 42" N., Long. 98° 41' W.
25 April, 1848

There hadn't been enough fish and seal on the sled to serve it as a main dish to ninety-five or a hundred men — a few were too ill to eat anything solid — and even Mr. Diggle's and Mr. Wall's record at routinely performing loaves-and-fishes miracles with the limited ships' stores did not allow them to fully succeed at this one (especially since some of the food on the Esquimaux sledge had been particularly putrid), but every man managed to get a taste of the savory blubber or fish along with the prepared Goldner soups or stews or vegetables.

Harry Peglar enjoyed the meal even though he was shaking with cold as he ate it and knew that it would only provoke the diarrhea that was already ripping him apart every day.

After the meal and before beginning their scheduled duties, Peglar and Steward John Bridgens walked together with their tin mugs of tepid tea. The fog muffled their own voices even as it seemed to amplify sounds from far away. They could hear men arguing over a card game in one of the tents on the far side of Terror Camp. From the northwest — the direction the two captains had walked before dinner — came the artillery rumble of thunder out over the pack ice. That sound had been going on all day, but no storm had arrived.

The two paused at the long line of boats and boat-sledges drawn up above the tumble of ice that would be the inlet's shoreline if there ever came a thaw to the sea.

"Tell me, Harry," said Bridgens, "which of these boats will we be taking if or when we must go to the ice again?"

Peglar sipped his tea and pointed. "I'm not certain, but I think Captain Crozier has decided to take ten of the eighteen here. We don't have men well enough to haul more these days."

"Then why did we man-haul all eighteen to Terror Camp?"

"Captain Crozier considered the possibility that we'd stay at Terror Camp for another two or three months, perhaps letting the ice around this point melt. We would have been better off with more boats, keeping some in reserve should others be damaged. And we could have hauled much more in the way of food, tents, and supplies in eighteen boats. With more than ten men in each boat now, it'll be damned crowded, and we'll have to leave too much of the stores behind."

"But you think we'll leave for the south with only ten boats, Harry? And soon?"

"I hope to Christ we do," said Peglar. He told Bridgens about what he had seen that morning, what Goodsir had said about the Esquimaux's stomachs being as full of seal meat as Irving's had been, and how the captain had treated those present, perhaps excepting the Marines, as a potential Board of Inquiry. He added that the captain had sworn them to secrecy.

"I think," John Bridgens said softly, "that Captain Crozier is not convinced that the Esquimaux killed Lieutenant Irving."

"What? Who else could . . ." Peglar stopped. The cold and nausea that were always with him now seemed to surge up and through him. He had to lean against a whaleboat to keep his knees from buckling. He had never considered for an instant that anyone other than the savages could have done what he'd seen done to John Irving. He thought of the frozen pile of grey entrails on the ridgeline.

"Richard Aylmore is saying that the officers have led us into this mess," said Bridgens in a voice so low it was almost a whisper. "He's telling everyone who won't inform on him that we should kill the officers and parcel out the extra food rations amongst the men. Aylmore in our group and that caulker's mate in yours say we should go back to *Terror* at once."

"Back to *Terror*..." repeated Peglar. He knew that his mind was dull with illness and exhaustion these days, but the idea made no sense at all. The ship was locked in the ice far out there and would be for months more, even if summer *did* condescend to appear this year. "Why don't I hear these things, John? I've heard none of this seditious whispering."

Bridgens smiled. "They don't trust you not to tell, my dear Harry."

"But they trust you?"

"Of course not. But I hear *everything* sooner or later. Stewards are invisible, y'know, being neither fish nor fowl nor good red meat. Speaking of which, that was a delightful meal, wasn't it? Perhaps the last relatively fresh food we shall ever eat."

Peglar didn't answer. His mind was racing. "What can we do to warn Fitzjames and Crozier?"

"Oh, they have this information about Aylmore and Hickey and the others," the old steward said nonchalantly. "Our captains have their own sources before the mast and around the scuttlebutts."

"The scuttlebutts have been frozen solid for months," said Peglar.

Bridgens chuckled. "That seems to be a very good metaphor, Harry, and all the more ironic for its literalness. Or at least an amusing euphemism."

Peglar shook his head. He still felt the nausea from the idea that amidst all this illness and terror, any man among them would turn on another.

"Tell me, Harry," said Bridgens, patting the inverted hull of the first whaleboat with his worn mitten. "Which of these boats might we be hauling with us and which will be left behind?"

"The four whaleboats will go for sure," Peglar said absently, still mulling over this talk of mutiny and what he had seen that morning. "The jolly boats are as long as the whaleboats, but damned heavy. If I were the captain, I might leave them behind and take the four cutters instead. They're only twenty-five feet long, but much lighter than whaleboats. But their draft may be too much for the Great Fish River if we can get there. The ships' smaller boats and dinghies are too light for the open sea and too flimsy for much hauling and river work."

"So it's the four whaleboats, four cutters, and two pinnaces, you think?" asked Bridgens.

"Yes," said Peglar, and had to smile. For all his years at sea and all his thousands of volumes read, Subordinate Officers' Steward John Bridgens still knew very little about some things nautical. "I think those ten, yes, John."

"At best," said Bridgens, "if most of the sick recover, that leaves only ten of us to man-haul each boat. Can we do that, Harry?"

Peglar shook his head again. "It won't be like the sea ice crossing from *Terror*, John."

"Well, thank the dear Lord for that small blessing."

"No, I mean that we'll almost certainly be man-hauling these boats over land rather than sea ice. It'll be much harder than the crossing from *Terror*, where we man-hauled only two boats at a time and could put as many men on a team as we needed to get over the rough parts. And the boats now will be even more heavily laden with stores and our sick than before. I suspect that we'll have twenty or more in harness for each boat hauled. Even then, we'll have to haul the ten boats in relays."

"Relays?" said Bridgens. "Dear heavens, it will take us forever to move even ten boats if we're constantly going back and forth. And the weaker and sicker we become, the slower we will go."

"Yes," said Peglar.

"Is there any chance that we shall get these boats all the way to the Great Fish River and then up the river to Great Slave Lake and the outpost there?"

"I doubt it," said Peglar. "Perhaps if a few of us survive long enough to get the boats to the mouth of the river and the right boats make it and they're rigged just perfectly for river running and . . . but, no, I doubt if there's any real chance."

"Then why on earth would Captains Crozier and Fitzjames put us through such labour and misery if there is no chance?" asked Bridgens. The older man's voice did not sound aggrieved or anxious or desperate, merely curious. Peglar had heard John pose a thousand questions about astronomy, natural history, geology, botany, philosophy, and a score of other subjects in precisely that same soft, mildly curious tone. With most of the other questions, it had been the teacher who knew the answer quizzing his student in a polite way. Here, Peglar was sure that John Bridgens did not know the answer to this question.

"What's the alternative? " asked the foretop captain.

"We could stay here at Terror Camp," said Bridgens. "Or even return to *Terror,* once our numbers have . . . decreased."

"To do what?" demanded Peglar. "Just to wait to die?"

"To wait in comfort, Harry."

"To *die?*" said Peglar, realizing that he was almost shouting. "Who the fuck wants to wait in comfort to die? At least if we get the boats to the coast — *any* of the boats — some of us may have a chance. There might be open water east to Boothia. We may be able to force passage up the river. At least *some* of us. And those who make it will at least be able to tell the rest of our loved ones what happened to us, where we were buried, and that we were thinking of them in the end."

"You *are* my loved one, Harry," said Bridgens. "The only man or woman or child left in the world who cares whether I am alive or dead, much less what I may have thought before I fell or where my bones will lie."

Peglar, still angry, felt his heart pounding inside his chest. "You're going to outlive me, John."

"Oh, at my age, and with my infirmities and proclivities toward illness, I hardly think . . ."

"*You're going to outlive me, John,*" grated Peglar. He shocked himself by the intensity of his voice and Bridgens blinked and fell silent. Peglar took the older man's wrist. "Promise me you'll do one thing for me, John."

"Of course." There was none of the usual banter or irony in Bridgens' voice.

"My diary . . . it's not much, I have trouble even thinking, much less writing these days . . . I'm quite sick with this God-damned scurvy, John, and it seems to addle my brain . . . but I've kept the diary for the past three years. My thoughts are in it. All of the events we've experienced are put down there. If you could take it when I . . . when I leave you . . . just take it back with you to England, I'd appreciate it."

Bridgens only nodded.

"John," said Harry Peglar, "I think Captain Crozier is going to decide to take us on the march soon. Very soon. He knows that every day we wait here we get weaker. Soon we won't be able to haul boats at all. We'll begin dying by the dozens here at Terror Camp before long, and it won't take that thing on the ice to carry us away or kill us in our beds."

Bridgens nodded again. He was looking down at his mittened hands.

"We're not on the same man-hauling teams, won't share the same boats, and may not even end up together if the captains decide to try for different escape routes," continued Peglar. "I want to say good-bye today and never have to do it again."

Bridgens nodded mutely. He was looking at his boots. The fog rolled over the boats and sledges and moved around them like some alien god's cold breath.

Peglar hugged him. Bridgens stood upright and brittle for a moment and then returned the hug, both men clumsy in their many layers and frozen slops.

The captain of the foretop turned then and walked slowly back toward Terror Camp and his tiny circular Holland tent with its group of off-duty shivering, unwashed men huddling together in inadequate sleeping bags.

When he paused and looked back toward the line of boats, there was no sign of Bridgens at all. It was as if the fog had swallowed him without a trace.

43

CROZIER

Lat. 69° 37' 42" N., Long. 98° 41' W.
25 April, 1848

He fell asleep while walking.

Crozier had been talking to Fitzjames about arguments for and against letting the men spend more days at Terror Camp as the two walked the two miles north through the fog to James Ross's cairn when suddenly Fitzjames was shaking him awake.

"We're here, Francis. This is the large white boulder near the shore ice. Victory Point and the cairn must be to our left. Were you really sleeping while walking?"

"No, of course not," rasped Crozier.

"Then what did you mean when you said, 'Watch out for the open boat with the two skeletons'? and 'watch out for the girls and the table rappings.' It made no sense. We were discussing whether Dr. Goodsir should stay behind at Terror Camp with the seriously ill men while the stronger ones try for Great Slave Lake with just four boats."

"Just thinking aloud," muttered Crozier.

"Who is Memo Moira?" asked Fitzjames. "And why should she not send you to Communion?"

Crozier pulled his cap and wool scarves off, letting the fog and cold air slap his face as he walked up the slow rise. "Where the hell is the cairn?" he snapped.

"I don't know," said Fitzjames. "It should be right here. Even on a sunny, clear day, I walk this inlet coastline to the white boulder near the bergs and then left up to the cairn at Victory Point."

"We can't have walked past it," said Crozier. "We'd be out on the fucking pack ice."

It took them almost forty-five minutes to find the cairn in the fog. At one point when Crozier said, "The God-damned white thing from the ice has taken it and hidden it somewhere to confound us," Fitzjames had only looked at his commanding officer and said nothing.

Finally, feeling their way along together like two blind men — not risking separating in the roiling fog, sure that they wouldn't even hear the others' calls over the constant drumbeat of approaching thunder — they literally stumbled into the cairn.

"This isn't where it was," croaked Crozier.

"It doesn't seem to be," agreed the other captain.

"Ross's cairn with Gore's note in it was at the top of the rise at the end of Victory Point. This must be a hundred yards to the west of there, almost down in this valley."

"It is very odd," said Fitzjames. "Francis, you've come to the arctic so many times. Is this thunder — and the lightning if it comes — so common up here so early?"

"I've never seen or heard either before midsummer," rasped Crozier. "And never like this. It sounds like something worse."

"What could be worse than a thunderstorm in late April with the temperature still below zero?"

"Cannon fire," said Crozier.

"Cannon fire?"

"From the rescue ship that came down open leads all the way from Lancaster Strait and through Peel Sound only to find *Erebus* crushed and *Terror* abandoned. They're firing their guns for twenty-four hours to get our attention before sailing away."

"Please, Francis, stop," said Fitzjames. "If you continue, I may vomit. And I've already done my vomiting for today."

"Sorry," said Crozier, fumbling in his pockets.

"Is there really any chance that it's guns firing for us?" asked the younger captain. "It *sounds* like guns."

"Not a snowball's chance in Sir John Franklin's Hell," said Crozier. "That pack ice is solid all the way to Greenland."

"Then where is the fog coming from?" asked Fitzjames, his voice more idly curious than plaintive. "Are you searching your pockets for something in particular, Captain Crozier?"

"I forgot to bring the brass messenger canister we brought from *Terror* for this note," Crozier admitted. "I felt the lump in my slops pocket during the burial service and thought I had it, but it's only my God-besotted pistol."

"Did you bring paper?"

"No. Jopson had some ready, but I left it in the tent."

"Did you bring a pen? Ink? I find that if I do not carry the ink pot in a pouch close to my skin, it freezes very quickly."

"No pen or ink," admitted Crozier.

"It's all right," said Fitzjames. "I have both in my waistcoat pocket. We can use Graham Gore's note . . . write on it."

"If this is the same damned cairn," muttered Crozier. "Ross's cairn was six feet tall. This thing hardly comes up to my chest."

Both men fumbled to remove rocks from a part of the cairn far down on the leeward side. They did not want to have to dismantle the entire thing and then have to rebuild it.

Fitzjames reached into the dark hole, fumbled around a second, and withdrew a brass cylinder, tarnished but still intact.

"Well I'll be damned and dressed in cheap motley," said Crozier. "Is it Graham's?"

"It has to be," said Fitzjames. Tugging his mitten off with his teeth, he clumsily unfurled the parchment note and began to read.

28 of May 1847. HM Ships Erebus and Terror . . . Wintered in the Ice in Lat. 70°05′ N. Long. 98°23′ W. After having wintered in 1846–7 at Beechey Island in Lat. 74°43′ 28″ N Long . . .

Fitzjames interrupted himself. "Wait, that's incorrect. We spent the winter of 1845 *to* '46 at Beechey, not the winter of '46 to '47."

"Sir John dictated this to Graham Gore before Gore left the ships," rasped Crozier. "Sir John must have been as tired and confused then as we are now."

"No one has ever been as tired and confused as we are now," said Fitzjames. "Here, later, it goes on — 'Sir John Franklin commanding the expedition. All well.'"

Crozier did not laugh. Or weep. He said, "Graham Gore deposited the note here just a week before Sir John was killed by the thing on the ice."

"And one day before Graham himself was killed by the thing on the ice," said Fitzjames. "'All well.' That seems like another lifetime, does it not, Francis? Can you remember a time when any of us could write such a thing with an easy conscience? There's blank space around the edge of the message if you want to write there."

The two huddled on the lee side of the stone cairn. The temperature had dropped and the wind had come up, but the fog continued to swirl around them as if unaffected by mere wind or temperature. It was beginning to get dark. To the northwest, the sound of guns rumbled on.

Crozier breathed on the tiny portable ink pot to warm the ink, dipped the pen through the scrim of ice, rubbed the nib against his frozen sleeve, and began writing.

(25th April) — HM's ships Terror and Erebus were deserted on the 22nd April 5 leagues NNW of this, having been beset since 12th Septr. 1846. The Officers and Crews, consisting of 105 souls, under the command of Captain F.R.M. Crozier landed here — in Lat. 69° 37' 42" Long. 98° 41'. This paper was found by Lt. Irving under the cairn supposed to have been built by Sir James Ross in 1831, 4 miles to the Northward, where it had been deposited by the late Commander Gore in June 1847. Sir James Ross' pillar has not however been found, and the paper has been transferred to this position which is that in which Sir J Ross' pillar was erected —

Crozier stopped writing. *What the hell am I saying?* he thought. He squinted to reread the last few sentences — *"Under the cairn supposed to have been built by Sir James Ross in 1831"? "Sir James Ross's pillar has not however been found"?*

Crozier let out a tired sigh. John Irving's first order upon ferrying the first load of matériel from *Erebus* and *Terror* long ago last August to begin the stockpile that would become Terror Camp was to find Victory Point and Ross's cairn again, then set up the cache for Terror Camp a few miles south of it along a more sheltered inlet. Irving had marked the cairn on their earliest crudely drawn maps as four miles from the cache point rather than the actual two miles, but they'd quickly discovered their mistake during subsequent man-haulings. In Crozier's fatigue now, his mind kept insisting that the canister with Gore's message had been moved from some false James Ross cairn to this real James Ross cairn.

Crozier shook his head and looked at Fitzjames, but the other captain was resting his arms on his raised knees and his head on his arms. He was snoring softly.

Crozier held the sheet of paper, pen, and tiny ink pot in one hand and scooped up snow with his other mittened hand, rubbing some on his face. The shock of the cold made him blink.

Concentrate, Francis. For the sake of Christ, concentrate. He wished he had another sheet of paper so that he could start over. Squinting at the cramped scrawl moving around the margins of the paper, words crawling like tiny ants — the center of the paper already filled with the official typeset information stating officiously **WHOEVER finds this paper is requested to forward it to the Secretary of the Admiralty,** then several more paragraphs repeating the instruction in French, German, Portugese, and other languages, then with Gore's scrawl above that — Crozier did not recognize his own handwriting. The script was palsied, cramped, tenuous, obviously the hand of a terrified or freezing or dying man.

Or of all three.

It doesn't matter, he thought. *Either no one is ever going to read this or they will read it long after we are all dead. It doesn't matter at all. Perhaps Sir John always understood this. Perhaps this is why he left none of the brass message canisters behind on Beechey. He knew all along.*

He dipped the pen in the rapidly freezing ink and wrote again.

Sir John Franklin died on 11th of June 1847 and the total loss by deaths on the Expedition has been to this date 9 officers and 15 Men.

Crozier stopped again. Was that correct? Had he included John Irving in the total? He couldn't do the arithmetic. There had been 105 souls under his care yesterday . . . 105 when he had left *Terror,* his ship, his home, his wife, his life . . . he would leave the number.

Upside down at the top of the sheet, on the bit of white space left, he scrawled *F. R. M. Crozier* and after it wrote *Captain and Senior Officer.*

He nudged Fitzjames awake. "James . . . sign your name here."

The other captain rubbed his eyes, peered at the paper but did not seem to take time to read it, and signed his name where Crozier pointed.

"Add 'Captain HMS *Erebus,*'" said Crozier.

Fitzjames did so.

Crozier folded the paper, slid it back into the brass canister, sealed it, and set the cylinder back in the cairn. He pulled his mitten on and fumbled the stones back into place.

"Francis, did you tell them where we are headed and when we're leaving?"

Crozier realized that he had not. He started to explain why . . . why it seemed to be a sentence of death for the men whether they stayed or went. Why he had not decided yet between man-hauling for distant Boothia or toward George Back's fabled but terrible Great Fish River. He started to explain to Fitzjames how they were fucked coming and fucked going and why no one was ever going to read the fucking note anyway, so why not just . . .

"Shhh!" hissed Fitzjames.

Something was circling them, just out of sight in the rolling, swirling fog. Both men could hear heavy footsteps in the gravel and ice. Something very large was breathing. It was walking on all fours, not more than fifteen feet from them in the thick fog, the sound of huge paws clearly audible over the heavy-gun rumble of distant thunder.

Hu-uf, hu-uf, hu-uf.

Crozier could hear the exhalations with each heavy footfall. It was behind them now, circling the cairn, circling them.

Both men got to their feet.

Crozier fumbled his pistol out. He pulled off his mitten and cocked the weapon as the footsteps and breathing stopped directly ahead of them but still out of sight in the fog. Crozier was certain he could smell its fish-and-carrion breath.

Fitzjames, who was still holding the ink pot and pen Crozier had given back to him and who had no pistol with him, pointed at the fog to where he thought the thing waited.

Gravel crunched as the thing moved stealthily toward them.

Slowly a triangular head materialized in the fog five feet above the ground. Wet white fur blended with the mist. Inhuman black eyes studied them from only six feet away.

Crozier aimed the pistol at a point just above that head. His hand was so firm and steady that he did not even have to hold his breath.

The head moved closer, floating as if it were unattached to any body. Then the giant shoulders came into view.

Crozier fired, making sure to shoot high so as not to strike that face.

The report was deafening, especially to nervous systems set on edge by scurvy.

The white bear, little more than a cub, let out a startled *woof,* reared back, wheeled, and ran off on all fours, disappearing into the fog in seconds. The scrabbling, running paw steps on gravel were audible for a long minute after, heading toward the sea ice to the northwest.

Crozier and Fitzjames started laughing then.

Neither man could stop. Every time one of them would slow in the laughter, the other would begin and then both would be caught up again in the mad, senseless hilarity.

They clutched their own sides from the pain of the laughter against their bruised ribs.

Crozier dropped the pistol and both men started laughing harder.

They clapped each other's backs, pointed toward the fog, and laughed until the tears froze on their cheeks and whiskers. They clutched each other for support while they laughed harder.

Both captains collapsed on the gravel and leaned back against the cairn, that action alone causing the laughter to return in force.

Eventually the guffaws turned to giggles and the giggles into embarrassed snorts, the snorts into a few final laughs, and finally those died into a mutual gasping for air.

"You know what I would give my left bollock for right now?" asked Captain Francis Crozier.

"What?"

"A glass of whiskey. Two glasses, I mean. One for me and one for you. The drinks would be on me, James. I'm standing you to a round."

Fitzjames nodded, wiping ice from his eyelids and picking frozen snot from his reddish mustache and beard. "Thank you, Francis. And I'd lift the first toast to you. I've never had the honour of serving under a better commander or a finer man."

"Could I please have the ink pot and pen back?" said Crozier.

Pulling his mitten back on, he fumbled the stones out, found the canister, opened it, spread the sheet of paper out upside down on his knee, tugged his mitten off again, cracked the ice in the ink pot with the pen, and in the tiny space remaining under his signature, wrote,

And start tomorrow, 26th, for Back's Fish River.

44

GOODSIR

From the private diary of Dr. Harry D. S. Goodsir:

Tuesday, 6 June — Captain Fitzjames has finally died. It is a Blessing.

Unlike the others who have died in the last Six Weeks since we first started Hauling the Boats south (a Living Hell of a vocation from which even the Ships' Only Surviving Surgeon is not exempted), the Captain, in my opinion, did not perish from the Scurvy.

He had Scurvy, there is no Doubt of that. I just Completed the post-mortem examination of that Good Man and the Bruises and Bleeding Gums and Blackened Lips all told the story. But I think Scurvy was not the Killer.

Captain Fitzjames's last three days were spent here; about 80 Miles south of Terror Camp, on a frozen point on a windswept bay where the bulk of King William Land curves sharply to the West. For the first time in Six Weeks, we have unpacked All the Tents — including the large ones — and used some Coal from the few sacks we brought along and the Iron Whaleboat Stove one crew has man-hauled so far. Almost all of our meals the past six weeks have been eaten cold or only Partially Heated over the tiny spirit stoves. For the last two nights we have had hot food — never enough, a third of the rations we need for the incredibly Strenuous Work we are Doing, but warm nonetheless. For Two Mornings we have wakened in the same place. The men are calling this place Comfort Cove.

Mostly we stopped to allow Captain Fitzjames to Die in Peace. But there was no Peace for the captain in his last days.

Poor Lieutenant Le Vesconte had evidenced some of the same Symptoms of Captain Fitzjames's last days. Lieutenant Le Vesconte died suddenly on our 13th Day on this terrible Voyage South — only 18 Miles from Terror Camp if I remember correctly, and on the same day that Marine Private Pilkington expired — but the Symptoms of Scurvy had been more Advanced in both the lieutenant and the private and their Final Agonies less excruciatingly drawn out.

I confess that I hadn't remembered that Lieutenant Le Vesconte's first name had been Harry. Our intercourse had always been quite Friendly but also quite Formal, and on the Muster Rolls I recalled his name had been listed as H. T. D. Le Vesconte. It bothers me now that I must have heard the Other Officers call him Harry from time to time — perhaps a hundred times — but I had always been too busy or preoccupied to notice. It was only after Lieutenant Le Vesconte's death that I paid attention to the other Men using his Christian name.

Private Pilkington's Christian name was William.

I remember that day in early May after Le Vesconte's and Private Pilkington's brief joint burial service, one of the men suggested that we name the small spur of land where they were buried "Le Vesconte Point," but Captain Crozier vetoed that idea, saying that if we named every place where one of us might end up buried after the dead person there, we'd run out of land before we ran out of names.

This Befuddled the men and I Confess that it Befuddled me as well. It must have been an Attempt at Humour, but it shocked me. It shocked the men into Silence as well.

Perhaps that was Captain Crozier's Purpose. It did put a stop to the men offering to name Natural Features after their Dead Officers.

Captain Fitzjames had shown a General Weakening for some weeks — even before we left Terror Camp — but Four Days ago he seemed to have been Struck Down by something more Sudden in its attack and far more Agonizing in its effects.

The Captain had been suffering Problems with his Stomach and Bowels for some weeks, but suddenly, on the Second of June, Fitzjames collapsed. Our protocol on the March is not to stop for sick men but rather to place them in one of the larger Boats and pull them along with the other Supplies and *dead weight. Captain Crozier made sure that Captain Fitzjames was made as comfortable as possible in his own Whaleboat.*

Since we are doing this Long March South in relays — working for Hours on End to pull 5 of the 10 Heavy Boats as little as a few hundred Yards across the terrible gravel and Snow, always trying to stay on the Land when possible rather than be forced to deal with Pack Ice and Pressure Ridges, sometimes covering less than a Mile in a Day on the resisting gravel and ice — I make it my practice to stay with the sickest men while the Man-hauling Teams go back for the other 5 Boats. Often Mr. Diggle and Mr. Wall, gamely preparing to cook Warm Meals for almost a hundred Starving Men on their little spirit stoves, and a few men with muskets to guard against the Thing on the Ice or Esquimaux are my only companions for those hours.

Other than the Sick and Dying.

Captain Fitzjames's nausea, vomiting, and diarrhea were terrible. Unrelenting. The Cramps curled him into a Fetal Position and made this strong and Brave man cry aloud.

On the Second Day, he tried to rejoin his team man-hauling his whaleboat — even the Officers pull from time to time — but soon he Collapsed yet again. This time the vomiting and cramps were Nonstop. When the Whaleboat was left on the Ice that afternoon as the able-bodied Men went back to man-haul forward the 5 Boats left behind on the First Haul, Captain Fitzjames confessed to me that his Vision was terribly blurred and that he was frequently seeing Double.

I asked him if he had been Wearing the Wire Goggles we use to block the sun. The men Hate them because they Obscure vision so terribly, and the Goggles tend to induce their own headaches. Captain Fitzjames admitted that he had Not been wearing them but pointed out that the day had been quite Cloudy. None of the other men were wearing them either. At that point our Conversation stopped as he was seized with diarrhea and vomiting yet again.

Late that night, in the Holland Tent where I was Attending him, Fitzjames gasped to me that he was having trouble swallowing and that his Mouth was constantly Dry. Soon he showed trouble Breathing and was no longer able to speak. By sunrise, a Paralysis had moved down his upper Arms to the point where he could no longer lift them or use his hands to Write messages to me.

Captain Crozier called a Halt that day — the first such full day's stop we had enjoyed since leaving Terror Camp almost six weeks earlier. All of the tents were pitched. The larger Sick Bay Tent was finally unpacked from Crozier's own Whaleboat — it took almost Three Hours to set it up in the wind and cold (and the men are much more Sluggish about such things these days) — and for the first time in almost a month and a half all the Sick were made comfortable in one place.

Mr. Hoar, Captain Fitzjames's long-suffering steward, had died on the Second Day of our March. (We had made less than a Mile that first Terrible day of Man-hauling, and the stack of Coal, Stoves, and other goods was still Horribly but Plainly Visible behind us at Terror Camp that first night. It was as if we had Achieved Nothing after twelve hours of Deadly Labour. Those first days — it took us Seven Days to cross the narrow iced Inlet south of Terror Camp and travel only Six Miles — almost destroyed our Morale and Will to go on.)

Marine Private Heather, who had lost a portion of his Brain months before, finally allowed his Body to Die on our Fourth Day out. His surviving fellow Marines played a bagpipe over his shallow, hastily dug grave that evening.

And so it went with the other Sick dying rapidly, but then there came a Long Period after the twin deaths of Lieutenant Le Vesconte and Private Pilkington at the end of the Second Week in which no one died. The men Convinced themselves that the truly Ill had died off and only the Strong remained.

Captain Fitzjames's sudden collapse reminded us that we were all growing Weaker. There were no longer any truly Strong among us. Except perhaps for the Giant, Magnus Manson, who lumbers along Imperturbably and who never seems to lose weight or energy.

To treat Captain Fitzjames's constant vomiting, I administered doses of asafetida, a gum resin used to control spasms. It helped very little. He was not able to Keep Down either solid food or liquids. I gave him limewater to settle his stomach, but it also did no good.

For his difficulty swallowing, I administered Syrup of Squills — a sliced herb set in tannin solution that is an Excellent Expectorant. Usually effective, it seemed to do little to lubricate the dying man's Throat.

As Captain Fitzjames lost the Use and Control of first his Arms and then his Legs, I tried Peruvian Wine of Coca — a powerful admixture of wine and cocaine — as well as solutions of hartshorn, a Medicine made from ground-up antlers of red deer which stinks strongly of ammonia, as well as Solution of Camphor. These Solutions, at Half the Dosage I gave to the captain, often Arrest and even Reverse paralysis.

They did not help. The Paralysis spread to all of Captain Fitzjames's extremities. He continued Vomiting and being Doubled Up by Cramps long after he could no longer speak or gesture.

But at least this Deadening of his Vocal Apparatus relieved the men of the Burden of hearing their Erebus Captain scream in pain. But I saw his convulsions and his mouth Open in silent screams that Long Last Day.

This morning, on the Fourth and Final Day of Captain Fitzjames's Agony, his lungs began to shut down as the paralysis reached his respiratory muscles. He Laboured all day to breathe. Lloyd and I — sometimes abetted by Captain Crozier, who spent many hours with his Friend at the End — would set Fitzjames in a Sitting Position or Hold Him Upright or actually Walk the paralyzed man around the Tent, dragging his Limp Stockinged Feet across the Ice-and-Gravel floor, in a vain attempt to help his failing lungs Continue to work.

In desperation, I forced Tincture of Lobelia, a whiskey-coloured solution of Indian tobacco that was almost pure nicotine, down Captain Fitzjames's throat, massaging it down his paralyzed gullet with my bare fingers. It was like feeding a dying Baby Bird. Tincture of Lobelia was the best respiratory stimulant left in my depleted Surgeon's apothecary, a Stimulant that Dr. Peddie had sworn by. It would raise Jesus from the dead a day early, Peddie used to blaspheme when in his cups.

It did no good whatsoever.

It must be Remembered that I am a mere Surgeon, not a Physician. My training was in Anatomy; my expertise is in Surgery. Physicians prescribe; Surgeons saw. But I am doing my Best with the supplies my Dead Colleagues left to me.

The most Terrible thing about Captain James Fitzjames's last hours was that he was Fully Alert through all of this — the vomiting and Cramps, the Loss of his Voice and ability to Swallow, the Creeping Paralysis, and the Final Terrible Hours of his lungs failing. I could see the panic and Terror in his eyes. His Mind was Fully Alive. His Body was Dying around him. He *could do Nothing about this Living Torture except to Plead with me through his Eyes. I was impotent to help.*

At times I wanted to Administer a lethal dose of *pure Coca* just to put an End to his Suffering, but my Hippocratic Oath and Christian belief did not allow that.

I went outside and Wept instead, making sure that none of the Officers or Men could see me.

Captain Fitzjames died at 8 minutes after 3:00 p.m. this afternoon, Tuesday the Sixth Day of June, in the Year of Our Lord Eighteen Hundred and Forty-Eight.

His shallow grave had already been Dug. The Covering Rocks had been Gathered and Stacked. All of the Men who could stand and dress themselves turned out for the Service. Many of those who had served under Captain Fitzjames the past three years wept. Even though it was warm today — five to ten degrees above Freezing — a cold wind Came Up out of the Relentless Northwest and froze many Tears to beards or cheeks or comforters.

The few Marines left in our Expedition fired a volley into the Air

Up the hill from the Grave, a Ptarmigan took to the air and flew out toward the Pack Ice.

A great Moan went up from the men. Not for Captain Fitzjames, but for the loss of the Ptarmigan for the evening's stew. By the time the Marines reloaded their Muskets, the bird was a hundred yards away and far out of Range. (And none of these Marines ever could have hit a bird on the wing at one hundred yards even when they were Well and Warm.)

Later — just a half hour ago — Captain Crozier looked in on the Sick Bay Tent and beckoned me outside into the Cold.

Was it Scurvy that killed Captain Fitzjames? *was his only question to me.*

I admitted that I did not think it was. It had been something more Deadly.

Captain Fitzjames thought that the steward serving him and the other officers since Hoar's death was poisoning him, *whispered the captain.* Is this possible?

Bridgens? *I said too Loudly. I was deeply shocked. I had always liked the Bookish old Steward.*

Crozier shook his head. Richard Aylmore has been serving the

Erebus officers the last two weeks, *he said.* Could it have been poison, Dr. Goodsir?

I hesitated. To say yes would certainly mean Aylmore would be shot at sunrise. The Gunroom Steward was the man who had been Given fifty Lashes in January for his Improvident participation in the Grand Venetian Carnivale. Aylmore was also a Friend and Frequent Confidant of Terror's Diminutive and sometimes Devious caulker's mate. Aylmore, we all knew, harboured a small and resentful Soul.

It could well have been poison, *I told Crozier not half an hour ago.* But not necessarily a Deliberately Administered poison.

What does that mean? *demanded Crozier. Our remaining captain looked so weary tonight that his white Skin actually glowed in the starlight.*

I said, I mean that the Officers have been eating the Largest Portions of the last of the Goldner's Canned Foods that we have brought along. There sometimes is an Unexplained but Deadly paralytic poison in foods that have gone bad. No one understands it. Perhaps it is some microscopic Animalcule we cannot Perceive with our Lenses.

Crozier whispered, Wouldn't we have smelled it if the canned foods had gone putrid?

I shook my head and grasped the captain's greatcoat sleeve to press home my point. No. That is the Terror of this Poison that Paralyzes first the voice and then the entire body. It cannot be Seen or Tested For. It is as invisible as Death itself.

Crozier thought for a long moment. I'll order everyone to go off the canned foods for three weeks, *he said at last.* The last of the rotten salted beef and poor biscuits will have to do us for a while. We'll eat it Cold.

The Men and officers will not be happy about this, *I whispered.* The canned soups and vegetables are as close as Anything comes to a Hot Meal on the March. They may become Mutinous at such Further Deprivation under such Harsh Conditions.

Crozier smiled then. It was a strangely chilling sight. Then I will not have everyone go off the canned foods, *he hissed.* Gunroom Steward Aylmore will continue eating it — out of the same cans he served James Fitzjames from. A good night to you, Dr. Goodsir.

I came back into the Sick Bay Tent then, attended to the sleeping sick men, and crawled into my Sleeping Bag with my mahogany Portable Writing Desk on my Knees.

My handwriting is so Difficult to read on the Page because I have been Shaking. And not just from the Cold.

Every time I believe I Know one of these men or Officers, I find that I am wrong. A Million years of Man's Medicinal Progress will never reveal the secret Condition and sealed Compartments of the Human Soul.

We leave before Dawn tomorrow. I suspect there will be no more stops such as the luxury of the last Two Days at Comfort Cove.

45

BLANKY

When Tom Blanky's third and final leg snapped off, he knew it meant the end.

His first new leg had been wondrous to behold. Shaped and whittled by Mr. Honey, *Terror*'s capable carpenter, it had been carved out of a single piece of solid English oak. It was a work of art and Blanky enjoyed showing it off. The ice master had peg-legged his way around the ship like a good-humoured pirate, but when Blanky had to go out onto the ice, he attached to the bottom of the peg a perfectly shaped wooden foot that snapped into a socket. The foot had a myriad of nails and screws on the bottom — better for traction on the ice than the hobnails in the men's winter boots — and the one-legged man, while not able to man-haul, had been more than able to keep up during their transfer to Terror Camp from the abandoned ship and then in the long haul south and now east.

No longer.

His first leg had broken off just below the knee nineteen days after they'd abandoned Terror Camp, not long after they'd buried poor Pilkington and Harry Le Vesconte.

That day, Tom Blanky and Mr. Honey, who'd been excused from man-hauling, both had ridden in a pinnace strapped to a sledge pulled by twenty straining other men while the carpenter carved a new leg and foot for the ice master from wood taken from a spare spar.

Blanky had never been sure whether or not to wear his foot when hobbling along with the procession of boats and sweating, swearing men. When they actually ventured out onto the sea ice — as they had the first days crossing the frozen inlet south of Terror Camp and again at Seal Bay and once more at the broad bay just north of the point where they'd buried Le Vesconte — the screwed and cleated foot worked wonders on the ice. But most of their march south and then west along and around the large cape and now back east again was made on land.

As the snow and ice on the rocks began to melt, and it was melting quickly this summer that was so much warmer than their lost summer of 1847, Tom Blanky's wooden ovoid of a foot would slide off slick rocks or be pulled off in ice crevices or would snap at the socket with every inopportune twist.

When out on the ice, Blanky tried to show his solidarity with his mates by hiking back and forth with the man-haulers, making both trips alongside the straining, sweating men, carrying small items when he could, occasionally volunteering to slip into the harness of an exhausted man. But everyone knew he could not pull his own weight with the hauling.

By the sixth week and forty-seven miles out, at Comfort Cove where poor Captain Fitzjames had died so hard, Blanky was on his third leg — a poorer, weaker substitute than the second one had been — and he tried manfully to hobble along on his peg through the rocks, streams, and standing water, although he no longer went back for the afternoon's hated second haul.

Tom Blanky realized that he had become just so much more dead weight for the exhausted and ill survivors — ninety-five of them now, not including Blanky — to haul south with them.

What kept Blanky going even when his third leg began to splinter — there were no more extra spars from which to whittle a fourth — was his rising hope that his skills as an ice master would be needed when they took to the boats.

But while the scrim of ice on the rocks and barren coastline melted during the day — sometimes the temperature rose as high as

40 degrees according to Lieutenant Little — the pack ice beyond the coastal bergs showed no sign of breaking up. Blanky tried to be patient. He knew better than any other man on the expedition that sea ice at these latitudes might not show open leads — even on a "more normal" summer such as this one — until mid-July or later.

Still, it was not only his usefulness that was being decided by the ice, but his survival. If they took to the boats soon, he might live. He did not need his leg to travel by boat. Crozier had long since designated Thomas Blanky as skipper of his own pinnace — commanding eight men — and once the ice master was at sea again, he would survive. With any luck at all, they could sail their fleet of ten little splintered and gouged boats right to the mouth of Back's Great Fish River, pause at the mouth to rerig for river running, and — with only the slightest help from northwest winds and men at the oars — head briskly upstream. The portages, Blanky knew, would be hard, especially hard for him since he could carry so little weight on his flimsy third peg, but a piece of cake after the man-hauling nightmare of the last eight weeks.

If he could last until they took to the boats, Thomas Blanky would live.

But Blanky knew a secret that made even his sanguine personality wane: the Thing on the Ice, the Terror itself, was after him.

It had been sighted every day or two as the straining procession of men had rounded the large cape and turned back east again along the shoreline, every day in the early afternoon when they turned back to haul the five boats they'd left behind, every twilight at around 11:00 p.m. as they collapsed into their wet Holland tents for a few hours' sleep.

The thing was still stalking them. Sometimes the officers saw it through their telescopes as they looked out to sea. Neither Crozier nor Little nor Hodgson nor any of the other few officers remaining ever told the man-hauling men that they'd seen the beast, but Blanky — who had more time than most to watch and think — saw them conferring and knew.

At other times, those hauling the last boats could see the beast clearly with their own unaided eyes. Sometimes it was behind them, trailing by a mile or less, a black speck against white ice or a white speck against black rock.

It's just one of them polar white bears, had said James Reid, the red-bearded ice master from *Erebus* and one of Blanky's closest friends now. *They'll eat you if they can, but mostly they're harmless enough. Bullets kill them. Let's hope it comes closer. We need some fresh meat.*

But Blanky knew at the time that it wasn't one of the white bears they shot for food from time to time. This was *it,* and while all men on the Long March feared it — especially at night or, rather, during the two hours of dimness that now passed for night — only Thomas Blanky knew that it was coming for him first.

The march had taken a toll on everyone, but Blanky was in constant agony: not from scurvy, which seemed to be affecting him less than most, but from the pain in the stump of the leg that the thing had taken. Walking on the ice and rock of the shore was so difficult for him that by midmorning of each day's sixteen- or eighteen-hour march, his stump would be streaming blood down over the wooden cup and leather harness that held it in place. The blood soaked through his thick canvas trousers and ran down his wooden peg, leaving a trail of blood behind. It soaked upward through his long underwear, trousers, and shirt.

During the first weeks of the march, while it was still cold, it was a blessing that the blood had frozen. But now, with the tropical warmth of days above zero, some above freezing, Blanky was bleeding like a stuck pig.

The long slops and greatcoats also had been a blessing — they hid the worst evidence of Blanky's bleeding from the captain and others — but by mid-June, it was too warm to wear the greatcoats while hauling, so tons of sweat-soaked slops and wool layers were piled in the boats they were hauling. The men often hauled in shirtsleeves through the warmest parts of the day, pulling on more layers as the afternoons cooled toward zero degrees. Blanky had joked with them when they asked him why he continued to wear his long coats. *I'm cold-blooded, boys,* he'd said with a laugh. *My wooden leg brings the chill of the ground up into me. I don't want you to see me shiver.*

But eventually he had to take off the greatcoat. Because Blanky was working so hard hobbling just to keep up, and because the pain of his tortured stump caused him to sweat even when he was standing still, he could no longer stand the freeze-and-thaw, freeze-and-thaw of all his layers of clothes.

When the men saw the blood pouring, they said nothing. They had their own problems. Most of them were bleeding from scurvy.

Crozier and Little often would pull Blanky and James Reid aside, asking the two ice masters their professional opinion about the ice just beyond the berg barrier of the shoreline. Once they'd come around to the east again, along the southern coast of this cape that had bulged out miles to the west and south of Comfort Cove — probably adding twenty miles to their haul south — Reid was of the opinion that the ice between this part of King William Land and the mainland, whether King William Land was connected to the mainland or not, would be slower breaking up than the pack ice to the northwest, where conditions were more dynamic come the summer thaw.

Blanky was more optimistic. He pointed out that the bergs piled here along this southern coast were becoming smaller and smaller. Once a serious barrier separating the shore from the sea ice, this wall of bergs was no more a hindrance now than a cluster of low seracs. The reason, Blanky told Crozier, and Reid had agreed, was that this cape of King William Land was sheltering this stretch of sea and coast, or perhaps of gulf and coast, from the glacierlike river of ice that had poured down so relentlessly from the northwest onto *Erebus* and *Terror* and even upon the coast near Terror Camp. That endless press of ice, Blanky pointed out, had been flowing down from the North Pole itself. Things were more sheltered here south of the King William Land southwestern cape. Perhaps the ice would break up sooner here.

Reid had looked at him strangely when Blanky delivered that opinion. Blanky knew what the other ice master was thinking. *Whether this is a gulf or a strait leading to Chantrey Inlet and the mouth of Back's River, ice usually breaks up last in a confined space.*

Reid would have been correct if he'd stated that opinion aloud to Captain Crozier — he hadn't, obviously not wanting to contradict his friend and fellow ice master — but Blanky was still optimistic. In truth, Thomas Blanky had been optimistic in his heart and soul every day since that dark night of 5 December of the previous winter when he'd considered himself a dead man as the Thing on the Ice chased him from *Terror* and into the forest of seracs.

Twice the creature had tried to kill him. And twice all that Thomas Blanky had lost had been parts of one leg.

He hobbled on, bringing cheer and jokes and the occasional shred of extra tobacco or sliver of frozen beef to exhausted, drained men. His tent mates, he knew, valued his presence. He took his turn at watch in the ever-shorter nights and carried a shotgun while painfully stumping alongside the morning boat procession as a guard, although Thomas Blanky knew better than any living man that no mere shotgun would stop the Terror Beast when it finally came in close to claim its next victims.

The tortures of the Long March were increasing. Not only were men slowly dying of starvation and scurvy and exposure, but there had been two other incidences of the terrible poisoning death that had claimed Captain Fitzjames — John Cowie, the stoker who had survived the thing's invasion of *Erebus* on 9 March, died screaming in cramps and pain and then silent paralysis on 10 June. On 12 June, Daniel Arthur, *Erebus*'s thirty-eight-year-old quartermaster, collapsed with abdominal pains and died from paralyzed lungs a mere eight hours later. Their bodies were not truly buried; the procession had paused only long enough to sew both bodies into the little remaining spare canvas and to pile rocks on them.

Richard Aylmore, the object of much speculation since Captain Fitzjames's death, showed almost no signs of illness. The scuttlebutt was that while everyone else had been banned from eating warm meals from the canned goods and suffered the scurvy worse for it, Aylmore had been ordered to share portions of his tinned meals with Cowie and Arthur. Other than the obvious answer of active and deliberate poisoning, no one could figure why the Goldner tins would horribly kill three men but leave Aylmore untouched. But while everyone knew that Aylmore hated Captain Fitzjames and Captain Crozier, no one could see a reason for the gunroom steward to poison his mates.

Unless he wanted their shares of food after they were dead.

Henry Lloyd, Dr. Goodsir's assistant in the sick bay, was one of the men dragged along in the boats these days — sick from scurvy that had him vomiting blood and his own loose teeth — so since Blanky was one of the few men other than Diggle and Wall who stayed with the boats after the morning haul, he tried to help the good doctor.

Oddly enough, now that it was getting tropically warm, there were more cases of frostbite. Sweating men who'd doffed their jackets and gloves would continue man-hauling into the chill of the endless evening — the sun hung in the south until midnight now — and be surprised to find that the air temperature had fallen to fifteen below during their exertions. Goodsir was constantly treating fingers and patches of skin turned white by frostbite or dead black from rot.

Sun blindness or screaming headaches caused by the sun's glare afflicted half the men. Crozier and Goodsir would move up and down the ranks of man-hauling men during the morning, cajoling them to put on their goggles, but the men hated the wire-mesh monstrosities. Joe Andrews, captain of the hold for *Erebus* and an old friend of Tom Blanky's, said that wearing the God-damned wire goggles was as difficult as trying to see through a pair of lady's black silk drawers but much less fun.

The snow blindness and headaches were becoming serious problems on the march. Some of the men begged Dr. Goodsir for laudanum after the headaches struck, but the surgeon told them that he had none left. Blanky, who was often sent to fetch medicines from the doctor's locked chest, knew that Goodsir was lying. There was a small vial of laudanum left there, unmarked. The ice master knew that the surgeon was keeping it for some terrible occasion — to ease Captain Crozier's last hours? Or the surgeon's own?

Other men suffered the torments of Hell from sunburn. Everyone was blistered red on their hands and faces and necks, but some men who would tug off their shirts for even the shortest periods during the intolerable heat of the midday, when temperatures were above freezing, would that same evening watch their skins, bleached white after three years of darkness and enclosure, burn red and quickly turn to suppurating blisters.

Dr. Goodsir popped the blisters with his lancet and treated the open sores with a salve that smelled to Blanky like axle grease.

By the time the ninety-five survivors were trudging east along the southern coast of the cape in mid-June, almost every man was on the edge of breakdown. As long as some men could man-haul the terribly heavy sledges with boats atop them and the full-packed whaleboats without sledges, others suffering could ride briefly, recover slightly, and rejoin the man-hauling within hours or days. But when there were too many sick and injured to pull, Blanky knew, their escape march would be at an end.

As it was now, the men were always so thirsty that every stream or trickle of water was a reason to stop and throw themselves on all fours to lap at the water like dogs. If it hadn't been for the sudden thaw, Blanky knew, they would have all died of thirst three weeks earlier. The spirit stoves were almost out of fuel. At first, melting snow in one's mouth seemed to assuage the thirst, but it actually drained more energy from the body and made one thirstier. Each time they dragged the boats and themselves across a stream — and there were more streams and rivulets running liquid now — everyone would stop to fill water bottles that no longer needed to be carried next to the skin to keep them from freezing.

But while thirst would not kill them soon, Blanky saw that the men were failing in a hundred other ways. Starvation was taking its toll. Hunger kept the exhausted men from sleeping through the four hours of twilight — if they did not have watch duty — which Crozier allowed for their sleeping time.

Setting up and taking down the Holland tents, simple acts that had been performed in twenty minutes two months ago at Terror Camp, now took two hours in the morning and two hours in the evening. Each day it took a little longer as fingers became more swollen and frostbitten and clumsy.

Few of the men's minds, not even Blanky's at times, were really clear. Crozier seemed the most alert of all of them most of the time, but sometimes when he thought that no one was looking, the captain's face became a death mask of fatigue and stupor.

Sailors who had tied off complicated rigging and shroud knots in the roaring darkness fifty feet out on a pitching spar two hundred feet above the deck on a stormy night off the Strait of Magellan during a hurricane blow could no longer tie their shoes in the daylight. Because there was no wood within three hundred miles — other than Blanky's leg and the boats and masts and sledges they'd hauled along with them and the remains of *Erebus* and *Terror* almost a hundred miles to their north — and because the ground was still hard-frozen an inch below the surface, the men had to gather heaps of stones at each stop to weigh down the edges of the tents and to anchor tent ropes against the inevitable nightly winds.

This chore also took forever. Men frequently fell asleep standing in the dimmed sunlight at midnight with a rock in each hand. Sometimes their mates did not even shake them awake.

So it came to pass that late in the afternoon of the eighteenth day of June, 1848, as the men were making their second haul of boats that day, when Blanky's third leg snapped off just below his bleeding knee stump, he took it as a sign.

Dr. Goodsir had little work for him that afternoon, so Blanky had turned back to peg his way alongside the last boats on the second haul of the endless day, when the foot and peg had caught between two immovable rocks and snapped the peg off high. He took the high break and his unusual presence near the end of the march as a sign from the gods as well.

He found a nearby boulder, made himself as comfortable as he could, dug out his pipe, and tapped in the last bit of tobacco he had been saving for weeks.

When a few of the seamen stopped in their hauling to ask what he was doing, Blanky said, "Just going to sit a spell, I reckon. Give my stump a rest."

When Sergeant Tozer, who was in charge of the Marine rear guard detail this sunny day, stopped to ask tiredly what Blanky was doing allowing the procession to pass him by, Blanky said, "Never you mind, Soloman." He had always enjoyed irritating the stupid sergeant by using his first name. "You just toddle off now with your remaining lobsterbacks and let me be."

Half an hour later, when the last boats were hundreds of yards to the south of him, Captain Crozier had come back with Mr. Honey, the carpenter.

"What the hell do you think you're doing, Mr. Blanky?" snapped Crozier.

"Just giving it a rest, Captain. I thought I might spend the night here."

"Don't be an ass," said Crozier. He looked at the snapped-off peg leg and turned to the carpenter. "Can you fix this, Mr. Honey? Make a new one by tomorrow afternoon if Mr. Blanky rides in one of the boats until then?"

"Oh, aye, sir," said Honey, squinting at the broken peg with an artisan's scowl at the failure — or mistreatment — of one of his creations. "We ain't got much spare wood left, but there's one extra jolly boat rudder we brought along as a spare for the pinnaces that I can turn into a new leg as easy as you like."

"D'you hear that, Blanky?" asked Crozier. "Now get off your ass and let Mr. Honey help you hobble to catch up to Mr. Hodgson's last boat there. Quickly now. We'll have you fixed up by tomorrow noon."

Blanky smiled. "Can Mr. Honey fix this, Captain?" He tugged off the wooden cup of the leg and detached the clumsy leather-and-brass harness.

"Oh, Christ damn it," said Crozier. He started to look more closely at the bleeding raw stump with the black flesh surrounding the white nub of bone but quickly pulled back his face from the smell.

"Aye, sir," said Blanky. "I'm surprised Dr. Goodsir ain't sniffed it out before this. I try to stay downwind of him when I'm helpin' him out in the sick bay. The boys in my tent know what's up, sir. There's nothing to be done for it."

"Nonsense," said Crozier. "Goodsir will . . ." He stopped.

Blanky smiled. It was not a sarcastic or sad smile but an easy one, filled with some real humour. "Will what, Captain? Take my leg off at the hip? The black bits and red lines run all the way up to my ass and private parts, sir, with apologies for being so picturesque about it. And if he did operate, how many days would I be lyin' in the boat like old Private Heather — God rest the poor bugger's soul — being hauled along by men who are as tired as I am?"

Crozier said nothing.

"No," continued Blanky, puffing contentedly on his pipe, "I think it'd be best if I rested here awhile on my own and just relaxed and thought some thoughts about this and that. My life has been a good one. I'd like to think about it some before the pain and stink get so bad I'm distracted."

Crozier sighed, looked at his carpenter and then at his ice master, and sighed again. He took a water bottle from the pocket of his great-coat. "Take this."

"Thank you, sir. I will. With gratitude," said Blanky.

Crozier felt in his other pockets. "I have no food with me. Mr. Honey?"

The carpenter came up with a moldy biscuit and a sliver of something more green than tan that might have been beef.

"No, thank you, John," said Blanky. "I am truthfully not hungry. But, Captain, would you do me a huge favor?"

"What is that, Mr. Blanky?"

"My people are in Kent, sir. Near Ightham Mote north of Tonbridge Wells. Or at least my Betty and Michael and old mum were when I set sail, sir. I was wondering, Captain, I mean if you have luck on your side and have the time later . . ."

"If I get back to England, I swear I'll look them up and tell them that you were smoking and smiling and sitting as comfortably on a boulder as a lazy squire when last I saw you," said Crozier. He pulled a pistol from his pocket. "Lieutenant Little's seen the thing through his glass — it's been trailing behind us all morning, Thomas. It'll be along presently. You should take this."

"No, thank you, Captain."

"You're sure about this, Mr. Blanky? Staying behind, I mean?" said Captain Crozier. "Even if you were . . . with us . . . for just another week or so, your knowledge of the ice might be very important to us all. Who knows what the conditions will be out on the pack ice twenty miles east of here?"

Blanky smiled. "If Mr. Reid weren't still with you, I'd take that to heart, Captain. I surely would. But he's as good an ice master as you could ask for. As a spare, I mean."

Crozier and Honey shook hands with him. Then they turned and hurried to catch up to the last boat disappearing over a distant ridge to the south.

———

It was after midnight when it came.

Blanky had been out of tobacco for hours and the water had frozen in the bottle where he'd foolishly left it sitting on the boulder next to him. He was in some pain, but he did not want to sleep.

A few stars had come out in the twilight. The wind from the northwest had come up, as it usually did in the evening, and the temperature had probably dropped forty degrees from its noontime high.

Blanky had kept the broken peg leg and its cup and straps on the boulder next to him. While his gangrenous leg tormented him and his empty stomach clawed at him, the worst pain tonight was from his lower leg and calf and foot — his phantom limb.

Suddenly the thing was just *there*.

It loomed up on the ice not thirty paces from him.

It must have come up through some invisible hole in the ice, Blanky thought. He was reminded of a tent fair in Tunbridge Wells he had seen as a boy, with a rickety wooden stage and a magician in purple silk with a tall conical hat embroidered with crude planets and stars. That man had appeared just like this, popping up through a trapdoor to the oohs and ahs of the country audience.

"Welcome back," said Thomas Blanky to the shadowy silhouette on the ice.

The thing reared up on its hind legs, a dark mass of hair and muscle and sunset-tinted claws and a faint gleam of teeth beyond anything, the Ice Master was sure, in mankind's racial memory of its many predators. Blanky guessed that it was more than twelve feet tall, perhaps fourteen.

Its eyes — a deeper blackness against the black silhouette — did not reflect the dying sun.

"You're late," said Blanky. He could not help it that his teeth were chattering. "I've been expecting you for a long time." He threw his peg leg and its rattling harness at the shape.

The thing did not try to dodge the crude missile. The shape towered there for a minute and then rushed forward like a wraith, the legs not even visibly moving to propel it, a monstrous mass sliding rapidly toward him across the rock and ice, the dark and terrible solidity of the shape finally opening arms to fill the ice master's vision.

Thomas Blanky grinned fiercely and clamped his teeth down hard on the stem of his cold pipe.

46

CROZIER

The only thing keeping Francis Rawdon Moira Crozier moving forward into the tenth week on the boat march was the blue flame in his chest. The more tired and empty and sick and battered his body became, the hotter and fiercer the flame burned. He knew it was not merely some metaphor of his determination. Nor was it optimism, as such. The blue flame in his chest had burrowed toward his heart like some alien entity, lingered like a disease, and centered in him as an almost unwanted core of conviction that he would do whatever he had to do to survive. *Anything.*

Sometimes Crozier came close to praying that the blue flame would just go out so he could surrender to the inevitable and lie down and pull the frozen tundra up over himself like a child under a blanket settling into his nap.

Today they were stopped — not pulling the sledges and boats for the first time in a month. And they had unpacked and clumsily pitched the large Sick Bay tent, although not the large mess tents. The men were calling this otherwise unremarkable place on a small bay along the southern coast of King William Land "Hospital Camp."

In the past two weeks they had just crossed the rugged ice of a huge bay that cut into the underside of the cape that seemed for weeks of hauling as if it would continue to bulge out to the southwest forever. But now they were headed southeast again, paralleling the coastline along the underside of that cape and then farther east — the correct direction if they were to get to Back's River.

Crozier had brought his sextant and theodolite along, and Lieutenant Little also had his sextant, as well as the dead Fitzjames's instrument as a spare, but neither officer had taken star sightings or sun sightings for weeks. It just wasn't important. If King William Land was a peninsula, as most of the arctic explorers, including Crozier's old commander James Clark Ross, had thought, then this coastline would lead them to the mouth of Back's River. If it was an island — which had been Lieutenant Gore's guess and Crozier's hunch as well — then they would soon see the mainland to their south and cross what should be a narrow strait to the mouth of Back's River.

Either way, Crozier — who had been content to follow the coast-line since they had no other real choice and navigate by dead reckoning for the time being — estimated that they were now about ninety miles from the mouth of Back's River.

On this march, they had been completing only a little better than a mile per day on average. Some days they did three or four miles, reminding Crozier of the fantastic rate of their crossing from the ships to Terror Camp on the ice highway they had laid down, but other days — when there was more rock than ice under the runners, when they had to ford sudden streams or in one case an actual river, when they were forced out onto the tortured sea ice when the coast-line became too rocky, when the weather was foul, when more men than usual were too sick to pull and ended up riding in the boat them-selves while their mates pulled the extra weight, first the sixteen hours of man-hauling the four whaleboats and a cutter, then back for the other three cutters and two pinnaces — saw them covering only a few hundred yards from their previous night's camp.

On 1 July, after weeks of warming weather, the cold and snow returned in earnest. A blizzard blew out of the southeast, directly into the eyes of the men hauling their sledges. Slops were pulled out of baled heaps in the boats. Welsh wigs were dug out of valises and packs. The snow added hundreds of pounds to the weight of the sledges and the boats atop them. The men so sick that they were being carried in those boats, lying atop supplies and folded tents, burrowed under the canvas covers for shelter.

The men hauled forward through three days of continuous driving snow out of the east and southeast. At night, lightning crashed and the men cowered low against the canvas floors of their tents.

Today they had stopped because too many of the men were sick and Goodsir wanted to administer to them, and because Crozier wanted to send parties ahead to scout and larger armed parties north into the interior and south out onto the sea ice to hunt.

They needed food badly.

The good news and the bad news was that they had finally finished the last of the Goldner canned foods. When the steward Aylmore, who on captain's orders had continued to eat and grow fat on the tinned foods, hadn't died from the terrible symptoms that killed Captain Fitzjames — although two other men who were not supposed to be eating from the cans had — everyone went back on the tinned foods to supplement the little remaining salt pork and cod and biscuits.

The 28-year-old seaman Bill Closson died screaming silently and convulsing from gut pains and paralysis, but Dr. Goodsir had no clue what might have poisoned him until one of his mates, Tom McConvey, confessed that the dead man had stolen and eaten a Goldner can of peaches that no one else had shared.

In the very brief burial service for Closson — his body lying without even a canvas shroud under the loose pile of rocks because Old Murray, the sailmaker, had died of scurvy and there was no extra canvas left anyway — Captain Crozier had quoted not from the Bible the men knew but from his fabled *Book of Leviathan*.

"Life is 'solitary, poor, nasty, brutish, and short,'" the captain had intoned. "It seems it is shorter for those who steal from their mates."

The eulogy, such as it was, was a hit with the men. Although the ten boats they had been dragging and hauling on sledges for more than two months all had old names assigned to them from when *Erebus* and *Terror* still sailed the seas, the man-hauling teams of seamen immediately renamed the three cutters and two pinnaces always hauled during the afternoon and evening stint of hauling — the part of the day they hated the most since it meant regaining ground already won through the sweat of the long morning. The five boats were now officially named Solitary, Poor, Nasty, Brutish, and Short.

Crozier had grinned at this. It meant the men were not so far gone into hunger and despair that their English sailors' black humour did not still hold a cutting edge.

———

The mutiny, when it came, was made vocal by the last man on earth that Francis Crozier would have imagined opposing his command.

It was the middle of the day and the captain was trying to get a few minutes' sleep while most of the men were out of camp doing reconnaissance or hunting. He heard the slow shuffle of many screw-heeled boots in the snow outside his tent, and he knew immediately that there was trouble outside the usual range of daily emergencies. The furtive sound of the footsteps as he came up from his light sleep warned him of the defiance to come.

Crozier pulled on his greatcoat. He always carried a loaded pistol in the right pocket of this coat, but recently he had begun carrying a smaller two-shot pistol in his left pocket as well.

There were about twenty-five men assembled in the open area between Crozier's tent and the large Sick Bay tent. The blowing snow, thick scarves, and filthy Welsh wigs made some of them hard to identify at first glance, but Crozier was not surprised to see Cornelius Hickey, Magnus Manson, Richard Aylmore, and a half dozen of the more vocal resenters in the second row.

It was the first row facing him that surprised him.

Most of the officers were off commanding the scattered hunting and scouting parties Crozier had sent out that morning — Crozier realized his mistake too late, sending away all of his most loyal officers, including Lieutenant Little and his second mate Robert Thomas, Tom Johnson, his faithful bosun's mate, Harry Peglar and some others, all at once, leaving the weaker men congregated here at Hospital Camp — but standing in front of this group was young Lieutenant Hodgson. Crozier was also shocked to see Reuben Male, captain of the forecastle, and *Erebus*'s captain of the foretop, Robert Sinclair, here. Male and Sinclair had always been good men.

Crozier strode toward the gathering so quickly that Hodgson actually took two steps back and collided with the giant idiot, Manson.

"What do you men want?" rasped Crozier. Wishing that his voice was not such a hoarse croak, he put as much volume and authority into it as he could. "What the hell is going on here?"

"We need to talk to you, Captain," said Hodgson. The young man's voice was trembling with tension.

"About what?" Crozier kept his right hand in his pocket. He saw Dr. Goodsir come to the opening of the Sick Bay tent and look out in surprise at the mob. Crozier counted twenty-three men in the group, and, despite the wigs pulled low and scarves pulled high, he noted who each man was. He would not forget.

"About going back," said Hodgson. The men behind him began muttering assent with the crowd murmur that was always the hive-mind sound of mutineers.

Crozier did not react at once. One piece of good news here was that if it was an active mutiny, if all the men including Hodgson and Male and Sinclair had already agreed to take control of the expedition by force, Crozier would be dead by now. They would have acted in the twilight dimness at midnight.

And the only other piece of good news was that while two or three of the seamen here were carrying shotguns, all the other weapons were out with the sixty-six men hunting today.

Crozier made a mental note never to allow all of the Marines to leave the camp again at the same time. Tozer and the others had been eager to hunt. The captain had been so tired that he had not thought twice about giving them permission to go.

The captain looked from face to face. Some of the weaker ones in the crowd looked down immediately, ashamed to meet his gaze. The stronger ones like Male and Sinclair stared back. Hickey looked at him with eyes so hooded and cold they could have belonged to one of the white bears they'd encountered — or perhaps to the thing on the ice itself.

"Go back to where?" snapped Crozier.

"To T-terror Camp," stuttered Hodgson. "There's canned food and some coal and the stoves there. And the other boats we left."

"Don't be a fool," said Crozier. "We're at least sixty-five miles from Terror Camp. It would be October — solid winter — before you reached it, if you ever did."

Hodgson wilted, but the captain of *Erebus*'s foretop said, "We're a hell of a lot closer to the camp than we are to this river we're killing ourselves to haul the boats to."

"That's not true, Mr. Sinclair," rasped Crozier. "Lieutenant Little and I estimate that the inlet to the river is less than fifty miles from here."

"The *inlet*," sneered a seaman named George Thompson. The man was known for drunkenness and laziness. Crozier could not cast the first stone at him for the drinking, but he despised laziness.

"The *mouth* of Back's River is fifty miles south down the inlet," continued Thompson. "More than a hundred miles from here."

"Watch your tone, Thompson," warned Crozier in a tone so low and deadly that even that lout blinked and looked down. Crozier looked around the crowd again. He spoke to all the men. "It doesn't matter if it's forty miles down the inlet to the mouth of Back's River or fifty miles, odds are good that it will be open water . . . we'll be *sailing* the boats, not dragging them. Now go back to your duties and forget this nonsense."

Some men shuffled, but Magnus Manson stood like a broad dam holding the lake of their defiance in place. Reuben Male said, "We want to go back to the ship, Captain. We think we'll have a better chance there."

It was Crozier's turn to blink. "Go back to *Terror*? Good Christ, Reuben, it must be more than ninety miles back to the ship, across *pack ice* as well as back through all that rough territory we've come through. The boats and sledges would never make it."

"We'll just take one boat," said Hodgson. The men murmured agreement behind him.

"What the hell are you talking about, one boat?"

"One boat," insisted Hodgson. "One boat on one sledge."

"We're sick of this man-hauling shite," said John Morfin, a seaman who had been seriously injured during the Carnivale.

Crozier ignored Morfin and said to Hodgson, "Lieutenant, how do you plan to get twenty-three men into one boat? Even if you steal one of the whaleboats, that will only hold ten or twelve of you, with minimal supplies. Or are you planning on having ten or more of your party die before you get back to the camp? They will, you know. More than that."

"There are the small boats at Terror Camp," said Sinclair, stepping closer and taking an aggressive stance. "We take one whale-boat back and use it and the jolly boats and ship's boats to ferry us out to *Terror*."

Crozier stared a moment and then actually laughed. "Do you think the ice has broken up there northwest of King William Land? Is *that* what you fools think?"

"We do," said Lieutenant Hodgson. "There's food on the ship. Lots of the canned food left. And we could sail for . . ."

Crozier laughed again. "You'd bet your lives that the ice has opened up enough this summer that *Terror* is afloat and just waiting for you to row your dinghies out to her? And that leads have opened up the entire way we came south? Three hundred *miles* of open water? In winter when you get there, if any of you do?"

"It's a better gamble than this, we think," shouted the gunroom steward, Richard Aylmore. The dark little man's face was contorted with rage, fear, resentment, and something like exhilaration now that his hour had come round at last.

"I'd almost like to go with you . . . ," began Crozier.

Hodgson blinked rapidly. Several of the men looked at one another.

"Just to see your faces when that gamble pays off with you walking *across the ice and pressure ridges* to find that *Terror* has been broken up by the ice just as *Erebus* was in March."

He let the effect of that image sink in for a few seconds before he said softly, "For Christ's sake, ask Mr. Honey or Mr. Wilson or Mr. Goddard or Lieutenant Little about what shape her *knees* were in. What shape her *rudder* was in. Ask First Mate Thomas about how badly her seams had started way back in April . . . it is *July* now, you fools. If the ice has melted around her even a wee bit, odds are greater that the old ship has sunk than floated. And if she hasn't, can twenty-three of you honestly tell me that you can man the pumps while sailing her through the maze of leads — if you get back in half the time it took you to get here just from Terror Camp, the winter freeze will already be setting in again. And how are you going to find your way through the ice if the ship can float, if it hasn't sunk, if you don't die manning the pumps day and night?"

Crozier looked around the mob again.

"I don't see Mr. Reid here. He's out with Lieutenant Little scouting our way south. With no ice master, you'll have a pretty time finding your way through the pancake ice and growlers and pack ice and bergs." Crozier shook his head at the absurdity of it all and chuckled as if the men had come to tell him a particularly good joke rather than foment a mutiny.

"Go back to your duties . . . *now*," he snapped. "I won't forget that you were foolish enough to bring this idea to me, but I'll try to forget the tone you used and the fact that you came like a mob of mutineers rather than like loyal members of Her Majesty's Royal Navy wanting to talk to their captain. Go on with you now."

"No," said Cornelius Hickey from the second row, his voice high and sharp enough to stop the wavering men in their tracks. "Mr. Reid will come with us. So will the others."

"Why will they?" asked Crozier, pinning the ferret with his gaze.

"They won't have any choice," said Hickey. He tugged at Magnus Manson's sleeve and the two stepped forward, past an alarmed-looking Hodgson.

Crozier decided that he would shoot Hickey first. His hand was on the pistol in his pocket. He would not even remove the weapon from the greatcoat for the first shot. He would shoot Hickey in the belly when he got three feet closer and then pull the pistol out and try to shoot the giant in the center of his forehead. No body shot was guaranteed to bring Manson down.

As if his thinking about shooting had made it happen, there came the crack of a shot from the direction of the coastline.

Everyone except Crozier and the caulker's mate turned to see what was happening. Crozier's gaze never left Hickey's eyes. Both men turned their heads only when the shouting started.

"Open water!" It was Lieutenant Little's party coming in from the pack ice — Ice Master Reid, Bosun John Lane, Harry Peglar, and half a dozen others, all carrying shotguns or muskets.

"Open water!" screamed Little again. He was waving both arms as he came across the rocks and ice of the shoreline and was obviously unaware of the drama going on in front of his captain's tent. "Not more than two miles south! Leads opening up large enough for the boats. Going on to the east for miles! Open water!"

Hickey and Manson stepped back into the ranks of cheering men where a mob had stood thirty seconds earlier. Some of the men started hugging one another. Reuben Male looked as if he was going to throw up at the thought of what he'd been about to do, and Robert Sinclair sat down on a low rock as if all the strength had gone out of his legs. The once-powerful foretop captain began to weep into his filthy hands.

"Get back to your tents and your duties," said Crozier. "We'll start loading the boats and checking the masts and riggings within the hour."

PEGLAR

*Somewhere in the Strait Between
King William Island and the Adelaide Peninsula
9 July, 1848*

The men waiting in Hospital Camp had been eager to depart ten minutes after Lieutenant Little's party brought in the word of the open water, but it was another day before they broke camp and another two days until the boats' hulls were actually slipped from the ice into the black water south of King William Land.

First they had to wait for all the other hunting and reconnaissance parties to return, and some came back after midnight, staggering into camp in the dim-yellow arctic twilight and collapsing into their sleeping bags without even hearing the good news. Very little game had been bagged, but Robert Thomas's group had killed an arctic fox and several white rabbits and Sergeant Tozer's team brought back a brace of ptarmigan.

On the morning of 5 July, a Wednesday, the Sick Bay tent all but emptied out as everyone who could stand or stagger wanted to lend a hand in preparations for putting to sea.

John Bridgens had taken the place of the dead Henry Lloyd and Tom Blanky as Dr. Goodsir's assistant in recent weeks, and the steward had watched the previous afternoon's near mutiny while standing next to the surgeon in the door of the Sick Bay tent. It was Bridgens who described the whole scene to Harry Peglar, who felt sicker than he already was by learning that his *Erebus* foretop counterpart, Robert Sinclair, had joined in the near uprising. Reuben Male, he knew, had always been a dependable man, but strong-willed. Very strong-willed.

Peglar had nothing but contempt for Aylmore, Hickey, and their sycophants. In Harry Peglar's eyes they were all men with busy little minds and — except for Manson — an abundance of words, but no sense of loyalty.

That Thursday, the sixth of July, found them out on pack ice for the first time in more than two months. Most of them had forgotten how terrible the man-hauling was on the open ice, even here in the lee of King William Land and the bulbous cape they'd just come around. There were still pressure ridges to haul the ten boats up and over. The sea ice was far less slippery under runners than the snow and shore ice were. There were no vales in which to shelter, no low ridgelines — not even the occasional boulder — in which to hide from the wind. Out here there were no trickling streams to drink from. The snowstorm continued and the wind grew stronger out of the southeast, blowing directly in their faces as they hauled the boats the two miles Lieutenant Little's hunting group had covered before coming across the open lead.

The first night out they were so exhausted that they did not even erect the Holland tents but pitched a few tent floors as tarps extending from the leeward side of the boats and boats on sledges and huddled together on the ice through the few hours of arctic summer dimness in their three-man sleeping bags.

Even with the storm, wind, and pack-ice difficulties, energized by their excitement, they covered the two miles by midmorning Friday, 7 July.

The lead was gone. Closed up. Little pointed out the thinner ice — none more than three to eight inches thick — where it had been.

With Ice Master James Reid in the lead, they followed the zigzag path of the recently frozen-over lead southeast then due east for much of that day.

Now, added to their disappointment and ever-present misery exacerbated by the snow in their faces and their thoroughly soaked clothing, came the tension — for the first time in years — of walking on thin ice.

A little after noon that day, Marine Private James Daly, who was one of six men sent ahead to test the ice by poking at it with long pikes, fell through. His comrades pulled him out, but not before he quite literally turned blue. Dr. Goodsir had Daly stripped naked on the ice, wrapped in Hudson's Bay blankets, and bundled under more blankets beneath the canvas cover of one of the cutters. Two other men had to stay with him, lying on either side of him in the canvas-yellow dimness beneath the boat cover so that their body warmth could keep him alive. Even then Private Daly's body shook and his teeth chattered uncontrollably and he ventured into delirium for much of the rest of the day.

The ice, as stable as a continent underfoot for two years, now rose and fell in low swells in a way that made everyone dizzy and caused some men to vomit. Pressure made even the thicker ice crack and groan with sudden explosions from far ahead, close ahead, to either side, behind, or directly underfoot. Dr. Goodsir had explained to them months before that one of the symptoms of advanced scurvy was a man's heightened sensitivity to sound — the blast of a gunshot could actually kill a man, he had said — and now the majority of the 89 men pulling the boats across the ice recognized those symptoms in themselves.

Even a near idiot like Magnus Manson realized that if any or all of the boats fell through the ice — ice that had failed to support a single skinny, starved scarecrow of a man like James Daly — there would be no hope for any of the men in harness. They would drown even before they froze to death.

Used to their tight procession across the ice, the men felt strange about their new man-hauling method of keeping the boats far apart and staggered. At times in the snowstorm each group would be out of sight of all the other groups and the sense of isolation was terrible. When they went back to haul the last three cutters and two pinnaces forward, they did not follow their old tracks and had to worry that the new ice they were on would not hold them.

Some of the men grumbled that they might have already missed the inlet leading south to the mouth of Back's River. Peglar had seen the charts and Crozier's occasional theodolite reading and knew that they were still a good distance to the west — thirty miles to the inlet, at the very least. Another sixty or sixty-five miles south then to the mouth. At the rate of their travel on land, even if food appeared and everyone's health miraculously improved, they would not reach the inlet until August and the mouth of the river until late September at the earliest.

The promise of open water made Harry Peglar's heart pound. Of course, his heart was pounding erratically much of the time these days anyway. Harry's mother had always worried about his heart — as a boy he had suffered scarlet fever and frequent pains in his chest — but he'd always told her such concerns were nonsense, that he was foretop captain in some of the world's greatest ships and that no man with a bad heart could hold such a position. Somehow he convinced her he was fine, but over the years Peglar felt occasional flutters in his chest, followed by days of pain and a sense of constriction and an ache down his left arm so bad that some days he had to climb to the foretop and upper spars with only one hand. The other foretopmen thought he was showing off.

These last weeks, his heart fluttered more frequently than not. He'd lost the use of his left fingers two weeks ago and the ache never left him. This, along with the embarrassment and inconvenience of the constant diarrhea — Peglar had always been a modest man, even about doing his business in the open over the side of a ship, which other men gave no thought to, had kept him constipated and waiting for darkness or the seat of ease.

But there was no seat of ease on this march. Not even a God-damned bush or shrub or large rock to hide behind. The men in Peglar's hauling team laughed that their petty officer would fall behind out of sight and risk being taken by the Terror rather than allow himself to be seen taking a shit.

It wasn't the friendly laughter that had bothered Peglar in recent weeks; it was the rushing to catch up with his team and to get back into harness. He was so exhausted from the internal bleeding and lack of food and heart flutters that he was having more and more trouble rushing to catch the receding boats.

So out of eighty-nine men this Friday, Harry Peglar was probably the only one who welcomed the blowing snow and the fog that came in after the snow began to abate.

The fog was a problem. Traveling so separately across the treacherous ice, it would have been easy for the boat teams to lose one another. Even backtracking to pick up the remaining cutters and pinnaces had been a problem, and that was before the fog grew thick as evening approached. Captain Crozier called a halt to discuss the matter. No more than fifteen men were allowed to congregate on a small area of ice at one time and that not too near a boat. They were pulling this evening with the fewest men it took to move the huge, heavy masses of boats and sledges.

The sledges were going to be a logistical problem if they ever reached the promised open water. The chances were great that they would need to load the deep-draft cutters and pinnaces with their keels and fixed rudders on sledges again before they reached the mouth of Back's River, so they couldn't just abandon the battered vehicles on the ice. Before leaving on Thursday, Crozier rehearsed taking the six sledged boats off, collapsing the heavy sledges as much as they had been designed to be collapsed or broken down, and stowing them properly in the boats. It took hours.

Setting the boats back up on their sledges before going out onto the pack ice was just within the men's failing strength and abilities. Fingers stupid with fatigue and scurvy fumbled with simple knots. A shallow cut kept bleeding. The slightest jostle left hand-sized bruises on their softening arms and in the thinning skin above their ribs.

But now they knew they could do it — unload, then load again the sledges, ready the boats for launching.

If they found the lead soon.

Crozier had each boat team light lanterns fore and aft. He called back the almost useless Marine ice-checkers with their pikes and appointed Lieutenant Hodgson as officer to lead the diamond of five boats, with one of the heavy whaleboats filled with the least essential items being pulled ahead of the others in the fog.

Every man there knew that this was young Hodgson's reward for throwing in with potential mutineers. His man-hauling team was led by Magnus Manson, while Aylmore and Hickey were also in harness, men who until now had been assigned to separate teams. If this lead boat team broke through the ice, the others would hear the screams and flailings through the heavy evening fog, but there would be nothing they could do except leave them and go a safer way.

The rest now must risk a near procession, staying close enough that they could see the others' lanterns in the growing gloom.

Around 8:00 p.m. there did come shouts and screams from Hodgson's lead team, but they had not fallen through. They'd found open water again more than a mile east and south of where Little had seen a lead on Wednesday.

The other teams sent men forward with lanterns, moving tentatively on what they assumed was thin ice, but the ice stayed firm and was estimated to be more than a foot thick right up to the edge of the inexplicable lead.

The cleft of black water was only about thirty feet wide, but it extended off into the fog.

"Lieutenant Hodgson," commanded Crozier, "make room in your whaleboat for six men at oars. Put the extra supplies out on the ice for now. Lieutenant Little will then take command of the whaleboat. Mr. Reid, you will go along with Lieutenant Little. You will proceed down the lead for two hours if that is possible. Don't raise your sail, Lieutenant. Oars only, but have the men put their backs into it. At the end of two hours — if you get that far — turn around and row back with your recommendation as to whether it's worth our effort to launch the boats. We'll use the four hours you are gone to unload everything here and pack the sledges into the remaining boats."

"Aye, sir," said Little and began barking orders. Peglar thought that young Hodgson looked as if he might weep. He knew how hard it must be to be in your twenties and know that your Naval career was over. *Serves him right*, thought Peglar. He'd spent decades in a navy that hanged men for mutiny and lashed them for the mere *thought* of mutiny, and Harry Peglar had never disagreed with either the rule or the punishment.

Crozier walked over. "Harry, do you feel well enough to go along with Lieutenant Little? I'd like you to handle the tiller. Mr. Reid and Lieutenant Little will be in the bow."

"Oh, yes, Captain. I feel fine." Peglar was shocked that Captain Crozier thought he looked or acted sick. *Have I been malingering in any way?* The very thought that he could have been made him sicker.

"I need a good man on the sweep oar and a third assessment as to whether this lead is a go," whispered Crozier. "And I need at least one man along who knows how to swim."

Peglar smiled at this even as his scrotum tightened at the thought of going into that black, cold water. The air temperature was below freezing, and the water, with all its salt content, would be as well.

Crozier clapped Peglar on the shoulder and moved on to talk to another "volunteer." It was obvious to the foretop captain that Crozier was carefully picking the men he wanted along on this scouting trip while keeping others, like First Mate Des Voeux, Second Mate Robert Thomas, Bosun's Mate and *Terror*'s disciplinarian Tom Johnson, and all the Marines, with him and alert.

In thirty minutes they had the boat ready to float.

It was a strangely equipped expedition within an expedition. They brought along a bag with some salt pork and biscuits, as well as some water bottles in case they became lost or otherwise extended the four-hour mission. Each of the nine men was handed an axe or pickaxe. If they should find a small berg overhanging and blocking the lead, or if a scrim of ice should block the way, they would try hacking their way through. Peglar knew that if a wider, thicker band of ice stopped them, they would portage the whaleboat to the next band of open water if they could. He hoped that he had the strength left to do his part in lifting, pulling, and shoving the heavy boat for a hundred yards or more.

Captain Crozier handed Lieutenant Little a two-barreled shotgun and a bag of cartridges. The items were stowed in the bow.

Should they somehow be stranded out there, Peglar knew, the heaps of supplies they kept onboard included a double-sized tent and a tarp for the floor. There were three three-man sleeping bags kept in the boat. But they did not plan to get lost out there.

The men crawled in and found their places as the ice fog curled around them. The previous winter, Crozier and the other officers and mates had discussed having Mr. Honey — and Mr. Weekes before his death on *Erebus* in March — raise the sides of all the boats. The small craft would have been better prepared for open seas that way. But in the end it was decided to keep the gunwales at their usual height to better facilitate river travel. Also to that end, Crozier had ordered all the oars cut down in length so that they might more easily be used as paddles on the river.

The remaining ton or so of bundled food and gear in the bottom of the boat made seating difficult; those six seamen at the oars had to prop their feet on the duffels and would be rowing or paddling with their knees as high as their heads, and as the man at the oar-sweep tiller, Peglar found himself sitting on a rope-wrapped bundle rather than on the stern bench — but everyone fit and there was room for Lieutenant Little and Mr. Reid to perch in the bow with their long pikes.

The men were eager to launch the boat. There was a chorus of "one, two, three" and several heave-hos, and the heavy whaleboat slid across the ice, the bow tipped and fell two feet into the black water, the oarsmen fended off nearby ice as Mr. Reid and Lieutenant Little crouched and gripped the gunwales, the men on the ice heaved again, oars found water, and they were moving away in the fog — the first boat from *Erebus* or *Terror* to feel liquid water under its hull in almost two years and eleven months.

A spontaneous cheer went up, followed by the more traditional three hip-hip-hurrahs.

Peglar steered the boat to the center of the narrow lead — never more than twenty feet across here, sometimes barely room for the shortened oars to find water on both sides — and by the time he glanced back over his shoulder, all the men on the ice were lost in the fog astern.

———

The next two hours were dreamlike. Peglar had steered a small boat through floe ice before — it had taken more than a week of poking into berg-ridden harbours and inlets before they'd found the right anchorage for the two ships at Beechey Island two autumns ago, and Peglar had been in command of one of those small boats for days — but that had not felt like this. The lead stayed narrow — never more than thirty feet wide and sometimes so tight they propelled the whaleboat by poling on the ice that scraped the sides rather than by rowing — and the narrow channel of open water would bend left and then right, but never quite so tightly that the boat could not make the turns. Tumbles of pressure-raised ice hid the view to either side and the fog continued to close on them, then open a bit, then close even more tightly. Sounds seemed to be muffled and amplified at the same time and the effect was unsettling; men found themselves whispering when they had to communicate.

Twice they encountered stretches where floating ice blocked the way or the lead itself was frozen over to the point that most of the men had to clamber out to shove floating ice ahead with pikes or to hack away at the frozen surface with pickaxes. Some of the men stayed on the ice on either side then, pulling at ropes tied to the bow and thwarts or grabbing the gunwales and shoving and pulling the screeching whaleboat through the narrow crevice. Each time the lead then widened enough that the men could clamber back in and shove, paddle, and row their way forward.

They had been creeping forward this way for almost their full allotment of two hours when suddenly the meandering lead narrowed. Ice scraped both sides, but they used the oars to pole as Peglar stood in the bow, his steering sweep useless. Then suddenly they popped out into what was by far the widest stretch of open water they had seen. As if confirming that all their troubles were behind them, the fog lifted so that they could see hundreds of yards.

They had either reached true open water or a massive lake in the ice. Sunlight streamed down from a hole in the clouds above and turned the seawater blue. A few low, flat icebergs, one the size of a respectable cricket pitch, floated ahead of them in the azure sea. The icebergs prismed the light and the weary men shielded their eyes from the painful glory of sunlight shimmering on snow, ice, and water.

The six men at the oars gave a loud, spontaneous cheer.

"Not yet, men," said Lieutenant Little. He was peering through his brass telescope, his foot up on the whaleboat's bow. "We don't know yet if this goes on . . . if there's a way out of this ice lake other than the way we came in. Let's make sure of that before we turn back."

"Oh, it goes on," shouted the seaman named Berry from his place at the oars. "I feel it in me bones. It's open water and fair breezes between here and Back's River, all right. We'll get the others, open our sails, and be there before supper tomorrow."

"I pray you're right, Alex," said Lieutenant Little. "But let's spend some time and sweat to make certain. I want to bring nothing but good news back to the rest of the men."

Mr. Reid, their ice master, pointed back at the lead from which they had emerged. "There are a dozen inlets here. We might have trouble finding the real lead when we come back unless we mark it now. Men, bring us back to the opening there. Mr. Peglar, why don't you take that extra pike and drive it into the snow and ice there at the edge where we can't miss it on our way back. It'll give us something to row toward."

"Aye," said Peglar.

With their return avenue marked, they rowed out into the open water. The large, flat iceberg was only a hundred yards or so from the opening to their inlet, and they rowed close to it on their way toward open water.

"We could camp on 'aton and have plenty of room left over," said Henry Sait, one of the *Terror* seamen at the oars.

"We don't want to camp," said Lieutenant Little from the bow. "We've had enough camping for a fucking lifetime. We want to *go home.*"

The men cheered and put their backs into it. Peglar at the sweep started a chantey and the men sang along, the first real singing they'd done in months.

———

It took them three hours — a full hour beyond the time they should have turned back — but they had to be sure.

The "open water" was an illusion: a lake in the ice a little more than a mile and a half long and a little more than two thirds of a mile wide. Dozens of apparent "leads" opened from the irregular southern, eastern, and northern ice edges of the lake, but they were all false starts, mere inlets.

At the southeastern terminus of the lake they tied up to the ice shelf, driving a pickaxe into the six-foot-thick ice and tying on to it, then cutting steps up the side as if it were a wharf; all the men clambered out and looked to the direction they'd hoped the open water continued.

Solid, flat white. Ice and snow and seracs. And the clouds were coming down again, swirling into a low fog. It was beginning to snow.

After Lieutenant Little looked in each direction, they boosted the smallest man, Berry, up onto the shoulders of the largest man there, thirty-six-year-old Billy Wentzall, and let Berry look through the glass. He boxed the compass with his search, telling Wentzall when to turn.

"Not so much as a fookin' penguin," he said. It was an old joke, referring to Captain Crozier's trip to the other pole. No one laughed.

"Do you see dark sky anywhere?" asked Lieutenant Little. "As one sees over open water? Or the tip of a larger berg?"

"Nay, sir. And the clouds is comin' closer."

Little nodded. "Let's head back, boys. Harry, you clamber down into the boat first and steady her, will you?"

No one said a word in their ninety-minute pull across the lake. The sunlight disappeared and fog blotted away the landscape again, but before long the cricket-pitch berg loomed out of the mist and showed them that they were going the correct direction.

"We're almost back to the lead," called Little from the bow. At times the fog was so thick that Peglar in the stern had trouble seeing the lieutenant. "Mr. Peglar, a little to port, please."

"Aye, sir."

The men at the oars did not even look up. To a man they seemed lost in the misery of their thoughts. Snow was pelting them again, but from the northwest now. At least the men at the oars had their backs to it.

When the fog did lift a bit, they were less than a hundred feet from the inlet.

"I see the pike," Mr. Reid said tonelessly. "A bit to starboard and you have it lined up nicely, Harry."

"Something's wrong," said Peglar.

"What do you mean?" called back the lieutenant. Some of the seamen looked up from their oars and frowned at Peglar. With their backs to the bow, they could not see ahead.

"Do you see that serac or big ice boulder near the pike I left at the mouth of the lead?" said Harry.

"Yes," said Lieutenant Little. "So?"

"It wasn't there when we came out," said Peglar.

"Back oars!" ordered Little, uselessly since the men had already ceased their rowing and were backstroking briskly, but the heavy whaleboat's momentum continued carrying it toward the ice.

The ice boulder turned.

GOODSIR

From the private diary of Dr. Harry D. S. Goodsir:

Tuesday, 18 July, 1848 —
Nine days ago, when our Captain sent Lieutenant Little and eight Men
ahead in a Whaleboat through the Lead in the Ice with orders to Return in
4 Hours, the rest of us Slept the best we could for a Pitiful Remnant of those 4
Hours. We spent more than 2 Hours loading the Sledges onto the Boats and
then, taking no Time to unpack Tents, we attempted to sleep in our Reindeer
Skin and Blanket bags atop waterproof tarps set down on the Ice next to the
Boats themselves. The days of the Midnight Sun were past now in early July
and we slept — or Tried to Sleep — through the few Hours of near
Darkness. We were very tired.
After the apportioned 4 Hours were up, First Mate Des Voeux woke the
men, but there was no Sign of Lieutenant Little. The Captain allowed most
to return to Sleep.
Two hours later, All were Wakened, and I tried to lend a Hand as best I
could — following the orders of Second Mate Couch as the Boats were made
ready to Launch. (As a Surgeon, of course, I always have some Fear of
injuring my Hands, although it is True that so far on this Voyage they have
Suffered every Insult short of Serious Frostbite and Self-Amputation.)
So it was that 7 Hours after Lieutenant Little, James Reid, Harry Peglar,
and the six seamen had set off on their Reconnaissance, 80 of us on the ice
prepared our own boats to follow. Due to movement of the Ice and lowering

*temperatures, the Lead had narrowed somewhat during the few hours
of Darkness and few more hours of Sleep, and getting the nine Boats
placed properly and launched correctly took some Skill. Eventually all of the
boats —the 3 whaleboats with Captain Crozier's in the lead (Second Mate
Couch's in second position with me aboard it) and then the 4 cutters
(commanded, respectively, by Second Mate Robert Thomas, Bosun John
Lane, Bosun's Mate Thomas Johnson, and Second Lieutenant George
Hodgson), followed by the two pinnaces under the command of Bosun's
Mate Samuel Brown and First Mate Charles Des Voeux (Des Voeux was
third in command of our overall Expedition now behind Captain Crozier
and Lieutenant Little and thus assigned the Responsibility of bringing up
the rear).*

*The weather had grown colder and there was Some light Snow falling,
but by and large the Fog had lifted to become a Low-Hanging layer of
Clouds moving only a Hundred Feet or so above the ice. While this allowed
us to see much farther than in the fog of the previous Day, the effect was
oppressive, as if all our Movements were taking place in some strange
Ballroom set in a deserted Arctic Mansion with a shattered White Marble
Floor underfoot and a Low Grey Ceiling with* trompe l'oeil *clouds just
above us.*

*At the moment the 9th and Final Boat was shoved into the water and its
Crew clambered in, there was a faint and Sad Attempt at a hurrah from the
men since it was the first time that most of these Deep Water Sailors had been
afloat in almost 2 Years, but the Cheer died aborning. Concern about
Lieutenant Little's Crew's Fate was too great to allow for any Sincere hurrahing.*

*For the first Hour and a half, the only sounds were the Groaning of the
Working Ice around us and the occasional Answering Groans of the Men
Working at the oars. But seated near the front of the second boat as I was,
sitting on the Thwart behind where Mr. Couch stood at the Bow, knowing that
I was Superfluous to all Locomotive Purposes, as much Dead Weight as the
poor comotose-but-still-breathing David Leys — whom the men had been
hauling in one of the pinnaces without Complaint now for more than 3 Months
and whom my new aide, former steward John Bridgens, duly fed and cleansed of
his own Filth every Evening in the medical tent we shared as if he was caring
for a Beloved but Paralysed Grandfather (ironic since Bridgens was in his early*

60's and comatose Leys was only 40) — my position thus situated allowed me to hear *Whispered Conversation between the Men at the Oars.*

Little and the Others must have got themselves Lost, *whispered a seaman named Coombs.*

There ain't no way that Lieutenant Edward Little got himself Lost, *shot back Charles Best.* He may be Stuck, but not Lost.

Stuck in what? *whispered Robert Ferrier at an adjoining Oar.* This Lead's open Now. It was open Yesterday.

Maybe Lieutenant Little and Mr. Reid found the way Open Ahead of them all the way to Back's River and just raised their Sail and went on, *whispered Tom McConvey from one Row back.* They're there already is my guess . . . eating Salmon that jumped into their boat and Trading beads for Blubber with the Natives.

No one said anything to this unlikely Suggestion. The mention of the Esquimaux had caused Quiet Consternation since the massacre of Lieutenant Irving and 8 of the Savages on 24 April last. I believe that most of the Men, however desperate for Salvation or Rescue from any Source, Feared rather than Hoped for another contact with the local Native People. Revenge, Some natural philosophers suggest and Sailors endorse, is one of the most Universal of human motivations.

Two and a half hours after leaving our campsite of the Previous Night, Captain Crozier's whaleboat broke out of the Narrow Lead into an Open Stretch of water. Men in the lead boat and my own boat let out happy shouts. As if left behind to Point the Way, a tall black ship's pike stood Upright, embedded in the Snow and Ice at the exit from this Lead. The Night's snow and freezing drizzle had painted the northwest side of the pike White.

These shouts also died Aborning as our Close Line of Boats pulled out into Open Water.

The water was Red here.

On shelves of ice to the Left and the Right of the Lead Opening, crimson streaks of what could only be Blood were smeared on the flat ice and down the Vertical Planes of the ice edges. The Sight sent a Shiver through me and I could see other men reacting with Open Mouths.

Easy now, men, *muttered Mr. Couch from the bow of our Boat.* This is just the sign of seals caught by the White Bears; we've seen such Seal Gore before in the Summers.

Captain Crozier in the lead boat was saying Similar Things to his Seamen.

A minute later we knew that these Crimson signs of Carnage were not the Residue of Seals butchered by White Bears.

Oh, Christ! *exclaimed Coombs at his oar. All the men quit rowing. The Three whaleboats, Four cutters, and Two pinnaces floated into a sort of circle in the choppy red-tinted water.*

The bow of Lieutenant Little's whaleboat rose vertically from the Sea. Its Name (one of the 5 boat Names not changed after Captain Crozier's Leviathan sermon in May) — The Lady J. Franklin *— was clearly Visible in black Paint. The boat had been Broken Apart about 4 feet Back from the bow so that only this Forward Section — the ragged End of shattered thwarts and splintered Hull just visible beneath the surface of the Dark and Icy Water — floated there.*

The men began Gathering other Flotsam as our 9 remaining Boats fanned out and rowed Slowly forward in a line: an Oar, more bits of Shattered Wood from gunwales and stern, a Steering Sweep, a Welsh wig, a bag that once held cartridges, a mitten, a bit of Waistcoat.

When Seaman Ferrier used a boat hook to pull in what looked to be a floating bit of Blue Peacoat, he suddenly cried out in Horror and almost dropped the long gaff.

A man's body floated there, his Headless Corpse still Garbed in sodden blue Wool, his Arms and Legs hanging down in the black water. The neck was a mere bit of severed Stump. His fingers, perhaps swollen by death and the cold water but looking strangely shortened into broad Stubs, seemed to move in the Currents, rising and falling on the Slight Swell like White Worms wriggling. It was almost as if, Voiceless, the Body was trying to tell us something via Sign Language.

I helped Ferrier and McConvey pull the Remains aboard. Fish or some Aquatic Predator had been nibbling at the Hands — the fingers were gone to the Second Joint — but the Extreme Cold had delayed the bloating and decomposition Processes.

Captain Crozier brought his whaleboat around until its bow was touching our side.

Who is it? *muttered a seaman.*

It's 'arry Peglar, *cried another.* I recognize the peajacket.

Harry Peglar didn't Wear no green Waistcoat, *interjected another.* Sammy Crispe did! *exclaimed a 4th Seaman.*

Silence! *bellowed Captain Crozier.* Dr. Goodsir, be so Good as to turn out our unfortunate Shipmate's pockets.

I did so. From the large pocket of the Wet Waistcoat, I pulled an almost-Empty tobacco Pouch tooled in red leather.

Ah, shite! *said Thomas Tadman, sitting next to Robert Ferrier on my Boat.* It's poor Mr. Reid.

And so it was. All the men then remembered that the Ice Master had been Wearing only his Peacoat and Green Waistcoat the previous evening, and All of Us had seen him refill his Pipe a thousand times from that faded red-leather pouch.

We looked to Captain Crozier as if he could explain what had Happened to our Shipmates, although in our Souls, we all knew.

Secure Mr. Reid's body under that Boat Cover, *ordered the Captain.* We'll search the area to see if there are any Survivors. Do not row or drift out of sight or shouting range.

Once again, the boats fanned out. Mr. Couch brought our boat back to the ice near the Inlet Opening, and we Rowed Slowly along the icy Shelf that rose about 4 Feet above the open water's Edge. We stopped at each smear of Blood on the surface of the Floe and on the Vertical Face, but there were no more bodies.

Oh, damn, *moaned 30-year-old Francis Pocock from his place at the Sweep in the Stern of our Boat.* You can see the bloody grooves of the man's Fingers and Nails in the Snow. The Thing must've dragged him backwards into the Water.

Batten down your Gob on such Talk! *called Mr. Couch. Holding his long pike easily in one hand like a True Whaleboat's Harpoon, he had one Booted Foot up on the whaleboat's Bow as he glowered back at the rowers. The men fell silent.*

There were three such Bloody Spots on the ice at this Nor'west End of the Open Water. The third One showed where Someone had been Eaten some 10 Feet back from the Edge of the ice. A few leg bones remained, as did some

*gnawed Ribs, a Torn Integument that might be Human Skin, and some
Strips of Torn Cloth, but no skull or identifiable features.*

Put me on the ice, Mr. Couch, *I said,* and I shall Examine the
Remains.

*I did so. Had this been ashore almost anywhere in the World but Here,
flies would have been buzzing around the Red Meat and Muscle left behind,
not to mention the strands of Entrails looking like a Gopher's Burrowing Ridge
beneath the thin Covering of last night's Snow, but here there was only the
Silence and the soft Wind from the northwest and the Groaning of the Ice.*

*I called back to the Boat — the seamen were averting their Faces — and
Confirmed that no identification was possible. Even the Few Remnants of
Torn Clothing could give no clue. There was no Head, no Boots, no Hands,
no Legs, not even a Torso other than the heavily gnawed Ribs, a Sinewed bit
of Spine, and half a Pelvis.*

Stay as you are, Mr. Goodsir, *called Couch.* I'm sending Mark and
Tadman to you with an emptied shot bag in which to put the poor
bugger's remains. Captain Crozier'll be wanting to give them a burial.

*It was Grim work, but done quickly. In the end, I directed the two
Grimacing Seamen to pack away only the Rib cage and bit of Pelvis into the
shot-bag Burial Shroud. The Vertebrae had frozen into the Floe Ice, and the
other remnants were too Grisly to bother about.*

*We had just shoved off from the ice and were Exploring along the South
rim of the Open Water when there came a shout from the North.*

Man found! *some Seaman cried.* And again, Man found!

*I believe that we all could feel our Hearts Pounding as Coombs,
McConvey, Ferrier and Tadman, and Mark and Johns pulled hard, and
Francis Pocock steered us to a cricket-pitch-sized patch of floating ice that had
drifted to the center of these Several Hundred Acres of Open Water amid the
Frozen Floes. We all wanted — we all needed — to find someone Alive
from Lieutenant Little's boat.*

It was not to be.

*Captain Crozier was already on the Ice and called me forward to the
Body lying there. I Confess that I felt slightly Put Upon, as if even the
Captain was unable to Certify Death unless I was forced to Inspect yet
another Undeniably Dead Corpse. I was very Tired.*

It was Harry Peglar lying there almost naked — his few remaining Clothes mere Underthings — Curled up on the Ice, Knees Raised almost to his Chin, Legs crossed at the Ankle as if his last energy had been spent trying to keep warm by pressing his body Tighter and Tighter, his Hands tucked under his Arms while he Hugged himself in what must have been an End in Violent Shivers.

His blue eyes were open and frozen. His flesh was also Blue and as Hard to the Touch as Carrera Marble.

He must've swum to the Floe, managed to Climb up, and froze to death here, *softly suggested Mr. Des Voeux.* The Thing from the Ice didn't catch or maul Harry.

Captain Crozier only nodded. I knew that the Captain had liked and much depended upon Harry Peglar. I also liked the Foretop Captain. Most of the men did.

Then I saw what Crozier was looking at. All around the Ice Floe in the recent snow — especially around the Corpse of Harry Peglar — were huge footprints, rather like a White Bear's with claws visibly indicated, only easily Three or Four times Larger than any white bear's paw prints.

The thing had Circled Harry many times. Watching as poor Mr. Peglar lay Shivering and Dying? Enjoying itself? Had Harry Peglar's last shivering Image on this Earth been of that White Monstrosity looming over him, its black, unblinking Eyes watching? Why had the thing not eaten our Friend?

The Beast was on two legs the entire time it was on the floe, *was all that Captain Crozier said.*

Other men from the Boats came forward with a piece of Canvas.

There was no exit from the Lake in the Ice except for the Rapidly Closing Lead from which we had come. Two circumnavigations of the Body of Open Water — five Boats rowing clockwise, four Boats rowing antiwiggens — offered the Discovery of only inlets, Ruptures in the Ice, and two more Bloody Swaths where it looked as if one of our reconnaissance whaleboats' crew pulled himself onto the ice and ran but was Cruelly Intercepted and pulled back. There were, thank God, shards of blue Wool but no more remains to be found.

It was early Afternoon by then, and to a Man I am sure that we had but

one Wish — to be Away from that accursed Place. But we had three
bodies of our Shipmates — or Parts of Same — and we felt the Need to
Dispose of them in an Honourable way. (Many of us assumed, I Believe,
and rightly so as it turned out, that these would be the last Formal Burial
Services the reduced Remnants of our Expedition would have the luxury
to perform.)

No useful Detritus was found floating in the ice lake save for an Expanse
of Soaked Canvas from one of the Holland Tents that had been aboard
Lieutenant Little's doomed whaleboat. This was used to Inter the body of our
friend Harry Peglar. The partial Skeletal remains I had investigated near the
Lead opening were left in the canvas Shot Bag. Mr. Reid's torso was sewn into
an extra blanket sleeping bag.

It is Custom at Burial at Sea for one or more pieces of Round Shot to be
placed at the Foot of the man being Committed to the Deep, ensuring that
the body will sink with Dignity rather than float Embarrassingly, but of
course we had no Round Shot this day. The seamen scrounged a Grapple
from the floating Bow of The Lady J. Franklin *and some metal from the last*
of the empty Goldner food tins to Weigh Down the various shrouds.

It took some time to pull the Nine Remaining Boats from the black water
and reset the cutters and pinnaces onto Sledges. The Assembly of these
Sledges and the lifting of the Boats onto them, with its concomitant Packing
and Unpacking of stores, drained the skeletal crewmen of the last of their
energy. Then the Seamen gathered near the edge of the Ice, standing in a
broad Crescent so as not to put too much Weight on any one part of the Ice
Shelf.

No one was in the mood for a Long Service and certainly not for the
Previously Appreciated Irony of Captain Crozier's fabled Book of
Leviathan, *so it was with some Surprise and not a small bit of Emotion that*
we listened to the Captain recite from Memory Psalm 90:

LORD, thou hast been our refuge: from one generation to another.

Before the mountains were brought forth, or ever the earth and
the world were made: thou art God from everlasting, and world without end.

Thou turnest man to destruction: again thou sayest, Come again,
ye children of men.

For a thousand years in thy sight are but as yesterday: seeing that is past as a watch in the night.

As soon as thou scatterest them, they are even as a sleep: and fade away suddenly like the grass.

In the morning it is green, and groweth up: but in the evening it is cut down, dried up, and withered.

For we consume away in thy displeasure: and are afraid at thy wrathful indignation.

Thou has set our misdeeds before thee: and our secret sins in the light of thy countenance.

For when thou art angry all our days are gone: we bring our years to an end, as it were a tale that is told.

The days of our age are three-score years and ten; and though men be strong that they come to fourscore years: yet is their strength then but labour and sorrow; so soon passeth it away, and we are gone.

But who regardeth the power of thy wrath: for even thereafter as a man feareth, so is thy displeasure.

So teach us to number our days: that we may apply our hearts unto wisdom.

Turn thee again, O Lord, at the last: and be gracious unto thy servants.

O satisfy us with thy mercy, and that soon: so shall we rejoice and be glad all the days of our life.

Comfort us again now after the time that thou has plagued us: and for the years wherein we have suffered adversity.

Shew thy servants thy work, and their children thy glory.

And the glorious Majesty of the Lord our God be upon us: prosper thou the work of our hands upon us, O prosper thou our handy-work.

Glory be to the Father, and to the Son, and to the Holy Ghost;

As it was in the beginning, is now, and ever shall be: world without end. Amen.

And all of us shivering survivors spake, Amen.

There was a Silence then. The snow blew softly against Us. The black water lapped with a Hungry Sound. The ice Groaned and Shifted slightly beneath our feet.

All of us, I believe, were Thinking that these words were a Eulogy and Farewell for each one of us. Up until this Day and the loss of Lieutenant Little's boat with all his men — including the irreplaceable Mr. Reid and the universally liked Mr. Peglar — I suspect that many of us still thought that we might Live. Now we knew that the odds of that had all but Disappeared.

The long awaited and Universally Cheered Open Water was a vicious Trap. The Ice will not give us up.

And the creature from the ice will not allow us to leave.

Bosun Johnson called, Ship's Company — OFF hats! *We tugged off our motley and filthy head coverings.*

Know that our Redeemer liveth, *said Captain Crozier in that Husky Rasp that now passed for his voice.* And that he shalt stand at the Latter Day upon the Earth. And though after our sin Worms destroy our bodies, yet in our flesh shall we see God: whom we shall see for ourselves, and our eyes shall behold, and not another.

O Lord, accept your Humble Servants here Ice Master James Reid, Captain of the Foretop Harry Peglar, and their Unknown Crewmate into your Kingdom, and with the two we can Name, please accept the Souls of Lieutenant Edward Little, Seaman Alexander Berry, Seaman Henry Sait, Seaman William Wentzall, Seaman Samuel Crispe, Seaman John Bates, and Seaman David Sims.

When our day comes to join Them, Lord, please allow us to join them in Thy Kingdom.

Hear our prayer, O Lord, for our Shipmates and Our Selves and for all Our Souls. And with thine ears consider our calling: hold not thy peace at our tears. Spare us a little, that we may recover our strength; before we also go hence and be no more.

Amen.

Amen, *we all whispered.*

The bosuns lifted the canvas Burial Shrouds and dropped them into the black water, where they Sank within Seconds. White bubbles rose like Final Efforts to Speak from our departed Shipmates, then the surface of the lake grew Black and Still again.

Sergeant Tozer and two Marines fired a single volley from their muskets.

I saw Captain Crozier stare at the black lake with an expression rich with suppressed Emotions. We will go now, he said Firmly to us, to all of us, to this slumped and sad and Mentally Defeated party. We can haul those sledges and boats a Mile before it is time to sleep. We will head Southeast toward the mouth of Back's River. The going will be Easier out here on the ice.

As it turned out, the going was much Harder on the ice. In the End, it was Impossible, not because of the usual Pressure Ridges and anticipated Difficulty transporting the boats, although that was Increasingly Problematic because of our Hunger, Illness, and Weakness, but because of the Breaking Ice and the Thing in the Water.

Moving in Relays as Usual but with Nine Fewer Men on our Expedition Muster that Long Arctic Evening of 10 July, we Progressed much less than a Mile before stopping to pitch tents on the Ice and to Sleep at last.

That sleep was Interrupted less than Two Hours later when the Ice suddenly began to crack and shift. The entire mass bobbed up and down. It was a most Disquieting Experience and we all scrambled to the exits of our Respective Tents and milled in some Confusion. Seamen began to strike the tents and make ready to pack the Boats until Captain Crozier, Mr. Couch, and First Mate Des Voeux shouted them into stillness. The officers pointed out that there were no signs of cracks in the ice near us, only this Movement.

After fifteen minutes or so of this, the ice Quieted until the Surface of the Frozen Sea under us once again felt as firm as Stone. We crawled back into our tents.

An hour later, the Bobbing and Cracking began again. Many of us repeated our earlier rush out into the Blowing Wind and dark, but the Braver Seamen stayed in their sleeping bags. Those of us who had Taken Fright crawled back into the Ill-Smelling and Crowded little tents — filled as they were with Snores, Sleeping Exhalations, Overlapping Bodies in Wet Bags, and the Ripeness of men who had not changed their Clothes in several months — with abashed countenances. Fortunately, it was too Dark for anyone to notice.

All that next day we struggled to haul the Boats forward to the Southeast across a Surface no more solid than a tightly drawn skin of India Rubber. Cracks were appearing — some showing six feet thickness of ice and more

*between the Surface and the Sea — but our sense of crossing a Plain of Ice
had disappeared, replaced with the Reality of moving from Floe to Floe on an
Undulating ocean of white.*

*I should Record here that on that Second Evening after we left the
Enclosed Ice Lake, I was catching up with my Duty of going through the
Dead Men's personal belongings, most of which had been Left Behind in our
General Stores when Lieutenant Little's reconnaissance group left in their
whaleboat, and had come to Captain of the Foretop Peglar's small pack
containing a few scraps of Clothes, some Letters, a few personal items such as
a Horn Comb, and several Books, when my Assistant, John Bridgens, said,*
Might I have a few of those things, Dr. Goodsir?

*I was surprised. Bridgens was indicating the Comb and a thick Leather
Notebook.*

*I had looked into the Notebook already. Peglar had written in a crude sort
of Code — spelling words in Reverse, Capitalizing the last letter of the last
word in each Sentence as if it were the first — but while the Summary of the
last Year of our Expedition might have held some Interest for a Relative, Both
the foretop captain's handwriting and sentence Structure, not to mention his
spelling, had grown more Laboured and Crude in the Months immediately
before and after our Abandoning of the Ships until it had all but disinte-*
grated. *One entry read,* O Death whare is thy sting, the grave at
Comfort Cove for who has any doubt how . . . *[an illegible line here
where the book had been Damaged by water]* . . . the dyer sad. . . .

*On the back side of that sheet, I had noticed where Peglar had drawn a shaky
circle and in that circle had written,* the terror camp clear. *The date had been
illegible, but it must have been around 25 April. Another page nearby included
such fragments as* Has we have got some very hard ground to heave . . .
we shall want some grog to wet houer . . . issel . . . all my art Tom for I
do think . . . time . . . I cloze should lay and . . . the 21st night a gread.

*I had Assumed upon Seeing this that Peglar had recorded that Entry on
the Evening of 21 April when Captain Crozier had told the Assembled Crews
of* Terror *and* Erebus *that the last of them would be Abandoning Ship the
next morning.*

*These were, in other Words, the scribblings of a semiliterate Man and no
Proud Reflection on the learning or Skill of Harry Peglar.*

Why do you want these? *I asked Bridgens.* Was Peglar a friend of yours?

Aye, Doctor.

You require a Comb? *The old Steward was almost bald.*

No, Doctor, just a Remembrance of the man. That and his Journal will serve.

Very strange, I thought, since everyone was lightening their Loads at this point, not adding Heavy Books to what they had to Haul.

But I gave Bridgens the Comb and Journal. No one needed Peglar's remaining Shirt or Socks or Extra Wool Trousers or Bible, so I left them on the Pile of discarded items the next morning. All in all, the Abandoned Final Possessions of Peglar, Little, Reid, Berry, Crispe, Bates, Sims, Wentzall, and Sait made for a sad little Cairn of Mortality.

That next morning, 12 July, we started coming Across more Bloody Patches in the Ice. At first the Men were Terrified that these were More signs of our Mates, but Captain Crozier led us to the Great Stained Areas and showed us that in the Centre of the Great Starbust of Crimson was the Carcass of a White Bear. They were all Murdered Polar White Bears, these Bloodstained areas, often with little More than a shattered Head, Great Bloodied White Pelt, Cracked Bones, and Paws left behind.

At first the men were Reassured. Then, of course, the Obvious Question set in — what was killing these Huge Predators just Hours before our Arrival?

The answer was Obvious.

But why was it slaughtering the White Bears? That answer was also Obvious: to deprive us of any possible Food Source.

By 16 July, the men seemed Incapable of going farther. In an 18-hour Day of Incessant Pulling, we would cover less than a Mile across the Ice. Often we could see the previous night's Pile of Discarded Clothing and Gear when we camped the Next Evening. We had found more Slaughtered White Bears. Morale was so low that if we had taken a Vote that Week, the Majority might have voted to Give Up, Lie Down, and Die.

That night of 16 July, as Others Slept and only One Man stood Watch, Captain Crozier asked me to come to his Tent. He now slept in the same Tent with Charles Des Voeux; his purser, Charles Hamilton Osmer (who was showing *signs of pneumonia); William Bell (*Erebus's *quartermaster); and Phillip Reddington, Sir John's and Captain Fitzjames's former captain of the fo'c'sle.*

The captain nodded and everyone except First Mate Des Voeux and Mr. Osmer left the tent to give us Privacy.

Dr. Goodsir, *began the Captain,* I need your advice.

I Nodded and Listened.

We have adequate Clothing and Shelter, *said Captain Crozier.* The extra boots I Had the Men Haul along in the Supply Pinnaces have saved Many Feet from Amputation.

I agree, Sir, I said, although I knew this was not the Item upon which he was asking for Advice.

Tomorrow morning I am going to tell the Men that we shall be Leaving One of the Whaleboats and two Cutters and one Pinnace behind and will be Continuing on only with the Five Remaining Boats, *said Captain Crozier.* Those two whaleboats, two cutters, and final pinnace are in the Best Condition and should suffice for Open Water, should we Encounter Any before the Mouth of Back's River, since our Stores are so Reduced.

The Men will be Heartily Glad to hear this, Captain, *I said. I certainly was. Since I now helped Man-haul the boats, the Knowledge that the days of Accursed Relaying were over quite Literally took some of the Ache from my shoulders and back.*

What I need to Know, Dr. Goodsir, *continued the Captain, his voice an Exhausted Rasp, his face Solemn,* is whether I can cut back on the Men's Rations. Or rather, when we *Do* cut back, will the Men still be Capable of hauling the Sledges? I need your Professional Opinion, Doctor.

I looked at the floor of the Tent. One of Mr. Diggle's Hoosh Pans — or perhaps Mr. Wall's Portable Contraption for Heating Tea back when we had bottles of Ether left for the Spirit Stoves — had burned a Round Hole there.

Captain, Mr. Des Voeux, *I said finally, knowing that I would be Stating the Obvious to them,* the men do not have enough Nourishment now to meet the Requirements of their Daily Labours. *I took a breath.*

Everything they eat is Cold. The last of the Canned Foods was

Consumed many Weeks ago. The Spirit Stoves and Spirit Lamps was left on the Ice with the Last Empty Bottle of Pyroligneous Ether.

This evening at Supper each man will get one Ship's Biscuit, a sliver of Cold Salt Pork, one Ounce of chocolate, a Palm Full of Tea, less than a Spoonful of Sugar, and his Daily Tablespoon of Rum.

And his Bit of Tobacco that we'd hoarded for them, *added Mr. Osmer.*

I nodded. Yes, and his bit of tobacco. And they do love their tobacco. That was a brilliant stroke to keep some hidden in the Stores. But no, Captain, I cannot say that the Men can get by on less than the Current Inadequate Amount of Food.

They must, *said Captain Crozier.* We shall be out of the salt pork in six days. Out of the Rum in ten.

Mr. Des Voeux cleared his throat. Everything depends upon us Finding and Shooting more seals on the Floes.

So far, I knew — everyone in the Tent knew, everyone on the Expedition knew — we had shot and Enjoyed precisely 2 Seals since leaving Comfort Cove two Months earlier.

I am thinking, *said Captain Crozier,* that heading North again for the Shore of King William Land — perhaps Three Days' pull, perhaps Four — might be Best. It is possible to eat Moss and Rock Tripe. I am told that the proper Varieties cook up into an Almost Palatable soup. If one can find the proper Varieties of Moss and Rock Tripe.

Sir John Franklin, *I thought in my weariness.* The Man Who Ate His Shoes. *My older Brother had told me That Story in the Months before our Departure. Sir John would have known, from Pathetic Experience, precisely which Moss and Rock Tripe to choose.*

The Men will be happy to get off the Ice, Captain, *was all that I could Say.* And they will be Overjoyed to Hear that we shall be Hauling Fewer boats.

Thank you, Doctor, *said Captain Crozier.* That is all.

I bobbed my head in a pathetic Sort of Salute, left, made the rounds of the worst Scurvy victims in their Tents — we no Longer Have a Sick Bay Tent, of course, and Bridgens and I nightly go from tent to tent to counsel and Dose our Patients — and then I staggered back to my own Tent (shared with Bridgens, the unconscious Davy Leys, the dying Engineer, Thompson, and the seriously ill carpenter, Mr. Honey), and fell Instantly Asleep.

That was the night that the Ice opened and swallowed up the Holland Tent in which Slept our Five Marines — Sergeant Tozer, Corporal Hedges, Private Wilkes, Private Hammond, and Private Daly.

Only Wilkes got out of the Tent before it Sank into the Wine-Dark Sea, and he was pulled from the Ice Crevice seconds before it Closed with a Deafening Crash.

But Wilkes was too Chilled, too Ill, and too Terrified to Recover, even when Bridgens and I wrapped him in the Last Dry Clothes in our Reserve and put him Between us in our Sleeping Bag. He died just before real Sunrise.

His Body was left behind on the Ice the next morning along with more Clothes and the Four Discarded Boats and their Sledges.

There was no Burial Service for him or the other Marines.

There was no Hurrah when the Captain announced that the four Sledges and Boats would no longer be hauled.

We turned North toward Land just over the Horizon. No retreat from Moscow ever felt such a sense of Defeat.

Three Hours Later, the Ice Cracked Again, and we were faced with Leads and Lakes to the North which were too small to justify launching the boats yet too large to allow us to haul the boats and sledges across.

49

CROZIER

When Crozier slept — even for a few minutes — the dreams returned. The two skeletons in the open boat. The intolerable American girls snapping toe joints to simulate a spirit rapping at a table in a darkened room. The American doctor posturing as a polar explorer, a pudgy man dressed in an Esquimaux parka and wearing heavy makeup on an overbright gaslit stage. Then the two skeletons in an open boat again. The night always ending with the dream that disturbed Crozier the most.

He is a boy and is with his Memo Moira in a vast Catholic cathedral. Francis is naked. Memo pushes him toward the altar rail, but he is afraid to go forward. The cathedral is cold; the marble floor under young Francis's bare feet is cold; there is ice on the white wooden pews.

Kneeling at the altar rail, young Francis Crozier can feel Memo Moira watching approvingly from somewhere behind him, but he is too frightened to turn his head. Something is coming.

The priest seems to rise up from some trapdoor set into the marble floor on the opposite side of the altar railing. The man is too large — far too large — and his vestments are white and dripping water. Smelling of blood and sweat and something ranker, he towers over little Francis Crozier.

Francis closes his eyes and, as Memo taught him while he knelt on the thin rug of her parlour, extends his tongue to receive the Eucharist. As important as this Sacrament is, as necessary as he knows it must be, Francis is terrifed to receive the Host. He knows that his life will never be the same after receiving the Papist Eucharist. And he also knows that his life will end if he does not receive it.

The priest looms closer and leans toward him . . .

Crozier awoke in the belly of the whaleboat. As always when he came up out of these dreams, even if he had caught only a few minutes' sleep, his heart was pounding and his mouth was dry from fear. And he was shaking hard, but from cold more than from fear or the memory of fear.

The ice had broken up in the part of the strait or gulf they were in on the 17th and 18th of July, and for four days after that, Crozier had kept the men together on the large ice floe where they had stopped — the cutters and pinnace removed from their sledges, all five of the boats fully loaded except for their tents and sleeping bags, and rigged for open water.

Each night the rocking of their large floe and the cracking and fracturing of ice sent them scurrying from their tents, half awake, sure that the sea was opening up beneath them and ready to swallow them as it had Sergeant Tozer and his men. Each night the gunshot explosions of the ice cracking eventually abated, the wild rocking fell into a more regular rhythm of swells, and they crawled back into their tents.

It was warmer, some days rising almost to the freezing point — these few weeks of late July would almost certainly be the only hint of summer this second frozen-in arctic year would see — but the men were colder and more miserable than ever. Some days it actually rained. When it was too cold to rain, ice crystals in the foggy air soaked their wool clothing since it was too warm now to wear waterproof winter slops over their peacoats and greatcoats. Sweat from their man-hauling soaked their filthy underwear, filthy shirts and socks, and their ragged, ice-crusted trousers; despite their almost-depleted stores, the five remaining boats were heavier than the ten boats they'd hauled before ever had been, for in addition to the eating, breathing, but still comatosely staring Davey Leys, more sick men had to be hauled along every day. Dr. Goodsir reported to Crozier each day that more feet — always soaked and in wet socks in spite of all the extra boots Crozier had thought to bring along — turned rotten, more toes and heels turned black, and more feet had grown gangrenous and were now in need of amputation.

The Holland tents were soaked and never dried. The sleeping bags they cracked open in the late evening and crawled into as darkness fell were soaked and frozen inside and out and never dried. When the men awoke in the morning after a few stolen minutes of fitful sleep — no amount of shivering could make one warmer — the inside of the circular and pyramid tents were lined with thirty pounds of hoarfrost that fell and dripped on the men's heads, shoulders, and faces as they tried to drink the tiny bit of lukewarm tea that was brought around to the tents each morning by Captain Crozier, Mr. Des Voeux, and Mr. Couch — a strange reversal of commanders as morning stewards that Crozier had instigated during their first week on the ice and which the men now took for granted.

Mr. Wall, *Erebus*'s cook, was sick with something like consumption and lay curled into the bottom of one of the cutters most of the time, but Mr. Diggle remained the same energetic, obscene, efficient, bellowing, and somehow reassuring figure he had been for three years at his post near the huge Frazer's Patent Stove aboard HMS *Terror*. Now, with the ether fuel depleted and the spirit stoves and heavy whaleboat coal stoves abandoned, Mr. Diggle's job was to portion out twice a day the small bit of cold salt pork and other victuals remaining, always under Mr. Osmer's and another officer's watchful supervision. But always the optimist, Diggle had cobbled together a crude seal-oil stove and cooking pot which he was ready to light if and when they shot more seals.

Every day, Crozier sent out hunting parties to find those seals for Mr. Diggle's pot, but there were almost none to be seen and those few sighted slipped back into their open leads or tiny holes before the hunters succeeded in shooting them. Several times, so the men on the hunting parties reported, the slippery black ring seals had been hit by buckshot or even a musket ball or rifle bullet but managed to slide back into the black water and dive out of reach before they died, leaving only a trail of blood on the ice. Sometimes the hunters knelt on the ice to lap at the blood.

Crozier had been in summer arctic waters many times before and knew that by mid-July the water and opening floes should be teeming with life: huge walruses sunning themselves on ice floes and flopping ponderously along the water's edge, their barks more a series of belches than barks; a proliferation of seals catapulting in and out of the water like children playing and bellying their way comically across the ice; beluga whales and narwhals spouting and rolling and submerging in the open leads, filling the air with their fishy breaths; female white bears swimming in the black water with their ungainly cubs and stalking seals on floes, shaking the water out of their strange fur as they pulled themselves from the ocean to the ice, avoiding the larger and more dangerous males, which would eat the cubs and the sow as well if their bellies were empty; finally, seabirds flying overhead in such profusion as to almost darken the blue arctic summer sky, birds on shore, on floes, and lining the irregular tops of icebergs like musical notes on a score, while more terns and gulls and gyrfalcons skimmed the water everywhere.

This summer, for the second year in a row, almost nothing living moved across the ice — only Crozier's diminished and diminishing men gasping in their man-hauling halters and their relentless pursuer, always briefly and partially glimpsed, always out of rifle or shotgun range. A few times in the evening, the men heard the yip of arctic foxes and frequently found their dainty tracks in the snow, but none ever seemed to make itself visible to the hunters. When the men did see or hear whales, they were always many floes and small leads over, too far to reach even by frenzied, careless running — men throwing themselves from rocking floe to rocking floe before the sea mammals casually breached and dove and disappeared again.

Crozier had no idea if they could kill a narwhal or beluga with the few small arms they carried, but he thought they could — a few rifle bullets to the brain should kill anything short of the Beast that stalked them (which the seamen had long since decided was no beast at all, but a wrathful God out of the captain's *Book of Leviathan*) — and if they somehow had the strength to drag a whale onto the ice and render it down, the oil would power Mr. Diggle's stove for weeks or months and they would eat blubber and fresh meat until they all burst.

What Crozier most wanted to do was to kill the thing itself. Unlike the majority of his men, he believed it was mortal — an animal, nothing more. Smarter, perhaps, than even the frighteningly intelligent white bear, but still a beast.

If he could kill the thing, Crozier knew, the mere fact of its death —

the pleasure of revenge for so many deaths, even if the rest of the expedition still were to die later from starvation and scurvy — would temporarily lift the morale of the survivors more than discovering twenty gallons of untapped rum.

The beast had not bothered them — not killed any of them — since the ice-enclosed lake where Lieutenant Little and his men had died. Each of the hunting parties the captain sent out had standing orders to return immediately should they find the thing's tracks in the snow; Crozier intended to take every man who could walk and every weapon that could fire out to stalk the beast. If he had to, he would use men banging pots and pans and shouting to flush the thing out, as if it were a tiger in the high grass of India being brought to bay by beaters.

But Crozier knew this would work no better than the late Sir John's bear blind. What they really needed to bring the thing closer was bait. Crozier had no doubt whatsoever that it was still keeping pace with them, moving in closer during the increasing hours of darkness, hiding wherever it hid, perhaps under the ice, during the day, and that it would come even closer if they could bait it in. But they had no fresh meat, and if they had even a pound of fresh kill, the men would devour it, not use it as bait to catch the thing.

Still, Crozier thought, while remembering the impossible great size and mass of the monstrous thing on the ice, there was more than a ton of meat and muscle there, perhaps several tons, since the larger male white bears weighed up to 1,500 pounds and the thing made its white bear cousins look like hunting dogs next to a large man in comparison. So they would eat well for many weeks if they *did* manage to murder their murderer. And with every bite, Crozier knew, even eating the thing-flesh as they were the salt pork while on the march, there would be the pleasure of revenge, even if it had to be a dish best served cold.

If it would work, Francis Crozier knew he would set himself out onto the ice as bait. *If it would work.* If it would save and feed even a few of his men, Crozier would offer himself to the beast as bait and hope that his men, who had proved themselves atrocious shots even before the last of *Terror*'s Marines died in the cold water, would be able to shoot the monster often enough, if not accurately enough, to bring it down, whether the Crozier bait survived or not.

With the thought of the Marines came, unbidden, the memory of Private Henry Wilkes's body left behind in one of the abandoned boats a week earlier. There had been no gathering of the men for Wilkes's nonburial, only Crozier, Des Voeux, and a few of the Marine's closer friends saying a few words over the body before dawn.

We should have used Wilkes's body for bait, thought Crozier as he lay in the bottom of the rocking whaleboat while the other men slept in heaped piles around him.

Then he realized — and not for the first time — that they had fresher bait with them. David Leys had been nothing but a burden for eight months, ever since the night in December of last year when the thing had given chase to the late Ice Master Blanky. Leys staring at nothing since that night, unresponsive, useless, hauled in the boat like a hundred and thirty pounds of soiled laundry for almost four months now, nonetheless managed to slurp down his salt-pork broth and rum ration every afternoon and to swallow his spoonful of tea and sugar each morning.

It was to the men's credit that none of them — not even the whispering Hickey or Aylmore — had suggested leaving Leys behind, or any of the other sick men who currently could not walk. But everyone must have had the same thought . . .

Eat them.

Eat Leys first, then the others when they die.

Francis Crozier was so hungry that he could imagine eating human flesh. He would not kill a man in order to devour him — not yet — but once dead, why should all that meat be left behind to rot in the arctic summer sun? Or worse yet, left behind to be eaten by the thing that was after them?

As a new lieutenant in his twenties, Crozier had heard — as all sailing men now heard sooner or later, usually as ship's boys before the mast — the true story of Captain Pollard in the U.S. brig *Essex* back in 1820.

Essex had been stove in and sunk, so the few survivors later reported, by an 85-foot sperm whale. The brig went down in one of the emptiest parts of the Pacific and the entire 20-man crew had been out in their boats hunting whales at the time and returned to find their ship sinking fast. Retrieving a few tools, some navigation instruments, and one pistol from the ship, the survivors set off in three whale-boats. Their only provisions were two live turtles they'd captured in the Galapagos, two casks of ship's biscuits, and six casks of fresh water.

Then they steered the whaleboats for South America.

First, of course, they killed and ate the large turtles, drinking the blood when the meat was gone. Then they managed to capture some hapless flying fish who leapt into the boat by accident; while the men had contrived to cook the turtle meat, after a fashion, the fish they ate raw. Then they dived into the sea, scraped the barnacles from the hulls of their three open boats, and ate those.

Miraculously, the boats encountered Henderson Island — one of those few specks on the endless blue that is the Pacific Ocean. For four days the twenty men captured crabs and stalked gulls and their eggs. But Captain Pollard knew that there were not enough crabs, gulls, or gull eggs on the island to sustain twenty men for more than another few weeks, so seventeen of the twenty voted to take to the boats again. They launched the boats and waved good-bye to their three remaining companions on 27 December, 1820.

By 28 January, the three boats had been separated from one another by storm, and Captain Pollard's whaleboat sailed eastward alone under the endless sky. Their rations now consisted of one and a half ounces of ship's biscuit per man a day for the five men in the whaleboat. By not so great a coincidence, this was precisely the reduced ration that Crozier had just secretly discussed with Dr. Goodsir and First Mate Des Voeux for when the last of the salt pork ran out in a few days.

The bit of biscuit and few sips of water had kept Pollard's men — his nephew Owen Coffin, a freed black man named Barzillai Ray, and two seamen — alive for nine weeks.

They were still more than 1,600 miles from land when the last of the biscuits ran out at the same time as the last of the water was drunk. Crozier had figured that if the biscuits lasted his men another month, they would still be more than 800 miles from human habitation in winter even if they reached the mouth of Back's River.

Pollard had no conveniently recently deceased men aboard his boat, so they drew straws. Pollard's young nephew Owen Coffin drew the short straw. Then they drew straws again to see who would do the deed. Charles Ramsdell drew the short straw this time.

The boy wished the other men a tremulous good-bye (Crozier always remembered his scrotum-tightening sense of horror the first time he heard this part of the story while on watch with an older man high in the mizzen of a warship far off Argentina, the old seaman terrifying Lieutenant Crozier by saying good-bye in a trembling boy's voice), and then young Coffin had laid his head on the gunwale and closed his eyes.

Captain Pollard, as he later testified in his own words, had given Ramsdell his pistol and turned his face away.

Ramsdell shot the boy in the back of the head.

The five others, including Captain Pollard, the boy's uncle, first drank the blood while it was warm. Although salty, it was — unlike the endless sea around them — drinkable.

Then they sliced the boy's flesh from his bones and ate it raw.

Then they broke open Owen Coffin's bones and sucked out the marrow to the last shred.

The cabin boy's corpse had sustained them for thirteen days, and just when they were considering drawing lots again, the black man — Barzillai Ray — died of thirst and exhaustion. Again the draining, drinking, slicing, cracking, and sucking of marrow sustained them until they were rescued by the whaler *Dauphin* on 23 February, 1821.

Francis Crozier never met Captain Pollard but he had followed his career. The unlucky American had retained his rank and gone to sea only once more — and once more was shipwrecked. After being rescued the second time, he was never again entrusted with command of a ship. The last Crozier heard, only a few months before Sir John's expedition sailed three years earlier in 1845, Captain Pollard was living as a town watchman in Nantucket and was universally shunned by both townspeople and whalers there. It was said that Pollard had aged prematurely, spoke aloud to himself and his long-dead nephew, and hid biscuits and salt pork in the rafters of his home.

Crozier knew that his people would have to make a decision about eating their own dead within the next few weeks, if not the next few days.

The men were approaching the point where they were too few and those few too weak to man-haul boats, but the four-day rest on the ice floe from the 18th to the 22nd of July had not renewed their energy. Crozier, Des Voeux, and Couch — young Lieutenant Hodgson, while technically the second in command, was given no authority by the captain these days — rousted men and ordered them out hunting or repairing sledge runners or caulking and rerepairing the boats rather than let them lie in their frozen sleeping bags in their dripping tents all day — but essentially all they could do was sit on their connected floes for days since too many tiny leads, fissures, small areas of open water, and patches of thin and rotten ice surrounded them to allow any progress south or east or north.

Crozier refused to turn back west and northwest.

But the floes were not drifting in the direction they wanted to go — southeast toward the mouth of Back's Great Fish River. They merely milled and circled upon themselves as the pack holding *Erebus* and *Terror* had for two long winters.

Finally, on the afternoon of Saturday, 22 July, their own floe began cracking up enough that Crozier ordered everyone into the boats.

For six days now they had floated, tethered together by lines, in patches and leads too short or small to row or sail in. Crozier had the one sextant left to them (he had left the heavier theodolite behind), and while others slept he took the best readings he could during the occasional short break in cloud cover. He reckoned their position to be about eighty-five miles northwest of the mouth of Back's River.

Expecting to see a narrow isthmus ahead of them any day now — the presumed peninsula connecting the bulb of King William Land to the previously mapped Adelaide Peninsula — Crozier had awakened in the boat at sunrise on the morning of Wednesday the 26th of July to find the air colder, the sky blue and cloudless, and glimpses of land darkening the sky more than fifteen miles away to both the north and south.

Calling the five boats together later, Crozier stood in the bow of his lead whaleboat and shouted, "Men, King William Land is *King William Island.* I'm certain now that there's sea ahead all the way east and south to Back's River, but I'll bet my last quid that there's no land connecting the cape you see far to the southwest there and the one you see far to the northeast. We're in a strait. And since we have to be north of the Adelaide Peninsula, we've completed the goal of the Sir John Franklin Expedition. *This is the North-West Passage.* By God, you've done it."

There was a weak cheer followed by some coughing.

If the boats and floes had been drifting south, weeks of man-hauling or sailing work might have been done for them. But the leads and areas of open water in which they floated continued to crack open only toward the north.

Life in the boats was as miserable as life on the floes in the tents had been. The men were crowded too close together. Even with boards on thwarts offering a second level for sleeping on those whaleboats and cutters with their sides built up by Mr. Honey (the disassembled sledges also served as a crossed-T deck amidships on the crowded cutters and pinnace), wet-wooled bodies were pressed against wet-wooled bodies both day and night. The men had to hang out over the gunwales to shit — an event that was becoming less and less necessary, even for the men with serious scurvy, as the food and water grew less — but while all the men had lost all vestiges of modesty, a sudden wave often soaked bare skin and lowered trousers, leading to curses, boils, and longer nights of shivering misery.

On the morning of Friday, 28 July, 1848, the lookout on Crozier's boat — the smallest man on each boat was sent up the short raised mast with a spyglass — spied a maze of leads opening all the way to a point of land to the northwest, perhaps three miles away.

The able-bodied men in the five boats pulled — and when necessary, polled between narrowing ice ledges, the healthiest men at the bow hacking away with pickaxes and fending off with pikes — for eighteen hours.

They landed on a rocky shingle, in a darkness broken only by short periods of moonlight when the returning clouds parted, a little after eleven o'clock that night.

The men were far too exhausted to dismount the sledges and lift the cutters and pinnaces onto them. They were too tired to unpack their soaked Holland tents and sleeping bags.

They fell onto the rough stones where they had ceased their dragging of heavy boats across the shore ice and rocks made slippery by high tide. They slept in clumps, kept alive only by their crewmates' failing body warmth.

Crozier did not even assign a watch. If the thing wanted them tonight, it could have them. But before he slept, he spent an hour trying to get a good sighting with his sextant and to work it out with the navigation tables and maps he still carried with him.

As best he could reckon, they had been on the ice for twenty-five days and man-hauled and drifted and rowed a total of forty-six miles to the east-southeast. They were back on King William Land somewhere north of the bulk of the Adelaide Peninsula and now even farther from the mouth of Back's River than they had been two days earlier — about thirty-five miles northwest of the inlet across the unnamed strait they'd been unable to cross. If they even crossed this strait, they would be more than sixty miles up the inlet from the mouth of the river, a total of more than nine hundred miles from Great Slave Lake and their salvation.

Crozier carefully stowed his sextant in his wooden case and set the case away in its oilskin waterproof bag, found a sodden blanket from the whaleboat, and threw it down on stones next to Des Voeux and three sleeping men. He was asleep within seconds.

He dreamt of Memo Moira shoving him forward toward an altar rail and of the waiting priest in dripping vestments.

In his sleep, as the men snored in the moonlight of this unknown shore, Crozier closed his eyes and extended his tongue to receive the Body of Christ.

50

BRIDGENS

> *River Camp*
> *29 July, 1848*

John Bridgens had always — secretly — compared the different parts of his life to the various pieces of literature that had formed his life.

In his boyhood and student years, he from time to time thought of himself as different characters from Boccaccio's *Decameron* or from Chaucer's ribald *Canterbury Tales* — and not all of his chosen characters were heroic by any means. (His attitude toward the world for some years was, *kiss my arse*.)

In his twenties, John Bridgens most identified with Hamlet. The strangely aging Prince of Denmark — Bridgens was quite sure that the boy Hamlet had magically aged over a few theatrical weeks to a man who was, at the very least, in his thirties by Act V — had been suspended between thought and deed, between motive and action, frozen by a consciousness so astute and unrelenting that it made him *think about everything, even thought itself*. The young Bridgens had been a victim of such consciousness and, like Hamlet, had frequently considered that most essential of questions — *to continue or not to continue?* (Bridgens's tutor at the time, an elegant don in exile from Oxford who was the first unabashed sodomite the young would-be scholar had ever encountered, had disdainfully taught him that the famous "to be, or not to be" soliloquy was not in any way a discussion of suicide, but Bridgens knew better. *Thus doth conscience make cowards of us all* had spoken directly to the boy-man soul of John Bridgens, miserable with the state of his existence and his unnatural desires, miserable when pretending to be something he was not, miserable when pretending and miserable when not pretending, and, most centrally, miserable that he could only *think about* ending his own life because the fear that thought itself might continue on the other side of this mortal veil, "perchance to dream," kept him from acting even toward quick, decisive, cold-blooded self-murder.)

Luckily, even as a young man not yet become himself, John Bridgens had two things besides indecision that kept him from self-destruction — books and a sense of irony.

In his middle years, Bridgens most thought of himself as Odysseus. It was not the wandering the world alone that made the comparison apt for the would-be scholar turned secondary officers' steward but rather Homer's description of the world-weary traveler — the Greek word meaning "crafty" or "guileful" by which Odysseus' contemporaries identified him (and by which some, such as Achilles, chose to insult him). Bridgens did not use his craft to manipulate others, or rarely did, but used it more like one of the round leather-and-wood or prouder metal shields behind which Homeric heroes sheltered while under violent attack by spear and lance.

He used his craft to become and to stay invisible.

Once, some years ago, during the five-year voyage on the HMS *Beagle* during which he had come to know Harry Peglar, Bridgens mentioned his Odysseus analogy — suggesting that all the men on such a trip were modern-day Ulysseses to some extent or another — to the natural philosopher aboard (the two played chess frequently in Mr. Darwin's tiny cabin), and the young bird expert with the sad eyes and sharp mind had looked penetratingly at the steward and said, "But how is it that I doubt you have a Penelope waiting at home, Mr. Bridgens?"

The steward had been more circumspect after that. He had learned — as Odysseus had learned after a certain number of years of his wanderings — that his guile was no match for the world and that hubris would always be punished by the gods.

In these last days, John Bridgens felt that the literary character with whom he had most in common — in outlook, in feeling, in memory, in future, in sadness — was King Lear.

And it was time for the final act.

———

They had stayed two days at the mouth of the river that drained into the unnamed strait south of King William Land, now known to be King William Island. The river here, in late July, was running freely in places and allowed them to fill all their water casks, but no one had seen or caught a fish from it. No animals seemed interested in coming down to drink from it . . . not so much as a white arctic fox. The best one could say about this campsite was that the slight indentation of the river valley kept them out of the worst of the wind and afforded them some peace of mind during the lightning storms that raged every night.

Both mornings at this camp, the men — hopefully, prayerfully — laid their tents, sleeping bags, and whatever clothing they could spare out on rocks to dry in the sunlight. There came, of course, no more sunlight. Several times it drizzled. The only day with blue sky they had seen in the past month and a half had been their last day in the boats and after that day, most of the men had to see Dr. Goodsir for their sunburns.

Goodsir — as Bridgens knew well, being his assistant — had very few medicines left in the box he'd put together from the supplies of his three dead colleagues as well as his own. There were still some purgatives in the good doctor's arsenal (mostly castor oil and tincture of jalap, made from morning-glory seeds) and some stimulants for the scurvy cases, camphor and Hartshorn being the last after the tincture of lobelia had been used so liberally in the first months of scurvy symptoms, some opium as a sedative, a bit of Mandragora and Dover's Powders left to dull pain, and only Sulphate of Copper and Lead remaining to disinfect wounds or deal with sunburn turned to blisters. Obeying Dr. Goodsir's orders, Bridgens had administered almost all of the Sulphate of Copper and Lead to the moaning men who had stripped their shirts off while rowing and added severe sunburn to their nightly misery.

But there was no sunlight now to dry the tents or clothes or bags. The men stayed wet and at night they moaned as they shook with cold and burned with fever.

Reconnaissance by their healthiest, fastest-walking shipmates had shown that while out of sight of land on boats they had passed a deeply indented bay less than fifteen miles to the northwest of this river where they had finally put in to shore. Most shocking of all, the scouts reported that the entire island curved back to the northeast only ten miles ahead of them to the east. If this was true, they were very close to the southeast corner of King William Island, their closest possible approach on this landmass to the Back River inlet.

Back River, their destination, lay southeast across the strait, but Captain Crozier had let the men know that he planned to continue man-hauling east on King William Island to the point where the coast of the island ceased its current southeastern slant. There, at this final point of land, they would set up camp again on the highest place possible and watch the strait. If the ice broke in the next two weeks, they would take to the boats. If it did not, they would try to haul them south across the ice toward the Adelaide Peninsula and, upon hitting land there, head due east the fifteen miles or fewer that Crozier estimated remained before they would reach the inlet leading south to Back's River.

The endgame had always been the weakest part of John Bridgens's chess skills. He rarely enjoyed it.

On the evening before they were scheduled to leave River Camp at dawn, Bridgens neatly packed away his personal gear — including the thick journal he had kept over the past year (he had left five longer ones on *Terror* the previous 22 April) — set it in his sleeping bag with a note that anything useful should be shared by his mates, took Harry Peglar's journal and his comb, added an old clothes brush that Bridgens had carried for many years, put them in his peacoat pocket, and went to Dr. Goodsir's small medical tent to say good-bye.

"What do you mean you're going for a walk and might not be back by the time we leave tomorrow?" demanded Goodsir. "What kind of talk is that, Bridgens?"

"I'm sorry, Doctor, I just have a strong desire to take a stroll."

"A stroll," repeated Goodsir. "Why, Mr. Bridgens? You are thirty years older than the average surviving seaman on this expedition, but you are ten times healthier."

"I've always been lucky when it came to health, sir," said Bridgens. "All due to heredity, I fear. No thanks to any wisdom I may have shown over the years."

"Then why . . . ," began the surgeon.

"It's just time, Dr. Goodsir. I confess to considering trodding the boards as a thespian long ago when I was young. One of the few things I learned about that profession was that the great actors learn how to make a good exit before they wear out their welcome or over-play a scene."

"You sound like a Stoic, Mr. Bridgens. A follower of Marcus Aurelius. If the emperor is displeased with you, you go home, draw a warm bath . . ."

"Oh, no, sir," said Bridgens. "While I admit I've always admired the Stoic philosophy, the truth is, I've always had a fear of knives and blades. The emperor would've had my head, my family, and lands for certain, I'm such a coward when it comes to sharp edges. I just wish to take a walk this evening. Perhaps a nap."

" 'Perchance to dream'?" said Goodsir.

"Aye, there's the rub," admitted the steward. The rue and anxiety — and perhaps fear — in his voice were real.

"Do you really think we have no chance to reach help?" asked the surgeon. He sounded sincerely curious and only a little sad.

Bridgens did not answer for a minute. Finally he said, "I truly do not know. Perhaps it all depends upon whether a rescue party has already been sent north from Great Slave Lake or one of the other outposts. I would think they might have — we have been out of touch for three years now — and if so, there may be a chance. I do know that if anyone on our expedition could get us home, Captain Francis Rawdon Moira Crozier is that man. He's always been under-rated by the Admiralty, is my humble opinion."

"Tell him that yourself, man," said Goodsir. "Or at least tell him that you're leaving. You owe him that."

Bridgens smiled. "I would, Doctor, but you and I both know that the captain would not let me go. He is stoic, I think, but no Stoic. He might put me in chains to keep me . . . going on."

"Yes," agreed Goodsir. "But you'll be doing me a favour if you stay, Bridgens. I have some amputations coming up that will require your steady hand."

"There are other young men who can help you, sir, and who have hands far steadier — and stronger — than mine."

"But no one as intelligent," said Goodsir. "No one I can talk to as I have with you. I value your advice."

"Thank you, Doctor," said Bridgens. He smiled again. "I didn't want to tell you, sir, but I've always been queasy around pain and blood. Since I was a boy. I've very much appreciated the opportunity to work with you these past weeks, but it's gone against my basically squeamish nature. I've always agreed with St. Augustine when he said that the only real sin is human pain. If there are amputations coming, it's best I'm going." He extended his hand. "Good-bye, Dr. Goodsir."

"Good-bye, Bridgens." The doctor used both of his hands to shake the older man's.

———

Bridgens walked northeast out of camp, climbed up out of the shallow river valley — as with everywhere else on King William Island, no hill or ridgeline was much higher than fifteen or twenty feet above sea level — found a rocky ridgeline free of snow, and followed it away from camp.

Sunset now came sometime around 10:00 p.m., but John Bridgens had decided that he would not walk until dark. About three miles from River Camp, he found a dry spot on the ridge, sat, and took a ship's biscuit — his day's ration — from his peacoat pocket and slowly ate it. Completely stale, it was one of the most delicious things he'd ever tasted. He had neglected to bring water with him, but now he scooped up a bit of snow and let it melt in his mouth.

The sunset to the southwest was beautiful. For an instant the sun actually emerged in the gap between low grey cloud and high grey gravel, hung there as an orange ball for a moment — the kind of sunset that Odysseus, not Lear, would have seen and enjoyed — and then disappeared.

The day and air grew grey and mellow, although the temperature, that had held in the twenties all day, was dropping very quickly now. A wind would come up soon. Bridgens would like to be asleep before the nightly wind howled out of the northwest or the nightly lightning storms rolled across the land and ice strait.

He reached into his pocket and removed the last three items there.

First was the clothes brush that John Bridgens had used as steward for more than thirty years. He touched the bits of lint on it, smiled at some irony understood only by himself, and set it in his other pocket.

Next was Harry Peglar's horn comb. A few light brown hairs still clung to the teeth of it. Bridgens held the comb tightly in his cold, bare fist for a moment and then set it in his coat pocket with the clothes brush.

Last was Peglar's notebook. He flipped it open at random.

Oh Death whare is thy sting, the grave at Comfort Cove for who has any doubt now . . . the dyer sad.

Bridgens shook his head. He knew that the last word should be "said," whatever else the water-stained and illegible part of the message should have read. He had taught Peglar to read but had never succeeded in teaching Harry how to spell. Bridgens suspected — since Harry Peglar was one of the most intelligent human beings he'd ever known — that there had been some problem with the constitution of the man's brain, some lobe or lump or grey area unknown to medical learning, that controlled the spelling of words. Even in the years after he'd learned to decode the alphabet and read the most challenging of books with a scholar's insight and understanding, Harry had been unable to pen the shortest letter to Bridgens without reversing letters and misspelling the simplest words.

Oh Death whare is thy sting . . .

Bridgens smiled a final time, set the journal in his front jacket pocket where it would be safe from small scavengers because he would be lying on it, and stretched out on his side on the gravel, laying his cheek on the backs of his bare hands.

He stirred only once, to tug his collar up and his hat down. The wind was coming up and it was very cold. Then he resumed his napping position.

John Bridgens was asleep before the last of the grey twilight died in the south.

51

CROZIER

They'd hauled for two weeks to the southeastern-most tip of the island — the point where the King William Island shoreline abruptly began curving north and east — and then they'd stopped to set up tents, send out hunting parties, and catch their breath while waiting and watching for openings in the sea-strait ice to the south. Dr. Goodsir had told Crozier that he needed time to deal with the sick and injured they'd been hauling in their five boats. They named the campsite Land's End.

When Crozier was informed by Goodsir that at least five men needed to have feet amputated during the stop there — which meant, he knew, that those men would never go farther than this place, since even the ambulatory seamen no longer had the strength to haul the extra weight of men in boats — the captain renamed the wind-whipped point Rescue Camp.

The idea, so far discussed only between Goodsir and himself although suggested by Goodsir, was for the surgeon to stay behind with the men recovering from the amputations. Four had been operated on already and so far none had died — the last man, Mr. Diggle, was to have his amputation this morning. Other seamen too sick or weary to continue on could opt to stay with Goodsir and the amputees, while Crozier, Des Voeux, Couch, Crozier's trusted second mate, Johnson, and any others with strength left would sail south down the inlet when — if — the ice relented again. Then this smaller group, traveling lightly, would head up Back River, returning with a rescue party from Great Slave Lake in the spring — or, with the help of a miracle, in the next month or two before winter arrived, providing that they ran into a rescue party moving north along the river.

Crozier knew that the chances of that particular miracle were so low as to be almost nil and that the chances of any of the sick men surviving at Rescue Camp until the following spring without help were not even worth discussing. There had been almost no easily hunted game all this summer of 1848, and August was proving to be no different. The ice had been too thick to fish through everywhere except in the few small leads and rare year-round *polynyas,* and they'd caught no fish even while in the boats. How could Goodsir and a few other attendants to the dying survive the coming winter here? Crozier knew that the surgeon had voluntarily signed his death warrant by volunteering to stay behind with the doomed men and Goodsir knew his captain knew it. Neither man spoke of it.

Yet that remained the current plan, unless Goodsir changed his mind this morning or a true miracle occurred and the ice opened up almost all the way to the shore this second week of August, allowing them all to set sail in two battered whaleboats, two battered cutters, and a single splintery pinnace, bringing the amputees, the injured, the starved, the too weak to walk, and the most advanced scurvy cases with them in the boats.

As potential food? thought Crozier.

This was the next issue that had to be dealt with.

The captain carried two pistols in his greatcoat whenever he went out of his tent now — his large percussion-cap revolver in his right pocket, as always, and the two-shot, twin-barreled little percussion pistol (what the American sea captain who'd sold it to him years ago had called "a riverboat gambler's belly gun") in his left pocket. He had not repeated his mistake of sending his best men — Couch, Des Voeux, Johnson, some others — out of camp at the same time while leaving such malcontents as Hickey, Aylmore, and the idiot giant Manson behind. Nor had Francis Crozier trusted Lieutenant George Henry Hodgson, his captain of the fo'c'sle, Reuben Male, or *Erebus* captain of the foretop Robert Sinclair since that day of near mutiny back at Hospital Camp more than a month earlier.

The view from Rescue Camp was depressing. The sky had been an unrelieved mass of low clouds for two weeks and Crozier hadn't been able to use his sextant. The wind had begun blowing hard from the northwest again and the air was colder than it had been for two months. The strait to the south remained a solid mass of ice, but not the flat ice interrupted by occasional pressure ridges such as they'd crossed on the trek from *Terror* to Terror Camp so very, very, very long ago. The ice in this strait south of King William Island was a total jumble of full-sized and shattered icebergs, crisscrossing pressure ridges, the occasional year-round *polynya* showing black water ten feet below the ice level but leading nowhere, and countless razor-edged seracs and ice boulders. Crozier didn't believe that any man in Rescue Camp — including the giant Manson — was up to man-hauling a single boat through that ice-forest and over those mountain ranges of ice.

The growls, explosions, crackings, blasts, and roars that now filled their days and nights were their only hope. The ice was agitated and torturing itself. Now and then, far out, it opened into tiny leads that sometimes lasted for hours. Then they closed with a thunderclap. Pressure ridges leapt to a height of thirty feet in a matter of seconds. Hours later, they collapsed just as quickly as new ridges thrust themselves up. Icebergs exploded from the pressure of the tightening ice around them.

It is only 13 August, Crozier told himself. The problem with that thinking, of course, was that instead of "only" 13 August, the season was now far enough along that it was time to be thinking, *It is* already *13 August.* Winter was fast approaching. *Erebus* and *Terror* had been first frozen in place off King William Land in September 1846, and there had been no respite after that.

It is only 13 August, Crozier repeated to himself. Time enough, if only a small miracle was granted them, to sail and row across the strait — probably man-hauling some short ice portages — the seventy-five miles he estimated to the mouth of Back's River, there to rerig the battered boats for travel upriver. With a bit more luck, the inlet itself beyond this visible ice jam would be free of ice — because of Back's Great Fish River's inevitable high summer flow northward and its warmer water — for as much as sixty miles of the way. After that, on the river itself, they would be racing the oncoming winter south each day while fighting their way upstream, but the voyage was still possible. In theory.

In theory.

This morning — a Sunday if the weary Crozier had not lost track — Goodsir was performing the last of the amputations with the help of his new assistant, Thomas Hartnell, and then Crozier planned to call the men together for a sort of Divine Service.

There he would announce that Goodsir would be staying with the crippled men and scurvy cases and he would bring into the open his plans to take a few of the healthiest men and at least two boats south within the coming week, whether the ice opened or not.

If Reuben Male, Hodgson, Sinclair, or the Hickey conspirators wanted to offer their alternate plans without challenging his authority, Crozier was ready not only to discuss them but to agree to them. The fewer men left at Rescue Camp the better, especially if it meant getting rid of the rotten apples.

The screaming started from the surgical tent as Dr. Goodsir began his operation on Mr. Diggle's gangrenous left foot and ankle.

A pistol in each pocket, Crozier went to find Thomas Johnson to tell him to assemble the men.

Mr. Diggle, the most universally liked man on the expedition and the excellent cook Francis Crozier had known and worked with for years on expeditions to both poles, died of blood loss and complications immediately after the amputation of his foot and just minutes before muster was called.

Each time the survivors spent more than two days at a camp, the bosuns dragged a stick through the gravel and snow in some relatively open, flat spot to create the rough outline of the *Erebus*'s and *Terror*'s top and lower decks. This allowed the men to know where to stand during muster and gave them a sense of familiarity. During the first days at Terror Camp and beyond, the muster positions had been crowded to the point of confusion, with more than a hundred men from two ships crowding into the footprint of a single ship's top deck, but now the attrition had reached the point where the gathering was appropriate for a single ship's mustering.

In the silence after the roll was called and before Crozier's brief reading of Scripture — and in the deeper silence in the aftermath of Mr. Diggle's screams — the captain looked out at the clusters of ragged, bearded, pale, filthy, hollow-eyed men leaning forward toward him in a sort of tired-ape slump that was meant to be a brisk standing at attention.

Of the thirteen original officers on HMS *Erebus,* nine were dead: Sir John, Commander Fitzjames, Lt. Graham Gore, Lt. H. T. D. Le Vesconte, Lt. Fairholme, First Mate Sergeant, Second Master Collins, Ice Master Reid, and Chief Surgeon Stanley. The surviving officers consisted of the first and second mates, Des Voeux and Couch; the assistant surgeon, Goodsir (who now joined the muster ranks late, his posture even more slumped than the other men's, his eyes downcast with exhaustion and defeat); and the purser, Charles Hamilton Osmer, who had survived a serious bout of pneumonia only to be prostrated in his tent now by scurvy.

It did not escape Captain Crozier's attention that all of *Erebus*'s commissioned Navy officers were dead and that the survivors were mere mates or civilians granted the honorary title of officer for wardroom purposes.

Erebus's three warrant officers — Engineer John Gregory, Bosun Thomas Terry, and Carpenter John Weekes — were all dead.

Erebus had left Greenland with twenty-one petty officers, and at today's muster, fifteen of them were still alive, although some of them — such as Purser's Steward William Fowler, who had never fully recovered from his burns at the Carnivale, were little more than mouths to be fed during the march.

A muster of *Erebus*'s able seamen on Christmas Day of 1845 would have heard nineteen sailors answering the call. Fifteen of them were still living.

Of seven Royal Marines who'd originally answered the muster call on *Erebus,* three had survived to this day in August of 1848 — Corporal Pearson and Privates Hopcraft and Healey — but all were too sick from scurvy even to stand guard or go hunting, much less haul boats. But this morning they stood leaning on their muskets among the other ragged, slumping forms.

Of the two ship's boys on *Erebus*'s muster — both actually men of eighteen when the two ships had sailed — both David Young and George Chambers had survived, but Chambers had been so heavily concussed by the thing from the ice during the Carnivale that he had been little more than an idiot since that night of fire. Still, he was able to haul when instructed and to eat when told to and to keep breathing without prompting.

So, according to the muster just finished, thirty-nine of *Erebus*'s original complement of sixty-five souls were still alive as of 13 August 1848.

The officers of HMS *Terror* had fared a bit better than those of *Erebus,* at least in the sense that two Naval officers — Captain Crozier and Second Lieutenant Hodgson — had survived. Second Mate Robert Thomas and Mr. E. J. Helpman, Crozier's clerk-in-charge and another civilian who served the expedition with officer's rank, were the other remaining officers.

Not answering muster today were Crozier's lieutenants Little and Irving, as well as First Mate Hornby, Ice Master Blanky, Second Master MacBean, and both his surgeons, Peddie and McDonald.

Four of *Terror*'s original eleven officers were still alive.

Crozier had started the expedition with three warrant officers — Engineer James Thompson, Bosun John Lane, and Master Carpenter Thomas Honey — and all three were still living, although the engineer had wasted away to a hollow-eyed skeleton too weak to stand, much less haul, and Mr. Honey not only showed advanced symptoms of scurvy but had had both feet amputated the night before. Incredibly, as of this assembly, the carpenter was still alive and even managed to shout, "Present!" from his tent when his name was called at muster.

Terror had sailed with twenty-one petty officers three years earlier and sixteen were still alive on this cloudy August morning — Stoker John Torrington, Captain of the Foretop Harry Peglar, and quartermasters Kenley and Rhodes had been the only casualties in that group until just moments ago when Cook John Diggle had joined the ranks of the dead.

Where nineteen able seamen had once answered *Terror's* muster, ten now did, although eleven had survived: David Leys still lay comatose and unresponsive in Dr. Goodsir's tent.

Of HMS *Terror's* contingent of six Royal Marines, none had survived. Private Heather, who had lingered for months with his shattered skull, finally died the day after they had left River Camp, and his body was left on the gravel without burial or comment.

The ship had recorded two "Boys" on its original muster, and now only one — Robert Golding, almost twenty-three years old and certainly no longer a boy, although gullible in a boy's way — answered to the roll.

Out of an original muster of sixty-two souls on HMS *Terror,* thirty-five had survived to see this Divine Service at Rescue Camp on 13 August, 1848.

Thirty-nine Erebuses and thirty-five Terrors remained, for a total muster of seventy-four men out of the one hundred twenty-six who had sailed from Greenland in the summer of 1845.

But four of these had suffered one or both of their feet being amputated in the last twenty-four hours and at least another twenty were almost certainly too sick, too injured, too starved, or too bone- and soul-weary to go on. A third of the expedition had reached their limit.

It was time for a reckoning.

———

"Almighty God," intoned Crozier in his exhausted rasp, "with whom do live the spirits of them that depart hence in the Lord, and with whom the souls of the faithful, after they are delivered from the burden of the flesh, are in joy and felicity: We give thee hearty thanks, for that it hath pleased thee to deliver this our brother John Diggle, age thirty-nine, out of the miseries of this sinful world; beseeching thee, that it may please thee, of thy gracious goodness, shortly to accomplish the number of thine elect, all of us here if it pleases thee, and thus to hasten thy kingdom; that we, with all those that are departed in the true faith of thy holy Name, may have our perfect consummation and bliss, both in body and soul, in thy eternal and everlasting glory; through Jesus Christ our Lord. Amen."

"Amen," croaked the sixty-two men still able to stand at muster stations.

"Amen," came a few voices from the other twelve lying in tents.

Crozier did not dismiss the assembled men.

"Men of HMS *Erebus* and HMS *Terror,* members of the John Franklin Discovery Service Expedition, shipmates," he rasped loudly. "Today we have to decide which way our paths shall carry us. You all remain — under both the Ship's Articles and the Articles of the Royal Discovery Service which you signed with your oaths of honour — under my command and will continue to be so until you are released by me. You've followed Sir John, Captain Fitzjames, and me this far, and you have done well. Many of our friends and shipmates have gone home to Christ, but seventy-four of us have persevered. I am resolved in my heart that every man of you here at Rescue Camp today should survive to see England, home, and your families again, and God shall be my witness that I have done my best to make sure that this shall be the outcome of our efforts. But today I release you to decide your own path by which to reach that goal."

The men murmured to one another. Crozier let that go on for a few seconds and then continued. "You've heard what we are doing — Dr. Goodsir to remain here with those too ill to travel, the healthier men to continue toward Back's River. Are there any among you who still wish to attempt to find some other way to rescue?"

There was a silence as men looked down and scuffled their booted feet on the gravel, but then George Hodgson hobbled forward.

"Sir, some of us do, sir. Want to head back that is, Captain Crozier."

The captain just looked at the young officer for a long moment. He knew that Hodgson was a stalking horse for Hickey, Aylmore, and a few of the more rebellious sea lawyers who had been stirring up the men with resentment for so many months, but he wondered if young Hodgson knew it.

"Back to where, Lieutenant?" Crozier asked at last.

"To the ship, sir."

"Do you think *Terror* is still there, Lieutenant?" As if to punctuate his query, the sea ice south of them exploded in a series of shotgun blasts and earthquake rumbles. An iceberg hundreds of yards from shore crumbled and fell.

Hodgson shrugged like a boy. "Terror Camp will be, Captain, whether the ship still is or not. We left food and coal and boats at Terror Camp."

"Aye," said Crozier, "so we did. And we'd all welcome some of that food now — even some of the tinned food that killed some of us so terribly. But, Lieutenant, that was some eighty or ninety miles and almost one hundred days ago when we left Terror Camp. Do you and the others really think you can walk or haul your way back there into the teeth of winter? It would be late November by the time you made your way even to the camp. Total darkness. And you remember the temperatures and storms of last November."

Hodgson nodded and said nothing.

"We ain't going to walk 'til no late November," said Cornelius Hickey, stepping out of the ranks to stand next to the slumped young lieutenant. "We think the ice is open along the shore back the way we come. We'll sail and row around that fuckin' cape we hauled five boats over like 'Gyptian slaves and be home in Terror Camp in a month."

The assembled men mumured furtively among themselves.

Crozier nodded. "It may indeed open for you, Mr. Hickey. Or it may not. But even if it does, it's more than a hundred miles back to a ship that may well be crushed and most certainly will be frozen fast by the time you get there. It's at least thirty miles closer to the mouth of Back River from here and the odds of the inlet being free of ice south of here, near the river, are much greater."

"You ain't talking us out of this, Captain," Hickey said firmly. "We talked it over 'mongst ourselves, and we're going."

Crozier stared at the caulker's mate. The captain's usual instinct to put down any insubordination immediately and with great strength and decisiveness rose in him, but he reminded himself that this was what he wanted. It was past time to get rid of the malcontents and to save those others who trusted his judgement. Besides, this late in the summer and in their escape attempt, Hickey's plan might even be workable. It all depended upon where the ice broke up — if it broke up anywhere before the winter set in. The men deserved to choose their own last, best chance.

"How many are going with you, Lieutenant?" asked Crozier, speaking to Hodgson as if he would actually be the commander of the group.

"Well . . . ," began the young man.

"Magnus is going," said Hickey, gesturing the giant forward. "And Mr. Aylmore."

The sullen gunroom steward swaggered forward, his face filled with defiance and visible contempt toward Crozier.

"And George Thompson . . . ," continued the caulker's mate.

Crozier was not surprised that Thompson would be part of Hickey's cabal. The seaman had always been insolent and lazy and — as long as the rum lasted — drunk whenever possible.

"I'm going along, too, . . . sir," said John Morfin, stepping up with the others.

William Orren, just turned twenty-six, stepped forward without a word and stood with Hickey's group.

Then James Brown and Francis Dunn — *Erebus*'s caulker and caulker's mate — joined the group. "We think it's our best chance, Captain," said Dunn and looked down.

Waiting for Reuben Male and Robert Sinclair to declare their intentions — realizing that if the majority of men standing at muster joined this group that all of his own plans for flight south were gone for good — Crozier was surprised when William Gibson, *Terror*'s subordinate officers' steward, and Stoker Luke Smith walked slowly forward. They'd been good men aboard ship and stalwart haulers.

Charles Best — a reliable *Erebus* seaman who had always been loyal to Lt. Gore — stepped forward with four other seamen in tow: William Jerry, Thomas Work, who had been sorely injured at Carnivale, young John Strickland, and Abraham Seeley.

The sixteen men stood there.

"Is that it then?" asked Crozier, feeling a hollow sense of relief that gnawed at his belly like the hunger that was always with him now. Sixteen men were standing there; they would need one boat, but they were leaving behind enough loyal men to head for Back River with him while also leaving enough to take care of the ill here at Rescue Camp. "I'll give you the pinnace," he said to Hodgson.

The lieutenant nodded gratefully.

"The pinnace is all busted up and rigged for river work and the sledge is a pain in the arse to drag," said Hickey. "We'll take a whaleboat."

"You'll get the pinnace," said Crozier.

"We want George Chambers and Davey Leys, too," said the caulker's mate, folding his arms and standing legs-apart in front of his men like a Cockney Napoleon.

"The hell you say," said Crozier. "Why would you want to bring two men who can't take care of themselves?"

"George can haul," said Hickey. "And we been takin' care of Davey and want to keep doin' so."

"No," said Dr. Goodsir, stepping forward into the tense space between Crozier and Hickey's men, "you haven't been taking care of Mr. Leys and you don't want George Chambers and him as fellow travelers. You want them as food."

Lieutenant Hodgson blinked in disbelief, but Hickey balled up his fists and gestured to Magnus Manson. The little man and huge man took a step forward.

"Stop exactly where you are," bellowed Crozier. Behind him, the three surviving Marines — Corporal Pearson, Private Hopcraft, and Private Healey — while visibly ill and shaky on their feet, had lifted and aimed their long muskets.

More to the point, First Mate Des Voeux, Mate Edward Couch, Bosun John Lane, and Bosun's Mate Tom Johnson were aiming shotguns.

Cornelius Hickey actually snarled. "We got guns, too."

"No," said Captain Crozier, "you do not. While you were at muster,

First Mate Des Voeux rounded up all weapons. If you leave peaceably tomorrow, you'll get one shotgun and some cartridges. If you take another step right now, you'll all get bird shot in your faces."

"You are all going to *die*," said Cornelius Hickey, pointing his bony finger at the men standing silently in muster formations while swinging his arm in a half circle like a scrawny weather vane. "You're going to follow Crozier and these other fools and you're going to *die*."

The caulker's mate wheeled toward the surgeon. "Dr. Goodsir, we forgive you for what you said about why we want to save George Chambers and Davey Leys. Come with us. You can't save these men here."

Hickey gestured contemptuously toward the sagging wet tents where the sick men lay.

"They're dead already, just don't know it," continued Hickey, his voice very large and loud coming from such a small frame. "We're going to *live*. Come with us and see your family again, Dr. Goodsir. If you stay here — or even follow Crozier — you're a dead man. Come with us."

Goodsir had absentmindedly worn his spectacles when he'd come out from the surgical tent and now he removed them and unhurriedly wiped moisture from them, using the bloody end of his woolen waistcoat as a rag. A small man with a boy's full lips and a receding chin only partially concealed under the hedge of curly beard that had grown down from his earlier unsuccessful side whiskers, Goodsir seemed completely at ease. He put his spectacles back on and looked at Hickey and the men behind him.

"Mr. Hickey," he said softly, "as grateful as I am for your boundless generosity in offering to save my life, you need to know that you do not need me along to do what you are planning to do with regards to dissecting the bodies of your shipmates in order to provide yourself with a larder of meat."

"I ain't . . . ," began Hickey.

"Even an amateur can learn dissective anatomy quite quickly," interrupted Goodsir, his voice strong enough to override the caulker's mate's. "When one of these other gentlemen you're bringing along as your private food stock dies — or when you help him die — all you have to do is sharpen a ship's knife to a scalpel's edge and begin cutting."

"We ain't going to . . . ," shouted Hickey.

"But I do strongly recommend that you bring a saw," overrode Goodsir. "One of Mr. Honey's carpenter saws will do nicely. While you can slice off your shipmates' calves and fingers and thighs and belly flesh with a knife, you shall almost certainly require a good saw to get the legs and arms off."

"God-damn you!" screamed Hickey. He started forward with Manson but stopped when the mates and Marines raised their shotguns and muskets again.

Unperturbed, not even looking at Hickey, the surgeon pointed toward the huge form of Magnus Manson as if the man were an anatomist's chart hanging on a wall. "It's not so different than carving a Christmas goose when one gets right down to it." He slashed vertical marks in the air toward Manson's upper torso and a horizontal one just below his waist. "Saw the arms off at the shoulder joints, of course, but you shall have to saw *through* each man's pelvic bones to cut off his legs."

Hickey's neck cords strained and his pale face grew red, but he did not speak again while Goodsir continued.

"I would use my smaller metacarpal saw to cut through the legs at the knees and, of course, the arms at the elbow, and then proceed with a good scalpel to slice away the choice parts — thighs, buttocks, biceps, triceps, deltoids, the meaty part behind the shins. Only then do you start the real butchering of the pectorals — chest muscles — and to get at any fat you gentlemen may have retained near your shoulder blades or along your sides and lower back. There shan't be much fat there, of course, nor muscle, but I'm sure Mr. Hickey wants no parts of you to go to waste."

One of the seamen in the back of the group behind Crozier dropped to his knees and began to dry retch into the gravel.

"I have an instrument called a tenaculum to crack the sternum and to remove the ribs," Goodsir said softly, "but I'm afraid I can't let you borrow it. A good ship's hammer and chisel — there's one in every boat kit, you've noticed — should serve that purpose almost as well.

"I do recommend you attend to rending the flesh first and set aside your friends' heads, hands, feet, intestines — all of the contents of the soft abdominal sac — for later.

"I warn you — it's more difficult than you think to crack open the long bones for their marrow. You'll need some sort of scraping tool, rather like Mr. Honey's wood-carving gouge. And do note that the marrow will be lumpy and red when it's forced from the center of the bones . . . and mixed with bone chips and fragments, so not terribly healthy to eat raw. I recommend you put each other's bone marrow into a pot for cooking straightaway and let yourselves simmer before trying to digest your friends."

"Fuck you," snarled Cornelius Hickey.

Dr. Goodsir nodded.

"Oh," the surgeon added softly, "when you get around to eating one another's brains, it will be simplicity itself. Simply saw off the lower jaw, throw it away with the lower teeth, and use any knife or spoon to gouge and hack your way up through the soft palate into the cranial vault. If you wish, you may invert the skull and sit around it, scooping out each other's brains like so much Christmas pudding."

For a minute there were no voices raised, only the wind and the groan, crack, and snapping of the ice.

"Is there anyone else who wants to leave tomorrow?" called Captain Crozier.

Reuben Male, Robert Sinclair, and Samuel Honey — *Terror*'s fo'c'sle captain, *Erebus*'s foretop captain, and *Terror*'s blacksmith, respectively — stepped forward.

"You're going with Hickey and Hodgson?" asked Crozier. He did not allow himself to show the shock he felt.

"Nay, sir," said Reuben Male, shaking his head. "We ain't with them. But we want to try walking back to *Terror*."

"No boat needed, sir," said Sinclair. "We're going to try hiking cross-country as it were. Straight across the island. Maybe we'll find some foxes and such inland, away from the coast."

"Navigation will be difficult," said Crozier. "Compasses aren't worth a damn here and I can't give you one of my sextants."

Male shook his head. "No worries, Captain. We'll just use dead reckoning. Most of the time, if the fuckin' wind is in our face — pardon my language, sir — then we're headed the right way."

"I was a seaman before I was a 'smith, sir," said Samuel Honey. "We're all sailors. If we can't die at sea, at least this way perhaps we can die aboard our ship."

"All right," said Crozier, speaking to all the men still standing there and making sure that his voice would reach to the tents. "We're going to assemble at six bells and divide up all the remaining ship's biscuits, spirits, tobacco, and any other victuals we still have. Every man. Even those who had their surgeries last night and today will be brought to the dividing-up. Everyone will see what we have, and every man will get an equal share. From this point on, each man — except those being fed and cared for by Dr. Goodsir — will be in charge of his own rationing."

Crozier looked coldly at Hickey, Hodgson, and their group. "You men will — under Mr. Des Voeux's oversight — go ready your pinnace for your departure. You'll leave at dawn tomorrow, and except for the divvying up of goods and food at six bells, I don't want to see your faces before then."

52

GOODSIR

For the two days after the amputations and Mr. Diggle's death and the muster of the men and the hearing of Mr. Hickey's plans and the pathetic dividing up of the food, the surgeon had no stomach for keeping his diary. He tossed the stained leather book into his traveling medical kit and left it there.

The Great Dividing Up, as Goodsir already thought of it, had been a sad and seemingly endless affair, extending into the shortening August arctic evening. It soon became obvious that — at least when it came to food — no one trusted anyone. Everyone seemed to harbour some bone-deep anxiety that someone else was hiding food, hoarding food, secreting away food, denying everyone else food. It had taken hours to unpack all boats, empty all stores, search all tents, go through Mr. Diggle's and Mr. Wall's stores, with representatives of each class of man on the ship — officers, warrant officers, petty officers, able seamen — sharing the search and distribution chores while the other men looked on with avid eyes.

Thomas Honey died during the night after the Dividing Up. Goodsir had Thomas Hartnell inform the captain and then he helped sew the carpenter's body into his sleeping bag. Two sailors carried it to a snowdrift about one hundred yards from the camp where Mr. Diggle's body already lay in cold state. The troop had begun forgoing burials and burial services, not because of an edict from the captain or some vote, but simply through silent consensus.

Are we preserving the bodies in the snowdrift so they won't spoil as future food? wondered the surgeon.

He could not answer his own question. All he knew was that while he was giving Hickey — and all the other assembled men (quite deliberately since he had spoken to Captain Crozier about the tactic before the muster assembly) — the anatomical details of carving up the human body to serve as sustenance, Harry D. S. Goodsir had been horrified to find himself salivating.

And he knew that he could not have been alone in that reaction to the thought of fresh meat . . . from whatever source.

Only a handful of men had turned out at dawn the next morning, Monday 14 August, to watch Hickey and his fifteen companions leave camp with their pinnace lashed onto its battered sledge. Goodsir had come back to see them off after making sure that Mr. Honey had been secretly buried in the drift.

Earlier, he had missed seeing the three walking men off. Mr. Male, Mr. Sinclair, and Samuel Honey — no relation to the recently deceased carpenter — had left before dawn on their proposed trek across the island to Terror Camp, carrying with them only their rucksacks, blanket sleeping bags, some ship's biscuits, water, and one shotgun with cartridges. They had not so much as a single Holland tent for shelter and planned to build caves in the snow if serious winter weather reached them before they reached Terror Camp. Goodsir thought that they must have said their good-byes to friends the night before, since the three men were out of camp before the first grey light touched the southern horizon. Mr. Couch later told Dr. Goodsir that the party headed north, inland and directly away from the coast, and planned to turn toward the northwest on their second or third day.

In contrast, the surgeon was amazed by how heavily Hickey's departing men had loaded their boat. Men all over camp, including Male, Sinclair, and Samuel Honey, had been abandoning useless items — hairbrushes, books, towels, writing desks, combs — bits of civilization they'd hauled for a hundred days and now refused to haul any farther, and, for some inexplicable reason, Hickey and his men had loaded many of these rejected pieces of junk into their pinnace along with tents, sleeping gear, and necessary food. One bag held 105 individually wrapped chunks of dark chocolate that was the shared accumulation of these sixteen men's allotment of a secret store hauled all this way as a surprise by Mr. Diggle and Mr. Wall — six and a half pieces of chocolate per man.

Lieutenant Hodgson had shaken hands with Crozier, and a few of the other men had said clumsy farewells to old shipmates, but Hickey, Manson, Aylmore, and the most resentful of the group said nothing. Then Bosun's Mate Johnson gave Hodgson the unloaded shotgun and a bag of cartridges and watched while the young lieutenant stowed them in the heavily loaded boat. With Manson in the lead and at least a dozen of the sixteen men lashed to the sledge and longboat by harnesses, they left the camp in silence broken only by the scrape of runners on gravel, then on snow, then on rock again, then again across ice and snow. Within twenty minutes they were out of sight over the slight rise to the west of Rescue Camp.

"Are you thinking about whether they'll make it, Dr. Goodsir?" asked Mate Edward Couch, who had been standing next to the surgeon and observing his silence.

"No," said Goodsir. He was so weary that he could only answer honestly. "I was thinking about Private Heather."

"Private Heather?" said Couch. "Why, we left his body . . ." He stopped.

"Yes," said Goodsir. "The Marine's corpse is lying under a shred of canvas by the side of our sledge tracks this side of River Camp, not twelve days' pull west of here — much less time than that at the rate Hickey's large team is pulling the single pinnace."

"Oh, Jesus Christ," hissed Couch.

Goodsir nodded. "I just hope they do not find the subordinate officers' steward's body. I liked John Bridgens. He was a dignified man and deserves better than to be devoured by the likes of Cornelius Hickey."

———

That afternoon, Goodsir was directed to come to a meeting near the four boats along the shore — the two whaleboats were inverted as always, the cutters still upright on their sledges but unloaded — out of the hearing of the men at their duties or drowsing in their tents. Captain Crozier was there, as were First Mate Des Voeux, First Mate Robert Thomas, Acting Mate Couch, Bosun's Mate Johnson, Bosun John Lane, and Marine Corporal Pearson, who was too weak to stand and had to half recline against the splintered hull of an overturned whaleboat.

"Thank you for coming so promptly, Doctor," said Crozier. "We're here to discuss ways to guard against the return of Cornelius Hickey's group and to look at our own options over the coming weeks."

"Surely, Captain," said the surgeon, "you don't expect Hickey, Hodgson, and the others to come back here?"

Crozier held up his gloved hands and shrugged. Light snow whipped around and between the men. "He still might want David Leys. Or the corpses of Mr. Diggle and Mr. Honey. Or even you, Doctor."

Goodsir shook his head and shared his thoughts about the bodies — starting with Private Heather — that lay along the return way to Terror Camp like frozen food caches.

"Aye," said Charles Des Voeux, "we've thought of that. It's probably the main reason that Hickey thought he could get back to *Terror*. But we're still going to mount a round-the-clock watch here at Rescue Camp for a few days and send Bosun's Mate Johnson here out with a man or two to follow Hickey's group for three or four days — just to be sure."

"As for our future here, Dr. Goodsir," rasped Crozier, "what do you see?"

It was the surgeon's turn to shrug. "Mr. Jopson, Mr. Helpman, and Engineer Thompson will not live more than a few days," he said softly. "Of my other fifteen or so scurvy patients, I simply do not know. A few might survive . . . the scurvy, I mean. Especially if we find fresh meat for them. But of the eighteen men who may stay here at Rescue Camp with me — Thomas Hartnell has volunteered to stay on as my assistant, by the way — only three, perhaps four, will be capable of going out to hunt seals on the ice or foxes inland. And they not for long. I would presume that the rest of those who remain here will have died of starvation no later than fifteen September. Most of us sooner than that."

He left unstated that some might survive awhile longer here by eating the bodies of the dead. He also did not mention that he, Dr. Harry D. S. Goodsir, had decided that he would not turn cannibal to survive, nor help those who found need to. His dissection instructions at the previous day's muster assembly were his last words on the subject. Yet he would also never cast judgement on the men here at Rescue Camp or on the expedition south who did end up eating human flesh to last a short while longer. If any man on the Franklin Expedition understood that the human body was a mere animal vessel for the soul — and only so much meat once that soul had departed — it was their surviving surgeon and anatomist, Dr. Harry Goodsir. Not extending his own life a few weeks or even months longer by partaking of such dead flesh was his own decision, for his own moral and philosophical reasons. He had never been an especially *good* Christian, but he preferred to die as one nonetheless.

"We may have an alternative," Crozier said softly, almost as if reading Goodsir's thoughts. "I've decided this morning that the Back's River party can stay here at Rescue Camp another week — perhaps ten days, depending upon the weather — in hopes that the ice will break up and that we can all depart here on boats . . . even the dying."

Goodsir frowned dubiously at the four boats around them. "Can so many of us fit in these few craft?" he asked.

"Don't forget, Doctor," said Edward Couch, "there are nineteen fewer of us now after the malcontents' departure this morning. And two more dead since yesterday morn. That's only fifty-three souls for four good boats, ourselves included."

"And, as you say," said Thomas Johnson, "more will die in the coming week."

"And we have almost no food to haul now," said Corporal Pearson from where he sprawled against the inverted whaleboat. "I wish to God it was otherwise."

"And I've decided to leave all the tents behind," said Crozier.

"Where will we shelter in a storm?" asked Goodsir.

"Under the boats on the ice," said Des Voeux. "Under the boat covers on open water. I did it during my attempt to reach the Boothia Peninsula last March, in the middle of winter, and it's warmer under or in a boat than in those fucking tents . . . excuse my language, Captain."

"You're excused," said Crozier. "Also, the Holland tents each weigh three or four times what they did when we started this voyage. They never dry out. They must have soaked up half the moisture in the arctic."

"So has our underlinens," said Mate Robert Thomas.

Everyone laughed to one extent or another. Two of them ended the laughter with coughs.

"I'm also planning to leave all but three of the big water casks behind," said Crozier. "Two of them will be empty when we set out. Each boat will have only one of the small casks for storage."

Goodsir shook his head. "How will your men slake their thirst while you're in the strait waters or on the ice there?"

"*Our* thirst, Doctor," said the captain. "If the ice opens, remember that you and the sick men will be coming along, not staying here to die. And we'll refill the casks regularly when we get to the fresh water of Back's River. Until then, I have a confession. We — the officers — *did* hoard one thing we did not confess to yesterday at the Dividing Up. A bit of spirit stove fuel hidden under the false bottom of one of the last rum casks."

"We'll melt ice and snow for drinking water on the ice," said Johnson.

Goodsir nodded slowly. He had been so reconciled to the certainty of his own death in the coming days or weeks that even the thought of potential salvation was almost painful. He resisted the urge to allow his hopes to rise again. Odds were overwhelming that everyone — Hickey's group, Mr. Male's three adventurers, Crozier's south-rowing group — would be dead in the coming month.

Again as if reading his thoughts, Crozier said to Goodsir, "What will it take, Doctor, to give us a chance to survive the scurvy and weakness for the three months it may take us to row upriver to Great Slave Lake?"

"Fresh food," the surgeon said simply. "I am convinced that we can beat back the disease in some of the men if we can get fresh food. If not vegetables and fruits — which I know are impossible up here — then fresh meat, especially fat. Even animal blood will help."

"Why will meat and blubber arrest or cure such a terrible disease, Doctor?" asked Corporal Pearson.

"I have no idea," said Goodsir, shaking his head, "but I am as certain of it as I am that we will all die of scurvy if we do *not* get fresh meat . . . even before starvation will kill us."

"If Hickey or the others reach Terror Camp," said Des Voeux, "will the tinned Goldner food serve the same purpose?"

Goodsir shrugged again. "Possibly, although I agree with my late colleague, Assistant Surgeon McDonald, that fresh food is always better than canned. Also, I am convinced that there were at least two types of poisons in the Goldner tins — one slow and nefarious, the other, as you remember with poor Captain Fitzjames and some others, very quick and terrible. Either way, we're better off seeking and finding fresh meat or fish than they are pinning their hopes on aging tins from the Goldner victuallers."

"We hope," said Captain Crozier, "that once out on the open water of the inlet, amidst the free-floating floes, seals and walruses will be available in plentitude before the real winter sets in. Once on the river, we'll put in from time to time to hunt deer, foxes, or caribou, but may have to pin *our* hopes on catching fish . . . a real probability according to such explorers as George Back and our own Sir John Franklin."

"Sir John also ate his shoes," said Corporal Pearson.

No one reprimanded the starving Marine, but neither did anyone laugh or respond until Crozier said, his rasping voice sounding totally serious, "That's the real reason I brought along hundreds of extra boots. Not just to keep the men's feet dry — which, as you have seen, Doctor, was an impossibility. But to have all that leather to eat during the penultimate portion of our trek south."

Goodsir could only stare. "We'll have only one cask of water but hundreds of Royal Navy–issued boots to eat?"

"Yes," said Crozier.

Suddenly all eight men began laughing so hard that they could not stop; when the others ceased, someone would begin laughing again and then everyone would join in.

"Shhh!" Crozier said at last, sounding like a schoolmaster with boys but still chuckling himself.

Men at their duties in the camp twenty yards away were looking over with curiosity painted on their pale faces staring out from under Welsh wigs and caps.

Goodsir had to wipe away tears and snot before they froze to his face.

"We're not going to wait for the ice to open all the way up to the shore here," Crozier said into the sudden silence in the group. "Tomorrow, as Bosun's Mate Johnson secretly follows Hickey's group northwest along the coast, Mr. Des Voeux will take a group of our ablest men south across the ice, moving with just rucksacks and sleeping blankets — with luck, traveling almost as quickly as Reuben Male and his two friends — going at least ten miles out onto the strait, perhaps farther, to see if there is any open water. If a lead opens to within five miles of this camp, we are all leaving."

"The men have no strength . . . ," began Goodsir.

"They will if they know for certain that there's only a day or two's haul between them and open water all the way to rescue," said Captain Crozier. "The two surviving men who've had their feet amputated will be on their bloody stumps and pulling with a will if we know the water is out there waiting for us."

"And with only a little luck," said Des Voeux, "my group will bring back some seals and walruses and blubber."

Goodsir looked out at the cracking, shifting, pressure-ridge surging ice jumble stretching south below low, grey snow clouds. "Can you haul seals and walruses back across that white nightmare?" he asked.

Des Voeux just grinned broadly in answer.

"We have one thing to be thankful for," said Bosun's Mate Johnson.

"What's that, Tom?" asked Crozier.

"Our friend from the ice seems to have lost interest in us and wandered away," said the still-muscular bosun. "We've not seen or heard him for certain since before River Camp."

All eight men, including Johnson, suddenly reached over to one of the nearby boats and rapped their knuckles on the wood.

53

GOLDING

Twenty-two-year-old Robert Golding rushed into Rescue Camp just after sunset on Thursday, the 17th of August, agitated, shaking, and almost too excited to speak. Mate Robert Thomas intercepted him outside of Crozier's tent.

"Golding, I thought you were with Mr. Des Voeux's group on the ice."

"Yes, sir. I am, Mr. Thomas. I *was*."

"Is Des Voeux back already?"

"No, Mr. Thomas. Mr. Des Voeux sent me back with a message for the captain."

"You can tell me."

"Yes, sir. I mean, *no*, sir. Mr. Des Voeux said I was to report only to the captain. Just the captain, sorry, sir. Thank you, sir."

"What in hell is all the commotion out here?" asked Crozier, crawling out of his tent.

Golding repeated his instructions from the second mate to report only to the captain, apologized, stuttered, and was led away from the ring of tents by Crozier. "Now tell me what's going on, Golding. Why aren't you with Mr. Des Voeux? Has something happened to him and the reconnaissance group?"

"Yes, sir. I mean . . . no, Captain. I mean, something *has* happened, sir, out there on the ice. I wasn't there when it did — we was left behind to hunt seals, sir, Francis Pocock and Josephus Greater and me, while Mr. Des Voeux went on farther south with Robert Johns and Bill Mark and Tom Tadman and the others yesterday, but this evenin' they come back, just Mr. Des Voeux and a couple of the others, I mean, about an hour after we heard the shotguns."

"Calm down, lad," said Crozier, setting his hands firmly on the boy's shaking shoulders. "Tell me what Mr. Des Voeux's message was, word for word. And then tell me what you saw."

"They're both dead, Captain. Both of them. I saw the one — Mr. Des Voeux had her body on a blanket, sir, it was all tore up — but I ain't seen the other one yet."

"*Who's* both dead, Golding?" snapped Crozier, although the "her" had already told him part of the truth.

"Lady Silence and the thing, Captain. The Esquimaux bitch and the thing from the ice. I seen her body. I ain't seen its yet. Mr. Des Voeux said it's next to a polyp about another mile out beyond where we was shootin' at seals, and I'm to bring you and the doctor out to see it, sir."

"Polyp?" said Crozier. "You mean *polynya?* One of the little lakes of open water in the ice?"

"Yes, Captain. I ain't seen that yet, but that's where the thing's carcass is according to Mr. Des Voeux and Fat Wilson, who was with him and carrying and pulling the blanket like it was a sled, sir. Silence, she was in the blanket, you see, all tore up and dead. Mr. Des Voeux says to bring you and the doctor and no one else and for me not to tell no one else or he'll have Mr. Johnson flog me when he gets back."

"Why the doctor?" said Crozier. "Are some of our people hurt?"

"I think so, Captain. I'm not sure. They're still out at the . . . the hole in the ice, sir. Pocock and Greater went on back south with Mr. Des Voeux and Fat Alex Wilson like Mr. D. V. said for them to, but he sent me back here and said to bring just you and the doctor, no one else. And not to tell no one else neither. Not yet. Oh . . . and for the surgeon to bring his kit with knives and such and maybe some larger knives for carvin' up the thing's carcass. Did you hear the shotgun blasts this evenin', Captain? Pocock and Greater and me heard 'em, and we was a mile away from the polyp at least."

"No. We wouldn't make out shotgun reports from two miles away over the damnable constant cracking and breaking of the ice here," said Crozier. "Think hard, Golding. Why exactly did Mr. Des Voeux say it should just be Dr. Goodsir and myself that come out to see . . . whatever it is?"

"He said he's fairly sure the thing's dead, but Mr. Des Voeux said it ain't what we thought it was, Captain. He said it's . . . I forget the words he used. But Mr. Des Voeux says it changes everything, sir. He wants you and the doctor to see it and know what happened there before anyone in the camp hears about it."

"What *did* happen out there?" pressed Crozier.

Golding shook his head. "I don't know, Captain. Pocock and Greater and me was hunting seals, sir . . . we shot one, Captain, but it slipped through its hole in the ice and we couldn't get to it. I'm sorry, sir. Then we heard the shotguns to the south. And a little later, an hour maybe, Mr. Des Voeux shows up with George Cann, who was bleeding on his face, and Fat Wilson, and Wilson was pulling Silence's body on a blanket he was draggin' and she was all torn to pieces, only . . . we're supposed to hurry back, Captain. While the moon's up."

Indeed, it was a rare, clear night after a rare, clear, red sunset — Crozier had been taking his sextant out of its box to get a star fix when he'd heard the commotion — and a huge, full, blue-white moon had just risen over the icebergs and ice jumble to the southeast.

"Why tonight?" asked Crozier. "Can't this wait for morning?"

"Mr. Des Voeux said it can't, Captain. He said to give you his compliments and would you be so kind as to bring Dr. Goodsir and come out about two miles — it ain't longer than two hours' walk, sir, even with the ice walls — to see what's there by the polyanna."

"All right," said Crozier. "You go tell Dr. Goodsir I want him and for him to bring his medical kit and to dress warmly. I'll meet the two of you at the boats."

———

Golding led the four men out onto the ice — Crozier ignored the message from Des Voeux to come just with the surgeon and had

ordered Bosun John Lane and Captain of the Hold William Goddard
to come along with their shotguns — and then into the jumble of
bergs and ice boulders, then over three high pressure ridges, and
finally through serac forests where Golding's earlier path back to the
camp was marked not only by his boot prints in the blowing snow but
also by the bamboo wands they'd hauled with them all the way from
Terror. Des Voeux's group had carried the wands with them two days
earlier to mark their way back and to show the best pathway through
the ice should they find open water and want the others to follow
them with the boats. The moonlight was so bright that it threw shadows. Even the narrow bamboo wands were like moon dials throwing
slashes of shadow lines onto the white-blue ice.

For the first hour there was only the sound of the laboured breathing, their boots crunching on snow and ice, and the cracking and
groans all around them. Then Crozier said, "Are you sure she's dead,
Golding?"

"Who, sir?"

The captain's frustrated exhalation became a small cloud of ice
crystals gleaming in the moonlight. "How many 'she's' are there
around here, God-damn it? Lady Silence."

"Oh, yes, sir." The boy snickered. "She's dead all right. Her titties
was all tore off."

The captain glared at the boy as they climbed another low pressure
ridge and passed into the shadow of a tall blue-glowing iceberg. "But
are you sure it's Silence? Could it be another native woman?"

Golding seemed stumped by that question. "Is there more
Esquimaux women out here, Captain?"

Crozier shook his head and gestured for the boy to continue leading.

They reached the "polyanna," as Golding continued calling it,
about an hour and a half after leaving camp.

"I thought you said it was farther out," said Crozier.

"I ain't never been even this far before," said Golding. "I was back
there hunting seals when Mr. Des Voeux found the thing." He gestured vaguely behind and to the left of where they now stood by the
opening in the ice.

"You said some of our people were injured?" asked Dr. Goodsir.

"Yes, sir. Fat Alex Wilson had blood on his face."

"I thought you said it was George Cann who had a bloody face," said Crozier.

Golding shook his head emphatically. "Uh-uh, Captain. It was Fat Alex who were bloody."

"Was it his own blood or someone or something else's?" asked Goodsir.

"I don't know," Golding replied, his voice almost sullen-sounding. "Mr. Des Voeux just told me to have you bring your surgeon's things. I figured someone had to be hurt, if Mr. Des Voeux needed you to fix 'im."

"Well, there's no one around here," said the bosun, John Lane, walking carefully around the ice edge of the *polynya* — which was no more than twenty-five feet across — and staring first down into the dark water eight feet lower than the ice and then back at the forest of seracs on all sides. "Where are they? Mr. Des Voeux had eight other men besides you with him when he left, Golding."

"I don't know, Mr. Lane. This is where he told me to bring you."

Captain of the Hold Goddard cupped his hands around his mouth and shouted, "Halloooo? Mr. Des Voeux? Hallooo?"

There came an answering shout from their right. The voice was indistinct, muffled, but sounded excited.

Motioning Golding back, Crozier led the way through the forest of twelve-foot-high ice seracs. The wind through the sculpted towers made a moaning, crooning sound, and they all knew that the serac edges were as sharp as knife blades and stronger than most ship knives.

Ahead of them in the moonlight, in the center of a small, flat ice clearing amid the seracs, the dark form of one man stood alone.

"If that's Des Voeux," Lane whispered to his captain, "he's got eight men missing."

Crozier nodded. "John, William, you two go ahead — slowly — keep your shotguns ready and on half-cock. Dr. Goodsir, please be so kind as to stay back with me. Golding, you wait here."

"Aye, sir," whispered William Goddard. He and John Lane tugged off their mittens with their teeth so they could use their gloved fingers, raised their weapons, half-cocked one of the heavy hammers on their double-barreled guns, and moved forward cautiously toward the moonlit clearing beyond the edge of the serac forest.

A huge shadow came out from behind the last serac and slammed Lane's and Goddard's skulls together. The two men went down like cattle beneath a slaughterhouse sledgehammer.

Another shadowy figure struck Crozier in the back of the head, pinned his arms behind his back when he tried to rise, and held a knife to his neck.

Robert Golding grabbed Goodsir and set a long blade alongside his throat. "Don't move, Doctor," whispered the boy, "or I'll do my own bit o' surgery on you."

The huge shadow lifted Goddard and Lane by the scruff of their greatcoats and dragged them out into the ice clearing. The toes of their boots made grooves in the snow. A third man came from behind the seracs, picked up Goddard's and Lane's shotguns, handed one to Golding, and kept the other for himself.

"Get out there," said Richard Aylmore, gesturing with the barrels of the shotgun.

With a knife still held to his throat by the shadowy shape Crozier now recognized by smell as the slackard George Thompson, the captain stood and half stumbled, was half pushed, out of the serac shadows and toward the man waiting in the moonlight.

———

Magnus Manson dumped the bodies of Lane and Goddard in front of his master, Cornelius Hickey.

"Are they alive?" rasped Crozier. The captain's arms were still pinned behind him by Thompson, but now that the muzzles of two shotguns were trained on him, the blade was no longer at his throat.

Hickey leaned over as if to inspect the men, and, with two smooth, easy moves, cut both their throats with a knife that had suddenly appeared in his hand.

"Not now they ain't alive, Mr. High-and-Mighty Crozier," said the caulker's mate.

The blood pouring out onto the ice looked black in the moonlight.

"Is that the technique you used to slaughter John Irving?" asked Crozier, his voice shaking with fury.

"Fuck you," said Hickey.

Crozier glared at Robert Golding. "I hope you got your thirty pieces of silver."

Golding snickered.

"George," said the caulker's mate to Thompson, standing behind the captain, "Crozier carries a pistol in his right greatcoat pocket. Pull it out. Dickie, you bring the pistol back to me. If Crozier moves, kill him."

Thompson removed the pistol while Aylmore kept his purloined shotgun aimed. Then Aylmore walked over, took the pistol and the box of cartridges Thompson had found, and backed away, shotgun raised again. He crossed the short moonlit space and handed the pistol to Hickey.

"All this natural misery," Dr. Goodsir said suddenly. "Why do you men have to add to it? Why does our species always have to take our full measure of God-given misery and terror and mortality and then make it worse? Can you answer me that, Mr. Hickey?"

The caulker's mate, Manson, Aylmore, Thompson, and Golding stared at the surgeon as if he had begun speaking Aramaic.

So did the only other living man there, Francis Crozier.

"What do you want, Hickey?" asked Crozier. "Other than more good men dead as meat for your trip?"

"I want you to shut the fuck up and then die slow and hard," said Hickey.

Robert Golding laughed a demented boy's laugh. The barrels of the shotgun he was holding beat a tattoo on the back of Goodsir's neck.

"Mr. Hickey," said Goodsir, "you do realize, do you not, that I shall never serve your purposes by dissecting my shipmates."

Hickey showed his small teeth in the moonlight. "You will, surgeon. I guarantee you will. Or you'll watch us cut *your pieces* off one at a time and then have us feed them to you."

Goodsir said nothing.

"Tom Johnson and the others are going to find you," Crozier said, never removing his gaze from Cornelius Hickey's face.

The caulker's mate laughed. "Johnson already found us, Crozier. Or rather, we found 'im."

The caulker's mate reached behind him and pulled a burlap bag from the snow. "What'd you always call Johnson in private, King Crozier? Your strong right arm? Here." He tossed a naked and bloody right arm, severed just above the elbow, white bone gleaming, through the air and watched it land at Crozier's feet.

Crozier did not look down at it. "You pathetic little smear of spittle. You are — and always have been — nothing."

Hickey's face contorted as if the moonlight were changing him into something nonhuman. His thin lips drew far back from his tiny teeth in a way that the others had seen only with scurvy victims in their last hours. His eyes showed something beyond madness, far beyond mere hatred.

"Magnus," said Hickey, "strangle the captain. Slow."

"Yes, Cornelius," said Magnus Manson, and shuffled forward.

Goodsir tried to rush forward, but the boy, Golding, held him fast with one hand while holding the shotgun to his head with the other.

Crozier did not move a muscle as the giant lumbered toward him. When Manson's shadow fell over both the captain and George Thompson holding him, Thompson himself flinched just a bit, Crozier sagged back, lunged forward, freed his left arm, and thrust his hand into the left pocket of his greatcoat.

Golding almost pulled the shotgun's trigger, thus almost blowing Goodsir's head off by accident, so startled was he as the captain's coat pocket burst into flame and the muted double boom of an explosion rolled past them and echoed back from the seracs.

"Ouch," said Magnus Manson, slowly raising his hands to his belly.

"God-damn it," Crozier said calmly. He had inadvertently fired both barrels of a two-shot pistol.

"Magnus!" cried Hickey and rushed forward to the giant.

"I think the captain shot me, Cornelius," said Manson. The big man sounded confused and a little bemused.

"Goodsir," shouted Crozier amid the confusion. The captain whirled, kneed Thompson in the bollocks and broke free. "Run!"

The surgeon tried. He pulled, shoved, and almost won his freedom before the younger Golding tripped him, knocked him onto his belly, and set the full pressure of his knee on Goodsir's back and the full force of two shotgun barrels against the back of Goodsir's skull.

Crozier was loping for the seracs.

Hickey calmly seized a shotgun from Richard Aylmore, aimed, and fired both barrels.

The top of a serac splintered and fell at the same time that Crozier was thrown forward on his face, sliding on the ice and on a film of his own blood.

Hickey handed the shotgun back and unbuttoned Manson's coats and waistcoats, ripping open the big man's shirts and filthy undershirt. "Bring the fucking surgeon over here," he shouted at Golding.

"It don't hurt much, Cornelius," rumbled Magnus Manson. "Tickles, more like."

Golding shoved, prodded, and dragged Goodsir over. The surgeon put on his glasses and inspected the twin wounds. "I'm not certain, but I don't believe the small-caliber bullets penetrated Mr. Manson's subcutaneous fat, much less his muscle layer. It's little more than two minor punctures, I fear. Now may I go attend to Captain Crozier, Mr. Hickey?"

Hickey laughed.

"Cornelius!" shouted Aylmore.

Crozier, leaving a trail of blood and shredded outer clothing, had gotten to his knees and begun crawling toward the seracs and serac shadows. Now he painfully got to his feet. He staggered drunkenly toward the ice columns.

Golding giggled and raised his shotgun.

"No!" cried Hickey. He pulled Crozier's big percussion-cap pistol from his coat pocket and took careful aim.

Twenty feet from the seracs, Crozier looked back over his shredded shoulder.

Hickey fired.

The bullet spun Crozier around and dropped him to his knees. His body sagged, but he flailed and thrust one hand down onto the ice in an attempt to rise.

Hickey took five steps forward and fired again.

Crozier was thrown backward and lay on his back with only his knees in the air.

Hickey took two more steps, aimed, and fired again. One of Crozier's legs was knocked aside and down as the bullet tore through the knee or the muscle just below the knee. The captain made no sound.

"Cornelius, honey." Magnus Manson's voice had the tone of an injured child. "My stomach is starting to hurt."

Hickey wheeled. "Goodsir, give him something for the pain."

The surgeon nodded. His voice, when he spoke, was very thin and very tight and very flat. "I brought an entire bottle of Dover's Powder — mostly made from a derivative of the coca plant, sometimes called cocaine. I'll give him that. All of it, if you like. With a chaser of Mandragora, laudanum, and morphine. That will take away the pain." He reached into his medical kit.

Hickey raised the pistol and aimed it at the surgeon's left eye. "If you even make Magnus sick to his stomach, much less if your fucking hand comes out of that bag with a scalpel or other blade, I swear to fucking Christ I'll shoot you in the balls and keep you alive long enough to make you eat them. Do you understand, Surgeon?"

"I understand," said Goodsir. "But it is the Hippocratic oath that determines my next actions." He brought out a bottle and spoon and poured out a tiny bit of liquid morphine. "Sip this," he said to the giant.

"Thank you, Doctor," said Magnus Manson. He slurped soundly.

"Cornelius!" cried Thompson, pointing.

Crozier was gone. Bloody smears led into the seracs.

"Oh, fuck me," said the caulker's mate with a sigh. "This arsehole is more trouble than he is worth. Dickie, have you reloaded?" Hickey was reloading the pistol as he asked the question.

"Aye," said Aylmore, lifting the shotgun.

"Thompson, pick up the extra shotgun I brought and stay here with Magnus and the surgeon. If the good doctor does anything at all that you don't like — even farts — blow his private parts off."

Thompson nodded. Golding giggled. Hickey with his pistol and Golding and Aylmore with their shotguns advanced slowly across the moonlit ice and then tentatively, single file, into the forest of seracs and shadows.

"He could be hard to find in here," whispered Aylmore as they stepped into the stripes of moonlight and darkness.

"I don't think so," said Hickey, and pointed at the broad smear of blood that led straight ahead between the ice columns like a telegraph code of black dots and dashes between the shadows.

"He still has a little pistol with him," whispered Aylmore, moving cautiously from serac to serac.

"Fuck him and fuck his pistol," said Hickey, striding straight ahead, his boots slipping a bit on the blood and ice.

Golding giggled loudly. "Fuck him and fuck his little pistol," he said in a singsong voice, snickering again.

The blood trail ended forty feet in at the black *polynya*. Hickey rushed forward and stared down at where the horizontal smears became vertical smears on the side of the eight-foot ice slab. Something had gone into the water here.

"God-damn it to God-damn fucking hell," cried Hickey, pacing back and forth. "I wanted to put that last bullet into the high-and-mighty king's fucking face while he watched, God-*damn* him. He robbed me."

"Look, Mr. Hickey, sir," said Golding, giggling. He pointed to what might be a body floating facedown in the dark water.

"It's only the fucking coat," said Aylmore, who had come cautiously out of the shadows with his shotgun raised.

"Only the fucking coat," repeated Robert Golding.

"So he's dead down there," said Aylmore. "Can we get out of here before Des Voeux or someone comes to the sound of all the shooting? It's two days back to the others and we still have the bodies to cut up before we can leave."

"No one's going anywhere yet," said the caulker's mate. "Crozier may still be alive."

"All shot up like that, without his coat?" asked Aylmore. "And look at the greatcoat, Cornelius. The shotgun tore it apart."

"He may still be alive. We're going to make sure he's not. And maybe the body will float to the surface."

"What are you going to do?" asked Aylmore. "Shoot his dead body?"

Hickey wheeled on the man and glared, making the much-taller Aylmore step back. "Yes," said Cornelius Hickey. "That's precisely what I'm going to do." To Golding he barked, "Go bring Thompson and Magnus and the surgeon. We'll tie up the doctor tight to one of them seracs while Aylmore and Thompson and me search and you watch over Magnus and cut Lane and Goddard into small enough to haul easylike bits."

"Me cut 'em up?" cried Golding. "You told me that's why we were grabbin' Goodsir, Cornelius. He was s'posed to do all the cutting up, not me."

"Goodsir will do the carving in the future, Bobby," said Hickey. "Tonight you have to do it. We can't trust Dr. Goodsir yet . . . not until we get him back with our people and many miles away from here. You be a good boy and go get the doctor and tie him up to a serac, tight, use your best knots, and tell Magnus to bring the carcasses over here where you can carve 'em. And get blades from Goodsir's kit and the big knives and carpenter's saw I brung that are over in the bag."

"Oh, all right," said Golding. "But I'd rather search." He trudged back out of the serac field.

"The captain must have left half his blood between where you shot him and here, Cornelius," said Aylmore. "If he didn't go into the water, he can't hide anywhere here without leaving a trail."

"That is precisely correct, Dickie my dear," said Hickey with a strange smile. "If he's not in the water he might crawl, but he cannot stop losing blood with wounds like that. We are going to search until we are sure he ain't under the water nor curled up somewhere here in the seracs where he crawled and hid and bled himself to death. You start over there on the south side of the *polynya*, I'll look to the north. We'll go clockwise. If you see any wee sign, even a drop of blood, even a scuff in the snow, shout and stop. I'll join you. And be careful. We don't want the dying fucker jumping out of the shadows and grabbing one of our guns now, do we?"

Aylmore looked surprised and alarmed. "Do you really think he could be strong enough to do that? With three bullets and all those shotgun pellets in him, I mean? Without his coat, he'd freeze to death in a few minutes anyway. It's getting much colder and the wind's getting stronger. Do you really think he's lying in wait for us, Cornelius?"

Hickey smiled and nodded toward the black pool. "No. I think he's dead and drowned and down there. But we're going to make fuckin' sure. We're not leaving here until we're sure, even if we got to search until the God-poxed sun comes up."

––––––––

In the end, they searched for three hours under the light of the rising and then descending moon. There were no signs at all near the *polynya* nor amid the seracs nor on the open ice fields beyond the seracs in all directions nor on the high pressure ridges to the north and south and east: no blood trails, no footprints, no drag marks.

It took Robert Golding the full three hours to hack John Lane and William Goddard into the size pieces that Hickey had asked for, and even then the boy made a dreadful mess of it. Ribs, heads, hands, feet, and sections of spinal cord lay around him on all sides as if there had been an explosion in an abattoir. And young Golding himself was so covered with blood that he looked like a player in a minstrel show by the time Hickey and the others got back. Aylmore, Thompson, and even Magnus Manson were taken aback by their young apprentice's appearance, but Hickey laughed long and hard.

The gunnysacks and burlap bags were filled with meat wrapped in oilcloths they'd brought. Yet still the bags leaked.

They untied Goodsir, who was shaking from the cold or shock.

"Time to go, Surgeon," said Hickey. "The other chaps are waiting ten miles west of here on the ice to welcome you home."

Goodsir said, "Mr. Des Voeux and the others will come after you."

"No," said Cornelius Hickey, his voice showing his absolute certainty, "they won't. Not with them knowing that now we got at least three shotguns and a pistol. And that's if they ever find out we was here, which I think they won't." To Golding, he said, "Give our new crewmate a sack of meat to carry, Bobby."

When Goodsir refused to accept the bulging sack from Golding, Magnus Manson knocked him down, almost breaking the surgeon's ribs. On the fourth attempt to hand him the dripping bag, after two more serious cuffings, the surgeon took it.

"Let's go," said Hickey. "We're done here."

54

DES VOEUX

First Mate Charles Des Voeux could not restrain himself from grinning as he and his eight men returned to Rescue Camp on the morning of Saturday, 19 August. For a change, he had nothing but good news to deliver to his captain and the men.

The ice pack had opened to floes and navigable leads only four miles out, and Des Voeux and his men had spent another day following the leads south until the strait became open water all the way to the Adelaide Peninsula and almost certainly to the inlet to Back River farther east around that peninsula. Des Voeux had *seen* the low hills of the Adelaide Peninsula less than twelve open-water miles away from an iceberg they'd climbed at their farthest-south extension of the ice pack. They could go no farther without a boat, which had made First Mate Des Voeux grin broadly then and which made him grin again now.

Everyone could leave Rescue Camp. Everyone there now had a chance at survival.

Almost better news to bring home was the fact that they had spent two days shooting seals on the floes at the edge of the new open sea out there on the strait. For two days and nights, Des Voeux and his men had gorged themselves on seal meat and blubber, their bodies craving the fat so much that even though the rich food made then sick — after weeks of only ship's biscuit and slivers of old salt pork — vomiting just made them hungrier, and they laughed and began gorging again almost immediately.

Each of his eight men was dragging a carcass of a seal behind him now as they followed the bamboo wands across the last mile of coastal ice to the camp. The forty-six men in Rescue Camp would eat well tonight, as would again the eight triumphant explorers.

All in all, Des Voeux thought as they came up the shingle past the boats, hallooing and hurrahing to get the camp's attention, other than the young squirt Golding turning back on his own that first day because of a belly ache, it had been almost a perfect expedition. For the first time in months — in *years* — Captain Crozier and the others would have news to celebrate.

They were all going home. If they left today, the healthy among them man-hauling the ill in the boats only the four miles on the winding trail through pressure ridges that Des Voeux had carefully charted, they would be afloat within three or four days, to the mouth of Back's Great Fish River within the week. And it was probable that the opening leads had advanced even closer to shore by now!

Filthy, ragged, slumped creatures emerged from their tents and left their desultory camp chores to come out to stare at Des Voeux's party.

The cheering of Des Voeux's men — Fat Alex Wilson, Francis Pocock, Josephus Greater, George Cann, Robert Johns, Thomas Tadman, Thomas McConvey, and William Mark — died as they looked at the dour, immobile, haunted-eyed faces of the men facing them. The men from the camp could see the seals being dragged, but they seemed to have no reaction.

Mates Couch and Thomas came out of their tents and down the shingle to stand in front of the line of Rescue Camp spectres.

"Did someone die?" asked Charles Frederick Des Voeux.

———

Second Mate Edward Couch, First Mate Robert Thomas, First Mate Charles Des Voeux, *Erebus* Captain of the Hold Joseph Andrews, and *Terror* Captain of the Maintop Thomas Farr were crowded into the oversized tent that had been used as Dr. Goodsir's hospital. The amputees, Des Voeux had learned, had either died in the four days he was gone or been moved back to smaller tents shared with the other sick men.

These five in this tent this morning were the last officers with any command authority left alive — or at least at Rescue Camp and well enough to walk — from the entire John Franklin Expedition. They had just enough tobacco left for four of the five — Farr did not smoke — to have their pipes going. The interior of the tent was filled with blue smoke.

"Are you sure it wasn't the thing from the ice that committed the carnage you found out there?" asked Des Voeux.

Couch shook his head. "We thought that might be the case at first — in fact, that was our assumption — but the bones and heads and remaining pieces of flesh we found. . . ." He stopped and bit down hard on the stem of pipe.

"Had knife marks on them," finished Robert Thomas. "Lane and Goddard were butchered by a human being."

"Not a human being," said Thomas Farr. "But some vile thing in the shape of a man."

"Hickey," said Des Voeux.

The others nodded.

"We have to go after him and the murderers with him," said Des Voeux.

No one spoke for a moment. Then Robert Thomas said, "Why?"

"To bring them to justice."

Four of the five men looked at one another. "They have three shotguns now," said Couch. "And almost certainly the captain's per-cussion-cap pistol."

"We have more men . . . guns . . . powder, shot, cartridges," said Des Voeux.

"Aye," said Thomas Farr. "And how many of them would die in a battle with Hickey and his fifteen cannibals? Thomas Johnson ne'er came back, y'know. His job was just to *track* Hickey's band, make sure they was leaving like they said they was."

"I can't believe this," said Des Voeux, removing his pipe and tamp-ing at the bowl. "What about Captain Crozier and Dr. Goodsir? Are you just going to abandon them? Leave them to Cornelius Hickey's whims?"

"The captain ain't alive," said Captain of the Hold Andrews. "Hickey wouldn't have no reason to keep Crozier alive . . . unless it was to torture and torment him."

"All the more reason to send a rescue party after them," insisted Des Voeux.

The others did not respond for a moment. The blue smoke swirled around them. Thomas Farr untied the tent door and opened it wider to let some air in and smoke out.

"It's been almost two days since whatever happened out on the ice happened," said Edward Couch. "It would be several more days before any party we sent could find and fight Hickey's group, even if they *could* find them. All the devil has to do is travel farther out on the ice or inland to throw us off. The wind obscures tracks in hours . . . even sledge tracks. Do you really think Francis Crozier, if he's alive now — which I doubt — would be alive or in any shape to be rescued in five days or a week?"

Des Voeux chewed the stem of his pipe. "Dr. Goodsir, then. We need the surgeon. Logic dictates that Hickey would keep *him* alive. Goodsir may be the reason Hickey and his accomplices came back."

Robert Thomas shook his head. "Cornelius Hickey may need Dr. Goodsir for his own infernal purposes, but we don't any longer."

"What do you mean?"

"I mean that most of our good surgeon's potions and instruments were left behind — he brought only his portable medical kit," said Farr. "And Thomas Hartnell, who's been his assistant, knows which potions to administer and how much and for what."

"What about actual surgery?" asked Des Voeux.

Couch smiled sadly. "Lad, do you really think that anyone who needs actual surgery from this point on in our travels is likely to survive, no matter what?"

Des Voeux did not answer.

"And what if Hickey and his men ain't goin' nowhere?" asked Andrews. "And never planned to? He come back to kill the captain, grab Goodsir, and take poor John Lane and Bill Goddard and carve 'em up like animals. He sees all of us as livestock. What if he's just waiting out there beyond the next rise, waiting to attack the whole camp?"

"You're turning the caulker's mate into a bogeyman," said Des Voeux.

"He done that to his self already," said Andrews. "But not a bogeyman, the Devil. The actual Devil. Him and his tame monster, Magnus Manson. They sold their souls — God-damn them — and received some dark power for it. Mark my words."

"You'd think that one real monster would be enough for any arctic expedition," said Robert Thomas.

No one laughed.

"It's *all* one real monster," Edward Couch said at last. "And not a new one to our race."

"So what are you all suggesting?" Des Voeux asked after another spell of silence. "That we run from a five-foot-tall demon caulker's mate and just head south with the boats tomorrow?"

"Me, I'm saying we leave today," said Joseph Andrews. "As soon as we load the boats with the few things we're takin'. Man-haul through the night. With luck, there'll be enough moonlight to guide by when she rises. If not, we use some of the lantern fuel we kept back. You said yourself, Charles, that the wands is still out there markin' the way. They won't be after the first real storm blows through."

Couch shook his head. "Des Voeux's men are tired. Our people are totally demoralized. Let's have a feast tonight — eat every one of those eight seals you brought in, Charles — then leave tomorrow morning. We'll all have more of a sense of hope after a big meal, some cooking and light using the seal oil, and a good night's sleep."

"But with men on watch tonight," said Andrews.

"Oh, aye," said Couch. "I'll stand watch myself. I'm not that hungry anyway."

"There's the question of command," said Thomas Farr, looking from face to face in the dim light filtering through the canvas.

Several of the men sighed.

"Charles is in overall command," said First Mate Robert Thomas. "Sir John himself promoted him as first mate of the flagship when Graham Gore got killed, so he's senior officer."

"But you were first mate on *Terror*, Robert," Farr said to Thomas. "You have seniority."

Thomas shook his head adamantly. "*Erebus* was the command ship. When Gore was alive, it was understood that he had overall expedition command above mine. Charles's got Gore's job now. He's in charge. I don't mind. Mr. Des Voeux is a better leader than me, and we're going to need leadership."

"I can't believe that Captain Crozier's gone," said Andrews.

Four of the five men smoked harder. No one spoke. They could hear men outside talking about the seals, someone laughing, and — beyond that — the cracking and rifle fire of ice breaking.

"Technically," said Thomas Farr, "Lieutenant George Henry Hodgson is in charge of the expedition now."

"Oh, fuck Lieutenant George Henry Hodgson up the arse with a hot poker," said Joseph Andrews. "If the little weasel were to come crawlin' back now, I'd strangle 'im with me own hands and piss on his corpse."

"I doubt very much if Lieutenant Hodgson is still alive," Des Voeux said softly. "It's decided then that I'm in overall command of the expedition now, with Robert second in command, Edward as third?"

"Aye," said the other four men in the tent.

"Then understand that I'm going to keep conferring with the four of you as we have to make decisions," said Des Voeux. "I've always wanted to be captain of my own ship . . . but not this fucking way. I'm going to need your help."

Everyone nodded behind their screen of pipe smoke.

"I have one question before we go out and tell the men to start preparing for the feast today and departure tomorrow," said Couch.

Des Voeux, who was bareheaded in the heat of the tent, raised his eyebrows.

"What about the sick men? Hartnell tells me that there are six who can't walk, even if their lives depended on it. Too far gone in scurvy. Take Jopson, the captain's steward, for instance. Mr. Helpman and our engineer, Thompson, are dead, but Jopson keeps hanging on. Hartnell says he can't even lift his head to drink — he has to be helped — but he's still alive. Do we take him with us?"

Des Voeux looked at Couch and then at the other three faces for unspoken answers, but they gave him nothing.

"And if we *do* take Jopson and the other dying ones," continued Couch, "what do we take 'em *as?*"

Des Voeux did not have to ask what the second mate meant. *Do we haul them along as shipmates or as food?*

"If we leave them here," he said, "they'll sure as hell be food if Hickey comes back the way some of you think he will."

Couch shook his head. "That isn't what I'm asking."

"I know," said Des Voeux. He took a deep breath, almost coughing because of the thick pipe smoke. "All right," he said. "Here is my first decision as new commander of the Franklin Expedition. When we drag the boats to the ice in the morning, any man who can walk to the boats and get into harness — or even into one of the boats — comes with us. If he dies on the way, we'll decide then whether to haul his body farther. *I'll* decide. But tomorrow morning, only those who can walk to the boats will leave Rescue Camp."

None of the other men spoke, but several nodded. No one met Des Voeux's gaze.

"I'll tell the men after we eat," said Des Voeux. "Each of you four choose one reliable man to join you on watch tonight. Edward will set the schedule. Don't let those men eat themselves into oblivion. We'll need our wits about us — at least some of us — until we get safely to the open water."

All four men nodded at this.

"All right, go tell your men about the feast," said Des Voeux. "We're done here."

GOODSIR

From the private diary of Dr. Harry D. S. Goodsir:

Saturday, 20 August, 1848 —
The Devil, Hickey, seems to have all the Good Fortune so denied to
Sir John, Commander Fitzjames, and Captain Crozier for so many Months
and Years.

They do not know that I had Inadvertently put my Diary into my
Medical Kit — or, rather, they probably know, since they thoroughly Searched
my kit two nights ago after taking me Captive, but they do not Care. I sleep
Alone in a tent except for Lieutenant Hodgson, who is as much Captive now
as I am, and he does not Mind my scribbling in the dark.

Part of me still cannot believe the Slaughter of my comrades — Lane,
Goddard, and Crozier — and had I not Seen with my own Eyes the Feast of
Human Flesh half of Hickey's party celebrated late Friday night upon our
return to this sledge Camp out on the Ice not far from our old River Camp,
I still might not Believe in such Barbarism.

Not all of Hickey's Infernal Legion have yet succumbed to the Lure of
Cannibalism. Hickey, Manson, Thompson, and Aylmore are Enthusiastic
Participants, of course, as are — it turns out — Seaman William Orren,
Steward William Gibson, Stoker Luke Smith Golding, Caulker James
Brown, and his mate Dunn.

But others abstain alongside Myself — Morfin, Best, Jerry, Work,
Strickland, Seeley, and, of course, Hodgson. We are all subsisting on Mouldy

Ship's Biscuits. Of those Fellow Abstainers, I suspect that only Strickland or Morfin and the Lieutenant may continue to Resist for long. Hickey's People have caught just one Seal on their voyage West along the coast, but that was enough to power a Stove with its Oil — and the smell of Roasting Human Flesh is Horribly Enticing.

Hickey has not Harmed me yet. Not even the past Two Nights when I have refused to partake of the Meal or to agree to Cut Other Bodies Up when the time comes. So far, Mr. Lane and Mr. Goddard's Parts have assuaged their appetite and Freed me from having to decide between becoming a Chef for Cannibals or being Maimed and Carved myself.

But no one is allowed to Touch the Shotguns other than Mr. Hickey, Mr. Aylmore, or Mr. Thompson — these Last Two have become lieutenants of the New Bonaparte that is our Diminutive Caulker's Mate — and Magnus Manson is a weapon of his own which only One Man — if he is indeed still a man — can Aim and Unleash.

But when I speak of Hickey's Fortune, I do not speak of just the Luck of his own Dark Making that brought him a source of fresh meat. Rather, I refer to today's Revelation when, just two miles northwest and offshore of our old River Camp where Mr. Bridgens went missing, we came upon Open Leads that stretched Westward along the Coast.

Hickey's Depraved Crew unsledged, Rigged, loaded, and Launched the pinnace almost at once, and we have been Sailing and Rowing quickly along to the West ever since.

You Might Ask, How can 17 Men fit into a 28-foot Open Boat meant to carry only 8 to a Dozen men comfortably?

The Answer is that we crowd upon each other Terribly and — even though we haul only Tents, weapons, cartridges, water casks, ourselves, and our Terrible Food supply — we are so Heavily Laden that the Sea rises almost to the Gunwales on either side, especially when the width of the Leads allows us to Tack into the wind without the Use of Oars.

I Heard Hickey and Aylmore whispering after we landed to pitch Tents this Evening — they made Little Effort to lower their Voices.

Someone will have to go.

The Water is Open ahead, the Way is Free — perhaps all the way back to Terror Camp, or even to Terror herself — just as the Prophet Cornelius

Hickey insisted during the confrontation with Crozier at the unnamed bay in July, where mutiny was avoided only by the shout of Open Water — and it may well Occur that Hickey and those who Remain with Him will be back at Terror Camp and the ship in three days of Easy Sailing rather than the Three and a Half Months of Brutal Man-hauling it took us to come the Same Distance in the Opposite Direction.

But now that they do not need Man-haulers, which Men will be Sacrificed to the Food stores so that the boat can be Lightened for tomorrow's Sailing?

Hickey and his Giant and Aylmore and the other Leaders are Walking Through Camp as I write, calling us peremptorily Out of Our Tents, although the Hour is Late and the night is Dark.

If I am Alive tomorrow, I will write more then.

56

JOPSON

Rescue Camp
20 August, 1848

T hey were treating him like an old man and leaving him behind because they thought he was an old man, used up, dying even, but that was ridiculous. Thomas Jopson was only thirty-one years old. Today, the twentieth of August, he turned thirty-one years old. It was his birthday, and none of them except Captain Crozier, who had quit coming to see him in his sick tent for some unknown reason, even knew it was his birthday. They were treating him like an old man because almost all of his teeth had fallen out from the scurvy and most of his hair had fallen out for some reason he did not understand and he was bleeding from his gums and eyes and hairline and anus, but *he was not an old man*. He was thirty-one years old today and they were leaving him behind to die on his birthday.

Jopson heard the revelries the afternoon and evening before — impressions and memories of the shouting and laughter and smell of roasting food were not connected since he had been shifting in and out of fevered consciousness all that previous day — but he had wakened in the twilight to find that someone had brought a plate holding a slab of oily sealskin, strips of dripping white blubber, and a fish-smelling stripe of almost-raw red seal meat. Jopson vomited — nothing had come up because he had not eaten for a day or days — and shoved the offending plate of offal out the open tent door.

He'd understood that they were leaving him when crewmate after crewmate came by his tent later in the evening, saying nothing, not even showing their faces, but each shoving in one or two rock-hard and half-green ship's biscuits, stacking them by his side like so many white rocks in preparation for his burial. He was too weak to protest then — and too preoccupied with his dreams — but he had known that these few lousy lumps of half-baked and fully stale flour were all he was to receive for his years of faithful service to the Navy, to the Discovery Service, and to Captain Crozier.

They were leaving him behind.

This Sunday morning he awoke more clearheaded than he had been in some days — perhaps in weeks — only to hear his shipmates' preparations to leave Rescue Camp forever.

There was shouting down by the boats as the two whaleboats were righted and as the two cutters were readied on their sledges and as all four boats were loaded.

How could they leave me behind? Jopson had trouble believing they could or would. Hadn't he stayed by Captain Crozier's side a hundred times during the captain's illnesses and moody low points and out-right bouts of drunkenness? Hadn't he quietly, uncomplainingly, like the good steward he was, hauled pails of vomit from the captain's cabin in the middle of the night and wiped the Irish drunkard's arse when he shat himself in his fever deliriums?

Perhaps that's why the bastard is leaving me to die.

Jopson forced his eyes open and tried to roll over in his sodden sleeping bag. It was very difficult. The weakness radiating out from his center consumed him. His head threatened to burst with pain every time he opened his eyes. The earth pitched against him as fiercely as any ship he'd ever ridden around the Horn in high seas. His bones ached.

Wait for me! he shouted. He thought he had shouted it, but it had been only a silent thought. He would have to do better than that . . . catch up to them before they shoved the boats out onto the ice . . . show them that he could man-haul with the best of them. He might even fool them by being able to force down some of their reeking, rotten seal meat.

Jopson could not believe that they were treating him like a dead man. He was a living human being with a good Naval record and excellent experience as a personal steward and with as solid a private history as a loyal citizen of Her Majesty's as any other man on the expedition, not to mention a family and a home in Portsmouth (if Elisabeth and his son, Avery, were still alive and if they'd not been evicted from the home they'd rented with Thomas Jopson's Discovery Service river-pay advance of 28 pounds against his first year's expedition salary of 65 pounds).

Rescue Camp now seemed empty except for a few low moans that could be coming from nearby tents or could be merely the incessant wind. The usual crunch of boots on gravel, soft cursing, rare laughter, the small talk of men going to and from watch, shouts between tents, echoes of hammer or saw, the smell of pipe tobacco — all were absent except for faint and receding noises from the direction of the boats. The men were really leaving.

Thomas Jopson was not going to stay here and die in this cold arse-end-of-the-world temporary camp.

Using all of the strength he had and some he knew he did not have, Jopson pulled his Hudson's Bay blanket sleeping bag down past his shoulders and began creeping his way out of it. The operation was made no simpler by the fact that strands of frozen sweat, blood, and other bodily fluids had to be ripped free of flesh and wool before he could crawl out of the blanket and toward the tent opening.

Moving what seemed like miles on his elbows, Jopson collapsed forward through the tent flap and gasped at how cold the air outside was. He had grown so used to the canvas-filtered dim light and stuffy air of his tent-womb that this openness and glare made his lungs labour and filled his squinted-shut eyes with tears.

Jopson soon realized that the sun's glare was illusory; indeed, the morning was dark and thickly fogged, with tendrils of icy vapour moving between the tents like the spirits of all those dead men they'd left behind. It reminded the captain's steward of the thick fog on the day they'd sent Lieutenant Little, Ice Master Reid, Harry Peglar, and the others forward down the first open lead in the ice.

To their deaths, thought Jopson.

Crawling over the ship's biscuits and seal meat — brought to him as if he were some damned pagan idol or sacrificial offering to the gods — Jopson pulled his unfeeling and unresponsive legs out through the circular tent opening.

He saw two or three tents standing nearby and for a second he was filled with the hope that the absence of ambulatory men here was temporary, that they were all busy doing something near the boats and would soon be back. But then Jopson saw that most of the Holland tents were missing.

No, not missing. He could see now, as his eyes adapted to the diffuse light leaking through the fog, that the majority of tents here on the south end of the camp — nearest to the boats and shoreline — had been collapsed, with rocks tossed atop them to keep them from blowing away. Jopson was confused. If they were actually leaving, wouldn't they be bringing the tents along? It was as if they planned to go out on the ice but then return soon. To where? And why? None of it made any sense to the sick and recently hallucinatory steward.

Then the fog shifted and lifted and he could see fifty yards or so to where the men were pulling, pushing, and tugging from the sides on the boats, hauling them out onto the ice. Jopson estimated that there were at least ten men per boat, which meant that all or almost all of the survivors here at camp were leaving him and the other really sick men behind.

How can Dr. Goodsir leave me behind? wondered Jopson. He tried to remember the last time it had been the surgeon who had lifted his head and shoulders to feed him broth or to clean him. It was young Hartnell yesterday, wasn't it? Or had that been several days ago? He could not recall the last time the surgeon had looked in on him or brought him medicine.

"Wait!" he called.

Only it had not been a call. It had hardly been a croak. Jopson realized that he had not spoken aloud for days — perhaps weeks — and the noise he'd just made sounded muted and muffled even to his own ringing ears.

"Wait!" That had been no better. He realized that he had to wave his arm in the air, make them see him, make them turn back for him.

Thomas Jopson could not raise either arm. Even trying to do so caused him to fall forward, his face striking the gravel.

There was nothing for it — he would just have to crawl toward them until they saw him and turned back. They wouldn't leave behind a fellow crewmate healthy enough to crawl a hundred yards after them onto the ice.

Jopson wriggled forward on his torn elbows another three feet and collapsed facedown onto the icy gravel again. The fog roiled around him, obscuring even his own tent a few paces behind him. The wind moaned — or perhaps it was more abandoned sick souls moaning in the few tents still standing — and the chill of the cold day cut right through his filthy wool shirt and soiled trousers. He realized that if he kept crawling away from his tent, he might not have the strength to crawl back and would die of the cold and damp out here.

"Wait!" he called. His voice was as weak and mewling as a newborn kitten's.

He crawled and wriggled and writhed another three feet . . . four . . . and lay gasping like a harpooned seal. His weakened, dragging arms and hands were of no more use than flippers would be . . . of less use.

Jopson tried digging his chin into the frozen earth to propel himself forward another foot or two. He immediately chipped one of his last remaining teeth in two but dug his chin in again for another try. His body was simply too heavy. It seemed attached to the earth by great weights.

I am only thirty-one years old, he thought fiercely, angrily. *Today is my birthday.*

"Wait . . . wait . . . wait . . . wait." Each syllable was weaker than the last.

Panting, gasping, his remaining strands of hair dabbing crimson streaks onto the rounded stones, Jopson lay on his belly, his dead arms at his sides, painfully cocked his neck, and settled his cheek against the cold earth so that he could see straight ahead.

"Wait . . ."

The fog swirled and then lifted.

He could see a hundred yards, past the odd vacuity where the boats had been lined up, past the shingle of shore gravel and the tumble of shore ice, out onto the ice itself where forty-some men and four boats — *where is the fifth?* — struggled southward deeper onto the ice, the men's own weakness evident even at this distance, their own progress not that much more efficient or elegant than Jopson's five-yard struggle had been.

"Wait!" This last shout had taken the penultimate ounce of draining energy — Jopson could feel his core's warmth flowing away into the icy ground beneath him — but it had come out as loud as any spoken word he had ever uttered.

"Wait!!" he finally shouted. It was a man's voice now, not a kitten's mewl or dying seal's squeak.

But it was too late. The men and boats were a hundred yards out now and disappearing fast — mere black, staggering silhouettes against an eternal background of grey and grey — and the cracking and groaning of ice and wind would have covered the sound of a rifle shot, much less a solitary voice of one man left behind.

For an instant the fog lifted more and a benevolent light fell on everything — as if the sun were coming out to melt the ice everywhere and to bring green tendrils and living things and hope back where none existed here before — but then the fog closed in and swirled around Jopson, blinding him and binding him with its clammy, cold grey fingers.

And then the men and the boats were gone.

It was as if they had never existed.

57

HICKEY

On the SW Cape of King William Island
8 September, 1848

Caulker's mate Cornelius Hickey hated kings and queens. He thought they were all bloodsucking parasites on the corpus-ass of the body politick.

But he found that he did not at all mind *being* king.

His plan to sail and row all the way back to Terror Camp or *Terror* herself went acropper when their pinnace — no longer so crowded — rounded the southwest cape of King William Land and encountered advancing ice pack. The open water narrowed to leads which led nowhere or which closed ahead of them even as their boat tried to creep along the coast that now stretched ahead to the northeast.

There was real open water much farther to the west, but Hickey could not allow the pinnace to be out of sight of land for the simple reason that no one left alive in their boat knew how to navigate at sea.

The only reason that Hickey and Aylmore had been so generous as to allow George Hodgson to come with them — actually, to seduce the young lieutenant into wanting to come with them — was that the fool had been trained, as all Naval lieutenants were, in celestial navigation. But on their first day of man-hauling away from Rescue Camp, Hodgson admitted that he could not fix their position or navigate their way back to *Terror* at sea without a sextant, and the only remaining sextants were still in the possession of Captain Crozier.

One of the reasons Hickey, Manson, Aylmore, and Thompson had doubled back and lured Crozier and Goodsir out onto the ice was to somehow get one of those God-damned sextants, but there Cornelius Hickey's native cleverness had failed him. He and Dickie Aylmore failed to come up with any convincing reason that their Judas goat — Bobby Golding — could ask Crozier to bring his sextant out onto the ice with him, so they'd discussed torturing that toff Irish bastard into somehow sending a note back demanding the instrument be sent out from camp, but in the end, actually seeing his tormentor on his knees, Hickey had opted to kill him at once.

So once they found open water, young Hodgson's usefulness, even as a man-hauler, was over, and Hickey soon had to dispatch him in a clean and merciful manner.

It helped to have Crozier's pistol and extra cartridges for just such a purpose. In the first days after they'd returned with Goodsir and a food supply, Hickey had allowed Aylmore and Thompson to keep the two extra shotguns they'd seized — Hickey himself had been given the third one by Crozier the day they left Rescue Camp — but he soon thought better of having the extra weapons around and had Magnus toss them into the sea. This way was better: the king, Cornelius Hickey, having the pistol and control of the only shotgun and its cartridges, with Magnus Manson by his side. Aylmore was an effete, bookish born conspirator, Hickey knew, and Thompson was a drunken lout who could never be fully trusted — Hickey knew such things by instinct and because of his innately superior intelligence — and when the Hodgson food supply ran short around the third day of September, Hickey sent Magnus to knock both men on the head, bind them up, and drag them half senseless before the other dozen assembled men where Hickey held a brief court-martial, found both Aylmore and Thompson guilty of sedition and of plotting against their leader and shipmates, and dispatched them both with a single bullet into the base of the brain.

With all three sacrifices for the greater good — Hodgson, Aylmore, and Thompson — the damned surgeon, Goodsir, still refused to fulfill his role as Dissector General.

So for each refusal, Commander Hickey had been forced to mete out a punishment for the recalcitrant surgeon. There had been three such punishments, so Goodsir was certainly having trouble walking now that they'd been forced ashore again.

Cornelius Hickey believed in luck — his own luck — and he'd always been a lucky man, but when luck failed him, he was always prepared to make his own.

In this case, when they'd come around the huge cape at the south-west corner of King William Land — sailing when they could, rowing hard when the leads grew narrow so close in to shore — and saw the solid pack ice ahead, Hickey had ordered the ship ashore and they'd reloaded the pinnace onto the sledge.

He didn't need to remind the men about how lucky they were. While Crozier's men were almost certainly dead or dying back there at Rescue Camp — or dying on the ice pack in the strait south of it — Hickey's Chosen Few had made it more than two thirds, and possibly as much as three quarters, of the way back to Terror Camp and all the supplies cached there.

Hickey had decided that a leader of his stature — the reigning King of the Franklin Expedition — should not be forced to man-haul. The men were certainly being fed well thanks to him (and thanks only to him) and should have no complaints about illness or lack of energy, so for this final part of the voyage he had decided to sit in the stern of the pinnace atop the sledge and to allow his dozen surviving subjects, excluding only the limping Goodsir, to pull him across the ice, gravel, and snow as they rounded the north curve of the cape.

For the last few days, Magnus Manson had ridden in the pinnace with him, and not simply because everyone now understood that Magnus was the king's consort as well as Grand Inquisitor and Execu-tioner. Poor Magnus was having stomach pains again.

The primary reason that Goodsir was limping but still alive was that Cornelius Hickey had a deep fear of disease and contagion. The other men's illnesses back at Rescue Camp and before — the bleeding scurvy especially — had disgusted and terrified the caulker's mate. He needed a doctor along to attend to him, even though he had not yet shown the slightest sign of illness that so plagued such lesser men.

Hickey's sledge team — Morfin, Orren, Brown, Dunn, Gibson, Smith, Best, Jerry, Work, Seeley, and Strickland — had also shown no signs of advancing scurvy now that their diet consisted of fresh or almost-fresh meat once again.

Only Goodsir was looking and acting sick, and that was because the fool insisted on eating only the last few ship's biscuits and water. Hickey knew that he would soon have to step in and *insist* that the surgeon partake of a healthier antiscorbutic diet — the fleshy parts such as thigh, calf, and fore- and upper arm were the best — so that Goodsir did not die on them because of his own perverse stubbornness. A doctor, after all, should know better. Stale ship's biscuits and water might sustain a rat if nothing else were available, but it was not a diet for men.

To make sure that Goodsir stayed alive, Hickey had long ago relieved the surgeon of all the medicines in his kit, watching over them himself and allowing Goodsir to dole them out to Magnus or others only under careful supervision. He also made sure that the surgeon had no access to knives, and when they were out at sea, he always had one of his men assigned to watch to make sure Goodsir did not throw himself overboard.

So far, the surgeon had shown no indications of choosing self-murder.

Magnus's stomachache was now severe enough not only to keep the giant riding in the sledge-raised pinnace with Hickey during the day, but to keep him awake some nights. Hickey had never known his friend to have trouble sleeping.

The two tiny bullet wounds were the cause, of course, and Hickey forced Goodsir to attend to them daily now. The surgeon insisted that the wounds were superficial and that any infection had not spread. He showed both Hickey and the innocently peering Magnus — holding up his shirttails to peek with alarm at his own belly — how the flesh around the stomach was still pink and healthy.

"Then why the pain?" Hickey insisted.

"It's like any bruise — especially a deep-muscle bruise," said the surgeon. "It may continue to hurt for weeks. But it's not serious, much less life-threatening."

"Can you remove the balls?" asked Hickey.

"Cornelius," whined Magnus. "I don't want my balls removed."

"I mean the bullets, darling," said Hickey, petting the giant's huge forearm. "The little bullets that are in your belly."

"Perhaps," said Goodsir. "But it would be better if I did not try. At least while we are on the march. The operation would require cutting through muscle that has already largely healed. Mr. Manson might have to lie down for several days of recovery . . . and there would always be the serious risk of sepsis. If we were to decide to remove the bullets, I would feel much more comfortable doing so at Terror Camp or when we are back at the ship. So the patient could recover in bed for several days or longer."

"I don't want my tummy to hurt," rumbled Magnus.

"No, of course you don't," said Hickey, rubbing his partner's huge chest and shoulders. "Give him some morphine, Goodsir."

The surgeon nodded and meted out a bit of the painkiller into a spoon.

Magnus always enjoyed his spoonfuls of morphine and would sit in the bow of the pinnace and smile sweetly for an hour or more before falling asleep after getting his doses.

So on this Friday, the eighth day of September, all was right with King Hickey's world. His eleven dray animals — Morfin, Orren, Brown, Dunn, Gibson, Smith, Best, Jerry, Work, Seeley, and Strickland — were well and free of disease and pulling hard each day. Magnus was happy most of the time — he enjoyed riding in the bow like an officer and looking back at the countryside they'd just crossed — and there was enough morphine and laudanum in the bottles to hold out until they reached Terror Camp or *Terror* herself. Goodsir was alive and limping along with the caravan and attending to the king and his consort. The weather was good, although growing colder, and there was absolutely no sign of the creature that had preyed on them in previous months.

Even with their vigorous diet, they had enough Aylmore and Thompson food stores left to provide stew over the next few days — they had found that human fat burned as fuel much as did whale blubber, although less efficiently and for shorter periods. Hickey had plans for a lottery after that if they needed one more sacrifice before they reached Terror Camp.

They could go on shorter rations, of course, but Cornelius Hickey knew that a short-straw lottery would instill terror into the hearts of his eleven already-compliant dray animals and reaffirm who was king of this expedition. Hickey was always a light sleeper but now slept with one eye open and his hand on the percussion-cap pistol, but one last public sacrifice — presumably with Magnus then having to dole out the fourth public punishment for noncompliance to Goodsir — should break any last hidden will to resist that might be left in his dray beasts' treacherous hearts.

Meanwhile, this Friday was beautiful, with temperatures in the pleasant twenties and a blue sky growing bluer to the north along their line of travel. The heavy boat sat high on the sledge while the wooden runners scratched and hissed as they slid across ice and gravel. In the bow, Magnus, recently dosed, was smiling, holding his belly with both hands and humming a soft tune.

It was less than thirty miles to Terror Camp and John Irving's grave near Victory Point, they all knew, and less than half that to Lieutenant Le Vesconte's grave along the coast. With the men strong, they were covering two to three miles each day and would probably do better if their diet improved again.

To that end, Hickey had just torn a blank page out of one of the multiple Bibles that Magnus had insisted upon gathering up and loading into the pinnace when they left Rescue Camp — never mind that the gentle idiot did not know how to read — and was now tearing that page into eleven equal little strips of paper.

Hickey, of course, would be exempt from the coming lottery, as would Magnus and the God-damned surgeon. But tonight, when they stopped to brew up tea and the evening stew, Hickey would have each man write his own name or put his sign on one of the slips of paper and all would be ready for the lottery itself. Hickey would have Goodsir look the slips over and publicly confirm that each man had signed his own true name or unique sign.

Then the names would go into the king's peacoat pocket in preparation for the solemn ceremony to come.

58

GOODSIR

On the SW Cape of King William Island
5 October, 1848

From the personal diary of Dr. Harry D. S. Goodsir:

6, 7, or perhaps 8 October, 1848 —

I have taken the Final Draught. It will be a Few Minutes before the Full Effect is Felt. Until it Is, I shall Catch Up on my diary.

These Last Few Days I have been recalling the Details of how young Hodgson confided in me and Whispered to me in the tent Weeks ago on that Last Night before Mr. Hickey shot him.

The Lieutenant whispered, I apologize for Disturbing you, Doctor, but I have to tell Someone I am Sorry.

I whispered back, You are not a Papist, Lieutenant Hodgson. And I am Not your Confessor. Go to Sleep and let me Sleep.

Hodgson Insisted, I apologize again, Doctor. But I have to tell someone how Sorry I am for Betraying the Captain — who was always Good to Me — and for Allowing Mr. Hickey to take you Captive like This. I sincerely Regret it and I am Dreadfully Sorry.

I Lay there Silently, Saying nothing, Giving the boy nothing.

Ever Since John was killed, *persisted Hodgson.* I mean, Lieutenant Irving, my Dear Friend from Gunnery School, I have been Convinced that Caulker's Mate Hickey committed the Murder and I have been Terrified of Him.

Why would You Throw in Your Lot with Mr. Hickey if you thought him a Monster? *I whispered in the Dark.*

I was . . . Afraid. I wanted to be on His Side because he was so Terrible, *whispered Hodgson. And then the Boy began to Weep.*

I said, Shame on you.

But I put my Arm around the Boy and patted his Back while he Wept until he fell Asleep.

The Next Morning, Mr. Hickey assembled Everyone and had Magnus Manson force Lieutenant Hodgson to kneel before Him while the Caulker's Mate brandished his Pistol and Announced how He — Mr. Hickey — would Brook no Shirking, explaining again How the Good Men Amongst Us would eat and live while the Shirkers would Die.

Then he set the long-barreled Weapon to the base of George Hodgson's skull and Blew his Brains out onto the Gravel.

I have to say that the Boy was Brave at his end. He showed no Fear at all that Morning. His last words before the Pistol's Explosive Discharge were, You can go to Hell.

I only wish that my End would be so Brave. But I know now for a Certainty that it Will Not.

Mr. Hickey's Theatricals were not at an End with the Death of Lt. Hodgson, nor when Magnus Manson stripped the Boy Naked and left his Corpse Lying there in front of the Assembly.

The Sight made my Chest hurt. Speaking as a Man of Medicine, poor Hodgson was Thinner than I would have Thought Possible with any Recently Living Human Being. His Arms were mere Sheaths of Skin along Bones. His Ribs and Pelvis pressed Outward so Fiercely against the Skin that they threatened to Burst Through. And everywhere, the Boy's flesh was Mottled with Bruises.

Nonetheless, Mr. Hickey called me Forward, handed me a Pair of Shears, and insisted that I Begin Dissecting the Lieutenant in front of the Assembled Men.

I demurred.

Mr. Hickey, his voice Pleasant, asked Again.

I demurred Again.

Mr. Hickey then commanded Mr. Manson to take the Shears from me and to Strip me as Naked as the Corpse at our Feet.

Once I was Without Clothing, Mr. Hickey paced back and forth in front of the men and Pointed to my Naked Features. Mr. Manson stood nearby holding the Shears.

There ain't no Room for Shirkers in our Band of Brothers — *said Mr. Hickey*. And while we *need* this Surgeon — for I do Plan to Take care of your Dear Men's health, every Man Jack of you — he must be Punished when he Refuses to Serve our Common Good. Twice he Has Refused this Morning. We shall Remove Two Unessential Appendages as a Sign of Our Displeasure.

And with that, Mr. Hickey Proceeded to prod at Different Parts of my Anatomy with the Pistol Barrel — my Fingers, my Nose, my Penis, my Testicles, my Ears.

Then he Raised my Hand.

A Surgeon *needs* 'is Fingers if he's going to be any Use to us — *he announced Theatrically and Laughed.* We'll save those for Last.

Most of the Men Laughed.

He don't need his Pizzle nor Bollocks, though, *said Mr. Hickey, prodding at the Aforementioned Parts with his Very Cold Pistol Barrel.*

The Men Laughed again. The Anticipation, I think, was very high.

But today we is Merciful, *said Mr. Hickey. He then ordered Mr. Manson to lop off Two of my Toes.*

Which two, Cornelius? *asked the large Idiot.*

You choose, Magnus, *said our Master of Ceremonies.*

The Assembled Men laughed yet Again. I could Sense their Disappointment that something so Banal as Mere Toes were being Removed, yet I could also Tell that they enjoyed seeing Magnus Manson as the Master of My Phalangeal Fate. It was not their Fault. The Average Seaman Turned out Here had no Formal Education Whatsoever and Disliked anyone who did.

Mr. Manson Chose my Two Big Toes.

The Audience laughed and applauded.

The Shears were Applied quickly and Mr. Manson's great Strength worked to my Advantage in the Procedure.

There was more Laughter — and great Interest — as my Medical Kit was brought and everyone watched as I Tied Off necessary Arteries, Stemmed the Bleeding as Best I could — all the while feeling rather Faint — and applied Preliminary Dressings to the Wounds.

Mr. Manson was directed to Carry me back to my Tent; his Ministrations were as Gentle as a Mother's to a sick Child.

That was also the Day when Mr. Hickey thought to Relieve me of My more *Efficacious Medicinal Bottles. But before that Morning, I had Already Poured the Majority of the Morphine, Opium, Laudanum, Dover's Powders, poisonous mercury Calomel, and Mandragora into a single Opaque and Innocent-Looking Bottle marked Sugar of Lead and hidden that somewhere Other than my Medical Kit. I had then used water to bring the Visible Levels of Morphine, Opium, and Laudanum up to previous Heights.*

The Irony here is that each time I Dose Mr. Manson for his "Tummy Aches," he is receiving more than Eight Parts water to Two Small Parts morphine. The Giant does not seem to notice the Loss of Efficacy, however, which once again reminds me of the Importance of Belief in the entire Medical process.

Since that Day of Lt. Hodgson's Demise, I have Demurred again to the Sum of Eight more Toes, One Ear, and my Foreskin.

The Last Operation created so much Mirth among the Assembled Men, despite the fresh Corpses lying in front of them, that one would have Thought that the Circus had come to Perform for them.

I know why Mr. Hickey has never made Good on his repeated Threats to relieve me of my Male Member or Testicles. The Caulker's Mate has seen enough Shipboard injuries to know that Bleeding from such Wounds often cannot be Stopped — especially when the Surgeon is the one bleeding and Quite Apt to be unconscious or suffering from Shock when the Operation must Necessarily be Performed — and Mr. Hickey does not want me dead.

Walking has been very Difficult since my Seventh through Tenth toes have been Removed. I had never truly Understood how Essential our Digits are for Balance. And the Pain, of course, over the past Month, has not been Insignificant.

I think I would be Committing the Sin of Pride — not to mention that of Lying — if I said Here that I had not considered Drinking from my hidden bottle of Morphine, Opium, and Laudanum (and other materia medica) all mixed into the hidden bottle I have Thought of for so many Weeks as my Final Draught.

But I never took the Bottle out of hiding.

Not until this Hour.

I Confess I had thought the Effect would be more Rapid than it is Proving.

I can no Longer feel my Feet — which is a Blessing — and my Legs have just gone Numb up to the Patella. But at this Rate, it will be another Ten Minutes or More before the Potion reaches and Stills my Heart and other Vital Organs.

I have just Drunk more of the Final Draught. I suspect I was a Coward for not Drinking it all down At Once to begin with.

I confess here — for Purely Scientific Purposes should someone someday discover this Diary — that the Mixture is not only Quite Potent but Quite Intoxicating. If anyone else here were alive this dark, stomy Afternoon — except for Mr. Hickey and possibly Mr. Manson up in their Throne Pinnace — they should see my Last Moments spent with Bobbing Head and Drunkard's Grin.

But I do not Recommend that this Experiment be Repeated for anything but the most Dire of Medicinal Purposes.

And this leads to a true Confession.

For the First and Only Time in my Medical Career and Life, I have not Served a Patient to the Utmost of my Ability.

I speak, of course, in regards to poor Mr. Magnus Manson.

My Initial Diagnosis of the twin Gunshot Wounds was a Lie. The Bullets were small of caliber, it is True, but the Tiny Pistol must have packed a Great Charge of Powder, for both Projectiles had — it was Obvious from my first Inspection — penetrated the Idiot Giant's skin, flesh, muscle layer, and stomach lining.

From my first Consultation, I had known that the Bullets were in Mr. Manson's Belly, Spleen, Liver, or some other Vital Organ, and that his Survival Depended upon Exploratory and then Removal Surgery.

I Lied.

If there is a Hell — in which I no longer Believe, since this Earth and some of the People in it are Hell enough for any Universe — I would be and should be Cast Down to the Worst Bolgia of the Lowest Circle.

I Don't Care.

I should say here — my Chest is now Cold and my Figners . . . fInGErS are also growing Cold.

When the Storm STRk about one Monf ago, I thank'd Gd.

It seemd at the Tim that we wer Actully going to Gt to Terrorr Camp. It Seemed that Mr. Hickey had won. We were — I believ — less than Twenty

MIls frm thatt Camp and Pogrssing 3 or 4 miiles a Day in nar-Perfect wether when the Fist of The Enlesss Storms Hit.

If there is a Godd . . . I . . . thank you, Deaare God.

Snowe. DAarknss. Terrrible winds Day and Nigt.

Even the Men who could Wlk dd not Pulll. The Harneesess were Abandoned. The Tents blew dwno, then bleww away. T he tempretre Droppped 50 degres.

Winter hd Strukc like Gd's Hammmer, and Mr. Hickey cuoold do Nothing but set Tarps aside his Thronepinacce and Shoot Half the Men to Feed the Other Half.

Some Men ran away into the Bolizzardds and Died.

Some Men stayed and were Shot.

Sme M Froze to Deth.

Sm Men Ate theother mn and Died Anwwyay.

Mr. Hickey and Mr. Masnsonn sit up There in Ther Boat in the Wind. I thinge, but donnot Know, that Mrr. Mansin is No Lngr Livvng.

OI killed him.

I kelled the Men I lff behing at Rescue Camp.

I am so Sorry.

I am so Sorry.

All my lfe, my Brother knows I wish my brther werehere now, Thmoshe knws, al my lifI hve lved Plato and the Dialogues of Sokrates.

Like the grete Sokates, but not rf not grete I, the Poisoin, mcuh Deservd, movs up throu my Torso and Deadeens my Limbs and Turns my Fingrs — Surgeons fingers — to Unfeellling Sticks and

So glad

Wrote the note nw pined to my Cheset befre this

EAT THESE MORTAL REMNAS OF DR HARRY D.S. GOOODSIRIFFF YO U WISSSH THE POISSSSN WITHINN THS BONES AND FELSH WIOL KILL YOOU ALSO

TheMen at Re   cm

Thomnas, if they Find this Upon my and Ret

I am So Sorry.
I did My Best But   never is en

Mr. Msnsns Wonds   I AM NOT S

Gd wac ov Th MEn

59

HICKEY

On the SW Cape of King William Island
18 October, 1848

Sometime in the last few days or weeks, Cornelius Hickey realized, he had ceased being a king.

He was now a god.

In fact — he suspected, was not yet certain, but suspected strongly
and was close to certain — Cornelius Hickey had become God.

Others died around him yet he lived. He no longer felt the cold.
He no longer felt hunger or thirst, much less the need to slake those
former appetites. He could see in the encroaching dark as the nights
lengthened toward the absolute, nor did the blowing snow and howling wind hinder his senses.

The mere mortal men had required a rigging of a tarp from the
boat and sledge when their tents ripped and blew away and they huddled there like sheep with their woolen asses turned to the wind until
they died, but Hickey was comfortable high on his throne in the stern
of the pinnace.

When, after more than three weeks of being unable to move
because of the blizzards, winds, and plummeting temperatures, his
dray beasts had whined and begged for food, Hickey had descended
among them like a god and provided them with their loaves and
fishes.

He had shot Strickland to feed Seeley.

He had shot Dunn to feed Brown.

He had shot Gibson to feed Jerry.

He had shot Best to feed Smith.

He had shot Morfin to feed Orren . . . or perhaps it was all the other way around. Hickey's memory could no longer be bothered with trivial matters.

But now those he'd so generously fed were dead, frozen hard into their blanket sleeping bags or contorted into the terrible claw shapes of their final throes. Perhaps he had become bored with them and shot them as well. He did vaguely remember carving up the choice parts of more men than he had shot to feed the others in the past week or two, back when he still needed to eat. Or perhaps it had just been on a whim. He could not recall the details. It was not important.

When the storms ended — and Hickey now knew that He could command them to cease at any time if it pleased Him to do so — he would probably bring several of the men back from the dead so that they could finish hauling Magnus and Him to Terror Camp.

The damned surgeon was dead — poisoned and frozen in his own little tarp tent some yards from the pinnace and the common graveyard tarp — but Hickey chose to ignore that unpleasant development — it was but a mild irritation. Even gods have phobias, and Cornelius Hickey had always held a deep fear of poison or contamination. After one glance — and after firing a single bullet into the corpse from the entrance to the tarp tent to make sure the damned surgeon was not feigning death — the new god Hickey had backed away and left the poisoned thing and its contaminated shroud-tarp alone.

Magnus had been mewling and complaining for weeks from his favored place in the bow but had been strangely quiet the last day or two. His last movement, during a lull in the blizzards when a dull winter light had illuminated the pinnace and the snow-buried tarp next to it and the low hill they were on and the frozen beach to the west and endless ice fields beyond, had been to open his mouth as if to make a request of his lover and God.

But instead of words issuing forth, or even another complaint, hot blood had first filled and then geysered from Magnus's open mouth, flowed down his bearded chin, and covered the big man's belly and gently folded hands, ending in a pool on the bottom of the boat near his boots. The blood was still there, but frozen now into waves and ripples, looking like nothing so much as some Biblical Prophet's flowing (but ice-covered) brown beard. Magnus had not spoken again since.

His partner's brief Death Nap did not disturb Hickey — he knew that He could bring Magnus back whenever He chose to — but the open eyes endlessly staring over that gaping mouth and frozen icefall of blood began to get on the god's nerves after a day or two. It was especially hard to wake up to. Especially after the eyes frosted over and became two white, icy, never-blinking orbs.

Hickey had stirred from his throne in the stern then, crawling forward past the propped shotgun and bag of powder-shot cartridges, over the centre thwarts past the heaps of wrapped chocolate (which He might deign to eat if hunger ever returned) and past the saws and nails and rolls of sheet lead, stepping over the towels and silk handkerchiefs stacked so neatly near Magnus's bloodied feet, finally kicking aside some of the Bibles that his friend had pulled close to him in the last days, stacking them like a little wall between Hickey and himself.

But Magnus's mouth would not shut — Hickey could not even snap off or chip away the thick river of frozen blood — nor would the white eyes close.

"I'm sorry, love," he whispered. "But you know how I hate being stared at."

He had used his ship's knife to pry out the frozen eyeballs and throw them far out into the howling darkness. He would fix that later when He brought Magnus back.

Finally, upon His command, the storm lessened and then died away. The howling ceased. The snow was piled five feet high on the westward, windward side of the pinnace high atop its sledge and had filled in much of the space under the death tarp on the leeward side.

It was very cold and Hickey's preternatural vision could see more dark clouds moving in from the north, but for this evening, the world was calm. He saw the sun set in the south and knew that it would be sixteen or eighteen hours until it rose again, also in the south, and that soon it would not rise at all. It would then be the Age of Darkness — ten thousand years of darkness — but that suited Cornelius Hickey's purposes well.

But this night was cold and gentle. The stars were bright — Hickey had been taught the names of some of the winter constellations now rising, but this night he had trouble even finding the Plow — and He was content to sit in the stern of his boat, his peacoat and watch cap keeping him perfectly warm, his gloved hands on the gunwales, his gaze locked forward in the direction of Terror Camp and even the distant ship He would reach when He chose to bring his dray beasts and consort back to life. He was thinking about months and years past and marveling at the inevitable miracle of his own transcendence.

Cornelius Hickey had no regrets about any part of his former mortal life. He had done what he had to do. He had repaid those arrogant bastards who made the mistake of ever looking down upon him and shown the others a hint of his divine light.

Suddenly, he sensed movement to the west. With some difficulty — it was very cold — Hickey turned his head left to look out to the frozen sea.

Something was moving toward him. Perhaps it had been his hearing — as preternatural and supernatural as all his other fine-tuned and augmented senses now — that had first detected the movement across the broken ice.

Something large was walking toward him on two legs.

Hickey saw the starlight glow on the blue-white fur. He smiled. He welcomed the visit.

The thing from the ice was no longer something to be feared. Hickey knew that it came now not as a predator but as a worshipper. He and the creature were not even equals at this point; Cornelius Hickey could order it into nonexistence or banish it to the farthest reaches of the universe with a sweep of his gloved hand.

It came on, sometimes dropping to lope forward on all fours, more often rising on two huge legs and striding like a man even while moving nothing like a man.

Hickey felt a strange disquiet disturb his deep cosmic peace.

The thing disappeared from his sight when it came very close to the pinnace and sledge. Hickey could hear it moving around by the tarp — under the tarp — worrying the frozen bodies there with its long claws, clicking teeth the size of knives, huffing its breath out from time to time — but he could not see it. He realized that he was afraid to turn his head.

He looked straight forward, meeting only Magnus's empty-eye-socketed gaze.

Then suddenly the thing was there, looming over the gunwales, the upper body rising six feet and more above a boat that was already raised six feet above the sledge and snow.

Hickey felt his breath catch in his chest.

In the starlight, with Hickey's new, improved vision, the beast was more terrible than he had ever seen it, more terrible than he could have ever imagined it. Just as He — Cornelius Hickey — had undergone a wonderful and terrible transformation, so had this creature.

It leaned its huge upper body over the gunwales. It huffed a fog of ice crystals into the air between Hickey and the bow and the caulker's mate inhaled the carrion breath of a thousand centuries of death-dealing.

Hickey would have fallen to his knees and worshipped the creature at that moment if movement had been an option, but he was quite literally frozen in place. Even his head would no longer turn.

The thing sniffed Magnus Manson's body, the long, impossible snout returning again and again to the icefall of brown blood covering Magnus's front. Its huge tongue gently licked at the frozen fall of brown blood. Hickey wanted to explain that this was the body of his beloved consort and that it must be preserved so that He — not Hickey the caulker's mate, but the He he had become — could restore his beloved's eyes and someday breathe life into him again.

Abruptly, yet almost casually, the thing bit off Magnus's head.

The crunching was so terrible that Hickey would have covered his ears if he had been able to lift his gloved hands from the gunwales. He could not move them.

The thing swung a white-furred forearm thicker than Magnus's massive leg had ever been and smashed the dead man's chest in — rib cage and spine exploding outward in a shower of white bone shards. Hickey realized that the thing had not *broken* Magnus the way Hickey had seen Magnus break a score of lesser men's backs and ribs; it had *shattered* Magnus the way a man would shatter a bottle or porcelain doll.

Looking for a soul to devour, thought Hickey, who had no idea why he had thought it.

Hickey could no longer move his head even an inch, so he had no choice but to watch as the thing from the ice excavated every inner part of Magnus Manson and ate them, crunching the bits in its huge teeth the way Hickey might have once chewed ice cubes. The thing then tore the frozen flesh from Magnus's frozen bones and scattered the bones throughout the bow of the pinnace, but only after cracking them open and sucking out the marrow. The wind came up and howled around the pinnace and sledge, creating distinct musical notes. Hickey imagined a mad god-thing from Hell in a white fur coat playing a bone flute.

It came for him next.

First it dropped to all fours, out of sight — which was somehow more terrifying than his being able to see it — and then, with a vertical motion like a pressure ridge rising, it loomed up and over the side of the gunwale and filled all of Hickey's vision. Its black, unblinking, inhuman, totally unfeeling eyes were inches from the caulker's mate's own staring eyes. Its hot breath enveloped him.

"Oh," said Cornelius Hickey.

It was the last word that Hickey ever spoke, but it was not so much a word as a single, long, terrified, speechless exhalation. Hickey felt his own last warm breath flowing out of him, out from his chest, up his throat, out through his open and straining mouth, hissing away between his shattered teeth, but instantly he realized it was not his *breath* leaving him forever, but his spirit, his soul.

The thing breathed it in.

But then the creature huffed, snorted, backed away, shook its huge head as if it had been befouled. It dropped to all fours and left Cornelius Hickey's field of vision forever.

Everything had left Cornelius Hickey's field of vision forever. The stars came down from the sky and attached themselves to his staring eyes as ice crystals. The Raven descended as a darkness upon him and devoured what the *Tuunbaq* would not deign to touch. Eventually Hickey's blind eyes shattered from the cold, but he did not blink.

His body remained sitting rigidly upright in the stern, legs splayed, boots firmly planted near the heap of gold watches he had plundered and the stack of clothing he had taken from the dead men, his gloved hands frozen to the gunwales, the frozen fingers of his right hand only inches from the loaded shotgun's barrels.

Late the next morning, before dawn, the storm front arrived and the sky began to howl again, and all that next day and all the next night the snow piled up in the caulker's mate's straining, open mouth and covered his dark blue peacoat and watch cap and terror-frozen face and shattered, staring eyes with a thin shroud-layer of white.

60

CROZIER

The beauty of being dead, he knows now, is that there is no pain and no sense of self.

The unhappy news about being dead, he knows now, is — just as he had feared many times when considering self-murder and rejecting it for just this reason — there are dreams.

The happy news about this unhappy news is that the dreams are not one's own.

Crozier floats in this warm, buoyant sea of nonself and listens to dreams that are not his own.

If any of his living, mortal-self's analytical powers had survived the transition to this pleasant floating-after-death, the old Francis Crozier might have wondered at his thought of "listening to" dreams, but it is true that these dreams are more like listening to another person's chant — although there is no language involved, no words, no music, no chant — than "seeing" dreams the way he always had when he was alive. Although there are most definitely visual images involved in this dream-listening, the shapes and colors are like nothing Francis Crozier ever encountered on the other side of Death's veil and it is this nonvoice, nonchant narrative that fills his death dreams.

There is a beautiful Esquimaux girl named Sedna. She lives alone with her father in a snow-house far north of the regular Esquimaux villages. Word of the girl's beauty spreads and various young men make the long trek across ice floes and barren lands to pay homage to the grey-haired father and to woo Sedna.

The girl's heart is not touched by any of the suitors' words or faces or forms, and in the late spring of the year, when the ice is breaking up, she goes out alone among the floes to avoid yet another year's fresh crop of moonfaced suitors.

Since this happened in the time when animals still had voices which the People understood, a bird flies over the opening ice and woos Sedna with its song. "Come with me to the land of the birds where all things are as beautiful as my song," sings the bird. "Come with me to the land of the birds where there is no hunger, where your tent will always be made of the most beautiful caribou skins, where you shall lie on only the finest and softest bearskins and caribou skins, and where your lamp will always be filled with oil. My friends and I will bring you anything your heart may desire, and you shall be clothed from that day forth in our finest and brightest feathers."

Sedna believes the bird-suitor, weds him in the tradition of the Real People, and travels with him many leagues over sea and ice to the land of the bird people.

But the bird had lied.

Their home is not made of the finest caribou skins but is a patched, sad place thrown together with rotting fish skins. The cold wind blows in freely and laughs at her for her gullible innocence.

She sleeps not on the finest bearskins but on miserable walrus hides. There is no oil for her lamp. The other bird people ignore her and she has to wear the same clothes she was wed in. Her new husband brings her only cold fish for her meals.

Sedna keeps insisting to her indifferent bird-husband that she misses her father, so finally the bird allows her father to come visit. To do so, the old man has to travel for many weeks in his frail boat.

When her father arrives, Sedna feigns joy until they are alone in the dark, fish-stinking tent, and then she weeps and tells her father of how her husband abuses her and of all she has lost — youth, beauty, happiness — by marrying the bird rather than one of the young males of the Real People.

The father is horrified to hear this story and helps Sedna devise a plan to kill her husband. That next morning, when the bird-husband returns with Sedna's cold fish for breakfast, the father and the girl fall upon the bird with the harpoon and paddle from the father's kayak and kill him. Then the father and daughter flee the land of the bird people.

For days they sail south toward the land of the Real People, but when the bird-husband's family and friends find him dead, they are filled with anger and fly south with a beating of wings so loud that it can be heard by the Real People a thousand leagues away.

The sea distance that took Sedna and her father a week to sail is covered by the thousands of flying birds in a few minutes. They descend upon the little boat like a dark and angry cloud made up of beaks and talons and feathers. The beating of their wings calls up a terrible storm that raises the waves and threatens to swamp the little boat.

The father decides to give his daughter back to the birds as an offering and throws her overboard.

Sedna clings to the boat for dear life. Her grip is strong.

The father takes his knife and cuts off the first joints of her fingers. As they fall into the sea, these finger joints are turned into the first whales. The fingernails become the white whalebone found on beaches.

Still Sedna clings. The father cuts off her fingers at the second joint.

These parts of her fingers fall into the sea and become the seals.

Still Sedna clings. When the terrified father cuts off the final stumps of her fingers, these fall onto the passing floes and into the water and become the walruses.

With no fingers left, only curved bone stumps like her dead bird-husband's talons where her hands had been, Sedna finally falls into the sea and sinks to the bottom of the ocean. She resides there until this day.

It is Sedna who is the mistress of all whales, walruses, and seals. If the Real People please her, she sends the animals to them and tells the seals, walruses, and whales to allow themselves to be caught and killed. If the Real People displease her, she keeps the whales, walruses, and seals with her down in the dark depths and the Real People suffer and starve.

What in the God-damned hell? thinks Francis Crozier. It is his self-voice that interrupts the slow no-self flow of the dream-listening.

As if summoned, the pain rushes in.

61

CROZIER

M*y men!* he shouts. But he is too weak to shout it. He is too weak to say it out loud. He is too weak even to remember what the two syllables mean. *My men!* he cries again. It emerges as a moan.

She is torturing him.

Crozier does not awaken all at once but rather comes awake through a series of painful attempts to open his eyes, stitching together separate tatters of attempted awareness stretching over hours and even days, always propelled up out of death-sleep by pain and by the two empty syllables — *my men!* — until he is, at last, conscious enough to remember who he is and to see where he is and to realize who he is with.

She is torturing him.

The Esquimaux girl-woman he had known as Lady Silence keeps cutting into his chest, arms, side, back, and leg with a sharp, heated knife. The pain is incessant and intolerable.

He is lying near her in a small space — not a snow-house as John Irving had described to Crozier, but some sort of tent made of skins stretched over curved sticks or bones — with flickering light from several small oil lamps illuminating the girl's bare upper body and, when he looks down, Crozier's own bare and torn and bleeding chest and arms and belly. He thinks she must be slicing him into small strips.

Crozier tries to scream but finds again that he is too weak to scream. He tries to bat her torturing arm and knife-hand away, but he is too weak to lift his own arm much less stop hers.

Her brown eyes stare into his, acknowledging that he is alive again, and then return to studying the damage her knife is doing as she cuts and slashes and tortures him.

Crozier manages the weakest of moans. Then he falls away into darkness, but not back into dream-listening and the pleasant no-self which he now only half remembers, but only into black wave-surges in a sea of pain.

———

She feeds him some sort of broth from one of the emptied Goldner tins she must have stolen from *Terror*. The broth tastes of some sea animal's blood. She then cuts strips of seal meat and blubber using a strange curved blade with an ivory handle, holding the slab of seal in her teeth and slicing dangerously close to her lips as she cuts downward, then chews the pieces well, finally pressing them between Crozier's chapped and torn lips. He tries to spit them out — he does not want to be fed like some baby bird — but she retrieves each fatty blob and presses it back into his mouth. Defeated, unable to fight her, he finds the energy to chew and swallow.

Then he falls back to sleep to the lullaby of howling wind but is soon awakened. He realizes that he is naked between furred sleeping robes — his clothes, all his many layers, are not in the little tent space — and that she has rolled him onto his belly now, setting some sort of smooth sealskin beneath him to keep the blood from his lacerated chest from soiling the soft hides and furs that cover the tent floor. She is cutting and probing his back with a long, straight blade.

Too weak to resist or roll over, all Crozier can do is moan. He imagines her slicing him to pieces and then cooking and eating the pieces. He feels her pressing strands of something moist and slimy onto and into the many wounds in his back.

At some point in the torture, he falls asleep again.

———

My men!

It is only after several days of this pain and of slipping constantly into and out of consciousness and of thinking that Silence is slicing him to pieces that Crozier remembers being shot.

He awakens with the tent dark except for a tiny amount of moonlight or starlight seeping through the tight-stretched hides. The Esquimaux girl is sleeping next to him, sharing his body heat even as he shares hers, and both of them are naked. Crozier feels not the slightest stir of passion or physical interest beyond his animal need for warmth. He is in too much pain.

My men! I must get back to my men! Warn them!

For the first time, he remembers Hickey, the moonlight, the gunshots.

Crozier's arm is lying across his chest and now he forces his hand to touch higher, where the shotgun pellets had struck his chest and shoulder. His upper left torso is a mass of welts and wounds, but it feels as if the shotgun pellets and any clothing driven into his flesh with them have been carefully dug out. There is something soft like moistened moss or seaweed pressed into the larger wounds, and while Crozier has the impulse to dig it out and throw it away, he does not have the strength.

His upper back hurts even more than his lacerated chest and Crozier remembers the torture as Silence dug there with her knife blade. He also remembers the slight squelching sound after Hickey pulled the trigger but before the shotgun cartridges fired — the powder had been wet and old and both shots had probably ignited with far less than full explosive force — but he can also recall the impact of the outer part of the widening pellet cloud hurling him around and then down onto the ice. He had been shot once from the back with the shotgun at extreme range and once from the front.

Has the Esquimaux girl dug out every pellet? Every shred of filthy clothing driven into me?

Crozier blinks in the dimness. He remembers visiting Dr. Goodsir's sick bay and the surgeon's patient explanations of how, in Naval warfare as well as with most of the wounds suffered on their expedition, it was usually not the initial wound that killed but the sepsis from the contaminated wounds that set in later.

He moves his hand slowly from his chest to his shoulder. He remembers now that after the shotgun blasts, Hickey then shot him several times with Crozier's own pistol and the first bullet had struck . . . *here*. Crozier gasps as his fingers find a deep groove in the flesh of his upper biceps. It is packed with the moldy, slimy stuff. The pain of touching it makes him dizzy and ill.

There is another groove from a bullet along his left rib. Touching that — just moving his hand that far exhausts him — makes him gasp aloud and black out for a moment.

When some consciousness returns, Crozier realizes that Silence has dug a bullet out of his flesh there in his side and also dressed this wound with whatever heathenish poultice she had applied elsewhere on his body. Guessing from the pain when he breathes and from the soreness and swelling in his back, he thinks that this bullet broke at least one rib on his left side, was deflected, and lodged under the skin near his left shoulder blade. Silence must have extracted it from there.

It takes endless minutes and the rest of his meager energy for him to lower his hand to touch his most painful wound.

Crozier does not remember being shot in the left leg, but the pain from the muscle there, just above and under his knee, convinces him that a third bullet must have passed through at that point. He can feel both the entrance and exit holes under his shaking fingers. Two inches higher and the bullet would have taken his knee, the knee would have cost him his leg, and his leg would almost certainly have meant his life. Again there is a poultice-bandage there, and although he can feel scabs, there seems to be no fresh flow of blood.

No wonder I'm burning up from fever. I'm dying of sepsis.

Then he realizes that the heat he feels may not be fever. These robes insulate so well and Lady Silence's naked body next to his is pouring out so much heat that he is completely warm for the first time in . . . how long? Months? Years?

With great effort, Crozier pushes back the top of the robe that covers both of them, allowing a little cooler air in.

Silence stirs but does not waken. Staring at her in the dim light in the tent, he thinks she looks like a child — perhaps like one of his cousin Albert's younger teenaged daughters.

With this thought in mind — remembering playing croquet on a green lawn in Dublin — Crozier falls asleep again.

———

She is in her parka and kneeling in front of him, hands about a foot apart, string made of animal sinew or gut dancing between her splayed fingers and thumbs. She is using her fingers to play a cat's cradle child's game with sinew as string.

Crozier watches dully.

The same two patterns keep appearing out of the complicated crisscross of sinew string. The first comprises three bands of strings creating two triangles at the top, just in from her thumbs, but with a double loop of string in the lower center of the pattern showing a peaked dome. The second pattern — her right hand pulled far away with just two bare strings running almost to her left hand where the string loops around just her thumb and little finger — shows a complex little loop of doubled string that looks like a cartoon figure with four oval legs or flippers and and a string-loop head.

Crozier has no idea what the forms mean. He shakes his head slowly to let her know that he does not want to play.

Silence stares at him for a silent moment, her dark eyes looking into his. Then she undoes the pattern with a graceful collapse of her small hands and sets the string in the ivory bowl he drinks his broth from. A second later she crawls out through the multiple tent flaps.

Shocked by the cold air blowing in for those seconds, Crozier tries to crawl to the opening. He needs to see where he is. Background groans and crackings have suggested that they are still on the ice —

perhaps very near where he was shot. Crozier has no sense of how long it has been since Hickey ambushed the four of them — himself, Goodsir, poor Lane and Goddard — but he has hopes that it has been only a few hours, a day or two at most. If he leaves now, he might still be able to get his warning to the men at Rescue Camp before Hickey, Manson, Thompson, and Aylmore show up there to do more damage.

Crozier is able to lift his head and shoulders a few inches but is far too weak to slither out from under the robes, much less to crawl to look out through the caribou-hide tent flaps. He sleeps again.

Sometime later — he is not even sure if it is the same day or if Silence has come and gone several times since he fell asleep — Silence wakes him. The dim light through the hides is the same; the interior of the tent is illuminated by the same blubber lamps. There is a fresh slab of seal lying in the snowy niche in the floor she uses for storage, and Crozier sees that she has just pulled off her heavy outer parka and is wearing only some sort of short pants with the fur side turned inward. The soft outer hide is lighter in color than Silence's brown skin. Her breasts bobble as she kneels in front of Crozier again.

Suddenly the string dances between her fingers again. This time the little animal design near her left hand is shown first, the string is loosened, retwisted, and the design of the peaked oval dome in the center comes next.

Crozier shakes his head. He does not understand.

Silence tosses the string into the bowl, takes her short, semicircular blade with the ivory handle looking like the handle of a stevedore's hook, and begins slicing up the slab of seal meat.

———

"I have to go find my men," whispers Crozier. "You have to help me find my men."

Silence watches him.

The captain does not know how many days may have elapsed since his first awakening. He sleeps much. His few waking hours are spent with him eating his broth, eating the scal meat and blubber that Silence no longer has to prechew for him but which she still lifts to his lips, and with her changing his poultices and cleaning him. Crozier is mortified beyond words that his basic elimination needs must be attended to him using another Goldner's can set into the snow, reachable through a gap between the sleeping robes beneath him, and that it is *this girl* who regularly must carry the can out to empty it somewhere out there on the ice floes. It does not make Crozier feel any better that the contents of the can freeze quickly and that there is almost no smell from it in the little tent that already smells so strongly of fish and seal and their own human sweat and presence.

"I need you to help me get back to my men," he rasps again. He feels that the odds are great that they are still close to the *polynya* where Hickey ambushed them — no more than two miles out on the ice from Rescue Camp.

He needs to warn the others.

It confuses him that every time he awakens, the dim light through the tent's hide walls seems the same. Perhaps, for some reason that only Dr. Goodsir could explain, he awakens only at night. Perhaps Silence is drugging him with her seal-blood soup to keep him sleeping during the day. To keep him from escaping.

"Please," he whispers. He can only hope that despite her muteness, the savage has learned a little English during her months aboard HMS *Terror*. Goodsir had confirmed that Lady Silence could hear, even if she had no tongue with which to speak, and Crozier himself had seen her start at some sudden loud noise when she was a guest on their ship.

Silence continues staring at him.

She's an idiot as well as a savage, thinks Crozier. He would be God-damned if he'd beg this heathen native again. He would have to keep eating, keep recovering, build up his strength, shove her aside one day, and walk back to camp himself.

Silence blinks and turns to cook the slab of seal meat over her little blubber stove.

He awakes on another day — or, rather, another night, since the light is as dim as always — to find Silence kneeling over him and playing her string game again.

The first pattern between her fingers shows the little peaked-dome shape again. Her fingers dance. Two vertical looped shapes appear, but with two legs or flippers now rather than four. She pulls her hands farther apart, and somehow the designs actually move — sliding farther from her right hand and toward her left hand, the balloon-leg loops moving. She undoes that design, her fingers fly, and the oval-dome shape appears in the center again, but — Crozier slowly realizes — it is not quite the same shape. The peak of the dome is gone and now it is a pure catenary curve such as he studied as a midshipman poring over geometry and trigonometry illustrations.

He shakes his head. "I don't understand," he rasps. "This game doesn't make any God-damned sense."

Silence looks at him, blinks, tosses the string into an animal-hide pack, and begins to pull him out of his sleeping furs.

Crozier still does not have the strength to resist, but neither does he use what little strength he has regained to help. Silence props him up and tugs a light caribou underjacket and then a thick fur parka over his upper body. Crozier is shocked to feel how light the two layers are — the cotton and wool layers he's worn for outside work the past three years weighed more than thirty pounds *before* they inevitably became soaked with sweat and ice, but he doubts if this upper outfit of Esquimaux clothing weighs more than eight pounds. He feels how loose both layers are on his upper body but how snugly everything fits at the neck and wrists — tight anywhere that heat might escape.

Embarrassed, Crozier does try to help pull on the light caribou pants over his nakedness — these are larger versions of the short pants that are all that Silence wears in the tent — and then the high caribou stockings, but his fingers get in the way more than not. Silence pushes his hands away and finishes dressing him with an impersonal economy of effort known only to mothers and nurses.

Crozier watches as Silence pulls liners that look to be made of woven grass onto his feet and pulls them tight over his feet and ankles. Presumably these are for insulation, and he has trouble even imagining how long it had taken her — or some woman — to weave the grass into such high, tight socks. Fur boots, when tugged on over his grass socks by Silence, overlap his fur stocking-pants, and he notices that the soles of these boots are made of the thickest hides of any of their clothing.

During the first hours he'd been awake in the tent, Crozier had wondered at the profusion of robes, parkas, furs, caribou hides, pots, sinew, the seal-oil lamps made of what looked to be soapstone, the curved cutting knife and other tools, but then he realized the obvious: it had been Lady Silence who had looted the bodies and packs of the eight dead Esquimaux killed by Lieutenants Hodgson and Farr. The rest of the material — Goldner tins, spoons, extra knives, marine mammals' ribs, pieces of wood, ivory, even what looked to be old barrel staves now used as part of the tent framework — must have been scavenged from *Terror* or the abandoned Terror Camp or during Silence's months alone on the ice.

When he is dressed, Crozier collapses onto one elbow and pants. "Are you taking me back to my people now?" he asks.

Silence pulls mittens over his hands, flips his hood with its white-bear fur trim up over his head, firmly grips the bearskin beneath him, and drags him outside through the tent flaps.

The cold air hits Crozier's lungs and makes him cough, but after a moment he realizes how warm the rest of his body feels. He can feel his own body heat flowing up and around him within the roomy confines of this obviously nonporous garment. Silence bustles around him for a minute — pulling him up into a sitting position on a pile of folded furs. He guesses that she does not want him lying on the ice, even on the bearskin, since it feels warmer in these strange Esquimaux clothes when one sits up and lets air warmed by one's own body heat circulate against the skin.

As if to confirm this theory, Silence whisks away the bearskin on the ice and folds it, adding it to the stack next to the one he's sitting on. Astonishingly — Crozier's feet have been cold every time he has ever gone up on deck or out onto the ice in the past three years, and have been *wet and cold* for every minute since he left *Terror* — neither the cold of the ice here nor moisture seems to penetrate the thick hide-soles and grass booties he's wearing now.

As Silence begins taking down the tent with a few sure movements, Crozier looks around him.

It is night. *Why has she brought me out here at night? Is there some emergency?* The caribou tent quickly being dismantled is, as he guessed from the noises, out on the pack ice, set amid seracs and icebergs and pressure ridges that reflect the little starlight thrown by the few stars peeking between low clouds. Crozier sees the dark water of a *polynya* not thirty feet from where he'd been lying in the tent, and his heart beats faster. *We've not left the area where Hickey ambushed us, not two miles from Rescue Camp. I know the way back from here.*

Then he realizes that this *polynya* is far smaller than the one Robert Golding had led them to — this patch of open, black water is less than eight feet long and only half that wide. Nor do the surrounding icebergs frozen into the pack ice here look right. They are much taller and more numerous than those near Hickey's ambush site. And the pressure ridges are taller.

Crozier squints at the sky, catching only glimpses of stars. If the clouds would part and if he had his sextant and tables and a chart, he might be able to fix his position.

If . . . if . . . might.

The only recognizable patch of stars he catches sight of look more like a winter constellation than one that should be in that part of the arctic sky in mid- or late August. He knows that he was shot on the night of 17 August — he had already made his daily log entry before Robert Golding had come running into camp — and he cannot imagine that more than a few days have passed since the ambush.

He looks wildly around the ice-jumbled horizons, trying to find a twilight glow that would hint of a recent sunset or imminent sunrise in the south. There is only the night and the howling wind and the clouds and a few trembling stars.

Dear Christ . . . where is the sun?

Crozier is still not cold, but he is trembling and shaking so badly that he has to use what little strength he has to grip the pile of folded furs to keep from toppling over.

Lady Silence is doing a very strange thing.

She has collapsed the hide-and-bone tent in a few efficient motions — even in the dim light, Crozier can see that the outer tent covers are made of sealskins — and now kneels on one of the sealskin tent covers and uses her half-moon blade to slice it down the middle.

Then she hauls the two halves of the sealskin to the *polynya* and, using a curved stick to lower the pieces into the water, thoroughly wets them. Returning to the site where the tent stood only moments ago, she pulls frozen fish from the storage area that had been cut into the ice in her half of the tent and briskly lays a line of fish, head to tail, along one side of each half of the quickly freezing tent cover.

Crozier has not the slightest clue as to what the wench is up to. It is as if she is performing some insane heathenish religious ritual out here in the rising night wind under the stars. But the problem is, Crozier sees, *she has cut up their sealskin tent cover.* Even if she rebuilds the tent from hides stretched over the scattered curved sticks and ribs and bones, it will no longer hold out the wind and cold.

Ignoring him, Silence rolls both halves of the sealskin tent cover tightly around the two lines of fish, pulling and tugging the wet sealskin to make it even tighter. It amuses Crozier that she has left half of one fish protuding from one end of both lengths of rolled sealskin, and now she concentrates on bending upward the head end of each fish ever so slightly.

In two minutes she can lift the two seven-foot-long lengths of sealskin-wrapped fish — each now frozen as solidly as a long, narrow piece of oak with a rising fish head at its tip — and she lays them parallel on the ice.

Now she sets a small hide under her knees and kneels to use bits of sinew and hide thongs to lash short lengths of caribou antlers and ivory — the former frame to the tent — to connect the two seven-foot-long wrapped-fish lengths.

"Mother of God," rasps Francis Crozier. *The frozen lengths of fish wrapped in wet sealskin are runners. The antlers are crosspieces.* "You're building a fucking sledge," he whispers.

His breath hangs as crystals in the night air as his bemusement turns to a sort of panic. *It wasn't this cold on 17 August and before — nowhere near this cold, even in the middle of the night.*

Crozier guesses that it has taken Silence half an hour or less to make the fish-runner, caribou-antler sledge, but now he sits on his stack of furs for another hour and a half or more — gauging the passage of time is difficult without his pocket watch and because he keeps drifting off into a light sleep even while sitting — as the woman works on the runners of the sledge.

First she removes something that looks like a mixture of mud and moss from a canvas bag that had come from *Terror.* Carrying Goldner cans of water from the *polynya,* she shapes this mud-moss into fist-sized balls and then lays these daubs the length of the ad hoc runners, patting and spreading them evenly with her bare hands. Crozier has no clue why her hands do not freeze solid despite her frequent breaks to stick her hands under her parka against her own bare belly.

Silence smooths the frozen mud with her knife, trimming it as a sculptor might cut his clay maquette. Then she brings more water from the *polynya* and pours it over the frozen layer of mud, creating an ice shoeing. Finally, she sprays mouthfuls of water onto a strip of bearskin and rubs that wet fur up and down the frozen mud along the length of each runner until the coating of ice there is absolutely smooth. In the starlight, it looks to Crozier as if the runners along the inverted sledge — just fish and strips of sealskin two hours earlier — are lined with glass.

Silence rights the sledge, tests the thongs and knots, puts her weight on the firmly lashed caribou antlers and short pieces of wood, and lashes the remaining antlers — two longer curved ones that had been the primary tent supports — up from the rear of the sledge to make rudimentary handles.

Then she lays several layers of sealskins and bearskins across the cross-antlers and comes to lift Crozier to his feet and help him over to the sledge.

He shakes off her arm and tries to walk to it by himself.

He has no memory of collapsing face-first into the snow, but his vision and hearing return as Silence is lifting him onto the sledge, straightening his legs, setting his back firmly against piled furs stacked against the rear antler handles, and setting several thick robes over him.

He sees that she has tied long strips of leather to the front of the sledge and woven the ends into a sort of harness that goes around her middle. He thinks of her finger-string games and sees what she had been saying — the tent (peaked oval) taken down, the two of them leaving (the walking figures in the sliding bits of string, although Crozier certainly was not walking this night), to another oval dome with no peak. (Another tent in the shape of a dome? A snow-house?)

With everything packed — the extra furs and canvas bags and hide-wrapped pots and seal-oil lamps all lying atop and around Crozier — Silence slips into harness and begins pulling them across the ice.

The runners glide with a glassy efficiency, far more silently and smoothly than the boat-sledges from *Terror* and *Erebus*. Crozier is shocked to discover that he is still warm; two hours or more of just sitting still out on the ice floe has not chilled him, except for the tip of his nose.

The clouds are solid overhead. There is no hint of sunrise on the horizon in any direction. Francis Crozier has absolutely no hint as to where the woman is taking him — back to King William Island? South to the Adelaide Peninsula? Toward Back's River? Farther out onto the ice?

"My men," he rasps at her. He strains to raise his voice and be heard over the wind sigh, snow hiss, and the groaning of the thick ice beneath them. "I need to get back to my men. They're looking for me.

Miss . . . ma'am . . . Lady Silence, *please*. For the love of God, please take me back to Rescue Camp."

Silence does not turn. He can see only the back of her hood and the white bear ruff gleaming in the faint starlight. He has no idea how she can see to proceed in this darkness or how such a small girl can pull his weight and the sledge's weight so easily.

They glide silently into the darkness of the ice jumble ahead.

62

CROZIER

Sedna at the bottom of the sea decides whether to send the seal up to the surface to face being hunted by other animals and the Real People, but in a real sense, it is the seal himself who decides whether to allow himself to be killed or not.

In another real sense, there is only one seal.

Seals are like Real People in that they each have two spirits — a life spirit that dies with the body and a permanent spirit that departs the body at the time of death. This longer-lasting soul, the *tarnic,* hides in the seal as a tiny bubble of air and blood that a hunter can find in the seal's gut and is the same shape as the seal itself, only much smaller.

When a seal dies, its permanent spirit departs and returns in exactly the same form in a baby seal descended from the seal who has decided to allow itself to be taken and eaten.

The Real People know that a hunter, over his lifetime, will be capturing and killing the same seal or walrus or bear or bird many times over.

Precisely the same thing happens to the permanent spirit of a member of the Real People when his life spirit dies with the body. The *inua* — the permanent spirit-soul — travels, with all of its memories and skills intact, only hidden, to a boy or girl in the line of the dead person's family. This is one of the reasons that the Real People never discipline their children, no matter how rowdy or even impertinent they may become. Besides the child-soul in that child, there resides an adult's *inua* — a father, uncle, grandfather, great-grand-father, mother, aunt, grandmother, or great-grandmother, with all its hunter's and matriarch's or shaman's wisdom — and it should not be rebuked.

The seal will not yield itself up to just any Real People hunter. The hunter must win them over, not just through his guile and stealth and skill but also through the quality of the hunter's own courage and *inua.*

These *inua* — the spirits of the Real People, seals, walruses, bears, caribou, birds, whales — existed as spirits before the Earth, and the Earth is old.

During the first period of the universe, the Earth was a floating disk beneath a sky supported by four pillars. Beneath the Earth was a dark place where the spirits lived (and where most live to this day). This early Earth was under water most of the time and without any human beings — the Real People or others — until two men, Aakulu-jjuusi and Uumaaniirtuq, crawled out of humps in the earth. These two became the first of the Real People.

There were no stars in that era, no moon, no sun, and the two men and their descendants had to live and hunt in total darkness. Since there were no shamans to guide the Real People in their behavior, the human beings had very little power and could hunt only the smallest of animals — hares, ptarmigan, the occasional raven — and they did not know how to live properly. Their only decoration was to wear the occasional *aanguaq,* an amulet made from a sea urchin shell.

Women had joined the two men on the Earth in this earliest of times (they came from the glaciers much as the men had come from the Earth), but they were barren and spent all their time walking the coastlines staring into the sea or digging into the ground in search of children.

The Second Cycle of the universe appeared after a long and bitter contest between a fox and a raven. The seasons appeared then, and then life and death itself; shortly after the seasons arrived, a new era began in which the life spirit of human beings would die with the bodies and the *inua*-spirit would travel elsewhere.

Shamans learned some of the secrets of the cosmic order then and were able to help the Real People learn how to live properly — creating rules which forbade incest and marrying out of the family or murder or other behavior which goes against the Order of Things. The shamans were also able to see back even into the time before Aakulujjuusi and Uumaaniirtuq crawled out of the Earth and to explain to the human beings about the origins of the great spirits in the universe — the *inuat* — such as the Spirit of the Moon, or about Naarjuk, the spirit of consciousness itself, or about Sila, the Spirit of the Air, who is also the most vital of all ancient forces; it is Sila who created and permeates and gives energy to all things and who expresses her wrath through blizzards and storms.

This is also the time when the Real People learned about Sedna, who is known in other cold places as Uinigumauituq or Nuliajuk. The shamans explained that all human beings — the Real People, the redder-skinned native human beings who lived far south of the Real People, the *Ijirait* caribou spirits, and even the pale people who appeared so much later — were born after Sedna-Uinigumauituq-Nuliajuk coupled with a dog. This also explains why dogs are allowed to have names and a name-soul and even share their master's *inua*.

The moon's *inua,* Aningat, had incest with and otherwise abused his sister, Siqniq, the *inua* of the sun. Aningat's wife, Ulilarnaq, loved to disembowel victims — animal or Real People — and so disliked the shamans' meddling in spirit matters that she would punish them by making them laugh uncontrollably. To this day, the shamans may be seized by uncontrollable laughter and frequently die from it.

The Real People enjoy knowing about these three most powerful spirits in the cosmos — the all-pervasive Spirit of the Air, the Spirit of the Sea, who controls all animals who live in the sea or depend upon the sea, and the final member of this trinity, the Spirit of the Moon — but these three original *inuat* are too powerful to pay much attention to the Real People (or to human beings of any sort) since these ultimate *inuat* are as far above the many other spirits as those lesser spirits are above human beings, so the Real People do not worship this trinity. Shamans rarely try to contact these most powerful of spirits — such as

Sedna — and content themselves with making sure that the Real People do not break taboos that would anger the Spirit of the Sea, the Spirit of the Moon, or the Spirit of the Air.

But slowly, over many generations, the shamans — known as *angakkuit* among the Real People — have learned more secrets of the hidden universe and of the lesser *inuat* spirits. Over many centuries, some of the shamans have acquired the gift that Memo Moira called the Second Sight — clairvoyance. The Real People call these abilities *qaumaniq* or *angakkua,* depending upon how they manifest themselves. Just as human beings once tamed their cousin-spirits, the wolves, to become dogs who shared their masters' *inua,* so did the *angakkuit* with the hearing-thoughts or sending-thoughts gifts learn how to tame and domesticate and control the smaller spirits who appeared to them. These helping-spirits were called *tuurngait,* and they not only helped the shamans see the invisible spirit world and look back to times before human beings, but also allowed them to look into other human beings' minds to see the faults committed by the Real People when they break the rules of the universe's order. The *tuurngait* helping-spirits aid the shamans in restoring order and balance. They taught the *angakkuit* their language, the language of the small spirits, which is called *irinaliutit,* so that the shamans could address themselves directly to their own ances-tors and to the more powerful *inuat* powers of the universe.

Once the shamans had learned the *irinaliutit* language of the spirit-helper *tuurngait,* the shamans could then help human beings confess their misbehavior and faults so as to cure diseases and to restore order out of the confusion that is human affairs, thus restoring the order of the world itself. This system of rules and taboos passed down by the shamans was as complex as the crisscross string patterns created between the fingers of Real People women to this day.

The shamans also acted as protectors.

Some minor evil spirits roam among the Real People, haunting them and bringing bad weather, but the shamans have learned how to create and consecrate a sacred knife and to kill these *tupilait.*

To stop the storms themselves, the *angakkuit* found and handed down a special hook that can cut the *silagiksaqtuq,* the vein of the wind.

The shamans can also fly and act as mediators between the Real People and the spirits, but they can — and frequently do — also betray the trust of their own powers and harm human beings by using *ilisi-iqsiniq,* powerful spells they cast which stir up jealousy and rivalry and which can even create a hatred sufficient to compel a Real Person to kill others for no reason. Frequently a shaman loses control of his *tuurngait* helping-spirits, and when that happens, if it is not remedied quickly, that incompetent shaman is like a large metallic rock calling down the summer's lightning and there is little choice except for the Real People either to bind up the shaman and leave him behind or to kill him, cutting off his head and keeping it separate from the body so that the shaman cannot bring himself back to life and pursue them.

Most shamans with any power at all can fly, heal people, families, and entire villages (actually by helping people heal themselves by finding balance again after confessing their faults), leave their bodies to travel to the moon or to the bottom of the sea (wherever the *inuat* most powerful of spirits might dwell), and — after the proper *irinaliu-tit* shamanic incantations, singing, and beating of drums — turn themselves into animals such as the white bear.

While most spirits who are not contained in souls are content to dwell down in the spirit world, there are creatures abroad who carry the *inua* spirits of monsters.

Some of the smaller of these monsters are called *tupilek* and were actually brought to life by people called *ilisituk* hundreds and thousands of years ago. These *ilisituk* were not shamans, but rather evil old men and women who learned much of the shamans' powers but used them to dabble in magic rather than in healing and faith.

All humans, and especially the Real People, live by eating souls — they know this well. What is hunting but one soul seeking out another soul and willing it into the ultimate submission of death? When a seal, for instance, agrees to be killed by a hunter, that hunter must honor the *inua* of the seal who has agreed to be killed, after it is killed but before it is eaten — since it is a creature of the water — by giving it a small ceremonial drink of water. Some of the Real People hunters carry small cups on a stick for that purpose, but some of the oldest and finest hunters still pass the water from their own mouths to the dead seals' mouths.

We are all eaters of souls.

But the evil *ilisituk* old men and women were soul-robbers. They used their incantations to take control of hunters, who often then took their families away from the village to live — and die — far away on the ice or in the interior mountains. Any descendants of these victims of soul-robbery were known as *qivitok* and were always more savage than human.

When families and villages began to suspect the old *ilisituk* of their evil, the sorcerers would often create small evil animals — the *tupilek* — to stalk, injure, or kill their enemies. The *tupilek* started out as lifeless things as small as finger-stones, but after being animated by the *ilisituk's* magic, they would grow to any size they wanted and take on terrible, unspeakable shapes. But since such monsters were easy for their victims to spot and flee from in the daylight, the stealthy *tupilek* usually chose to take the approximate shape of any true living thing — a walrus, perhaps, or a white bear. Then the unsuspecting hunter who had been cursed by the evil *ilisituk* would become the hunted. Human beings very rarely escaped the murderous *tupilek* once they were sent out to do their killing.

But there are very few evil, old *ilisituk* sorcerers left in the world today. One reason for this is that if the *tupilek* did not succeed in killing its assigned victim — if a shaman intervened or if the hunter was so clever as to escape by his own devices — the *tupilek* invariably returned to slaughter its creator. One by the one, the old *ilisituk* became victims of their own terrible creations.

Then there came a time, many thousands of years ago, when Sedna, the Spirit of the Sea, became infuriated with her fellow spirits, the Spirit of the Air and the Spirit of the Moon.

To kill them — these other two parts of the Trinity that made up the basic forces of the universe — Sedna created her own *tupilek*.

This spirit-animated killing machine was so terrible that it had its own name-soul and became a thing called *Tuunbaq*.

The *Tuunbaq* was able to move freely between the spirit world and the Earth world of human beings, and it could take any shape it chose. Any form it took was so terrible that even a pure spirit could not look upon it directly without going mad. Its power — concentrated by Sedna only on the goals of wreaking havoc and death — was pure terror itself. On top of that, Sedna had granted her *Tuunbaq* the power of commanding the *ixitqusiqjuk,* the innumerable smaller evil spirits abroad.

By itself, one on one, the *Tuunbaq* could have killed either the Spirit of the Moon or Sila, the Spirit of the Air.

But the *Tuunbaq,* while terrible in every aspect, was not as stealthy as the tinier *tupilek.*

Sila, the Spirit of the Air, whose energy fills the universe, sensed its murderous presence as it stalked her through the spirit world. Knowing that she could be destroyed by the *Tuunbaq* and also knowing that if she was destroyed the universe would be thrown down into chaos again, Sila called on the Spirit of the Moon to help her defeat the creature.

The Spirit of the Moon was not interested in helping her. Nor was he concerned about the fate of the universe.

Sila then beseeched Naarjuk, the Spirit of Consciousness and one of the oldest *inua* deep-spirits (who, like Sila, had appeared when the chaos of the cosmos had been separated from the thin but growing living green reed of order so very long ago), to help her.

Naarjuk agreed.

Together, in a battle that lasted for ten thousand years and which left craters and rents and vacuums in the fabric of the spirit world itself, Sila and Naarjuk defeated the terrible *Tuunbaq*'s attack.

As all *tupilek* who have failed in their assassination assignments are destined to do, the *Tuunbaq* then turned back to destroy its creator . . . Sedna.

But Sedna, who had learned all of her lessons the hard way since even before her father had betrayed her so long ago, had understood the danger the *Tuunbaq* posed to her even before she created it, so now she activated a secret weakness she had built into the *Tuunbaq,* chanting her own spirit-world *irinaliutit* incantations.

Instantly the *Tuunbaq* was banished to the surface of the Earth, never able to return to the spirit world nor to the deep bottom of the sea nor to hold pure spirit form in either place. Sedna was safe.

The Earth and all its denizens, on the other hand, were no longer safe.

Sedna had banished the *Tuunbaq* to the coldest, emptiest part of the crowded Earth — the perpetually frozen region near the north pole. She chose the far north rather than other distant, frozen areas because only the north, the center of the Earth to the many *inuat* gods, had shamans there with any history of dealing with angry evil spirits.

The *Tuunbaq*, deprived of its monstrous spirit form but still monstrous in essence, soon changed form — as all *tupilek* do — into the most terrible living thing it could find on Earth. It chose the shape and substance of the smartest, stealthiest, most deadly predator on Earth — the white northern bear — but was to the bear in size and cunning as a bear itself is to one of the dogs of the Real People. The *Tuunbaq* killed and ate the ferocious white bears — devouring their souls — as easily as the Real People hunted ptarmigan.

The more complicated the *inua*-soul of a living thing is, the more delicious it is to a soul-predator. The *Tuunbaq* soon learned that it enjoyed eating men more than eating *nanuq*, the bears, enjoyed eating man-souls more than it enjoyed eating walrus-souls, and enjoyed eating men more even than it enjoyed devouring the large, gentle, and intelligent *inua*-souls of the orca.

For generations, the *Tuunbaq* gorged itself on human beings. Large parts of the snowy north that once were thick with villages, areas of the sea that once saw fleets of kayaks, and sheltered places that had heard the laughter of thousands of the Real People were soon abandoned as human beings fled south.

But there was no fleeing the *Tuunbaq*. Sedna's ultimate *tupilek* could outswim, outrun, outthink, outstalk, and outfight any human being alive. It commanded the *ixitqusiqjuk* bad spirits to move the glaciers farther south, making the glaciers themselves follow the human beings who'd fled into green lands so that the white-furred *Tuunbaq* would be comfortable and concealed in the cold as it continued to eat human souls.

Hundreds of hunters were sent out from the Real People villages to kill the thing, and none of the men returned alive. Sometimes the *Tuunbaq* would taunt the families of the dead hunters by returning parts of their bodies — sometimes leaving the heads and legs and arms and torsos of several hunters all mixed together so that the families could not even carry out the proper burial ceremonies.

Sedna's monster soul-eater looked as if it might eat all the human-being souls on Earth.

But, as Sedna had hoped, the shamans of the hundreds of groups of the Real People huddled around the periphery of the cold north, sent verbal messages, then met in *angakkuit* shaman enclaves and talked, prayed to all their friendly spirits, conferred with their helping-spirits, and eventually came up with a plan to deal with the *Tuunbaq*.

They could not kill this God That Walked Like a Man — even Sila, the Spirit of the Air, and Sedna, the Spirit of the Sea, could not kill the *talipek Tuunbaq*.

But they could contain it. They could keep it from coming south and killing all of the human beings and all of the Real People.

The best of the best shamans — the *angakkuit* — chose the best men and women among them with shamanic abilities of clairvoyant thought-hearing and thought-sending, and they bred these best men with the best women the way the Real People today breed sledge dogs to create an even better, stronger, smarter generation.

They called these beyond-shamanic clairvoyant children the *sixam ieua,* or spirit-governors-of-the-sky, and sent them north with their families to stop the *Tuunbaq* from slaughtering the Real People.

These *sixam ieua* were able to communicate directly with the *Tuunbaq* — not through the language of the *tuurngait* helping-spirits as the mere shaman had attempted, but by directly touching the *Tuunbaq*'s mind and life-soul.

The spirit-governors-of-the-sky learned to summon *Tuunbaq* with their throat singing. Devoting themselves to communicating with the *Tuunbaq,* they agreed to allow the jealous and monstrous creature to deprive them of their ability to speak to their fellow human beings. In exchange for the *tupilek* killing-creature no longer preying on human souls, the spirit-governors-of-the-sky promised the God Who Walks Like a Man that they — the human beings and Real People — would no longer make their dwelling places in its northernmost snowy domain. They promised the God Who Walks Like a Man that they would honour it by never fishing or hunting within its kingdom without the monster-creature's permission.

They promised that all future generations would help feed the God Who Walks Like a Man's voracious appetite, the *sixam ieua* and other Real People catching and bringing fish, walruses, seals, caribou, hares, whales, wolves, and even the *Tuunbaq*'s smaller cousins — the white bears — for it to feast on. They promised that no human being's kayak or boat would trespass on the God Who Walks Like a Man's sea-domain unless it was to bring food or to sing the throat songs that soothed the beast or to pay homage to the killing-thing.

The *sixam ieua* knew through their forward-thoughts that when the *Tuunbaq*'s domain was finally invaded by the pale people — the *kabloona* — it would be the beginning of the End of Times. Poisoned by the *kabloonas'* pale souls, the *Tuunbaq* would sicken and die. The Real People would forget their ways and their language. Their homes would be filled with drunkenness and despair. Men would forget their kindness and beat their wives. The *inua* of the children would become confused, and the Real People would lose their good dreams.

When the *Tuunbaq* dies because of the *kabloona* sickness, the spirit-governors-of-the-sky knew, its cold, white domain will begin to heat and melt and thaw. The white bears will have no ice for a home, so their cubs will die. The whales and walruses will have nowhere to feed. The birds will wheel in circles and cry to the Raven for help, their breeding grounds gone.

This is the future they saw.

The *sixam ieua* knew that as terrible as the *Tuunbaq* was, this future without it — and without their cold world — would be worse.

But in the times before this should come to pass, and because the young clairvoyant men and women who were the spirit-governors-of-the-sky spoke to the *Tuunbaq* as only Sedna and the other spirits could — never with voices but always directly, mind to mind — the still-living God Who Walks Like a Man listened to their propositions and their promises.

The *Tuunbaq,* who — like all the greater *inuat* spirits — loves to be pampered, agreed. He would eat their offerings rather than their souls.

Over the generations, the *sixam ieua* clairvoyants continued to breed only with other human beings with the same skill. At an early age, each *sixam ieua* child gave up his or her ability to speak with his or her fellow human beings to show the God Who Walks Like a Man that they were devoted to speaking only to him, to the *Tuunbaq.*

Over the generations, the small families of the *sixam ieua* who live so much farther north than the other villages of Real People (who are still terrified of the *Tuunbaq*), always making their homes on the permanently snow-and-glacier-covered earth and ice pack, became known as the God-Walking People, and even their speaking-families' language became a strange blend of the other Real People's tongues.

Of course, the *sixam ieua* themselves can speak no language — except for the clairvoyant speech of *qaumaniq* and *angakkua,* thought-sending and thought-receiving. But they are still human beings, they still love their families and belong to their larger family groups, so to speak to the other Real People, the *sixam ieua* men use a special sign language and the *sixam ieua* women tend to use the string-shape games that their mothers taught them.

> Before leaving our village,
> and going out onto the ice
> to find the man I must marry,
> the man my father and I dreamt of,
> back when the paddles were clean,
> my father took a dark stone, *aumaa,*
> and he marked each paddle.
>
> he knew that he would not return
> alive from the ice
> we had both seen in our *sixam ieua* dreams,
> the only dreams that are true,

that he, my beloved Aja,
would die out there,
at the hands of a pale-person.

since coming off the ice,
I've looked for that stone
in the hills
and on the river-beds,
but I have never found it.

upon my return to my people
I will find the paddle on which the *aumaa*
made its grey mark.
birth was a short line
at the blade tip.
but longer and above this,
death was drawn parallel.

come again! shouts the Raven.

63

CROZIER

C rozier awakes with one hell of a splitting headache.

He wakes most mornings these days with a splitting headache. One would think that with his back and chest and arms and shoulders peppered by shotgun blasts and with no fewer than three bullet wounds in his body, he'd have other pains to notice upon awakening, and while those agonies descend on him quickly enough, it's the terrible headaches he notices first.

It reminds Crozier of all the years he drank whiskey every night and regretted it every morning after.

Sometimes he wakes, as he did this morning, with nonsense sylla-bles and strings of meaningless words echoing in his aching skull. The words are all clickety-clack-sounding, like children making up vowel-heavy clucking noises just to find the right number of syllables for a jumping-rope song, but they *seem* to mean something in those few painful seconds before he comes fully awake. Crozier feels mentally tired all the time these days, as if he's spent his nights reading Homer in Greek. Francis Rawdon Moira Crozier has never in his life attempted to read Greek. Nor wanted to. He's always left that to scholars and to poor book-obsessed souls like the old steward, Peglar's friend, Bridgens.

This dark morning he's awakened in their snow-house by Silence, who is using the string shapes shifting between her fingers to tell him that it is time to go seal hunting again. She is already dressed in her parka and disappears out the entrance tunnel as soon as she's finished communicating with him.

Grumpy that there is to be no breakfast — not even some cold seal blubber from last night's dinner — Crozier dresses himself, pulling on his parka and mittens last, and crawls downhill out through the entrance passage that faces south, away from the wind.

Outside in the dark, Crozier gets carefully to his feet — his left leg still sometimes refuses to accept his weight in the morning — and looks around. Their snow-house glows slightly from the blubber lamp that is left burning to keep the temperature up inside even while they are away. Crozier clearly remembers the long sledge voyage that brought them to this place. He remembers watching, fur-bundled on his sledge and as helpless as he had been those many weeks ago, with something like awe as Silence had spent hours digging out and then constructing this snow-house.

Since then, the mathematician in Crozier had spent hours lying beneath his robes in the snug little space and admiring the catenary curve of the thing and the absolute and seemingly effortless precision that went into the woman's cutting of the snow blocks — in starlight — and the near perfection of the rising, inward-tilting walls made from those snow blocks.

Even as he watched from beneath his furs that long night or dark day — *I'm as useless as tits on a boar,* had been his thought — he'd also thought, *This thing should fall.* The upper blocks were almost horizontal. The last blocks she'd cut had been trapezoidal, and she'd actually shoved that final block — the key block — out from the inside and then trimmed the edges and tugged it into position from within the new snow-house. Finally Silence had come out and climbed onto the catenary-curve almost-dome of snow blocks, scrambled to the top, jumped up and down, and actually slid down its sides.

At first Crozier thought she was just acting like the child she sometimes looked to be, but then he realized that she was testing the strength and stability of their new home.

By the next day — another day without sunlight — the Esquimaux woman had used her oil lamp to melt the inside surface of the snow-house, then let the walls freeze again, coating it with a thin but very hard glaze of ice. She then thawed the sealskins that had been used first for the tent and then for the sledge and rigged them with sinew cords punched through the walls and ceilings of the snow-house, hanging the skins a few inches from the inside walls to provide an inner lining. Crozier had seen immediately that this protected them from dripping even while raising the temperature inside their living space.

Crozier was astonished at how warm their snow-house seemed: always, he guessed, at least fifty degrees warmer than the outside temperature and frequently warm enough that neither of them wore anything but their caribou-skin shorts when out from under the robes. There was a cooking area on the snow ledge to the right of the entrance, and the antler-and-wood frame there not only suspended their various cooking pots over seal-oil flames but was used as a clothes-drying frame as well. As soon as Crozier was able to crawl and go outside with her, Silence explained through her string-language and gestures that it was imperative that they always dry out their outer clothing upon coming back into the snow-house.

Besides the cooking platform to the right of the entrance and a sitting shelf to the left of it, there was the broad sleeping platform at the rear of the snow-house. Edged with what little wood Silence had brought — reused from the tent and then from the sledge — that wood, frozen in place, kept the platform from being worn down. Silence then spread the last of the moss from her canvas bag on the shelf, presumably as an insulating material, and then took great care spreading the various caribou and white-bear skins on the shelf. She then showed him how they should sleep with their heads toward the door and with their now-dry clothing bunched up as pillows. *All* of their clothing.

For the first days and weeks, Crozier insisted on wearing his caribou shorts under the sleeping robes even though Lady Silence slept naked every night, but soon he found that so warm as to be uncomfortable. Still weakened by his wounds to the point that passion was not yet a temptation, he soon became accustomed to crawling naked between the sleeping robes and re-donning the perspiration-free shorts and other clothing only when he rose in the morning.

Whenever Crozier awoke naked and warm under his robes next to Silence in the night, he tried to remember all the months aboard *Terror* when he was always cold, always wet, and when the lower deck was always dark and dripping and ice-rimed and reeking of paraffin and urine. The Holland tents had been even more miserable.

Now outside, he pulls his ruffed hood forward to keep the deep cold away from his face and looks around.

It is dark, of course. It had taken Crozier a long time to accept that somehow he had been unconscious — or dead? — for weeks between the time he was shot and his first conscious awareness of being with Silence, but there had been only the shortest, dimmest glow in the south during their long sledge trip to this place, so there was no doubt that it was now November, at the very least. Crozier had been trying to keep track of the days since they had come to the snow-house, but with the perpetual darkness without and their strange cycles of sleeping and waking within — he guessed that they sometimes slept twelve hours or more at a stretch — he could not be sure how many weeks had passed since they came to this place. And storms outside often kept them inside for unmeasurable days and nights, subsisting on their cold-stored fish and seal.

The constellations wheeling around — the sky is very clear today, and thus the day very cold — are winter constellations, and the air is so cold that the stars dance and shake in the sky just as they have all those years Crozier has watched them from the deck of *Terror* or some other ship he'd taken to the arctic.

The only difference now is that he is not cold and he does not know where he is.

Crozier follows Silence's tracks around the snow-house and toward the frozen beach and frozen sea. He doesn't really have to follow her tracks since he knows that the snow-covered beach is a hundred yards or so to the north of the snow-house and that she always goes to the sea to hunt seals.

But even knowing his basic directions here does not tell him where he is.

From Rescue Camp and his crew's other camps along the south coast of King William Island, the frozen straits were always to the south. He and Silence could now be on the Adelaide Peninsula south across the straits from King William Island, or even on King William Island itself, but somewhere along its uncharted eastern or northeastern coasts where no white man has ever been.

Crozier has no memory of Silence transporting him to the tent site after he was shot — or of how many times she might have moved the tent before he returned to the world of the living — and has only the haziest recall of how long their journey on the fish-runner sledge was before she built the snow-house.

This place might be anywhere.

They didn't have to be on King William Island at all, even if she has brought them north; they might be on one of the islands in the James Ross Strait somewhere to the northeast of King William Island or on some uncharted island off either the east or west coast of Boothia. On moonlit nights, Crozier can see hills inland from their snow-house site — not mountains, but hills larger than any the captain has ever seen on King William Island — and their campsite itself is more sheltered from the wind than any place he or his men ever found, including Terror Camp.

As Crozier crunches his way across the snow and gravel of the beach and out onto the jumbled sea ice, he thinks of the hundreds of times in the past few weeks when he has tried to communicate his need for leaving to Silence, for finding his men, for getting back to his men.

She always looks at him without expression.

He has come to believe that she understands him — if not his words in English, then the emotions behind his pleas — but she never answers by either expression or string-sign.

Her understanding of things — and his own growing understanding of the complex ideas behind the dancing designs in the string between her fingers — borders, Crozier thinks, on the uncanny. He sometimes feels so close to the odd little native girl that he awakes in the night not knowing which body is his and which hers. At other times, he can hear her shout to him across the dark ice to come quickly or to bring an extra harpoon or rope or tool . . . even though she has no tongue and has never made a sound in his presence. She understands much, and sometimes he thinks that it is her dreams he dreams every night and wonders if she also has to share his nightmare of the priest in white vestments looming over him as he awaits Communion.

But she will not lead him back to his men.

Three times Crozier has left on his own, crawling out the passage as she sleeps or pretends to sleep, bringing just a bag of seal blubber to sustain him and a knife with which to defend himself, and three times he has become lost — twice in the interior of whatever land-mass they are on, once far out onto the sea ice. All three times Crozier has walked until he can walk no more — perhaps for days — and then collapsed, accepting death as his just and proper punishment for abandoning his men to die.

Each time, Silence has found him. Each time, she has bundled him onto a bearskin, set robes over him, and silently pulled him the cold miles back to the snow-house, where she warms his frozen hands and feet against her naked belly under the robes and does not look at him while he weeps.

Now he finds her several hundred yards out onto the ice, bent over a seal's breathing hole.

Try as he might — and he has tried — Crozier can never find these damned breathing holes. He doubts if he could find them in summer daylight, much less by moonlight, starlight, or in the full dark as Silence does. The stinking seals are so clever and so *sly* that he does not wonder that he and his men killed only a handful in all their months on the ice and never one through its breathing hole.

Through the talking strings, Crozier has been made to understand that a seal can hold its breath under water for only seven or eight minutes — perhaps fifteen at the most. (Silence explained these units of time in heartbeats, but Crozier thought he had successfully trans-lated them.) Evidently, if he understands Silence's strings correctly, a seal has territorial boundaries — like a dog or wolf or white bear. Even in the winter, the seal must defend those boundaries, so to make sure that he has enough air within his under-ice kingdom, the seal finds the thinnest ice around and scoops out a dome-shaped breathing hole large enough to hold his entire body, leaving only the tiniest possible actual hole penetrating the thin-shaved ice through which he can breathe. Silence has shown him the sharp scraping claws on a dead seal's flipper and actually clawed at the ice with them to illustrate how well they work.

Crozier believes Silence when she strings that there are dozens of such breathing-hole domes within a single seal's territory, but he's damned if he can find them. The domes she shows so clearly in her strings and which she finds so easily out here in the ice jumble are all but invisible amid the seracs, pressure ridges, ice blocks, little bergs, and crevasses. He's sure he's stumbled over a hundred of the damned things and never noticed one except as an irregularity in the ice.

Silence is squatting near one now. When Crozier is a dozen yards away, she gestures for him to be quiet.

To hear Silence tell of it with the string patterns making pictures between her hands, the seal is one of the most cautious and wary creatures alive, so silence and stealth are the essence of hunting seal. Here Lady Silence earns her name.

Before approaching a breathing hole — how *does* she know they're there? — Silence sets down small squares of caribou skin that she retrieves after each step, setting her thick-booted feet carefully onto them so as not to make the slightest crunch on the snow and ice. Once next to the breathing-hole dome in the dark, moving in slow motion, she softly pushes several forked antlers into the snow and sets her knife, harpoon, lines, and other hunting bric-a-brac on them so that she can retrieve them without making a noise.

Before leaving the snow-house, Crozier has tied sinew thongs around his arms and legs the way Silence has shown him, in an attempt to keep his clothes from rustling. But he knows that if he walks closer to the hole now, he'll sound, in his white-man clumsiness, like a collapsing tower of tin cans to the seal below — if there *is* a seal below — so he strains to see the ice surface beneath him, makes out the inevitable two-foot-by-two-foot-thick caribou skin that Silence leaves for him, and slowly, carefully, goes to his knees on it.

Crozier knows that before he arrived, after Silence found the breathing hole, she carefully and slowly removed the snow over that hole with her knife and widened the hole itself with a bone pick set into the butt of her harpoon shaft. She then inspected the hole to confirm that it was directly above a deep channel in the ice — if not, the chances of a good harpoon thrust were low, he understood now — and then she built the tiny mound up again. Since the snow was blowing, she put a narrow gauze of skin over the hole to prevent it from being filled in. Then she took a very thin point of bone fastened by a long piece of gut string to the tip of another bone and slid this indicator down into the hole, setting the other end on one of her antler twigs.

Now she waits. Crozier watches.

Hours pass.

The wind comes up. Clouds begin to obscure the stars, and snow blows across the ice from the land behind them. Silence stands there, hunched over the breathing hole, her parka and hood slowly being covered with a film of snow, her harpoon with its ivory tip in her right hand, its weight being supported at the rear by the forked antler in the snow.

Crozier has seen her catch seals in other ways. In one, she hews two holes in the ice and — with Crozier's help using one of two harpoons — literally beguiles the seal to her. She has taught him that while the seal may be the animal kingdom's soul of caution, its Achilles' heel is its curiosity. If Crozier gets the head of his specially prepared harpoon near Silence's hole under the ice, he moves the harpoon up and down ever so slightly, causing two small bones rigged with split-feather shafts near the head of the harpoon to vibrate. Eventually, the seal cannot resist its curiosity and pops up to investigate.

In the full moonlight, Crozier has gaped as Silence has moved across the ice on her belly, pretending to be a seal herself, moving her arms like flippers. On those times he can't even see the seal's head protruding from a hole in the ice until there is a sudden, impossibly fast motion of her arm, and then she is pulling back the harpoon attached to her wrist by a long cord. More often than not, there is a dead seal on the other end.

But this dark night-day there is only the seal's breathing hole to watch and Crozier stays on his skin pad for hours, watching Silence standing bent over the almost indiscernible dome. Every half hour or so, she reaches back slowly to her antler-twigs and removes a strange little instrument — a curved bit of driftwood about ten inches long with three bird claws attached — and scratches so lightly at the ice over the breathing hole that he can't hear the noise even from a few feet away. But the seal must hear it clearly enough. Even if the animal is at another breathing hole, perhaps hundreds of yards away, it seems — eventually — to be overcome by the curiosity that will doom it.

On the other hand, Crozier has no idea how Silence can see the seal to harpoon it. Perhaps in the sunlight of summer, late spring, or autumn its shadow might be visible under the ice, its nose visible beneath the tiny breathing-hole opening . . . but in starlight? By the time her warning device vibrates, the seal could have turned and dived deep again. Can she smell its presence as it rises? Can she sense it in some other way?

He is half frozen — a symptom of lying on the caribou pad rather than sitting upright — and dozing when Silence's little bone-and-feather indicator must have vibrated.

He comes awake in an instant as she blurs into action. She lifts the harpoon from its butt rest and flings it straight down through the breathing hole in less time than it takes for Crozier to blink awake. Then she is leaning back, pulling hard on the thick cord disappearing through the ice.

Crozier struggles to his feet — his left leg aches abominably and does not want to support any weight — and hobbles to her side as quickly as he can. He knows that this is one of the trickiest parts of the seal hunt — pulling the thing up before it can writhe off the barbed ivory harpoon head if it is only injured, or just tangle in ice or slip away to the depths if it is dead. Speed, as the Royal Navy had never tired of telling him, is of the essence.

Together they wrestle the heavy animal up through the hole, Silence pulling at the cord with one surprisingly strong arm and hacking away at the ice with her knife in the other hand, enlarging the hole.

The seal is dead but more slippery than anything Crozier has ever encountered. He gets his mittened hand under the base of a flipper, taking care to avoid the razor-sharp claws at the end, and heaves to leverage the dead animal up onto the ice. All the while, he is gasping and cursing and laughing — relieved from his duty to remain silent — and Silence is, of course, silent except for the occasional soft hiss of breath.

When the seal is safe on the ice, he stands back, knowing what will come next.

The seal, barely visible in the little starlight that's made its way between the low-scudding clouds, lies with its black eyes unblinking and looking vaguely censorious, its open mouth leaking only a trace of black-looking blood onto the blue-white snow.

Panting a bit from the exertion, Silence goes to her knees on the ice, then to all fours, and then she lies on her belly with her face next to the dead seal's.

Crozier takes another silent step back. Strangely, he feels now much the same way he did when he was a boy in Memo Moira's church.

Reaching under her parka, Silence pulls out the tiniest stopped flask made of ivory and fills her mouth with water from it. She has kept the flask next to her bare breasts under the fur so as to keep the water liquid.

She leans forward and sets her lips to the seal's in a strange parody of a kiss, even opening her mouth the way Crozier has seen whores do with men on at least four continents.

But she has no tongue, he reminds himself.

She passes the liquid water from her mouth to the seal's mouth.

Crozier knows that if the seal's living soul, not quite departed from this body, is pleased with the beauty and workmanship of the harpoon and barbed ivory spearhead that killed it, is pleased with Silence's stealth and patience and her other hunting methods, and especially if it enjoys the water from her mouth, it will go tell the other seal-souls that they should come to this hunter for the chance to drink such fresh, clear water.

Crozier does not know how he knows this — Silence has never signed it to him with strings or suggested as much through any other gestures — but he knows it is true. It's as if the knowledge comes from the headaches that plague him every morning.

The ritual over, Silence gets to her feet, brushes the snow from her pants and parka, gathers up her precious instruments and harpoon, and together they drag the dead seal the two hundred yards or so to their snow-house.

———

They eat all evening. It seems that Crozier can never get his fill of fat and blubber. Their faces are both as greasy as a greased pig's arse by the end of the evening, and he points to his face, points to Silence's equally greasy face, and bursts into laughter.

Silence never laughs, of course, but Crozier thinks he sees the slightest hint of a smile before she scrambles down the entrance passage and returns — naked except for her caribou shorts — with fresh handfuls of snow for them to wipe their faces with before wiping them again with soft caribou skins.

They drink icy water, heat and eat more seal, drink again, go outside to separate places to relieve themselves, drape their damp clothing over the drying rack above the low-burning blubber flame, wash their hands and faces again, brush their teeth with fingers and string-wrapped twigs, and crawl naked under the sleeping robes.

———

Crozier has just dozed off when he awakens to the feel of Silence's small hand on his thigh and private parts.

He reacts immediately, stiffening and rising. He has not forgotten his previous physical pain and scruples about having relations with the Esquimaux girl: these details simply are not in his mind as her small but urgent fingers close around his penis.

They are both breathing hard. She flings her leg over his thigh and rubs up and down. He cups her breasts — so warm — and reaches down behind her to fiercely grab her round behind and pulls her crotch tighter against his leg. His cock is almost absurdly hard and pulsating, its swollen tip vibrating like the seal-indicator feathers at every fleeting contact with her warm skin. His body is like the curious seal, rising quickly toward the surface of sensations in spite of its wiser instincts.

Silence throws aside the top sleeping robe and straddles him, reaching down in a motion as quick as her harpoon-throwing movement to seize him, position him, and slide him inside her.

"Ah, Jesus . . . ," he gasps as they begin to become one person. He feels the resistance against his straining cock, feels it surrender to their motion, and knows — with deep shock — that he is bedding a virgin. Or that a virgin is bedding him. "Oh, God," he manages as they start moving more wildly.

He pulls her shoulders down and tries to kiss her, but she turns her face away, setting it against his cheek, against his neck. Crozier has forgotten that Esquimaux women do not know how to kiss . . . the first thing any English arctic explorer is told by the old veterans.

It does not matter.

He explodes within her in a minute or less. It has been so long.

Silence lies still on him for a while, her small breasts flattened and sweaty against his equally sweaty chest. He can feel her rapid heartbeat and knows she can feel his.

When he can think, he wonders if there is blood. He does not want to soil the beautiful white sleeping robes.

But Silence is moving her hips again. She sits straight up now, still straddling him, her dark gaze holding his. Her dark nipples seem to be another pair of unblinking eyes watching him. He is still hard inside her, and her motions, impossibly — this has never happened in Francis Crozier's encounters with doxies in England, Australia, New Zealand, South America, and elsewhere — are making him come alive again, grow harder, begin to move his own hips in response to her slow grinding against him.

She throws her head back and sets her strong hand against his chest.

They make love like this for hours. Once, she leaves the sleeping shelf, but only long enough to return with water for them to drink — snowmelt from the small Goldner's tin they leave suspended over the clothes-drying flame — and she matter-of-factly cleans the small smears of blood from her thighs when they've finished drinking.

Then she lies on her back, opens her legs, and pulls him over her with her hand strong on his shoulder.

There is no sunrise, so Crozier will never know if they have made love all that long arctic night — perhaps it has been entire days and nights without sleeping or stopping (it feels this way to him by the time they sleep) — but sleep they eventually do. Moisture from their sweat and breathing drips from the exposed parts of the snow-house walls and it is so warm in their home that for the first half hour or so after they fall off into sleep, they leave the top sleeping robe off.

64

CROZIER

After he made land,
when the world was still dark,
Tulunigraq, Raven, heard the Two Men dream about
    light.
But there was no light.
Everything was dark, as it had always been.
No sun. No moon. No stars. No fires.

Raven flew inland until he found a snow-house
where an old man lived with a daughter.
He knew they were hiding light,
hoarding a bit of light,
so he entered.
He crawled up through the passage.
He looked up through the *katak*.
Two skin-bags were hanging there,
one holding darkness,
and the other holding light.

The man's daughter sat there awake
while her father slept.
She was blind.

Tulunigraq used his thought-sending
to make the daughter want to play.
"Let me play with the ball!" the daughter cried,
waking the old man.
The man awoke and took down the bag that held
the daylight.
The light was wrapped in caribou skin which was
made warm by the daylight inside
wanting to get out.

Raven used his thought-sending to make
The girl push the daylight-ball toward the *katak*.
"No!" cried the father.
Too late.
The ball went down the *katak*, bounced down
the passage.

Tulunigraq was waiting.
He caught the ball.
He ran out the passage,
ran with the daylight ball.

Raven used his bill.
He tore the skin-ball.
Tore at daylight.
The man from the snow-house was
chasing him through willows
and ice, but the daylight-man was no man.
The man was a falcon.
"Pitqiktuak!" screamed Peregrine, "I will
kill you, Trickster!"

He flew down on Raven,
but not before Raven tore the skin-ball open.

Dawn rose.

Light spilled everywhere.

Quagaa Sila! Dawn rose!

"Uunukpuaq! Uunukpuagmun! Darkness!"
shrieked the Falcon.
"Quagaa! Light everywhere!"
cried Raven.

"Night!"
"Daylight!"
"Darkness!"
"Daylight!"
"Night!"
"Light!"

They went on shouting.
Raven cried —
"Daylight for the earth!"
"Daylight for the Real People!"
It will be no good
if we have one but not the other.

So Raven brought daylight to some places.
And Peregrine kept darkness fast in other places.
But the animals fought.
The Two Men fought.
They threw light and darkness at one another.
Daylight and night came into balance.

Winter follows summer.
Two halves.
Light and darkness complete one another.
Life and death complete one another.
You and I complete one another.

Outside, the *Tuunbaq* walks in night.
Where we touch,
there is light.

Everything is in balance.

65

CROZIER

They leave on their long sledge trip shortly after the sun makes its first hesitant, midday, and only-minutes-long appearance on the southern horizon.

But Crozier understands that it is not the return of the sun that has determined their time for action and his own time of decision; it is the violence in the skies the other twenty-three and a half hours each day that has decided Silence that the time has come. As they sledge away from their snow-house forever, shimmering bands of colored light coil and uncoil above them like fingers opening out from a fist. The aurora grows stronger in the dark sky every day and night.

The sledge is a more serious device for this longer trip. Almost twice as long as the jury-rigged fish-runnered six-foot sled Silence had used to transport him when he could not walk, this vehicle has runners made up of small and carefully shaped pieces of scavenged wood interlinked with walrus ivory. It uses shoes of whalebone and flattened ivory rather than just a layer of peat paste on its runners, although Silence and Crozier still reapply a layer of ice to the runners several times a day. The cross sections are made up of antlers and the last bits of wood they had, including the sleeping-shelf slat; the rising rear posts are composed of heavily lashed antlers and walrus ivory.

The leather straps are now rigged for both of them to pull — neither will ride unless there is an injury or illness — but Crozier knows that Silence has built this sledge with great care in the hopes that it may be pulled by a dog team before this year is over.

She is with child. She has not told Crozier this — by the strings or by a glance or by any other visible means — but he knows it and she knows he does. If all goes well, he estimates that the baby will be born in the month he used to think of as July.

The sledge carries all of their robes and skins and cooking gear and tools and skin-sealed Goldner tins to hold water once thawed and a supply of frozen fish, seal, walrus, fox, hare, and ptarmigan. But Crozier knows that some of this food is for a time that may not come — at least for him. And some of it may be for presents, depending upon what he decides and what then happens out on the ice. He knows that, depending upon what he decides, they will both be fasting soon in preparation — although, as he understands it, he is the only one who *must* fast. Silence will join him in the fast simply because she is his wife now and will not eat when he doesn't. But if he dies, she will take the food and the sledge and come back to land to live her life and continue her duties here.

For days they travel north along a coastline, skirting cliffs and too-steep hills. A few times the severe topography forces them out onto the ice, but they do not want to be out there for long. Not yet.

The ice is breaking up here and there, but only into small leads. They do not stop to fish at these leads or to pause at *polynyas,* but press on, pulling ten hours a day or more, moving back to land as soon as they can to continue the hauling there even though it means much more frequent refreshening of the ice on the runners.

On the evening of the eighth night, they pause on a hill and look down at a cluster of lighted snow-domes.

Silence has been careful to approach this little village from the downwind side, but still one of the dogs staked into the ice or earth below begins to bark madly. But the others do not join him.

Crozier stares at the lighted structures — one is a multiple dome made up of at least one large and four small snow-houses connected by common passageways. Just the thought, much less the sight, of such community makes Crozier ache inside.

From far below, muffled by snow blocks and caribou skin, comes the sound of human laughter.

He could go down there now, he knows, and ask this group to help him find his way to Rescue Camp and then to find his men; Crozier knows this is the village of the band belonging to the shaman who escaped the massacre of eight Esquimaux on the other side of King William Island and it is also Silence's extended family, as were the eight murdered men and women.

He could go down and ask them to help, and he knows that Silence will follow and translate with string-signs. She is his wife. He also knows the odds are great that unless he does what he will be asked to do out on the ice — Silence's husband or no and whatever their reverence and awe and love for her — these Esquimaux may well greet him with smiles and nods and laughter and then, when he is eating or asleep or unwary, will slip tight thongs over his wrists and a skin bag over his head and then stab him again and again, women stabbing along with the hunters, until he is dead. He has dreamt about his blood flowing red on white snow.

Or perhaps not. Perhaps Silence does not know what will happen. If she has dreamt that particular future, she has not stringed the outcome to him nor shared those dreams.

He doesn't want to find out now anyway. This village, this night, tomorrow — before he has decided about the other thing — is not his immediate future, whatever else his future and his fate may or may not be.

He nods to her in the darkness and they turn away from the village and drag the sledge north along the coast.

———

During the days and nights of travel — they rig only a protective caribou skin to hang above them from the sledge-antlers as they huddle together under hides for the few hours they sleep — Crozier has much time to think.

In the last few months, perhaps because he has had no one to speak to — or at least no interlocutor who can respond with actual out-loud speech — he has learned how to let different parts of his mind and heart speak within him as if they were different souls with their own arguments. One soul, his older, more-tired soul, knows that he has been a failure in every way a man can be tested. His men — the men who trusted him to lead them to safety — are all dead or scattered. His mind hopes that some have survived, but in his heart, in his soul of his heart, he knows that any men so scattered in the land of the *Tuunbaq* are already dead, their bones bleaching on some unnamed beach or empty ice floe. He has failed them all.

He can, at the very least, follow them.

Crozier does not yet know where he is, although he suspects more each day that they have wintered on the western coast of a large island northeast of King William Island, at a point on almost the same latitude as Terror Camp and *Terror* herself, although those sites would be a hundred miles or more west from here across the frozen sea. If he wanted to return to *Terror* he would have to travel west across this sea and perhaps across more islands and then across all of the north of King William Island itself and then twenty-five more miles out onto the ice to reach the ship he abandoned more than ten months earlier.

He does not want to return to *Terror*.

Crozier has learned enough about survival in the past months that he thinks he can find his way back to Rescue Camp and even to Back's River given enough time, hunting as he goes, building snow-houses or skin tents when the inevitable storms arise. He can seek out his scattered men this summer, ten months after he abandoned them, and find some trace of them, even it if takes years.

Silence will follow him if he chooses this path — he knows she will — even though it means the death of everything she is and everything she lives for here.

But he wouldn't ask her to. If he were to go south after his crew, he would go alone because he suspects that, despite all his new knowledge and skills, he would die on such a search. If he doesn't die on the ice, there will be an injury on the river he would have to follow south. If the river or injury or illness along the way doesn't kill him, he might encounter hostile Esquimaux groups or the even more savage Indians farther south. Englishmen — especially the old arctic hands — love to believe that Esquimaux are primitive but peaceful people, slow to anger, always resistant to war and strife. But Crozier has seen the truth in his dreams: they are human beings, as unpredictable as any other race of man, and often descend into warfare and murder and, in hard times, even cannibalism.

A much shorter and surer route to rescue than going south, he knows, would be to head due east from here across the ice before the ice pack opens for the summer — if it opens at all — hunting and trapping as he goes, then crossing the Boothia Peninsula to its eastern coast, traveling north to Fury Beach or the old expedition sites there. Once at Fury Beach he could just wait for a whaler or rescue ship. The chances for his survival and rescue in that direction are excellent.

But what if he makes it to civilization . . . back to England? Alone. He will always be the captain who let all his men die. The court-martial will be inevitable, its outcome predetermined. Whatever the court's punishment might be, the shame will be a lifelong sentence.

But this is not what dissuades him from heading east or south.

The woman next to him is carrying his child.

Of all his failures, it is Francis Crozier's failures as a man which hurt and haunt him the most.

He is almost fifty-three years old and he has loved only once before this — proposing marriage to a spoiled child, a mean-spirited girl-woman who had teased him and then used him for her pleasure the way his sailors used dockside chippies. *No,* he thought, *the way I used dockside chippies.*

Every morning now and often in the night he awakens next to Silence after sharing her dreams, knowing that she has shared his, feeling her warmth against him, feeling himself responding to that warmth. Every day they go out into the cold and fight for life together — using her craft and knowledge to prey on other souls, to eat other souls, so that their two life-spirit souls can live awhile longer.

She is carrying our child. My child.

But that is irrelevant to the decision he must make in the next few days.

He is almost fifty-three years old and he is now being asked to believe in something so preposterous that the very thought of it should make him laugh. He is asked — if he understands the strings and the dreams, and he believes he does at long last — to *do* something so terrible and so painful that if the experience does not kill him, it may drive him mad.

He has to *believe* that such counterintuitive insanity is the right thing to do. He has to *believe* that his dreams — mere dreams — and that his love for this woman should make him surrender a lifetime of rationality to become . . .

Become what?

Someone and something else.

Pulling the sledge next to Silence under a sky filled with violent color, he reminds himself that Francis Rawdon Moira Crozier believes in nothing.

Or rather, if he believes in anything, it is in Hobbes's *Leviathan*.

Life is solitary, poor, nasty, brutish, and short.

This cannot be denied by any rational man. Francis Crozier, in spite of his dreams and headaches and strange new will to believe, remains a rational man.

If a man in a smoking jacket in a coal-fire-heated library in his manor house in London can understand that life is solitary, poor, nasty, brutish, and short, then how can it be denied by a man pulling a sledge stacked with frozen meat and furs across an unnamed island, through the arctic night under a sky gone mad, toward a frozen sea a thousand miles and more from any civilized hearth?

And toward a fate too frightening to imagine.

On their fifth day pulling along the coast, they come to the end of the island and Silence leads them northeast out onto the ice. The going is slower here — there are the inevitable pressure ridges and shifting floes — and they have to work much harder. They also travel more slowly so as not to break the sledge. They use their blubber stove to melt snow for drinking water but do not pause to catch fresh meat, despite the many breathing-hole domes Silence points out in the ice.

The sun now rises for thirty minutes or so each day. Crozier cannot be sure of the time. His watch disappeared with his clothing after Hickey shot him and after Silence rescued him . . . however she did that. She has never told him.

That was the first time I died, he thinks.

Now he is being asked to die again — to die as what he was in order to become something else.

But how many men get such a second chance? How many captains who have watched one hundred twenty-five men in their expedition die or disappear would want it?

I could disappear.

Crozier has seen the mass of scars on his arm, chest, belly, and leg each night when he strips to crawl beneath the sleeping robes, and he can feel and imagine how terrible the bullet and shotgun-pellet scars are on his back. They could be an explanation and excuse for a life-time of silence about his past.

He can hike east across Boothia, hunt and fish in the rich, warming waters off the east coast there, hide from Royal Navy and other English rescue ships, and wait for an American whaling ship. If it takes two or three years there before one comes, he can survive that long. He is sure of it now.

And then, instead of going home to England — has England ever been home for him? — he can tell his American rescuers that he has no memory of what has happened to him or what ship he belonged to — he can show his terrible wounds as evidence — and go to America with them at the end of the whaling season. There he can start a new life.

How many men get a chance to start such a new life at his age? Many men would want to.

Would Silence go with him? Would Silence bear the stares and laughter of sailors and the harsher stares and whispers of "civilized" Americans in some New England city or New York? Would she trade her furs in for calico dresses and whalebone corsets, knowing that she would always be the ultimate stranger in the ultimate strange land?

She would.

Crozier knows this as surely as he knows anything.

She would follow him there. And she would die there — and die soon. Of misery and of the strangeness and of all the vicious, petty, alien, and unbridled thoughts that would pour into her like the poison from the Goldner tins poured into Fitzjames — unseen, vile, deadly.

He knows this as well.

But Crozier could raise his son in America and have a new life in that almost-civilized country, perhaps captain a private sailing ship there. He has been a total failure as a Royal Navy and Discovery Service captain and as an officer and as a gentleman — well, he was never a gentleman — but no one in America would ever need to know that.

No, no, a serious sailing ship would take him to places and ports where he might be known. If he is recognized by any English Naval officer, he would be hanged as a deserter. But a small fishing ship . . . fishing out of some small New England harbour village, perhaps, with an American wife waiting in port to raise his child with him after Silence dies.

An American wife?

Crozier glances at Silence straining in the sledge harness to his right, pulling with him. The crimson and red and purple and white light from the aurora overhead paints her furred hood and shoulders. She does not look at him. But he is sure that she knows what he is thinking. Or if she does not know now, she will when they curl up together later in the night and dream.

He cannot go home to England. He cannot go to America.

But the alternative . . .

He shivers and pulls his hood forward so that the polar-bear fur on either side of his face can better capture the warmth of his breath and body.

Francis Crozier believes in nothing. *Life is solitary, poor, nasty, brutish, and short.* It has no plan, no point, no hidden mysteries that make up for the oh-so-obvious miseries and banalities. Nothing he has learned in the last six months has persuaded him otherwise.

Has it?

Together, they pull the sledge farther out onto the pack ice.

———

On the eighth day they stop.

This place looks no different than most of the other pack ice they have crossed in the previous week — a bit flatter, perhaps, fewer large ice blocks and pressure ridges, perhaps, but essentially just pack ice. Crozier can see a few small *polynyas* in the distance — their dark water like blemishes in the white ice — and the ice has broken up here and there into several small, impermanent going-nowhere leads. If the spring breakup is not actually coming two months earlier this year, it is doing a good impersonation of it. But Crozier has seen such false spring thaws many times before in his arctic experience and knows that the real breakup of pack ice will not begin until late April or later.

In the meantime, they have patches of open water and seal breathing holes galore, perhaps even the chance to hunt walrus or narwhal should they appear, but Silence is not interested in hunting.

Both of them get out of their harness and look around. They have stopped hauling in the brief interlude of midday southern twilight that passes for daytime.

Silence steps in front of Crozier, removes his mittens, and then removes her own. The wind is very cold and their hands should not be exposed for more than a minute, but in that minute she holds his hands in hers and looks at him. She moves her gaze to the east, then looks south, and then looks back at him.

The question is clear.

Crozier feels his heart pounding. He cannot remember any time in his adult life — certainly not the night that Hickey ambushed him — when he has felt so frightened.

"Yes," he says.

Silence puts her mittens back on and begins unpacking the sledge.

As Crozier helps her unpack things onto the ice and then break down parts of the sledge itself, he wonders again how she has found this place. He has learned that while she sometimes uses the stars or moon to navigate by, more often than not she just pays great attention to the landscape. Even on seemingly barren snowy terrain, she is counting the mathematically precise snow ridges and snow mounds created by the wind, even while noting which way these ridges run. Like Silence, Crozier has begun measuring time not so much in days as in sleepings — how many times they have stopped to sleep, whatever time of day or night that might have been.

Out here on the ice, he has been more aware than ever — that is, he has shared some of Silence's awareness — of the subtleties of hummocked ice and old winter ice and new pressure ridges and thick pack ice and dangerous new ice. He now can see a lead many miles away just by the slight darkening of clouds above it. He now avoids dangerous but almost invisible fissures and rotten ice without actively noticing that he is doing so.

But why this place? How did she know to come here for what they are about to do?

I am *about to do it,* he realizes and his heart pounds more wildly.

But not yet.

In the quickly dimming light, they connect some of the slats on the sledge and the unlashed vertical posts to build a crude framework for a small tent. They will be here only a few days — unless Crozier remains here forever — so they do not try to find a drift in which to construct a snow-house, nor do they spend energy on making the tent fancy. It will serve as shelter.

Some of the skins are set in place for the outer wall of the tent, most go inside.

While Crozier is arranging their floor furs and sleeping furs, Silence is outside, quickly and efficiently cutting blocks of ice from some nearby jumble block and building a low wall on the windward side of the tent. That will help some.

Once inside, she helps Crozier rig the blubber-flame cooking lamp and antler frame in the caribou-skin vestibule of the tent and they begin melting snow for drinking. They will also use the frame and flame for drying their outer clothes. The wind blows snow around the abandoned and empty sledge, which is little more than runners now.

For three days they both fast. They eat nothing, drinking water in an attempt to quell their belly's rumblings; they leave the tent for long hours each day, even when the snow comes, to exercise and relieve tension.

Crozier takes turns throwing both harpoons and both lances at a large snow-and-ice block; Silence had recovered them from her dead family members at the massacre site and prepared one heavy harpoon with its long cord and one lighter throwing lance for each of them months ago.

Now he throws the harpoon with such force that it buries itself ten inches into the block of ice.

Silence walks closer and removes her hood, peering at him in the shifting light from the aurora.

He shakes his head and tries to smile.

He has no signs for *Isn't this what you do to your enemy?* Instead, he reassures her with a clumsy hug that he is not leaving or planning to use the harpoon on anything or anyone anytime soon.

———

He has never seen the aurora like this.

All day and night the cascading curtains of color dance from horizon to horizon with the center of the displays directly overhead. Not in all of his years of expedition near the north or south poles has Crozier seen anything remotely resembling this explosion of light. The hour or so of wan daylight does almost nothing to lessen the intensity of the aerial display.

And there is ample acoustical accompaniment to the visual fireworks.

All around them, the ice groans, cracks, moans, and grinds from pressure, while long series of explosions under the ice begin like scattered artillery fire and quickly move to an unceasing cannonade.

Already unnerved by anticipation, Crozier is more deeply shaken by the noise and movement of the ice pack under them. He sleeps now in his parka — perspiration be damned — and is out of the tent and onto the ice a half dozen times each sleeping period, sure that their broad floe is breaking up.

It never does, although cracks open here and there within fifty yards of their tent and send fissures racing faster than a man could run through seemingly solid ice. Then the cracks close and disappear. But the explosions continue, as does the violence in the sky.

In his last night in this life, Crozier sleeps fitfully — his fasting-hunger makes him cold in a way that even Silence's body heat cannot compensate for — and he dreams that Silence is singing.

The ice explosions resolve themselves into steady drumbeats that serve as background for her high, sweet, sad, lost voice:

> *Ayaa, yaa, yapape!*
> *Ayaa, yaa, yapape!*
> *Ajâ-jâ, ajâ-jâ-jâ . . .*
> *Aji, jai, jâ . . .*
> *Tell me, was life so beautiful on earth?*
> *Here I am filled with joy*
> *Whene'er the dawn comes up above the earth*
> *And the great sun*
> *Glides up into the sky.*
> *But there where you are*
> *I lie in fear and trembling*
> *Of maggots and teeming vermin*
> *Or sea creatures with no souls*
> *That eat into the hollow of my collar bone*
> *And bore out my eyes.*
> *Aji, jai, jâ . . .*
> *Ajâ-jâ, ajâ-jâ-jâ . . .*
> *Ayaa, yaa, yapape!*
> *Ayaa, yaa, yapape!*

Crozier awakes trembling. He sees that Silence is already awake, staring at him with her dark, unblinking eyes, and in a moment of pure terror deeper than terror, he realizes that it was not her voice that he has just heard singing this dead man's song to him — literally a song from a dead man to his previous living self — but the voice of his unborn son.

Crozier and his wife rise and dress in mutual ceremonial silence. Outside, though perhaps morning, it is still night, but a night of a thousand thrusting colors laid over the shaking stars.

The shattering ice still sounds like a drumbeat.

66

The only paths left now are surrender or death. Or both.

All of his life, the boy and man he was and has been for fifty years would rather die than surrender. The man he is *now* would rather die than surrender.

But what is death itself other than the ultimate surrender? The blue flame in his chest will accept neither choice.

In their snow-house the past weeks, under their sleeping robes, he has learned about another type of surrender. A sort of death. A change from being one to being something else that is neither self nor not-self.

If two such different people who have no words at all in common can dream the same dreams, then perhaps — even with all dreams set aside and all other beliefs ignored — other realities can merge as well.

He is very frightened.

They leave the tent wearing only their boots, shorts, leggings, and the thin caribou-skin shirts they sometimes wear under their parkas. It is very cold tonight, but the wind has died down since the day's brief glimpse of midday sun.

He has no idea what time it is. The sun has been set for many hours, and they have not slept yet.

The ice breaks under pressure with the steady beat of drums. New leads are opening nearby.

The aurora casts curtains of light from the starry zenith to the white-ice horizon, sending shimmers to the north, to the east, to the south, and to the west. All things, including the white man and brown woman, are tinted alternately in crimson, violet, yellow, and blue.

He goes to his knees and raises his face.

She stands over him, bending slightly as if watching a breathing hole for a seal.

As taught, he keeps his arms at his side, but she grips him firmly by his upper arms. Her hands are bare in the cold.

She lowers her head and opens her mouth wide. He opens his. Their lips are almost touching.

She inhales deeply, seals her mouth over his, and begins blowing into his open mouth, down his throat.

This is where — in their practice during the long winter darkness — he had so much trouble. Breathing in another person's breath is like drowning.

His body tense, he concentrates fiercely on not gagging, on not pulling away. He thinks — *surrender.*

Kattajjaq. Pirkusirtuk. Nipaquhiit. All clack-clack names he half remembers from his dreams. All names the Real People around the world's circle of northern ice have for what they are doing now.

She begins with a short rhythmic series of notes.

She is playing his vocal cords like a bank of woodwinds' reeds.

The low notes rise out over the ice and blend with the pressure-cracking and the pulsing aurora light.

She repeats the rhythmic motif but this time leaves a short gap of silence between the notes.

He takes her breath from his lungs, adds his own, and blows back into her open mouth.

She has no tongue, but her vocal cords are intact. The notes they produce with his breath fluttering them are high and pure.

She blows music from his throat. He brings music from hers. The opening rhythmic motif quickens, overlaps, hurries itself. The range of notes becomes more complex — as much flute as oboe, as distinctly human as any voice, the throat-song can be heard for miles across the aurora-painted ice.

Every three minutes or so in the first half hour, they pause and gasp for breath. Many times in practice they have broken up in laughter here — he understands through her string-signs that this was part of the fun when it was only a woman's game, making the other throat-singer laugh — but there can be no laughter tonight.

The notes begin again.

The song takes on the quality of a single human voice singing, simultaneously bass-deep and flute-high. They can shape words by breathing through each other's vocal cords like this and now she does — speaking words in song through the night; she plays his throat and vocal cords like a complex instrument and the words take shape.

They improvise. When one changes rhythm, the other must always follow. In that sense, he knows now, it is very much like making love.

He finds the secret space to breathe in between sounds so that they can go longer and make deeper, purer notes. The rhythm quickens toward an almost climactic point, then slows, then quickens again. It is follow the leader, back and forth, one changing the tempo and rhythm, the other following like a lover responding, then the other taking the lead. They throat-sing each other this way for an hour, then two hours, sometimes going twenty minutes and more without stopping for a breath.

The muscles of his diaphragm hurt. His throat is on fire. The notes and rhythm now are as complicated as those created by any dozen instruments, as interlaced, complex, and ascending as the crescendo of a sonata or symphony.

He lets her lead. The single voice the two of them make, the sounds and words the two of them speak, are hers, through him. He surrenders.

Eventually she stops and falls to her knees next to him. They are both too exhausted to hold their heads up. They pant and wheeze like dogs after a six-mile run.

The ice has stopped its noises. The wind has ceased its hum. The aurora pulses more slowly overhead.

She touches his face, gets to her feet, and goes away from him, pulling the tent flap shut behind her.

He finds enough strength to stand and to shed the rest of his clothes. Naked, he does not feel the cold.

A lead has opened to within thirty feet of where they made their music, and now he walks toward this. His heart will not slow its pounding.

Six feet from the edge of the water he goes to both knees again and raises his face to the sky and closes his eyes.

He hears the thing rising from the water not five feet from him and hears the scraping of its claws on ice and the huff of its breath as it pulls itself out of the sea onto the ice and hears the ice groaning under its weight, but he does not lower his head nor open his eyes to look. Not yet.

Water from its coming out of the sea laps against his bare knees and threatens to freeze him to the ice he kneels on. He does not move.

He smells the wet fur, the wet flesh, the bottom-of-the-ocean stink of it, and senses its aurora shadow falling over him, but he does not open his eyes to look. Not yet.

Only when his skin prickles and goose bumps rise at the heavy-mass presence seeming to surround him and only when its meat-eater's breath envelops him does he open his eyes.

Fur dripping like a priest's wet and clinging white vestments. Burn scars raw amid the white. Teeth. Black eyes not three feet from his own and looking deep into him, predator's eyes searching for his soul . . . searching to see if he has a soul. The massive triangular head bobs lower and blots out the throbbing sky.

Surrendering only to the human being he wants to be with and to the human being he wants to become — never to the *Tuunbaq* or to the universe that would extinguish the blue flame in his chest — he closes his eyes again, tilts back his head, opens his mouth, and extends his tongue exactly as Memo Moira taught him to do for Holy Communion.

67

TALIRIKTUG

In the spring of the year that their second child was born, a girl, they were visiting Silna's family in the God-Walking People's band headed by the old shaman Asiajuk when word came from a visiting hunter named Inupijuk that a band of the Real People far to the south had received *aituserk,* gifts, of wood, metal, and other precious objects from dead *kabloona* — white men.

Taliriktug signed to Asiajuk, who translated the signs into questions for Inupijuk. It sounded as if the treasure might be knives, forks, and other artifacts from *Erebus*'s and *Terror*'s ship's boats.

Asiajuk whispered to Taliriktug and Silna that Inupijuk was a *qavac* — literally, "a man from the south," but also a term in Inuktitut that denoted stupidity. Taliriktug nodded his understanding but continued to sign questions that the sour shaman passed on to the stupidly grinning hunter. Part of Inupijuk's social discomfort, Taliriktug knew, was that the hunter from the south had never been in the presence of *sixam ieua* spirit-governors before and was not quite sure if Taliriktug and Silna were human beings or not.

It sounded as if the artifacts were real. Taliriktug and his wife went back to their guests' *iglu,* where she nursed the baby and he thought about it. When he looked up, she was using string to sign.

We should go south, said the strings between her fingers. *If you want to.*

He nodded.

In the end, Inupijuk agreed to guide them to the southeastern village and Asiajuk decided to come with them — very unusual, since the old shaman rarely traveled far these days. Asiajuk brought his best wife, Seagull — young Nauja of the *amooq* big tits — who also carried her scars from the band's lethal encounter with the *kabloona* three years earlier. She and the shaman were the only survivors of that massacre, but the girl showed no resentment toward Taliriktug. She was curious about the fates of the final *kabloona* whom everyone knew had headed south across the ice three summers ago.

Six hunters of the God-Walking People's band also wanted to come along — mostly out of curiosity and to hunt along the way, since the ice was breaking up very early in the strait this spring — so eventually they set out in several boats since leads were opening along the coastline.

Taliriktug, Silna, and their two children chose to travel — as did four of the hunters — in their long double *qayaq,* but Asiajuk was too old and had too much dignity to paddle a *qayaq* anymore. He sat with Nauja in the center of a spacious, open *umiak* as two of the young hunters paddled for him. No one minded waiting for the *umiak* when there was no wind for its sails since the thirty-foot-long craft carried enough fresh food in it that they rarely had to stop to hunt or fish unless they wanted to. This way they could also bring their own *kamatik* sledge in case they needed to travel across land. Inupijuk, the southern hunter, rode in the *umiak,* as did six *Qimmiq* — dogs.

Although Asiajuk generously offered to let Silna and her children ride in his now-crowded *umiak,* she string-messaged her preference for the *qayaq.* Taliriktug knew that his wife would never want any child of hers — certainly not Kanneyuk, the two-month-old — to be so close to the vicious dogs in such a tight space. Their two-year-old son, Tuugaq — "Raven" — had no fear of dogs, but he also had no choice in the matter. He rode in the niche in the *qayaq* between Taliriktug and Silna. The baby, Kanneyuk (whose secret *sixam ieua* name was Arnaaluk), rode in Silna's *amoutiq,* an oversized baby-carrying hood.

The morning they left was cold but clear and as they shoved off from the gravel beach the fifteen remaining members of the God-Walking band chanted their farewell-come-back song:

Ai yei yai ya na
Ye he ye ye yi yan e ya quana
Ai ye yi yai yana.

———

On their second night, the last before paddling and sailing south through leads from the *angilak qikiqtaq,* or "biggest island," that James Ross had named King William Land so long ago, ignoring the fact that the natives who had told him about it had kept calling it *qikiqtaq, qikiqtaq, qikiqtak* — they camped less than a mile from the site of Rescue Camp.

Taliriktug walked there alone.

He'd been back before. Two summers ago, only weeks after Raven was born, he and Silna had come here. That was only a little less than one year after the man Taliriktug used to be had been betrayed and ambushed and shot down like a dog, but already there was little sign that this had been a major campsite for more than sixty Englishmen. Except for a few tatters of canvas frozen into the gravel, the Holland tents had torn and blown away. All that remained were campfire rings and a few stone tent rings.

And some bones.

He had found some long bones, bits of chewed vertebrae, only one skull — the lower jaw missing. Holding the skull in his hands two summers ago, he had prayed to God that this was not Dr. Goodsir.

These scattered and *nanuq*-gnawed bones he had gathered up and interred with the skull in a simple stone tomb, setting a fork he'd found among the stones atop the heap of rocks the way the Real People, even the God-Walking People he'd spent the summer with, liked to do, sending helpful tools and beloved-by-the-dead possessions to the spirit world with the dead.

Even as he did this, he'd realized that the *Inuit* would have thought this an obscene waste of precious metal.

He'd then tried to think of a silent prayer he could say.

The prayers in Inuktitut he'd heard in the past three months were not appropriate. But in his awkward attempt to learn the language — even though he would never be able to utter a syllable of it aloud — he'd played a game that summer trying to translate the Lord's Prayer into Inuktitut.

That evening, standing by the cairn holding his crewmates' bones, he'd tried to think the prayer.

Nâlegauvît kailaule. Pijornajat pinatuale nuname sorlo kilangme . . .
Our father, which art in heaven, hallowed be thy name.

That was as far as he'd been able to get two summers ago, but it felt like enough.

Now, almost two years later, walking back to his wife from a Rescue Camp that was even emptier — the fork was gone and the cairn had been opened and plundered by Real People from the south, even the bones scattered where he could not find them — Taliriktug had to smile at his dawning realization that even if he were granted his biblical threescore and ten years, he was never going to master this language of the Real People.

Every word — even the simple nouns — seemed to have a score of variants, and the subtleties of the syntax were far beyond a middle-aged man who'd gone to sea as a boy and never learned even his Latin. Thank God he would never have to speak this language aloud. Straining to understand the click-clack flow of it gave him the kind of headaches he used to have when Silna first shared her dreams with him.

The Great Bear, for instance. The simple white bear. The God-Walking People and the other Real People he'd encountered in the past two years called it *nanuq*, which was simple enough, but he also heard variants that might be written down — in English, since the Real People had no written language — as *nanoq, nänuvak, nannuraluk, takoaq, pisugtooq,* and *ayualunaq.* And now, from Inupijuk, this hunter from the south (who, he now knew, was not as stupid as Asiajuk insisted), he had learned that the Great Bear was also called *Tôrnârssuk* by many of the southern bands of the Real People.

For a period of a few painful months — he was still healing then and learning how to eat and swallow all over again — he had been perfectly satisfied to have no name at all. When Asiajuk's band began calling him Taliriktug — "Strong Arm" — after an incident during a white-bear hunt that first summer when he had single-handedly hauled the carcass of the dead bear out of the water when a team of dogs and three hunters had failed (it had not been his superhuman strength, he knew, just that he'd been the only one to see where they'd snarled their harpoon line on a projection of ice), he hadn't minded the new name even though he had been happier without one. Asiajuk told him that he now carried the soul-memory of an earlier "Strong Arm" who had died by the hand of the *kabloona*.

Months earlier, when he and Silence had come to the *iglu* village so that she could have the help of the women during the birth of Raven, he had not been surprised to learn that the Real People Inuktitut name of his wife was Silna. He could see how she embodied the spirit of both Sila, the goddess of the air, and Sedna, the goddess of the sea. Of her secret *sixam ieua* spirit-governor name, she would not or could not share it with him through her string-signing or dreams.

He knew his own secret name. On that first night of great misery after the *Tuunbaq* had taken his tongue and older life away, he had dreamt his secret name. But he would never tell anyone, even Silna, whom he still called Silence in his sent-thoughts during their love-making and in their dreams.

———

The village was named Taloyoak and consisted of about sixty people and a scattering of more tents than snow-houses. There were even some snow-covered sod homes projecting out from the cliffs that would have grassy roofs come summer.

The people here were called Oleekataliks, which he thought meant "Men with Capes," although the outer skins they wore on their shoulders looked more to him like Englishmen's woolen comforters than real capes. The head man was about Taliriktug's age and was handsome enough, although he had no teeth left, which made him look older than his years. The man was named Ikpakhuak, which Asiajuk told him meant "the Dirty One," although as far as Taliriktug could see and smell, Ikpakhuak was no dirtier than the rest of them and cleaner than some.

Ikpakhuak's much-younger wife was named Higilak, which Asiajuk smirkingly explained meant "the Ice House." But Higilak's manner was not in any way cold toward the strangers; she helped her husband welcome Taliriktug's band with warmth and an outpouring of hot food and gifts.

He realized that he would never understand these people.

Ikpakhuak and Higilak and their family served them *umingmak,* musk ox steak, as their feast meal, which Taliriktug enjoyed well enough but which Silna, Asiajuk, Nauja, and the rest of his band had to choke down, since they were *Netsilik,* "People of the Seal." After all the meeting ceremonies and meals were over, he managed through his interpreted signs to move the conversation to the *kabloona* gifts.

Ikpakhuak acknowledged that the People of the Cape had such treasures, but before showing his guests, he asked that Silna and Taliriktug show everyone in the village their magic. The Oleekataliks had not met any *sixam ieua* in the lifetimes of most of the villagers — although Ikpakhuak had known Silna's father, Aja, decades ago — and Ikpakhuak politely asked if Silna and Taliriktug would fly around the village a little bit and perhaps turn themselves into seals, not bears, please.

Silna explained — through her string-signs interpreted by Asiajuk — that the two spirit-governors-of-the-sky chose not to do that, but that they would both show the hospitable Oleekataliks where the *Tuunbaqs* had taken their tongues, and that her *kabloona sixam ieua* husband would give them the rare treat of seeing his scars . . . scars inflicted in a terrible battle with evil spirits years ago.

This completely satisfied Ikpakhuak and his people.

After this dog-and-pony cum scar show was over, Taliriktug managed to get Asiajuk to bring the subject back to the *kabloona* gifts.

Ikpakhuak instantly nodded, clapped his hands, and sent boys to gather the treasures. They were handed around the circle.

There were various pieces of wood, one of them split from a well-handled marlin's spike.

There were gold buttons bearing the Naval anchor motif of the Discovery Service.

There was a fragment of a lovingly embroidered man's undervest.

There was a gold watch, the chain it may have hung from, and a handful of coins. The initials on the back of the watch, CF^DV — Charles Des Voeux.

There was a silver pencil case with the initals EC on the inside.

There was a gold-medal citation once presented to Sir John Franklin from the Admiralty.

There were silver forks and spoons bearing the crests of Franklin's various officers.

There was a small china plate with the name SIR JOHN FRANKLIN written out on it in colored enamel.

There was a surgeon's knife.

There was a mahogany portable lap writing desk that the man now holding it recognized because it had been his own.

Did we really haul all this shit hundreds of miles in our boats? thought Crozier. *And before that, thousands of miles from England? What were we thinking?* He felt that he might throw up and had to close his eyes until the nausea passed.

Silence touched his wrist. She had sensed the tilt and shift in him. He looked into her eyes to assure her that he was still there, although he wasn't. Not really. Not completely.

———

They paddled along the coast to the west, toward the mouth of Back's River.

Ikpakhuak's Oleekataliks had been vague, even evasive, about where they had found their *kabloona* treasures — some said they were from a place called Keenuna, which sounded like one of a series of islets in the strait just south of King William Island — but the majority of hunters said they had come across the riches west of Taloyoak at a place called Kugluktuk, which Asiajuk translated as "Place of Falling Waters."

To Crozier, it sounded like the first small waterfall he'd read about that Back had said was just upriver from the mouth of Back's Great Fish River.

They spent a week searching there. Asiajuk and his wife and three of the hunters stayed with the *umiak* at the mouth of the river, but Crozier and Silence with their children, the still-curious hunter Inupijuk, and the other hunters paddled their *qayaqs* upriver the three miles or so to the first low falls.

He found some barrel staves there. A leather boot sole with holes where screws had been driven through. Buried in the sand and mud of the riverbank, he uncovered an eight-foot length of curved and once-polished oak that might have been from the gunwale of one of the cutters. (It would have been pure treasure to the Oleekataliks.) Nothing else.

They were leaving in defeat, paddling downstream to the coast, when they came upon an older man, his three wives, and their four runny-nosed children. Their tent and caribou skins were on the wives' backs and they had come to the river, so the man said, to fish. He had never seen a *kabloona* before, much less two *sixam ieua* spirit-governors without tongues and was very frightened, but one of the hunters with Crozier calmed his fears. The old man was named Puhtoorak and was a member of the Qikiqtarqjuaq band of the Real People.

After food and pleasantries had been exchanged, the old man asked what they were doing so far from the God-Walking People's northern lands, and when one of the hunters explained that they were looking for living or dead *kabloona* who might have come this way — or their treasures — Puhtoorak said that he hadn't heard of *kabloona* on this river but mentioned between large bites of their gift of seal meat, "Last winter I saw a big *kabloona* boat — as large as an iceberg — with three sticks coming up out of it, stuck in the ice just off Utjulik. I think there were dead *kabloona* in its stomach. Some of our younger men went into the thing — they had to use their star-shit stone axes to chop a hole in its side — but they left all the wood and metal treasures where they were because they said the three-sticks house was haunted."

Crozier looked at Silence. *Did I understand him correctly?*

Yes. She nodded. Kanneyuk began to cry, and Silna parted her summer parka and gave the baby her breast.

———

Crozier stood on a cliff and looked out at the ship in the ice. It was HMS *Terror.*

It had taken them eight days of travel from the mouth of the Back River west to this part of the coast of Utjulik. Through the God-Walking People hunters who understood his signs, Crozier had offered bribes to Puhtoorak if the old man would agree to bring his family with him and come along to show them the way to the *kabloona* boat with the three sticks rising from its roof, but the old Qikiqtar-qjuaq wanted nothing more to do with the haunted *kabloona* three-stick house. Even though he had not gone in with the young men last winter, he had seen that the thing was tainted with *piifixaaq* — the kind of unhealthy ghost-spirits that haunted a bad place.

Utjulik was an Inuit name for what Crozier had known from maps as the west coast of the Adelaide Peninsula. The open-water leads had ended not very far west of the inlet leading south to Back's River — the narrowing strait there was solid ice pack — so they'd had to beach and hide the *qayaqs* and Asiajuk's *umiak* and continue on with the six dogs pulling the heavily solid thirteen-foot *kamatik*. Using the kind of inland dead reckoning that Crozier knew he would never master, Silence led them the twenty-five miles or so straight across the interior neck of the peninsula to the area of the west coast where Puhtoorak had said he'd seen the ship . . . even, he confessed, stood on its deck.

Asiajuk had not wanted to leave his comfortable boat when it came time to head cross-country. If Silna, one of the God-Walking People's most revered spirit-governors, had not signed her sincere request that he join them — a request from a *sixam ieua* was a command to even the surliest of shamans — Asiajuk would have ordered his hunters to take him home. As it was, he rode in style under furs in the *kamatik* and even helped from time to time by throwing pebbles at the straining dogs and shouting, "Haw! Haw! Haw!" when he wanted them to go left and "Gee! Gee! Gee!" when he wanted them to go right. Crozier wondered if the old shaman was rediscovering the youthful pleasures of sledge travel by dog team.

Now it was late afternoon of their eighth day and they were looking down at HMS *Terror*. Even Asiajuk seemed intimidated and subdued.

Puhtoorak's best description of the precise location had been that the three-stick house "was frozen in the ice near an island about five miles due west" of a certain point and that he and his hunting party "then had to walk about three miles north across smooth ice to reach the ship after crossing several islands on their walk from the point. They could see the ship from a cliff at the north end of the large island."

Of course, Puhtoorak had not used the term "miles" nor "ship" nor even "point." What the old man had said was that the three-stick *kabloona* house with an *umiak's* hull was a certain number of hours' walk west of *tikerqat,* which means "Two Fingers," which the Real People called two narrow points along this stretch of the Utjulik coastline, and then somewhere close to the north end of a large island there.

Crozier and his band of ten people — the hunter from the south, Inupijuk, was sticking with them to the bitter end — had walked due west across rough ice from the Two Fingers and crossed two small islands before reaching a much larger one. They found a cliff dropping almost a hundred feet to the ice pack at the north end of that large island.

Two or three miles out in the ice, the three masts of HMS *Terror* rose at a raked angle toward the low clouds.

Crozier wished he had his old telescope, but he didn't need it to identify the masts of his old command.

Puhtoorak had been right — the ice for this last part of the walk was much smoother than the jumbled shore and pack ice between the mainland and the islands. Crozier's captain's eye saw why: there lay a string of smaller islands to the east and north, creating a sort of natural seawall sheltering this fifteen- or twenty-nautical-square-mile patch of sea from the prevailing winds out of the northwest.

How *Terror* could have ended up here, almost two hundred miles south of where she had been frozen fast near *Erebus* for almost three years, was beyond Crozier's powers of speculation.

He would not have to speculate much longer.

The Real People, including the God-Walking People, who lived in the shadow of a living monster year in and year out, approached the ship with obvious anxiety. All of Puhtoorak's talk of haunting ghosts and bad spirits had worked its effect on them — even on Asiajuk, Nauja, and the hunters who'd not been there to hear the old man. Asiajuk himself was muttering incantations, ghost-chasing chants, and keeping-safe prayers all during their walk out onto the ice, which added to no one's sense of security. When a shaman gets nervous, Crozier knew, everyone gets nervous.

The only one who would walk next to Crozier at the lead of the procession was Silence, carrying both the children.

Terror was listing about twenty degrees to port, her bow aimed toward the northeast and her masts raking to the northwest, with too much of her starboard-side hull showing above the ice. Surprisingly, there was one anchor deployed — the port-side bow anchor — its hawser disappearing into the thick ice. Crozier was surprised because he guessed the bottom to be at least twenty fathoms deep here — perhaps much more — and because there were little inlets all along the northern curves of the islands behind him. At the very least — unless there was a storm — a prudent captain seeking safe harbour would have brought the ship into the strait on the east side of the large island he'd just walked from, dropping anchor between the big island — whose cliffs would have blocked the wind — and the three smaller islands, none more than about two miles long, east of there.

But *Terror* was here, about two and a half miles out from the north end of that large island, with her anchor dropped into deep water and all of her exposed to the inevitable storms from the northwest.

One walk around the ship and a look up at her canted deck from the lower northwest side solved the mystery of why Puhtoorak's hunting band had been forced to chop their way through the hull on the raised starboard side, probably a splintered and battered and already near-breached hull, in order to gain entry: all the top-deck hatches were battened and sealed.

Crozier returned to the man-sized hole the band had smashed into the exposed and weathered hull. He thought he could squeeze through. He remembered Puhtoorak saying that his young hunters had used their star-shit axes to force their way in here, and he had to smile to himself despite the surge of painful emotions he was feeling.

"Star shit" was what the Real People called falling stars and the metal they used from the falling stars they found lying on the ice. Crozier had heard Asiajuk talk about *uluriak anoktok* — "star shit falling from the sky."

Crozier wished he had a star-shit blade or axe with him right now. The only weapon he carried was a basic work knife with a blade made from walrus ivory. There were harpoons on the *kamatik* but they weren't his — he and Silence had left theirs with their *qayaq* a week ago — and he didn't want to ask to borrow one just to go into the ship with it.

Back at that sledge, forty feet behind them, the *Qimmiq* — the large dogs with their uncanny blue and yellow eyes and souls they shared with their masters — were barking and growling and howling and snapping at one another and at anyone who came close to them. They did not like this place.

Crozier signed to Silence, *Sign Asiajuk to ask them if anyone wants to come in with me.*

She did so quickly, using just her fingers without string. Even so, the old shaman always understood her much more quickly than he could make out Crozier's clumsy signs.

None of the Real People wanted to go through that hole.

I will see you in a few minutes, Crozier signed to Silence.

She actually smiled. *Do not be stupid,* she signed. *Your children and I are coming with you.*

He squeezed in and Silence followed a second later, carrying Raven in her arms and Kanneyuk in the soft-hide baby-holder she sometimes carried on straps against her chest. Both children were sleeping.

It was very dark.

Crozier realized that Puhtoorak's young hunters had hacked their way in to the orlop deck. This was lucky for them since if they'd tried a bit lower amidships here, they would have run into the iron of the coal bins and the water-storage tanks on the hold deck and never could have chopped their way through, even with star-shit heads on their axes.

Ten feet in from the hole in the hull it was too dark to see, so Crozier found his way by memory, holding Silence's hand as they walked ahead down the canted deck and then turned aft.

As his eyes adapted to the dark, there was just enough light filtering in for Crozier to make out that the heavy padlocked door to the Spirit Room and to the Gunner's Storeroom farther aft had been smashed open. He had no idea whether this had been the work of Puhtoorak's men, but he doubted it. Those doors had been left padlocked for a reason and they were the first place any white men returning to *Terror* would want to go.

The rum casks — they'd actually had so much rum they'd had to leave casks of it behind when they took to the ice — were empty. But casks of gunpowder remained, as well as boxes and barrels of shot, canvas bags of cartridges, almost two bulkheads' lengths of muskets still set in their grooved places — they'd had too many to carry — and two hundred bayonets still hanging from their fittings along the rafters and beams.

The metal in this room alone would make Asiajuk's band of Real People the richest men in their world.

The remaining gunpowder and shot would feed a dozen large bands of the Real People for twenty years and make them undisputed lords of the arctic.

Silence touched his bare wrist. It was too dark to sign, so she thought-sent. *Do you feel it?*

Crozier was astonished to hear that — for the first time — her shared thoughts were in English. She had either dreamt his dreams even more deeply than he'd imagined, or she had been very attentive during her months aboard this very ship. It was the first time they'd shared thoughts in words while awake.

Ii, he thought back to her. *Yes.*

This place was bad. Memories haunted it like a bad smell.

To lighten the tension, he led her forward again, pointed toward the bow, and thought-sent her an image of the forward cable locker on the deck below.

I was always waiting for you, she sent. The words were so clear that he thought they might have been spoken aloud in the darkness, except for the fact that neither of the children awoke.

His body began to shake with emotion at the thought of what she had just told him.

They went up the main ladder to the lower deck.

It was much brighter up here. Crozier realized that — finally — daylight was actually coming through the Preston Patent Illuminators that punctuated the deck above them. The curved glass was opaque with ice, but — for once — not covered with snow or tarps.

The deck looked empty. All of the men's hammocks had been carefully folded and stowed away, their mess tables cranked up between the beams to the overhead deck, and their sea chests pushed aside and carefully stowed. The huge Frazer's Patent Stove in the center of the forward berthing area was dark and cold.

Crozier tried to recall if Mr. Diggle was still alive when he, the captain, had been lured onto the ice and shot. It was the first time he'd thought of that name — *Mr. Diggle* — in a long time.

It's the first time I've thought in my own tongue for a long time.

Crozier had to smile at that. "In my own tongue." If there really was a goddess like Sedna who ruled the world, her real name was Bitch Irony.

Silence tugged him aft.

The first officers' cabins and mess rooms they looked into were empty.

Crozier found himself wondering which men could have possibly reached *Terror* and sailed her south.

Des Voeux and his men from Rescue Camp?

He felt almost certain that Mr. Des Voeux and the others would have continued south in the boats toward Big Fish River.

Hickey and his men?

For Dr. Goodsir's sake, he hoped so, but he did not believe it. Except for Lieutenant Hodgson, and Crozier suspected he had not lived for very long in that company of cutthroats, there was hardly a man in that pack who could sail, much less navigate, *Terror.* He doubted if they had been able to sail and navigate the one small boat he'd given them.

That left the three men who had left Rescue Camp to hike over-land — Reuben Male, Robert Sinclair, and Samuel Honey. Could a captain of the fo'c'sle, a captain of the foretop, and a blacksmith sail HMS *Terror* almost two hundred miles south through a maze of leads?

Crozier felt dizzy and a little nauseated from thinking about the men's names and faces again. He could almost hear their voices. He *could* hear their voices.

Puhtoorak had been correct: this place was now home to *piifixaaq* — resentful ghosts that stayed behind to haunt the living.

———

There was a corpse in Francis Rawdon Moira Crozier's bunk.

As far as they could tell without lighting lamps and going down into the hold and orlop deck, this was the only dead body on board.

Why did he decide to die in my bunk? wondered Crozier.

He had been a man about Crozier's height. His clothes — he'd died under blankets in a peacoat and watch cap and wool trousers, which was odd since they must have been sailing in full summer — gave no clue to his identity. Crozier had no wish at all to go through his pockets.

The man's hands, exposed wrists, and neck were brown and mum-mified, shriveled, but it was his face that made Crozier wish that the Preston Patent Illuminator overhead was not allowing in as much light as it did.

The dead man's eyes were brown marbles. His hair and beard were so long and wild that it seemed quite possible that they had continued growing for months after the man's death. His lips had shriveled away to nothing and been pulled back far from the teeth and gums by tendons stretching and contracting.

It was the teeth that were so upsetting. Rather than having fallen out from scurvy, the front teeth were all there and very broad and an ivory yellow and impossibly long — three inches long, at least — as if they had grown the way a rabbit's or rat's teeth continue growing until, unless worn down by gnawing something solid, they curve in and cut the creature's own throat.

These dead man's rodent teeth were impossible, but Crozier was looking at them in the clear, grey evening light coming down through the domed skylight of his old cabin. It was not, he realized, the first impossible thing he had seen or experienced in the last few years. He suspected it might not be his last.

Let's go, he signed to Silence. He did not want to thought-send here where things were listening.

————

He had to use a fire axe to hack his way up through the sealed and nailed-shut main hatch. Rather than ask himself who had sealed it and why — or if the corpse below had been a living man when the hatch had been sealed so tightly above him — he threw the axe aside, clambered up, and helped Silence up the ladder.

Raven was fussing himself awake, but Silence rocked him and he began to snore softly again.

Wait here, he signed and went below again.

First he brought the heavy theodolite and several of his old manuals up, took a quick reading of the sun, and jotted his bearings in the margin of the salt-stained book. Then he carried theodolite and books below and tossed them aside, knowing that fixing this ship's position one last time was perhaps the most useless thing he'd ever done in a long life of doing useless things. But he also knew he'd had to do it.

Just as he had to do what he did next.

In the dark Gunner's Storeroom on the orlop deck he split open three successive kegs of gunpowder — pouring the contents of the first on the orlop deck and down the ladder into the hold deck (he would not go down there), the contents of the second keg everywhere on the lower deck (and especially inside the open door of his own cabin), and the contents of the third keg in black trails along the canted upper deck where Silence waited with his children. Asiajuk and the others on the ice had come around to the port side and now watched from thirty yards away. The dogs continued to howl and strain to get away, but Asiajuk or one of the hunters had staked them to the ice.

Crozier wanted to stay in the open air, even with the afternoon light waning, but he made himself go below to the orlop deck again.

Carrying the last keg of lamp oil left on the ship, he spilled a trail of it on all three decks, taking care to douse the door and bulkhead of his own cabin. His only hesitation was at the entrance to the Great Room where hundreds upon hundreds of spines of books stared back at him.

Dear God, would it hurt if I took just a few of those to help get through the dark winters ahead?

But they now carried the dark *inua* of the death-ship in them. Almost weeping, he dashed lamp oil across them.

When he was finished pouring the last of the fuel on the upper deck, he flung the empty cask far out over the ice.

One last trip below, he promised Silence with his fingers. *Go on to the ice now with the children, my beloved.*

The Lucifer matches were where he had left them in the drawer of his desk three years earlier.

For a second he was sure that he could hear the bunk creak and the nest of frozen blankets stir as the mummified thing behind him reached for him. He could hear the dry tendons in the dead arm stretching and snapping as the brown hand with its long brown fingers and too-long yellow nails slowly rose.

Crozier did not turn to look. He did not run. He did not look back. Carrying the matches, he left his cabin slowly, stepping over the lines of black gunpowder and deck boards stained by the whale oil.

He had to go down the main ladder to throw the first match. The air was so bad here that the match almost refused to light. Then the gunpowder lit with a *whump,* ignited a bulkhead he'd soaked with oil, and raced forward and aft in the dark along its own trail of fire.

Knowing that the orlop deck fire alone would have been enough — these timbers were dried to tinder after six years in this arctic desert — he still took time to light the lines of powder on the lower deck and open upper deck.

Then he jumped the ten feet to the ramp of ice on the west side of the ship and cursed as his never fully recovered left leg announced its pain. He should have clambered down the rigged rope ladders here as Silence obviously had had the sense to do.

Limping like the old man he was sure he would soon be, Crozier walked out onto the ice to join the others.

The ship burned for almost an hour and a half before it sank.

It was an incredible conflagration. Guy Fawkes Day above the Arctic Circle.

He definitely wouldn't have needed the gunpowder or lamp oil, he realized while watching. The timbers and canvas and boards were so leached of moisture that the entire ship went up like one of the incendiary mortar bombs it had been designed to launch so many decades ago.

Terror would have sunk anyway, as soon as the ice thawed here in a few weeks or months. The axe-hole in its side had been its death wound.

But that is not why he burned it. If asked — which he never would be — he could not have explained why it had to be burned. He knew that he did not want "rescuers" from British ships poring over the abandoned ship, carrying tales of it home to frighten the ghoulish citizens of England and to spur Mr. Dickens or Mr. Tennyson on to new heights of maudlin eloquence. He also knew that it wouldn't have been only tales these rescuers would have brought back to England with them. Whatever had taken possession of the ship was as virulent as the plague. He had seen that with the eyes of his soul and smelled it with all his human and *sixam ieua* senses.

The Real People cheered when the burning masts collapsed.

They'd all been forced to move back a hundred yards. *Terror* burned its own death-hole in the ice, and shortly after the flaming masts and rigging fell, the burning ship began hissing and bubbling its way to the depths.

The noise from the fire woke the children and the flames so heated the air out here on the ice that all of them — his wife, scowling Asiajuk, big-titted Nauja, the hunters, happily grinning Inupijuk, even Taliriktug — took off their outer parkas and piled them onto the *kamatik*.

When the show was over and the ship was sunk and the sun was also sinking toward the south so that their shadows leapt long across the greying ice, still they stayed to point and enjoy the steam rising and celebrate the bits of burning debris still scattered here and there on the ice.

Then the band finally turned back toward the big island and then the smaller islands, planning to cross the ice to the mainland before they would make camp for the night. The sunlight shining until after midnight helped their march. All of them wanted to be off the ice and away from this place before the few hours of dimness and full darkness came. Even the dogs quit barking and snarling and seemed to pull harder when they passed the smaller island on their way back in to the land. Asiajuk was asleep and snoring under his robes on the sledge, but both the babies were wide awake and ready to play.

Taliriktug took the squirming Kanneyuk in his left arm and put his right arm around Silna-Silence. Raven, still being carried by his mother, was petulantly trying to slap her arms away and force her to put him down so he could try to walk on his own.

Taliriktug wondered, not for the first time, how a father and mother without tongues were going to discipline a headstrong boy. Then he remembered, not for the first time, that he now belonged to one of the few cultures in the world that did not bother to discipline their headstrong boys or girls. Raven already had an *inua* of some worthy adult in him. His father would just have to wait to see just how worthy it was.

The Francis Crozier *inua* still alive and well in Taliriktug had no illusions about life being anything but poor, nasty, brutish, and short.

But perhaps it did not have to be solitary.

His arm around Silna, trying to ignore the raucous snores from the shaman and the fact that baby Kanneyuk had just pissed on her father's best summer parka, while also ignoring the petulant swats and mewling noises from his squirming son, Taliriktug and Crozier continued walking east across the ice toward solid ground.

ACKNOWLEDGMENTS

I wish to acknowledge the following sources for providing information in my writing of *The Terror*:

The idea to write about this era of Arctic exploration came from a short comment, almost a footnote, about the Franklin Expedition that I encountered in Sir Ranulph Fiennes *Race to the Pole: Tragedy, Heroism, and Scott's Antarctic Quest* (Hyperion, © 2004), the pole being raced to in this instance being the South Pole.

Three books that were especially important to me in the early stages of research were *Ice Blink: The Tragic Fate of Sir John Franklin's Lost Polar Expedition* by Scott Cookman (John Wiley & Sons, Inc., © 2000); *Frozen in Time: The Fate of the Franklin Expedition* by Owen Beattie and John Geiger (Greystone Books, Douglas & McIntyre, © 1987); and *The Arctic Grail: The Quest for the Northwest Passage and the North Pole, 1818–1909* by Pierre Berton (Second Lyons Press Edition, © 2000).

These books led me to some of their invaluable sources, including *Narrative of a Journey to the Shores of the Polar Sea* (John Murray, © 1823) and *Narrative of a Second Expedition to the Shores of the Polar Sea* (John Murray, © 1828), both by Sir John Franklin; *Sir John Franklin's Last Arctic Expedition* by Richard Cyriax (ASM Press, © 1939); *The Bomb Vessel* by Chris Ware (Naval Institute Press, © 1994); *A Narrative of the Discovery of the Fate of Sir John Franklin* by F. L. M'Clintock (John Murray, © 1859); *In Quest of the Northwest Passage* (Longmans, Green & Co, © 1958); *Journal of a Voyage in Baffin's Bay and Barrow Straits, in the Years 1850–51, Performed by H.M. Ships "Lady Franklin" and "Sophia"*

Under the Command of Mr. William Penny, in Search of the Missing Crew of H.M. Ships "Erebus" and "Terror" by Peter Sutherland (Longman, Grown, Green, and Longmans, © 1852); and *Arctic Expeditions in Search of Sir John Franklin* by Elisha Kent Kane (T. Nelson & Sons, © 1898).

Other sources frequently consulted include *Prisoners of the North: Portraits of Five Arctic Immortals* by Pierre Berton (Carroll & Graff, © 2004); *Ninety Degrees North: The Quest for the North Pole* by Fergus Fleming (Grove Press, © 2001); *The Last Voyage of the Karluk: A Survivor's Memoir of Arctic Disaster* by William Laird McKinlay (St. Martin's Griffin Edition, © 1976); *A Sea of Words: A Lexicon and Companion for Patrick O'Brian's Seafaring Tales* by Dean King (Henry Holt & Co., © 1995); *The Ice Master: The Doomed 1913 Voyage of the* Karluk by Jennifer Niven (Hyperion, © 2000); *Rowing to Latitude: Journeys Along the Arctic's Edge* by Jill Fredston (North Point Press, a Division of Far-tar, Straus and Giroux, © 2001); *Weird and Tragic Shores: The Story of Charles Francis Hall, Explorer* by Chauncey Loomis (Modern Library Paperback Edition, © 2000); *The Crystal Desert: Summers in Antarctica* by David G. Campbell (Mariner Books, Houghton Mifflin, © 1992); *The Last Place on Earth: Scott and Amundsen's Race to the South Pole* by Roland Huntford (The Modern Library, © 1999); *North to the Night: A Spiritual Odyssey in the Arctic* by Alvah Simon (Broadway Books, © 1998); *In the Land of White Death: An Epic Story of Survival in the Siberian Arctic* by Valerian Albanov (Modern Library, © 2000); *End of the Earth: Voyages to Antarctica* by Peter Matthiessen (National Geographic, © 2003); *Fatal Passage: The Story of John Rae, the Arctic Hero Time Forgot* by Ken McGoogan (Carrol & Graf, © 2001); *The Worst Journey in the World* by Apsley Cherry-Garrard (National Geographic, © 1992 and 2000); and *Shackleton* by Roland Huntford (Fawcett Columbine, © 1985).

Other sources consulted include *The Inuit* by Nancy Bonvillain (Chelsea House Publications, © 1995); *Eskimos* by Kaj Birket-Smith (Crown, © 1971); *The Fourth World* by Sam Hall (Knopf, © 1987); *Ancient Land: Sacred Whale — The Inuit Hunt and Its Rituals* by Tom Lowenstein (Farrar, Straus and Giroux, © 1993); *The Igloo* by Charlotte and David Yue (Houghton Mifflin, © 1988); *Arctic Crossing* by Jonathan Waterman (Knopf, © 2001); *Hunters of the Polar North — The Eskimos* by Wally Herbert (Time-Life Books, © 1981); *The Eskimos* by Ernest S. Burch Jr. (University of Oklahoma Press, © 1988); and *Inuit: When Words Take Shape* by Raymond Brousseau (Editions Glénat, © 2002).

My sincere thanks to Karen Simmons for finding ... and returning ... many of these later sources.

Internet sources were too many to list, but they include The Aujaqsquittuq Project: Documenting Arctic Climate Change; Spiritism On Line; The Franklin Trial; Enchanted Learning: Animals — Polar Bear (Ursus martimus); Collections Canada; Digital Library Upenn; Radiworks.cbe; Wordgumbo — Canadian Inuit-English Dictionary; Alaskool English to Iñupia; Inuktitut Language Phrases; Darwin Wars; Cangeo.ca Special Feature — Sir John Franklin Expedition; and SirJohnFranklin.com.

The Internet was also my primary access route to primary source materials, including the Francis Crozier Collection, held at Scott Polar Research Institute, University of Cambridge; the Sophia Cracroft Collection (ibid); Sophia Cracroft correspondence; Notes for the Memoir of Jane Franklin. Also included are details of ships' musters, dates, and official documents from the Records of the British Admiralty, Naval Forces, and Royal Marines; records from the Home Office (UK), and legal documents concerning the investigation into the Goldner food canning irregularities from the Supreme Court of Judicature (UK).

Useful illustrations and maps came from *Harper's Weekly* (April 1851), *The Athenaeum* (February 1849), *Blackwood's Edinburgh Magazine* (November 1855), and other sources.

The letter from Dr. Harry D. S. Goodsir to his uncle, 2 July 1845, is in the collection of the Royal Scottish Geographical Society and was quoted in *Frozen in Time: The Fate of the Franklin Expedition* by Owen Beattie and John Geiger.

Finally, my sincere thanks to my agent, Richard Curtis; to my first editor at Little, Brown, Michael Mezzo; to my current editor, Reagan Arthur; and — as always — to Karen and Jane Simmons for encouraging me to go on and then waiting for me while I *was* on this particularly long Arctic expedition.

ABOUT THE AUTHOR

Dan Simmons is the Hugo Award–winning author of *Hyperion* and *The Fall of Hyperion* and their sequels, *Endymion* and *The Rise of Endymion*. He has written the critically acclaimed suspense novels *Darwin's Blade* and *The Crook Factory*, as well as other highly respected works including *Summer of Night*, its sequel, *A Winter Haunting*, and *Song of Kali*, *Carrion Comfort*, *Ilium*, and *Olympos*. Simmons makes his home in Colorado.